Downfa

DOWNFALL

WILL JORDAN

CANELO

First published in the United Kingdom in 2019 by Canelo

Canelo Digital Publishing Limited
57 Shepherds Lane
Beaconsfield, Bucks HP9 2DU
United Kingdom

A CIP catalogue record for this book is available from the British Library.

Print ISBN 978 1 78863 463 2
Ebook ISBN 978 1 910859 73 5

This book is a work of fiction. Names, characters, businesses, organizations, places and events are either the product of the author's imagination or are used fictitiously. Any resemblance to actual persons, living or dead, events or locales is entirely coincidental.

The publishers have made efforts to locate any copyright holders whose works feature in this novel. Any legitimate rights holder is welcome to contact the publisher.

Look for more great books at www.canelo.co

For Ian and Trish,
whose support and encouragement meant so much.

Prologue

Afghanistan – January 14th, 2011

Drake inhaled, taking a breath of the chill morning air as he surveyed the great panoramic vista stretching before him. To the north, the great snow-capped peaks of the Pamir Mountains rose high into the dawn sky, their summits glowing red and orange in the first light of the new day. To the south lay the mighty Karakoram range, still shrouded in shadows, and beyond them the unmarked border with Pakistan.

Sandwiched between these great bastions of rock lay the winding river valley of the Wakhan Corridor. For a thousand years it had been a vital trade route between East and West, carrying spices and silks from China, and traders and explorers from Europe. Marco Polo himself had travelled its mountainous paths on his great journey eastwards. In later centuries, this place had become a pawn in the Great Game between the Russians and British: two empires locked in a battle for supremacy, with Afghanistan caught in the middle.

Generations of conflict had seen this thriving trade route shut down, its eastern borders closed and its once prosperous population reduced to scattered, impoverished settlements.

But for all its dark history and troubled present, it remained one of the most starkly, uncompromisingly beautiful places Drake had ever laid eyes on.

'I wish you could see this,' he said quietly. 'I always used to volunteer for last watch of the night, so I could watch the sun rise over the mountains. On a clear morning, it was so quiet, so empty. You could almost forget there was anyone else in the world.'

He glanced over at the woman standing by his side.

'Was it the same for you?'

She didn't reply, and he knew she couldn't. But he asked the question anyway, because he wanted her to think about it. He wanted her to reflect on the events that had brought them both here: two very different lives that had become bound up in this place. Two people who had fought and bled in this beautiful, troubled, lonely place, their deeds a generation apart and their experiences tempered by different wars.

He wanted her to think on that, and on him.

It started with a familiar sound that disturbed the predawn silence: a distant, rhythmic thump of rotor blades. Well accustomed to the vagaries of acoustics in mountains like this, Drake knew that there were two choppers inbound, just as he knew exactly where they were coming from.

Sure enough, the aircraft appeared a few seconds later from behind a towering rock escarpment, roaring up the valley from the west at high speed. One flying higher and some distance behind to cover the lead aircraft.

Drake recognized the wide, squat profile of the UH-60 Black Hawk right away. Bringing his binoculars up, he could see that the trailing aircraft had been outfitted with the full fire-support package: rocket pods, air-to-ground missiles and rotary cannons for high-speed strafing runs. Between them, the two aircraft carried enough troops and ordnance to obliterate an entire company.

And it was all for him.

There was a good chance they'd already spotted him and his companion, exposed as they were in the middle of an open plain. If they didn't already have unmanned aerial vehicles orbiting overhead, he'd have been very surprised.

Still, there was no sense taking chances. Removing a signal flare from his pocket, he pointed it skyward and pulled the release pin.

A single red projectile shot upwards, reaching about 100 feet before igniting, spewing sparks and orange-coloured smoke as it drifted slowly back to earth on its miniature parachute.

The choppers soon changed course, the lead aircraft quickly angling towards him while its counterpart turned more sluggishly, weighed down by heavy weapons and armour.

'This is it,' Drake said as the choppers closed in on them. 'It'll be over soon.'

The woman made no attempt to flee or resist as the lead aircraft's nose flared upwards, slowing its forward momentum and engulfing them both in a hurricane of dust and tiny rocks from the rotor downwash.

Drake threw up an arm to shield his eyes, watching as the big chopper slowly settled on the ground about 50 yards away.

The rough, mountainous terrain that dominated the eastern swathe of this country had always been difficult to pacify, its heights and tortuous valleys naturally lending themselves to ambushes and guerrilla warfare, allowing the inhabitants to confound invading armies for centuries. Death by a thousand cuts.

His companion had made a career out of doing just that, but that had been a different time. A different war.

Anyway, ambushes were the last thing on Drake's mind now. He'd made sure to choose a wide and relatively flat plateau where he knew a helicopter could set down without difficulty.

The second Black Hawk gunship continued to orbit overhead, its cannons and rockets standing by to decimate any enemy that dared present itself. Drake could actually see the barrels of its 20mm guns tracking around to keep him in their sights.

As the main engines of the first Black Hawk powered down, Drake watched the side door slide open and six men in full combat gear pile out, quickly establishing a perimeter around the landing site, the barrels of their M4 assault rifles sweeping the surrounding rocks and cliff faces. Drake could just hear their hushed voices as they called out to each other over their radio net, confirming the area was clear.

He made no moves as this was happening, just let them get on with their task. He'd been in their position many times in his life, and knew they'd be nervous, edgy, hyped up on adrenaline, expecting the worst. No sense provoking a fight he couldn't win.

Aside from this, he paid the fire team little attention. They were just grunts, here to test the waters and absorb the first hits if they came. Drake was more interested in the small group still lingering aboard the chopper, protected by its armoured hull while their underlings secured the area.

Seconds ticked by as he waited for them to make their move, waited for the leader of this formidable display of military power to finally show themself.

It happened a full minute after the chopper had landed. The side door slid open once more, and two people emerged.

First out was an operative like the others who had come before him. Tall, well built and imposing, his considerable physical presence enhanced by the Kevlar vest and webbing that covered his torso, he moved with the natural confidence of a predator. This was a man born to end lives.

His face might have been called handsome but for the conspicuous scar that trailed down one side, extending from his jawline to above his left eye in a single straight gash. The result of a knife fight that had ended before either he or his opponent could claim victory.

The M4 carbine at his shoulder was lowered but held in a firm grip, ready to be swung into action at a moment's notice. His face, so often given to expressions of malicious glee, was cold and stony in that moment. All business.

Even he looked fearful of what might happen next.

Jason Hawkins was intimately familiar to Drake, and all too dangerous in his own right, but they both knew it was the woman he was protecting who was really in charge here. The woman who had exited the chopper not with the solid, confident leap of a trained operative, but with the more cautious and tentative step of a civilian. The woman who was wearing an expensive tailored suit instead of camo fatigues, and who looked as uncomfortable in her Kevlar vest and winter jacket as any VIP or government dignitary forced to visit conflict zones.

The woman who was watching him now, her expression caught between wariness, curiosity and burgeoning excitement. Just the sight of her was enough to stir similar feelings in Drake.

Tall, dark skinned and with her shoulder-length hair arranged in a sleek side parting, she projected an air of calm, precise, calculated intellect. Her trim physique, straight back and confident stride spoke of an active life that permitted few indulgences. She must have been at least 50 by now, yet there was an agelessness to her that wasn't the result of vanity, cosmetics or surgery, but rather some great inner well of energy, discipline and drive to excel in everything she did.

The pair halted about five yards away, Hawkins covering Drake with his assault rifle now that he was so close. Taking no chances in case Drake was wearing a suicide vest or clutching a pair of grenades with the pins removed.

'You know the drill,' the big man said. 'Let's see those hands. Slowly.'

Drake smiled in amusement. 'Nervous, Jason?'

'Should I be?'

'Depends what you came here for.'

He said nothing to that, but kept Drake covered with the carbine, though Drake noticed his finger edge a little closer to the trigger. Just looking for an excuse to fire.

Letting him sweat just a little longer, Drake raised his hands into view, palms open, fingers outstretched. He had come to this meeting with nothing. No concealed firearms or blades, no hidden body armour, nothing with which to defend or attack.

No tricks. No backing out now.

'That's enough,' the woman commanded. 'Ryan came here in good faith, and so have we. Lower your weapon.'

'Ryan caused a lot of problems for us.'

She gave him a sharp look, repeating her command. 'Lower your weapon.'

Reluctantly the lead operative complied.

Drake smiled again, amused by this show of forced obedience. Like an attack dog eager to get stuck in, but more afraid of his master than his potential enemy. As well he should be.

Both Drake and Hawkins knew what she was capable of.

Satisfied, she nodded to Drake's prisoner. 'Well, let's see her.'

Her head was covered with a black hood that rendered her blind and, of course, kept her face hidden. Reaching up, Drake grasped the fabric and yanked it off with a quick, efficient motion.

There was a moment of tension as the hood came away, and Drake saw Hawkins instinctively raise his weapon despite his orders to stand down. He watched as the man's fleeting look of surprise shifted rapidly into disbelief at the sight that confronted him, then finally the growing realization of what this moment truly meant.

Drake had lived up to his reputation and more, had justified the trust shown in him and repaid it a hundredfold. And he'd returned with the biggest prize of all. The woman who had eluded the CIA's best hunters time and again, who had given Hawkins the facial scar he bore today, who had fought her way out of every trap laid for her and countered every attempt to defeat her.

Anya.

'I'll be damned,' Hawkins said under his breath, his familiar sneer returning. 'I told you I'd be seeing you again.'

Anya could do nothing but glare at him in impotent fury, her mouth gagged, her hands bound. The cuts and bruises marking her face attested to the fact she hadn't come quietly. And here she was, her options exhausted, her reserves spent, her time up.

Anya, defeated by the one man she trusted above any other.

'Oh, Ryan,' the older woman whispered, shaking her head in wonder as she surveyed the bound and gagged prisoner standing before her. 'It's good to have you back.'

Drake's smile was triumphant as he tossed the hood away.

'It's good to be back, Elizabeth.'

Part I

Memory

In 1953, the CIA began the top-secret project known as MK-Ultra to investigate the use of psychoactive drugs, mental conditioning and hypnosis for the purpose of mind control, information gathering and psychological torture. The programme was officially discontinued in 1973.

Candidate B-16 was waiting for her as the door slid back into the wall and she stepped through into the silent, blank room beyond, seated patiently at the metal table in the centre of this perfect white cube. Another blank canvas waiting for her to paint upon.

This one looked like a good prospect, she thought. She'd read his file, analysed his assessment reports, but she always deferred her final judgement until she'd had a chance to speak with them face to face. Thirty years old, in excellent physical condition, intelligent and quick to learn. A man in the prime of his life, at the peak of his physical prowess.

But she would help him to become so much more.

'Good morning, candidate,' she said, sliding into a chair opposite him. The echo of her voice was oddly deadened by the sound-absorbing materials covering every surface, designed to filter out all ambient noises and distractions so that they could be truly alone.

He looked at her, his expression neither hostile nor welcoming. He was assessing her, just as she was assessing him. 'It's afternoon, actually.'

She ignored this.

'This will be our first session together; the first of many, I hope. It's a chance for us to... get to know each other a little. I'd like to ask you a few questions before we begin, and I need you to answer them fully and truthfully. Would that be okay?'

He shrugged. 'Ask away.'

She smiled faintly, laying down a file folder on the table. It contained a summary of every aspect of this man's personality, codified and analysed and broken down into data, tables, dry facts and figures. She had a selection of predefined questions to draw from, but she didn't need them now. She'd written the list herself and knew every one of them by heart.

'What's the date today?'

'February 4th, 2002.' No hesitation, no difficulty in recollection. Not yet, at least.

'And who is the president of the United States?'

'Are you serious?'

'Answer the question, candidate.'

He sighed impatiently. 'Last I checked, it was George W. Bush.'

'Good.' Attitude, a little defiance and impatience with trivialities, just as his psych profile had indicated. 'Do you know where you are?'

'Fort Bragg, North Carolina.' He tilted his head. 'Would you like to know my favourite colour too, Doctor?'

'I'll ask the questions.' She leaned forward a little, studying his reactions carefully. 'Tell me, why are you here?'

'I'm supposed to begin training for a new special forces group being developed. But so far all I've done is sit around in hospitals and padded rooms. So, either I've lost my mind and this is all a delusion, or there's something you guys aren't telling me.' He leaned forward too, matching her posture. 'That's my story. Now why don't you tell me why you're here?'

She smiled faintly, looking at him across the table. The tense posture, powerful body, the bright-green eyes focussed on her. The keen and dominant mind seeking to understand her.

Well, he would understand soon enough. She'd make sure of it.

'I'm here to help you, candidate,' she replied. Yes, this one was going to make an excellent subject, she'd decided. 'I'm here to make you more than you are, more than you ever thought

you could be. And I think you and I are going to get along very well indeed.' She reached *for the folder in front of her and flipped it open. 'So, let's get started.'*

Chapter 1

CIA headquarters, Langley – January 8th, 2011

As the acting director of the CIA, it wasn't often that Marcus Cain found himself summoned to meetings these days. In reality, there was now only one man within the Agency that had the authority to demand an audience with him.

That man was Inspector General Frank Hogarth.

For the past six months, Hogarth and a specially selected team within his directorate had been investigating the sudden death of Cain's predecessor, Robert Wallace. The Department of Justice and the FBI had of course been conducting their own inquiry, but protocol and pride demanded that the CIA itself investigate the possibility of foul play. After all, it wasn't every day that their most senior officer died in the line of duty.

Today was the day Hogarth's team delivered its conclusions.

'Director Cain, thank you for coming in,' Hogarth said, rising from his chair and rounding the small conference table to shake Cain's hand.

Hogarth wasn't a big man by any means; in fact, Cain stood a good six inches taller than him. Short and rotund, his fleshy face hidden behind a thick beard and wire-rimmed glasses, his curly dark hair reduced to a few thin, wiry patches on top, Hogarth's appearance was that of a bank manager at some quiet out-of-town branch, coasting comfortably to retirement with no aspirations to rise any higher.

In short, he was a genial and unassuming man who was easy to underestimate, as many had done to their cost. Cain had known him for more years than he cared to remember, and while he considered their relationship fairly cordial, he was always aware that Hogarth was not someone to be trifled with.

He had an eye for detail that bordered on obsessive, and when it came to investigating possible wrongdoing, he left absolutely nothing to chance. Every testimony and piece of evidence was thoroughly and ruthlessly examined, every inconsistency exposed and cross-referenced. And no amount of political pressure or bribery would convince him to expedite or curtail an investigation.

'Always a pleasure, Frank,' Cain lied, well aware that a great deal rested on what happened in this room today.

Technically Hogarth reported to the CIA director and was therefore subordinate to Cain himself, but his remit to investigate potential crimes, corruption or misconduct within the Agency was effectively unlimited, allowing him access to any person, department or information deemed pertinent. Within the confines of this room at least, Hogarth now outranked Cain.

Even worse, Cain's extensive network of informants and loyal subordinates within the Agency had all failed to find dirt on Hogarth: no skeletons in his closet, nothing that could be used as leverage. He was, in a rare departure from the norm within the intelligence community, both uncorrupted and untouchable, which made him extremely dangerous.

'Would you like a coffee?' Hogarth offered as he took a seat back at the table, slipping on a pair of reading glasses to consult the file laid out before him. A second officer, his adjutant, was also seated, there to act as a witness to the meeting.

Cain was also permitted a representative of his own choosing, but he'd declined. The fewer people present for this, the better.

'I'd rather get right down to it, if you don't mind.' When Hogarth glanced up over the rim of his glasses, Cain added, 'Got a backlog of reports to work through.'

The inspector general smiled, though it didn't quite reach his deep-set eyes. 'Well, we'll try to make this as painless as possible.' Glancing at his adjutant, he added. 'Steven, would you start the tape?'

All of Cain's previous interviews had been similarly recorded. They had been voluntary meetings on his part, so the tone hadn't been as heated as an official interrogation, but the questions had been no less probing. Cain was the last man to have seen Director Wallace alive, and therefore a great deal of the investigation into the man's death had focussed on him.

As the digital recorder did its thing, Hogarth raised his voice, assuming a more official tone. 'For the record, meeting reference SI224/7, presentation of investigation findings and recommendations. The date is January 8th, 2011. Present are Acting Director Marcus Cain, Investigator General Frank Hogarth and Special Investigator Steven Burke.'

With this minor record-keeping task out of the way, Hogarth turned to Cain. 'Now, Director Cain, protocol normally requires that this meeting be chaired by an officer at least one rank higher than the subject of the investigation. Given that you're currently serving as acting director and this therefore isn't possible, please confirm for the record that you waive the regulation in this instance.'

'I do,' Cain agreed.

'Good, then we can proceed.' Glancing down at his printed report, Hogarth began to read. 'Now, in the matter of Special Investigation 224 regarding the death of former CIA Director Robert Wallace, the investigation team has concluded that some anomalies in terms of forensic evidence were present at the scene of his death. These anomalies are summarized in Section 3 of the report. The investigation team also found minor inconsistencies in witness testimonies provided by Acting Director Marcus Cain regarding Director Wallace's state of health at the time of their last meeting, this occurring at approximately two pm on the day of his death. These inconsistencies are summarized in Section 4.'

Cain could feel himself tensing up as Hogarth went on. He had taken every possible step to make Wallace's death appear like an accident, employing a clean-up team to retrieve his body, prepare it and stage it to make it look like the man had died in a car accident. But such endeavours were by nature rushed jobs, hurriedly carried out before the victim was reported missing and a search begun. And in the case of a high-profile government employee like Wallace, time had truly been against them.

Hogarth and his people by contrast had had all the time in the world to pore over every detail, analyse every fibre and shred of evidence. Inevitably they would find holes in the story. Any subterfuge, no matter how well constructed, would eventually collapse if it was poked and prodded enough. The only question remaining was whether any of the holes were big enough to undermine the narrative he'd constructed.

Hogarth paused, knowing that this was the critical moment.

'With these factors taken into account, none of these inconsistencies offer a compelling alternate explanation for Director Wallace's death. Also, given the recent personal loss suffered by Director Cain shortly before the incident, it would be unreasonable to expect a perfect recollection of events on his part,' he concluded, giving Cain a faint nod.

'It's therefore the determination of this investigation that Director Wallace suffered a severe myocardial infarction shortly after departing his meeting with Director Cain, lost control of his vehicle and crashed into a ravine running parallel to the road where he was driving at the time. This hypothesis is consistent with the results of his autopsy carried out shortly after his death, and with Director Wallace's medical assessments in the months leading up to his death, indicating he was experiencing high levels of stress and anxiety associated with his position. Cause of death was determined as a combination of the aforementioned heart attack, and blunt force trauma caused by the crash. Our investigation therefore concurs with our colleagues at the FBI that Director Wallace's death was accidental, and recommends no further investigative action be taken at this point.'

Laying down his report, he regarded Cain, his gaze cool and assessing. 'Do you have any comment regarding these findings, Director Cain?'

Cain shook his head, careful to keep his expression neutral. To show even a hint of relief now could well give Hogarth enough ammunition to rethink his findings.

'For the record, Director Cain has indicated negative.' Hogarth cocked an eyebrow before adding, 'And do you agree with the recommendations of this investigative summary?'

'I do.'

'In that case, sir, we consider the matter concluded. The complete findings of the investigation are in the report in front of you. If you have any questions about any aspect then please contact my office. Meeting concluded at approximately 10.30.'

'Great work as always, Frank,' Cain said as he stood up with a copy of Hogarth's report tucked under his arm, easily a couple of hundred pages long. Both men knew he was never going to read it in any depth, but Hogarth was the kind of man to cross every T and dot every I, even if no one ever saw them. 'Pass on my compliments to your team.'

'Will do, Marcus. It'll mean a lot coming from the acting director,' Hogarth remarked, slipping into a slightly less formal mode now that they were no longer discussing official business. However, Cain hadn't missed the emphasis he'd put on the word 'acting', reminding him that his new position was by no means permanent. But that was a battle he had no interest in fighting today.

He was about to wrap things up when Hogarth took a step closer and lowered his voice. 'There's just one thing that keeps... niggling me.'

'Really? What's that?' Cain asked, faking benign interest.

'Oh, nothing much. Just one of those loose ends we never quite managed to tie up. I mean, it's not like this is on the record or anything...'

He was fishing; Cain felt a flash of irritation towards the rotund man who simply wouldn't let it alone. Of course he could end the conversation right here, make his excuses and leave like nothing had happened. But it had happened. And he knew such an abrupt dismissal would leave a lingering suspicion in Hogarth's mind. Nothing more than a tiny scratch, barely noticed, but one which might slowly fester over time.

The only choice was to deal with it now.

'Try me.'

'Well, it's Wallace's personal secretary,' Hogarth admitted. 'She was one of the last people to speak with him before he logged out of Langley the day he died. He told her not to transfer any calls through to him for the rest of the afternoon, said he was going to be out of town for a while.'

Cain shrugged. 'Makes sense. He was coming to speak with me. I guess he didn't want to be disturbed.'

'Exactly, but it's the instruction he gave her afterwards that bothers me. He told her that he might need to schedule a meeting with the director of national intelligence the following day, "depending on how it goes". Those were his words. Any idea what he might have been referring to?'

Cain could guess what the investigator general was thinking. Hogarth knew the two men had had a turbulent working relationship, and he suspected there was more to their meeting than a simple personal visit. But he couldn't prove it. He was reaching, giving Cain one last prod to see if he might slip up.

Cain managed to adopt a patient, understanding expression. 'We've been over this in my debriefing, Frank,' he pointed out calmly, rationally. 'Like I said in my statement, we didn't talk about work. He came to offer his condolences for the death of my daughter.' Cain composed himself, and for once his expression of pain wasn't entirely fake. 'He said I should take as much time off as I needed, then he left. That was the last time I saw him.'

Hogarth studied him, before nodding and spreading his hands in a gesture of finality and acceptance. 'Well, like I said, it's just one of those little things.'

Cain laid a hand on his shoulder. 'Not every question gets to be answered, Frank. We both know that.'

Letting go, he turned and strode out of the room with the folder under his arm, fully intending to dispose of it at his earliest convenience. The investigation was concluded, and finally he was in the clear. He could put all this bullshit behind him and focus on the real work that lay ahead.

That was enough for him.

Chapter 2

Zurich, Switzerland

Alex Yates was running, pounding up the snow-covered slope, his legs driving him onwards with grim, almost frantic determination. The soft *crump* of freshly fallen snow beneath his boots was interspersed with the rasp of his breathing as he eagerly sucked fresh, cold air into his lungs. Beneath his heavy winter jacket, he was already perspiring as he pushed his body harder and harder, refusing to give in to the burning fatigue in his muscles.

There!

Spotting a target to his right, he whirled around, dropped to one knee, then raised the MP5 submachine gun up to his shoulder. The bulky suppressor unit attached to the barrel made it heavier, differently balanced than it should have been, but he was learning to compensate for this.

Get a good sight picture. Don't fire until you're ready. It's more important to shoot true than to shoot first.

His target, nothing more than a sheet of paper with the outline of a human body printed on it, drifted into the centre of his weapon's iron sights. Bracing himself, he depressed the trigger and felt the rattling, jarring recoil as the suppressed weapon spat out a burst of 9mm rounds. The centre of his target disintegrated into a ragged hole as the bullets tore through it, while ejected shell casings disappeared, sizzling, into the snow beside him.

Good hit. Keep moving. Faster!

Rising to his feet, his breath misting in the cold air, he resumed his charge up the hill. Another target fell to his deadly accurate fire as he pushed on, pounding through the snow, slowing only to eject the magazine from his weapon and press another one home. He couldn't tell how many rounds remained in it, but it didn't feel like many judging by the weight. Better to have a full mag at the ready.

He caught movement at the edge of his vision and instinctively turned towards it, coming within an instant of firing before realizing it was nothing but a hare bounding away from the commotion. The small animal leapt nimbly between the drifts, its white fur blending easily with the winter terrain, before disappearing amongst the pine trees that lined the slope.

Stay calm. Don't fire unless you're sure of your target. Move!

Sweating and breathing hard, Alex resumed his ascent, eyes sweeping constantly left and right, eagerly seeking the next target.

He soon spotted not one but two enemies about 30 yards to his left. One was rising from behind a fallen tree trunk as if it were a sniper about to take a shot at him, while the other stood in open ground to its right.

Alex went for the sniper first. Another innocuous paper target with bullseyes in the centre of the chest and head to measure the shot pattern, the kind found on rifle ranges the world over. But Alex wasn't seeing a simple paper target. He never did.

What Alex saw was a man, tall and big and powerful. A man whose face was marked with a scar that left the corner of his mouth turned upwards in a sneering, disparaging smile.

Raising the weapon again, Alex sighted this target and opened fire.

Too soon! You fired too soon!

His shots fell too low, chewing up the tree trunk but missing his intended target. Adjusting his aim and cursing his lapse of judgement, he held the trigger down, expending the remainder of his magazine in a single, continuous stream of automatic fire that tore a dozen finger-sized holes in the paper surface.

Click.

Out of ammo. No time to change mags.

Allowing the submachine gun to fall on its sling, he reached for the Beretta 9mm semi-automatic at his waist, drew it and brought it up into firing position. He thumbed off the safety catch, braced himself for the noise and recoil, then fired.

Unlike the MP5, this weapon wasn't silenced, and the crack of each shot seemed to reverberate inside his skull, leaving his ears ringing and his head aching. But that didn't stop him firing. Again and again he squeezed the trigger, the weapon snapping back against his wrists, the rounds tearing through his target to impact in the snow field beyond.

But Alex didn't see that. Instead he saw...

...the barrel of an assault rifle rise towards him, and the smiling visage of his adversary as his finger tightened on the trigger. Alex tensed up, frozen in terror, waiting for the first shot to slam into his unprotected body.

Then in a blur of movement, someone stepped in front of him just as the rifle spat a crackling, thunderous burst.

The young woman stiffened suddenly, looking down in surprise at the red stains spreading across her chest. Then slowly her legs crumpled beneath her and she fell.

'Lauren!' Alex cried in horror and...

...anger as he advanced towards the target, the Beretta clutched in both hands, pumping round after round into it. Oblivious to the noise, the pain in his wrist, the pounding of his heart and the aching fatigue in his body.

He saw his enemy with that scarred, twisted smile of his. Mocking him, mocking the young life he'd just ended, the future he'd just destroyed—

Alex jerked back suddenly as a figure moved out from behind a tree right in front of him. A hand shot out and grasped the Beretta, forcing it skywards, away from his target. Away from his enemy.

'That's enough!' Anya said, her voice as hard and commanding as her severe expression. 'Cease fire.'

Alex blinked, reality seeming to snap back into place around him as if he'd just been awoken from a nightmare. He tried to calm himself, regain his composure.

'I'm fine,' he replied, lowering his gun and engaging the safety just as she'd taught him. 'Change the targets over and I'll do it again.'

The woman shook her head. 'You've been at this all afternoon, Alex. You're exhausted, you need to rest.'

'Soldiers don't get to choose when they fight. You told me that.'

If anyone could use her own words against her, she supposed Alex was the prime candidate. That didn't mean his interpretation of her words was correct, however.

'You're not a soldier. And pushing yourself to breaking point will not change that.'

He wasn't listening, concentrating instead on removing the spent clip from the MP5 and finding a fresh one from the bandolier he was carrying. 'Just get the fucking targets set up.'

He was making to return down the slope when Anya stepped in front of him, blocking his path. 'That wasn't a suggestion,' she said, her tone quiet but firm. 'Stand down now.'

Alex's frustration and resentment threatened to break his self-control. She could almost feel the anger, the rage simmering inside him like a pressure cooker unable to find release. This was a situation that had been building for some time, and which she knew she'd have to deal with sooner or later.

It might as well be now.

'Come back to the house with me,' she said. 'There's something I want to show you.'

The young man cocked an eyebrow. 'Is *that* a suggestion?'

'An invitation, but I hope you'll accept it.'

Alex bowed to the inevitable. 'Fine.'

Anya's home was about a quarter of a mile further down the mountainside, overlooking the shores of an Alpine lake near the Swiss border. A pleasant, remote spot that afforded remarkable views on a clear day, and far enough from the nearest town that the dense woodland could be used as a makeshift shooting range without attracting unwanted attention. It had served her well over the past few years, providing not only a measure of security and defence, but some much-needed isolation from an increasingly hostile and chaotic world.

Alex was sitting uncomfortably on an armchair in one corner of the living room when Anya returned from her brief foray into the cellar. Broodingly silent, he looked like an errant schoolboy that had just been sent to the principal's office.

Anya pulled up a chair opposite him, reached into her pocket and laid a single photograph on the armrest of his chair. Its edges were a little frayed, and it was starting to curl a little, but the picture was still quite recognizable.

It was a picture of a young woman in desert combat fatigues, perched on the edge of a sand dune with a weapon cradled in her lap. She was looking at the camera, but there was no playful smile on her face. Instead there was an almost ferocious determination coming from her, as if she were about to go into battle.

'Do you recognize her?'

Alex looked down at the youthful, serious face beside him, then up at the woman seated opposite. Twenty years of trials and hardships might have separated the two of them, but the resemblance was unmistakable.

'That picture was taken during Desert Storm. About a year after I came back from Afghanistan. I weighed about 80 pounds when I returned, could barely walk across the room without help.'

Anya leaned back in her chair, searching for the right way to express what she needed to say. 'But I was determined to get back in the fight. I trained every day, worked so hard that I threw up, ignored what the doctors told me, convinced myself I needed to be better than I was before. I thought if I trained hard enough, I could... erase everything that had happened, somehow leave it behind.'

Alex's eyes were still on the picture. 'Why show me this now?'

'Because, Alex, I see the young woman in that picture sitting in front of me now,' she explained. 'And I don't want you to make the same mistakes I did.'

This situation was partly of her own making, she knew. Alex had come to her a few months ago, asked her to teach him how to fight, to protect himself, so that he wouldn't be a liability or a burden on anyone again. And after some deliberation, she had recognized the merits of this request and agreed.

She'd done it partly to give him the knowledge and skills he'd need to survive in this dangerous and unforgiving world he'd become part of. But mostly she'd hoped to divert his mind from the dark thoughts that weighed heavy on him since their deadly confrontation with Cain in Berlin the previous year.

In the first respect at least, she had been extremely successful. Alex had proven not only a willing but an able pupil, throwing himself into every task set for him with a fierce, almost obsessive dedication that was quite out of character.

The results spoke for themselves. Once weak and unfit from a life of bad food and little exercise, his body had hardened and strengthened over the past several months. He could strip down and reassemble weapons, shoot to a reasonable standard, even defend himself hand to hand after many painful but instructive lessons on her part.

He had worked hard all right. Perhaps a little too hard.

'And you think I'm trying to forget?'

Anya sighed. 'I know what Lauren meant to you. I know you blame yourself for what happened—'

'Blame myself?' His lips drew back in a grim, bitter smile. 'You've got it all wrong, Anya. I don't blame myself. I blame that fucking sadistic bastard Hawkins for gunning her down right in front of me. And I blame Cain for putting her there in the first place. And sooner or later I'm going to kill them both for what they've done.'

And there it was. Anya couldn't blame him for feeling like that, but such a path only had one end for someone like Alex. The enemies he'd set himself against were far beyond his abilities, no matter how much she might train or prepare him.

'Alex, I understand why you want them dead. But... that's a fight you can't win.'

'We'll see about that.'

'No we won't, because this goes no further,' she informed him firmly. Whatever deluded fantasy he was harbouring needed to be squashed now. 'Your training is finished.'

'Then what the hell was this all for?' he demanded. 'Why teach me all this stuff?'

'You asked for my help, I gave it to you.'

'You bullshitted me to keep me busy.'

Anya gave him a sharp look. 'I taught you to defend yourself, not to go looking for a fight. Believe me, the Agency will give you a fight you can never hope to win.' She sighed. 'Lauren gave her life to save yours. Throwing it away on a lost cause won't bring her back.'

Alex seemed to wilt at the mention of her name. Anya saw a moment of doubt in him, a moment of begrudging understanding. But it was quickly masked, turned into something that would serve him better. Defiance, anger, rebellion.

'So what's *your* plan?' he challenged her. 'Wait? We've done nothing but sit on our arses for six months, and where has it gotten us? Cain's the director of the CIA now. Fuck me, he'll probably be president by this time next year. How long do you really think it'll be before he finds us?'

For that, Anya had no answer. She and the rest of the group had escaped the confrontation in Berlin by the skin of their teeth. They'd been broken, both mentally and physically, by their brutal ordeal and left in no shape to mount any kind of offensive operation for some time. Instead they had retreated into hiding to rest and recuperate.

But this isolation had slowly lapsed into inertia as the days and weeks drifted by, as summer waxed and waned, the leaves turned brown and died, and the first snows of winter began to fall. Time had passed, and their desire to strike back at their enemies had faded.

They'd tried to make plans at first, of course. Meeting almost every day to discuss recent events and snatches of news that had reached them, trying to plan their next move. But these gatherings frequently descended into bitter arguments and recriminations that achieved nothing, and no firm consensus was ever reached.

Eventually they'd grown less frequent as their futility became obvious, and now it was almost unknown for the whole group to gather together. They were drifting apart, she knew, going their separate ways as the shared purpose and leadership that united them sputtered and failed.

Anya had rarely sought to question their lack of action, but deep down she knew the truth. They were afraid. Afraid they would gamble and lose again. Afraid none of them would make it back next time.

It was a fear that even she wasn't immune to.

'We have survived this long,' she replied. It was a weak retort and they both knew it.

'Is that all we're doing now? Surviving? That's what our glorious leader decided?'

Anya had no good answer for him. What the group needed now was strong leadership to reunite them. She herself couldn't provide it; too many of them had served under another, been through too much with him to answer to an outsider like her now.

What they needed was Ryan Drake.

But he was no longer with them. The Ryan Drake they needed hadn't been present since their escape from Berlin. The man left behind in his place had become sullen, withdrawn and uncommunicative, spending most of his time isolated in his apartment in Zurich, brooding on his past decisions and failures.

'It hasn't been an easy time for any of us. Ryan included.'

Alex's expression made it plain he wasn't convinced by that remark, or impressed by Drake's conduct thus far.

'Then help him,' he said, telling her what she already knew. 'Or get rid of him and move on. But do something, because we can't keep going like this any longer. Someone needs to lead us out of this, and if he can't do it any more...' Alex shrugged. 'Well, I don't suppose you need me to tell you.'

She didn't, and she also didn't appreciate his insinuation that Drake was some lost cause that they should simply abandon. She wouldn't allow herself to entertain such a notion. But that didn't mean she was able to refute it either.

Feeling he'd made his point, Alex rose stiffly from the chair, his legs starting to cramp up now he'd been sitting immobile for a while, and handed her back the photograph.

'It's a nice picture,' he said quietly. 'You should take better care of it.'

Anya leaned back as Alex departed, staring at the snow-covered mountains beyond her window but seeing nothing. Her thoughts were turned inwards, weighing up everything Alex had said. She hardly considered the young man a fountain of wisdom under normal circumstances, but even she was obliged to see the truth in his warning.

As difficult as it was to face up to, she knew deep down that something had to be done. The group needed a leader. It couldn't be her, so that left only one possibility. The only question was whether he still had it in him.

Well, we'll find out soon enough, she thought as she reached for her cell phone and set about composing a message.

Chapter 3

It was barely an hour after his meeting with Hogarth that Cain's personal cell phone chimed with an incoming message. There weren't many people who had access to his number, and he had a hunch who it might be.

The message was brief, direct and to the point.

NEED TO TALK. USUAL PLACE. 13.00.

And that was it. The sender didn't bother asking for acknowledgement, because there was no doubt about who held the power in this particular relationship. For now at least.

Cain knew exactly what the topic of discussion would be at today's meeting, and that was fine with him. For once, he had good news to deliver.

Thus, at one pm that day he found himself out in the woodland of Fairfax County, about ten miles from central DC. It was an unseasonably mild January afternoon in Virginia, the sun valiantly striving to break through the barrier of cloud that had hung low for most of the morning. The air smelled of moss and wet earth, the ground still covered by a carpet of last year's leaves.

It was a remote spot with only a few trails threading their way through the lichen-covered tree boles, lacking much in the way of scenery and offering little incentive for hikers or tourists, which made it ideal for meetings like these. However, a protective screen of armed agents patrolled the woods at a discreet distance just in case.

His contact was right on time, as always. Some men might have made Cain wait, but Richard Starke wasn't that kind of man. He was as precise and punctual as a Swiss watch, his mind structured around a world of mathematics, codes, ciphers and algorithms. As the director of the National Security Agency, America's premier codebreaking and electronic surveillance organization, these things were as vital to his daily life as oxygen.

His appearance mirrored his fastidious personality. Neither tall nor short, not overweight nor athletic, he was as thoroughly average a physical specimen as one could conceive. His face often wore a thoughtful, pensive expression, as if his mind was immersed in bigger issues, never quite in the here and now. A man who spoke less than he listened, who never sought the limelight and functioned best alone with his own thoughts.

His suit, shoes and tie were of good quality but conservative and practical, lacking any hint of style, flair or personality. Even his greying hair was cut short and neatly side parted, always in the same style, never a hair out of place.

Cain had known Starke for over a decade, and his appearance had changed so little that he often felt like he'd travelled back in time whenever they met. A grey man in grey clothes. To a casual observer, he was a nobody. Just another one of DC's anonymous government drones toiling away in some cubicle or windowless basement office. Easy to overlook, easy to forget, easy to underestimate.

That was exactly how he liked it.

'Marcus,' Starke said as he approached, which was about as close as he came to a welcome. He didn't offer to shake hands, and neither did Cain.

'You wanted to talk,' he mentioned.

Starke didn't break stride, instead brushing right past him. 'Walk with me.'

Cain fell into step beside him as he strolled along the forest path. He said nothing further, knowing that Starke spoke and acted only when he was ready.

They'd been walking almost a full minute before he considered it time to begin the conversation.

'Hogarth's finished his investigation.'

His tone made it plain this wasn't a question.

Cain nodded. 'Wallace's death was an accident. No further action will be taken.'

'Of course it won't,' Starke snorted. When Cain glanced at him, he carried on. 'Who do you think made that happen?'

Cain didn't respond.

'The group has people in his department. We always have,' Starke explained patiently. 'We made sure they were on his investigative team, and the right evidence found its way to him.'

'The group', as Starke referred to it, was the collective organization made up of prominent figures in each of the country's major intelligence, military and even executive agencies. A powerful assemblage of like-minded individuals united by a common goal, as influential and dangerous as it was secretive and insular.

For those on the outside, or foolish enough to believe they understood its nature and purpose, it was known by many names: the Section, the Circle, even the Syndicate. Each moniker was as true and as false as the other, since that was the very nature of the group. Deceit and subterfuge were its modus operandi, misdirection its greatest weapon.

To their uneasy allies and those coerced into doing their bidding, they represented a shifting entity of uncertain goals and identity, a dangerous combination of risk and reward that stifled insurrection and sowed the seeds of mistrust and paranoia. To their enemies or anyone unlucky enough to be caught in their path, they were a terrifying foe that could strike from any direction, thwart any stratagem and strike at any weakness.

They were everywhere and nowhere, as impossible to locate as they were to guard against.

Cain had been associated with this group for the best part of two decades, had risen slowly through their ranks via careful political manoeuvring and displays of skill, yet even he didn't know their full size and capabilities. They employed a great many people, but each was told only what they needed to know and no more. Few, if any, understood their ultimate goals and motivations.

For men like him, who had been lucky enough to find favour and rise from the lowest levels, actually earning their trust was a long and arduous process. Only now, with his rise to director of the CIA, did Cain stand a chance of interacting directly with the inner circle: the men at the very top of the pyramid who controlled the vast organization beneath.

'I'm grateful for their loyalty,' Cain said at last, his voice measured.

'Don't be,' Starke replied. 'This was damage limitation, nothing more. We both know Wallace didn't come to you that day to offer his condolences for the death of your daughter. The clean-up crew you used were sloppy, they left evidence behind that we had to deal with. You should have contacted me, we could have arranged better mitigating actions.'

'Time was a factor. I didn't want to—'

'You didn't want us to know, you mean?' Starke interrupted. 'Surely you realize that about the group by now, Marcus? We know everything.'

Cain reconsidered his approach. There was little to be gained by feigning innocence. 'Wallace could have compromised us. I had to take action, and I didn't want to risk contacting you.'

'That's a mistake I suggest you don't make again,' Starke informed him coldly. 'The group doesn't appreciate members acting on their own initiative. We haven't survived as long as we have by tolerating loose cannons.'

It was a sobering reminder that his position was far from safe, no matter what Hogarth's investigation had decided. Cain knew all too well that careers and even lives had been ended by the group for acts of insubordination.

'So why did you help me?'

Starke paused. 'We've got a lot invested in you. For now at least you're still considered useful, but think carefully on that, Marcus. Investments are only maintained while they continue to pay off.'

Cain clenched his fists, well aware of the implicit threat. But at the same time, he began to perceive a tension in Starke's posture, a strain in his voice that hadn't been there before. Starke possessed many admirable traits – a ferocious intellect, a ruthless ability to solve problems and a formidable political savvy, to name but a few – but to Cain's trained eye he had always been a poor liar, preferring to obfuscate and reinterpret rather than fabricate a new reality. Starke's was a profession that dealt in facts, numbers, calculations, probabilities, not active deceit and subterfuge. That was Cain's domain, and he was very good at it.

He began to perceive the man beside him in a new light, to understand that the source of his unease was more personal than collective.

'It was you, wasn't it?' he said suddenly, deciding to play his hand. 'You did this.'

'What?'

'You're the one who's got too much invested in me, not them,' Cain said, his tone harder and more forceful now. '*You* vouched for me, brought me into the group, helped me rise through the ranks. If I go down, then ultimately you're the one they'll blame. That's why *you've* kept this from the group. It was damage control of your own reputation, wasn't it, Richard?'

Starke stopped walking and turned to face him. His thoughtful expression had been replaced by a look of anger. And Cain knew he had him. After all these years, he finally had the measure of the man.

'Be careful, Marcus,' the NSA director warned him. 'You're forgetting yourself.'

Cain raised his chin. 'I know exactly who I am. I'm the director of the CIA.'

'*Acting* Director,' Starke reminded him. 'Until they find someone permanent.'

'You're looking at him.'

'The office of CIA director is a political appointment, not an executive one,' Starke informed him tersely. 'You need the president and congress behind you. There will be hearings, investigations, confirmations.'

'So what? My record speaks for itself, and the group owns enough of congress to get me confirmed. I can do so much more without some asshole wannabe politician watching over my shoulder. So what's the problem, Richard?'

'The problem is *we* haven't given you permission!' Starke snapped. 'After all this time, don't you understand that? You don't get to decide when things like this happen – *we do*. We always have. That's the way this works. That's how the group operates.'

'I've served the group's interests for 20 years, Richard,' Cain said, taking a step towards him. He was well aware of the risks of openly challenging this man, but he was committed now. There was no going back. 'Twenty fucking *years* of my life I've given to you. Now you're going to give something back.'

'You think you're the only one who's made sacrifices for us?' Starke took a breath. 'Men have served a lot longer than you and been rewarded with a lot less.'

'Other men, not me. I want this, Richard. I *deserve* this.'

'You *deserve* nothing,' Starke hit back. 'People are promoted if and when it serves the group's interests, not their own personal ambitions or what they think they deserve. There's a plan, and for now at least you have a part to play in it. I strongly advise you to be content with that.'

'A plan can change.'

Starke was resolute. 'Ours won't. You of all people should know that.'

He was leaving Cain with no option. 'Then maybe you should take a minute to consider what might happen if it doesn't.'

'What exactly are you saying?'

'Come on, Richard. You're the numbers man here. You deal in probabilities and risk analysis. What do you think I might do if you screw me over? I have no close friends, no wife, no family. My only child's dead.' His throat tightened. 'What do you think the chances are that I might just snap and cash in all my chips, tell Hogarth everything, destroy that precious reputation you've worked so hard to protect?'

Cain stared at him, standing just a foot or so away. Starke didn't often make eye contact, and Cain knew he was uncomfortable with such direct engagement, which was why he made a point of doing it now. He wanted Starke to know the kind of man he was dealing with.

'You wouldn't do something as stupid as that. You've played this game too long.' He tried to phrase it as a firm, conclusive judgement, but there was a slight waver, a hint of uncertainty in his voice.

'In the past 20 years I've lost everything and everyone I ever cared about. I've sacrificed everything I have for the group,' Cain admitted. 'If I wanted to, I could destroy a dozen different operations, cripple your plans for years to come, burn the entire group to the fucking ground. Because I have nothing left to lose. You do. You should think very carefully on *that*, Richard.'

Cain thought Starke was going to physically attack him. He tensed up, waiting for the inevitable explosion.

It never came. Instead, Starke showed a flicker of a smile – hard and derisive.

'Well, how about that?' he said, his tone faintly mocking. 'Marcus Cain, finally ready to step up to the big leagues. Didn't think you had it in you.'

Cain waited in threatening silence, knowing there was more coming.

'All right, Marcus,' Starke said at last. 'But if you really want a seat at the big table, I suggest you bring something worthwhile with you.'

'I already have something.'

'Something?'

'Some*one* we've been after for a long time.'

Starke's posture shifted a little at that. He knew who Cain was referring to.

It was a man the Agency, the group, the whole Western world had been hunting for the past decade. A man who had overseen the deadliest terror attack in human history, whose actions had triggered two wars and resulted in hundreds of thousands of casualties. It had taken a plethora of clandestine operations, assassination and even tense personal negotiation on Cain's part, but at last the prize was within his grasp.

The leader of al-Qaeda. Usama bin Mohammed bin Awad bin Ladin, better known by his Westernized title.

Osama bin Laden.

Even Starke looked impressed by this claim, though it was tempered by his typical wariness. 'If you're screwing with me—'

'I'm not. The intel is credible.'

He considered this before nodding. Cold and analytical as he was, Starke had watched those haunting images of the towers coming down, the bodies on the streets, the dust clouds covering Manhattan. This was a prize even he couldn't ignore.

'I'll make some calls,' he said at length. 'But before I do, I suggest you get your house in order.'

'Meaning?'

Starke cocked an eyebrow. 'The thorn in our collective side. It's starting to look like a loose end you just can't tie up. Would that be right?'

Cain was all too aware of the thorn that Starke was referring to. Actually, two thorns. The first was Ryan Drake, a former CIA operative whom Cain had viewed as nothing more than a pawn to be used and sacrificed. But the man had somehow slipped from his grasp and continued to pose a threat.

The second was a ghost from Cain's more distant past. Anya, once the most promising of protégés, had turned against him, coming after him again and again, leaving a trail of bodies in her wake. Her pursuit of vengeance had even resulted in the death of his own daughter last year.

Either of these threats he could deal with alone, but together they represented a growing problem that was requiring more and more effort to contain. Worse, they were attracting others to their cause.

'I don't leave loose ends. You should know that about me by now.'

The only question was how to find them. Both Drake and Anya had effectively disappeared, dropping off the map and maintaining a low profile for more than six months. But he knew they would come after him again sooner or later. They had to.

This was a fight that only one side would survive.

'Then handle this, Marcus,' Starke said, leaning in close and lowering his voice. 'Handle it before you waste all that capital you've just earned. Don't force the group to do it for you.'

Chapter 4

Zurich, Switzerland

Fists raised and body taut with anticipation, Ryan Drake circled his opponent with slow, deliberate steps, trying to focus his thoughts and control his breathing. Breathing was the key to movement, which in turn was the key to controlling the fight.

Nearby, his opponent matched his position, fingers tensing and relaxing. Only a sheen of sweat coated her skin in the dim glow of the overhead electric lights, and she gave little outward sign of fatigue. Despite being in her mid-forties now, her body was still lean and muscular from a lifetime of active service, and more agile than many soldiers a decade younger. Her thick blonde hair was tied back with a single band at the nape of her neck, while her steely blue eyes were locked on him, waiting for an opening.

Anya wasn't by nature an offensive fighter. Lacking the brute strength and size needed to dominate a fight, she preferred to let her opponent make the first move, using her superior experience and skill to frustrate their attacks. But when she did decide to retaliate, it was as lethal as it was explosive.

'Again,' she said, her voice calm and composed.

They had been at it for nearly an hour now. Drake had received a message from her earlier this afternoon requesting a meeting at the run-down boxing gym on the eastern edge of the city that he was known to attend on occasion. Usually out of hours by paying the owner a little extra, allowing him to train alone.

It had been obvious enough what she had in mind tonight. Anya had sparred with him before, using the physical activity to reach out to him as he became increasingly withdrawn. He'd been reluctant to come at all, but he knew she wouldn't be put off.

'So are you going to tell me what this is all about?' he asked.

'I could ask the same of you, Ryan.'

'What's that supposed to mean?'

'You know exactly what it means.' Her tone was sharp and accusing. 'You have not been with us for months. You shut yourself away, you don't talk to any of us, you leave the group without a leader. Why?'

Drake lunged at her, feinting left before sidestepping right. He swung with a punch that was both hard and fast – she had urged him never to hold back in training. His fist missed her by mere inches, but it was enough for her to move forward, sweep her leg behind his and slam him into the canvas. Like most boxing rings, there was a certain amount of give to the floor to prevent serious injury, but it was still a painful experience.

'You're hiding, Ryan,' the older woman said as she circled him, muscles bunching and releasing with each step. 'But what are you really hiding from?'

Drake rose stiffly, angered at being taken down so easily. Even more angered by her line of questioning. 'You don't know what you're talking about.'

If he'd hoped to defuse the situation, he was wrong. 'I know *you*,' she chastised him. 'This isn't who you are. This isn't the man I know.'

Again he came at her, ducking below her guard, lunging left and sweeping his fist upwards in a vicious uppercut. Anya dodged it, but only just. As she backed off a pace, he launched a roundhouse kick aimed at her midsection. Unable to avoid it entirely, she instead twisted sideways, absorbing some of the energy then grabbing his leg and trying to yank him off his feet.

He was ready for this, shoving her backwards before she had a chance to take him down. Anya went with it, taking the impact as she hit the canvas and using her momentum to roll into a crouch, ready to spring to her feet again.

'Then maybe you don't know me as well as you think.'

'Don't I?' Anya challenged him. 'I think you don't know yourself.'

Drake hesitated, struck by her candour. The last few months had drifted by as a vaguely remembered blur, the monotony of each day blending into the next so that Drake had found himself losing track of time. Losing track of himself. Some days he'd wander out of his apartment and return with no recollection of where he'd gone or what he'd done. One time he'd awoken in his bed and discovered, to his shock and disbelief, that almost a week had passed.

You're not yourself – that's what people said. Maybe there was more truth to that statement than they knew. If Drake wasn't himself, then who exactly was he? Might he fall asleep one night and awaken as a different man for ever?

'I could have killed you a dozen times over today, Ryan,' she said, pacing back and forth like a caged lion. 'You fight like you're in a dream. Well, *wake up now!*'

Drake glared at her. Their training sessions were always strenuous, but there was a line they didn't cross. They were both trained killers, and the potential for an accident in unrestricted combat was all too real. Why was she pitting herself against him like this?

'I don't want to hurt you,' he cautioned her.

'Hurt me?' Her voice was almost mocking now. 'You're not even worthy of my time.'

Anger flared up inside him as he moved in on her, fists clenched, muscles tight and coiled, poised to strike. If she wanted a fight, he'd give her one.

Their confrontation was short but vicious, both of them throwing and landing blows that hit with bruising force. Both were tiring after nearly an hour of such punishment, but Drake's greater size and strength combined with his growing frustration gave him an edge. Managing to sidestep and avoid a hard strike, he caught Anya's outstretched arm and twisted it behind her back. She would have

27

no choice but to submit now if she didn't want a dislocated shoulder, and he tightened the pressure to remind her of that fact.

'Had enough?' he asked as she tried to free herself.

He could feel the warmth radiating from her skin, smell the faint tang of sweat and hear her rapid breathing. And he became acutely conscious of her body pressed against his: the smooth muscles of her legs, the soft mounds of her buttocks, the pounding of her pulse.

Anya turned her head a little to look at him and he caught a glimmer of something in her eye. A sensual, almost primal look of attraction, of need and desire, that elicited an instinctive response.

His lapse was brief, but it was enough. Lashing out with her other arm, she drove an elbow into his side, winding him and loosening his grip enough to pull her arm free, before pivoting around and throwing him to the ground once more.

She was breathing a little harder from the exertion, and a loose tendril of hair had escaped the tie to fall in front of her face. The look of attraction and arousal had vanished, replaced by one of anger and disappointment.

'Are you really so easy to manipulate?' she demanded, pacing again. 'Thinking with your balls instead of your brain. Is that how McKnight was able to fool you so long?'

Drake rose slowly to his feet, his expression hardening. Forceful sparring was one thing, but reminding him of past failures and betrayals was something very different. Samantha McKnight had been a trusted member of his team for over two years. More than that, she'd been someone very special to him. The fact she'd proven to be a spy working for their enemies, and that her betrayal had resulted in the death of one of his team, still cut deep more than six months later.

'You don't want to do this.'

She didn't back down, because she knew she was getting the reaction she wanted at last. 'Don't tell me what I want, Ryan. I told you to fight me, so fight. For once, do something like you mean it!'

She was right, of course. Drake had been holding back, pulling his punches and carefully limiting his aggression. But Anya was wrong about his motives, perceiving his lack of commitment as condescension. She couldn't know the real reason he was reluctant to fight.

'What are you afraid of?' Anya demanded, jabbing him in the chest. 'Afraid I'm wrong, and I can't stop you? Or that I'm right, and you don't have what it takes any more?'

'Let's not find out,' he cautioned her. 'Back off.'

She moved in to push him again, but this time his hand swept upwards and batted her arm forcefully away. That was all the excuse Anya needed, coming in hard and fast with a flurry of kicks and punches, intent on knocking him down properly.

A hard strike to the side of his face knocked him off balance, and for a few seconds the world seemed to blur and he felt darkness close in around him.

That was when it happened. A blur of confused and disjointed images exploded inside his mind, bursting into life like flashes of lightning.

He saw fire and smoke, charred bodies and heard the cries of dying men. Silent figures stalking through the black haze with drawn weapons, the sun bathing the entire scene blood red. Drake was stalking through this chaos with a rifle up at his shoulder, gunfire ringing out all around him, eagerly searching for a target.

Anya was closing in to strike him again, but he barely noticed. His mind was consumed by the sounds and images tumbling before his eyes, each one coming faster and more vividly.

Drake was moving again, stinging smoke and heat rasping his throat. The sun casting a crimson glow on everything. Silent, faceless men with drawn weapons surrounded him. Enemies or friends, he couldn't tell.

A blood-red sun, growing stronger and darker. Becoming like a black hole sucking in everything, until the world itself was swallowed up around him.

Screams echoed in the darkness.

Even as Anya drew back her arm to hit him again, he whirled around and lashed out, parrying the strike and retaliating with a speed and power that caught even the veteran operative off guard. Drake was barely even aware of what he was doing; it was as if his body had developed a will of its own and he was merely observing its terrible actions.

He saw himself going on the attack, advancing on her, vaguely felt the jarring blows as they slipped through her guard and began to land. He saw himself reach out, lift her off the floor and throw her to the canvas.

He should have felt shock and horror at seeing the woman he cared for so deeply hurt at his own hands, but that wasn't how he felt at all. Instead he was filled with joy, elation and excitement at seeing an enemy down and vulnerable. He felt a great upwelling of satisfaction in knowing he'd beaten her, along with an overwhelming desire to finish the job.

Never leave your enemy standing. Never let them rise again. Finish her now!

He was on top of her, using his size and strength to pin her down. Experienced and tough she might have been, but even Anya couldn't stop him as he clamped a hand around her throat and squeezed. His eyes met hers, and for the first time he saw fear in them. The fear of a hunted animal.

Kill her!

'Ryan,' she managed to gasp before his grip closed off her airway. 'Ryan… stop.'

The sound of her voice seemed to cut through the fog of rage that had enveloped him, and Drake came back to himself with a startled groan, then released his grip.

He was vaguely aware of something sharp pressing into his side, and looked down to see Anya holding a knife against his abdomen, just below the protective bone wall of his ribcage. A single upward thrust would be enough to puncture lungs, sever arteries, inflict an injury that would kill him in a matter of minutes. She must have had the weapon concealed throughout the sparring session, ready and waiting.

'Are you going to use that?' he asked.

'Only if I must. Now back off.' He could see red marks around her neck where he'd very nearly choked her unconscious.

Drake rose slowly to his feet, keeping his hands where she could see them. He wanted to reach out to her, to tell her not to be afraid, to reassure her that he was himself again. He wanted to, but he couldn't. Because she would know he was lying.

Anya too stood up, lowering the knife but keeping her grip on it all the same. The seconds stretched out as they watched each other across the open training area, afraid to move, neither one saying a word.

Finally she broke the silence.

'You wanted to kill me.' It came out not as an accusation or a rebuke, but a simple statement of fact.

He had nothing to give but the truth.

'Yes.'

'Why?'

Drake shook his head, trying to gather his confused thoughts. 'It was... I felt like a different person. Like someone else was in control.'

'Do you recognize this person?'

He wanted to say no, wanted to tell her it had been a fluke, an aberration, but he knew it wouldn't be true. And Anya would know it too. The person he'd momentarily become, the murderous thoughts that filled his mind had felt chillingly familiar. And worst of all, welcome.

His silence told its own story, and Anya nodded in sad acceptance.

'You knew, didn't you?' he prompted. 'You knew this would happen. That's why you pushed so hard, why you had the knife.'

'I had to, Ryan. There is another side to you, a side I don't understand, and I don't think you do either. I saw it once before, in Berlin. You have been different ever since that day, and I needed to understand why. I thought I could... make you face it. Drive it out somehow and bring back the man I remember, the man we need now. But I don't think I can. It's worse than I thought.'

'So that's what I am now?' he asked. 'A threat? An enemy?'

Anya shook her head. 'I have risked my life for you before, and I would do it again. But this is something I can't protect you from. There's a... darkness inside you. I don't know what it is or where it came from, but it is there. And I'm afraid it's getting stronger.'

Drake didn't say anything to this. Every word was a great weight settling on him, and instinctively his mind rebelled against it, screaming that she was wrong, that he knew himself, what he was capable of and who he was.

He'd been a soldier for much of his adult life, had fought, killed and very nearly been killed on many occasions. He accepted those risks, made peace with the life he'd chosen, knowing that it might well end before his time. But not to know one's own mind, to feel as if there were another Ryan Drake living within him – that was something else entirely.

'What if that darkness is who I really am?' he asked, voicing a question neither of them had dared articulate until now. 'What if I've been living a lie?'

For once, Anya was at a loss. 'I can't give you those answers, Ryan. But one way or another you need to find them and face them.'

The finality of that statement made him feel even worse than before.

Anya turned away and withdrew from the room, leaving Drake alone.

Chapter 5

George Breckenridge had sensed this meeting coming for a while now, the way an antelope can sense a lion watching it from the long grass.

His foot tapped nervously on the carpet as he awaited his summons to the divisional leader's office. He was uneasy, agitated, and unable to hide either fact. Though he'd never served as a field operative, he'd been with the Agency long enough to know that the bureaucracy and power struggles at Langley could be just as ruthless and unforgiving as any mission behind enemy lines.

Or so he liked to tell himself.

The desk phone nearby buzzed, and the efficient, middle-aged secretary stationed there picked it up.

'Yes, sir?' She listened for a moment or two, then set it down again.

'Go on in, Mr Breckenridge,' she said, her manner brisk and unemotional. 'Mr Franklin will see you now.'

Might as well get it over with, he thought bleakly. Rising from his chair, Breckenridge squared his shoulders and crossed the outer office with what he hoped was a confident, purposeful stride.

The office of the director of the CIA's Special Activities Division was surprisingly small and austere for such a senior position. The desk and other furniture were basic and unadorned. The carpet was simple and hard-wearing, the windows facing out across the sprawling Langley campus to the Old Headquarters Building and the extensive parkland that lay beyond. Neat and efficient, but starkly impersonal.

Nonetheless, it was an office Breckenridge had once held ambitions of occupying.

'George, good to see you,' Dan Franklin said, crossing the room to shake his hand. *Getting around a lot better these days*, Breckenridge noted with sour grace.

Franklin's military career had been cut short by a roadside bomb in Afghanistan nearly ten years ago, leaving him with spinal injuries and chronic pain which had gradually worsened over the years, eventually forcing him to undergo major surgery. His recovery had been laborious, and for a while it had seemed he might be forced into early retirement.

But Franklin was nothing if not determined, throwing himself into rehab, chipping away at it day by day, and it seemed his efforts were now paying off.

His posture recalled something of the strength and vigour of the soldier he'd once been, with only a barely noticeable limp hinting at the extent of his old injuries.

'And you, Dan,' Breckenridge replied, knowing it was a complete lie. But thinking it best to take the initiative, he added, 'You asked to see me?'

'Please, take a seat,' he said, indicating a chair facing his desk.

Both men sat down, with Franklin opening a drawer in his desk and lifting out a bottle of whisky, followed by a pair of glasses. He glanced up questioningly at his subordinate. Breckenridge shook his head. He wasn't exactly a teetotaller, but neither was he fond of malt liquor. It never sat well on his stomach.

'Suit yourself,' he conceded, pouring himself a glass. 'Personally, I find a drink takes the edge off at times like this. Little habit I picked up from my predecessor.'

Breckenridge considered that. Franklin's predecessor was now acting director of the CIA. However, he was more concerned at the man's choice of words.

'Times like this?'

Here it comes, he thought. *I'm being cut loose.*

It wasn't exactly surprising, he supposed. Breckenridge had once been head of the Agency's Shepherd programme – the highly trained paramilitary group tasked with finding and rescuing compromised CIA assets. If a spy or valuable informant went missing, it was the Shepherd's job to bring them home. It was difficult and dangerous work, and in many cases their missing asset came home in a casket, but they'd also had their share of spectacular successes.

Until two years ago, at least. That was when Ryan Drake and his team had gone rogue during a mission in Libya, prompting Marcus Cain to unceremoniously terminate the Shepherd programme pending a review of its conduct and personnel. And leaving Breckenridge stranded without a job.

He'd bounced around various administrative roles since then, most of which had been a step down from his previous position, and none of which entailed any real responsibility or authority. Nobody had said it out loud, but it was clear. He was tainted by his association with Drake and the Shepherd teams, damaged goods. A man whose once promising career was on a fast track to nowhere.

The director of Special Activities Division took a sip of his whisky.

'I guess there's no point beating around the bush on this one,' he said.

Breckenridge tensed like he was about to absorb a punch to the face. 'The fact is, George, I'm planning on reactivating the Shepherd programme,' Franklin stated firmly, laying down the sentence as if it were a rubber stamp on some official form. 'On a small scale at first, using a pool of carefully vetted operatives, but it's not going to be easy to get this thing up and running again. It's been two years since we closed it down, and a lot of the specialists we used to draw from have been poached by other programmes or moved into the private sector. There's not the operational experience that there used to be, so we'll need a man who's familiar with the old protocols to oversee it.' He tilted his glass towards his subordinate. 'I want that man to be you, George.'

Breckenridge blinked, stunned by what he'd just heard. Franklin's revelation was the exact opposite of what he'd expected to be told today. He'd prepared himself to lose his job. He'd been facing up to the unhappy prospect of looking for a new career at 50 years old, with a mortgage he couldn't afford and a retirement plan in tatters, but at least he'd been ready for it in his own way.

But not this. This changed everything.

'I… think I'll have that drink after all,' he managed to say.

Smiling in amusement, Franklin poured him a measure. He downed a mouthful, shuddering as it went down. Still, it did serve to calm his thoughts a little, allowing him to formulate a better response. 'But I thought Director Cain shut down the Shepherd programme? It was done.'

'It was, but the need for it hasn't changed. Even Cain recognizes that.'

What he didn't add was that over the past couple of years, Cain had methodically removed any case officers or specialists who were potentially still loyal to Ryan Drake. He might have agreed to resurrect the Shepherd programme, but only with 'reliable people' in the mix. And one of those people was George Breckenridge.

Franklin leaned forward, his smile gone now. 'But let's be clear about one thing. You report in to me, and me alone now. You keep me informed about everything that happens, and I decide what goes further up the chain. Are we absolutely clear on that?'

Even Breckenridge was savvy enough to take his meaning. There would be no going over his head, no clandestine reports to people above him. The buck stopped with Dan Franklin from now on, or Breckenridge's career would sure as shit stop with him too.

'Clear.'

Franklin's smile returned, a little more relaxed and genuine than before. The two men clinked their glasses and finished their drinks.

Breckenridge was in a considerably better mood driving home from Langley that evening than he'd been when he'd left for work that morning. He even stopped off at a 7-Eleven just off Maple Avenue in Fairfax to pick up a bottle of champagne on a whim. Their selection was limited and their prices overinflated, but he didn't care too much. Screw the ulcers for one night: he was in the mood for celebrating.

He felt energized, invigorated, confident like he hadn't been in a long time. Even the overcast winter skies and gathering darkness couldn't dampen his mood. He was back on top again. That fucking asshole Drake might have derailed his career for a year or two, but he'd been given a second chance now. His talents had been recognized, his contributions valued, his—

He was passing through an intersection, about to turn south for the last leg of his journey, when the bomb placed on the underside of his 2010 Ford Fusion detonated. Placed right beneath the driver's footwell, Breckenridge barely had time to process the orange flash, the sudden storm of metal and debris and fire before he was consumed by the blast and killed. The fuel tank ruptured a second or so later, adding about 30 gallons of gasoline to the inferno that consumed both car and passenger.

The stricken vehicle rolled on for another 50 yards or so under its own momentum, slewing off the road and into a street light, flames roaring from the shattered windows. Other cars swerved and skidded to avoid it, the few pedestrians who were out and about on that winter evening unable to get within 20 yards due to the intense heat. At least a dozen people reached for their phones within seconds of the crash, most dialling 911, a few switching their cameras to video mode to record the whole thing.

It would be a further nine minutes before the first fire truck arrived on the scene, by which time George Breckenridge and the bottle of champagne he'd been looking forward to opening that evening would be reduced to ash.

Chapter 6

Thirteen, fourteen, fifteen, sixteen…

Keira Frost exhaled as she pulled herself up again, muscles straining to raise her body weight up above the chin-up bar she'd installed in the door frame of her cramped, low-rent apartment.

Seventeen, eighteen, nineteen…

Her arms were burning with the effort, biceps straining against the pull of gravity, but still she persisted, forcing her tired body to comply with her demands. Her vest was damp with sweat, the fabric clinging uncomfortably to her skin.

Twenty, twenty-one…

Almost there. Twenty-five. She wanted twenty-five.

Twenty-two…

She tried to raise herself one last time, but her arms would no longer oblige. She hung there, half-raised, trembling with the effort as she sought some reserve of strength that no longer existed, before finally letting go and dropping to the floor.

'God-fucking-damn it,' she muttered, reaching for the bottle of beer on the table nearby and draining what was left in a single gulp.

As she slammed the bottle back down, she caught sight of her right hand. A small, straight line of scar tissue about an inch long marked both the palm and the back of it. A little reminder of the knife blade that had been driven straight through it six months earlier, pinning her hand to a table.

That had hurt, she reflected. Hurt like a son of a bitch. Even now, all this time later, it still pained her during cold weather. And the weather was cold indeed in this part of the world.

Raising the hand up, she slowly tensed and extended her fingers, testing the grip, seeing how well the nerves and muscles and tendons responded. They moved, but not as easily as the other hand. Took more conscious effort on her part. The tips of the last two fingers were still a little numb. The digits were no longer a natural extension of her mind, but rather a tool that required focussed attention to operate.

She clenched the hand into a fist, wishing she could drive it into the face of the man who had done this to her. Pay him back in some small measure.

The TV was playing on the other side of the room at low volume, tuned to CNN, the expertly coiffed anchor recapping the news headlines now that they were at the top of the hour.

'More protests in Tunisia today as demonstrators turned out in force on the streets of the capital, calling for political reform and the resignation of President Ben Ali, who has been in power since taking office in 1987.'

The report switched to show images of massed civilian demonstrators marching through the streets of Tunis, clutching banners and handwritten signs, most of them calling for Ben Ali to step down and make way for new leadership.

'Many of these protests were sparked by the dramatic revelations at the end of November of corruption and embezzlement of public funds by the Ben Ali regime, which has become increasingly repressive and hard line in recent years, with police frequently intervening to break up demonstrators.'

Once again the images changed, this time showing protestors hurling bricks and petrol bombs at police lines, police responding with tear gas and riot shield charges, and demonstrators being beaten and hauled into custody.

Another impoverished state struggling in vain to escape from beneath another dictator. Frost was still young, but shit like that was already getting old for her.

'Yeah, good luck with that,' Frost mumbled, heading to the fridge for another beer.

She'd just swung the door open and was surveying the paltry selection of ready meals inside when the news feed abruptly switched back to the studio. 'We interrupt this report to bring you an update on the car bomb explosion in Washington DC earlier this evening, which left one person dead and several others with minor injuries. The victim of this attack has now been named as George Breckenridge, a 51-year-old employee of the Central Intelligence Agency.'

Frost swung around as the man's driving licence picture appeared on screen next to the news anchor. *It couldn't be*, she thought to herself. *It just couldn't.*

But it was. Same greying hair, same fleshy face, same look of condescension that she'd come to know all too well.

'The CIA has yet to comment on the death of Mr Breckenridge, but already there is heavy speculation that his death was a terrorist act. We now go live to Gina Harkness, who is on the scene...'

'Fuck me!' Frost whispered, reaching for her phone.

Chapter 7

Drake took another gulp of whisky straight from the bottle as he paced back and forth across his small apartment. The walls seemed to be closing in, the air claustrophobic and suffocating. He felt like a caged animal, burning with energy that he couldn't expel.

His unrestrained sparring session with Anya earlier had only made the problem worse.

Over and over he saw himself knock her to the ground, felt his hands close around her throat, imagined himself choking the life out of her. The exhilaration, the primal bloodlust was so strong and immediate even now that he had to consciously fight it back.

Anya's words echoed in his ears, mocking his refusal to accept the truth.

'There's a... darkness inside you. I don't know what it is or where it came from, but it is there. And I'm afraid it's getting stronger.'

The buzz of his cell phone jolted him away from these dark thoughts, at least temporarily. Normally he would have been irritated and reluctant to answer, but tonight he welcomed the distraction. He was surprised to see Frost's number.

What the hell could she want at such a late hour?

'Keira, what—'

'Turn your TV on,' the young woman blurted out. 'Go to CNN now.'

He frowned. 'Why?'

'Just fucking do it, Ryan!'

Swearing under his breath, he snatched up the TV remote and searched for CNN. His eyes danced across the headline ticker scrolling along the bottom, the image of a twisted, charred vehicle surrounded by police and forensics teams, the file photo of a man, believed to be the victim of a terrorist attack. He understood it all in the space of a couple of seconds.

'Jesus,' he whispered.

George Breckenridge, dead. Killed by a car bomb on his way home from work.

Drake was hardly the man's biggest fan, finding him to be arrogant and obstructive at the best of times. In fact, in the time he worked with Breckenridge as a Shepherd operative, he couldn't recall ever having a favourable impression of him, but that didn't mean he wanted to see the man dead.

'It gets worse, Ryan.' She sounded shaken. 'The guy who did this has released a video claiming responsibility.'

'What do you mean? Who?'

Frost was silent, searching for the right words, the right way of explaining what she'd just witnessed. But she didn't have to. The news anchor beat her to it.

'The group claiming responsibility for this attack has released a video to CNN and several other news outlets.'

Drake stood rooted to the spot as the footage began to play.

It depicted a lone man seated in front of a plain black background, his face covered by a balaclava that left only his eyes and mouth exposed. The poor sound and video quality made it obvious this clip had been recorded on a basic camera set-up, perhaps even a phone. There seemed to be an odd flicker to the image, as if the frames were slightly out of sync with the audio, which itself contained a lot of static noise: electronic buzzing, unusual pops and bleeps, and snatches of some kind of music that faded in and out.

The result was a discordant jumble of low-level noise that caused the hairs on the back of Drake's neck to prickle, and a chill to run through him. It wasn't a chill of foreboding, but rather recognition. He'd heard these sounds before.

'Now you've seen what I can do, but what you don't understand is why,' the man began. His voice had been digitally altered to change the tone and inflection. 'This is the first strike in a new war, a war against people who want to keep you weak and ignorant and afraid. People who live in the shadows, hiding behind veils of secrecy and lies. If those people are watching now, I have a message for them.' He leaned in closer to the camera. 'Your time is over. I have no demands, I'm not interested in negotiation or compromise. I can't be silenced, and I will not stop until every one of you is made to pay. This is my promise to you.'

His next words would haunt Drake for the rest of his days.

'My name is Ryan Drake,' he said. 'And this is just the beginning.'

'Ryan, tell me you just saw what I saw,' Frost said urgently, her voice sounding curiously far off. 'What the fuck is going on?'

But Drake wasn't hearing her. Something was happening to him, something deeper and more frightening than having his name used by an impostor. He felt as if a hole had been torn in his psyche and all kinds of dark things were pouring through it.

Another flash, a memory. An old memory that had haunted him for a long time. Old but terrifyingly vivid, as if the past had leaked into the present, becoming real and tangible again.

Fire and smoke, charred bodies, the cries of dying men. Silent figures stalking through the black haze with drawn weapons, the sun bathing the entire scene blood red. Drake moving through this chaos with a rifle up at his shoulder, gunfire ringing out all around him, eagerly searching for a target.

Until at last he found one.

Drake ran a shaking hand through his hair, squeezed his eyes shut in a vain effort to block it out. It made no difference. The flashes were coming faster now, stronger. He couldn't stop them.

'What if that darkness is who I really am? What if I've been living a lie?'

39

Dropping the phone, he stumbled through to the bathroom. He leaned over the sink as the pulse pounded in his ears and a maelstrom of images whirled through his mind, faster and faster, unstoppable in their intensity.

He looked at his reflection in the mirror, expecting to see his own face, flushed with drink and anger. But he didn't. The man staring back at him was a stranger, a monster who had been lurking in the darkness. A monster whose lips slowly parted to reveal a triumphant smile.

The smile of the victor over the vanquished.

Drake was moving again, stinging smoke and heat rasping his throat. The sun casting a crimson glow on everything. Silent, faceless men with drawn weapons surrounded him. Enemies or friends, he couldn't tell.

Drawing back his fist in a sudden, uncontrollable explosion of fury, Drake slammed it into that mocking smile, wanting to crush it, destroy it, purge that monster from his mind for ever.

Hot pain blossomed from his hand and shattered glass tumbled into the sink.

A blood-red sun, growing stronger and darker. A black hole sucking in everything, until the world itself was swallowed up around him.

Screams echoed in the darkness.

He squeezed his eyes shut as the memories cascaded together into an unbearable crescendo, and his world collapsed around him into darkness.

Darkness and silence.

Drake drew in a breath, long and slow, filling his lungs with new life. He exhaled, revelling in the simple sensation that seemed to have been denied him for so long.

When he opened his eyes, he was himself again. The fear and anger and conflict had vanished. Drake's mind felt perfectly clear and focussed.

He could feel warmth on his hand, and glanced down to see blood trickling from several deep cuts, deep crimson staining the white porcelain. It should have hurt, but the pain didn't trouble him. Reaching for a nearby towel, he wrapped it around the injured hand to slow the bleeding, then turned away from the broken mirror.

He was himself again, whole and perfect and ready. And he knew what he had to do.

Chapter 8

Anya woke to the sound of hammering on her front door, the hard thump of fists on wood echoing through the quiet night-time stillness of the house. Her eyes snapped open immediately, her mind rousing itself to full alertness in seconds. The thumping continued. Whoever was out there wasn't taking no for an answer, leaving her with little choice but to venture out.

Reaching beneath the bed, she pulled out the Colt M1911 semi-automatic she always kept there and racked back the slide to chamber the first round. M1911s were single-action weapons, meaning the first round had to be manually drawn into the breech and the hammer pulled back before they could be fired.

They could be carried in a number of configurations, with many people favouring a full magazine and empty chamber with no safety engaged. Anya however preferred to carry the weapon 'cocked and locked' with a round chambered and the safety on. It was more intuitive to her, and allowed the weapon to be primed and fired with one hand.

Armed and ready, she swung her legs over the edge of the bed. She was barefoot and wearing only her nightclothes, but she could move quickly and quietly like this.

Advancing into the corridor with the weapon, she made it as far as the small wall-mounted screen that displayed the feed from the hidden camera at her front door. A young woman was hammering impatiently on her door, dressed in bike leathers, her short dark hair in disarray.

'Anya, open the goddamn door!' Keira Frost demanded. 'Quit screwing around!'

Letting out an exasperated breath, Anya laid the weapon down on a nearby shelf, then unlocked the door.

Frost pushed her way inside, accompanied by a chill gust of wind. The younger woman flashed Anya an irritable look as she passed.

'Jesus, would it kill you to turn your cell phone on?' Frost called over her shoulder as she made for the living room. 'I've been trying to call you for the past hour.'

Anya slammed the front door shut with rather more force than necessary. 'I appreciate an uninterrupted sleep,' she remarked. 'What do you want, Frost?'

'Bad shit's going down.' Dumping her backpack on the coffee table, she unzipped it and removed a laptop computer.

Anya frowned, running her fingers through her tangled hair. 'Be specific.'

'Figured this is something you might want to see.' Powering up the laptop, she spun the machine around for Anya to see. 'Watch this.'

She hit play, and a CNN news article appeared on screen, with an aerial view of a destroyed vehicle, smoke still rising from the wreckage. To a casual observer it might have seemed like simple destruction by fire, but Anya recognized explosive damage when she saw it.

As if to confirm, the headline for the piece read: 'One Killed in Terrorist Attack in Washington DC'.

'Who is George Breckenridge?' Anya asked as the name of the victim flashed up.

'Used to be our CO when we were in the Shepherd programme,' Frost hurriedly explained. 'Kind of an asshole, as it happens.'

Anya would have to take her word for that. 'I don't understand. Why is this so important to us?'

Frost's mouth twitched, a sure sign that she had bad news to deliver. 'Not long after the story broke, someone released a video claiming responsibility.'

Opening a second video file, Frost hit the play button.

Anya watched as the man on screen ranted against mysterious enemies lurking in the shadows and the war he was going to bring to them, typical ramblings of a conspiracy theorist or political radical. There were many such men these days, and she paid the embittered words little heed.

Only when the man concluded his tirade with two brief, chilling sentences did she understand why Frost had come here in the middle of the night.

My name is Ryan Drake. And this is just the beginning.

The screen went dark as the clip ended. Anya carried on staring at the screen for several seconds, her mind racing as she tried to process what she'd just seen. 'Has Ryan seen this?'

Frost nodded.

'Tell him to come here.'

If someone was out there killing people in Drake's name, then they needed to understand who was doing it and why.

'I can't. He's gone.'

Anya turned to look at her. 'What do you mean, gone?'

'Well, the opposite of "here".' When Anya's expression darkened, she went on. 'He was the first person I called when I saw the news report. I told him to watch, then he just hung up in the middle of the call. So I went straight to his apartment, but it was already empty. He'd taken his bug-out bag and disappeared.'

This situation was getting more serious by the minute. Such bags contained enough money, clothes, equipment and supplies for an operative to disappear at the drop of a hat and be able to survive for at least a week.

'Can't you track him?'

It was Frost's turn to look annoyed. 'I've got a two-year-old Sony laptop, not the Starship Enterprise. It's not like I can scan for the son of a bitch.' She looked away, perhaps realizing that barbed comments weren't going to help. 'What do you wanna do?'

Anya ran a hand along her jaw, deep in thought. If Drake had vanished after seeing that news report, it suggested one of two things. Either he knew who had made that recording in his name and was going to confront them, or he was in league with them and this was a planned operation.

She couldn't decide which prospect worried her more.

'Call the others,' she said. 'Tell them to come here right now.'

Chapter 9

Zurich Hauptbahnhof, despite being one of the busiest train stations in the country, was almost deserted at this time of night. Only weary commuters and a few unruly drunks drifted along the platforms waiting for their ride home.

Still, trains departed from there at every hour of the day, and it didn't take Drake long to find one going in his direction. He slipped on board, making sure nobody was following him, and chose a seat well away from the handful of other passengers in the carriage.

Dumping his bug-out bag on the seat beside him, he eased in close to the window, facing down the carriage so he had a decent view of anyone approaching. Satisfied that nobody was remotely interested in him, he released his grip on the concealed Browning automatic and reached for his cell phone.

As the brightly lit station receded into the distance, Drake dialled a number from memory.

The call was answered swiftly, but no voice spoke to greet him. They were waiting for him to make the first move.

'Asset B-16 reporting in,' he said automatically, surprised at how easily it slipped out. His old designation, which had become as much of an identity to him as the name he'd grown up with. Batch B, recruit number 16.

'Status?'

The voice that spoke to him was exactly like the one in the video he'd watched earlier. Low pitched, distorted, electronically disguised. Its owner could have been any age, gender or nationality and he wouldn't know.

'Mobile.'

'Location?'

'Zurich.' He glanced out the window, watching the sleeping city slip by. 'Awaiting instructions.'

He heard an odd, electronic warbling coming down the line. It took him a moment to realize that it was laughter.

'Perfect, Ryan. You didn't miss a beat,' his anonymous contact complimented him. 'It's good to know my message found the right person.'

Drake seemed to snap out of the familiar, almost robotic mindset that had taken hold.

'You killed Breckenridge. And you framed me for his death.' There was no need to phrase it as a question. The answer was obvious enough.

'Only way I could make sure you saw my message. And from what I've heard, the world won't miss that guy,' he explained. 'I've been looking for you for a long time.'

'Congratulations, you've got my attention. Now who the fuck are you?'

'A concerned citizen.'

'I'm going to need more than that.'

'Patience, Ryan. All in good time.'

Drake felt his pulse quicken. 'I'm all out of patience. Right now I want answers. Why did you contact me?'

'I'm here to help you.'

'Help me do what?'

'Fill in the blanks, you might say. There are things missing from your life, memories you can't access. A certain mission you can't remember no matter how hard you try?'

Drake closed his eyes and whispered a single word. A word that had haunted him for years now. 'Hydra.'

'Exactly. Someone doesn't want you to know what really happened that day, and they've gone to great lengths to cover it up. Unfortunately, the mental block is starting to degrade, and pretty soon it's going to collapse entirely. Frankly, I'm surprised you've held out this long. You're a man living on borrowed time, Ryan.'

'Bullshit,' he countered.

'Is it? You've been having… episodes lately, haven't you? Flashbacks? Insomnia? Mood swings, depression, anxiety?' Drake didn't answer. 'You're in the final stages now. Believe me, it's only going to get worse from here if we don't deal with it soon.'

Drake started as the carriage door hissed open and a pair of young women covered in tattoos and piercings sauntered by, one of them giving him a disdainful look as she passed. Drake ignored them both, concentrating intently on his call.

'So deal with it,' he barked. 'Fill in the blanks. I'll wait.'

Another one of those unnerving electronic laughs. 'I'm afraid it's not as easy as that.'

'It never is,' Drake replied cynically.

His contact ignored the remark. 'I can't give you the answers you need, but I can show you the way to them.'

'What way would that be?'

'You're going on a journey, Ryan. It's not going to be easy, and time is very much against you. But if you act fast and follow my instructions, you just might make it to the end with your mind intact. And you'll get the answers you've been looking for.'

'And why the hell should I trust a man who won't identify himself?'

'You shouldn't,' his new friend countered. 'I probably wouldn't in your situation. But the way I see it, you don't have much alternative.'

'I could ditch this phone right now and disappear. You'd never see or hear from me again. How's that for an alternative?'

'Then leave. Pretend this never happened. By my estimates, you'll lapse into psychosis within a couple of weeks anyway. You'll spend the rest of your life trapped in a permanent nightmare you can't wake up from, never knowing what's real and what isn't. Is that what you want, Ryan?'

Drake couldn't suppress the shudder of dread that passed through him at this dire prediction, because he'd already experienced a measure of it tonight. The thought of living in such a state permanently was worse than death itself.

'But if that's not enough to persuade you, maybe this will be.'

Drake's phone bleeped with an incoming message, containing a single image file. Opening it, Drake felt his blood run cold at the sight that confronted him. A photograph, clearly taken from a concealed position, of a woman in her mid-thirties as she exited a doorway. A woman whose features bore a certain similarity to his own.

His sister Jessica.

'You just made the biggest mistake of your life, son,' he growled into the handset, struggling to contain his fury at the implied threat to the only family he had left.

'You're missing the point, Ryan,' his contact retorted. 'I'm not doing this to threaten you, but if *I* can find her, do you really think our enemies will have trouble tracking her down?'

Drake had no answer for that.

'Look, I know this isn't what you wanted to hear. You're in a shitty situation, and believe me when I say it's going to get worse before it gets better, but I'm not your enemy. In fact, I know what you're going through better than anyone.' Despite the distortion, there was an earnest, emotional undertone to his voice now. He wasn't trying to command or intimidate Drake, but rather to persuade him. 'We both want the people who fucked you over to pay for what they've done. And they will, but first you have to show a little faith in me.'

Drake wasn't in the habit of accepting deals from anonymous parties with unknown goals or intentions, but neither could he abandon the only real lead he might have to the question that had haunted him for years.

What happened to me?

'What do you want me to do?' he asked.

'Every journey starts with a first step,' the caller explained. 'Yours is in South America.'

Chapter 10

The calls went out, asking the others to convene at Anya's home with the greatest urgency. Alex was first to arrive, showing up at her door bleary eyed and dishevelled after literally getting up and throwing some clothes on. Olivia Mitchell wasn't far behind him, looking a little more presentable. Coming from a military background, she was no stranger to early morning wake-up calls and seemed to have little problem with Anya's summons.

Only Jonas Dietrich, typically, kept them waiting, taking almost an hour to show up. His clean-shaven face and neatly combed hair confirmed he'd taken the time to shower and wash before departing, much to Anya's chagrin.

Nonetheless, he still managed to grumble as he stepped over the threshold and slunk into the living room, warning that unless lives were at stake, he considered it a wasted trip.

His doubts were soon silenced as Frost replayed the news clips she'd shown to Anya and the others. Dietrich sat staring at the screen, his face a mask of puzzlement and growing disbelief. He spoke only once, requesting that she play it through a second time.

As the video clip terminated, he looked up at the others. 'So… things have pretty much gone to shit.'

'Breckenridge is dead,' Frost reminded him. As a former Shepherd team leader himself, Dietrich had worked with the divisional leader for a couple of years.

The man shrugged without concern. 'He was an asshole. At least somebody saved me the trouble,' he said coldly. 'The question is, why frame Ryan for it?'

'It gets better,' the young woman went on, relating Drake's sudden disappearance.

Dietrich closed his eyes and sighed. The kind of long, weary sigh that a parent might make when they find their kid scribbling on the walls with a crayon.

'*Verdammte Scheiße*,' he muttered in German. 'The man sits on his ass for six months, then out of nowhere he pulls shit like this.'

'You're assuming he's actually guilty of this attack?' Frost asked.

Dietrich looked at her. 'And you're assuming he's not. Ryan's been acting weird for months, barely talking to anyone. And it's no secret he had no love for Breckenridge. Then he vanishes right after the news breaks. What other conclusion can you draw?'

'That he went into hiding to avoid reprisals?'

'Bullshit.' Dietrich's dismissal was immediate and unequivocal. 'He'd have found a way to tell us what was going on. He wouldn't just split without explanation.'

'His disappearance might be a reaction to what he saw,' Mitchell reminded him. 'We shouldn't write the guy off before he has a chance to explain himself.'

'Has anyone actually tried contacting him?' Alex suggested.

Frost looked at him with about as much disdain and irascibility as it was possible for one person to level at another. 'Genius detective work, Yates. Wish I'd thought of it.'

'Fuck off, at least I'm putting ideas out there. What's *your* big play, Poirot?'

Frost was stumped, but unwilling to let him have the last word. 'Dumb ideas aren't an improvement over no ideas. Of course I tried to contact him, but he's gone dark. That means he's not using any devices I can track,' she added pedantically.

Ignoring the bickering, Dietrich levelled a suspicious look at Anya. 'You're the last one to see him. Did you know anything of this?'

'Nothing,' Anya answered truthfully.

'But you suspected something,' he pressed.

Dietrich had never enjoyed a good relationship with Anya, not least because he'd once been leader of the Shepherd team assigned to hunt her down. He might have become a reluctant ally of the group since then, mostly through circumstances and mutual interest, but generally Dietrich seemed to regard her every action and motive as questionable.

'He was… different.' Anya trailed off, unsure how to voice her thoughts. 'It was a difficult meeting. We fought, and he left.'

She'd expected a reaction from the others at a revelation like this, and sure enough she got one.

'What do you mean, you fought?' Alex asked. 'About what?'

'When did this happen?' Frost asked at the same time.

'Quiet!' Dietrich commanded them, raising his voice above the flurry of questions. 'Tell us what happened. No bullshit.'

Anya let out a breath. 'We were training together. I pushed him, and it… got out of hand.' Briefly she related the events of their sparring session, the sudden change that had come over Drake, and even his attempt to strangle her.

'Jesus Christ, Anya! And you're just telling us this now?' Frost interjected. 'Ryan tried to kill you, and you didn't think it was worth mentioning?'

'What happened was between us,' she said heatedly. 'I was trying to help him.'

'How? By provoking him?' Dietrich shook his head. 'You brought this on yourself.'

Mitchell leaned forward, ignoring the hostile atmosphere. 'How did you think this would help him?'

'I have noticed a change in him since we escaped Berlin, just as you have. He has been distant, preoccupied, he doesn't sleep properly. I confronted him about it. I had hoped Ryan would… get help, talk to someone. I never imagined he would do something like this.'

Alex threw up his hands. 'So basically he's flipped his shit, gone all Manchurian Candidate and turned into our own personal Osama bin Laden.'

'Hey!' Frost cut in, with real animosity. 'Most of us are only alive right now because of Ryan, so show some goddamn respect.'

Alex said nothing. Like Mitchell, he was a relative newcomer to the team and knew almost nothing of its other members, save for Anya, so his loyalties naturally tended towards her. He felt no such attachment to Drake.

'Take it easy, both of you. Bitching isn't going to help,' Mitchell warned her younger and more hot-headed teammates. 'Whatever Drake's motivations, this attack wasn't the work of some raving lunatic. It was planned. And if the man responsible chose to expose himself on TV like that, there must be a reason behind it.'

It didn't take Dietrich long to reach the obvious conclusion. 'He wanted Drake's attention. He wanted to make sure Drake saw that news report.'

Mitchell nodded. Solving crimes and apprehending suspects had once been a way of life for her, and as far as she was concerned this was no different.

'This still doesn't tell us where Drake's gone, or what he's planning,' Alex pointed out.

Anya was inclined to agree. In her mind, Ryan hadn't been himself for some time, but it seemed that news report had pushed him over the edge. Much as she hated to contemplate it, there was a very good chance he might have snapped somehow. In which case, he was a danger not only to himself, but to others as well.

'There has to be something we're not seeing yet,' she decided. 'I want to look at his apartment, see if there are any clues to his next move.'

'I'm coming with you,' Mitchell said.

Anya nodded agreement. As a former CID officer, Mitchell's skills might prove useful. 'Alex, Keira, find out if there is anything about the attack online,' she added. 'And look for any digital trace of Ryan. Credit cards, cell phone pings—'

'We know the drill,' Alex assured her, packing up to leave. 'I'm going to work from my place. I've got a better set-up there. And the atmosphere's better.'

'Tie in with me once you're online so we can coordinate,' Frost called after him. 'And try not to jerk off too much.'

Alex gave her the finger over his shoulder as he departed.

'Where do you want me?' Dietrich asked, cornering Anya as she was grabbing her jacket and preparing to leave.

Anya looked at him. 'Stay here and keep watch. If that's not too much trouble.'

The man gave her a hostile look.

Outside in the chill night air a few minutes later, Mitchell unlocked her car. 'We're pretty screwed right now, aren't we?' she said, speaking candidly now they were alone.

Anya's expression confirmed her suspicions. 'Ryan was trained to hunt people who don't want to be found. He knows how to avoid us. Until he makes his next move, we have nothing to work with.'

Mitchell fired up the engine. 'What makes you think there's a next move?'

'If I'm right, we'll know when it happens.'

49

Chapter 11

It was a hot night.

Hot, damp and humid, the air still and stifling.

Outside, the chirp of crickets and other night insects echoed through the steaming darkness, a strange nocturnal music of changing rhythm and intensity. A dog barked somewhere off in the distance, and a car drove by on the wet road, tyres rumbling on the tarmac.

Thomas Hayes lay sprawled on his expansive bed, the covers thrown back, chest rising and falling as he slept. But it was a troubled sleep that brought little rest.

A faint breeze, imperceptible but for the slight stirring of the curtains it caused, sighed through the room.

Hayes stirred, his unconscious mind alerted that something had changed, some tiny shift in his surroundings that might be important. His dark lashes flickered, held still, then parted.

For several seconds he lay there, wondering what had disturbed him. His eyes scanned the shadows of the room, looking for anything out of the ordinary. There was nothing obvious, and yet his instincts told him to be alert.

Then he heard something – a soft, muted thump from somewhere in the big house. Against the background of insects outside it was almost indistinguishable, but his hearing was keen. Something was wrong, and that realization soon drove away the last vestiges of sleep.

Easing himself out of bed, he reached into the bedside drawer and felt his fingers close around the cold metal grip of a pistol. He hefted the weapon, checking the safety was disengaged and that a round was chambered, just as he'd been taught.

Armed, he rose from the bed and crept across the room. Eyes by now accustomed to the darkness, he advanced into the hallway, keeping the pistol low. The only sounds he could hear were the faint tread of his bare feet on the thick carpet and the beating of his own heart, strong and steady despite his growing unease.

Another tiny shift in air pressure carried with it the scent of grass and flowers outside. An open window? An open door? He was sure he'd checked everything before retiring to bed, and the alarm system would surely have warned him if an entrance had been missed.

The first room on his left was the office. Gripping the pistol in sweating hands, he paused outside the door for a moment before opening it. Within stood his antique desk, shipped here from the States at considerable expense, its surface cluttered with papers and reports, his computer's indicator lights flashing in sleep mode. Nothing out of place.

He repeated the same process in the spare bedroom and bathroom, clearing each room in turn. In short order, the building's first floor was secure.

Maybe he was imagining things.

As he reached the end of the corridor, he moved down the sweeping flight of curved stairs to the entrance hall below. The stairs were solid, constructed of stone inlaid with marble, the elaborately carved baluster providing a firm support even for unsteady feet. Easy for a man like him to descend without making much noise.

Emerging into the main hallway, the front door came into view. It was standing ajar, open just a few inches, the warm night air seeping in.

Hayes felt a tiny bead of sweat forming at his temple. Someone was in here. How the hell had they been able to defeat that lock without triggering the alarm? The security system in this building was supposed to be state of the art. He should know; he'd paid enough for it.

He was just turning to reach for his house phone when a voice spoke, hard and commanding. 'Don't move.'

Fear charged through him. He froze, glanced down at the pistol, wondering whether the intruder knew he was armed. Maybe, if he was quick…

'Don't even think about it,' the voice warned. 'Drop the gun and slide it towards me.'

Shit.

He did as commanded, hearing the echo as the weapon skittered across the stone floor before coming to rest. If his adversary had the drop on him, there was no use provoking him. Rio was a dangerous city at the best of times, and robberies were commonplace. His palatial house, recently restored and situated in an upmarket part of town, no doubt presented a tempting target.

'Put your hands behind your head and interlock your fingers.'

Again he complied. 'Listen, we can work something out. You've probably guessed I'm a rich man. There's at least 20 grand in the—'

'I'm not interested in money. Turn around.'

Heart pounding, he turned to face the corridor leading towards the kitchen. The intruder was standing there, face hidden in the shadows. For several moments he remained like that, silent and unmoving.

'What do you want?' Hayes asked, trying to keep his voice calm. He was torn between anger and apprehension. If this was a robbery, then so be it. He could live with the loss of a few dollars or other valuables. He had plenty to spare.

But what if it was something else?

'Your access key card and system passcodes.'

Hayes' stomach knotted as he began to perceive this man's true intentions. 'You can't be serious. You know you'll never get in there, it's—'

He jumped as a silenced round slammed into the door frame beside him, splinters of wood prickling his arm.

'Time isn't on your side tonight, Doctor,' he warned, training the gun on Hayes' abdomen. 'Now, the key card.'

With a trembling hand, Hayes pointed back up the stairs. 'It's in the safe in my office.'

'Then let's go.'

Keeping his hands up, he ascended the stairs once more, stumbling once in his haste. His captor followed a few paces behind: close enough to keep him covered, but far enough away that he couldn't turn suddenly and knock the gun out of his hand. As if he'd be foolish enough to try.

Returning to his office, he crossed the room and approached the small safe set into the wall. It wasn't big enough to hold much, but then it didn't need to be. The item inside was more valuable than mere money.

Punching his access code into the numeric keypad on the side, Hayes listened for the telltale hum as the bolt inside was automatically withdrawn, then unlatched the door and swung it open.

'Step back,' his captor ordered.

He did as instructed, watched as the armed man moved forward, reached inside and removed the single item inside – an electronic access card set within a protective frame, with his name and photograph printed on it.

'Thanks for your help,' he said, slipping the card into his pocket.

'You're wasting your time,' Hayes warned him. 'The security system's biometric as well as electronic, and the facility's guarded 24 hours a day. You'll never get inside.'

His captor turned to him, eyes gleaming in the darkness, cold and hard and without mercy.

'Don't worry about that. It's not your problem,' he said, raising his weapon.

'Wait, you don't have to—'

His sentence was cut short by a brief flash, followed by a dull wet thump as the round slammed into his chest. A moment later, a second projectile struck.

He staggered back against the wall and slid down to the floor, leaving a bloody mark on the pristine white wallpaper. Gasping, choking on blood, he looked up through bleary eyes to see the darkened figure standing over him, motionless for a moment, watching his final breaths.

'You won't be around to see how this ends, but I want you to know the truth before you die. I want you to know that you're all going to answer for what you did.' The pistol was raised again, pointed at his head. 'This is just the beginning.'

Hayes closed his eyes as another dull thud resounded, and then he knew no more.

Chapter 12

'Ah, come on, you asshole. Pass the goddamn ball!' security guard Patrick Tarver muttered, staring intently at the small TV mounted in the corner of his hut where an NFL game was being broadcast. It was a repeat of the live game from earlier in the day, but he'd avoided watching it until now. Why watch at home when he could be paid to watch it here?

It wasn't like there were many other demands on his time during the long and usually uneventful night shift. The research facility he was assigned to protect effectively shut down when the scientists and lab technicians drifted off home to their expensive apartments, leaving behind a skeleton security staff. The most exciting event he'd encountered in his six months here had been a cougar prowling around outside the perimeter fence in search of food, but the animal had quickly vanished when it discovered the fence was electrified.

Thus Tarver had slipped into a dull and largely unchanging routine of reading, doing crossword puzzles and, of course, catching his home team the Pittsburgh Steelers whenever they played. Now he was starting to wish he hadn't bothered.

The Steelers had tried to make another break for it on their fourth down instead of playing it safe and punting it upfield, only to run into a solid Bengal defensive line that stopped them cold. Unable to progress beyond the ten-yard line, they'd been forced to hand possession over. Their opponents wasted no time capitalizing on their mistake.

'Goddamn it.' He took a gulp of coffee, wishing he had something stronger and colder. A man at least deserved a beer if he had to watch his team get their asses kicked.

An electric fan hummed away behind him, the monotonous drone of its motor almost drowned out by the steady drumming of rain on the roof. Rain was heavy and frequent in Brazil at this time of year, combining with the near constant heat to create a humid, sweltering environment that was a pain in the ass to work in. Already he could feel damp patches under his arms and in the small of his back.

Fucking country, he thought disdainfully. Just as well the pay was good.

Trying to filter out the ambient noise and the uncomfortable heat, Tarver watched as the Bengals' quarterback suddenly broke and made a run on the end zone. Son of a bitch looked for a good position to score.

His attention was distracted from the screen by the glare of headlights as a vehicle turned off the main road and approached his security gate. He glanced at his watch, already sure it was too early for the first day shift.

As it drew nearer and slowed down, he recognized the general shape and outline as a new model Ford Explorer belonging to the facility manager, Thomas Hayes. Working night shift as he did, Tarver had only encountered the man on occasion, and that was quite enough for him. He had a reputation as a hard-ass who punished even minor infractions, particularly amongst the lower-ranked staff.

What the hell was he doing here tonight?

Irritated by the bad timing, he muted the TV and sat up straighter in his chair as the vehicle rolled to a stop opposite his security hut. The engine was still rumbling away, rain pattering off the bodywork. The windows were firmly closed to let the air conditioning do its thing. Just the thought of cool, dry air blasting over him was enough to make Tarver green with envy.

Leaning out of his window, he made a winding motion with his hand, indicating for Hayes to roll his window down. Plant manager or not, Tarver needed to check his ID before he opened the gate.

The window began to roll down, accompanied by the hum of electric motors. But at the same time, Tarver noticed the Steelers making a sudden interception that was deftly passed to their quarterback, who made a run on the end zone with a blocker running interference. The Bengals' defence, caught unprepared by this sudden break, were all over the place trying to intercept him.

Turning back towards the vehicle, he switched on some fake enthusiasm to greet the new arrival.

'Evening, sir. Can I see your ID card and—'

He didn't get a chance to finish. The sight of a silenced automatic pointed at him was enough to make the words die in his throat. And the man holding it most definitely wasn't Thomas Hayes.

Tarver hesitated for a second or so as his brain tried to process what he was seeing, then instinctively reached for the hidden alarm button fixed beneath his console.

'Don't even think about it,' the driver warned. 'Move away from the terminal. And get your hands up where I can see them.'

Tarver froze, then dumbly complied, too shocked and frightened to resist.

'That's better. Now, Tarver,' he said, reading the name tag on his shirt. 'How many men are on duty tonight?'

'S-six,' Tarver replied, trying to keep the tremble from his voice.

'Including you?'

'Yeah.'

'Good. Now I want you to reach out and open the main gate.'

'Look pal, there's no money here. This is just a research lab. We don't have anything worth stealing.'

Brazil was an impoverished country with a violent history, and many desperate men willing to risk it all to escape to a better life. If that was what his friend in the car was planning, he was going to be very disappointed.

'Open the gate, Tarver. Don't make me ask again.'

Sighing, Tarver reached out and pressed the gate control switch, causing it to retract automatically and opening the way ahead.

'It's done. Please, just let me—'

A single bright flash lit the interior of the car, illuminating the driver's face. Tarver jerked once as the silenced 9mm projectile penetrated his forehead before blasting out the back of his skull, taking a good portion of his brain with it.

The security guard slumped backwards and toppled off his chair, blood and cranial matter painting the back wall of his hut.

On the blood-spattered TV screen, the Steelers quarterback broke through the last defensive line, throwing himself down in the end zone to score a touchdown. The home crowd erupted in applause just as Tarver's killer eased off the brake and drove slowly towards the facility.

-

At the main reception desk, Carl Swafford looked up as the front doors buzzed and unlocked, and a new arrival strode in, soaked through from the heavy rain outside. His hood was still up and his head down, so Swafford couldn't identify the man, but presumably he was one of the researcher staff, perhaps come to check up on some experiment or retrieve a forgotten personal item.

'Goddamn,' the man grumbled, shaking the worst of the water off. 'It is raining cats and dogs out there tonight!'

Swafford offered a fake chuckle as the new arrival bustled towards the desk. 'One of the advantages of being stationed in here, sir.' He turned a little more serious as the man drew closer. 'Can I check your ID so I can log you in?'

'Sure, let me just grab it here,' he rep lied, fumbling through his jacket pockets. 'Never can remember where I put the damn thing.'

'That's why it's a good idea to use a lanyard,' Swafford pointed out, indicating his own access card hanging around his neck. *Fucking asshole*, he thought beneath his patient smile. *Probably earns three times what I do, and couldn't tie his shoelaces without help.*

'Hate the things, always make me feel like I'm being strangled. Ah, here we are,' he said, lifting his card triumphantly from his pocket as if it were a major achievement, only for the corner to catch on the jacket's lining and slip from his grasp. It fell and skittered across the smooth floor, coming to rest just behind Swafford's desk. 'Oh, damn it! Sorry, butterfingers tonight.'

'It's okay, sir. I got it,' Swafford hastily said as he bent down to pick it up.

Only as he leaned in close and reached out to pick up the card was he able to make out the name and picture on it. Thomas Hayes, the director of the facility, and most certainly not the man standing in front of him.

He heard movement on the other side of the desk, rapid footsteps coming at him, and instinctively turned towards them. He was just in time to see the man swing something down towards his head, followed by a jarring impact, an explosion of white light and an odd sensation of falling. Falling into nothingness.

As the unconscious guard slumped sideways and collapsed with a trickle of blood staining the back of his neck, Drake holstered the pistol he'd struck him with, hurried behind the desk and hooked his hands under the man's armpits. He was a big guy, easily a couple of hundred pounds of dead weight, and moving such a man any distance was no easy task. Still, he wasn't unfamiliar with transporting unconscious prisoners.

A small office was positioned behind the reception desk, mostly for admin and storing stationery goods judging by the cardboard boxes lining the shelves, but it would do just fine to keep the man out of sight. With no telltale bloodstains on the floor or walls, it might take the others a while to realize anything was amiss.

Whether the guy survived was another matter. There were few reliable ways to knock someone unconscious without risking skull fractures or even brain damage. The man might wake up in ten minutes, fully conscious and pissed off, or he might never wake at all. Time would tell, but Drake didn't plan on being around to find out.

Drake dumped him on the floor inside and closed the door behind him. Assuming the guard manning the main gate hadn't been lying, that was two down and four to go.

Drawing his automatic once more, Drake strode away from reception, heading towards the real target of his mission tonight.

Chapter 13

In the secure monitoring room in the centre of the building, Chief of Night Security Luis Garcia frowned, leaning in closer to the terminal that allowed him to observe and control virtually every aspect of the facility.

According to the access logs, the facility manager Thomas Hayes had just swiped in through the main entrance, yet he'd received no word from the perimeter security gate of this unexpected arrival. Normally any visitors were called in by the night watchman on duty at the gate, so the other staff could be made aware.

The arrival of the facility manager was an even bigger deal. Garcia's night shift could hardly be described as negligent – he was a trained professional who took his job seriously – but his men were only human. Months of monotonous inactivity had brought about a certain complacency. And if Hayes spotted them being less than professional, the blame would inevitably fall on him.

Surveying the bank of monitors built into the wall above him, he caught sight of Hayes traversing the overhead corridor linking one building to another, his nose deep in a file folder. He was dressed in dark trousers, an open shirt and rain jacket, his head covered by a baseball cap that was still dripping with water. Garcia had noticed previously that Hayes' hair was thinning on top, requiring careful arrangement to disguise a growing bald spot. The heavy monsoon-like rainfall would have ruined all that hard work, and Hayes was too vain to be out looking dishevelled.

The question however remained – what the hell was he doing here, and why hadn't Garcia been notified?

The facility was divided into two main structures, imaginatively titled Buildings A and B. Building A was the administrative section, containing offices, conference rooms, eating areas, storage spaces, machine rooms and of course, his security station. For all intents and purposes it looked like any other bland, mid-sized office block in most parts of the world, save for a rather more stringent and sophisticated security system.

Building B was where the real work went on. It was where the small army of researchers and scientists locked themselves away, working on God only knew what.

Unlike its blandly corporate neighbour, B was a big monolithic unit with only one way in or out, hermetically sealed and guarded by a full biometric security system. No windows, no cameras, no other doors. He didn't fully understand what they did in there, save that it involved medical research and new drug treatments, but that was just fine by him. He was content to do his own job and let the eggheads do theirs.

Curious and a little annoyed that Tarver hadn't seen fit to warn them of Hayes' arrival, Garcia reached for his radio. 'Main gate, come in.'

There was no response.

'Tarver, you'd better not be jerking off in there,' Garcia warned. 'Answer your goddamn radio.'

His forceful request was met with radio silence. Checking the camera feeds overlooking the gate, he could see nothing out of the ordinary. The gate itself had closed as part of its automatic cycle, and the rain was still falling heavily, but he could make out the pale flicker of TV images from within the security hut.

There was no sign of Tarver.

'Fuck,' he said under his breath, switching channels. 'Lopez, come in.'

'Go,' Hector Lopez, assigned to patrol the facility perimeter, replied.

'Tarver's not answering his radio. Go take a look and kick his ass, would you?'

Lopez snorted in amusement. 'Copy that.'

–

Having reached the end of the elevated walkway that connected the two buildings, Drake halted before the big steel door now barring his way. A small glass viewing port permitted limited visibility into the room beyond, where a similar door stood about ten feet away, forming a combined airlock and decontamination chamber. There were no handles or latches of any kind on either door, and he didn't doubt that forcing them open would require nothing less than high explosives.

The only means of access was a keycard reader fixed into the wall, with a small indicator screen mounted above it. Removing Hayes' card from inside his jacket, he carefully inserted it into the reader and waited for it to scan. The machine buzzed for a few seconds as it did its thing, then the reader flashed green to indicate the card had been accepted.

A text prompt appeared on the screen above.

Welcome, Doctor Hayes. Please verify ID with retinal scan.

A circle had appeared on the screen, indicating where he was to place his eye. Retinal scans worked by measuring the pattern of veins and blood vessels within the human eye, comparing it to a stored database of authorized users. Since they stayed the same throughout one's life and no two humans shared identical patterns, they were nearly impossible to falsify.

Reaching into his pocket, Drake produced a small plastic Ziploc bag containing a single round, fleshy orb that he'd been obliged to bring with him tonight. Opening the bag, he held Hayes' eyeball up to the scanner and waited while the flickering red beams of light danced across its surface.

Removing a human eye without rupturing it is no easy process, requiring a lot of cutting and damage to the surrounding tissue for a clean extraction. It had been a messy job, to say the least, and combined with the gunshot wound, Hayes' funeral was definitely going to be a closed-casket affair after Drake's grisly handiwork. He'd also had to act quickly, making his way here before the veins and arteries started to collapse and deteriorate. Now he'd find out if his work had paid off.

There was another crisp beep, and the door retracted into the wall on hydraulic power, a loud buzzer sounding to warn anyone nearby that the airlock was about to cycle. Stepping inside, he waited patiently while the door slid back into place.

The airlock was a big white-walled chamber about ten feet square, with enough space to accommodate a dozen people at a time if necessary. White hazmat suits hung in rows along one wall, with boxes of gloves, boots and respirators carefully laid out beneath. He imagined the lab beyond dealt with all manner of dangerous substances, making respirators a priority.

'Stand by for decontamination,' a computerized voice warned him. 'Please stand in the centre of the room with your arms raised. Decontamination in five, four, three, two, one.'

–

As luck would have it, Lopez was already circling back around towards the security hut when the call came in from Garcia. A minute or so of brisk walking brought the small wooden structure into sight. Nothing seemed out of place, and the gate had cycled closed.

'Hey, Tarver! You in there?'

No answer.

This didn't feel right. Failure to answer his radio could be down to faulty equipment, but Lopez couldn't imagine his colleague abandoning his post altogether.

Frowning, the security guard reached for the radio affixed to his shoulder. 'It's me. I can see the hut, but there's no sign of Tarver. I'm gonna take a look.'

'Copy that. Keep your eyes open,' Garcia instructed him.

Lopez clicked his radio off. 'Yeah, great advice,' he mumbled, drawing his sidearm.

Chapter 14

The moment the air shower finished blasting Drake to remove loose particles from his clothes and skin, the inner airlock door buzzed and swung open, granting him access to the world beyond. Motion-activated lights blinked on, revealing the interior of Building B.

Clutching one of the hazmat respirators, Drake stepped carefully inside this technological sanctum like a pilgrim entering a holy shrine, pausing briefly to take it all in. This place was, in comparison to the blandly functional admin block he'd just left behind, a haven of medical precision, order and pristine cleanliness.

Most of it was given over to a series of glass chambers, clearly research labs of some kind. Electron microscopes, mass spectrometers, centrifuges, powerful desktop computers and countless other pieces of sophisticated lab equipment he didn't even recognize gleamed in the stark electric light, while racks of chemicals and biological samples sat in neat rows within glass-fronted refrigeration units.

It was a clean, sterilized environment carefully isolated from the outside world, free from contamination that could impair the work being done here. The air felt cool and unnaturally dry, the kind of dryness that irritated the throat and made the eyes feel gritty. More than that, it smelled of absolutely nothing, not even the disinfectant so often associated with medical facilities, every particle having been filtered out by the building's sophisticated air processing system.

Drake strode past the isolation chambers and the powerful workstations, heading for the bank of offices at the far end of the floor. The chemicals and equipment in this room were worth millions of dollars in their own right, but he was here for something far more valuable: information.

Each office was marked with a tag denoting the name and function of its owner, with most of them belonging to chief researchers, team leaders and other senior positions, but he ignored them. The one he was looking for was at the end of the row, and marked with a simple tag.

Thomas Hayes – Facility Director

The door was locked and secured with the same keycard system as the building itself. Running his access card through the machine, he waited until he heard the click of a lock disengaging, then eased the door open and stepped inside.

–

Hitting the override switch on his side of the fence, Lopez waited while the chain-link gate trundled back, then cautiously stepped through, his eyes scanning the darkened jungle that lay about 50 yards beyond the perimeter fence.

Tightening his grip on the sidearm, he approached the hut. He could see the glow of a TV playing against the interior walls, and hear the monotonous hum of a cooling fan.

His thumb moved upwards slightly, feeling for the safety catch. Like all the night security guards, he'd been through firearms training and was even a half-decent marksman, but he'd never fired a gun outside a range before. The prospect of trouble left him tense and anxious.

He rounded the hut's doorway, the barrel of his weapon sweeping from left to right. Then he saw the blood-coated wall, the body of his comrade lying sprawled on the floor. He could feel his stomach knot, and bile rising into his throat.

'Oh fuck,' he gasped, turning away from the horrific scene and reaching for his radio.

–

Hayes' office was pretty much what Drake had expected: spotless, precisely ordered, logically laid out, and entirely lacking in personality. No family photos on his desk, no awards or paintings on the walls. Everything as clinical and sterile as the high-tech labs just outside.

The workstation housed a top-of-the-range set-up operating a pair of big flat-screen monitors. Hurrying over, he sat down on the plush leather office chair and hit a few random keys to bring the unit out of hibernation. A password screen was the first thing to appear.

Quickly tapping in a sequence of random letters and numbers that he'd committed to memory, his finger hovered over the 'enter' key for a second or so, before finally hitting it.

The password window promptly gave way to the system's desktop, which was cluttered with various files and folders dedicated to different projects and administrative tasks, on a background of what looked like the Grand Canyon at sunset. Drake was surprised. Based on Hayes' personality, or lack thereof, he'd expected to see the standard Windows backdrop. Maybe there was more to the guy than he'd imagined – not that it mattered much now.

Reaching into his pocket, he fished out a little black memory stick, found a port on the front of the terminal and inserted it. It took only a second or so for the program stored on the drive to automatically boot up and get to work, presenting him with a simple dialogue window.

Initiate file transfer? Y/N

The program was a little gift from Frost, created months ago for quickly gathering electronic intel. At a single keystroke, it would automatically scan and copy the entire contents of the target machine's hard drive onto the memory stick, effectively creating a clone of the system that could be dissected and examined later. The information he was after might be deeply buried within the labyrinthine file network, or might not exist at all. Either way, finding it would take time he didn't have right now.

Hitting the 'Y' key, he watched as the prompt screen was replaced with a progress bar that slowly began to fill up as the program worked feverishly to transfer the data over. The memory stick was pretty much the highest capacity device of its kind available, or so Frost had assured him.

Time would tell whether it was up to the task.

–

Garcia was busy cycling through the various camera feeds situated around the facility when the frantic radio call came through from Lopez.

'Garcia, we've got an armed intruder! Hit the alarm now!'

'Lopez, slow down, for Christ's sake,' Garcia ordered him. 'What's going on?'

'Tarver's dead! That asshole must've killed him and stolen his key card. We've got a hostile inside the building.'

'Fuck,' Garcia snapped, leaning over his terminal and hitting the panic button to trigger a full security lockdown of the facility. As alarms started blaring throughout the building and the emergency system automatically notified key company personnel of the security breach, he reached for his radio again.

'All units, we have a hostile in Building B. He is armed and should be considered extremely dangerous. Tarver is dead. I repeat, Tarver is dead. Move in and lock it down!'

He was immediately met with a chorus of affirmatives, some of them a little hesitant and edgy, others hardened with anger. Having nobody else to interact with, night security teams tended to become close-knit groups, and Tarver had been popular amongst his colleagues. They would want payback.

There were three remaining security guards, plus himself in the monitoring station to coordinate their efforts. Backup units would be scrambling to assist them now that the alarm had been triggered, but they would take time to arrive. Until then, they would have to handle the situation themselves.

This might have been a cause for real concern had the facility been under attack by a larger group, but a quick check of the perimeter sensors confirmed nobody else had tried to make entry. Four of them against a single intruder. Why would one man think he could get in and out of a high-security compound like this alive?

Those were questions they'd be sure to ask him once he was secured. For now, the question was how to isolate him so they could take him down.

There were no surveillance cameras inside Building B; Hayes had specified from the outset that he didn't want anyone, even his own security chief, eavesdropping on the work going on in there. As a result, their mysterious intruder had vanished beyond Garcia's electronic sight the moment he cycled the airlock.

But his escape would be fleeting at best. Building B had been designed as a hermetically sealed, climate-controlled cube – the airlock system was the only way in or out. Whether he knew it or not, their enemy was now trapped inside.

That building was now his prison, and if Garcia and his men had their way, it would soon become his tomb.

–

Drake glanced up from the computer as alarms blared throughout the building. His entry had been discovered, and rapid response teams would be on their way. Normally an emergency call would automatically notify local police units, but he doubted the owners of this place would want police snooping around.

He turned his attention back to the file transfer window – 43 per cent complete.

At best he figured he had 15 minutes to get what he needed and get out, with the small matter of the remaining security guards still to deal with.

If they were smart, they would barricade the airlock to prevent him escaping, and simply wait him out until backup arrived. Containment was usually the best option in situations like this. But these guys weren't smart. They were predictable, inexperienced and most of all, angry. They'd want payback for their dead comrade.

No, they were coming in. He would have to meet them when they did.

–

Flexing his fingers in nervous anticipation, Garcia watched as his three-man security team, led by Lopez, advanced down the overhead walkway to the airlock outside Building B. Their weapons were raised and it was clear from their body language that they were nervous and edgy.

'We're outside the airlock,' Lopez called in over the radio net. 'It's still secure. Nobody's getting out without going through us.'

'Copy that,' Garcia replied.

'What are your orders?'

Garcia didn't respond right away. Logically, they had their adversary bottled up in there, unable to escape. They could wait him out until backup arrived, but doing so would give him free rein to cause as much damage as he desired. The equipment in that building was worth millions, and its destruction would likely have dire repercussions for all of them.

Worse, it would confirm that he and his men weren't up to the task of apprehending one man. They would be seen as cowards who had failed to do their duty – himself most of all. He was chief of the night watch. This failure was on him.

'Let's get in there and take this asshole down,' urged Jacob Williams, the youngest member of his team. Williams was a macho blowhard at the best of times, always out to prove something, and tonight he was well and truly fired up.

'He killed Tarver already, and he's armed,' Lopez reminded him. 'You really want to fuck with this guy?'

'There's one of him and three of us,' Williams retorted. 'I ain't scared to go in there, even if you are.'

'Hold it,' Garcia commanded. The situation was tense enough, it wouldn't take much for tempers to flare. Anyway, an idea had just occurred to him.

Building B was protected against all manner of emergencies, from security breaches to chemical spills, and especially fires. It was fitted with a sophisticated fire suppression system that employed carbon dioxide rather than water so as not to damage the equipment in there. In the event of a fire, the system would saturate the air with carbon dioxide, effectively starving any fire of oxygen and smothering it.

The downside to such a system was that it invariably caused anyone trapped inside to lose consciousness, and in high enough doses they could go into cardiac arrest. It could even be operated remotely from his security station.

'Get ready to move in,' he said, turning to the fire suppression controls on his left. 'This guy shouldn't give you any trouble.'

'What makes you so sure?' Lopez asked.

'Because he'll be unconscious by the time you get to him.'

Reaching out, he flipped back the plastic cover on the fire suppression master switch, glanced at his team on the monitor, then pressed it.

–

The first thing Drake was aware of was a sudden loud, urgent alarm tone that started blaring out from every speaker in the building, drowning out even the security breach klaxon that had been running for the past ten seconds or so. This was a new one, and it meant something was about to happen. He had a feeling he knew what it was.

A few seconds later, he was hit by a jet of cold, misty vapour that began to pour down from vents in the ceiling, settling like stage mist over everything in the room and blurring his view of the world around him. Similar vents were dispensing their load throughout the building, filling every room, office and experimentation chamber with the same toxic gas.

Normally CO_2 makes up just a fraction of a percent of normal, breathable air. However, anything over 1 per cent concentration would begin to induce the first symptoms of carbon dioxide poisoning.

If the air's CO_2 content rose to 4 per cent it would be virtually impossible for him to move or function, while 10 per cent or more would quickly induce unconsciousness and finally asphyxiation. Fire-suppression systems like this could jack that concentration up to 30 or 40 per cent, killing anyone who wasn't protected.

Clever. He didn't expect them to have thought of it so quickly.

He imagined they would give the gas a minute or so to do its thing before popping the airlock and storming the place in strength, ready to finish him off. Which meant he was out of time.

He glanced at the computer terminal, and the progress bar on which this all depended – 52 per cent complete.

The fire-suppression system continued pumping CO_2 into Building B for 30 seconds before depleting its reserves and automatically shutting down. In Garcia's monitoring station, various warning messages had appeared on his screen advising that the atmosphere inside the building was now toxic, that anyone trapped inside would need urgent medical treatment, and that he should trigger immediate ventilation with outside air.

He ignored this warning, waiting while the seconds ticked by. The gas would incapacitate a human in a matter of seconds, but he was taking no chances. Maybe the guy was tougher than normal, or just good at holding his breath. Garcia tried to imagine him desperately fumbling through the haze, searching in vain for an exit as his brain slowly succumbed to the gas. That thought gave him some consolation.

After a full two minutes had passed, he reached for his radio again. 'All units, move in now. Use the respirators in the airlock chamber.'

Accessing the airlock manual override, he enabled the command for it to open, and watched as the big door slowly slid backwards to allow his team access.

'Copy that,' Lopez acknowledged. 'We're going in.'

—

In the airlock, Lopez shivered a little as the air shower blasted him and his two comrades, the chilled oxygen rippling through his clothes and raising the hairs on the back of his neck. He was breathing a little harder now, his respirator unit working to supply the demands of his lungs. Still, the faceplate was uncomfortable and claustrophobic, and he had to fight the urge to rip it off.

With the decontamination cycle complete, the inner door buzzed once before sliding silently back into the wall. Lopez raised his weapon, safety off and finger on the trigger, ready to open fire on anything that moved.

Straight away a wall of pale grey mist drifted into the chamber, reducing visibility to just a few yards. His comrades were visible only as vague, indistinct shapes through the haze. Garcia had shut down the alarm sirens as the team entered the airlock to make communications easier, but the emergency lights were still flashing, their intermittent red glow turning the swirling mist around them crimson.

'Christ, this stuff's everywhere,' Oliver DaForte, the third member of his team said, his voice muffled by his respirator.

'CO_2's heavier than air. It'll settle as we move,' Lopez explained. 'Follow me, stay close.'

As the team advanced warily into the lab, Lopez spoke into his radio again. 'We're in. No sign of movement. You got a location?'

Though there were no surveillance cameras in here, Garcia was still able to remotely monitor most other aspects of the building, including the use of access cards on locked doors.

'Last recorded access was Hayes' office,' Garcia reported. 'He hasn't used the keycard again. Must still be in there. North-west corner, end of the row.'

That made sense at least. If this man had gone to the trouble of impersonating Director Hayes and stealing his access card, there must have been something in his office that he wanted. Likely the gas had overpowered him before he'd made it out of the room.

'Copy. Moving to intercept.'

'Roger. I'm purging the atmosphere now.'

Deep within the building's complex air filtration system, powerful fans went to work sucking the toxic CO_2 build-up out of the air and replacing it with fresh oxygen.

Advancing through the silent, ghostly lab in which none of them had ever set foot, the team glanced left and right at the unfamiliar machinery and medical paraphernalia.

'What the fuck is this place?' DaForte wondered. 'Shit I've never seen before.'

'Nobody touch anything,' Lopez growled. 'You break it, it's your ass.'

Tracking an armed hostile was dangerous enough without worrying about accidentally releasing some toxic chemical or deadly virus that might be stored here.

Leaving the main research space behind, the team advanced along the row of offices reserved for senior facility personnel, all of which were closed and locked. They were moving slower and more cautiously now, weapons sweeping left and right, the hiss of their respirators growing faster as nerves and adrenaline took hold.

Hayes' office was directly ahead, closed and locked like all the others. Approaching it, Lopez removed his security keycard and held it out towards the electronic reader. His clearance allowed him to override lockouts and access any room in the facility, though doing so would be automatically logged in the system and questioned later.

'We go in on three,' he said, turning to his two comrades. 'Stay close, move fast and for Christ's sake watch where you point your weapons. I don't want friendly fire. Understand?'

Both men nodded.

'One,' he said, reaching out with the card. 'Two.'

He swiped it through the reader. There was a single beep as the security override kicked in and the lock was disabled.

Lopez reached for the door handle, gripping his weapon tight. 'Three!'

Chapter 15

The next few seconds passed in a blur of movement and frantic, heart-pounding energy. Throwing the door open, Lopez advanced inside the office, his weapon sweeping the murky confines of the room, still partially fogged with CO_2. DaForte and Williams went in right behind him, each shouting out a challenge to anyone who might be listening.

'Don't move! Don't fucking move!'

'Hands up!'

There was no response, no movement of any kind. The barrel of Lopez's weapon swept across the darkened room, seeking a target but finding none. There wasn't even a body lying sprawled on the floor.

'Anybody got eyes-on?' he called out, wondering if his faceplate was fogged up.

DaForte shook his head. 'Nothing.'

'Where the fuck is he?' Williams asked.

A glow was coming from Hayes' work terminal. It was powered up, meaning someone must have been in here recently. Edging around the desk, Lopez examined the screen to see what it was doing, and frowned when he caught sight of the dialogue box in the centre of the monitor.

File transfer complete

'What the hell...?'

His question was interrupted by a sudden crash on the other side of the office, and he whirled around in time to see a dark figure leap down from the ceiling, broken chunks of ceiling tile raining down around him.

Like most offices, the ceiling in here was fake, made up of thin ceramic tiles suspended from a metal grid for support. It was there for aesthetic reasons, to cover up the network of ventilation ducts, cabling and other apparatus that snaked across the real ceiling of a facility like this. The crawl space above it was mostly empty, and often a couple of feet deep. Plenty of room for a man to hide if he was able to remove one of the tiles and clamber up, waiting for the unsuspecting team to pass below him. Then all he had to do was let go and allow gravity to do the rest.

He landed almost on top of Williams, knocking the young man to the ground with a well-placed kick to the small of his back. As Williams cried out and fell, DaForte instinctively turned towards the commotion with his weapon raised. He hadn't seen the initial attack happen and it therefore took him a moment to process the scene before him.

His hesitation would prove fatal.

Before he could sight his target and open fire, his adversary reached out and ripped the respirator from his face, causing him to throw up his hands to try to protect himself. Coughing and gasping for air that wouldn't come in the heavy, CO_2-laden atmosphere, he tried to shoot, only for his enemy to grab his outstretched arm and twist it behind him.

'Fuck you!' Williams shouted, rolling over on the floor and turning his weapon on his assailant.

In the time it took for the young man to take aim and fire, their enemy had turned the now helpless DaForte towards Williams. A trio of gunshots rang out, there was an agonized scream, and DaForte fell to the ground with blood pumping from three separate wounds to his torso.

Williams barely had time to realize his mistake. Before DaForte had even hit the ground, a single low-pitched thud answered his hail of gunfire, accompanied by the dull wet crunch of bone and flesh giving way beneath the onslaught of a silenced high-velocity projectile.

Only Lopez was afforded a clean shot at him, and he wasted no time in taking it. Training his weapon, he opened fire, the sharp crack of his Smith & Wesson automatic echoing off the walls.

But even as he pulled the trigger and the gun's muzzle flare lit up the room like lightning, his target seemingly vanished into the CO_2 haze, throwing himself aside to land behind the desk. Hyped up on adrenaline, Lopez put three more rounds into the desk, each tearing a fist-sized hole in the wooden frame as they punched through it.

He ceased fire, and a second or so of unnatural silence descended on the room as he frantically planned his next move. He had to move, had to get around that desk and put this bastard down for good. It was just the two of them now.

He didn't get the chance to move. A pair of dull thuds resounded from beneath the desk, and his legs exploded in agony as the shots hit home, shattering both tibias like matchwood. Unable to support himself, he toppled and fell backwards, the gun clattering from his grasp as his body started to go into shock.

The respirator unit was barely able to keep up with his gasping, frantic breathing as he groaned in pain. Torn muscle and broken pieces of bone were visible through the holes in his trousers, his blood leaving twin crimson trails in the carpet beneath him as he vainly tried to drag himself backwards.

Vaguely, through his fogging vision, he saw his attacker rise up from behind the desk and approach him, saw the automatic fitted with a bulky suppressor in his right hand.

'Please,' he gasped as the weapon swung towards him. 'I just work here.'

'Worked,' the man corrected him.

A heavy thump was the last noise he heard.

Drake lowered his weapon, wisps of smoke still trailing from the barrel as he surveyed the dead bodies that now littered the room. He didn't feel an ounce of sympathy for the three men he'd just killed. They'd died the moment they entered that airlock; it was simply a matter of how long they held him up.

With the security taken care of, Drake returned to the office workstation and removed the memory stick, tucking it carefully into his pocket. He had what he'd come here for; now all he needed was an exit.

'Lopez, what's happening over there?' a harsh voice crackled from the dead man's short-range radio unit. 'Give me a report, goddamn it!'

Drake knelt down and unhooked it from the man's bloodstained uniform.

'Williams, DaForte! Someone talk to me!'

Taking a moment to concentrate on the terrified voice he'd heard before pulling the trigger, Drake pressed the transmit button.

'It's Lopez,' he said, imitating the man's accent and tonal inflection. The muffling quality of his respirator unit would almost certainly disguise any discrepancies. 'We got him! Bastard was wearing a respirator, tried to jump us when we made entry. I had to put him down.'

'He's dead?' His relief was almost tangible.

'Man's got half a dozen rounds in him. He isn't going anywhere.'

'I guess there was no choice. You okay?'

'Yeah, but DaForte took one in the leg,' Drake replied, looking at the man who had been inadvertently gunned down by his own comrade. 'We need a medical evac ASAP.'

'Stand by, I'm opening the airlock now.'

'Copy that. We're en route.' Drake clicked the radio off for now and placed it in the pocket of his shirt.

The air filtration system had almost finished dispersing the CO_2 gas, allowing him to remove his respirator and breathe unaided. Opening the office door, he swept the area with his silenced Browning automatic, just in case a fourth member of the team had lingered outside. When he didn't see anyone, he strode back down the corridor and into the main lab area.

Like most research facilities, this place was well stocked with medical equipment, pharmaceutical supplies, a multitude of chemicals and compressed gasses and liquids. Many of which, if mixed together in the proper proportions, would provide him with exactly what he needed. Drake could improvise a primitive explosive compound from even the most basic of household chemicals, so this place was a treasure trove of possibilities by comparison.

His first targets were several big cylinders of compressed oxygen fixed to the wall, used to supply air to the isolation chambers. Using his knife, he severed the hoses leading from the cylinders to the chambers, then manually cranked open the valves to maximum so that pure oxygen began to vent into the room. It wouldn't take long for the combustible gas to propagate throughout the building, greatly increasing the effectiveness of what he'd planned.

This done, he turned his attention to the chemical supplies carefully arranged in refrigerators and storage cabinets around the room.

The first component was nitromethane, of which he found several large plastic containers stacked at the base of one of the chemical storage lockers, all sporting urgent red stickers warning that it was both highly flammable and corrosive.

Nitromethane was one of the most versatile compounds in the world, used in everything from pharmaceuticals to textile manufacture and even as a fuel for model aircraft. As an intermediary in organic synthesis, it was widely employed in the manufacture of certain drugs and medical compounds, which explained why this lab had stockpiled large quantities of it.

What was less well known was that under the right conditions, it could be caused to detonate with even greater force than TNT. A mixture of nitromethane and ammonium nitrate had even been used in the Oklahoma City bombing in 1995. Drake however didn't have the time to properly synthesize such explosives, and would have to rely on something a little more primitive.

Stacking several of the containers together, he turned his attention to the second ingredient. Hydrazoic acid, a colourless, odourless liquid, was stored in glass flasks inside one of the deep freezer units. It was an innocuous-looking chemical at first sight, but it made up for that with explosive potential and sheer instability. All it took was a hard impact, or for its base temperature to rise a few degrees above zero, to trigger explosive decomposition.

Carefully removing one of the flasks from its freezer, he carried it over to an equipment sterilizer that had been set up on a nearby desk. Basically a powerful steam oven, it was designed to blast implements, beakers, containers or any other contaminated objects, destroying every trace of bacteria so that they could be safely used again.

Setting the flask of acid inside, he unscrewed the lid on the first container of nitromethane and poured it in, quickly followed by a second until the sterilizer unit was filled to the brim with the viscous, oily liquid. He stacked the remaining containers next to the sterilizer, closed and latched the lid to form a seal, then set the machine's digital timer for two minutes.

It was ready.

Taking one last look around, Drake flicked the unit's power switch to start the timer, then enabled the stopwatch function on his wrist watch. With his task complete, he turned away and made for the airlock.

As promised, the inner door was already open to the decontamination chamber beyond. Replacing his respirator, Drake removed the stolen radio and pressed transmit once more.

'We're in,' he reported, injecting the right amount of urgency. 'Open it up!'

As the big door slid closed behind him and the re-pressurization process began, he glanced at his watch – 1 minute 35 seconds left.

Chapter 16

As the airlock cycled and re-pressurized, Garcia turned his attention to the monitor covering the elevated walkway leading from Building B back to A, wondering what kind of condition DaForte would be in when the doors opened. There was a medical kit in his monitor room which would probably be enough to stabilize his condition until—

'Oh shit,' he gasped as a single figure stepped out of the airlock.

He watched in horror as the man calmly strode down the corridor towards his building, discarding the respirator unit he'd been carrying and drawing a silenced automatic from his jacket, ready to use it on anyone who opposed him.

Only now did the chief of security understand the extent of his mistake.

He'd released the man who had just murdered four of his comrades, and who might well be on his way to killing the fifth. He looked over at the locked door that barred entrance to his monitor room. It was a good two inches thick, reinforced with steel and Kevlar, able to withstand even an explosive breaching charge. It should have made him feel safe, but it didn't.

Nothing did now.

Pausing at the end of the corridor, the killer looked up at the surveillance camera. Garcia had the unnerving impression that the man was somehow looking directly at him.

He saw the man reach for something in his pocket, saw him raise it to his mouth, and jumped when his radio crackled. 'Are you listening?'

With a trembling hand, Garcia pressed his own transmitter. 'Yes.'

'What's your name?'

'Luis,' he answered, too shocked to think about holding back.

'Well, Luis, you have a choice. You can try to stop me, or you can stand aside. If you stand aside, you'll never see me again. But if you try to stop me, I'll be the last thing you ever see.' He let that sink in. 'Your call.'

It took Garcia all of three seconds to make his decision. Reaching for the door controls, he disabled the magnetic locks holding it closed.

As the door buzzed, the intruder inclined his head slightly in a gesture of acknowledgement, then held up the radio again.

'You made a good choice, Luis. Now do me a favour and tell your employers what happened here tonight. Tell them Ryan Drake is coming for them.'

Dropping the radio, the man eased the door open and exited the overhead corridor. Garcia watched as he continued his calm, measured journey through the building, heading for the main exit.

Even if he'd harboured thoughts of trying to impede the man's progress, he wouldn't have had the chance. His security room was suddenly rocked by a violent, thunderous explosion that reverberated through the building and caused the monitors to flicker and finally shut down. The main lights blew out as the circuits were cut. Streams of dust fell from the ceiling panels as Garcia took cover beneath his desk, certain the intruder had detonated a bomb right outside.

As the red emergency lights powered up, Garcia cautiously emerged from his hiding place to stare at his bank of monitors. Many had been knocked out by the blast, but one or two external cameras were still active, and the scene they displayed was one of absolute devastation.

Building B was gone, torn asunder by some terrific internal explosion. The roof had already collapsed in on itself, and the external walls were leaning inwards. Bright orange flames at least 50 feet high licked up into the night sky, occasionally turning blue and green as various chemicals ignited, while a pall of hazy smoke drifted across the entire scene. More explosions erupted as compressed cylinders cooked off in the intense heat.

When Garcia turned his attention back to the cameras, he found no sign of the intruder. The man had departed as suddenly as he'd arrived, leaving only death and destruction in his wake.

Chapter 17

It was a beautiful evening on the west coast of California, the sun slowly setting in a near-cloudless sky, gentle waves stirring the blue waters of the Pacific to break and crash in fountains of white foam just offshore. The kind of evening that made one feel delighted simply to be alive.

Elizabeth Powell turned off the winding coastal road, slowing her silver Mercedes-Benz convertible long enough for the automated gates to roll back, then stomped on the gas again to bring her into the big paved courtyard beyond. Parking up, she shut down the powerful V8 sports engine and just sat there, allowing the breeze to sigh past her, carrying with it the distant crash of waves and the calls of seagulls.

Such peace and tranquillity was rare in her life, but she'd learned to appreciate it when she could.

Her home was a sprawling, two-storey, contemporary-styled villa situated on the rocky cliffs overlooking the Pacific coast. It was one of many in this area, though few were as grand or commanded as impressive a view. Malibu was where the rich and famous set up home, and her neighbourhood was one of the most desirable locations of the lot. Hollywood movie stars, European business tycoons, Russian oligarchs and even Arab royalty were all to be found within a half-mile of her home.

It amused her that she'd procured a better spot for herself than they had. Then again, she'd made it her philosophy in life to excel where others faltered, to go just a little further than others were able or willing to.

Stepping into the cool, air conditioned reception hallway, she kicked off her heeled shoes and strode purposefully through to the kitchen, her footsteps barely audible on the polished marble. Opening out onto a sweeping balcony that over-looked the endless ocean, she'd had the kitchen specially designed to take full advantage of the view.

Dumping her purse, keys and cell phone on the kitchen island, she selected a bottle of white wine from the fridge – Beringer Chardonnay, nearly a hundred dollars a bottle but more than worth it – and poured herself a moderate glass. She didn't take too much just yet, thinking she might go for a run before sunset, but there were few better ways of quietening her restless thoughts after a long day.

The problem with being at the top of the pile was that everyone looked up to you. There was no one else to turn to, nobody to give you guidance or advice.

That was just fine with her, but it did require a high degree of mental discipline that could become wearying.

She had just taken her first sip when her cell phone started ringing and vibrating on the hard kitchen worktop. She ignored it, letting it go to voicemail. She employed plenty of subordinates to look after her company when she was off the clock.

Turning towards the balcony, she was about to open the big sliding doors and take a seat outside when the phone rang again.

'Goddamn it,' she said under her breath, retrieving the phone to check the caller ID. It was Mike Brody, her head of South American operations. This was enough to get her attention. It had to be the early hours of the morning there, so he was unlikely to be calling over some trivial issue that could be resolved tomorrow.

'This had better be good, Mike,' she warned him, taking another sip. 'There are roughly eight hours of the day when I'm off the clock, and this is one of them.'

Brody got straight to the point. 'We have a problem, Liz. Can you talk freely?'

'Yeah. Go.'

Powell listened as he explained everything he knew about an incident at their research facility in Rio de Janeiro, which wasn't much at this point. But the basics of his report were enough to jump her heartbeat up a gear. An armed raid, men dead, explosions on site.

'What's the extent of the damage?'

'Not good,' he said, sounding decidedly shaken. 'Right now it looks like a total loss.'

Powell closed her eyes and rubbed the bridge of her nose, as she was prone to doing when she received bad news. 'We had security. You assured me that place was airtight.'

Brody cleared his throat. 'Like I say, we're still getting information in. But it seems whoever did this was able to circumvent our security protocols.'

'You don't say. I need you to lock the area down, and keep local police out. Spin a cover story if you have to, say it was a gas explosion. I want full containment and a news blackout on this. Understand?'

'Liz, this is—'

'Make it happen, Mike,' she cut in. 'And get someone on site who knows what the hell they're doing. I want a full situation report in one hour.'

Brody hesitated, clearly thinking to protest her order, but soon thought better of it. 'Of course. We'll get our best men on it.'

'People, Mike,' she corrected him. 'Sometimes the best person for the job isn't a man. You should keep that in mind.'

Hanging up the phone, she looked down at the glass of wine in her hands, gently swirling the amber liquid around and watching the play of sunlight across its surface.

'Fuck!' she shouted, hurling the glass against the wall.

–

Bringing the stolen Ford Explorer to a halt in a patch of waste ground, Drake exhaled slowly, calming himself after the events of the past hour or so. After an op like this, some reflection helped to bring the adrenaline under control.

Just breathe, listen to the sound of it, let everything else fall away. That's what he'd been taught, and it had never failed him.

The rain had eased off now, allowing him to discard the raincoat stolen from Hayes' home. In the distance, he could just make out the bright orange glow of the fires from the destroyed facility and hear the wail of fire engines sent to tackle the blaze. The thought of the damage he'd caused tonight gave him a fleeting sense of satisfaction.

That should be enough to get their attention, he thought.

His compact rucksack was right where he'd left it earlier in the night, hidden beneath a pile of rocks and broken wooden planking. Tossing this discarded rubble aside, he pulled out the rucksack, opened it up and retrieved his own clothes. After quickly changing, he dumped the used items in the vehicle.

In under a minute, it was done. The only things he kept were the Browning automatic with the silencer removed for easier concealment, and the memory stick he'd obtained with such effort.

He held the device up, contemplating the wealth of information contained within. Enough perhaps to answer the questions that had dogged him for the past seven years, to finally shed light on the darkened recesses of his past, perhaps even save his sanity.

Slipping the device into his pocket, he took Hayes' shirt from the driver's seat, strode around to the rear of the vehicle and unscrewed the fuel cap, then stuffed it into the opening. He reached for the flint lighter in his pocket, ignited it and held the flickering flame against the fabric. The expensive cotton caught within seconds, and that was all he needed.

Drake had covered about 100 yards when the fireball lit up the night sky, accompanied by the boom of an explosion. Even from this distance, Drake could feel the heat of the flames. By the time local fire crews, already occupied with the destruction at the facility, made their way here, there would be nothing left of the Explorer worth retrieving.

He didn't bother to look back as he slipped through a gap in the chain-link fence at the edge of the waste ground and vanished into the night. Drake had other tasks now.

Chapter 18

It was well into the afternoon of the following day by the time the team got their first big break. Anya and Mitchell had made their sweep of Drake's apartment as agreed, finding nothing out of the ordinary save for his discarded cell phone on the floor, and a half-finished bottle of whisky on the kitchen counter. No clues as to why he'd disappeared so suddenly and, more importantly, no indication of where he'd gone.

The pair had returned to Anya's place with little to go on. Frost likewise had been unable to find any digital trace of Drake so far. If he'd booked travel out of the country, he'd done it with ID and payment details that none of the team were aware of.

In the end it was Alex who found the first clue, turning up at the front door unannounced, clutching his laptop, looking like he'd gone too long without sleep.

'You need to see this,' he said. The others gathered around to observe as he set up his computer, then hit play on a video file. Once again the message from the man claiming to be Drake began to play.

'There was a reason he wanted Ryan to see this,' Alex explained as the clip carried on playing. 'I didn't notice it at first, but there was something off about the audio. I thought it was just ambient noise or poor recording equipment, but there's a lot more to it than that. Listen closely.'

He'd adjusted the sound composition on this version, minimizing the spoken dialogue in favour of the background noise. Sure enough, the pops and crackles and oddly lilting tones had become more pronounced, blending together into a more coherent spectrum of sound, forming what could almost be described as a melody.

'There's a hidden audio layer in this recording,' Alex explained, clearly excited by his discovery. 'I had to mess around with the balance and pull the different ranges apart to find it, but it's there. You might not have noticed it when the video originally played, but your brain did. It's like subliminal messaging.'

'What the hell do you know about hidden audio layers and subliminal messaging?' Frost asked, looking more than a little put out that he'd been the one to spot this.

'More than you, apparently,' Alex fired back. 'Listen to it when you isolate it completely from the other layers.'

Replaying it again with the filter engaged, the group was startled to hear a definite musical composition, the pitch rising and falling slowly, following a beat that even the least musically gifted could follow. It was still slightly garbled, but it was unmistakable.

'It's a song,' Dietrich said, frowning as he tried to identify it.

'Sounds like classical music,' Frost added, unable to elaborate further. Her knowledge of the form left much to be desired.

'It's a hymn,' Mitchell corrected her, straining to pick up the vaguely familiar tune. 'A church hymn. I think it's… yeah, it's "Will the Circle Be Unbroken".'

Alex looked at her. 'How on earth do you get that?'

The woman shrugged. 'My family were big churchgoers when I was a kid. Guess it must have rubbed off on me.'

Anya shook her head. 'What's the significance of this song?'

'Search me,' Alex admitted. 'It could be some kind of trigger or a warning that more information is coming, like those weird numbers station things they used in the Cold War.'

Having served with the CIA during that period, Anya was well acquainted with numbers stations and the seemingly baffling streams of random letters and words they would broadcast, their true meanings known only to a select few who were ready and waiting for them. Many such stations would begin and end their broadcasts with music to allow listeners to properly calibrate their receivers before the main message was sent.

'Anyway, it gets better,' Alex went on. 'It wasn't just hidden audio cues in this video. There were static images hidden inside the visual display, just single frames roughly every three or four seconds. You can't see them with the naked eye, but watch what happens when you slow it down.'

Once again he replayed the video, this time with the sound muted and the frame rate reduced so that instead of broadcasting at around thirty frames per second, it was down to just two or three. The result was a jerky, unwatchable experience, but one which allowed them to process each frame as they saw it.

Frame after frame, they saw only the masked man standing against the black background, his mouth moving with glacial slowness as he spoke each word. And then, suddenly, his image was gone, replaced by a single symbol set against a lighter background. The number 5.

'There!' Alex said, pausing the video.

'Okay, so it's a number 5,' Dietrich observed sarcastically. 'Doesn't tell us much.'

'Not on its own, so I went to the trouble of isolating the rest of the hidden frames.' Alex opened a new window on the laptop. 'Check this out.'

They watched as each of the hidden frames played out in sequence, each one of them a number, 11 in all.

'Son of a bitch. It's a cell phone number,' Frost exclaimed.

'With an international prefix,' Anya added, searching her memory. '55. That's South America.'

'Brazil, to be more specific,' Alex confirmed.

Mitchell looked at him. 'Does it work? Have you tried it?'

Alex shook his head. 'It's an unregistered number, and it's inactive now. My guess is it was a one-time burner for Ryan to make contact on. After that, our friend here must have tossed it.'

Anya nodded. It was unfortunate, but not unexpected given what little they knew about the man behind this attack. Whatever he might be, he certainly wasn't an amateur.

'Then that should be where we focus our efforts,' she decided. 'Look for anything out of the ordinary in Brazil. Attacks, murders, terrorist strikes—'

'That could be a bloody long list,' Alex remarked. With widespread corruption, gang violence and drug dealing, Brazil had some of the highest crime and murder rates in the world.

'Then we'd better get started,' Frost said, already turning to her computer.

Chapter 19

Los Angeles, California

The headquarters of Unity Medical Research Group were situated in Santa Monica on the western outskirts of Los Angeles, not far down the coastal road from Elizabeth Powell's private villa. A big ultra-modern edifice of glass and steel, its mirrored windows reflected the California sunset and the distant skyscrapers of central LA. It was designed in the shape of a giant triangle – the symbol of the company it housed.

To most casual observers it seemed little different, if perhaps a bit more ostentatious, than the countless other corporate buildings in that district of the city. Everything from aerospace companies to financial analysts and even videogame development houses had made Santa Monica their home. But none of them did what Unity could do. None of them were helping reshape the world.

Powell's office was on the third floor at the north-eastern corner, facing the sprawling cityscape on one side and the peaceful tree-covered hills of Topanga State Park on the other.

She had driven straight here from her home the second she'd ended the call, breaking half a dozen speed limits along the way and not caring one bit. She needed to be here. This wasn't the kind of situation that could be managed from her kitchen.

She leaned in close to her computer screen, reviewing the security camera footage from their facility in Rio de Janeiro, hastily compressed and sent to her via secure email. She watched the assailant advance through the supposedly secure facility with infuriating ease, the security team's inept attempts to respond, their idiotic choice to flood the research building with CO_2 suppressors, and their fatal decision to go in after him rather than wait for backup.

She watched as the man emerged from the containment building a couple of minutes later, advancing along the overhead corridor that ran between the two buildings, and halt when he encountered a locked door.

He turned his head upwards then, looking directly into the camera and showing his uncovered face for the first time.

Elizabeth felt her heart beat faster as she took it all in. That rugged, handsome face, the short dark hair, the lips drawn back in a faintly mocking smile. It was a face she'd once known very well indeed, that she'd believed she would never see again. And here it was, staring right back at her.

She watched as Ryan Drake raised a radio unit to his mouth and spoke, calmly conversing with the building's security chief. The radio conversation itself hadn't been recorded, but she could just make out his end of the exchange through the camera's own microphone.

'You made a good choice, Luis. Do me a favour, tell your employers what happened here tonight. Tell them Ryan Drake is coming for them.'

Closing down the video, Powell leaned back in her chair, her mind whirling through the implications of what she'd just seen.

Finally making a decision, she reached for her desk phone and hit the speed dial button for Walter Harris, her personal assistant. Given the heavy demands of her work, the man was effectively on call 24/7.

'Walter, I need to fly to DC right away. Have the corporate jet fuelled up and ready to go,' she said, her calm voice concealing the turmoil in her head. 'And contact our friends at Langley. I want to speak with Marcus Cain.'

–

Drake had taken a room at a local hotel: a cheap place in an even cheaper part of town that took payment in cash and didn't ask too many questions. The fat, elderly woman working the front desk hadn't even asked for a name as he parted with his small wad of notes, instead handing him an old-fashioned key chained to a block of wood to deter theft.

The rooms were also available to rent by the hour, and judging by the strained grunts and exaggerated female moans coming from behind one door, some people were still making use of them. Drake ignored the sounds of rented pleasure as he passed along the dingy corridor.

Unlocking his door, he bent down and checked for the piece of paperclip he'd left in the doorjamb. It hadn't moved. Nobody had been snooping around here in his absence.

Locking the door behind him, he dumped the backpack on the bed, removed his jacket and withdrew the Browning automatic he'd kept concealed during his walk back to the hotel.

With the automatic in hand, Drake lowered himself into a chair over by the window. The blinds were drawn but light from the street lamps outside was still seeping in, orange and sickly. Ejecting the magazine, he thumbed out the remaining .40 calibre rounds, laying them in a neat line on the desk. Magazine springs could lose their strength if kept under tension for too long.

A lot of soldiers experienced the shakes, but it was usually after an engagement. You never really got a chance to get scared while it was all going on. You felt a rush, to be sure, and the instinct to fight and stay alive, but not real fear. There was too much running, too much shouting and frantic fumbling with weapons and ammunition to let yourself think about it. It was only later, after the firing stopped and the wild confusion died down, that your mind got a chance to process the shit-storm you'd just passed through.

Then you realized you could have died at any moment. Any one of those rounds that had whizzed over your head could have had your name on it. And everything you were, everything you'd done and everything you might do would be snuffed out like a candle.

It had been like that for Drake once too, but not any more. Now the prospect of fighting stirred a different emotion in him, one that was even more deeply buried than fear. It was an emotion that shouldn't rightly have had a word; it was too ingrained, too primitive for that. But if he had to pick a word that best summed up what he'd felt, he would describe it as joy.

It was perhaps the same feeling his distant ancestors had experienced when they brought down some great beast with spears and clubs. The satisfaction of having prevailed against an enemy, the raw ecstasy of survival in the face of death.

He'd left a couple of items in his room ahead of his return tonight, both of which were resting on the small desk. The first was a bottle of *cachaça*, some shitty local spirit that tasted a little like rum that had gone off. Still, it did the job well enough.

Drake poured himself half a glass and downed it in one gulp, grimacing as it settled reluctantly in his stomach.

The second item was a laptop computer. A basic model he'd brought with him from Switzerland in his go-bag. He'd disabled all the network options and even removed the wireless card, so it was impossible for the machine to communicate with the outside world. Conversely, there was also no way to track its location.

Powering up the laptop, he retrieved the memory stick from his jacket and carefully inserted it into the USB port. It took nearly 30 seconds for the machine to scan the contents of the memory stick and present an overview of them on screen – a testimony to how much raw data Frost's program had transferred over. Pouring himself another glass of *cachaça,* Drake got to work.

Many of the files and directories dealt with simple administrative tasks. Others were allocated specific project names and designations, signifying at least some of the work that had gone on within that facility. The less important ones seemed to have been allocated a numeric reference, but the more serious undertakings were given proper code names.

DAYBREAK
MERCURY
CASCADE
WHIRLWIND
TEMPEST
AURORA

On and on they went, more than he could easily peruse even if he spent the rest of the night trawling through it all. Pulling up a search tool, he input the name 'HYDRA', and hit the 'enter' key.

No results found

Frowning, Drake inputted the search again, wondering if he'd entered it incorrectly, only to be met with the same blunt, frustrating response.

It couldn't be, he told himself. It had to be there somewhere. This couldn't have been for nothing.

For several minutes he tried every variation on Hydra or anything associated with it that he could think of, yet still nothing happened. Why was it not there? Had he been wrong? Had his contact lied to him?

Then, switching tacks, he tried a different search parameter: 'Ryan Drake'.

And this time, he got the hit he'd been looking for.

1 result(s) found

A file inside a hidden directory within the complex system architecture. A file dedicated solely to him.

That was enough to send a shiver of foreboding through him. It *was* here. Somehow he *had* come under their influence, and this file could tell him everything. It could tell him what they'd done to him, how they'd changed him, and how he might free himself of their insidious influence.

Forcing himself to remain patient, Drake selected the file and opened it.

But it didn't open. Instead a dialogue box appeared.

Access restricted (Executive level only). Enter password.

Drake hurriedly typed Hayes' password, only to be met with the same message. He tried again, working methodically even as he felt the anger and frustration building, but the file remained locked.

Hayes didn't have access. Drake could enter the man's password until the laptop ceased to function, but it would make no difference. The only person who could open it was the director of the company herself.

Very clever, Elizabeth.

His cell phone was ringing inside his jacket. Retrieving it, he checked the caller ID and found, as before, that the number was unknown.

'I'm here.'

'And you've been busy,' his contact remarked. 'You don't waste any time, I see.'

'I'm not here to play games. Let's hope you're not either.'

His thinly veiled anger was not lost on the caller. 'I'm guessing you didn't find what you were looking for.'

You fucker, Drake thought, realizing why this man already knew he'd failed.

'And you knew I wouldn't.'

He didn't respond.

'You'd better hope I don't catch up with you,' Drake warned.

'Wait,' the caller implored. 'I promised you answers, and I meant it. Tonight was the first step, but not the last. Your next is—'

'Spare me,' Drake cut in. 'I warned you about playing games. Well, I know exactly who I need. I'm going to get my own answers from her.'

82

'You're making a mistake,' the caller said, his voice more insistent. 'This isn't going to work—'

Drake ended the call, then powered down the phone to prevent further contact and dumped it beside the laptop, which still displayed the same password screen.

He would find the answers he needed, and he'd do it his way. Nobody else could help him now, and nobody controlled him either. The plan might have changed, but his resolve to see it through hadn't. The only difference was how many people would have to die first.

Chapter 20

'Whoa, I got something!' Frost called out, beckoning the others over to her laptop. It didn't take the group long to cluster around her.

'What is it?' Mitchell asked.

'An explosion at a medical research facility in Rio de Janeiro,' Frost said, quickly scanning the headlines. 'A big one, by the looks of it.'

The footage was a shaky, handheld recording, probably taken from someone's smartphone. It showed a scene of destruction, the wreckage of a building that looked like half the USAF had just carpet-bombed it.

'Shit, someone really made a mess,' Alex remarked.

'There's conflicting reports bouncing around. The company says it was a gas explosion, but there's testimony from the fire crews on the scene that they found gunshot victims in the facility. Local news reporters are already suggesting it might have been a drug cartel hit.'

Dietrich cocked an eyebrow. 'Could be right. Place is a fucking war zone. What makes you think this was Ryan's work?'

The young woman looked up at him. 'I did some snooping on local police databases and found a separate report of a murder victim found in his home this morning. Shot to death by a silenced weapon: two in the chest, one in the head. Standard execution protocol for Agency operatives, not the blood-and-guts routine the cartels go in for. I'll give you ten bucks if you can tell me where the guy works.'

The answer was obvious enough. If this theory was correct, Drake had killed that man, perhaps to steal his ID or access, and used them to infiltrate the facility and destroy the place. The question that remained was why he'd done it.

'Shit, Frost. I think you might have actually impressed me for once,' Dietrich conceded.

She offered a decidedly fake smile. 'Well, fortunately I don't base my self-worth on what some asshole thinks.'

'This could be a lead,' Mitchell allowed. 'Or it could still be a coincidence. Tough call.'

Anya however had already made up her mind. She'd never been a believer in coincidence. In any case, she sensed Drake's handiwork at play here. The phone trace, the murder, the explosion all pointed to one place – Rio.

Mitchell looked at her. 'What are you thinking?'

To say Anya had a plan would be a wild exaggeration. All she had right now was an objective. 'This feels like Ryan,' she decided. 'I have to go there, find out what happened and track him down.'

'Then you're going to need help,' Mitchell said.

Anya shook her head. If Drake had truly reverted to that ruthless, bloodthirsty man then there was no telling what he might be capable of.

'Not with this. Ryan could kill any one of you if he wanted,' she declared. 'I can't put you in that kind of danger.'

'So what's your plan? You're going to march in there at high noon, the lone gunslinger, and take him down all by yourself?' Dietrich scoffed. 'Good luck with that.'

Anya folded her arms. 'If I have to.'

'Listen to what you're saying. He kicked your ass once already,' Frost reminded Anya with her typical bluntness. 'If Ryan's as dangerous as you say, what makes you think it'll turn out any different next time?'

'I underestimated him before. I won't make that mistake again.'

Anya would never admit it to anyone, but Frost's declaration had exposed a deep-seated fear. A fear that perhaps it wasn't just lack of preparation that had allowed Drake to get the better of her, but something more inescapable – time.

'You might not get the chance,' Mitchell said. 'If he kills you and there's nobody around to back you up, then we've blown our best shot at bringing him in. Together we might have more luck.'

Anya didn't respond. Much as their assistance might improve her chances, this was hardly some highly disciplined military unit who would follow her orders without hesitation. The thought of working with this eclectic group of people who either didn't trust her, didn't respect her or didn't understand her was hardly an appealing one.

And the thought of one or all of them following her to their deaths was even less palatable. Too many people had put their faith in Anya during her long career, had trusted her to lead them into battle and bring them out alive. Most were now dead.

'I'm no leader,' she warned them. 'Not any more.'

'We don't need you to be. We just need you to let us help,' Alex added, sensing her resolve wavering. 'When it comes to slapping the handcuffs on him… well, you guys can fight it out amongst yourselves. I'll be at the nearest pub.'

It was a weak attempt at humour, and Anya was in no mood for laugher. Instead she turned from the group to stare out at the sweeping panorama of the Alps. Many times she'd found solace in that view, but not today. Today she knew she would only find peace when they brought Drake in.

And she knew she stood a better chance with their help.

'All right,' she decided, finally bowing to the inevitable. 'We do this together.'

Between them they possessed a wide range of different skills, many of which could prove invaluable in tracking down Drake. The question was how best to use them. She could make life-or-death choices in the heat of battle without any difficulty, but when it came to winning the cooperation of others, especially those who wouldn't follow without question, she was quite out of her depth.

They were looking at her now, waiting for her to say something, Dietrich most of all, his natural inclination towards command and authority asserting itself. If she didn't do something now, he would likely step in and do it for her.

'We will divide into two groups. The first group will be responsible for intel gathering,' she decided, then turned her attention to Alex.

Out of all of them, he was the one she'd spent the most time with, and therefore felt most comfortable around. He was also a formidable computer expert, able to hack into systems others believed impregnable and secure information most considered inaccessible.

'We need to know more about the target of this attack. I doubt it was chosen at random, so see what you can find out about the facility and its owners.'

He nodded. 'On it.'

'Frost, do what you can to help him,' Anya carried on, speaking more decisively now as she fell into the once familiar rhythm of issuing instructions. 'And see if there was any security footage of the attack that would confirm Ryan's presence.'

'I know the drill.' Already she was opening up new windows on screen. 'What are you going to do?'

'Find a way to get to Brazil at short notice without the Agency knowing,' she replied, her mind already racing ahead as she contemplated and discarded various plans. Leapfrogging across the Atlantic Ocean was no small task, even for someone with her resources.

To her surprise, Dietrich spoke up. 'I might be able to help with that.'

Part II

Rationalization

The MK–Ultra programme involved more than 80 universities, 200 researchers and 150 human experiments involving psychedelic drugs, paralytics and electroshock therapy. Most participants were never informed of the true purpose of these experiments.

As before, the candidate was seated at the table in the centre of the interview room when the door slid open and she stepped through. But he wasn't sitting with the composed stillness he had before. Now his hands and feet were securely strapped to the chair, preventing him from moving, preventing him from lashing out at her.

And the face that had held an expression of casual interest during their first session was now gaunt and haggard, etched with pain and exhaustion. Those green eyes were on her now, alight with anger and defiance. This was always the most difficult stage in the process, when the conscious mind made one last great effort to defend itself.

'Good morning, candidate,' she said, reciting the exact greeting she used each time. It was in fact early evening in the real world by now, but that didn't matter. What mattered was the routine, the solid and unchanging foundation of reality that it represented.

And as each of the candidates was learning in his own way, the real world no longer existed.

He didn't respond, but she noted his confused, questioning look. He was searching his memory, trying to decide if that was true. Trying to decide which version of reality he believed more.

'This is our fifth session together, candidate,' she informed him. 'We've talked together at great length, and I think we've come to know each other well. Would you agree?'

'What the fuck are you people doing to me?' he demanded, his voice strained like a rope stretched to breaking point.

She paced slowly around him, studying his reactions, his appearance, the changes she'd wrought on him. She took note of the beads of sweat standing out on his face, the muscles straining against his bonds, the desperation and defiance that still burned bright.

'I'm helping you, candidate,' she replied. 'I want to make you more than you are. But you have to help me. You're strong, maybe the strongest we've ever dealt with. And you're fighting us. We can't help you until you stop resisting.'

'You're torturing people!' he snapped. 'You're fucking sick!'

She nodded sympathetically, understanding his suffering, his inner conflict. If only he could begin to understand what she was doing here, the potential she was releasing, the future she was helping to bring about. If only he could see beyond these walls.

'Did you know we almost never came to be, candidate?' she asked, moving around behind him so that only her voice reached his conscious mind. 'Humanity was once an endangered species. Seventy thousand years ago, Neanderthals dominated all Eurasia. Hundreds of thousands of them, spread all across the continent. Then came the Cro-Magnons – us. Just a few thousand of them, a little evolutionary offshoot that started in Africa and spread northwards. And within twenty thousand years, the Neanderthals that had once outnumbered us so overwhelmingly were gone, and we were all that was left. Why do you think that was, candidate?'

He didn't respond. She could see him trembling, struggling within himself.

'Evolution,' she stated. 'They had advanced as far as they could. We were smarter, faster, more inventive than they could ever be. We out-competed them, and in the end there could only be one winner. Evolution can be a painful process, and only the strong survive it.' She laid her hands gently on his shoulders. 'And so here we are, fifty thousand years later. Now we live in a world where there are no competing species to fight, where nature's been tamed by science and progress, where there's nothing left to challenge us. And do you know what that means? This is it. This is as high as we're going to climb, as good as we're ever going to be. And with nothing left to challenge us, all we have left to fight is each other. We've lost our purpose. Evolution has brought humanity to a dead end, just like the Neanderthals.'

She let go and knelt down in front of him so that she was looking him dead in the eye. She needed him to see her now, needed him to understand the strength of her desire to succeed.

'We can change that,' she whispered. 'You and I, together. We can give the world new purpose. We can make things better, give humanity a fresh start. But it all begins right here, in this room. You have to make a choice, candidate. Are you going to be part of that future, or another one of evolution's dead ends?'

When she left the room a short time later, she was met by Thomas Hayes, her leading pharmaceutical researcher. The man whose brilliant mind had developed the compounds they were now using to such effect. He'd observed the entire session via concealed surveillance camera. All such sessions were recorded for later review.

'You're wasting your time,' he warned, speaking with the solemn assurance of a doctor proclaiming a patient's time of death. 'There's too much resistance. We've seen it before — sometimes the mind just won't accept the conditioning.'

'Increase his dosage by 50 per cent,' she instructed him.

His eyes opened wide at this. 'That's well beyond the safety threshold. You'll kill him.'

'Just do it,' she snapped. 'He can take it. I know he can.'

Chapter 21

International airspace

Anya stretched, the muscles in her back tightening and the vertebrae popping audibly as she tried to find a comfortable seating position. It wasn't easy given that the McDonnell Douglas DC-10 transport aircraft they were travelling in was designed to accommodate cargo rather than passengers. Comfort was at a premium here.

Dietrich had indeed lived up to his word to lay on transport for them, pulling various strings and calling in more than a few favours with his former colleagues at the BND, the Federal Intelligence Service of Germany. Somehow they'd arranged for a cargo hauler bound for Brazil to make an unscheduled stopover at Zurich international airport.

Once it had taxied into a hangar reserved for German haulage companies, the five travellers had been hustled aboard, squeezing in amongst long lines of squat metal freight pallets. And that had been it; the idling engines had spun up and the big aircraft was airborne again and en route to its destination. The whole thing had been accomplished in under 20 minutes. Even Anya was impressed.

The flight crew, all gruff and decidedly unfriendly in character, had said almost nothing except to instruct them to strap themselves in and not to venture up to the flight deck unless there was an emergency. They clearly had no idea why this group had been shunted aboard their aircraft, but they knew an illegal operation when they saw one, and wanted nothing to do with it.

Anya had her reservations about the whole plan, partly because it went against her nature to trust her security to someone else's arrangements, but mostly because it went against her better judgement to trust Dietrich with anything. The man was undoubtedly resourceful, even intelligent, but she didn't care for his haughty and suspicious personality one bit.

Nonetheless, the journey had gone as smoothly as a cargo flight over the Atlantic in squally weather could be expected to go, and by her calculations they should be touching down in under two hours.

The rest of the group had made the best of the situation, exchanging conversation at times and even playing a few card games with the deck Mitchell had had the foresight to bring. But as the flight dragged on, the talk had petered out and most of them had gone their separate ways. Alex was now lying stretched out on the deck with his jacket rolled beneath his head as a makeshift pillow, while Frost was sitting cross-legged on the opposite side of the hold, earphones in, face set with concentration as she tapped away at her laptop.

Every so often she would pause in her work, slowly tensing and flexing the fingers of her right hand before resuming her task. Jason Hawkins, one of Cain's men, had impaled her hand with his knife six months earlier. Though the injury seemed to have healed well, Anya guessed she'd experience a slight loss of dexterity in that hand for the rest of her life.

Dietrich by contrast had remained aloof throughout, saying little and keeping to himself as much as possible. Anya was hardly the biggest conversationalist, but in his case she sensed a different motive. When she looked at him, she saw a man planning his own actions and serving his own agenda. Whether or not that agenda aligned with the group's, only he knew.

But the biggest dilemma facing her was how to begin their search for Drake once they were on the ground. Brazil was a big country, and an easy place for a man like him to disappear. It had been nearly eight hours since news of the attack broke, giving him a considerable head start on them. It was entirely possible that he'd fled Brazil altogether and that his trail would be long cold.

Her introspection was disturbed when Mitchell approached, gripping one of the cargo pallets for support as the aircraft rode through another patch of turbulence.

'Got a minute?'

Anya nodded, privately relieved to have something to distract her. 'What do you need?'

'A sense of purpose would be good,' Mitchell admitted, taking a seat. 'I was wondering what I can do.'

Anya considered the question carefully. In truth, she knew little of this woman, save that she'd risked her life to protect Anya and Alex from an Agency kill team in Istanbul. The encounter had left Mitchell critically injured and very nearly ended her life. Only prompt medical care and a hastily organized rescue mission on Drake's part had spared her from life imprisonment or death.

'You seem to know a few things about Ryan's motives.'

Mitchell chuckled. 'You kidding? I've been winging it ever since this started.'

Anya recognized false modesty. Whether or not this situation was outside her normal experience, the fact remained that Mitchell had previously demonstrated good instincts and a cool head – two factors that would serve them well in the days ahead. And unlike Alex and Frost, who were still young and temperamental, or Dietrich who was experienced but cynical and uncooperative, Mitchell seemed more balanced and stable. Her methodical manner of thinking also suggested a very specific line of work.

'You were a police officer once,' she said. 'Before you served in the Agency.'

'More or less,' Mitchell confirmed. 'Army CID.'

The US Army Criminal Investigation Division was a small but highly trained unit assigned to investigate major crimes within the military – everything from rape to murder to extortion and terrorism. They were soldiers trained to outsmart and out-think other soldiers, to be a cut above their contemporaries. That being the case, she might well be the perfect person to have on side at a time like this.

'Were you good at your job?'

'I had my moments.'

That was good enough. 'Then what do you make of Ryan's actions?'

'Well, this is a pretty unusual situation.' Mitchell took a deep breath, searching for the right way to summarize her thoughts. 'Normally when a crime's been committed we look for motive, method and opportunity to help identify the perp. In this case, we know the last two. We have our suspect, we know what he looks like and, to some extent, how he operates. Unfortunately he knows the same about us, and he's been trained to avoid capture. If he's determined to stay one step ahead, he'll use that against us. That's what I'd do.'

Anya could see no reason to question that assessment. 'So how do we find him?'

'Like I said, we know Drake's method of attack and the opportunity he had. It's the motive that's missing. That's going to be key to understanding what Drake's thinking, and what he might do next. The video implied there's going to be more attacks, and I'm guessing Drake will be the one to carry them out. That's our best lead. If we want to find him, we need to figure out what his next target might be.'

'Or who,' Anya remarked thoughtfully.

Mitchell nodded. 'The video mentioned something about people who live in the shadows.' She was watching Anya carefully. 'Any idea what that might refer to?'

Anya certainly had her suspicions, but she'd been reluctant to voice them earlier.

'It could be nothing,' she evaded.

'Or it could be something,' Mitchell prompted her. 'Generally I'd settle for having more information over less.'

Anya had a feeling she'd say that. She looked the woman hard in the eye. 'You have heard of a group called the Circle.'

'Only what Drake told me. Bad guys meeting in dark rooms, shadow governments secretly ruling the world. Illuminati-type bullshit.'

Anya snorted with amusement, though explaining the whole truth would take more time than they had. 'Something like that. Ryan and I both had dealings with them in the past. He may be trying to attract their attention now.'

'But why? He's just one man, and by his own admission these people have the power to topple governments and reshape countries. What does he expect to do?'

Anya could only shrug. 'If I know Ryan, he will have a plan.'

But maybe you don't know him as well as you thought, a voice in her head warned her. She tried not to think about that moment his hands had closed around her throat.

'I guess it fits with our previous theory. He wouldn't have staged an attack like this unless he expected a reaction. Whether or not he's ready for it is anyone's guess.'

Anya sighed in exasperation. Drake was resourceful, but he couldn't possibly comprehend the magnitude and power of the enemy he'd pitted himself against.

The Circle had crushed more men like Drake than even they could keep track of, and wouldn't hesitate to do so again.

'I need to take a walk,' she decided, rising from her seat.

Mitchell watched her go, saying nothing.

Slipping through the gap between the long line of freight pallets, Anya made her way to the rear of the cargo bay, where there was at least a little more space to move around. Good; she needed to move, to pace back and forth, to try to expend some of the nervous tension in her body.

Four years spent inside a jail cell in a Siberian prison would be enough to make anyone wary of confined spaces.

But it was more than simple claustrophobia. She was anxious to get on the ground, to start their search for Drake before it was too late. She could feel time running against them. Little by little, minute by minute, she could feel him slipping away, and it hurt.

It hurt more than she imagined it ever could.

'Never took you for the emotional sort.'

Anya spun around, startled out of her thoughts. A male voice, faintly accented, faintly contemptuous.

Dietrich was watching her, standing in the shadows between two freight pallets with his arms folded, leaning nonchalantly against one of the steel frames.

'What do you want?'

Dietrich took a step into the open space. She suddenly had the impression of a boxer taking the centre of the ring, dominating the space around him. 'To talk to you, as it happens.'

'About what?'

'About who is really in charge here.'

'We had an agreement.'

'*You* had an agreement,' he corrected her. 'I never said I would follow your orders.'

Anya felt herself bristling at his condescending attitude. But more than that, she was beginning to realize the problem he presented. She'd encountered plenty like him. In fact, she could pretty much guarantee that every large group had at least one: the alpha male, the dominant force, the decision maker who wouldn't accept anyone else's authority. Least of all hers.

Unfortunately, she couldn't do the things she used to do with such people. She'd been in enough fights lately, and beating him down and humiliating him would only arouse thoughts of violent revenge rather than respect.

'What makes you think you're the better choice to lead?' she asked instead, attempting to reason with him.

'This isn't the first time I've been sent to hunt people like Drake. I found both Ryan *and* yourself. Twice,' Dietrich reminded her.

'And we both escaped you. Twice.'

She saw a glimmer of something behind his grey eyes then. Something dark and unpleasant. 'You escaped because Drake was dumb enough to let you go. I wouldn't have made the same mistake.'

'He couldn't stop me. Neither could you.'

'Then maybe that's something you have in common now. He couldn't stop you back then because he was weak and sentimental, and you couldn't stop him now. But the thing I keep asking myself is why. Is it because your history with him clouded your judgement, or is it something else?'

Anya could feel her hands curling into fists as Dietrich took another step towards her. She didn't normally rise to such petty provocations, but this man was an exception. He seemed to see right to the heart of people, to know their weaknesses better than they knew themselves.

'You were quite something in your day, from what I've heard. And that's what makes it so difficult to accept, isn't it? Knowing your day is almost over,' he said, adopting a tone of false empathy.

'Then do it,' she challenged him. Ally or not, there were some things she wouldn't stand from anyone. 'Be man enough to try what you're thinking. Then we'll find out whose day is over.'

Dietrich didn't back down, but neither did he come any closer. Instead his lips curled into a sardonic smile, and somehow she understood this was exactly the reaction he'd been aiming for.

'You've just answered my question,' he said. He was still looking at her with that contemptuous expression. 'You might have the others fooled, but I know your kind.'

'And what kind is that?' she asked, daring him to say the wrong thing.

'You're the eye of a storm, Anya. Everything around you is chaos and death and destruction, but somehow it never quite reaches you. People fight and die for you, they sacrifice everything in the war you started, and for what? You don't care. As long as you survive to fight another day, that's all that matters. You're a curse, a curse on us all. We'd all be better off if you'd never existed.'

Anya was no stranger to insults. She'd taken plenty – racial and sexual and everything in between – and had grown numb to them. Dietrich certainly wasn't the first one to try to break her down in this way, but the sting of his criticism was made worse because she perceived the grain of truth in it.

'Good,' she said evenly, her fear and anger gone now. 'Good. You are at least man enough to be honest with me, so I'll be honest with you. You're a selfish, arrogant, spineless coward. You may think you've met my sort before, but I have definitely met yours. You're the kind who gets people killed, and blames his own shortcomings on others. I have not lived without making mistakes, Dietrich, but at least I have been honest about them. And I can tell you that a man like you is the opposite of what we need now. If you go after Ryan, your arrogance will get you both killed. Throw your life away if that's what you want – I can't stop you, and frankly I don't care anyway – but I won't let you do that to him.'

The seconds stretched out as they remained in an uneasy stand-off, two forceful personalities matched against one another, silently vying for dominance.

Then at last she saw Dietrich smile again, cold and mocking.

'Well then, I suggest you stay out of my way in Brazil, because I'm not turning my back on you for a second. Do we understand each other?'

Anya offered him no smile, cold or otherwise. 'Perfectly.'

Dietrich turned away and slipped back into the shadows between the cargo crates.

Anya knew trouble was brewing, but whereas in the past she'd had free rein to ruthlessly purge such men from any unit under her command, she wielded no such power now. Casting Dietrich loose would only encourage him to take matters into his own hands. Since he was plainly unwilling to work *for* her, the only choice was to work *with* him. For now at least.

Chapter 22

Elizabeth Powell was no stranger to the corridors of Langley. She had visited more than once in her career, always in secret, always for clandestine meetings that would never be officially acknowledged. Always answering the summonses of men who could make or break her future, who demanded results and cared nothing for the sacrifices required to fulfil their mandates.

Well, today she was the one calling the meeting, and she would not be delayed. After receiving security footage of the attack in Rio and learning the identity of the man responsible, she had flown overnight, arriving at Dulles International in the early hours.

This was one meeting that needed to be face to face.

Cain had at least done her the courtesy of clearing her through the building's security protocols. Now sporting a red ID badge marked VISITOR – ESCORTED AT ALL TIMES, she was conducted upstairs to a private conference suite, where she was advised Cain would meet with her as soon as possible. Instead she had bypassed the meeting room and made straight for Cain's personal office, ignoring the protests of the young staff officer assigned as her chaperone.

'Ma'am, you can't go this way,' he said, struggling to keep up with her fast, purposeful strides. 'Ma'am, I'm going to have to ask you to turn back now or I'll be forced to call security.'

'What's your name, son?' Powell asked without breaking stride.

'Lewis, ma'am.'

'Great. Fuck off, Lewis. I'll take it from here.'

Shoving open the door to Cain's outer office, she was met by a stern, middle-aged woman with ash-blonde hair whom she assumed was his private secretary. The woman glanced up from her computer, peering over the rims of her reading glasses.

'Can I help you?' she asked, in a tone that might as well have said 'who the fuck do you think you are, marching in here like you own the place?'

'No, you can't,' Powell replied. 'I'm here for your boss.'

'Director Cain isn't available right now,' the secretary warned. 'Have a seat and I'll advise him you're here.'

'Trust me, he'll make himself available for this.'

She saw the secretary's right hand moving towards something under her desk, either a panic button or a concealed weapon. Personal assistants to high-ranking

Agency executives, no matter how stuffy and bureaucratic their appearance, were all firearms trained and prepared to give their lives to protect their bosses if necessary.

Before this stand-off deteriorated, Cain's door opened. 'It's all right, Janet,' he said reasonably. 'Go ahead and let her through. I had a feeling Ms Powell would make her own way here.'

Powell watched as the hand relaxed, moving away from whatever lay beneath her desk. Turning to a sweating and out of breath Lewis, who had only just caught up with her, she gave him a withering look.

'Go get yourself a glass of water, Lewis. You look like you could use it.'

She strode into Cain's inner sanctum. In all the times she'd visited Langley, she'd never been in the office of the director himself.

It was not to her taste. The wood-panelled walls and low ceiling induced a mild claustrophobia, not helped by the fact the blinds were half closed, keeping the early morning sunlight out. The furniture was old fashioned. Even the carpet was a drab grey colour.

A framed photograph of the president hung on the wall to the right of Cain's cluttered desk – pretty much a mandatory feature of government buildings like this. At least Obama was a little easier on the eye than his idiotic predecessor, she reflected as she made for the sideboard beneath it.

'You're looking well, Elizabeth,' Cain remarked stiffly as he closed the door.

'Fuck you, Marcus,' she snapped back, opening the crystal decanter and inhaling the amber-coloured contents. Lagavulin malt whisky. At least Cain had half-decent taste in liquor.

Cain watched as she poured herself a generous glass. 'A little early, isn't it?'

'Not for me,' she countered, tossing back a mouthful. She'd flown overnight from California, but hadn't slept a wink. The spirit blazed a trail down to her otherwise empty stomach, lighting a fire that matched the heat of her temper. 'You know why I'm here.'

Cain nodded. 'How bad is it?'

'How bad?' she repeated. 'Total, Marcus. Years of work gone up in smoke, not to mention that it'll take months to rebuild and cost millions of dollars. And it's not like we can claim this on insurance.'

'Are you here for a loan?' he taunted.

Powell took another gulp of whisky and rounded on him. 'I'm here for answers, you arrogant asshole. We both know who did this. You assured me Drake was under control, that he would never be a problem for us again, so explain to me how the fuck this happened.'

Cain approached her slowly, taking his time, a tall and imposing presence, but she didn't shrink away. She had faced down plenty of intimidating men without being cowed, and today was no exception.

'Maybe you should be asking the same question of yourself, Elizabeth,' he suggested, his voice annoyingly patronizing.

'What?'

'You've done well for yourself these past few years. The great Elizabeth Powell, CEO of one of the fastest growing medical research groups on earth. Entrepreneur, scientist, philanthropist − and a multimillionaire to boot. But I remember when you were just a dirt-poor research assistant with big ideas that nobody was prepared to fund. Nobody but us.'

'And I'm eternally grateful to you all,' she said sarcastically. 'But maybe you'd like to skip to the point?'

'You made a lot of assurances to win our support. You promised us results.'

'And I delivered.'

'You promised your work was flawless.'

'It was. The men it was applied to weren't. That being the case, maybe you should have provided better men.'

Cain ignored her. 'You promised Drake would never remember what happened.'

'I did.'

'And yet here we are. You're in the hole, and Drake's out for blood. Not a very pleasant feeling, is it? Knowing there's someone out there who wants to kill you. Knowing that despite all the money, all the layers of protection, eventually there will come a day when that person takes a shot at you.'

If he was trying to frighten her, it wasn't going to work. Powell knew something about Drake that even Cain wasn't aware of.

'Spare me the ghost stories, Marcus,' she said. 'I came here for answers, but I'll be leaving with a little more than that.'

'What exactly do you have in mind?'

She took another drink of whisky, a slower one this time. She was drawing it out, making him wait, making him wonder what she was planning.

'You know the problem with little boys?' she said. 'They're messy. They love having their toys to play with, but they never do learn to clean up after themselves. And pretty soon that causes problems for everyone around them.'

'I'm waiting for that point.'

'My point is, you've had plenty of chances to deal with Drake. You've had every opportunity anyone could ask for, and somehow you just keep leaving those toys lying around, Marcus. That was just fine as long as the mess was confined to your own little playroom, but it's not. Now other people are caught up in your failures. I'm here because I've come to clean up your mess for you.'

Cain smiled. 'You think you're going to take on Drake alone?'

'Not alone,' she corrected him. 'You'll give me some of the resources you've been misusing for so long, so I can put an end to this. You're going to give me back control of Operation Hydra.'

Cain's smile faltered. 'That's not going to happen, Elizabeth.'

'Isn't it?' she challenged. 'Maybe you're forgetting who created them in the first place, who they really answer to? Maybe you'd like a reminder?'

'They aren't yours any more. They have other tasks now.'

'They'll always be mine.' Powell tilted her head questioningly. 'Anyway, I wonder what our "mutual friends" would make of this, if they knew the man you failed to contain is now threatening one of their most successful projects? How do you think that would play out?'

Cain might have been the first to recognize her potential, but it was the group who had given her the resources she needed to make her plans a reality. They were the ones who had rewarded her success with huge financial bonuses, allowing her to build Unity from a struggling research firm into the multinational conglomerate it was today. Her work was helping to change the world, and of course they were right there beside her, making sure she changed it in a way that most benefitted them.

She might answer to Cain after a fashion, but Cain ultimately answered to the group.

'What exactly would you do with them?' he asked.

Powell smiled, sensing victory. 'They're insurance, in case outside influences come into play. Once I have Drake, he'll tell us everything he knows. Then I'll put an end to it once and for all.'

Clearly Cain wasn't displeased with what she was suggesting, even if he doubted her ability to accomplish it. That was just fine with her. People had doubted and underestimated her most of her life, and it simply made it all the more satisfying when she proved them wrong.

'What makes you think you can even find Drake?' he asked.

Her smile broadened as she drained the last of the whisky. 'Don't worry about that. If I'm right about him, he'll find me.'

Chapter 23

Rio de Janeiro, Brazil

'Jesus Christ, this place is a fucking sauna,' Alex remarked, wiping the sweat from his brow as the group hurried across the busy pedestrian area just outside Galeão international airport, passing businessmen seeking air conditioned sanctuary, and harassed-looking parents hastening to catch their flights with disgruntled children in tow.

The heat and humidity had hit them as soon as they were smuggled out of their aircraft. Alex had grown acclimatized to the cold weather and fresh, high-altitude air of Switzerland over the past few months. Stepping into the wilting tropical heat of Brazil was like setting foot on a different planet.

'Dry your eyes, snowflake,' Dietrich called over his shoulder as he headed to the nearby parking lots in search of a taxi rank. 'I don't want to have to hit you on our first day here.'

'Prick,' Alex said under his breath.

At least their arrival had gone smoothly. After disembarking, they'd been met by a Brazilian immigration official who had escorted them through customs with the most perfunctory checks of their documentation, and no interest whatsoever in their baggage (which was just as well, as most of them were armed). Alex was already starting to suspect that such favours could be bought and sold easily enough here.

Now that they were through international arrivals, their support from the BND had abruptly ended. They were in Brazil all right, and free to begin their search for Drake, but they were on their own.

The taxi pick-up area lay just beyond a row of towering palm trees swaying gently in the breeze. Scanning the lines of bright yellow cars and minivans, Dietrich selected a vehicle big enough to accommodate the group and made for it.

The driver was a short, amiable-looking man in a baggy white shirt and dark trousers, standing by his door idly smoking while he awaited his next fare.

'Where to, my friend?' he asked.

Dietrich opened his mouth to reply, but Anya beat him to it. 'Gamboa neighbourhood,' she said briskly, opening the front passenger door. 'I'll tell you where to stop once we get there.'

Alex caught Dietrich's annoyance, though it was quickly masked. If the taxi driver noticed it, he gave no indication. 'Okay. No problem.'

Dumping their gear in the trunk, aside from Dietrich and Anya who kept their packs conspicuously close by, the group settled into the vehicle and off they went, merging into the busy traffic that surged along the main drag.

Their progress was far from sedate however. Drivers in Brazil, as Alex quickly discovered, used their horns as liberally as most drivers used turn signals. The result was a cacophony of noise and confusion at nearly every traffic snarl-up, which meant pretty much everywhere in a city with a population of nearly six million people, all fighting for space on a road system designed to accommodate half that number.

Nonetheless, they eventually fought their way clear of the airport, at which point the road opened out, the terminal buildings receded into the distance and their view improved considerably.

Their resolutely utilitarian transport aircraft had had no windows in the cargo bay, so Alex had been unable to observe the city during their descent. Only now, as they drew onto a wide bridge that connected the airport island with the mainland, was he afforded his first proper look at Rio de Janeiro, and what he saw was breathtaking.

Rio, like many coastal cities, had begun its existence as a simple maritime port, chosen by Portuguese colonists because its sheltered bay offered good anchorage for their shipping. There had been little planning and no consideration for how such a colony might expand in the decades to come. The result was a twenty-first-century metropolis that was both bafflingly impractical and stunningly beautiful, its inhabitants hemmed into narrow valleys that lay between the three massive coastal mountains dominating the area: Corcovado, Sugarloaf and Two Brothers.

Sitting in the back of that hot, cramped taxi with a group of people he barely knew, Alex stared out at it all, mesmerized by the hundreds of yachts and pleasure craft plying the shimmering waters of Guanabara Bay, the white beaches dotted with tourists and locals alike, the tall buildings crowded right up against the shoreline, their mirrored glass windows gleaming in the bright sunshine. And most prominent of all, the famous statue of Christ the Redeemer atop the peak of Corcovado mountain, his arms spread wide as if to encompass the entire city.

This place was the stuff dreams were made of, at least to him. The kind of city he'd seen on TV a million times but never could have imagined visiting. And yet here he was: Alex Yates, computer hacker, part-time smartarse, with no clue what he was getting into.

'You guys are here for vacation?' the driver asked. The question came out so smooth, so easy, that it was obvious he'd asked it a thousand times and probably didn't much care about the answer. But good banter got you better tips, as most cab drivers the world over knew.

'Business,' Anya replied, neglecting to elaborate.

Alex saw the man's eyes survey the group in the back, perhaps wondering what sort of business people like this might be involved in. 'You staying in Rio for long?'

'Just drive the car, man,' Dietrich advised him. If there was one thing Anya and he had in common it was their dislike of small talk.

The driver knew better than to argue with the mean-looking German, and wisely set to his task.

Crossing the road bridge into the city proper, they once more found themselves deep in a concrete jungle, thronging with activity and traffic, while great square office blocks and residential complexes thrust high into the afternoon sky. This was downtown Rio, the business and financial heart of the city, where the tallest buildings and the most expensive real estate was located.

This, however, was not where they were heading. Their driver charted a generally south-western course, bearing away from the city centre and down towards the residential districts that fringed the coastline. The buildings took on a distinctly older, more colonial style as they progressed, the wide boulevards narrowing into cobbled single-lane roadways.

Unsurprisingly scooters, mopeds and motorbikes were the predominant form of transport in this part of town. Their cab was like an unwelcome invader.

At one point they came within inches of a collision with one of these bikes. The young driver, and the girl in a short skirt clinging to him, responded as pretty much everyone in this country responded to almost being crushed into the sidewalk – by shouting abuse and giving him the finger, then zipping off in a plume of dirty grey exhaust smoke and indignation.

Alex had tried to keep track of their course, but his mind soon became lost in the maze of side streets, alleyways, courtyards and dead ends. Fortunately at least one member of their party seemed to know where they were going.

'Here,' Anya declared. 'Stop here.'

The driver did just that, not trying to pull into the sidewalk and apparently not bothered that he was blocking the road behind. Mopeds and bikes soon began to flow around the parked car, like a boulder tossed into a stream.

Stepping out of the cab Alex was once again assailed by the heat, made all the more intense by the still air in the close confines of the street, and the heady combination of exhaust fumes, cooking smells and the sheer press of humanity.

Dietrich paid off the driver with what little local currency he had to hand, then grabbed his backpack and glanced around, apparently not pleased by what he saw.

'Illuminate me,' he prompted Anya. 'What the fuck are we doing here?'

Anya, already striding down the street, called back. 'We may be here for a while. We need money.'

Frost looked around. 'I'm not seeing any banks around here.'

'Trust me.'

Her destination soon came into view: a big warehouse-style building set back from the main road. The signs were all in Portuguese, but judging by the warehouse's general appearance and the images of men carrying heavy boxes, Alex guessed it was a self-storage facility.

He was proven right as Anya led them inside, apparently operating from memory, the rest of the group following her down several long corridors.

She stopped beside one particular lock-up and bent down to examine the combination padlock. A few twists of the three wheels and the lock disengaged, allowing her to retract the metal roller door.

The storage room was a basic six-by-eight cinderblock cell with a single light fitting. It was entirely devoid of features, and its only contents were a single military-style metal briefcase pushed up against the far wall. There was enough space to accommodate them all, allowing Anya to pull the doors closed behind them while she inspected the case.

Inside they found a neatly packed survival cache: some spare clothes, passports and other official documents, and several stacks of Brazilian reals.

It was clear this cache hadn't been touched in many years. The passports had long since expired, and the folded civilian clothes gave off the musty odour of things that have been left too long. Dietrich and Mitchell exchanged a glance as Anya sifted through this obsolete detritus.

However, it wasn't all useless documents and moth-eaten clothes. The Heckler & Koch VP70 automatic pistol wrapped in greaseproof paper and stowed away in one corner of the case was perfectly serviceable, as evidenced when Anya pulled back the slide and tested the firing mechanism. The click of the firing pin hitting an empty chamber was as crisp and precise as the day the gun had come off the assembly line. Two spare magazines and a box of 9mm Parabellum rounds had been packed in next to it, ready to be loaded.

'How many of these places do you have?' Mitchell asked, examining the hefty wad of bank notes in her hands. Brazilian reals weren't worth much against the US dollar, but it was clear she was still holding a sizeable sum.

Anya shrugged as she quickly refilled both magazines with the boxed ammunition, their brass casings rendered slightly dull by age. 'Fifteen years ago the unit I commanded had operatives all over the world, so we set up emergency caches like this wherever they were needed. Most were never used.'

'How do you know where they are?' Alex asked.

Anya reached up and tapped the side of her head.

'Jesus,' Mitchell said, quietly wondering how many millions of dollars had been left sitting in storage lockers like this all across the world, forgotten and abandoned until their leases eventually ran out and they were repossessed.

'We need money, and this was the quickest way,' Anya explained, tucking the pistol into the back of her jeans. Taking the money from Mitchell, she transferred it to her own backpack.

'Great, but what's next?' Alex asked.

Anya shouldered her pack. 'Next we need a place to work from. Let's go.'

Chapter 24

Jason Hawkins watched as the Gulfstream executive jet taxied into the private hangar on the edge of Santos Dumont airport, its engines putting out a powerful high-pitched whine that was enough to make the man beside him wince. Hawkins paid it no heed; he was quite used to noises like this.

As the aircraft came to a stop barely 20 feet away, he felt a trickle of sweat running down between his shoulder blades to pool at the small of his back. He tried to tell himself it was just the heat, but recognized that was a lie.

He was nervous about meeting the woman on that plane, nervous as a small child when they hear heavy footsteps on the stairs, knowing that Dad is coming with his bad mood and his sour whisky breath and his fists like boulders.

No other person on this earth could evoke these kinds of childlike emotions in Jason Hawkins. But then, no other person knew him quite like Elizabeth Powell did.

He watched as the jet's forward hatch opened and the little set of stairs unfolded. A few seconds of inactivity followed, during which Hawkins held his breath and waited.

Then she appeared.

It had been a good few years since he'd last seen Powell, years that had certainly left their marks on him. Time barely seemed to have touched Powell. Dark skinned and vibrant, she was tall and graceful as an athlete. Her height was amplified by the heels she wore, while her perfectly tailored suit matched the contours of her body – strong but sleek. As always, not a hair out of place, not even a momentary show of hesitation as she descended the stairs. Hollywood movie stars could have learned a few things from her.

Gliding down the stairs, she strode across the hangar's concrete floor towards them. Hawkins held his position but she didn't look at him. Her attention was focussed on the man by Hawkins' side. The man in the expensive suit who was always fidgeting uncomfortably, never able to find quite the right posture or position.

He took a step towards her, one hand thrust out in a terse attempt at a greeting. 'Elizabeth, good to see you. How was your—'

'Spare me the pleasantries. This isn't a social call, Mike,' she said briskly. 'I want to see Thomas Hayes' body, then I want an inspection of the lab.'

Hawkins noticed the muscles of Brody's fleshy throat working. His complexion seemed to have grown even more florid.

'Liz, I'm not sure that's a good idea. Tom is—'

'Dead,' Powell finished for him. 'I noticed. But I want to see him. Make it happen.'

'O-of course. We've laid on some cars to take you there,' he said, turning away and reaching for the cell phone in his jacket pocket.

Only then did Powell turn her attention to Hawkins, looking him up and down as if he were a piece of artwork laid on for her to appraise. He couldn't rightly tell whether she approved of what she saw or not.

'Well, it's been a long time, B-13,' she said, addressing him by his old designation. Testing cycle B, candidate number 13. 'So you're all they sent me, huh?'

She was already walking towards the black SUV waiting a short distance away, the *click-click* of her heels echoing around the big hangar.

'The rest of the team is maintaining a perimeter around the lab,' Hawkins explained, falling into step beside her. 'But Director Cain thought it best if I met you here.'

'Did he, indeed?'

'I'm their CO. I'm best placed to brief you on our current situation.'

He saw a smirk. 'You're in command?'

'That's right.'

'Not any more. All tactical decisions come through me from this point onwards,' she announced. 'But by all means, deliver your briefing, Jason. I want to know what I've got to work with here.'

Hawkins hoisted himself into the back of the SUV beside her. Within seconds they were off, leaving the hangar and the private jet behind.

Chapter 25

'You know, this city has some of the best beaches in the world,' Alex pointed out wistfully. 'I just wanted to put that out there.'

They had indeed found a place to stay and operate from. Before departing Switzerland, Anya had discreetly called ahead and reserved an apartment less than a mile from the emergency cache. It was a prudent move that had saved them precious time.

However, if he'd been hoping for some glamorous modern residence over-looking Copacabana Beach, Alex was to be truly disappointed. This was a dusty, run-down looking place that smelled of tobacco smoke and spilled drinks, with ancient decor that looked like the owners had declared the 1960s the height of architectural style and vowed never to move on. The only view beyond the shuttered windows was another line of tall buildings on the opposite side of the narrow busy street below. The blare of car horns and shouted conversations was a constant background clamour that seemed to reverberate through the building.

'We're not here for sightseeing.' Anya dumped her pack on the threadbare couch. 'Now if you're finished complaining, we have work to do.'

Dietrich, for once, seemed to be of like mind. 'Our priority should be to scope out the site of the attack, see if we can learn anything about the people involved. In the meantime, you and Frost finish digging into the owners of the facility.'

'Still working on that, but so far it's been one brick wall after another,' Frost admitted. 'The site is officially registered to a company called Plastico Research.'

'And they are?' he prompted.

'A fake plastics manufacturer.'

Dietrich cocked an eyebrow. 'As in fake plastic dog shit?'

'As in, they don't exist,' she clarified. 'They've been around for nearly eight years but in that whole time they've produced nothing, and they develop nothing.'

Which was an instant red flag for anyone. 'They look pretty successful for a business that doesn't make anything.'

'They're also owned by a shell company in Panama called ANC Trading,' Alex chimed in. 'Again, there's nothing about them online, but I'd be willing to bet ANC Trading leads to another shell company.'

'So we've got a facility that produces nothing, owned by a company that doesn't exist except on paper. Where does this all lead us?' Mitchell asked.

'Up shit creek, as far as I can tell,' Alex confirmed reluctantly. 'Whoever really owns that place has gone to a lot of trouble to keep it a secret. It's not going to be an easy one to unravel.'

Anya had heard enough. 'We'll learn nothing more sitting here,' she decided. 'Keep at it. In the meantime, we need to get moving. Mitchell, I assume you've been trained in recon and covert observation?'

The former CID operative nodded. 'Of course.'

'Good. Go to their facility and see what you can find there. But don't get too close; they will have security on site.' Reaching behind her, she withdrew the VP70 pistol and held it out. 'I hope you don't need to use this, but take it just in case.'

'Likewise,' Mitchell agreed, checking the safety.

'What about you? Where are you going?' Dietrich asked.

Anya's expression was grim but resolute. 'I'm going to speak with a man who may know something.'

'Then I'm coming with you.'

Anya shook her head. 'No, Dietrich. You're not.'

Naturally this flat refusal didn't go down well. 'And we're supposed to just trust you?'

'No, you're supposed to stay out of the way and let me do what I have to. This man doesn't meet with outsiders. He'll only talk with me, assuming I find him in a good mood.'

Frost caught her expression. 'Didn't think you had friends in this part of the world.'

'I don't,' Anya assured her.

Chapter 26

Morgues hold a kind of gruesome fascination for most people. Rows of cold metal cabinets, each door opening into a little chamber of death, enough to fill even the most pedestrian of imaginations with uneasy feelings of darkness and confinement.

The reality was practical and clinical, stainless steel worktops and gleaming implements that reminded Hawkins more of an industrial kitchen than any medical facility. The dead held no fear for him.

The plastic sheet was pulled back, exposing the naked body of Thomas Hayes stretched out on the mortuary trolley, and the gruesome handiwork of his killer. It was immediately apparent that he'd been shot three times at close range, twice in the chest and then in the centre of the forehead. The chest wounds, just inches apart, would likely have killed him regardless, but it was the shot to the head that had wreaked the most catastrophic damage. The low-velocity slug, probably fired from a silenced weapon, had shattered the back of his skull on exit. The resulting collapse in air pressure had literally sucked out a good portion of his brain matter.

He'd been cleaned up by the morgue technicians, of course, and his head was resting on a little pillow that hid the worst of the damage, but Hawkins knew all too well the grisly results of close-range head shots.

One thing the technicians couldn't hide however was Hayes' right eye, or lack thereof. The socket was empty, leaving nothing but a bony cavern streaked with blood and muscle fibres that had been severed from the eyeball.

Brody, the fat man in the expensive suit who seemed to be Powell's subordinate, let out a strangled breath and recoiled.

Powell was oblivious. Pulling on a pair of rubber gloves, she probed the twin entry wounds in Hayes' chest. The impacts would have caused massive internal damage, severing arteries and collapsing his lungs.

'Well, this explains how he was able to fool our biometrics,' she remarked, regarding the empty eye socket with mild annoyance. 'Make a note to include active blood flow sensors in our next security upgrade, would you Mike?'

'Yes… Yes, of course,' Brody replied thickly.

'What's the matter? Never seen a dead body before?' she asked.

'Not like this,' he managed to say, loosening his tie. 'This is absolute brutality.'

Removing the gloves, Powell tossed them into a nearby waste bin. 'Drake knew he'd need Hayes' keycard and biometrics to enter Building B. He also knew where Hayes lived, and how to get in without triggering his home security.'

Hawkins shrugged. 'Ryan's been trained in close target recon. He might have been scoping the place out for weeks.'

'Or he had insider knowledge,' Powell added, allowing the unspoken question to hang in the air. 'He didn't target the facility manager at random, and he didn't go to all this trouble just to blow the lab up. He needed high-level access.'

'So he was looking for something,' Hawkins concluded.

'Come on, I want to take a look at the site.' Leaving the body uncovered, she turned to leave, sparing an ill-looking Brody a brief glance as she passed. 'If you need to throw up, do it now, Mike. Either way, we're leaving.'

-

Olivia Mitchell swore under her breath and slapped the mosquito that had started to feed on her arm, leaving behind a tiny crumpled body and a little crimson smear. The fucking things were everywhere, especially in the steaming, jungle-covered hillside she'd hiked up to get a decent view of the destroyed facility.

It was about the only location she could find to carry out her recon without risking exposure. Security teams had established a wide cordon around the compound, preventing anyone getting within 100 yards of the perimeter. They were dressed in civilian clothes, but she knew professionals when she saw them. Buzz-cut hair, muscular build, tense and alert posture – these guys were military through and through.

So here she was in a makeshift OP (observation point) about half a mile from the target of Drake's attack, sweating her ass off on a muddy, densely forested hillside while the local wildlife slowly ate her alive, despite the liberal doses of mosquito repellent she'd slapped on.

Still, at least the place offered good cover, dense enough to render her invisible from 20 yards away, never mind half a mile. Even if there were men patrolling, they could walk right by and never see her. Mitchell had heard plenty of stories about tourists going for short walks in primary rainforest like this, only to lose their bearings amongst the thick foliage and end up wandering aimlessly for days.

Fortunately she was better prepared, having brought plenty of water, camou-flage clothing and a cell phone with inbuilt GPS. She hadn't exactly been top of her class at tactical navigation, but if she couldn't find her way out with that combination of training and technology, she didn't deserve to be here in the first place.

Aside from the automatic that Anya had given her, Mitchell's only tools were a pair of binoculars and a high-powered digital camera. In truth, the camera could magnify almost as well as the binoculars, with the added bonus that the focus auto-adjusted and compensated for changing lighting conditions.

She could also immediately snap anything of interest, and had already captured about a dozen shots of the compound, as well as the security presence around it. The facility seemed to consist of two main structures connected by a covered overhead walkway. At least, it used to. The first building had been torn apart by some great explosion from within, leaving pieces of debris scattered in a wide arc. The overhead walkway lay in twisted ruins, and fire had gutted whatever had survived the initial detonation.

Only the second building was relatively intact, though its roof and side wall had clearly been damaged in the explosion, shattering windows and probably starting minor fires.

Once the initial flurry of activity had subsided, little else had occurred in the past hour. Static observations like this could be some of the most mind-numbing and uncomfortable exercises imaginable, testing endurance and patience as you waited for something to happen.

She took a swig from her water bottle and considered her options. The sun was already going down as afternoon faded into evening, and soon she would lose the light. Not only would it be harder to observe the target area, but navigating in zero visibility would be a nightmare, GPS or no GPS.

The potential for slipping down a muddy slope and breaking a leg, or twisting an ankle on an exposed root was all too real. If that happened then she was screwed.

After deliberating for a time, she resolved to stay on station for another 30 minutes. If nothing happened by then, she would withdraw from the OP and return to the safe house. As it happened, she caught a sudden increase in activity barely five minutes later. New arrivals, by the looks of things. Focussing her zoom lens on the compound, she watched as a pair of black SUVs – late model Toyotas – pulled into the parking lot of the relatively undamaged secondary building.

The rear door of the lead vehicle opened, and out stepped one of the passengers. A man, tall and well built like so many of the others, his dark hair cut short, his rugged face that could have been called handsome but for a prominent scar running down one side...

Mitchell knew this man, knew the cruelty and malice of which he was capable. She knew he was responsible for the death of her former partner, and many more besides. She knew he was the reason she'd ended up in an intensive care ward in Istanbul, and very nearly an early grave. And now he was here, surveying the very place Drake had destroyed hours earlier.

'Son of a bitch,' she whispered, wishing she held a sniper rifle and not a camera. For a split second she imagined pulling the trigger, feeling the weapon kick back painfully against her shoulder – a good, solid pain that she could happily take – and a second or so later, the little explosion of red and grey mist as his head was blasted open like a ripe watermelon.

She would risk being discovered, risk being killed, risk anything if it meant taking that bastard down.

But he was down there, and she was up here, and for now there was no way to alter that state of affairs. The best thing she could do was to observe and report back.

She snapped a few pictures as he moved around, speaking with a couple of the security operatives who had come forward to report to him, then she switched her attention back to the SUV as a second passenger emerged.

This one, whatever her function, was clearly not a soldier. A woman, tall and elegant, well dressed and corporate-looking, had slid out of the SUV and was now walking towards Hawkins and his subordinates. The way they seemed to snap to attention told her the woman was a major player.

'Well, hello there,' Mitchell whispered, focussing her lens and snapping several rapid-fire pictures.

Once she was confident she had enough, she connected the camera up to her cell phone, selected the best pictures and promptly sent them to Alex and Frost, who were standing by at the safe house. It took several minutes for the device to transmit the high-resolution images, but finally the cell phone pinged to let her know the file transfer was complete.

With her initial objective accomplished, Mitchell hurriedly stowed the camera and other gear, slithered out of her OP and began to retrace her steps through the jungle while there was still some light left.

–

'I don't know how he did it,' Luis Garcia, the security chief of the night watch said, his head down and his voice hushed. 'I sent three of my best guys in there, and he went through them like they didn't even exist.'

He was sitting in a small observation room in Building A, where he'd been held since the attack the previous night. He'd already given his account of events to several different company men, but this new group frightened him almost as much as that insane son of a bitch who had so brazenly killed his entire security team.

'And you let him go,' Powell said, her tone accusing, her gaze withering.

She had already been on a tour around the perimeter of Building B, had seen the scale of the destruction. She couldn't venture into the ruins since they were still saturated with toxic and volatile chemicals. She'd said nothing during the brief tour, her expression hard and closed off as the cost of reconstruction ran through her mind. But no amount of money could restore Thomas Hayes, their head researcher.

Garcia looked up, his eyes those of a cornered animal.

'Nothing we did could even slow him down,' he protested. 'I thought if I could at least report back on what happened—'

'You could save your own ass,' Powell interrupted. 'Don't feel bad about it, Luis. Self-preservation is one of the strongest of all human instincts.'

'This guy wasn't human. He killed everyone. He...' He was shaking, his voice trembling as he tried and failed to go on.

'Hey, it's all right, Luis. Calm down,' Powell said, laying a hand on his heaving shoulder. 'You did your best. No one can ask more of you than that.'

Garcia swallowed, fighting to compose himself, feeling weak and stupid for almost losing it like that. He was head of security, supposed to be made of stronger stuff. He nodded, letting her know he'd be okay.

Withdrawing her hand, Powell rose from her seat and turned to leave the room. Passing Hawkins, who was standing guard at the door, she gave him a faint but noticeable nod.

She didn't bother to look back as she heard the weapon being drawn, the half-formed cry of protest from Garcia, or the gunshot as Hawkins fulfilled his order without hesitation. Her mind was already on other matters.

'Mike,' she said, catching up with Brody who was waiting nervously in the corridor outside. He knew what had just gone on in there, and he was frightened. Frightened of Powell and the armed men who now answered to her. If she could so easily order the execution of one of their own, what was to stop her killing any others she deemed unworthy?

'Yes?' he said.

'I want some time to review the security footage again. The full version, not just the highlights. And activate the Clean Slate protocol. Put the shell company into liquidation and terminate all of their assets, then give me a list of alternate sites within the hour. We're pulling out of Brazil.'

'Are you sure?' he asked, following her as she strode down the corridor.

'I haven't slept in 24 hours, Mike, and my time is very precious. Do *not* make me repeat myself,' she said.

Brody suppressed a shudder as Hawkins emerged from the office, wiping a splash of blood from his cheek. 'Of course. It'll be done.'

'Those security guards. They had families, I presume?'

Brody nodded. 'They did.'

He didn't rightly know the details of their personal lives – they were just grunts, hired because they met the job requirements – but all men had families in some form or another.

Powell thought for a moment. 'Make sure they get a decent compensation package. And make sure they understand it'll stay that way as long as they keep their mouths shut.'

'I will.'

'Now that we're done here, I want to get out of this shithole,' she said, looking around the damaged office building. 'And I want dinner and a place to stay for the night. Think you can manage that?'

'We already have a penthouse suite reserved for you in Rio. Fully secured.'

She flashed a disarming smile. 'I knew there was a reason I kept you around, Mike.'

Hawkins had caught up with them, and Brody seemed to shrink away from the big man's presence. 'You want some of my guys to escort you?'

'*My* guys,' Powell corrected him. 'Until this is over, they're my guys. And no, I don't need them. I've got other work for you tonight, Jason.'

Hawkins' scarred face twisted into a smile. 'I'm listening.'

Chapter 27

'Fuck,' Alex said as a warning appeared on his computer screen, advising him the scanning tool he'd deployed had failed to find any viable options. Another dead end.

Frost, returning from the kitchen with a bottle of beer in hand, looked over with mild interest. 'What you working on?' she asked, popping the cap.

'The research building Drake blew up. The company that owns it might not exist online, but they've definitely got a shielded network that's active,' he said. 'I'm trying to access it directly through the IP address, but the firewall's giving me trouble.'

'Forget it, I tried already.' She sat down on the other side of the dining table that had become their workstation, its scratched and chipped surface already covered with discarded food cartons and crumpled cans of energy drink. 'That thing is tighter than a duck's asshole.'

He raised an eyebrow at the colourful metaphor. 'Yeah, but you're not me. I've never found a firewall I couldn't break through.'

Keira snorted in amusement before placing her feet up on the table. Without further word from any of their scouting parties out in the field, neither of them had much to do.

'That's pretty arrogant, considering who you're sharing a room with.'

'It's also true. I used to make a living breaking into systems like this.'

'That's how you met Anya, right? She hired you to hack into the Agency.'

'Something like that.'

Frost took another swig of her beer. 'You run with any of the big clans?'

He glanced at her disparagingly. 'Nobody you'd know.'

'Whoa there, son.' She smiled, but it wasn't a friendly smile. It was the kind of hostile baring of teeth that she reserved for those in real danger of provoking her ire. 'That kind of attitude will get you in trouble.'

'I'm not your son, and I'm not here to make friends,' he shot back. 'Do us both a favour and mind your own business.'

Frost knew it was petty to provoke him like this, but part of her couldn't resist. He stirred her sense of pride and competitiveness. While he'd learned his trade in expensive universities, mixing with the best and brightest, she'd spent much of her teenage years homeless and well outside the law.

However, before she could respond with another barb, both of their computers pinged with incoming messages from Mitchell.

Frost eagerly opened them, scrolling through the half-dozen high-res images, noting the security on site, the destruction caused by the explosions, and most interestingly the shot of the female executive. Clearly she was a major player.

'Looks like we've got someone to snoop on,' she said, glancing over at Alex. 'Whoever this woman is, she's important.'

But Alex didn't reply. He was staring at his screen, the colour drained from his face.

Frowning, Frost opened up the last image to find a man she instantly recognized. A man who had taken both herself and Drake captive last year, who had executed one of their team, tortured them both, impaled her hand with his knife.

'Oh shit,' she muttered.

Alex had nothing to say. He stood up and strode away from the table, heading for the bedrooms. Frost likewise jumped to her feet, sensing trouble.

'Hey, where the hell are you going?' she asked as he marched back into the room with his backpack slung over one shoulder. The look of cold, resolute anger on his face made it plain he had nothing good in mind.

'Get out of my way.'

He made to push past but Frost sidestepped him, blocking his path.

'Forget what you're thinking, Alex,' she warned, guessing his intentions. 'Not going to happen. You wouldn't get within half a mile of him.'

'Fuck off,' he snapped, shoving her into the wall opposite. Clearly he was in no mood to debate the issue rationally.

She blocked the door with her foot just as he was reaching for it. Alex had had enough. Dropping his bag, he whirled to face her, his right arm shooting out like a piston, aiming for a gut punch that would wind her long enough for him to leave.

The young woman slipped deftly aside, caught his arm, turned his momentum against him and locked it behind his back. Downward pressure, applied none too gently now that she'd been obliged to defend herself, forced him to his knees.

'I'm only going to say this one time. Stand the fuck down or learn to type with one arm.' She put a little more pressure into it to emphasize her point, straining the tendons in his shoulder.

'Take your fucking hands off me, Frost,' he hissed.

He wasn't getting it, and part of her wondered if he'd accept a dislocated shoulder out of sheer stubbornness. 'Do you *want* to die? Is that it?'

'Why do you care?'

'Because this is about more than just you, you dumb fuck!' she shouted. 'You go on some revenge trip and get yourself killed, you've just compromised all of us. I'm not gonna let you screw this up. You hear me? I'm doing this to keep us alive.'

She let go and he twisted around to face her, his fists clenched. But he didn't try to attack her again. He'd already learned she wasn't someone he could steamroll through.

'He killed Lauren. He murdered her right in front of me.'

Some of the anger and frustration seemed to have left him now, replaced by something more raw and painful.

'I know,' Frost said, pushing her hair away from her eyes. 'Fuck me, of course I know. He killed someone close to me too.'

'Then come with me, let's kill this prick together.'

She shook her head sadly. If only he knew how many times she'd fantasized about that very thing. 'Believe me, I want him dead just as much as you, but we have to be smart about this. Going in guns blazing is a quick way to get ourselves killed. And even if we didn't, we might lose our one chance at finding Ryan.' She looked at him across the short expanse of hallway. 'So we stick to the plan and do our jobs. Okay?'

Alex slunk back into the apartment's living room. He didn't say a word, just sat down at his laptop and went back to work. But it was clear this wasn't over.

Sighing, Frost released her grip on the Beretta 9mm concealed at the small of her back. She was glad at least that she hadn't had to resort to drawing the weapon on him.

Chapter 28

Anya had operated in some of the harshest and most dangerous conflict zones on the face of the earth, from the burning deserts of Iraq to the windswept mountains of Afghanistan, the tundra of Siberia to the sprawling forests of Estonia. But the terrain she found most difficult was the tropical jungle she was now creeping through.

The heat and cloying humidity contributed greatly to her unfavourable opinion. Anya was accustomed to colder climates, having spent her first 20 years in the Baltic States where summers were short and warm, and winters long and bitterly cold. She could endure the cold with stoicism and resilience, but this damp, sultry warmth sapped her stamina.

She had operated in true rainforests before, where the near-impenetrable canopy encompassed a strange world of haunting twilight and deep shadow. By the time she and the rest of her team had emerged after a couple of weeks, they'd each been about a stone lighter and pale as corpses from lack of sunlight.

But this secondary jungle was the worst: a claustrophobic world of snaking vines, towering stands of bamboo and her personal favourite, the 'five-minute plant', so named because of its ability to snag clothing, loose hair or even exposed skin with its purplish, wickedly sharp hooks, delaying travellers for several minutes as they laboriously untangled themselves.

She'd caught a taxi ride to the north-western outskirts of town, travelling through the colourful *favelas* that characterised the northern districts of Rio. These were the slum areas where crime, drug trafficking and prostitution were rife, and where law and order had effectively ceased to exist. The driver had been reluctant even to venture there, requiring some financial incentive to convince him.

After leaving her grateful driver behind, she'd promptly headed for the hills, charting a course northwards through the jungle. And now here she was, a couple of hours later, barely three miles from her start point, tired and sweating.

Stopping in a shallow, muddy gully carved out by spring runoff, she sat down on a log that was slowly decomposing into the forest floor, unscrewed the cap of her water bottle and took a drink.

Finding the person she was looking for wasn't going to be an easy task, but the deeper her course took her into the hills north of the city, the closer she sensed she was getting.

That feeling was confirmed less than a minute later when her keen hearing detected the faint rustle of feet. The creak of a root taking weight but stopping just short of snapping. The metallic rattle of moving parts inside a weapon casing, so characteristic of crudely assembled Russian weapons.

Carefully laying down the water bottle, she tensed her muscles, preparing herself for what was coming.

And come it did. Noise and movement erupted all around her as several armed men burst out of the foliage from different directions, all with weapons trained on her.

'Don't move!'

'Hands up! Hands up!'

Anya did as instructed. As she did so, her eyes darted from one man to the next, quickly assessing their origins, possible training and the likely threat they posed. One look was enough to confirm they were neither military nor professional operatives. All four were dressed in gaudy civilian clothes – cargo pants, loose shirts and vests were the order of the day here. One was even wearing a Brazilian national soccer shirt.

Three of them were young, barely out of their teens, which was a bad sign. Young men, inexperienced, pumped up on adrenaline and with something to prove often had itchy trigger fingers. She would have to handle this one carefully.

They were all armed with AK-type weapons, though she doubted they were of Russian origin. Judging by the enclosed forward sight on one of them (all Russian AKs had an open sight arrangement), Anya guessed they were actually Type 56s: crude Chinese copies made with cheaper, lower-quality parts, resulting in a gun that was less reliable and with a shorter service life.

However, the chances of all four weapons failing were pretty slim. She was under no illusions that if she made a wrong move, one or all of her new friends would open fire.

'Please don't kill me!' she cried out, putting on a show of absolute terror. 'Oh God, please don't shoot! I'm an American! I'm unarmed!'

'Get down!' one of them yelled. 'Down on your knees!'

'Okay! Okay, I'll do it. Just please don't hurt me.'

She lowered herself to her knees, keeping her head down and her hands up where they could see them. That seemed to have the desired effect, as the shouting quietened down considerably. She watched as the four-man scouting party abandoned their firing positions and closed in without even leaving one man to cover their approach.

Sloppy, and amateurish. She made a mental note of that, but didn't count herself as lucky just yet. Professionals are dangerous but predictable, while amateurs are the worst of both worlds.

The four men had closed in, moving in front of her so they could get a good look at her face. Good – that way she could see them too.

The eldest of the four stepped forward, using the barrel of his weapon to raise Anya's face up towards him. She could feel the recoil compensator pressing into her jaw and had little choice but to comply, staring fearfully into his eyes.

He was about 40 years old, short and squat, with a prominent gut clearly visible beneath his loose T-shirt. His dark hair was receding from a high forehead, his teeth yellowed by age and tobacco. His chin seemed almost non-existent, his face disappearing into his neck so that it was hard to tell where one ended and the other began.

'You are American?' he asked, speaking surprisingly good English.

Anya sniffed and nodded.

'And what's a pretty American like you doing all alone in the jungle? This is a dangerous place, many bad men around here.'

A few of his companions sniggered.

'I... I was hiking towards one of the hills near my hotel, I lost my way,' Anya stammered. 'Please, I just want to go home. I just want to get out of here.'

'Maybe we can take you back,' he suggested, and she could practically see the new thoughts forming in his mind. Thoughts of what he might do with this woman who had stumbled into his territory, miles from anyone who might hear her cries. 'Or maybe not. What will you give us if we do?'

Her eyes flitted between them, lingering on the weapons. 'I don't have any money.'

Kneeling down beside her so that their eyes were level, he smiled, his teeth like old weathered tombstones leaning at precarious angles.

'Then you'll have to give us something else,' he said, running his hand up her side until he reached her breast, squeezing it through her vest. She gasped and looked away, feigning fear and disgust. 'We're all good men here, and we deserve a reward for helping you. Isn't that right, guys?'

There was some laughter from the others. He was their leader all right, and he was out to show how big a man he was.

'So what do you say, beautiful?' he asked, cupping her face. 'Are you going to give me my reward?'

Anya hesitated, looking for another way out but finding none, then finally nodded.

Grinning, her captor laid his rifle aside, then stood up, unzipped his trousers and proudly pulled his already engorged member out, accompanied by nervous encouragement from the others. They were young still, and likely hadn't done anything like this before, but they were going along with it because to back out now would be cowardly, unmanly.

None of them wanted to be the weak link, the one who didn't have the guts to go through with it. So they would watch, and they would laugh and egg each other on, and when it was their turn they'd pretend to enjoy it. Maybe some of them even would.

Maybe they'd get a taste for this sort of thing and go out looking for another victim, seeking that same thrill. Not one who was lost and alone in the jungle, but one who walked down the wrong alley, cut through the wrong park, turned the wrong corner.

Maybe.

'You guys can wait your turn,' the leader said. 'When I'm done with her, I don't care who goes next.' He looked down at Anya, trembling. 'Don't keep a man waiting, beautiful. Give me my reward.'

Anya leaned closer, her lips parted, and saw him close his eyes in anticipation. It happened fast, just as it had to.

Clenching her fist, she drove it upwards between his legs, right into his exposed and vulnerable genitals. It was an awkward angle to swing from and she didn't manage to get as much force into it as she'd hoped, but it didn't matter. The fleshy impact as her fist struck home was followed by a kind of yielding, crumpling sensation, as if she'd just punched a freshly baked loaf of bread.

He let out a tearing, high-pitched sound that was something between a groan and a scream, but more profound than either. He began to buckle, falling forward so that he was in danger of landing on top of her, but she was faster.

Springing up from her knees, she reached behind her back for the Colt M1911 and whipped the weapon out of its holster. At the same time, she hooked her arm around her captor's neck and yanked him around in front of her, forming a shield of flesh and bone between herself and the others, who were only now starting to react.

People, especially untrained kids who have been given guns and told to play at soldiers, are slow to react to things they're not expecting. This gave Anya enough time to gain the advantage. By the time the barrels of their cheap Chinese knock-off assault rifles started to rise towards her, Anya already had them covered with the M1911, and a hostage to boot.

And in the face of this sudden threat, they did what no trained soldier should ever do in a three-on-one situation: they froze.

'Drop the guns,' Anya ordered them calmly. 'Drop them or I start shooting.'

She saw a couple of questioning looks exchanged, saw the wheels starting to turn as they sized up the situation. There were three of them, and one of her. No matter how good she was, she couldn't kill all three before they opened fire.

'I have the drop on you. And I'm a good shot, my friends,' she promised. 'I don't think you are. If you want to make this a fight, at least two of you will die.'

Her human shield was still moaning pitifully. She knew he was of little use as a real shield – the 7.62mm rounds would go through his body like paper – but she wanted them to see him, wanted them to see what she'd done to their fearless leader.

That more than anything proved to be the clincher.

The kid in the soccer shirt was first to go, laying his assault rifle down as if it had suddenly become red hot. He was quickly followed by the other two, who dropped their guns and backed away with their hands up. Unarmed, they suddenly looked very different – just a trio of skinny, frightened adolescents clustering together for support.

'Please don't kill us,' the one with the soccer shirt said. 'We wouldn't have done it.'

Sure you wouldn't, Anya thought to herself. But retribution would have to take a back seat today. She'd allowed these men to track and close in on her, had allowed them to think she was a helpless, lost tourist so that she could get them in this position, so that they could take her to their employer.

'I want to speak with Rojas,' she said. 'Take me to him.'

Their faces reflected shock and fear at the mention of that name.

'We don't know any Rojas.'

Anya might have laughed at the absurdity of that lie, given their very obvious reaction. As it was, she kept her tone flat and controlled.

'Then you're no use to me,' she said, aiming her weapon at the young man to his left, who threw up his arms and turned away, as if bullets were like punches that could be deflected by the right posture.

'No!' football shirt cried out. 'Okay, okay! We know him.'

'How far is his base?' Anya asked, keeping the weapon levelled. As far as interrogations went, this was a contender for the easiest of her career.

'A couple of miles. We have a jeep at the head of this valley, it can get us there no problem.'

Anya sensed no hint of deception. His was the openness and honesty of youth, easily exploited.

'Then take me there.' Releasing her grip of the human shield, she planted a kick squarely in his ample rear, causing him to collapse into a foetal position at their feet. 'He's your friend, you carry him.'

Keeping the group covered while they helped the injured man to his feet, Anya removed the magazines from the discarded assault rifles and tossed three of the weapons into the muddy creek, retaining what seemed to be the best one for herself. It hadn't been very well looked after, but at least the firing mechanism and ammunition feed seemed in good order.

'Let's go,' she instructed once she was ready. The leader of the group was on his feet, barely, his clothes streaked with mud and his genitals still dangling stupidly from his open fly. 'And zip him up while you're at it. I've seen enough already.'

Chapter 29

Frost and Alex were sitting on opposite sides of the dining table, hunched over their laptops, looking and feeling like the world's most dysfunctional couple.

Neither of them had said much about their earlier confrontation, because they were each absorbed in their own thoughts, dark memories and fantasies of revenge. But one thing was clear: if Hawkins was in the country, it confirmed Drake's involvement.

Their task was interrupted by a knock at the door. 'Stay here,' Frost warned, standing up and drawing her Beretta 9mm.

She advanced to the front door, which was locked and barred. Not enough to stop a determined assault, but enough to provide some warning. And perhaps buy a few vital seconds to escape.

Leaning in close to the spyhole, she was relieved to find Mitchell standing in the hallway, looking tired and impatient at the delay. Removing the barricade and unbolting the door, she stepped aside to let her in.

Mitchell headed straight for the kitchen and grabbed a bottle of water from the fridge. Her clothes were stained with mud and sweat, her dark hair hanging in limp tangles, her skin damp with perspiration. She looked like she'd just returned from a month-long expedition through the Amazon.

'How did it go out there?' Frost asked, closing and relocking the door.

Mitchell didn't reply until she'd tipped about half the bottle down her throat.

'Peachy,' she replied with a false smile. 'I'm thinking about doing it again tomorrow.'

'There's something stronger in there if you want,' Frost added, nodding to the bottles of Brahma beer that she'd insisted on purchasing earlier.

Mitchell shook her head and took another gulp of water. 'Later. Did you find anything on our new friend?'

'You might be in luck,' Alex called through. 'Facial recognition turned up a hit.'

Intrigued, Mitchell strode through and leaned over him to examine his screen. The picture wasn't one of the long-range, hastily aimed photos she'd taken earlier, but a different image lifted from some profile piece run by an American business magazine. It was definitely the same woman – same tall and confident posture, same striking features, same perfectly styled hair.

'Her name's Elizabeth Powell,' Alex explained. 'A medical pioneer, entrepreneur, CEO and all-round genius based out of California.'

It was clear from Mitchell's blank expression that the name meant nothing to her.

'Yeah, that was pretty much my reaction,' Frost concurred.

'*Should* I know her?' Mitchell asked.

'Depends on the circles you move in. Liz there is CEO and sole owner of the Unity Medical Group, one of the most successful private pharmaceutical companies in the US. They hit the scene big time about six or seven years ago and they've been growing ever since. Some of the stuff these guys are coming up with is cutting edge: stem cell therapies, new cancer treatments, antiviral drugs—'

'Okay, you can stop jerking off now,' Mitchell said, sensing her verbose companion was getting carried away.

'The point is, they're a big deal. And Powell is at the centre of it. According to a couple of the profiles I've read, her personal wealth is estimated at anywhere from 50 to 100 million dollars. And they were written a couple of years ago.'

'Sounds like a high roller,' Mitchell acknowledged, unable to suppress a twinge of envy. 'So how come we've never heard of her?'

'Hard work, from what we can tell,' Frost interjected. 'Her company's structured in a weird way – lots of subsidiaries and semi-independent divisions all concentrating on their own thing. Seems Unity Medical Group is the umbrella company for the whole operation. When one division releases a big new drug or medical breakthrough, it's given a bit of publicity and everyone gets a pat on the back, but not many people bother to connect the dots.'

'Plus Powell herself has kept a low profile right from the start,' Alex added. 'Avoided publicity, never gives interviews or press access. Very little is known about her private life. When one magazine tried to run a piece on her, they were hit with multiple injunctions and gag orders. A few months later they were out of business.'

'In short, Elizabeth Powell is the most powerful person you've never heard of,' Frost finished.

Mitchell ran a hand through her unpleasantly damp and greasy hair. 'So what the hell is she doing here?'

'It's safe to say the facility Drake blew up was important to her,' Alex reasoned. 'Since it's not officially connected to Unity as far as I can work out, I'd guess they were doing some kind of dodgy work down here, away from oversight. The kind of stuff for which Powell wanted… what's the term you spooks use? Plausible deniability?'

'Sounds about right.'

'It all adds up to a giant shitstorm in the making,' Frost said, echoing all their thoughts. 'And Ryan's right in the centre of it.'

Mitchell sighed, feeling like she had more questions than answers after her little foray into the jungle. 'Any word back from Anya?'

'Nothing, she's gone dark. Same with Dietrich.' Frost shook her head in exasperation. 'Only thing worse than a lone wolf is *two* fucking lone wolves.'

There wasn't much that Mitchell could say to that. Both Dietrich and Anya seemed to have their way of doing things, and interfering with either of them would be a bad move. For now, all they could do was trust that the two operatives knew what they were doing.

Anyway, she had more immediate matters to attend to.

'Stay on it, see what else you can find on Powell. Right now, I need a shower.'

Moving away from the table, she gave Frost a significant look. The young woman came over to join her, out of earshot of their colleague.

'Everything okay here?' Mitchell asked. The charged atmosphere in the apartment wasn't lost on her.

'Yeah. Why?' Frost evaded.

She shrugged. 'Just a feeling, that's all.'

A brooding air seemed to hang around Alex particularly.

'It's fine. Nothing I can't handle.'

Mitchell lingered a moment longer before deciding to let the matter drop for now, heading instead for the bathroom.

Chapter 30

Anya's new-found guides gave her remarkably little trouble on the short hike through the jungle, leading her to a winding but apparently well-used trail to the far end of the valley, where a dirt road had been carved into the hillside. As promised, an open-topped 4 x 4 was waiting there, partially hidden behind a stand of bamboo.

It was an old Jeep Wrangler, its dull red paintwork covered with mud and spotted with rust in places. They quickly reversed back out onto the road and were on their way, bumping and jolting along the unpaved surface.

The kid in the football shirt did the driving, since Anya needed her hands free and none of the others seemed willing or able. The senior member of the group had recovered sufficiently to walk unaided, albeit with a noticeable limp, and was glaring at her from the other side of the rear passenger compartment. However, she doubted he was going to give her any further trouble.

At her direction, football shirt drove slowly, keeping the gears in low ratio just in case he was tempted to plough into a tree and make a break for it. Again, she doubted any of them were brave enough to try something like that, but it didn't hurt to take precautions.

The road climbed steeply, ascending the ridge at the head of the valley before descending just as sharply down the other side, zigzagging down the forested slopes to reduce the incline a little. Now there was no choice but to go slowly unless they wanted to plunge right over the edge, and Anya could see the tension in their driver as he pressed heavily on the brakes at every turn.

Too inexperienced to downshift, she thought.

The road levelled out somewhat after several hairpin turns, allowing them to make rapid progress across the plateau beyond. And, sure enough, after a mile or so the jungle receded, revealing a grand, colonial-style villa perched atop a low hill. Set within a couple of acres of carefully manicured lawns with marble statues and sculpted hedgerows, it looked like the kind of place a Colombian drug lord might take up residence.

And in Rojas' case, that wasn't too far from the truth.

Anya directed the driver to pull up at the main entrance, since they'd already been spotted by a couple of armed men guarding the approach road.

Slowing down, football shirt brought them into the paved courtyard then halted near the villa's arched entrance. The two guards on duty there, both of whom were dressed in suits and open collars complete with radio earpieces, looked considerably more professional than the scouting party she'd encountered. Both were big men, one of them sporting a shaved head and goatee with tattoos running down his neck, the other wearing his hair slicked back.

They approached warily with their weapons drawn. They were armed with Heckler & Koch MP7 submachine guns – expensive military-grade weapons that couldn't have been easy to come by in this part of the world.

If this turned into a firefight, she didn't like her chances.

'Who is this, Pacho?' the one with the goatee asked, directing his question to the man Anya had injured earlier.

Pacho didn't respond. He glanced nervously at Anya, unsure of what to say in case he started a gun battle with his boss's bodyguards.

Anya answered for him. 'I'm here for Rojas. Tell him I want to speak with him.'

Goatee man frowned. 'You'll speak with me, or you answer to this,' he said, indicating the submachine gun. 'Who the hell are you?'

Anya had no time for this. 'Tell him Maras is here. He will see me.'

If in doubt, always appeal to a man's self-interest. Guarding against threats was one thing, but incurring his boss's wrath by delaying an important visitor was quite another. Sure enough, after a few seconds' deliberation, self-interest won out.

Retreating a few paces while his companion kept Anya covered, he spoke quietly into his concealed radio. Anya waited, saying and doing nothing. No sense provoking people that she needed to cooperate with her.

Finally the bodyguard returned and spoke a few mumbled words to his colleague, interspersed with a hostile look in her direction. Nonetheless, the decision had apparently been made.

'The boss will see you,' goatee man said. 'Step down and hand over your weapons.'

Anya ejected the magazine from the assault rifle and tossed the clip away, then handed the empty weapon to her former captor. The man accepted it with sour grace, and it was plain from his expression that he would have used it against her if he'd had the chance.

'Be careful with that in future,' she warned him, before jumping down from the Jeep. The M1911 she handed over to goatee man on the promise that he return it to her in perfect order when she left.

He stood by while his colleague patted Anya down for hidden weapons, working with quick and professional efficiency. Finding none, he gave a curt nod.

'Follow me,' goatee man ordered.

She was escorted inside under the watchful eyes of her chaperone. Passing through the big double doors that barred the main entrance, she crossed into an expansive and ornately decorated reception hall beyond. Roughly oval shaped, the decor matched the exterior of the building: marble floors that gleamed under the lights overhead, expensive furniture, walls adorned with massive gold-framed paintings, and a staircase that ascended to the upper level in a graceful, sweeping arc along the curved wall.

Anya's boots left muddy prints on the otherwise pristine floor as she walked, and she wondered how long it would be before some servant or underling came scurrying out to clean up the mess.

On the opposite side of the hallway lay an opulent dining room, similarly decorated in a style she found quite overbearing, its long mahogany table set but unused. A big set of French doors opened out onto a patio area, and she could make out the glimmer of a pool in the centre of it.

'He is waiting for you out there,' goatee man prompted. 'Go.'

Anya skirted around the dining table, pausing only once to look back at her escort.

'What about the others?' she asked, pointing towards the main entrance. 'I don't want to see those men again.'

Frowning, he glanced in the direction she'd pointed. And as he did so, Anya snatched one of the knives from the table, pocketing it before he noticed anything amiss. It was a standard table knife, more useful as an implement than a weapon, but it would do in a pinch.

'Never mind them,' goatee man said, irritated by her question. 'Go now.'

She shrugged. 'Fair enough.'

As she'd thought, the dining room opened out onto an expansive terraced garden, the private space ringed by a stone parapet and sculpted topiaries. A swimming pool was located in the centre, the illuminated waters casting glimmering beams of light against the side of the villa.

And the pool was not empty.

Anya watched as a figure, sleek and graceful, pushed off from the far side and glided beneath the surface towards her – a half-glimpsed shape that moved seemingly without effort. And a few seconds later, a young woman's head emerged by the edge of the pool.

Pushing the long dark locks back from her face, she glanced up at Anya and smiled pleasantly, then hoisted herself out of the water and padded around the patio towards her, water dripping from her naked skin. She was young, mid-twenties at most, with the full lips, rounded face and olive skin common to those of Portuguese ancestry. And she was quite perfectly beautiful.

Anya tensed up, suspicious of this unexpected arrival. She moved with a subtly enticing sway of the hips, a carefree ease that betrayed no hostile intentions. Her modest musculature, full breasts that bobbed slightly in time with her steps, and hourglass figure suggested a body honed for attractiveness rather than practicality.

The fact she was wearing not a shred of clothing seemed to be of no concern to her at all. She walked proudly naked around the pool, and while Anya was certainly not embarrassed by such things, such brazen confidence in front of a total stranger was curious all the same.

'Where are my manners?' she purred in a sultry voice that was deeper than her age suggested. 'A new guest, and I haven't even offered you a drink.'

'I'm here for Rojas,' Anya said coldly as the young woman drew near. A little nearer than necessary. 'Where is he?'

'All business, I see.' She affected an unhappy pout, then smirked as a new idea came to her. 'A shame.'

There was a look in her eyes, of simmering attraction and desire that Anya genuinely couldn't decide was real or affected. If it was the latter, then she was a good actress.

A droplet of water trickled down the smooth curve of her breast, hung briefly suspended from a taut nipple before falling to the stone by Anya's foot. She reached up one delicate hand to touch a lock of blonde hair that had fallen in front of Anya's face, leaning in a little closer.

'Business is so boring, and I can be so much fun...'

Anya grabbed her by the wrist then, eliciting a gasp of surprise and pain. The look of disquiet in her smoky dark eyes definitely wasn't fake this time.

'I came to speak with Rojas, not to play games with his whore. Now where is he?' Anya demanded, tightening her grip. She could snap this foolish girl's arm like a dry twig if she chose, and her patience was already wearing thin. 'Don't make me ask again.'

That was when she heard the click of a hammer being drawn back, the sound coming from so close that she almost expected to feel the barrel of a weapon pressed into the side of her head.

'That is no way to talk to a lady,' a voice – smooth and deep and distinctly masculine this time – chided her. Rojas' voice. 'You must learn better manners.'

Anya froze, understanding why Rojas had used the young woman – his mistress, his girlfriend, his wife – as a very effective distraction. He was good – that much even she would acknowledge. Distraction or not, she hadn't detected his approach, and if he really wanted her dead then she would have been. That thought didn't sit well with her.

'Maras,' he said, saying her old Agency code name like it was something dredged from the depths of an old cupboard, moth-eaten and decaying. 'When I heard that name, I didn't believe it was really you. You have a lot of balls coming back after all this time. Give me a good reason I shouldn't just kill you and save myself a lot of aggravation.'

'You agreed to meet with me,' Anya pointed out without turning around or releasing her grip on the young woman. 'It would be... impolite to kill me without at least hearing me out.'

How much time passed before he responded, Anya couldn't rightly say. It might have been two seconds, or ten. Time was always difficult to gauge when you had a gun pointed at your head.

'I'll give you that,' he finally conceded. 'Let Valeria go, and we'll talk.'

Anya released her grip on the young woman, who backed away a step, glaring at Anya and rubbing her wrist. Valeria bent over and retrieved a silk robe that was resting on a sun lounger by the side of the pool, wrapping it around herself. The thin material clung to the damp contours of her body in such a way that it seemed almost a wasted effort.

'Good girl,' Rojas said. 'Now run along, Valeria. Maras and I are going to talk.'

Anya watched as she padded barefoot across the patio and disappeared in through the French doors. Then came the sound she'd been waiting for – the click of a hammer as it was eased back into place, meaning Rojas was wielding a single-action weapon. Anya was willing to bet he was holding her hostage with her own gun.

Her suspicions were confirmed when she turned around, finding herself facing down the barrel of an M1911. But the weapon interested her less than who was holding it. This was the first time she'd properly laid eyes on him in nearly ten years.

Now in his mid-forties at least, Cesar Rojas still possessed the lean and vigorous physique of a man a decade younger, with only a few wisps of grey in his otherwise dark, shoulder-length hair. This minor concession to maturity certainly didn't diminish his appearance however; if anything it enhanced it. His facial features were sharp and finely formed and distinctly Latin in arrangement, with the long straight nose, square chin and high forehead characteristic of his people.

Had she known nothing of his history, Anya might well have considered him attractive. Unfortunately, she knew plenty.

Rojas had been an Agency asset for the better part of ten years, starting his career in Colombia as a 'freelance consultant' in the war on drugs. In reality, Rojas had been nothing but a paid assassin, one of many hired by the CIA to take down prominent cartel leaders, no questions asked.

There were rumours that he was responsible for killing two of Pablo Escobar's top lieutenants, and that he'd helped himself to some of the enormous sums of cash hidden away by the Medellín cartel after its collapse. Of course, the truth of this would likely never be known.

After Escobar's downfall, the Agency had tasked him with hunting down communist guerrilla groups and other far-left revolutionaries operating in the country, and he'd gone on to carve a bloody trail across Central and South America. Anya had even worked with him on a couple of operations in Venezuela in the late 1990s. As she'd soon discovered, Rojas wasn't an obedient soldier or a tactical planner who cared for the bigger picture, but he was very, very good at killing people.

Then, just like that, he'd retired, cashing in the considerable capital he'd built up with the Agency and using it to start a new life in Brazil. She'd even helped facilitate his resettlement. But to her knowledge, he'd never explained why he had suddenly chosen to leave what was apparently a very successful and lucrative profession.

'It's been a long time,' he said, studying her reactions.

'It has.'

'You look old.'

She looked him up and down. 'And you look soft.'

'That's the Maras I remember.' Flashing a broad, wolf-like grin, Rojas lowered the weapon, turned away and gestured for her to follow him. 'Come, let's have a drink.'

A table was set up near the edge of the terrace, with a bottle of tequila and several glasses already laid out. Rojas took a seat and poured a couple of shots. Anya neglected to touch the drink, however. Aside from the fact this most definitely wasn't a social call, she had little liking for tequila at the best of times.

'Not going to force a man to drink alone, are you? That's a rotten trick for any woman to play.'

Sensing he was unlikely to let the matter drop, Anya plucked up her glass, resigned herself to the inevitable and tipped it down her throat. It was harder than the liquor she was used to drinking, and far less enjoyable. Still, it seemed to be enough to mollify Rojas, who downed his shot with considerably more enthusiasm and leaned back in his chair, surveying her across the table.

Holding up the weapon that he'd taken from her, Rojas turned it over slowly in his hand, light from the house gleaming across its surface.

'This gun has seen too many wars,' Rojas decided, shaking his head as if the weapon were an intriguing puzzle, then looking up at Anya. 'Just like its owner. Haven't you ever considered changing with the times, trying something new?'

'It suits me just fine,' Anya replied.

He grinned, laying the automatic on the table, just out of her reach, so that she'd have to stretch across to take it. He wasn't ready to return it just yet.

'First things first. How did you find me?'

'It wasn't hard,' Anya admitted. 'You were always a smart man, Cesar. And smart men are predictable. That's why the Agency hired you in the first place.'

For once his smile faltered, and that gave her a measure of satisfaction. 'So why come looking for me after so long?' he asked, changing the subject a little. 'I'm retired. You know that.'

'Nobody retires from this business. *You* know *that*,' Anya reminded him. Her implication was clear – you might be living the high life here, but I can change that all very quickly. 'Anyway, I didn't come looking for a hired gun. All I want is information.'

This prompted a look of intrigue. Reaching for the bottle, he poured them another round. 'Information on what?'

'On whom,' she corrected him. 'You've heard about the bombing in Rio.'

'The lab some crazy gringo blew up?'

She nodded. 'An… associate of mine was involved. British, ex-SAS, ex-Agency. A man by the name of Drake.'

'Ex-lover?' he asked, taking a sip.

Anya wisely avoided the question. 'He has gone rogue. I came here to find him and bring him home. For that, I need your help.'

Rojas chuckled and spread his arms to encompass his surroundings. 'I'd love to oblige, but what do I know of such things?'

It was Anya's turn to smile. She stared him down, elbows on the edge of the table. 'Bill Clinton was president when you left the CIA, Cesar. That's ten years without any income. Do you really expect me to believe your Agency severance package paid for this house, the cars, the security… the women?'

'Valeria came free of charge, as it happens.'

'Enough jokes,' she cut in. 'I know you have connections in Rio. I don't care what business you are involved in, but I want you to put the word out on Drake, see if anyone knows anything.'

'What do you expect to find?'

'I don't know yet,' she conceded. 'But if he arrived here on a commercial flight, he would have needed weapons, tactical clothing, equipment. Especially if he is planning further attacks. I need to find him before he goes through with it.'

Rojas took another sip of tequila. She could sense his shrewd mind assessing her, trying to get the measure of her. 'You speak to me as if I owe you a favour,' he said. 'But my account with the Agency, with *you*, was settled a long time ago. So by my reckoning you have no favours to call in.'

She knew this would happen. Rojas had been a talented assassin, but an even better negotiator. Nothing was free of charge where he was concerned.

'Of course not,' Anya admitted. 'But the question you should ask yourself is what will happen if you don't help me. I wonder how the Agency would feel, knowing their golden boy has become one of the very men he was hired to assassinate?'

Rojas twirled the shot glass in his hand. 'Times change, Maras. A smart man changes with them.'

'No more games, Cesar. I need to find that man, and you are going to help me.'

A slow smile began to spread across his face – the smile of a man who has finally found the solution to a troubling problem. Downing the remainder of his drink, he laid the glass carefully down on the table and straightened up in his chair.

'You know what, Maras? I think you're overplaying your hand,' he said, mockingly. 'I think this man means more to you than you're ready to admit.'

He glanced down at the gun. So close to him, so far from her.

'The Agency are after him too, aren't they? He made enemies of them when he blew up that facility. That's why you're so eager to find him now – you're trying to get to him before they do.'

He was testing her to see how long it took before she broke. Though he didn't share her skill at interpreting subtle body language and shifts in expression, Rojas nonetheless had a striking ability to read people's characters. That was what had made him such an effective killer – he understood the men he'd been assigned to assassinate.

He knew their strengths, and their weaknesses.

'I think they'd be *very* interested to know you were here tonight. I think they'd pay handsomely for that information. Perhaps we should find out?'

Anya could sense the pressure building as Rojas prepared to act. She could tell what was about to happen just as one knows thunder will follow lightning.

Everything seemed to go into slow motion as the tension reached a peak, then finally broke. Rojas went for the gun, closing his hand around the butt and bringing the weapon up towards her. It was too far for her to intervene, too close for him to miss.

But before he could fire, he had to arm the weapon. He'd disabled the action when their stand-off by the pool ended, meaning he either had to pull back the slide or, more likely, manually cock the hammer with his thumb.

But Anya had no intention of letting him open fire. Grabbing the edge of the wooden table, she heaved it upwards with an explosive effort, throwing it into his line of sight just as he was cocking the action. The timing was perfect, the solid mass of the table knocking the weapon from his grasp, causing it to clatter across the stones and come to rest near the edge of the pool. Glasses and the bottle of tequila shattered on the patio slabs as the table toppled.

Anya wasn't concerned with the weapon now. Leaping up from her chair just as Rojas did the same, she threw a punch aimed at his larynx, intending to both disable him and prevent him calling out for help. But he was ready, expertly twisting aside to avoid the hit and catching her outstretched arm, hoping to hyperextend the elbow joint. She drove a knee into his midsection that elicited a grunt of pain and broke his hold.

She saw the next hit coming and threw out both hands to parry his chest punch, then slipped aside to evade another blow that came in hard and fast. Her adversary was relentless, forcing her to go on the defensive. As he swept in with a high kick, Anya shifted her weight to absorb some of the impact. It was still enough to knock some of the wind out of her, but she managed to wrap her arm around his leg just as he made contact, preventing him from withdrawing it.

Knowing she had him off balance, she was already reaching for the table knife in her trouser pocket. A second more, and she might have plunged it into the fleshy part of his thigh, aiming for the big femoral artery that ran along the inside close to the bone. If she severed that, he would bleed out within a matter of minutes.

She never got the chance. Rojas leapt into the air with an agility that surprised even her, bringing his other foot up in a powerful kick aimed at her head. Knowing such a blow would certainly knock her unconscious, she abandoned her effort and threw herself aside. She instinctively rolled with the momentum of her fall, finishing in a crouch, ready to spring at him again.

But Rojas wasn't interested in resuming his offensive. Having freed himself from her grip, he dashed towards the automatic that lay by the edge of the pool. Anya tore after him, drawing the knife from her pocket just as he snatched up the gun and swung it towards her.

Their timing couldn't have been more perfect if they'd tried. The barrel of the weapon came up level with Anya's face just as the knife met his throat, its serrated point just touching the skin above the carotid artery. And at that moment of mutually assured death, both combatants froze.

Rojas' eyes flicked down to the blade. 'One of mine, if I'm not mistaken,' he said, sounding remarkably calm for a man seconds from a very bloody and painful death. 'What are you going to do with that? Spread butter on me?'

'Make one move and you'll find out,' Anya promised, tightening her grip on the improvised weapon. Cutlery or not, she was certain she had enough to deal him a fatal injury.

'So this is how it ends? You killed by your own gun, me by my own knife?'

'I did not come here to kill you, Cesar,' Anya said. 'But I will. I'll kill everyone in this building, burn it to the ground if I have to.'

'All this for one man?'

She could feel her chest tightening. 'He would do the same for me.'

What Rojas did next surprised even her. His lips curled into a smile, and without a second thought he withdrew the weapon, pointed it skyward and pulled the trigger.

Click.

The click of a hammer striking an empty chamber. The gun wasn't loaded, she realized. The gun had never been loaded.

His smile grew into a warm, genuine laugh, as if he'd just pulled off some ingenious prank that she'd yet to recognize. Anya lowered the knife, feeling both confused and somehow foolish.

'Well, who would have thought it? The great Maras has a heart after all,' Rojas said, dusting off his trousers and smoothing his hair back. 'It's been a while since I've had a fight like that. Thank you for the entertainment.'

Rather than a man who had narrowly escaped death at the hands of a trained killer, he looked invigorated and excited, as if he'd just returned from a good session at the gym.

'I could have killed you,' Anya said, angered and perplexed by his actions.

'And I could have killed you,' Rojas countered, unconcerned. 'Stimulating, isn't it? Staring death in the face and telling him to go fuck himself.' He looked down at the smashed bottle and glasses, and his smile faltered a little. 'You owe me a bottle of good tequila, though.'

Anya tossed the knife away in disgust. 'Why, Rojas? What do you want from me?'

'I wanted to know what you were really made of,' he said, turning more serious. 'Why you were really here, and what this man meant to you. Now I do.'

'And?'

He left her hanging, just because he could. 'Who am I to stand in the way of star-crossed lovers? I'll make a few calls, see if anyone knows anything. If he's in Rio, we'll find him.'

Anya let out the breath she hadn't known she'd been holding. Rojas wasn't trying to deceive her; she would have known if he was. It was hardly a definitive lead, but Rojas' assistance just might yield the vital clue that led her to Drake. He had, after all, made a career out of hunting men others couldn't find.

'Call me on this number when you have something,' she said, handing him a piece of paper with her number on it. 'I'm leaving. And I'm taking one of your vehicles.'

'As you wish,' he conceded with a shrug. 'The boys you ambushed out in the jungle don't deserve a vehicle anyway.'

They deserve a few other things, she thought. Petty revenge was the least of her concerns tonight.

Instead she held out her hand, waiting for something. When Rojas frowned in puzzlement, Anya nodded to the weapon in his hand.

'You have something of mine.'

Looking down at it, he smiled and held it up to the light, as if it were a sculpture offered up for appraisal. Anya however was annoyed to see that the weapon had been damaged during the fight, the Parkerization coating chipped and scratched from when it landed on the rough stonework.

'But of course,' he said, handing it over with an exaggerated bow. 'I trust you won't use it just yet.'

It would have been a poor show to have killed him right after winning his cooperation, but she'd have been lying if she said she wasn't tempted.

Anya pushed the weapon down the back of her trousers. She was about to leave when she paused and turned towards him again, her curiosity piqued.

'Why did you retire?' she asked.

Rojas looked up from the smashed bottle. 'Why do you ask?'

'You were good at what you did. Better than most. What made you leave?'

For perhaps the first time, she saw the cocky veneer slip a little. 'A man shouldn't keep doing bad things just because he's good at them.' He gave her a meaningful look. 'Think on that.'

'I'm not a man.'

'No,' he acknowledged. 'No, you're not.'

Turning away, Anya left without further comment.

Chapter 31

Hector 'Cuatro' Aguilar worked with the precision of a surgeon, using the razor-sharp edge of his knife to break up the little mound of white powder on his desk. Cocaine granules had a tendency to stick together, especially in humid climates like this, so it was important to separate the grains as finely as possible.

Satisfied, he used the blade to carefully sculpt the powder into a perfectly straight line, starkly white against the dark brown wood of the table. Just one this evening – two would produce more profound effects, elevate his mind to greater heights, but it might also make him lose control, and a real man never lost control. Especially not when he was working.

There were deals to be done, deliveries to be made and money to be collected, and he'd been charged with overseeing it all. Making sure everything ran smoothly, every dollar accounted for. A big responsibility, and one that experience had taught him to take very seriously.

He glanced at his right hand, as he often did. The tanned skin was marked with tattoos that extended all the way up his arm, but in most respects his hand was perfectly normal: square, broad and strong. Except for the fourth finger, which ended in a short, abrupt stump before the first knuckle, still pink with scar tissue.

He could still feel the blinding sheet of pain as the knife sliced his digit off – the same knife he was holding right now – followed by the white-hot agony of the iron he'd used to cauterize the wound. It had been a brutal but very effective reminder of what happened to men who fucked up.

Leaning in close, he held one nostril closed and inhaled through the other, closing his eyes as he waited for the drug to work its magic. It happened fast, as it always did. The synapses in his brain started to light up like a Christmas tree, filling him with a wave of euphoria that rose to a crescendo before breaking and crashing.

Grabbing the knife, he swung it back and plunged it into the table, leaving the point embedded half an inch in its surface. He let out a gasp of excitement, his heart pounding in his chest, filling his body with strength and power. He felt good, he felt invincible. He wished he could feel this way for ever.

'Boss?'

Cuatro looked up, seeing a big man standing in the doorway, though 'big' was scarcely a sufficient word to describe him. The man was massive, his neck thicker than most men's thighs, his hulking shoulders and voluminous gut barely concealed within the loose shirt he wore. A human mountain who looked like he could pick up regular men and toss them around like rag dolls. His nickname was Oso, literally meaning 'bear'.

'What's up?' Cuatro asked, wiping the traces of powder from his nostrils. 'If it's that motherfucker Vidal asking for more money again, tell him I'll cut his balls off and feed them to him.'

Oso shook his head. 'This is something else, man. A new buyer. A gringo.'

Cuatro perked up immediately. Most of his clients were by necessity Brazilian, with a smattering of Colombians, Bolivians and even a few from Venezuela. White men were usually smart enough to stay out of places like this. But it wasn't just his ethnicity that caught Cuatro's interest.

'What does he look like?'

Oso shrugged his wide, heavy shoulders. 'About my height, dark hair. Looks like he stays in shape.'

'You checked him out?' he asked.

Oso nodded, his face almost swallowed by the fleshy mass of his neck. 'No wires, no weapons. Fucker's clean.'

The police in Rio rarely moved into the favelas, but every so often – usually around election time – they got it into their heads they were going to clean up the district, and would launch another short-lived initiative to tackle organized crime. They'd arrest a few low-level dealers, pat themselves on the back and enjoy the glowing headlines for a while, and life in the favelas would carry on as normal.

He paused. 'Dante's got him downstairs. You want me to cut him loose?'

Cuatro knew he had to make his decision. To deliberate would risk looking indecisive and weak, and those were two things he most definitely wasn't. Especially with a line of cocaine still working its magic. He felt relaxed, confident, able to take on anything.

'Show him up.'

In short order, the new arrival was escorted up to the dilapidated room with its sagging old couches and knife-marked table that served as Cuatro's office. Cuatro looked over as he entered, closely followed by Dante, the skinny little Bolivian who served as the third member of his crew.

He was a big guy, Cuatro realized right away. Tall, well built, not muscular but clearly no stranger to exertion. His hair was cut short, his jaw coated with several days' growth. He was dressed in simple, cheap and hard-wearing clothes: a pair of old jeans, hiking boots coated with mud, and a grey T-shirt with sweat patches beneath the arms. Smart, Cuatro knew. Any man who had the balls to walk through a neighbourhood like this in fancy clothes might as well paint a target on his back.

'What's up, brother?' Cuatro said in English, pasting on a veneer of charm. 'The boys tell me you want to do a deal.'

'I didn't come here for the scenery.'

Even with his mind still riding the wave of cocaine, Cuatro couldn't help thinking there was something unnerving about this guy. He was a little too still, too controlled. Not that he'd ever voice such fears, of course.

'You're a funny guy. Question is, how did you find me?'

'I asked around. People said you could get what I need, no questions asked.'

'Right on both counts. You're lucky, friend. I can hook you up with any shit you need,' Cuatro acknowledged with no trace of modesty. 'So tell me what you want.'

'One MP5K with laser sight and integrated suppressor, four spare mags with 200 rounds of ammunition, one tactical ballistic vest, two stun and two fragmentation grenades, one fast-rope descent harness and a night-vision scope.'

Cuatro leaned back in his chair, taking it all in. 'That's quite a list.' He glanced up at Oso. 'You planning to start a war?'

'I plan on finishing one.'

'Gear like that is specialized, my man. Takes a lot of permits to get hold of. Shit's going to cost you big time.'

It was the oldest of old sales tricks, and one that his new friend was apparently wise to. 'There are no permits for gear like this. You either have it or you don't, so let's do a deal or I walk now.'

Cuatro's smile waned. 'You know, when I sell weapons to a man, I make a point of learning what he plans to do with them. After all, this is a dangerous city. Men get shot, women go missing, buildings get blown up...'

He saw those green eyes widen in sudden recognition, and knew then he'd found his man. 'Hold him!' he snapped in Portuguese.

Oso might have been the size of a mountain, but he could move quickly when the need arose. At Cuatro's command, he sprang forward and seized the man by the arms, virtually lifting him off the ground. He tried to resist, but it was a wasted effort. Oso could snap both his arms if he chose.

'I knew there was something off about you, man,' Cuatro said as he rounded his desk, strutting slowly and confidently. 'My boss warned me about you, said some crazy white boy was going around causing trouble and I should put the word out to find you.' He searched his memory for the name. 'Ryan Drake, that was it, right? Shit, I never thought you'd walk right into my office, *Ryan*. Fucking bonus right there, boys!'

Both Dante and Oso laughed, more because they feared Cuatro's volatile temper than because they found his comment amusing.

'You're making a mistake,' Drake warned. 'It doesn't have to go down like this.'

Grinning, Cuatro drew back his fist and rammed it into Drake's exposed stomach, dropping him to his knees as he coughed and gasped, frantically trying to suck some air back into his lungs. Soft as dog shit, just as Cuatro had suspected.

He pulled his cell phone out of his pocket and quickly dialled his boss's number. This was one call he couldn't wait to make. 'Boss? It's me. I've got your guy,' he reported, looking over at Drake and grinning. 'Yeah, I'm sure it's him. Ryan Drake. Stupid gringo walked straight into my office trying to buy weapons.'

He paused, listening.

'Yeah, he's alive. You want us to kill him?' He looked disappointed with the answer. 'Okay, no problem. Give us about 20 minutes.'

Finishing up the call, he slipped the phone back into his pocket.

'Never got a chance to introduce myself, *Ryan*,' Cuatro went on, enjoying himself now. 'Name's Hector, but everyone calls me Cuatro. It means "four". You knew that, right?'

Kneeling down in front of the prisoner, Cuatro held up his maimed hand, giving him a good view of the missing digit.

'Back when I was just starting out, I fucked up on a job. And I disrespected my boss trying to cover it up, and *that's* the worst thing a man can do. Everything in life comes down to respect, and when you don't have that...' He snapped his remaining fingers. 'You're nothing. So he gave me a choice: take my punishment like a man, or die like a fucking dog. One mistake, one finger. So I did it myself, with my own knife, and I didn't even cry out. Not fucking once, man.'

He wrenched his knife point free from the table and looked at Dante. 'Give the man a hand.'

Grabbing the prisoner's right arm and pulling it free from Oso's hold, Dante wrestled it onto the table, pressing down on it so that the palm was forced flat against the surface, the fingers splayed like the legs of a spider. His struggles increased as it became obvious what was about to happen, but he was still weakened by the blow to his stomach, and Oso was easily able to keep him under control.

'One mistake, one finger, my friend,' Cuatro said as he leaned in with the knife. He could see fear in the man's eyes, and relished it. It would be even more satisfying when that fear turned into wild pain. 'I wonder if you'll take it like a man or a little bitch?'

Oso watched as Cuatro brought the knife down. This wasn't the first time Cuatro had done this to those who had crossed him, and likely it wouldn't be the last. But it was always interesting to see how they reacted when the blade bit into their flesh. Some cried out before the cutting even started, others managed to hold out until the bone snapped or the finger was detached entirely.

But they all gave in eventually. And somehow he doubted this one would last long.

So intent was he on his boss and the knife he wielded, he didn't notice his prisoner shift his right foot slightly so that the instep pressed against his left leg, didn't hear the faint mechanical click as a spring-loaded blade was deployed, and didn't see the man raise his foot up.

What he did notice was the sudden explosion of pain in his right foot as the prisoner drove his leg downwards, impaling it with the blade protruding from his boot. Barely a second later the blade struck again, this time gouging a bloody path down his shin that parted skin and laid open the fat and muscle beneath.

Caught completely off guard, Oso gave vent to a bellowing howl of pain and fury that stopped his two comrades in their tracks. Both men instinctively turned towards him, neither understanding yet what had happened, as the giant loosened his grip on the prisoner and began to keel over.

Drake capitalized on their confusion with brutal efficiency. With his arms now freed, he lashed out at Dante, catching the bridge of the man's nose with his elbow. Drake felt the satisfying crunch as bone and cartilage snapped, and heard a muffled scream from behind. He didn't waste time looking, for there was one more opponent to be taken care of.

Cuatro swung furiously with his machete, slashing at Drake's face and throat, missing only because Drake managed to lean out of its deadly arc. With Cuatro off balance because of his failed strike, Drake gripped a handful of his lank hair and shoved downwards with all his strength, kicking the man's feet out from under him at the same time. Cuatro's head hit the desk with such force that the entire unit shuddered under the impact.

Plucking the machete from his loosened grasp, Drake reversed his grip on the hilt and raised it up above his head. Steel flashed for an instant, followed by a thud and a scream of pain as the three remaining fingers of Cuatro's hand were severed.

Drake let him fall to the floor, moaning and clutching at the bleeding stumps of what was left of his hand. He had other matters to attend to, chief amongst them Dante, who had backed up against the wall, blood soaking down the front of his vest. Still, he had recovered enough from the shock of his broken nose to draw a weapon from the waistband of his baggy jeans.

Taking a step forward just as he whipped the gun out with a snarl, Drake once again lashed out with the heavy, long-bladed knife, aiming for anywhere along his arm. The blade met with flesh, there was a feeling of jarring resistance, then a moist thump, and Dante's right hand fell to the floor along with the weapon it was still clutching.

The gun barked on landing, the thunderous shot echoing, though the projectile went well wide of its target. With spurts of arterial blood erupting from his arm in time to his pulse, Dante could only stare at him in blank terror as Drake raised his right foot, the spring-loaded knife still protruding from it, and drove the blade deep into his neck.

Dante had opened his mouth at that last moment before impact. Drake couldn't decide whether it was to beg for mercy, shout in defiance or to scream in fear. Most likely the latter, he judged. But whatever his intent, all that came out was a kind of strangled, rasping, bubbling sound. His body began to convulse, fighting against the death that was closing around him.

Drake spared him only a brief look before the sound of footsteps charging up the stairs alerted him to a new threat. He'd counted two additional men downstairs when he'd been escorted inside, and they'd clearly been alerted by the gunshot.

Withdrawing the knife from Dante's throat, he bent down and snatched the gun from his severed hand, surprised by what he found. It was a Beretta 93R, a variant of the popular 9mm handgun, externally identical to it in most ways save the extended magazine and collapsible foregrip beneath the barrel. An odd choice of weapon for a low-level gang member like Dante, but it would do in a pinch.

Sliding the foregrip downwards, he flicked the fire selector on the side to burst-fire mode and dropped to his knees just as the door flew open and a pair of men stormed in, weapons drawn.

They didn't even get a chance to take in the bloody scene that confronted them. Drake put three rounds into the first man, dropping him like a stone. Adjusting his aim, he tightened his grip and unleashed two more bursts into his second target.

The 93R was a lightweight weapon and not really designed for sustained fire like this. It kicked furiously, spitting brass across the room, but its effectiveness was undiminished. A couple of shots went wide as even Drake struggled to control the weapon, but several found their mark, and the second man stumbled and fell backwards down the stairs.

Drake peered through the grey gun smoke at the results of his grim work. The big man who had been holding him was still alive, trying to crawl stupidly into a corner of the room as if he thought he could hide there. Switching the Beretta back to single-shot mode, Drake took aim and fired, putting a round through his skull. The fleshy thud as his massive body hit the floor seemed to reverberate through the beams beneath.

All that remained now was Cuatro, who lay curled up on the floor near his desk, whimpering pathetically, his mutilated hand pressed in tight against his body. Blood was pooling, and though he was unlikely to bleed to death, there was a pretty good chance he'd go into shock, especially given how high he'd been earlier.

Approaching the injured man, Drake hunkered down beside him, looking into his eyes, which were wild and filled with terror.

'Looks like we'll need to call you Uno from now on,' he said. 'It didn't have to be this way, you know. We could have done a deal and gone our separate ways.'

'D–don't kill me, man,' he stammered. 'I wasn't going to—'

'Shh,' Drake said almost soothingly. 'It's all right now. All I need you to do is answer a few questions. Okay?' Cuatro nodded emphatically. 'Good man. First of all, tell me why your boss was looking for me.'

Chapter 32

With the wind whipping through the Jeep's open driver compartment, Anya block-changed into third gear and leaned hard on the gas, swinging the wheel to overtake an ancient truck lumbering along the narrow road ahead. The Jeep had been built in a different age, when power steering was just a crazy dream in some engineer's mind, forcing her to rely on brute strength to complete the dangerous manoeuvre.

Rojas had made good on their agreement, allowing her to drive off with one of his vehicles. She couldn't guarantee he'd get it back in the same condition, but she didn't care too much. The man was living in the kind of house that would make a film star jealous; he could certainly afford to lose one Jeep.

Her journey back through the network of jungle trails had been difficult, to say the least. It might have been quicker than hiking through the steaming rainforests, but the hard seat and jolting suspension hadn't exactly offered a comfortable ride.

Still, after a few wrong turns her path had at last intersected with an actual paved road, and she was now on her way back towards Rio. Her meeting with Rojas had used up precious time, but with luck it might prove to be a worthwhile gamble.

Now she needed to find out what the others had been doing. Fishing out her cell phone, she dialled Alex.

'Anya, where the hell have you been?' he demanded as soon as the call connected.

'No names, this is an open line.'

Even the CIA or NSA couldn't monitor every phone conversation, especially unregistered cells like hers, but their eavesdropping capabilities had been formidable even in her day. Using a system known as ECHELON – a joint intelligence-sharing agreement between the US, UK, Canada, Australia and New Zealand – they had been able to intercept and decode everything from encrypted emails to phone calls and text messages on a global scale.

ECHELON had almost certainly been upgraded in the years since. There was a good chance Cain had directed some of this system's resources towards her part of the world, so there was no sense in giving them more ammunition.

'Fine,' Alex conceded. 'But answer the question.'

'I met with someone. He's agreed to help us,' she explained, deciding the details could wait until later. 'Did you find anything at the facility?'

'Lots of things.'

She listened while he outlined their findings about Elizabeth Powell, the head of Unity Medical Group. Her mind was racing as she worked to digest this new information and somehow integrate it into the puzzle facing them. Clearly there was more to learn if they were to understand what was driving Drake, but it was a start.

However, it was obvious that Alex was holding something back.

'Say whatever you have to say,' she pressed, zipping close by a young woman on a moped, and ignoring the shout of indignation that echoed over her shoulder. Given how much work it took just to control the Jeep, she should have been thanking her lucky stars Anya didn't nudge her into the vegetation at the side of the road.

'All right, but you're not going to like it,' he cautioned. 'Powell brought a friend out to play with her. Starts with H and ends with awkins.'

Anya's hold on the wheel tightened involuntarily, the knuckles standing out like white rocks just beneath the skin.

'He was working for her?'

'*For* her or *with* her,' he confirmed. 'Hard to tell from the photos. Either way, he's here and I'm guessing he didn't come for the beaches. Watch your arse out there.'

Anya shook her head, angered by this new and most unwelcome development. Hawkins was as dangerous and unpredictable as he was sadistic and cruel. Each time they'd encountered him, he'd left a trail of bodies in his wake.

However, his presence did tell her something very important about this woman Elizabeth Powell. Whoever she was, whatever she was involved in, she had a connection to Cain and the Agency. Drake, Cain, Hawkins, Powell... all four of them were linked.

'Thanks for telling me,' she said.

'By the way, have you seen our friendly neighbourhood German lately?'

She frowned. 'No. Why?'

'He's been dark all night. I'd say we're getting worried, but that implies we give a shit about him. Thought you should know, though.'

Anya wasn't inclined towards profanity, otherwise she'd have been turning the air blue right now. Dangerous, unpredictable enemies outside their team she could deal with. Dangerous and unpredictable 'allies' within were a whole different matter. It was possible Dietrich was simply conducting his own line of investigation, free from the group's interference. Then again, it was equally possible he'd run into trouble, and now needed their help.

Neither possibility made her happy. She had hoped to snatch a few hours' sleep when she returned to the safe house – it was late, and she'd been awake well over 24 hours – but the prospect of one of their team being MIA put the brakes on that idea.

'I'm on my way back now,' she said. 'Stay alert, and call me if he returns.'

'Nah, it's happy hour here,' he replied sarcastically. 'Tequila slammers all round.'

'I've had enough tequila tonight,' she said, grimacing. 'Just call me.'

Chapter 33

'Fucking city,' Jonas Dietrich mumbled as he looked out over the distant skyscrapers of downtown Rio, lit by the glow of a million electric lights.

It was an impressive view, but his immediate surroundings were far less agreeable. The sprawling favelas that constituted the city's northern districts made the eastern European slums he'd become so familiar with look like the Playboy mansion. Most were little more than shacks with corrugated roofs, many with no electricity or running water. He'd watched women dumping buckets of raw sewage into gutters at the side of the street while barefoot children ran by. The heat and the stink were overpowering.

The favelas were a lawless world unto themselves – a fiery and dangerous city within a city where even the Brazilian government feared to tread.

As he'd quickly come to appreciate, districts, neighbourhoods or even individual streets often fell under the control of a local gang or minor criminal boss. Protection rackets, prostitution, drug dealing and intimidation were a way of life here. Strength and ruthlessness were the only qualities that offered a chance of survival. These were kings and warlords ruling over their own miniature fiefdoms, always plotting to overthrow their rivals.

He might have felt sorry for the locals caught up in this endless struggle for survival and dominance. They hadn't asked for such a life, and likely few of them wanted it, but here they were and here they would certainly stay. But he felt little pity for them, because they lacked the initiative, the intelligence or the imagination to strive for anything better.

'I want to make a confession,' he said, turning to look at the man seated before him. He had little choice but to sit: Dietrich had duct-taped his arms and legs to the chair. 'It's been a long day. I was woken up early, and I really don't appreciate being woken early. Then I flew halfway around the world to this shithole country you live in. I've been working with a group of retards that I don't respect or trust. And to top it off, I've had to spend most of my afternoon with the smell of shit in my nose, speaking with assholes like you.' He leaned forward. 'Needless to say, patience is not one of my virtues. So if I choose to let you speak, you should make use of that to say something of value.'

The man wasn't going to be saying anything just yet. A second piece of duct tape covered his mouth, preventing all but a muffled groan coming out.

Dietrich's day had indeed been long, but it hadn't been entirely unproductive. After making his way to the favelas on foot and taking stock of the area, he'd approached whatever local gang members he could find for information. It wasn't hard: just pick the meanest, most aggressive-looking assholes you could find. Anyway, most were branded with tattoos loudly proclaiming their affiliation, and many openly carried weapons in the street. No cops, no worries.

He'd made it known to these dubious contacts that he was looking for a 'friend', a white man who might have passed this way looking to buy guns or explosives, and that he was willing to part with a hefty wad of cash – his share of Anya's money from the emergency cache – if anyone could point him in the right direction.

Many had been unwilling or unable to help, others openly hostile, and one of two had even tried to lure him into what his instincts told him were traps. Any time a stranger suggested going somewhere 'more private' to talk, it was unlikely to end well. Needless to say, he'd avoided such encounters.

And after several hours of fruitless and frustrating searching, he'd finally turned up a lead. From a kid, of all people, no more than ten years old. He'd heard about Dietrich's enquiries in the neighbourhood, and informed him that he had indeed seen a white man in this part of town that very day, seeking out someone who could sell him weapons.

'It's good, it's good,' he'd kept saying in haphazard English, as if that somehow lent his story a stronger element of credibility.

'Yeah, it's really good,' Dietrich had replied suspiciously. It had sounded promising, but in his experience, impoverished kids and bullshit stories went comfortably hand in hand. 'Where did he go?'

That was when the kid had given him *that look*. The kind of knowing, crafty look a used car salesman gives you when he knows you're going to be driving one of his shit cars by the end of the day.

'You pay, I tell you,' he said, holding out a skinny, grubby hand. 'It's good, it's good.'

Dietrich had reluctantly unrolled about ten dollars' worth of local currency and handed it over, though he'd kept most of the notes back.

'I pay, now you tell.'

The kid had promptly directed him to a local man known as Rata – the Rat – given him a description and a rough idea of where to find him. According to him, Rata was a fixer who could get things for people, and therefore a logical choice for a foreigner looking to buy a weapon at short notice.

It sounded plausible, but stuff like this often did. Dietrich had parted company with him on the agreement that if his story turned out to be bullshit, he'd return and take back a great deal more than his ten dollars. The kid however had seemed completely unperturbed, and went on his way without a care in the world.

In the event, his tip had turned out to be good. Dietrich had quickly located the man known as Rata at an outdoor cantina several blocks away. His nickname must have been assigned ironically because the short, stocky man was built like a tank, his chest and arms bulked out by heavy weightlifting, his bull-like neck thick with corded muscle. Listening to his description over a beer bought by Dietrich, Rata had confirmed that he'd indeed made contact with the man Dietrich sought, and that he'd referred this client on to his boss to handle the deal barely an hour ago.

And that had been where the flow of information stopped. Sensing Dietrich's urgency, Rata had given him *that look* and promptly demanded payment of five hundred dollars US before he'd say another word. Dietrich had politely invited him to go somewhere 'more private' to talk.

The resulting tussle hadn't amounted to much. Rata's muscle was all for show, relying on intimidation rather than actual fighting prowess. Dietrich had subdued him with a few quick, well placed blows.

And now here they were, with Rata tied to a chair in the centre of a small apartment above the cantina, and Dietrich trying to decide how best to get the information out of him.

'You've heard of the Colombian necktie before, yes?' he said, producing the knife that Rata had tried to pull on him during the fight.

It was a good weapon, he decided, eyeing it with professional objectivity as he watched the light glint along its edge. The blade was short but made of good steel, and precisely shaped.

'You begin by making an incision along the throat, just below the jaw,' he said, miming cutting in slow motion. 'Then when you've got your man nice and opened up, you reach up through the hole and pull his tongue down through the gap.'

Rata was bucking and kicking in the chair as if he expected to break free. For all his brute strength, he couldn't gain the leverage needed to make use of it. He was going nowhere.

'Relax, man! It's nonsense, of course,' Dietrich assured his prisoner. 'Just Hollywood bullshit that sounds cool. I even tried it once myself on a guy in Poland just to prove the point. Complete waste of time.

'In your case, I think we'll play a little game,' he decided. 'Right now you can see, hear, smell and speak. You're a lucky man having all those senses, Rata. The question is, how many are you willing to lose before you tell me what I want to know? Obviously you'll be needing your tongue, for now. But those ears of yours... they look pretty big to me. I bet the kids used to tease you, right? Maybe that's why they call you Rata. Well, I know what to do with ears like those.'

Grasping Rata's right ear, he pulled it away from the side of his head and brought the edge of the knife down against it. One quick slice, like a butcher carving a piece of ham, and the skin and cartilage would separate, leaving him with a single bloody earlobe in his hand.

If Rata had been frightened before, he was positively shitting himself now, screaming and thrashing with such frantic energy that he was actually in danger of breaking free. But it didn't matter now, Dietrich knew he'd made his point. And if he hadn't been able to read the man's obvious panic, the spreading urine stain across his jeans was all the evidence he needed.

Withdrawing the knife, he reached up and tore away the duct tape from his mouth.

'Whatever comes out of your mouth in the next three seconds had better be very interesting to me,' he warned. 'Now speak.'

'I'll tell you!' Rata pleaded. 'Cuatro. My boss's name is Cuatro! That's where I sent your guy.'

Dietrich wasn't letting him off that easy. 'And who is this Cuatro?'

'He's connected, man. He runs all the gangs around here. Guns, drugs, women… Cuatro controls it all. He can get you any shit you need.'

Another petty tyrant, Dietrich thought. Still, it made sense. If Drake had gone in search of heavy weaponry or specialized equipment, he'd need a man who was well connected.

Placing his foot on the chair between Rata's legs, Dietrich leaned in close.

'Tell me where I can find Cuatro.'

Chapter 34

Having fought her way along minor roads for the past 20 minutes, and incurred the wrath of half of Rio's road users, Anya was deep in the sprawling northern outskirts of the city when her cell phone went off. This time, however, it wasn't Alex calling.

'What is it?' she asked, having to work twice as hard to control the heavy steering with one hand.

'Greetings to you, too,' Rojas said sarcastically. 'We have something.'

Anya's brows rose in surprise. It had been barely an hour since their meeting.

'What, exactly?'

'One of my… associates in Rio. A man by the name of Cuatro. He called me half an hour ago to say a man matching Drake's description came into his safe house, looking to buy weapons.'

Anya's heart skipped a beat. 'He has seen Ryan?'

'Better than that. He captured him.'

She couldn't believe what she was hearing. More than that, she simply *didn't* believe Drake would allow himself to be taken prisoner by a low-level street thug.

'Call him and tell him I'm on my way. Tell him not to take any chances.'

'That's the problem, I can't tell him anything. He's not answering his cell,' Rojas admitted, his unease apparent. 'I'm sending some of the boys to check on him.'

'Don't,' Anya cut in quickly, guessing the cause of Cuatro's sudden silence. 'They'll just die.'

'You have a better suggestion?' he prompted.

'Give me the location of Cuatro's safe house.'

–

Elizabeth Powell had to admit, her deputy Mike Brody might have been a weak-hearted asshole, but he'd at least found her respectable accommodation. Her home for the evening was a penthouse suite at the Emiliano Rio hotel, complete with private rooftop pool and sundeck overlooking the famous Copacabana Beach. The suite was accessible only via a private elevator, and was guarded by four armed men from Unity Group's security service.

The food wasn't bad either, she decided after sampling the filet mignon, cooked rare and prepared with minimal sauces and seasoning, as it should be. She took a sip of 2003 Shiraz, savouring the taste but taking care not to overindulge. There was much to be done and, if her suspicions proved correct, she would need all her faculties about her before this night was over.

As she dined, her company was hard at work liquidating their financial and logistical resources in Brazil, making provisions to decommission the research facility and relocate the surviving scientists and technicians to a new site. The machines and labs they could rebuild, but the loss of Hayes and his expertise wasn't so easily undone.

She was finishing up when her cell phone rang.

Laying down her cutlery, she picked it up. 'Yes?'

'Not catching you at a bad moment, am I?' Marcus Cain asked, his tone suggesting he didn't much care.

'For you, Marcus, it's never a bad moment,' she lied.

He got right to it. 'What's the situation there?'

'We're working on it.'

Cain knew when he was being stonewalled. 'You told me you were there to… what was the phrase you used? Clean up my mess? I'd hate to think you were making one of your own.'

Powell took another sip of wine. 'I hope that's not some veiled threat. I think you and I are past that point now.'

'Consider it some professional advice. If you're hunting a man like Drake, don't fuck around. Finish it when you have the chance.'

'You know your problem, Marcus? Men like you never learn the value of patience. Always trying to *make* things happen, trying to force the issue. Sometimes all you have to do is sit back and wait, and the answers have a way of coming to you.'

'Be careful, Elizabeth. You might not like the answers that come your way.'

'Don't judge others by your own low standards,' she chided. 'I'll call you when I have what we need. Until then, stay out of my business.'

Ending the call, she thought on it, then dialled another number. It rang for several seconds before it was answered.

'Yeah?' Hawkins said, speaking through a head-mounted comms rig. Powell could hear the high-pitched whine of helicopter engines and the *whop-whop-whop* of rotor blades in the background.

'How far out are you?'

'We're en route now. ETA five minutes.'

That was good news, she thought. 'And you're sure the target is there?'

'We've got a drone orbiting overhead – we can see it all. There's been a lot of cell phone activity from that location in the past hour,' Hawkins responded. 'All encrypted and untraceable, at least for now. We'll know more once we're inside.'

Powell didn't question this, content to leave such military matters to military professionals. Anyway, Hawkins would never lie to her. He couldn't even if he wanted to.

'All right. Call me when it's done.'

'Copy that.'

People were going to die tonight, many of them because of the decisions she'd made. That should have made her feel something, but she only felt a lingering sense of anticipation. Everything else was just a distraction.

Chapter 35

Cesar Rojas stepped out onto the paved terrace overlooking the gardens below. It was a peaceful night, with not a breath of wind stirring the trees nearby. Save for the chirp of cicadas and other nocturnal insects, all was quiet.

The tranquil evening was a marked contrast to the conflicted thoughts and concerns raging in his mind. The arrival of Anya had been a sharp and sudden reminder of a very different time. It was a life that he'd long since turned his back on, believing he could bury it and leave it behind for ever.

He should have realized nothing stayed buried for ever.

Looking out over the life he'd built for himself – a good life, even if it was founded on bad deeds – he could almost feel the changes starting. His dark, amorphous past was reaching out for him, hoping to ensnare him, pull him down with it.

He heard the quiet pad of feet approaching, felt a pair of arms slide around his waist, a warm body pressed close.

'What's on your mind?' Valeria asked, her voice soft and husky in his ear. She was dressed now, but he could feel the soft, insistent swell of her breasts against his back.

'Just business,' he replied absently.

Valeria wasn't a fool; it had been obvious enough that he hadn't acquired his wealth by staying on the right side of the law. He'd never pretended otherwise, but neither had he given her the full truth, and she hadn't pressed him for the details. She was pragmatic enough to accept there were some things he was never going to share.

'The woman?'

'An old acquaintance.'

'Nothing more?' Her grip tightened a little.

Rojas smiled faintly. The female capacity for suspicion and jealousy towards their own sex never ceased to impress him. 'We worked together. Nothing more.'

That seemed to placate her a little.

'I heard you talking on the phone,' the young woman said. 'About Cuatro. Has something happened?'

'I don't know yet.'

'But you're worried.'

Rojas didn't respond. Sharing his fears with her was unlikely to make them less real.

'I can tell this doesn't sit well with you,' she said, her hands moving up to his shoulders. 'It's been a long time since I've felt you this tense.' Her breath warmed his ear as she whispered, 'I can think of a few ways to loosen you up.'

Her hands slid around to his front, moving lower, her touch bold and arousing.

'Not now,' he said, gently but firmly moving her hand away. 'When this business is finished. Until then, I have...'

He trailed off then, straining to listen. He'd caught the sound of something in the night air, something deeper and more rhythmic than the random background chirps and cricks of insects. Had there been a breeze or anything to stir the jungle, he might have missed it.

But he could hear it drifting across the plateau, from beyond the tree-lined ridge about a mile away. A low, powerful *thump-thump-thump*. An engine.

An aircraft engine.

And it was closing in.

'Come with me!' he commanded, taking the young woman by the hand and dashing towards the house just as the sound of rotor blades rose in intensity and the dark shape of a chopper appeared over the ridge, lit only by flashing recognition lights.

They were met by Matias, head of the villa's security team and Rojas' personal bodyguard, who emerged from the villa with his weapon drawn.

'Boss, we've got incoming!' he shouted, beckoning the pair over. 'The car's ready to—'

He was abruptly silenced when a high-velocity projectile ripped through his skull, his bald dome shattering like an eggshell. His mouth hung open, his eyes suddenly unfocussed, and his body jerked and went rigid. It seemed like he would remain frozen, standing obscenely upright like a statue, until his legs went limp and he collapsed like a rag doll, his blood and brains painting the white flagstones.

Valeria was too stunned even to scream, but Rojas simply pulled her past him and into the villa. If they were to survive the night, they had to move fast.

He could hear the sharp report of weapons fire coming from around the compound, the staccato thunder reverberating through the stone walls. He didn't hear any return fire from the jungle, and he knew he wouldn't. Their enemies were almost certainly using silenced weapons, standard practice for an Agency assault team.

There was no chance of fending off such an attack. The guards posted around the perimeter were fine for seeing off local criminals or lost tourists, but the enemy they faced now was out of their league. At best, his men might delay their adversaries, but that was all.

Goddamn you, Maras, he thought bitterly. She had brought this on him.

'Follow me! Move!' he shouted, jerking Valeria towards the main hallway where a doorway led to the basement.

'Where are you going?' she screamed, her voice almost drowned out by the roar of the chopper and the crackle of gunfire. 'We have to get to the car. We have to leave!'

He was about to respond when the front door burst open and another one of his men backed inside, snapping off single shots from his assault rifle that resounded off the walls in a deafening clamour, empty shell casings pinging off the marble floors. He was putting down some cover fire while he tried to fight his way inside, but he'd barely crossed the threshold before a silenced burst tore through the wooden door and cut him down. He let out a cry and fell backwards, the door swinging closed behind him.

A couple of rounds sailed right past him, burying themselves in the wall just a few feet away and scattering broken chunks of brickwork. Valeria, who had by now recovered from the shock of watching Matias' death, let out a squeal of terror.

'Fuck this!' she cried, pulling away from him. 'Die here if you want!'

'Valeria! Stop!' Rojas shouted, throwing himself towards the fallen guard. The floor of the reception hallway was made of polished marble, the smooth surface allowing him to slide several feet on his knees and snatch up the dead man's assault rifle.

Glancing back the way he'd come, he was just in time to see the young woman sprinting down the opposite corridor towards the villa's parking garage. She didn't look back, didn't hesitate for a second.

'Wait!' he called after her. 'You won't—'

With the sounds of gunfire and the scream of the helicopter and the thudding of his own heartbeat loud in his ears, he simply didn't notice the faint whoosh of an incoming rocket.

All he was aware of was a sudden, dazzling flash coming from the direction of the dining room, the sight of broken glass and bricks and pieces of furniture rushing past him, and the oddly dizzying sensation of flying through the air.

Then darkness.

Chapter 36

Anya had visited many exotic and far-flung places in her life, had experienced a rich and bewildering array of unusual cultures, bizarre religions and outlandish customs. She had witnessed the full spectrum of human nature and society, from the sublime to the depraved and everything in between. But never had she encountered anything like the favelas of Rio.

Simultaneously vibrant and colourful, the neighbourhoods were stricken with the most abject poverty, yet their inhabitants were strikingly, defiantly alive. Music blared from car speakers and open windows, couples argued in full view, food was roasted on open grills, men drank and gambled and smoked, women gossiped and giggled, children played and cavorted and fought. Life, precarious and unforgiving though it was, went on here as it did everywhere else.

The built environment in which these people lived had to be seen to be believed. None of it, from the street layout to the construction of homes, shops and bars, had been laid down according to any plan or design. Everything was improvised, thrown together, jerry-rigged and somehow made to work. Power and telephone lines were strung across roads, water pipes were haphazardly plumbed into those homes lucky enough to afford them, generators hummed and coughed, their fumes adding to the reek of car and bike exhausts.

Buildings were extended, modified, gutted, then extended again with teetering rows and storeys of bricks that would have given most builders nightmares. It was one of the most confusing, irrational and overcrowded places Anya had ever seen. It was also the perfect environment for a man like Drake to disappear.

Bringing the Jeep to a stop outside a shop crammed with handbags and shoes of every size and description, she killed the engine and began to survey a building about 50 yards back. It was next to impossible to navigate by addresses or street names, but it did match the description of Cuatro's safe house.

Three storeys tall, and modelled in the Spanish colonial style, it had obviously been a structure of some importance, more substantial in its construction and elegant in design. Decades of repurposing and neglect had seen it gradually take on the appearance of its surroundings, the dun brown rendering marked by graffiti in places and peeling away entirely in others to expose the stonework beneath.

Yet for all the obvious signs of decay, the place wasn't derelict. Thin shafts of light were visible through gaps in the shuttered windows, and the main door appeared stout and well maintained.

The question was, who might she encounter in there?

Only one way to find out. Removing the keys, she opened the door and stepped down from the Jeep. Suspecting some local hotshot might have a go at hotwiring it in her absence, she popped the hood and removed the fuse from the ignition system.

She walked back up the crowded street, which sloped steeply towards the west. She kept to the opposite side of the road and tried her best to blend in – no easy task given her ethnicity.

She was more or less parallel with the building's crumbling façade, and could now see that it was separated from its neighbours by narrow alleyways on both sides. Again, an unusual set-up in this part of town, but it gave more weight to this being a safe house. The fewer connections to other buildings, the harder it was for people to eavesdrop.

Changing direction, she angled across the street towards it, picking her way past the cavalcade of scooters, mopeds and other small bikes, and slipped into the alleyway running down the building's right side.

It was dark. Though there were few working street lights anywhere in the favelas, the main roads were brightly illuminated by shop fronts, bars festooned with garish neon signs, and the headlights from passing traffic. But just a few yards beyond lay a gloomy world of crumbling brickwork, shallow fetid pools, discarded trash and rotting garbage. The stench alone was almost enough to drive her back, but she ventured resolutely forward.

It didn't take long for her eyes to adjust, though what she saw was hardly encouraging. If she'd hoped for a conveniently placed fire escape or similar external access, she was to be disappointed. The building reared up tall and daunting and frustratingly inaccessible, with no windows, doors, ladders or obvious handholds. No good.

However, the same was not true of the building that backed onto it. It was a residential block that had probably started as a single-storey unit, but which had been gradually built upon and extended like everything else around here. Each level was slightly smaller than the one below. The result was a building that resembled a steep, lopsided pyramid angled towards the safe house, like an unsteady drunkard leaning on a friend for support.

Following the alleyway around towards the rear, Anya found her path barred by a solid breeze-block wall and locked metal gate, the small courtyard behind shrouded in shadow. Since she didn't have the tools or the time to pick the lock, the only choice was up and over.

Leaping up, she grasped the top of the wall and pulled herself up, balancing then dropping down quietly into the yard on the other side. It wasn't paved; she could feel bare earth beneath her feet. Perhaps a garden of some kind.

A cat hissed at her then darted away – a sleek feline shape that scaled the wall before vanishing in search of a quieter spot to spend the night. A flight of stairs led directly to the level above, suggesting the locked gate was the main point of entry. Creeping up, she froze at the top, alerted by the distinctive rattle of automatic gunfire, muffled shouts and warning cries from inside.

Ascending the last few steps, she moved over to the grimy, curtained-off window of the upper apartment, raising her head just enough to peek in through one corner where the curtain didn't reach. A small, old-fashioned TV was gleefully playing a very loud and very violent action movie.

A pair of fat, naked, hairy legs were stretched out on a foot stool facing the TV. She couldn't tell if the owner was asleep or simply engrossed, but it seemed he was oblivious to her presence. She was happy to leave it that way, and retreated from her vantage point.

There were no stairs or ladder access to the uppermost level. It was possible the final stairwell was internal, or perhaps it was located around the front of the block. Anything was possible here.

She didn't want to risk being seen from the street below. Anyway, the roof here was low compared to the ground floor, and easy enough for her to scale.

She was getting tired of clambering up walls tonight, but could think of no better way to make entry. Muscles straining with the exertion, Anya hauled herself up, boots scraping against the bare brick walls, then crawled across the rooftop to survey the safe house opposite.

As she'd hoped, she was now level with the roof of the target building, the two structures separated by about six feet of open space. It didn't sound like much, but one slip or mistimed leap would mean a fatal fall down to the alley below.

Don't think about it, just get it done, she told herself. That had been her mantra for most of the foolish and dangerous things she'd been obliged to do in her life, and it had held up fairly well thus far.

Backing up, she took a couple of deep breaths, then rushed at the gap and leapt.

For a dizzying moment she saw the darkened alleyway sail by beneath her, light reflecting off the distant pools of water as she flew through the air. Then in a heartbeat the opposing rooftop rushed at her.

Anya had parachuted into more than a few hostile environments, and knew how to execute a controlled landing. Tucking her head in, she allowed her legs to absorb some of the impact, rolled forward and over as her momentum carried her several yards beyond the edge of the roof.

She was in.

Reaching behind, she drew the M1911 and looked around, checking for hostiles. She'd seen none from the opposite rooftop, but that didn't mean she was alone. If she'd been in charge of security, she would certainly have kept men posted up here.

Still, no targets presented themselves. The rooftop was as quiet as a building in the middle of the favelas could be, with nothing but the hum of vehicle engines and music and chatter drifting up to her on the warm night breeze. She relaxed, satisfied the first stage was complete.

Staying crouched, she made for the stairwell at the far corner of the roof. She discovered the rusted steel access door was unlocked – another sign that all was not as it should be. Swinging it open and grimacing as the corroded hinges squealed, she raised her weapon and advanced into the darkness.

154

The stairwell was nothing but bare stone steps and brick walls, her footfalls echoing with that hollow, dusty sound peculiar to old buildings as she descended.

There was an interesting mixture of odours in the air. The first was a rich, pungent aroma that didn't take much effort to identify. It wasn't surprising given the kind of men who worked here, and she'd have been surprised if cannabis was the most potent substance they consumed.

The second was the stale, lingering scent of alcohol. Lots of it, of many different varieties. Again, no big surprises.

The last was the most significant. Sharper, bitter and chemical-like, it was a smell she'd inhaled on countless battlefields during her 20-year career, a smell that stung the eyes and irritated the back of the throat. The smell of burned cordite.

Someone had discharged weapons in here recently.

Emerging from the stairwell into the upper floor, Anya found herself in a wide corridor lit by a flickering bulb. Either it was defective or the power was unreliable. Shuttered windows were located at each end, through which she caught glimpses of neon signs outside, while several doors led off into smaller rooms. Likely the corridor encircled the building's core since this place, unlike its ramshackle neighbours, seemed to adhere to some kind of architectural logic.

Crates of liquor and cigarettes were stacked against the wall, mostly Mexican and American brands. She saw the distinctive Jack Daniel's logo printed on several of them. There must have been hundreds of bottles on this floor alone. Creeping along the corridor, dry old floorboards creaking beneath her boots, she paused beside one of the doors. It had been forced open, the lock destroyed by a close-range gunshot. She eased it open a few inches and glanced inside. More wooden packing boxes of varying sizes were stacked against the walls, all painted olive drab and emblazoned with black-and-white letters denoting their contents.

This wasn't another room full of booze, but of weapon and ammunition crates that looked like a mixture of Russian and Brazilian military stock, with a few American ones mixed in. Several of these containers had been thrown on the floor with no concern for their contents, while others had been crudely levered open, the wood splintered and cracked.

She didn't have time to examine them in more detail, but even a cursory glance confirmed that the room contained a sizeable arsenal. Between weapons, alcohol and tobacco, it seemed Cuatro and his friends had their fingers in many illegal pies.

The smell of cordite was growing noticeably stronger as she advanced. Backing up against the wall, Anya closed her eyes for a second to focus her mind and senses, then opened them and advanced around the corner.

A scene of slaughter greeted her.

First and most obvious was a pair of dead men lying sprawled on the floor just outside a doorway up ahead. Both had been killed by multiple gunshot wounds to the chest and torso, their blood soaking into everything around them.

More bodies lay in the next room. Picking her way past them, she surveyed what had clearly been a decidedly one-sided fight. Three more corpses were in there, all showing signs of being attacked repeatedly with a sharp, bladed weapon.

The resulting injuries had left blood everywhere, and even Anya was struck by the sheer ferocity of it.

She paused briefly to examine one man lying atop a crude wooden desk. All the digits of his right hand had been severed, and a long machete protruded from his chest, the haft pointing straight up at the ceiling in almost comical fashion, as if this were some fake murder mystery scene set up for her to puzzle over.

But it wasn't fake. The blood, the spent shell casings, the burned cordite, it was all real. Whoever had killed these men had done so with a combination of technical skill and sheer brutality that was becoming frighteningly familiar. Drake had been here all right.

Such was her fixation, she almost didn't notice the shadow that fell across the body as a figure moved across the flickering glow cast by the hallway lights. Only when she heard the faint creak of floorboards did she whirl around, bringing her weapon up to bear.

Too late.

Chapter 37

Hawkins strolled slowly around the villa's grand hallway, surveying the paintings that adorned the walls like a patron touring an art gallery, his boots scattering spent shell casings and crunching pieces of broken plaster.

'Never did go in for this classical stuff myself,' he remarked, pausing to consider some elaborate painting of an eighteenth-century general astride his horse. Just another idealized vision of warfare to flatter the vanity of some rich asshole.

However, he smiled when his gaze rested on the item mounted beneath the painting.

'But this. *This* is what I'm talking about,' he said, reverently removing the cavalry sabre and withdrawing the weapon from its ornate metal scabbard. 'This is something beautiful.'

The blade was notched and dented in places, confirming that it had seen action. A real weapon wielded by real soldiers, the way battles were supposed to be – up close and personal, where you could see the anger and fear and hatred in your opponent's eyes, trade real blows, feel the fleshy resistance as your blade bit.

He made a few practice swings, listening to the *whoosh* as its keen edge parted the air, marvelling at how well balanced and solid the weapon still was. Not just a weapon, but a work of art.

Damn, a man could have the time of his life with a blade like this.

He handed the scabbard to the woman who stood by his side, dressed in the same black combat fatigues as himself. Riley, his protégé, the eager and dangerous young woman who had served him so well in Berlin several months earlier. She had gone in with the rest of the assault team tonight, right at the vanguard of the attack. As beautiful and deadly as the sword he now held.

Two prisoners knelt on the floor in the centre of the room behind them. A man and a woman, their hands bound, staring up at him like rabbits caught in a snare.

The woman was young, dark haired and beautiful despite the streaks of blood across her face. They'd captured her trying to flee the compound in an armoured Toyota SUV, its bulletproof glass and Kevlar chassis proving remarkably resilient to small-arms fire. It had made it nearly 100 yards until a well placed M203 high-explosive round had blown apart the front axle and disabled the engine, allowing his team to move in and extract the frightened passenger.

The man, short and squat, his thinning hair falling in greasy tangles, had taken cover during the attack and surrendered at the first opportunity. Smart guy: the rest of his comrades were dead, some resisting more than others, but all meeting the same fate. Hawkins hadn't lost a single operative in return.

Unfortunately, their true target had eluded them. Cesar Rojas was not counted amongst the dead. A search of the basement had uncovered an escape tunnel hidden behind a shelving unit, which exited into the jungle a couple of hundred yards away. Far enough from the battle to escape their notice until it was too late, with the heavy canopy also helping him evade the Reaper drone's thermal-imaging cameras.

Rojas was smarter than Hawkins had given him credit for.

'I want to congratulate you both,' he began, allowing the tip of the sword to rest on the marble floor. 'You're alive. Not many of your friends can say the same, so already you're doing pretty well in my book. Now let's see if you keep that winning streak going. First one to give me a decent answer gets to stay alive. Ready?'

He relished moments like these. He'd never seen the point in trying to break people down when it was so much easier to turn them against each other. A little lesson he'd learned early in his life.

'Where is Rojas?'

'I-I don't k-know where he is,' the fat man stammered.

Hawkins smiled and looked over at Riley. 'You hear that? He doesn't *k-k-know*.'

'I was o-outside. I didn't s-see him,' the man went on, stumbling over his words in his eagerness to prove his ignorance. Maybe he wasn't so smart after all, Hawkins conceded. 'I j-just work for him. Please, I don't know anything. I—'

Hawkins had already heard enough. He drew the sword tip back just a few inches, then calmly plunged it into the man's throat. The wonderfully sharp blade went through his windpipe, arteries and tendons as if it wanted to do it, and Hawkins merely had to let it happen.

The man's eyes went wide, his mouth open as if to scream, yet barely a sound emerged. Several inches of the blood-covered sword were now protruding through the back of his neck.

'Holy shit!' Hawkins exclaimed, marvelling at the ease with which the weapon had completed its task. 'You know, I've killed people all kinds of different ways in my time, but I've never used a goddamn sword before.'

The man hung there for a second or two, his spinal column waiting for signals from his brain that would never arrive, before Hawkins withdrew the blade and he slumped to the floor in a limp, fleshy heap.

Hawkins allowed the tip of the blade to rest on the floor, blood trickling down its edge, before turning to the remaining prisoner. She hadn't reacted to her companion's gory death.

'How about you, beautiful? You've been playing it cool so far, and I respect that. Hell, I like that in a woman. So what have you got to tell us?'

The young woman's eyes darted from the dead body on the floor to the bloody blade that had made it happen, before settling on the man who wielded it. She was thinking, rationalizing, weighing up her choices.

'How do I know I won't end up like him?' she asked.

'I give you my word.'

She spat contemptuously at his feet. 'Your word is worth shit to me, *idiota*. You let me go, give me a cell phone and I'll call you with everything I know once I'm in the clear. Not before.'

Hawkins smiled. 'Did you somehow miss what I just did to your buddy there?' he asked, pointing his sword at the corpse.

She stared up at him without fear. 'Kill me if you want. Then you'll never find out what I know.'

'Shit, you've got some big shiny lady balls on you, trying to negotiate at a time like this.' He glanced over at Riley. 'What do you make of this?'

'Give me five minutes alone with her. She'll talk,' Riley promised.

He considered it for a moment or two. 'I like your positive attitude, but we're on kind of a timetable tonight.'

Glancing up at the two operatives standing guard, he gave them a brief nod. The big men rushed forward, seizing hold of Valeria. She let out a furious cry and tried to kick free, but her efforts were wasted. Her captors were far stronger, and well versed in prisoner restraint.

'Wouldn't struggle if I were you,' Hawkins warned as he tossed the sword to Riley, who caught it by the hilt. 'We wouldn't want you to get hurt.'

Reaching into a pouch in his webbing, he produced a small Autoject compressed air syringe, its transparent barrel filled with a pale-green liquid.

'Sometimes during interrogations we run into little snags like this,' he explained, approaching Valeria with the syringe. 'People who have a little... trouble coming around to our way of thinking. Lucky for you, my employer developed a little something to clear that mind of yours.'

'*Foda-se!*' she cried, trying to back away.

He held the syringe up, letting her look at it.

'You should feel honoured. Not many people get a chance to experience this.' He smiled. 'Night, night.'

Her head was yanked sideways, exposing her neck and allowing Hawkins to administer the Autoject. There was a faint hiss, a sharp cry of pain, and that was it. The drugs had been discharged. Hawkins stepped back and waited for them to take effect.

It was about 20 seconds before they migrated up through her bloodstream and into her brain. Twenty seconds before her struggles eased, her eyes lost focus, and the fear left her. Now her face had taken on a serene, dreamlike expression, her full lips turned up a little at the corners as if with the beginnings of a smile. At Hawkins' instruction, the guards let go of her and she simply sat there, staring off into nothingness.

Stepping in front of her, Riley waved a hand before her eyes. There was no reaction.

'The fuck is that stuff?' she asked, curious and a little unnerved.

Hawkins held a finger in front of his mouth, appealing for silence.

'Can you hear me?' he asked, speaking gently and slowly.

'Yes.' Her voice was distant, disconnected.

'I want you to think back to earlier tonight. Do you remember what happened?'

'There was a woman. She came here tonight to speak with Rojas.'

Hawkins raised an eyebrow. 'What did this woman look like?'

'She was a white woman, with yellow hair. Rojas used the name Maras.'

'And what did Maras want?'

'She wanted his help finding someone. A man called Drake.'

'Did Rojas agree to help her?'

'Yes. He spoke with his contacts in the city, asking if they had heard of this man.'

'And had they?' Hawkins pressed her.

'There was one… his name is Cuatro. He said Drake had come to his place.'

'Do you know where Cuatro's place is?'

The unnerving, dreamy smile was still there. 'Yes.'

'Good. Tell me.'

The drugs Powell had developed to tap into the human subconscious were incredible, able to cause a person not only to recall events and situations with perfect clarity, but to actually relive them as if they were happening again. It was amazing what a person could remember without their conscious mind interfering.

'Well done,' he said, laying a hand on her shoulder. 'You did real good.'

Her smile broadened, becoming an expression of childlike joy at his praise. 'Now I want you to do one more thing for me. I want you to forget everything that happened here tonight. Sit down, close your eyes and forget.'

The young woman tucked her feet beneath her and closed her eyes, her expression of absolute peace and serenity a macabre contrast to the death and destruction all around.

Satisfied, Hawkins turned away and spoke into his radio. 'Fire up the chopper. We're out of here in two minutes. Saddle up, boys!'

'What about her?' Riley asked, still carrying the sword he'd given her. 'Want me to finish her?'

'Why? I gave her my word I wouldn't kill her. A man's word still counts for something in my book.' He glanced at the bloody weapon. 'Don't worry, there's plenty to go around tonight.'

Riley grinned as she followed him outside with the rest of the assault team, their Black Hawk chopper already stirring into life.

Chapter 38

Anya's enemy was right on her, big and dark and partially silhouetted by the flickering light from the hallway. Was it Drake trying to ambush her? A survivor of this massacre? Or someone else entirely?

As Anya raised the automatic, a hand shot out and seized the weapon, jerking back the slide so that the hammer was blocked and unable to fire.

Aware of how vulnerable she suddenly was, Anya went for the knife at her waist, yanking it free of its sheath, and swept it upwards.

'Stop!' a familiar voice commanded.

Her arm halted, holding the blade an inch or two from his throat. For a tense, heart-stopping moment they remained like that, locked in a frozen embrace. The hallway light flickered, allowing Anya to see the man's face. It was a stern, arrogant face with thin lips drawn back in an angry grimace.

'Dietrich,' she spat, neglecting to lower the blade. 'What are you doing here?'

The big German didn't move a muscle. 'Looking for Ryan. What the fuck do you think I'm doing here?'

'How did you get inside?'

'Through the front door,' he answered. 'It was open and unlocked.'

Anya didn't say anything, though privately regretted not trying to enter that way first. She might have avoided her acrobatics up on the roof.

Letting out a breath, Anya slowly lowered the knife. With the stand-off broken, he released his grip on the automatic and they both stepped back a pace.

'Did you do this?' Anya asked, gesturing at the carnage around them.

The German snorted, glancing at the man literally impaled on the desk. 'A little excessive, don't you think? Whatever happened here, it seems we both missed the party.'

'And Ryan,' she remarked, her frustration obvious. 'Where have you been all day? You have not answered your cell phone.'

'Neither have you,' he pointed out. 'And for your information, I work better alone.'

Sheathing the knife with a certain reluctance, Anya glared at him. 'I told you not to interfere with this.'

'I don't take orders from you. And I'm not inclined to sit on the sidelines.'

'Watch yourself, Dietrich,' she warned. 'I did not spend all day getting here to have you blunder in and ruin it.'

'Well, that proves how slow you are, because I've been working on this for about...' he looked at his watch, 'two hours now, and I'm still ahead of you.'

Tempted as she was to bite back, this was no time for petty bickering. Instead she turned to more urgent matters.

'Tell me something useful. Since you got here first, what have you found?'

'Same as you. A load of dead guys, a stash of weapons and booze, and no Ryan.' He shrugged. 'Pretty tough to question a bunch of dead men.'

On this at least Anya was in full agreement. Knowing what Drake had taken from this place might have offered some clues about his intentions.

'Damn,' she said under her breath.

She was about to speak when the uncomfortable silence was broken by a bleep. Anya searched for the source of the noise, quickly narrowing it down to the dead man lying on the desk. She could see the phone's illuminated screen through the bloodstained fabric of his shirt.

Someone was calling.

Chapter 39

The kitchen and service area of the Emiliano Rio hotel was a hotbed of frenetic activity, shouted orders, chefs labouring over grills and ovens, servers and porters moving rapidly around with trays of food in an elaborate, constantly changing dance.

In such a hectic environment, cooks and waiters scarcely had time to take notice of the person standing next to them, never mind observe the fleeting passage of a new arrival who strode through the place like he had worked there his whole life.

Tall, good looking and clean cut, his dark hair neatly combed, he looked much like the rest of the waiting staff. It was common throughout Rio that nobody fat or ugly was selected for customer-facing roles in places like this.

A young kitchen assistant, busy washing and peeling the next tray of vegetables, glanced up briefly as he passed by, helping himself to one of the spare grey server tunics that hung along the wall. Spillages and dropped plates weren't unknown even among skilled waiting staff, and stained uniforms had to be changed immediately.

She didn't recognize him, but that wasn't surprising. A small army of people worked here on various shift patterns, and many staff were brought in at short notice to cover busy periods. Maybe he was a temp, though she caught herself hoping she'd see him around here more often. Brushing that thought aside, she looked back down at the food awaiting preparation and resumed her task.

Barely breaking his stride, the new arrival slipped the tunic over his shoulders, buttoned it up as he hurried on through the service area and took one of the room service trolleys with him. In under 30 seconds, he had taken what he needed and departed.

The access corridors beyond the kitchens were, unlike the rest of the lavishly appointed hotel, simple breeze-blocked rectangles with bare concrete floors, cheap fluorescent strip lighting, and pipes and ductwork snaking across the ceilings overhead. The walls were painted plain white with occasional arrows and printed directions to important areas to help staff navigate.

Ryan Drake required no such assistance. He knew exactly where he was going, and quickly and efficiently wheeled the service trolley along to the bank of elevators at the far end. Most of them were for the main guest levels, but one was set aside for the penthouse suite.

This elevator required an access key which only a few staff members possessed. Fortunately, for tonight at least, Drake had managed to become one of this privileged group. It was amazing how easy it was to pickpocket an employee distracted by a local teenager, bribed into acting belligerent about not being allowed to use the hotel restrooms. Best 50 dollars Drake had ever spent.

A black holdall was stowed discreetly between a pair of water pipes set into a recessed alcove about halfway along the corridor. Not terribly well hidden, but people coming this way were usually too busy to take much notice. Drake snatched it up and slid it onto the lower shelf of his serving trolley.

Stopping in front of the penthouse elevator, Drake fished in his pocket for the stolen key, then inserted and turned it. The doors pinged and swung open, revealing a spotlessly clean elevator car reserved for the hotel's richest and most valued customers. Even the carpet was thick and expensive.

As the doors slid closed, Drake picked up the holdall, dumped it on top of the serving trolley and unzipped it.

First out was a pair of Russian MP-443 Grach automatics chambered with 9 x 19mm cartridges. Reliable and well-engineered weapons introduced less than ten years ago, they had quickly proven themselves in the field and become standard sidearms for most branches of the Russian military. Drake had liberated them from Cuatro's sizeable arsenal earlier, relieved to have found something to suit his needs. He'd also brought with him a pair of attachable suppressors, which he quickly screwed in place at the end of each barrel.

After checking the safeties were engaged and a round was in each chamber, he slid both pistols down the back of his tunic. The garment was already tight given the Kevlar body armour he was wearing, but he wasn't complaining.

Better to have it than not.

His other weapons of choice were less lethal but equally useful. Despite a thorough search of Cuatro's safe house, he'd been unable to procure any stun grenades, which was unfortunate. He'd just have to make do with a couple of M18 smoke grenades, their cylindrical bodies coloured olive green but their tops painted bright red to designate the smoke colour.

Last out was a long coil of dark nylon rope with a grappling hook affixed to one end. The rope he stowed below, while the grenades were hooked into his belt at the back. Anyone walking behind him would see them and the grips of the automatics right away, but that didn't matter. He only needed to appear normal from the front.

Thus prepared, he reached out for the control panel and pressed the button for penthouse level.

Chapter 40

'Well?' Dietrich said impatiently. 'You going to answer it?'

Anya glanced at him, then back at the phone. Given that the phone apparently belonged to Cuatro, it was most likely Rojas trying to make contact again.

Reaching into the dead man's shirt pocket, Anya withdrew the phone, its plastic casing slick with blood, and pressed the green icon. She didn't speak, just waited and listened. She could hear various static pops, crackles and digital distortion on the line, characteristic of a scrambler unit.

'Aren't you going to say hello?'

The voice was low pitched, lower than a normal human's, and slightly garbled and warped as if not quite in sync. The caller was using software to disguise their identity.

'That depends who I'm talking to,' she said. 'Do we know each other?'

'There was a time when I felt you knew me better than I knew myself.'

Holding her free hand up, she snapped her fingers several times to get Dietrich's attention. When he looked, she silently mouthed an instruction.

He can see us.

As Dietrich hurried to the nearest window, Anya decided to try her luck. 'Then you knew I would find this place, Ryan. You knew I would come looking for you.'

She heard a discordant jumble of sounds that might have been a laugh. 'Nice try, bad guess. The man you're looking for has other tasks tonight.'

–

As the elevator rose smoothly, Drake kept his eyes forward, his head tilted slightly downwards away from the camera, his face impassive. A security camera was looking down on him from just above the door, vetting him to make sure he was an authorized member of staff. If her minders suspected anything was wrong, they would shut down the elevator, lock the doors and call security.

But they didn't. To them, he was just another anonymous waiter on his way up to collect the leftovers from their boss's meal.

Drake took a slow, deep breath and closed his eyes. What he was about to do called for cool, calculated decisions under pressure, not fury and raw aggression. That was the only way he was going to get to her.

He opened his eyes as the elevator slid to a graceful halt, the chime sounded once and the doors automatically slid open to reveal a pair of men waiting for him. Both were tall and heavy-set, and dressed in the kind of cheap, nondescript suits that always reminded him of limousine drivers. Neither man was overtly carrying, but he spotted the distinctive bulge of weapons concealed inside their suit jackets.

Drake's eyes darted from one man to the other, gauging the distance between them, carefully working out the mechanics of what he was about to do. The one with the reddish hair was looking at him questioningly, perhaps sensing something wasn't quite right. He would probably err on the side of caution and go for the weapon inside his jacket.

Now.

Reaching behind him, Drake clapped his hands around the grips of both weapons and pulled them smoothly free of their improvised holster. He didn't yank them out forcefully or with excessive speed, because that would risk snagging them on a belt or piece of fabric, but instead drew them out in a single, fluid motion and brought them out in front of him.

Both bodyguards saw the initial movement and threw their jackets aside to expose weapons mounted in shoulder holsters, their bodies moving in such perfect unison that it was almost like watching a choreographed dance routine.

They were good, reacting quickly and keeping their cool, but they were too late. Drake only took a fraction of a second to judge the angle of his shots.

Getting what he believed to be a good line of sight on both men, Drake squeezed the triggers simultaneously. Both weapons kicked back against his wrists, quickly followed by a second volley in case his aim was off.

It wasn't.

Both men jerked and crumpled to the ground, the red-haired man with a round in the forehead and another just below his left eye, shattering most of the bones in his face. Not a pleasant way to go, but at least it had been quick.

His colleague meanwhile had been caught with Drake's first shot, a glancing blow to the side of his head. The round had ripped away the skin and a sizeable chunk of skull along with it, exposing the bloody, delicate organ within. He wasn't quite dead yet, but neither did he present much of a threat now, thrashing weakly on the floor and making odd choking noises that were probably meant to be screams. Drake put another pair of rounds into him to finish the job.

Wheeling the trolley halfway out of the elevator to block the doors and prevent anyone calling it, Drake unbuttoned the restrictive grey tunic and tossed it aside, then snatched up the coiled nylon rope from his holdall and looped it over his shoulder.

With both silenced Grachs at the ready, he advanced along the short corridor that led from the elevator bank to the suite itself. It was, as he'd expected, luxuriously appointed and ultra-modern in design. Lots of plate glass windows, with the rooftop pool and sun terrace situated just outside.

'Linford? Deverell?' a voice called from around the corner.

Drake could hear footsteps approaching – rapid, concerned by the noise. He backed up against the wall just as a third man in similar attire appeared around the corner, gun already drawn.

As he started to swing the weapon around towards the two dead men over by the elevator, Drake reached out and clamped his hand down on the gun, jerking it upwards to prevent him getting a shot in, then raised the Grach, positioned the bore of the silencer beneath his chin and pulled the trigger.

The resultant spray of blood reached all the way to the ceiling, painting the white surface vivid red.

With his enemy neutralized, Drake let go and allowed the man to fall to the ground like a sack of potatoes as he carried on, making for the suite's living area. His shirt and face were speckled with blood, but that didn't matter now. All that mattered was *her*.

She was exactly where he knew she'd be. Standing over by the window, her back to him, a glass of wine in hand as she surveyed the city below. Tall, graceful, elegant, perfect. He watched as one slender arm reached up, tilting the glass of wine to her lips.

Drake edged into the room, covering her with the automatic. His eyes swept left and right in search of other threats, other obstacles to be overcome. None presented themselves.

'You don't need to be afraid,' Powell said softly. 'It's just the two of us now.'

Drake had the weapon trained on her. She couldn't have been more than ten yards away. A perfect shot. If she so much as twitched, all he had to do was squeeze the trigger.

'Turn around,' he instructed. 'Slowly.'

He heard a chuckle, low and husky. 'Worried that I'm armed?' she asked. 'You really have forgotten, haven't you?'

Laying the wine glass down on the dining table, Elizabeth Powell raised her chin and turned around to face him. And at last he was afforded his first proper view of her face.

Far from being afraid or astounded by his sudden intrusion into her world of luxurious harmony, she was smiling at him. The smile of a parent reunited with a wayward child.

'It's good to see you again, Ryan.'

–

'Would you like to try again?' the voice on the phone taunted.

Anya's jaw tightened. If not Drake or Rojas, then who else would have gone to this kind of trouble?

'Stop toying with me,' she said tersely. 'Tell me what you want.'

She expected a response that would answer her question. Whoever this man was, he wouldn't have made this call just to taunt her. But even Anya, for all her years of experience and cunning, couldn't have foreseen what came next.

'Forgive me, I should have known.' A pause, perfectly timed. 'You never did enjoy playing games, did you, *sesele*?'

The word hit home with such force that it felt like a physical blow. Her mouth dropped open, she let out a strangled gasp, and she seemed to sag visibly, bracing her hand against the desk for support. It was all she could do to keep from dropping the cell phone.

Sesele. Such a benign, simple word on the face of it. An affectionate term of endearment used by the people of her homeland towards friends and family members alike. An epithet, playful and perhaps mildly teasing, but to her it meant so much more. It spoke of a powerful and abiding bond, a bond forged through shared peril, hardship, glory, loss and tragedy.

Sesele – little sister.

Only one man had ever called her by that nickname in her entire adult life, because only one could have gotten away with it. He had earned that right the hard way, as a man should. He had done it by fighting beside her on dozens of battlefields, risking his life alongside hers, protecting her as she'd protected him. And in time she'd come to think of him as the older brother she'd never had.

But that time had passed.

That man was gone now. They were all gone.

'Where did you hear that name?' she managed to say, her voice as brittle as ancient parchment.

'Hear it? I gave it to you, *sesele*,' he explained. 'Do you really forget so easily?'

'No,' she said, shaking her head vehemently. 'No, it's not possible. You can't be him. The man who gave me that name is dead.'

'You were dead once.' Even through the distortion she could sense his change in tone. 'All of us mourned you, myself most of all. But you came back, even though we gave up hope. You came back, and so have I.'

Anya squeezed her eyes shut as if to block out the emotion, the pain, the joy and sorrow of that moment. Not just that moment, she realized, which was separated from her by long, cold years of loss and longing, but this moment right here, right now. She tried in vain to hold on to her crumbling denial, to block out the growing realization, the sudden explosion of *hope*, that he was telling the truth.

When she opened her eyes again, the lashes were wet with tears.

'How can this be?' she whispered. 'How did you…?'

'How did I find you?' he finished for her. 'You still don't understand, do you? I didn't have to find you. Your hunt for Drake brought you right to me.'

Anya could barely comprehend what she was hearing. Somehow this man was connected to Drake's destructive presence here. Were the two men working together? Was he controlling and directing Drake's actions?

'As for how I survived, you would be surprised what a man can endure when he has something to live for. And *I* have something to live for.'

Her heart was beating so hard and fast that it seemed to be swelling beyond the confines of her ribcage. Anya's mouth was dry, her throat constricted as her mind raced to understand it all.

'What do you mean?'

'We wasted our lives waging other men's wars, *sesele*. We fought and killed and bled for ideologies, flags, governments who cared nothing for us. We sacrificed everything we had until there was nothing left to give… and where did it get us?'

He allowed the question to hang. 'This will be my final mission. For me, for you, for all our fallen brothers. And when my work is finished, you'll know exactly what I had to live for.'

'Wait.' She was pacing the room now. 'If you really are the man I once knew, then meet with me. We can talk face to face, like we should. You can tell me everything. Meet me.'

'And if I did? Would you greet me as a friend, or with the barrel of a gun?'

Anya swallowed with difficulty, her throat suddenly dry. 'If you are still the man I remember, I would greet you as I always have.'

Silence greeted that statement. She could hear only the muted pop and crackle of static distortion in the background.

'No. Not yet,' he said. 'I have work to do first. But when the time is right, when you are ready to know the truth, we will meet again, *sesele*.'

She could sense he was about to end the call. 'Wait, I—'

'One more thing,' he interrupted. 'If I were you, I would leave soon. I am not the only one who knows you're there.'

The line cut out then, leaving Anya alone.

She was given no time for contemplation. No sooner had the call ended than Dietrich called out to her from his window vantage point.

'Anya, you'd better get over here!'

Slipping the phone into her pocket, she hurried out of the room and along the corridor to join him.

'What is it?' she asked.

'Company,' he replied, edging aside so that she could peer through the narrow gap between the window shutter and the frame.

Looking down into the street below, she spotted a pair of black SUVs parked up. High quality, powerful, late-model vehicles with darkened windows. Definitely not the kind one would normally find in this part of town.

As she watched, the doors on both SUVs were thrown open and black-clad men piled out, making no attempt to hide their assault rifles as they converged on the building. These men were trained tactical operatives, and they had one objective in mind.

They were coming inside.

Chapter 41

Drake could do nothing but stare at her, drinking in the details of her face as it regarded him with a cool, gentle, quizzical expression. A face that had become like a half-remembered dream, felt and experienced but never truly understood and rationalized. A face that was perfect in its symmetry, the elegant harmony of its features, beautiful in a way that so few others were.

So many times he'd felt that he could almost picture what she looked like, as if the memory of her were a hazy, intangible thing that would dissipate if he ever tried to reach out for it. He wondered then if she had changed since their last encounter. Had she always looked this way, or was his mind playing tricks on him? And if this memory of her, which had had such a profound impact on his life, was so unreliable, then what other aspects of his memory, of *himself*, might he not understand?

'Well?' Powell prompted. 'You've gone to a lot of trouble to find me. Here I am, Ryan. Don't you have anything to say?'

Drake had a great many things he wanted to say, yet in that moment he found it hard to single any of them out. A thousand thoughts and questions and confusing memories whirled through his mind seemingly all at once, bursting in and out of his consciousness like flashes of lightning. It was as if a carefully constructed dam had given way inside his mind, and everything held back by it had all come tumbling out at once.

In a flash, he saw visions of hospital clinics, of clean and sterile rooms and people in white coats. He saw machines, syringes, drugs, bright lights and jarring, deafening sounds. He saw Thomas Hayes leaning in to examine him, asking him questions, then an instant later the man was at the other end of the room, talking with *her*.

Drake saw her glance at him, saw her smile encouragingly. That same smile she was showing him now.

'I never knew your name,' he heard himself say, almost without being aware of it. 'In all that time, you never told me your real name.'

There it was. Out of all the things he could have said, could have asked, could have railed and ranted about, that was what he chose. Drake couldn't have truly explained why that troubled him so much. Perhaps it was because it went against his natural sense of order, his instinctive feeling of *rightness*. How can you truly have any meaningful relationship with someone who has no name, no foundation on which to base your sense of them?

Or perhaps it was something else, something less rational. Perhaps it was a lingering sense of jealousy, of antipathy. Why hadn't she told him? Wasn't he worthy of it?

Powell nodded patiently, showing that she understood his anger, his frustration, his pain. Of course she understood. She always had understood him.

'It must be very difficult for you to appreciate now, but there were choices, sacrifices we had to make back then. We did it so you could become what you are now.'

'What I am,' he repeated.

And what exactly am I? What did you create?

'Yes, Ryan. *What you are.* You're something very special. You've done remarkable things – things other men never could have achieved. And you did these things because of the gifts I gave you. Even back then, I saw what you had the potential to become.'

Once again a series of flashbulb memories flickered. He saw himself kicking down a door of some house at night, saw himself raise a weapon, felt the familiar and comforting kick of it against his shoulder, heard screams in the darkness.

Powell took a step towards him, as if she wanted to reach out and embrace him. Jolted out of his memories, Drake raised his weapon.

'Stay back!' he warned. 'Don't come any closer.'

Powell shook her head. 'There's no need for that now. You can put the weapon down.'

He wanted to put it down. Drake couldn't explain it, but as the words left her mouth he was seized by a compelling urge to lay his gun down. He *had* to put it down, he was certain of that. Of course she was right. She knew what was best for him, she always had.

No! his mind screamed at him, as if there were two warring forces at work inside his head and Drake, the essence of him, were merely a bystander.

The gun trembled, the barrel dipping just slightly before he managed to drag it back up again, using every ounce of willpower to keep it pointed at her. What was wrong with him? Why was he listening to her?

Powell was watching this inner struggle play out too, and tilted her head slightly as if trying to rationalize this minor problem.

'You've grown stronger, I see,' she remarked. 'Interesting. A different man would have complied without question. But you're not like the others, are you, Ryan?'

She took another step towards him, her heels clicking on the hardwood floor.

'Stop,' Drake said. 'I'll fire.'

'No, you won't,' she promised, taking another step. 'But please, try if you must.'

The part of his mind that still remained his own now flared with anger and righteous fury. Of course he should fire. *Kill her now, and be rid of her for ever! Pull the trigger and end it. Do it now!*

Drake tried to tighten his finger on the trigger, tried to force his body to obey, but it wouldn't listen. It was as if the nerves that transmitted signals from his brain to his hand were no longer working. The gun was trembling visibly in his grip now as the woman approached him, and he tried to keep her in his sights.

But there was another part of his mind, a deeper and stronger part, that was telling him to put the gun down. He couldn't kill her. She was everything to him, the centre of his world, the foundation upon which his entire being was built.

Kill her now! his conscious mind screamed.

You can't kill her, the other voice whispered. *You never could.*

It happened almost without Drake being consciously aware of it. Moving almost of its own volition, his arm slowly lowered, the barrel of the silencer now pointed to the floor.

Powell smiled that same gentle, encouraging smile. Part of him revelled in it, rejoiced to have won her praise. Another part of him railed in horror and disgust.

'That's good, Ryan. You did the right thing,' she assured him. She was only a few feet away now. 'The only thing. You can no more kill me than you can stop the sun from rising. Think of it as an... insurance policy, to help you remember where your loyalties truly lie. Every candidate like you was given it.'

He felt rooted to the spot, unable to escape, unable to resist. Still that part of his mind cried out for him to fight her, but it was growing smaller and weaker by the minute. 'What did you do to me?'

'I *made* you, Ryan. I broke down every little piece of who you were, and I remade it into something better.' She brushed past him then, standing so close that he could smell her perfume. 'Every man has his own unique strengths and weaknesses, and they can all be taught to excel in their own way, but you were different. You were so much more than the others. Even from the beginning you were my favourite, and I made sure the best of my work went into you. I wanted you to be something perfect, something beautiful.'

Reaching down, she gently prised the gun from his hands. He didn't try to stop her. He couldn't anyway. He felt himself falling more and more under her spell. Her voice was mesmerizing, her presence intoxicating. 'I knew one day you would come back to me. You would find me again.' Her voice was barely a whisper. 'You didn't know why, you couldn't explain what you were looking for, but I know what brought you here. You wanted to come, didn't you, Ryan?'

Drake felt that she wasn't simply speaking to him, she was speaking for him. She was articulating the thoughts and emotions that he hadn't consciously acknowledged.

'You've been so lost, so alone all this time,' that persuasive voice carried on. 'All you wanted to do was come home, to belong again.'

Drake could feel tears stinging his eyes. As if every moment of grief, sadness, longing and loneliness he'd ever experienced had suddenly coalesced together into an overwhelming swell of emotion that crashed devastatingly against him.

'But you *are* home now,' Powell promised him. 'You've come back to me, and you don't have to feel alone any more. Because I'm going to help you, Ryan.'

–

'Let me get this straight,' hotel manager Mateo Carbrera said, sitting up straighter in his chair. 'You saw this man's face for... what? Three, four seconds?'

The young, nervous-looking kitchen hand – he thought her name might be Paola – nodded, looking at the stains on her chef's apron rather than face his accusing stare. 'About that long, sir.'

'So, three or four seconds in the middle of a busy kitchen, with people running back and forth.' Carbrera rested his elbows on the desk, his fingers steepled in a manner he believed lent him a thoughtful, diplomatic air. 'And in that time you were able to identify him as the man who blew up that factory the other day? The one whose picture has been on the news?'

Again she nodded. 'I think so, yes.'

Carbrera let out a weary sigh. Managing a large hotel like this could be a trying experience even on the best days, and he had little time for staff members reporting every little problem as if there were no one else who could deal with it.

'Why not notify security?' he asked. 'Why come to me?'

'I didn't recognize him right away,' she confessed. 'It was only once my shift ended, and I happened to see his face on the TV again that I made the connection.'

Carbrera smiled with exaggerated patience, convinced the silly girl had confused an innocent member of staff with the man on TV, or more likely was just looking for attention.

'And what would a terrorist want with one of our porter uniforms?'

She swallowed and at last made eye contact. 'Our porters can move all around the hotel. Including the guest rooms.'

Carbrera's smile was still there, only now it didn't look so confident. Now there was a certain edge, a doubt that crept in with those words. A doubt, and a recollection of another little incident that had made its way up the chain to him in the last half-hour. A report from one of the waiters about a missing elevator key.

A key that gave access to the penthouse suit.

Carbrera rose from his chair with a speed that was surprising for a 60-year-old man on the wrong side of 240 pounds, rounded his desk and took the young woman by the arm.

'Come with me,' he said, his voice hard and imperious as he led her out of the office.

Chapter 42

It took Anya less than a second to assess the situation, the forces deployed against them, their own – limited – options.

'We need to get out of here,' she said, backing away from the window.

No sooner had she spoken than the lights suddenly blinked out, plunging them into near darkness. Only the thin shafts of orange light filtering through the window shutters provided any illumination.

'Really, you think?' Dietrich replied sarcastically.

Anya paused, listening. She could hear something against the exterior of the building. The sound of movement, the squeal of a descent harness unwinding at full speed, the flick of a rope uncoiling.

'Move!' Anya shouted, sprinting across the floor and sliding beneath the wooden desk with Cuatro's body still impaled on top.

But even as she did this, the old and partially rotten wooden shutters on the other side of the room exploded inwards, caved in by the booted feet of an operative who had fast-roped down the side of the building.

Propelled by his own momentum, he swung in through the window and executed a textbook entry, landing solidly on the floor and bringing his Heckler & Koch UMP submachine gun into play within seconds.

His eyes swept the room, spotted Anya, and brought his weapon to bear just as she reached up and heaved the desk over onto its side with a violent crash. Anya flattened herself against the floor as a volley of suppressed .45 rounds tore through this improvised barricade, punching holes all along its length and even ripping into the body of Cuatro which now lay sprawled on the floor in front of it.

'Dietrich! Covering fire!' she shouted. She needed him to suppress this man while she changed position.

There was no response. Dietrich appeared to have vanished.

Gritting her teeth in anger, Anya pushed the barrel of her weapon through one of the ragged holes that had been punched out, and fired a trio of rounds blindly through the gap. An ejected cartridge pinged off the table leg beside her, burning her arm. She ignored it, concentrating on putting maximum firepower on her target.

She heard a couple of dull thuds, including the distinctive *whang* as one of the rounds struck a section of armour plate and ricocheted away, but no cry of pain. It didn't matter, it was enough to put him off balance.

She scrambled up from her hiding place, vaulted over the top of the table and charged. Taking hasty aim, Anya fired on the move, the dull crack of the M1911's .45 calibre rounds echoing off the walls.

The .45 calibre slugs were big and heavy, but at low velocity they were unable to defeat her adversary's body armour and flattened harmlessly against it. However, the impact of the shots was enough to knock him backwards, disrupting his aim just as he squeezed the trigger.

A burst of automatic fire sailed over Anya's right shoulder as she grabbed the barrel of the weapon and twisted it upwards, the rattle of the firing mechanism jarring her arm with each blast. The barrel was heating up rapidly, and she could feel the burning heat even through the shielded foregrip.

Driving her knee into the man's crotch, she heard a snarl of pain. Exerting himself, he pulled the gun free and swung it like a club, trying to catch her across the face. Anya barely managed to duck away, but instead of retaliating she reached behind her back, drew the knife from its sheath and swiped, slicing through the descent harness he was still latched onto.

Dropping the submachine gun, which was too big and awkward to use at such close quarters, her adversary reached for his waist and unholstered a pistol.

Anya had less than a second to act. Leaping up, she planted a kick solidly in the centre of his chest, knocking him back towards the window. His legs slammed against the windowsill and, caught off balance, he pitched over backwards and fell out through the gap with a startled cry. Anya heard the thump as he landed in the street about 30 feet down.

There was no time to celebrate. Anya crouched down and snatched up the submachine gun, pulling back the primer handle far enough to check there was a round in the breech. The UMP was essentially a scaled-up version of the old MP5 9mm, chambered with high velocity .45 calibre rounds to give it an edge against modern body armour. She couldn't tell how many rounds were left, and there wasn't time to check.

The crash of splintering wood from the other end of the hallway told her a second operative was on his way. Clutching the UMP to her shoulder, she sprinted to the doorway to face this new enemy just as he swung in through the window and landed lightly on the floor.

Except it wasn't a *he* at all.

Anya could tell from the short stature and slender frame that she was facing a woman. Unlike the enemy she'd just knocked out through the window, this one was wearing no mask, revealing a youthful face that might have been considered pretty were it not for the expression of sadistic malevolence. It was a face that Anya had encountered only once before, during the desperate gun battle in Berlin as she and Drake's team fought to escape.

She raised her submachine gun, the beam from its under-barrel laser sight tracing a path through the air towards Anya.

Without having to worry about unhooking herself from a descent harness, Anya was half a second faster on the draw. Raising the UMP, she took aim at the young woman's head. It was a more difficult target to hit, but even the powerful submachine gun was unlikely to penetrate her body armour.

She squeezed the trigger, and the weapon spat out a burst of fire. UMPs have a relatively slow rate of fire compared to most submachine guns, partly to offset the greater recoil of their cartridge. She could feel the jarring punch of each shot as the energy was transferred from the weapon to her body.

But her target was moving even as Anya opened fire, dropping into a crouch so that her shots sailed over the young woman's head, shattering cases of whisky and other spirits that were stacked against the walls. With the weapon's potent recoil trying to pull the barrel upwards, Anya was unable to compensate in time.

The laser sight was on her. Her enemy was about to return fire.

If unable to attack, then defend. If unable to defend, then retreat. Sun Tzu had said that about 2,500 years ago, and it still held just as true today.

Anya threw herself behind the doorway. A long burst of gunfire hit the wall mere feet away from her, shattering the thin plaster before ricocheting off the solid brick beneath. In such close quarters, the chances of being hit and wounded by a ricochet were dangerously high.

She backed up against the wall as more projectiles struck, and looked down at the weapon. The charging handle had flown back and locked, exposing the empty breech and magazine beneath. She was out of ammunition.

Her opponent had no such problems. Something heavy and metallic landed against the door, and she knew immediately that her enemy had just increased the tempo of her attack.

Scrambling away from the door, Anya ducked as a concussive boom reverberated down the hallway, blowing the door right off its hinges, shattering the cases of alcohol stacked nearby and very nearly ruining Anya's eardrums at the same time. Only by clapping her hands over her ears had she prevented herself being deafened. As it was, she felt dizzy and light-headed.

This was one fight she wasn't going to win.

Further down the corridor, Riley carefully ejected her spent magazine lest Anya hear the distinctive clatter and realize she was reloading.

'We haven't been introduced,' she called out as she withdrew a fresh mag from her webbing. 'I'm Riley. I'm looking forward to killing you tonight.'

Inserting the mag, she yanked back the cocking lever and heard the click as the first round was drawn into the breech.

'I had to wait a long time for this. Might as well enjoy ourselves,' she said as she advanced from cover with the UMP ready. As she crept forward along the smoke-filled corridor, she spoke quietly into her tactical radio. 'Move in. Capture only.'

Not far away, Anya dropped the empty submachine gun and reached for the M1911 at her hip, quickly checking the mag. As she'd feared, it too was out of ammunition.

Replacing it, she drew out her knife, the only weapon she had left.

176

Dietrich wasn't coming back, she knew now. He must have used the distraction she provided to make a break for it, either clambering out a window or perhaps finding some means of ascending to the roof. Whatever he'd done, he had better hope she didn't make it out of here, otherwise there would be a reckoning when she caught up with him.

If she even made it that far. Right now, her chances were perilously slim.

The crash of a door being kicked open drew her attention to a new threat coming from the stairwell. Anya leaned in close to the doorway and peered around the edge. She could just make out armoured figures moving through the gloomy hallway towards her, almost certainly equipped with night-vision goggles.

The rest of the assault team that had piled out of the SUVs outside must have secured the lower floor and ascended the stairwell. She couldn't recall how many she'd seen, but it must have been half a dozen at least.

'Tango in sight,' one of them hissed.

Anya tensed up as a trio of submachine guns turned on her, the green beams of their laser sights arcing towards her through the cordite smoke. Unarmed save for the knife in her left hand, she could do little to stop them now.

That was when something happened that Anya neither expected nor understood. A door popped open between her and the assault team, a dark figure momentarily blocking her view. Then she heard a dull pop as red light shot down the corridor, striking the lead member of the assault team and bursting apart into separate pieces, all burning with such ferocious intensity that she was forced to look away.

She heard the man's agonized scream as the incandescent chemical reaction ignited his clothes. His submachine gun spat fire in all directions as he flailed and thrashed in his panic, slamming into walls and igniting the alcohol that had already been spilled. High-proof spirits don't need much incentive to ignite, and within seconds the floor was ablaze.

His comrades were forced to back off, their infrared visors overwhelmed by the bloom of heat and light, not to mention the danger of being engulfed in the growing inferno or by his wild, unaimed gunfire. His agony was only ended when Riley took matters into her own hands and opened fire at point-blank range, putting him down.

Anya stared at the most incongruous sight: Dietrich standing in the corridor just a few yards away, clutching what appeared to be a bulky snub-nosed rifle that resembled a giant six-shooter pistol.

She watched as Dietrich triggered a second shot, the massive ammunition cylinder rotating to cycle the next round into the breech. A second bright-red signal flare shot towards their opponents, this time missing its target and impacting the wall at the far end before falling to the floor in multiple pieces. It was immediately followed by a third round that went high, hit the ceiling and broke apart. The combination of pyrotechnics and alcohol-soaked floors created an impenetrable wall of fire, sparks and red chemical smoke.

Lowering the cumbersome weapon, Dietrich turned to look at her.

'What the fuck are you waiting for?' he shouted. 'Move!'

Without waiting for her response, he disappeared into the stairwell the assault team had emerged from. Anya knew the opportunity wouldn't last long, and quickly forced herself to her feet to race after him.

He was heading up, making for the roof, since there were almost certainly more operatives waiting downstairs. Their best chance was to try to escape across the rooftops.

Turning around at the top of the first flight, he levelled the big weapon at the doorway they'd just passed through and fired two more rounds at it. Intense flares shot past Anya's face then exploded against the wall, showering them with sparks and spewing bright red smoke that began to fill the stairwell. Combined with the rounds he'd already expended, they now had the makings of a destructive inferno on their hands.

'Watch your fire!' she shouted furiously. She'd be lying if she didn't feel a measure of gratitude for what he'd done in the corridor, but that didn't mean she wanted to get her face burned off for her troubles.

The weapon's ammunition was depleted. Snapping the top open in the same way one would open a break-action revolver, Dietrich emptied out the spent 40mm shell casings, which clattered down the stairs around him. He started to reach into the satchel he was carrying, then seemed to think better of it and dumped the heavy weapon.

'You know, I'm getting a little tired of saving your ass,' he remarked as he resumed his run up the stairs. 'When are you going to return the favour?'

Anya decided not to voice her immediate thoughts on that. 'What was that thing?' she asked instead.

'Grenade launcher, American.' He glanced at her over his shoulder. 'This building is a weapons cache, don't you know?'

Of course she knew. She'd seen the crates for herself when she entered, but hadn't been able to get to the armoury with the assault team blocking her path. Dietrich clearly had used the distraction of their entry to arm himself with whatever he could find.

'A little excessive, even by your standards,' she remarked sourly.

She didn't understand why he'd loaded it with signal flares of all things. Launchers like that were compatible with all kinds of rounds, from high explosive to fragmentation and tear gas. Most of which would have been far more effective, given the situation.

'Not like I had time to pick and choose. It was the only weapon I could find with ammo.' When she didn't respond, he added, 'You can thank me later, by the way.'

'Assuming we don't blow up first. The building is on fire,' she pointed out. 'It's a weapons cache, don't you know?'

Dietrich didn't respond, but he did pick up his pace.

Chapter 43

Manuel Sergeoni, the chief of hotel security, rose hastily from his desk as Carbrera strode into his office with the young kitchen assistant in tow.

'What can I do for you, sir?' the man asked, straightening his shirt and looking like a kid caught with his hands in the cookie jar. The impression was heightened by his fresh, youthful complexion, which was quite at odds with the 41 years he'd seen.

Carbrera wasted no time. 'Pull up the security feeds for the north corridor outside the kitchen area,' he instructed.

As the security chief cycled through the camera feeds, Carbrera glanced at the young woman. 'What time did you say this happened?'

She opened her mouth, feeling deeply self-conscious under his intense stare. 'A-about ten thirty,' she managed to stammer.

The hotel manager turned to his chief of security. 'Do it.'

Bringing up the camera feeds on the bank of monitors, he scrolled back through the stored footage until he'd reached the right time stamp. The corridor was empty.

'Fast forward,' Carbrera said impatiently.

The footage began to move more rapidly and it wasn't long before various porters and waiters hustled through. Each time one of them passed, Carbrera would look searchingly at his young female companion, but each time she would shake her head, feeling more and more foolish with each passing second.

Maybe she'd been wrong about the whole thing. Maybe she'd caused all this fuss, gotten everyone worked up and agitated over nothing.

If so, it could well mean the end of her employment here…

'There!' she said, jabbing a finger at the screen. 'That's him!'

Sergeoni froze the image, giving them a good view of the man mid-stride as he advanced down the corridor with a serving trolley in front of him.

'You're certain?' Carbrera asked, squeezing her arm hard. 'You are sure it's him?'

The young woman nodded. She didn't consider herself a confrontational person, and all too often in her life she'd deferred to others rather than speak her mind. But not this time.

'That's the man I saw.'

Carbrera nodded, and it seemed as if something had come over him, his entire tempo and demeanour changing. Now he was sober and serious as he gave Sergeoni a nod to resume the footage.

They watched as the intruder continued his journey, retrieving a pack or holdall stowed in an alcove and placing it on the serving trolley. His route took him to

179

the far end of the corridor, past the doors leading into the hotel's main restaurant, and onwards to the bank of service elevators at the end.

They watched as he selected the penthouse elevator, produced a key from his tunic and calmly unlocked it. The doors swung open, he pushed the trolley inside, and within seconds he was gone.

'The penthouse suite,' Carbrera said under his breath.

Sergeoni spoke up. 'I just got off the phone with Maintenance. They say the elevator is jammed at the penthouse level, it's not responding to floor calls. The doors won't close.'

Carbrera was facing up to a terrifying reality.

'Bring up the penthouse cameras,' he ordered.

Sergeoni's eyes widened. 'Sir, that's against—'

'Do it now!' the hotel manager snapped.

It wasn't widely known, but a number of discreet cameras had been placed in the hotel's penthouse suite, partly as an extra security measure for the high-profile guests who sometimes resided there, and partly to guard against the kind of 'impropriety' that had occasionally been experienced in the past. The rich people of the world could host some of the most lavish – and hedonistic – parties imaginable, some of which had resulted in damage and personal injury when they got out of hand.

Naturally, access to these cameras was strictly policed and automatically logged to prevent abuse. They were to be used only in the event of criminal proceedings or emergencies where lives were endangered. In Carbrera's mind, this qualified.

The camera feed abruptly switched to the reception hallway of the penthouse level, where a pair of suited men were standing opposite the private elevator. Both men looked big, serious, intimidating. Paola watched as the elevator doors slid open to reveal the man with the trolley.

One of the guards took a step forward, then a whole lot of things happened at the same time. Both men reached for something inside their jackets, but before they could do a thing, a pair of twin flashes came from inside the elevator.

Paola covered her mouth with her hand and turned away in horror as both men were gunned down right before her eyes. Even the slightly grainy black-and-white image couldn't detract from the shock of what she'd witnessed.

'My God,' Sergeoni whispered.

–

Drake was losing himself. With each passing second, with each whispered word, he could feel the walls of protection and self-control that he'd erected around his mind vanishing. Not being destroyed by assault from without, but something more insidious and far more alarming. They were being peacefully dismantled from within.

Part of him – a large, growing part that he hadn't even known existed until mere minutes ago – wanted to submit to her, wanted to follow her every command, wanted to earn her praise and gratitude. 'I'm so glad that you've come back, Ryan,' she said in that low, breathy, softly persuasive voice that was at once magnificently and horrifyingly compelling.

She didn't shout, she never shouted, never tried to force or command. All she did was help you understand that there was no other way, no other truth beyond the one she offered. Once you understood that, everything made sense.

'I knew you would, in the end. I can help you become the man that you were, I can help to heal you again. You'd like that, wouldn't you? You want to feel whole again, not fractured like you are now.'

Drake closed his eyes. Both opposing aspects of his psyche, surging with the desperate resolve to defy and obey, had reached a perfectly balanced peak. All it would take was the tiniest nudge to send them tumbling over in absolute surrender.

'Yes,' he whispered. And suddenly he was utterly convinced he'd never wanted anything more desperately in his entire life. He was broken, and she would fix him. 'I do.'

'Good, then all you have to do is help me,' she went on. 'There's something I need you to do...'

Something happened then to change the balance of their struggle, something neither of them had anticipated. Instead of Powell's quiet and wonderfully convincing voice being in his ear, Drake was abruptly assaulted by the deafening blare of a fire alarm.

The woman drew back, startled, angered, casting around for the source of the noise. The effect on Drake was even more profound, akin to throwing a bucket of freezing water over a man just as he's drifting off to sleep. He started with shock, his mind torn out of the hypnotic, dreamlike state that it had lapsed into.

His head snapped around and he stared at Powell with a dawning comprehension, as if seeing her in an entirely different light. But before the woman could speak, the emergency stairwell door behind her was thrown open and several men poured into the room, all with drawn weapons.

Drake was moving even as they stopped to take in the sight of three of their comrades lying dead on the floor, their blood painting the walls and expensive carpet. Drake was running, sprinting for the doors leading outside to the penthouse observation deck. As he moved, he yanked one of the smoke grenades from the belt of his trousers, pulled the pin and tossed it on the ground.

He heard a shout from one of them, 'Target in sight!'

'No!' Powell called out, but it was too late.

A volley of automatic fire resounded through the big open room, the crackle of gunshots drowning out even the persistent blare of the alarms. Several of the plate glass windows in front of Drake shattered under the onslaught, broken fragments tinkling across the floor as he leapt through the newly opened gap.

He felt something slam into his right shoulder blade. It felt like someone had just swung a sledgehammer at him, and he stumbled momentarily before regaining his balance and tearing out onto the rooftop terrace.

Brock Schultz, the head of Powell's security team which had just stormed the penthouse suite, paused to check that his charge was alive and unharmed. He was sure he'd scored at least one hit on his target, which would certainly slow him down. Now he was eager to close in and finish him, to avenge the death of his three colleagues.

'Target's on the sun deck!' he called out, watching as Drake disappeared into the swirling mass of red smoke spewing from the grenade. 'He's got nowhere to go. Gossard, secure the VIP. Everyone else with me. Let's go!'

Flanked by his two fellow operatives, he raced out through the haze of smoke, past the shattered windows and over to the railing that demarcated the upper section of the observation deck. A swimming pool shimmered below them, its pristine blue waters reflecting against the side of the building.

And at the far side of this pool, standing atop the wall that encircled the entire sun deck, was their intruder, seemingly trying to decide whether to jump. Let him, Schultz thought. It was easily 150 feet down to ground level.

'Freeze!' he yelled, training his Smith & Wesson automatic on his target. 'Nowhere left to go, pal. Come down from there and give yourself up.'

As satisfying as it would be to gun the fucker down right now, he wanted to take him in alive. Once they had him in a locked cell, he'd make sure he got five or ten minutes alone with the son of a bitch.

The man glanced up from his precarious vantage point and they made eye contact. Schultz found himself looking into the eyes of a trained killer, and what he saw there was enough to take the edge off his desire for revenge. Suddenly the prospect of being alone with him in a locked room didn't seem quite so appealing.

But it was only a passing glimpse, as the man took a bold step backwards and disappeared over the edge without a sound.

'Goddamn it,' Schultz said through clenched teeth, leaping over the railing and sprinting over to the spot he'd jumped from.

He leaned out over the edge, expecting to see a broken body lying sprawled amongst the decorative trees that encircled the hotel. What he saw was their enemy detaching himself from the rope harness he'd just used to scale the side of the building.

By now well out of range of their sidearms, Schultz could do nothing but watch with impotent rage as their quarry turned and vanished into the night.

Hearing the click of heels approaching on the terrace, he turned to face Elizabeth Powell. The night breeze whipped across the exposed terrace, lifting loose tendrils of dark hair across her face.

'Ma'am, you shouldn't be out here—' Schultz began.

'Shut up,' she replied, silencing him with a raised hand. Her eyes were fixed on the direction of Drake's escape, her expression caught between disappointment and excitement.

'See you soon, Ryan,' she said quietly.

Chapter 44

Throwing open the stairwell access door, Dietrich burst out onto the rooftop, coughing as smoke billowed around him. He drew his weapon and looked around, quickly taking stock of their surroundings.

Anya was right behind him, breathing a little harder after their rapid ascent from the lower floor. Searching amongst the discarded detritus that littered the rooftop, she found a metal pole that might once have been used for stringing out laundry to dry, rammed one end beneath the door handle and the other into the rooftop.

It wouldn't hold their pursuers for long, assuming the assault team were able to fight their way past the blaze and up through the smoke-filled stairwell, but it might buy them time to escape.

Even from up here, it was obvious that the blaze was spreading rapidly. Smoke was now drifting up from the lower windows, and the stench of flammable materials being consumed was heavy in the air. Sooner or later the growing conflagration would reach one of the weapons caches, and when it did this building was history.

'Let's go before we cook,' Dietrich said, having concluded that the best means of escape was to leap across the gap to the residential block that backed onto this building.

Just as he was moving towards the edge of their own rooftop however, Anya grabbed his arm, pulling him back.

'What the fuck?'

'Wait,' Anya whispered, scanning the opposite rooftop with its clutter of chimney stacks, satellite dishes, washing lines and ventilation ducts. Something wasn't right. This was too easy.

She felt it then. The change in the air, the breathless sense of anticipation that comes before a thunderclap. The instinctive certainty that something is about to happen.

'Get down!' she cried just as a muzzle flash erupted on the opposite rooftop.

Both operatives hit the ground as the first burst of suppressed gunfire cut through the air. A second volley hammered against the low retaining wall that marked the rooftop boundary, shattering bricks and sending chunks of cement flying in all directions.

Both were obliged to flatten themselves against the roof, crawling as close to this meagre cover as possible.

'Fuck,' Dietrich snarled, tilting his weapon over the lip of the retaining wall and returning fire, capping off half a dozen shots in the same general direction that the gunfire had come from.

The .40 calibre Glock 22 that Dietrich was using was a powerful handgun, but with only 13 rounds in the mag he simply couldn't put down enough volume of fire to have much hope of scoring a hit. Anya knew he was doing little more than wasting ammo.

A shorter, sharper burst of fire answered this furious show of defiance. The shooter's aim was frighteningly accurate, and Anya heard a loud *whang* as a round struck the retaining wall and ricocheted off the frame of Dietrich's weapon.

'*Scheisse!*'

Dropping the Glock, Dietrich clutched his injured hand, hit by bullet fragments. Lucky for him he'd only been hit by shrapnel rather than the round itself, otherwise he'd probably have lost most of his fingers.

Anya could see a long dent in the Glock's frame where the round had struck it, buckling it inwards. Whether the weapon still functioned was anyone's guess.

With neither side firing, an eerie sense of calm settled over both rooftops, disrupted only by the growing roar of the fires downstairs as they slowly consumed the building.

The silence was broken by a peal of laughter from the opposing roof.

'Well, shit. Guess this isn't what you had in mind,' a voice taunted. 'Out of the frying pan and into the fire, huh?'

Anya should have known Hawkins would have been the one overseeing tonight's assault. Cain's personal attack dog, always spoiling for a chance to kill.

'You still alive over there, Anya?' he called out. 'Hate to think I'd killed you so easy.'

Anya looked around for something, anything that might aid their escape. Reaching out, she picked up the damaged Glock and pulled back the slide. It moved, but only with considerable force on her part. The barrel might also have been compromised, making the weapon as dangerous for its user as its intended target.

'I'm happy to disappoint you,' she replied, hoping to stall him.

'Goddamn, if you don't have a sense of humour after all,' he acknowledged. 'But you've got to admit you're in a tight spot right now. I'd say it won't be long before that rooftop starts cooking right beneath you.'

Anya glanced at Dietrich, who had ripped a section of his shirt away and was wrapping it around his injured hand. He had shuffled off the satchel he'd been carrying so he could work unencumbered.

'What's in the bag?' she whispered.

Dietrich looked up at her, dark brows furrowed. 'What?'

'Your satchel.' She pointed at the simple canvas bag beside him. 'What's in it?'

Opening it up, he held out a couple of spare 40mm rounds for the flare gun he'd discarded earlier, intending to reload it before deciding it had served its purpose.

Such a weapon might have provided the ideal distraction right now, but without the launcher they had no means of setting the flare rounds off.

'So listen, I've got a better idea. What do you say you lay down your guns and come on over here?' Hawkins shouted. 'Can't promise happy endings all round, but it's better than burning to death, right?'

'How about you come over *here*, you redneck prick?' Dietrich retorted. 'Then we'll see how happy your end is.'

Their adversary was silent for a few seconds as he considered his next words. 'Tell you what, *mein herr*. I've got no beef with you, so I'm gonna make you a deal. You hand that little lady over to me, and I'll consider us all square. No harm, no foul, right? You can go your own way, and I'll go mine. How does that sound?'

Dietrich didn't respond to this dubious offer right away, but Anya could see that his focus had slowly shifted to the weapon that now lay between them, that he was weighing up his chances of survival either way. *Don't do it*, she silently urged him. *Don't make me kill you.*

On the opposite rooftop, Hawkins shifted position slightly while keeping the M4 assault rifle up at his shoulder. He had a clear line of sight over most of the building, and was well protected by the solid bulk of the chimney stack he was crouched behind. And if need be, he could just sit here and watch the fireworks display.

Down below, traffic had ground to a halt. The losers who called this dump their home were gathering round the burning building to watch the drama play out, many taking pictures and footage on their cell phones. Had Hawkins been remotely concerned for their welfare, he might have warned them of the danger they were in.

'Tick-tock, Adolf. It's getting warm up here, and we've both got places to be,' he shouted. 'What's your answer?'

His radio earpiece crackled with an incoming transmission. 'Bravo team to all units, recommend you pull back now,' Riley said, her voice dry and rasping from smoke inhalation. 'The fire's spreading fast in there.'

'Copy that, Bravo,' Hawkins replied calmly. 'Spread out and secure the perimeter. I've got them.'

'I'm coming up—'

'Negative, follow my instructions,' Hawkins said, an edge of sharp steel in his voice. Riley was a promising student, one of his favourites, but sometimes she needed reminding who was in command. 'Clear?'

It was a second or two before she responded. 'Clear.'

Anya was all for him tonight. And just as he'd thought, she wasn't going to give up easily. Stubborn to the end.

He raised his voice. 'Okay, pal. You had your chance. If you want to die for her, that's fine with me.'

Just then, a loud boom echoed from deep inside the building, rumbling up towards the rooftop like some great belch rising from a distended stomach. Hawkins glanced down as sparks and bursts of flame erupted from one of the windows into the street below. The spectators cried out in alarm and awe, scattering as pieces of burning debris landed amongst them. The initial blast was quickly followed by smaller bursts and firework-like pops as ammunition started to cook off.

His distraction was only momentary, but it was enough. Catching movement on the opposing rooftop, Hawkins looked up as a small metallic object was hurled over the edge of the parapet, sailing towards him. A grenade or other explosive device, or perhaps even a smoke bomb.

Either way, he turned his M4 towards it, squeezing off several rounds in quick succession. Hitting such a small, fast-moving target would have been a difficult proposition even for a skilled marksman, but Hawkins was more than just a skilled soldier. A natural affinity with weapons had been tempered by decades of intensive training and experience, both on the battlefield and on the rifle range, and the results spoke for themselves.

The first two rounds missed their target, and the third barely grazed the device as it tumbled through the air towards him. But the fourth projectile hit it square on.

The effect was as sudden as it was violent. A blindingly intense light exploded, and the projectile seemed to burst apart into multiple pieces that rained down all around him, trailing vivid red smoke and sparks. Clearly it was a pyrotechnic device of some kind, and the impact of his shot had set it off.

Hawkins was forced to throw his arm up to shield himself from this incendiary debris, and felt a piece bounce off his sleeve, burning right through the fabric and setting it aflame before he batted it away.

He heard the light thud of footsteps on his own rooftop, and looked up to see a demon charging at him through the smoke and flying sparks. A demon whose face glowed crimson in the red light of the burning flares, her eyes two points of icy hatred focussed solely on him.

He saw her arm drawn back, saw the flash of steel glinting in the red light as she hurled a blade at him, and only then did his reactions kick in as he attempted to twist aside. A burning flash of pain told him the blade had struck home, embedding itself in his chest just below the left shoulder.

His ballistic vest had offered some protection, but the point had nonetheless carved its way into the skin and muscle layer beneath.

Not enough to seriously injure him, but enough to give Anya time to close the distance between them. Realizing it was no help in close-quarters battle, Hawkins dropped the unwieldy assault rifle like a broken toy and rushed forward to meet her, yanking the knife from his chest. They met roughly in the centre of the rooftop, him swiping wildly with the already bloodstained blade, and her slipping aside to avoid the strike.

She wasn't fast enough. The knife sliced through fabric and skin alike, leaving a thin trail of blood across her left side.

The two adversaries circled each other amidst the smoke and the wildly flickering red glow of the flares, their eyes locked, bodies tense. Hawkins tightened his grip on the blade, smiling with malicious delight. He couldn't have asked for a better way to end it.

Just the two of them, up close and personal. The way it should be.

'You know something? Cain wanted you brought in alive. He wants to be the one who pulls the trigger,' he said, preparing to strike. 'Can't say I blame the man, after you murdered his daughter and all.'

Anya's eyes shone with anger. But more than anger, he saw pain and guilt. 'That's a lie.'

'You killed her the moment you brought her into this. She was safe, living her own life, but *you* chose to use her. Her blood is on your hands, Anya.' He shook his head in mock sorrow. 'You should have seen the look on the old man's face when I told him what happened. Damn near broke my heart.'

Hawkins let the words sink in, let her really process what he'd said. He could feel her resolve slip, her self-control falter, her focus waver. He knew then how deep that wound went.

He went for it, moving in fast, his powerful muscles coiling and releasing as he launched himself at his prey. He swept the blade upwards, saw her right arm move instinctively to counter, then quickly reversed his direction and came in on her left side. Her vulnerable side.

Unable to deflect the blow from that angle, she instead threw up both arms and managed to catch his knife hand, her legs almost buckling beneath her as he exerted all his force downwards. He had her now. She was having to use all her strength just to hold him off, her muscles straining with the effort.

He swung with his free hand, aiming to strike at her throat, but she ducked aside and retaliated with a knee to the stomach. It hurt, but she lacked the strength to seriously injure him.

Digging his feet in, he drove her backwards across the rooftop, straight into the chimney stack. It seemed to shake under the impact, and Anya grunted in pain.

Hawkins clamped his hand around her throat before she could recover. Anya could hold the knife off all she wanted, but she couldn't stop him choking the life out of her. Hawkins felt a surge of exhilaration and triumph as his grip tightened, constricting her airway.

'Cain will be pissed at me for killing you, might even take a shot at me,' he told her, straining to bring the blade in closer. Anya couldn't reply, but she could hear his words. 'But you want to know something? For this, it'll be worth it.'

This was what he'd wanted for so long. This was what he'd fantasized about, staring into those vivid blue eyes as the fear and panic took hold, as the life slowly faded from them. Knowing that he was the one who had finally killed her.

'I'm glad it ended this way, Anya,' he whispered, leaning in close as she struggled in vain to break his hold. 'I wanted to be with you at the end, to send you on your way.'

It was because he was leaning in so close, staring so intently into Anya's eyes as he slowly starved her body of oxygen that he saw something reflected in them.

Not some stirring of terror or the slow loss of focus as hypoxia took hold, but something else. Movement. Movement behind him.

Releasing his hold on Anya, who fell to her knees gasping for breath, Hawkins turned just as Dietrich swung a piece of wood down against him. The heavy piece of lumber struck his shoulder, cracking the wood and knocking him off balance.

Dietrich swung again, hoping to finish his adversary off, but Hawkins had by now recovered and caught the weapon in mid-air, wrenching it from his grip and responding with a kick to the midsection that doubled him over. Pressing his advantage, Hawkins leapt in with a crushing hook that knocked Dietrich flat.

He was just raising his boot to stamp on the dazed man's head when Anya barrelled straight into him, tackling him around the waist like a football player. She was a good 50 pounds lighter than Hawkins, but momentum and desperate, furious aggression gave her enough to knock him off balance. Pitched backwards by the unexpected impact, he toppled over the edge of the roof to land heavily on the level below.

He was down, but not out. Already he was moving, his face twisted in anger. Anya had nothing to offer in return but a defiant glare.

'Get up, Dietrich! Move!' Anya yelled, hauling Dietrich to his feet and retreating from the edge just as Hawkins opened fire, the bullet whizzing past her head. A second shot ricocheted off the wall just below her.

Sprinting for the edge of the building, Dietrich and Anya leapt over the gap, ignoring the drop to the alleyway below.

Landing on the other rooftop, which was now smoking as the fire ate away at it beneath, the pair made for the opposite side where a similar residential block backed onto it. Behind them, a section of roof gave way and collapsed, flames shooting upwards through the ragged gap.

Clambering back up to the rooftop level and sighting his rapidly receding targets, Hawkins took aim at Anya and squeezed the trigger. The weapon barked and a round sailed through the night air, narrowly missing the woman as she reached the edge of the rooftop and gathered herself up to leap again.

Adjusting his aim, Hawkins fired a second time, but just as he did so a violent explosion erupted from within the building. The roof seemed to bulge upwards, straining to hold in the vast release of energy, then suddenly broke apart and erupted in a great detonation, throwing fire and smoke up into the air.

Even he was forced to turn away from the sudden blast of searing heat, wary of being caught by flying debris. As pieces of flaming wood rained down across his rooftop, Hawkins peered through the smoke and raging fires that now licked up at the night sky, seeking his enemy.

Both Anya and Dietrich were gone.

'Alpha to all units,' Hawkins said. 'Targets are on the move, heading west across the rooftops. Close them down.'

'Copy that, Alpha. We're on it.'

–

'That's twice I've saved your ass tonight,' Dietrich said as he vaulted over a low wall, barely slowing down in his haste to flee the scene. Pillars of smoke, lit from below by the raging inferno, had already risen hundreds of feet into the night sky.

Because they were now lower than the roof of the safe house, they were out of Hawkins' line of sight. If they were lucky, he might assume they'd been killed in the collapse. If not, he would send his agents out to hunt them down. Either way, their best option was to get the hell out of here as quickly as possible. With no weapons left, they certainly wouldn't survive another pitched battle.

Traffic was at a standstill, cars and vans sitting idle as drivers leaned out of their windows, while residents poured out of bars and homes to gawk at the burning building. With their attention on the distant inferno, they paid little heed to the man and woman sprinting across the rooftops.

'You would still be trapped on that roof if it wasn't for me,' Anya reminded him, pulling ahead as she leapt down onto the sheet steel roof of the next building. The thin metal groaned and flexed a little as it took her weight, but held firm. 'Maybe you could show a little gratitude for once?'

In truth, she was relieved he'd come to her aid during her brief confrontation with Hawkins. It had been part of their hastily concocted plan for her to keep him occupied while Dietrich got into position, but it could have very easily gone wrong.

'Keep dreaming,' he shot back. 'Consider yourself lucky I didn't sell you out.'

'Why didn't you?'

Dietrich didn't get a chance to answer. The wall beside him exploded in a shower of brick dust and sharp fragments, quickly followed by several more impacts that tore into the rooftop around them. Dietrich ducked down, trying to present as small a target as possible.

'Fuck! They're on us!' he called out, veering sharply right.

Anya stole a glance at the street, scanning the sea of humanity until her eyes alighted on a young woman with blonde hair staring up at them. A young woman with a silenced submachine gun up at her shoulder, unleashing another burst of fire.

'Follow me!' she cried, quickly changing direction and leaping across a wider gap between her building and the next.

On the street below, Riley lowered her weapon and sprinted for the nearest alleyway, heading in the same direction, angrily shoving a rotund older woman out of her way.

'Tangos heading north across the rooftops!' she called into her radio, running through the narrow gap between buildings.

She might have been slight of build and lacking the brute strength of her fellow operatives, but Riley had been a promising athlete once. A sprinter, able to muster startling bursts of energy when the situation called for it, and she was still young and fit. No way were Anya and her accomplice, both well into their forties, going to outrun her.

'Willard, Alverez, left flank,' she ordered, vaulting nimbly over a fallen trash can. 'Patton, MacKinnon, swing north and cut them off. Everyone else on me. Go! Go!'

A pair of operatives pounded down the alley just behind her, following Riley's orders to stay close, though both were hard pressed to keep up with the punishing pace she was setting.

Spotting movement above, she looked up as Anya leapt between buildings, her silhouette momentarily visible against the night sky. Too quick to get a decent shot, but it didn't matter. They had the manpower. It was only a matter of time until her team cut them off.

Anya leapt down from one rooftop to the next, rolling to cushion the impact before leaping back up. Their course was carrying them generally downhill, so that each rooftop was lower than the one before. It made their progress easier, but the constant impacts were taking a toll.

Behind her, she heard Dietrich make the same leap, landing hard, struggling to his feet and pushing on.

'Keep moving!' she commanded. 'Move, or I leave you here!'

A voice called out from somewhere off to her right. 'Tango in sight!'

Anya was just turning towards it when Dietrich tackled her from behind, knocking her behind a partially constructed wall, his not inconsiderable weight and momentum adding to the force of the impact. She heard the whine of shots ricocheting off the steel roof around them.

Down in an alleyway not far from their position, Riley heard the news she'd been waiting for. 'Tangos are pinned down! Rooftop, 50 yards north-west of your position.'

'Copy that, we're inbound,' she replied, redoubling her efforts. 'Keep their heads down. Do *not* fucking lose them!'

Up on the rooftop, Anya struggled out from beneath Dietrich. She could feel something warm and wet against her chest, and looked down to find blood smeared across her shirt. It wasn't hers.

'You're hit,' she informed her companion.

Dietrich had backed up against the brick wall, his face contorted in pain, one bloodied hand pressed against his side. 'I'm glad you noticed.'

'We have to get out of here,' she said, flinching as another round hit the wall. Their enemies were putting down a slow but constant rain of fire, conserving ammunition but keeping them pinned down. 'They'll surround us if we don't move.'

'We're pinned down. It's too far to the next rooftop.' Their path to the next building would mean crossing at least ten yards of open ground, leaving them totally exposed.

The only possible escape route Anya could think of was straight down, over the side of this building and onto the next row of dwellings about 20 feet below. A fall from that height onto a hard roof could well be fatal, but if Anya's guess about these houses was accurate, it might just be possible.

Dietrich followed her gaze and seemed to see the same possibility, though his reaction was far more decisive.

'Fuck that,' he said. 'You want to get us killed?'

'Staying here won't keep us alive.' She tilted her head behind them, in the direction the shots were coming from. 'We jump or we die. Your choice.'

Dietrich weighed it up for a second or so.

'*Gottverdammt*,' he muttered.

That was good enough for her. 'On three. One…'

Anya moved into a crouch position.

'Two…'

She braced herself against the wall, body taut and ready.

'Three!'

Both operatives pushed off from the wall at the same time, racing for the edge of the roof, bent nearly double to keep themselves hidden as long as possible. The edge of the rooftop rushed forward to meet them, and at the last instant they threw themselves off into the void beyond.

Two full seconds of sickening, terrible weightlessness followed as they tumbled through the air, the world passing by in a blur of electric lights, car horns, shouts from below, brightly coloured walls, rusty metal roofs and snaking, trailing power lines everywhere.

The rooftop seemed to hover in the distance, as if encroaching on them only at a laborious, glacial pace. Then in a heartbeat it all seemed to change, rushing straight up at them like a giant fist seeking to punch them both out of the air.

They landed at the same time, hitting the corrugated steel roof like a pair of boulders hurled by some medieval siege machine. The thin sheet metal broke away from its supporting crossbeams with a wrenching screech and the roof collapsed beneath their weight. Once again they were falling, now inside the building below.

This fall was over much quicker, however. Anya plunged straight onto a wooden table, which buckled beneath the impact, the legs bowing outwards and breaking. She took the landing as best she could, trying not to tense up too much, hoping to avoid snapping bones or tearing ligaments. As she rolled away from the ruined piece of furniture, her body bursting with pain, pieces of roofing and support materials tumbled down around her like metal rain.

She heard a scream from somewhere nearby, but it wasn't Dietrich. This was a female scream. Opening her eyes, she looked up into the startled face of a little girl. She was dressed in shorts and a T-shirt that was too big for her, staring at Anya in open-mouthed disbelief.

A glance around the room revealed its purpose clearly enough. An old fashioned TV, a rickety looking wooden cabinet, a couple of chairs, potted plants and kids' toys everywhere. A family lived in this house, or what was left of it after their destructive entry. It was lucky for the girl that she hadn't been beneath them when they landed.

Anya moved her limbs experimentally, half expecting to feel the hideous, grinding pain of broken bones crunching against one another, but mercifully everything still seemed to be working. She didn't doubt she would regret this plunge tomorrow morning, assuming she was still alive then, but for now at least she was still able to move.

'I'm sorry,' Anya said as she rose unsteadily to her feet, knowing immediately how foolish that must have sounded. 'It's all right. We won't hurt you.'

'Yeah, we're too busy hurting ourselves,' Dietrich groaned. He'd landed on an old floral-patterned couch which had cushioned his fall better than any crash mat, leaving him with just a few minor cuts and bruises.

Lucky him, Anya thought with sour grace. She felt as if she'd been sealed inside a tumble drier with a pallet of bricks for a couple of spin cycles.

She heard footsteps in the small dwelling, and looked over as a figure emerged into the room, pulling the little girl backwards to place his substantial bulk between her and the intruders. A man, her father no doubt, short and sturdy and wearing only a vest and a pair of boxer shorts, his thinning hair sticking out from the sides of his head. He looked like he'd just stumbled out of bed, awoken by the commotion. He was clutching a baseball bat in both hands.

He was shouting something and waving the bat around, flecks of spit flying from his mouth. Anya imagined that burglaries were a common occurrence in the favelas, and that most home owners had to be ready to defend their property.

Anya held up a hand, trying to placate him, but that only seemed to incense him further. He took a step towards her, the bat raised high, ready to take a swing, then abruptly stopped in his tracks.

'Don't take another step,' Anya warned, thumbing back the hammer on her M1911. It didn't matter that the gun was out of ammunition – not to him at least.

'Dietrich, can you move?' she asked. She was tired and hurting, and trying to hide both facts at that moment.

'I hope so,' Dietrich retorted sarcastically. 'Otherwise you'll leave me behind.'

'Don't tempt me. Just get up.' The threat of force was holding the home owner off, but she couldn't say how long that would last.

Rolling off the couch, Dietrich managed to stand and limped over to the door, unbolted it and threw it open. Keeping the father and his daughter covered, Anya backed away, threading a path through the ruins of the living room.

'Don't follow us,' she warned, before disappearing into the night.

The house opened out onto a gloomy side street, maybe 20 yards back from the main drag. They were far enough away from the burning safe house that the traffic was moving more freely, though many windows had been thrown open so that the locals could gawk at the two lunatics who had just thrown themselves through the roof of their neighbour's house.

Dietrich was already moving towards the main road, hoping to flag down or hijack a vehicle out of here. 'Come on, let's go before they—'

He stopped, the words dying in his throat as his eyes rested on the operative standing at the entrance to their street. His submachine gun was trained on Dietrich, the green splash of his laser sight painting the man's chest.

'Freeze!' he called out, leaning into the weapon, ready to fire. 'Don't fuckin' think about it, asshole.'

Anya turned away, seeking a possible escape route in the other direction, only to meet with an even worse sight. Riley, along with two other operatives. All of whom now had Anya covered.

No way out.

The young woman's face was flushed with the exertion of her frantic pursuit, her brow coated with a sheen of sweat, but nonetheless she flashed a smile of triumph. She'd hunted her prey down.

'Not bad. You gave us a good chase,' she said as her two comrades advanced on Anya with their weapons raised. 'But you're all out of tricks. Now drop the weapon and get on your knees, bitch.'

Anya hesitated, seeking any way out, any option left untried. There was nothing.

She slowly lowered herself to her knees. Dietrich did likewise, both placing their hands behind their heads.

Riley reached for her comms unit. 'We've got them. Roll in the ground transport.' Clicking the transmitter off, she looked down at Anya, who glared back at her with cold hatred. 'You might think I want to just kill you myself, but I don't need to. I'm going to be there, Anya. I'm going to be there watching when they finally break you, and I'm going to enjoy it.'

She looked over at the operative covering Dietrich. 'We don't need that piece of shit,' she decided with casual disdain. 'Kill him.'

Even as the operative readied his weapon to fire, Anya could hear the rumble of a vehicle pulling in from the main road, saw the flash of its headlights as it turned onto their street. No doubt it was here to ferry her out of the favelas, perhaps to a private airfield where an unregistered flight would be standing by to return her to the States. Or whatever deep, dark hole Cain had set aside for her.

But the vehicle didn't pull to a stop. Instead it suddenly increased speed, the engine ramping up in tempo as the driver stomped on the gas. The operative, suddenly caught in the blinding headlights, turned towards the source of the disturbance, bringing his weapon around with him.

He was too late.

In a storm of metal and squealing brakes, the car ploughed into him. There was a sickening crunch, a scream as he was thrown up over the hood, then a clatter as he landed on the ground several yards away.

Blinded by the headlights, Anya couldn't see what was happening, but she heard the sound of a door opening, followed by a voice calling out to her.

'Get down, Maras!'

She didn't have to be told twice. Anya dropped to the ground just as a loud, sustained burst of automatic gunfire echoed down the street.

Caught out in the open, Riley and her teammates were left without cover and caught the full force of this deadly assault. The young woman reacted instinctively, grabbing the man closest to her by the straps of his webbing and pulling him in front of her just as the heavy-calibre slugs slammed into him.

Even his sophisticated body armour couldn't withstand such punishment, and he let out an agonized groan as the rounds punched through the steel plates and Kevlar lining to wreak devastating damage on the soft body within. Dragging this human shield with her even as his legs faltered and he collapsed, Riley threw herself in through the doorway that Anya and Dietrich had so recently emerged from.

The deafening hail of gunfire carried on for a good three or four seconds – easily expending a full magazine – during which Anya and Dietrich could do nothing but lie in the mud and fetid puddles amongst the discarded detritus of the favela. Whatever this weapon was, it was firing heavy-calibre shells. Anya could feel the movement of air around her as they zipped past right above her head.

When at last the carnage came to an end, Anya's ears were ringing. But she heard a voice.

Rojas' voice.

'Well? You going to lie there all night, or do you want to get out of here?'

Anya and Dietrich scrambled to their feet and sprinted towards the headlights, one of which was cracked where it had struck the unfortunate operative. Anya paused just long enough to snatch up the pistol she'd dropped, refusing to leave it behind.

The vehicle was in fact a Toyota Hilux, its bodywork smeared with mud but its engine still rumbling with defiant power. Dietrich reached the vehicle first, throwing open the rear door and clambering inside, and Anya was right behind him.

Rojas had already returned to the driver's seat and slammed his door shut. On the passenger seat, Anya saw the long, dark-grey shape of a light machine gun, its bipod mount now folded away. That certainly explained the ferocious rain of fire he'd been able to put down.

'What are you doing here?' she demanded, heaving the door closed.

Rojas flashed her a look in the rear-view mirror.

'A good question,' he replied, throwing the transmission into reverse and accelerating out of the side street. 'You and I have much to talk about tonight.'

With that, he slipped the Hilux into drive and stamped on the gas. The big 4 x 4 shot forward, accelerating downhill and away, horn sounding the whole way as panicked scooters and bikes veered aside to make way.

In under a minute they were clear of the scene, though Anya didn't relax. She knew this night was only getting started.

Chapter 45

Drake shrugged his jacket off and dumped it on the floor of his grimy guest room.

He'd made good his escape from Powell's penthouse suite, disappearing into the urban sprawl of downtown Rio and ultimately making his way back to his hotel, bruised and hurting and furious at his failure. Worse, he was frightened. Frightened of Powell and the power she had wielded over him, frightened of himself for falling so easily under her spell.

Drawing the silenced automatic from the back of his trousers, he turned the gun over in his hand, watching as the sickly orange glow of electric lights glinted across its dark polished surface. How easy it should have been to point that gun at her head and pull the trigger.

How easy it seemed now. Pull a trigger, end a life. He'd done it many times already tonight without the slightest difficulty. Yet standing in her presence, smelling the scent of her perfume, listening to the sound of her voice, it had been a daunting, impossible task.

Setting the weapon down on the bed, Drake snatched up the bottle of *cachaça* from the little table by the window and ventured through to the cramped bathroom. There he unbuttoned the formal shirt he'd used to infiltrate the hotel, wincing with pain as his injured muscles began to stiffen and contract. He dropped the shirt on the floor, then undid the Velcro straps of the Kevlar vest beneath, gratefully shrugging out of the cumbersome garment.

He twisted around to get a decent look at himself in the mirror. As he'd thought, a round had struck him on the right shoulder. The vest had absorbed the worst of it, but the considerable impact had left a large bruise that had already turned purple and black. Removing the vest had left a streak of blood down his shoulder and arm where the skin had split and ruptured.

Hardly a major injury, but one that would need attention all the same. In a temperate zone such a wound presented little difficulty, but Rio was situated in a tropical climate with all kinds of air- and water-borne parasites just looking for a way in. Drake had served in such places before, and knew from experience that even minor cuts could swell up into throbbing, pus-filled mounds within hours if left untreated.

Holding the bottle of *cachaça* up, he clamped his teeth down on the cork and yanked it free, then poured the spirit directly onto the wound. Drake closed his eyes and bit down hard, letting out a low, animalistic growl as the potent alcohol soaked into his torn flesh. He thumped his fist against the wall hard enough to rattle the mirror above the sink.

Good. He wanted, *needed* the pain right now. He needed it to clear his mind, to cleanse himself of the memory of what had happened earlier.

When at last it was done, he spat the cork out into the sink and downed a mouthful of the spirit himself. Its sweet fire blazed a path down his throat, but he wasn't complaining.

A buzzing sound was coming from his discarded jacket. The vibration of his cell phone.

Still clutching the bottle, he returned to the bedroom and retrieved the phone.

'Didn't work, did it?' the voice asked. 'I warned you. We could have avoided this.'

'What the fuck did you bastards do to me?' Drake demanded. His adrenaline was spiking as if preparing for another fight. He was desperate for an enemy to lash out at, for a face he could pound into mush.

But he couldn't. The awful truth had already dawned on him.

You want to see your real enemy, Ryan? Go look in the mirror again.

'The answer to that question can't come from me,' the voice explained, infuriatingly calm. 'But I can tell you this much: Powell took no chances with the weapons she created. She made sure they could never turn against her.'

'Weapons?'

'Yes, weapons. That's what you are, Ryan. That's what you were made to be, what *she* made you. Obeying her commands is the first, most fundamental thing you were taught.'

'Then how do I change that?' Drake asked.

'You don't.'

His grip on the bottle tightened. Once more he felt that primal fury rising inside him, the overwhelming urge to fight, to kill, to grapple with something tangible.

'You're going to have to do better than that,' Drake warned.

'I can't undo the things she did to you. But I *can* help you.'

'How?'

'I can't remove her control, but I can put a stop to the woman herself. *If you listen to me.*'

His meaning was plain. Further acts of insubordination were unlikely to be tolerated. 'Say I agreed. What do you need from me?'

'Does the name Tenbrook mean anything to you?'

The bottle slipped from Drake's hand as the hotel room around him receded into darkness and his mind transported him to a different place. A memory. A memory of something he'd never thought of before.

He was in a briefing room, little more than a partitioned section of tent, dust blown in through gaps in the canvas by the warm, fitful wind. Men sitting all around him, the smell of unwashed bodies and gun oil and old leather. The sound of vehicle engines outside. The sigh of the wind so unique to that hot, lonely place called Afghanistan.

He saw a man pointing to satellite images on the board behind him. A man in civilian clothes.

My name's Tenbrook. That's the first, last and only thing you need to know about me. Right now, I'm here to brief you on the situation. This mission is going to call for the best we have, and as of now, that is you.

'I know that name,' Drake said, speaking slowly as if rousing from a deep sleep. 'He… he was there. He delivered our briefing that day.'

'Tenbrook is the key to this. Find him and bring him in alive, and you'll get the answers to your questions, Ryan.'

'Will I find you too?'

'When the time's right, you will.'

Drake could feel it now, that focus, that determination, that desire to strike back. All of it had found a new target, and he knew with absolute certainty that Tenbrook would give him the answers he sought, the truth he'd been denied for so long. Even if Drake had to rip them from him one at a time.

'Tell me where he is.'

Chapter 46

Rojas drove the Toyota Hilux through the busy streets of central Rio like a man possessed, often taking insane chances and narrowly avoiding head-on collisions.

Buildings whizzed past at frightening speed, the shacks and poorly constructed buildings of the favelas gradually giving way to more organized and settled neighbourhoods.

Both passengers busied themselves trying to address their numerous injuries, wrapping crude bandages around cuts and gashes, and extracting pieces of broken glass and other debris embedded in their flesh.

'How's that wound?' Anya asked Dietrich. He'd taken a round during their escape across the rooftops, though the extent and severity of the injury was unknown.

'Hurts,' he replied tersely, a hand still pressed against it to slow the bleeding.

'Let me look at it.' Leaning over, Anya ripped his bloodied shirt open and switched on the car's internal light to get a better look.

She quickly discovered that the round had impacted the left pectoral muscle with a glancing blow, carving a gory furrow about three inches long and partially damaging the exposed muscle tissue beneath. He needed medical attention soon.

'Breathe in as far as you can,' she instructed. He did, and she watched his chest expand without difficulty as the lungs filled with air. Knowing he was unlikely to die from the wound left her feeling oddly relieved, an emotion she hadn't expected where he was concerned. 'I don't think you have broken ribs or internal bleeding. Keep pressure on the wound for now until we can get proper treatment. You were lucky, Dietrich.'

He gave her a sour look. 'I've been shot before. I've never felt lucky about it.'

Their erstwhile saviour remained stubbornly silent, intent on pushing the car as hard as possible. The barely repressed rage radiated from him, and Anya was uncertain how to deal with him. They were alive because Rojas had come to their aid, but how and why had he sought them out?

It was Dietrich who decided to break this uneasy stand-off. 'Not that I'm ungrateful for what you did back there, but who the hell are you?'

Rojas didn't respond.

Dietrich leaned closer to Anya. 'Friend of yours?'

'Not quite,' she replied, then suddenly tensed up as their driver veered sharply left, throwing the big Hilux around as if it were a sports car. Anya and Dietrich had almost exhausted their fear quota for the night, but even they flinched when a truck laden with logs roared past only inches away, horn blaring indignantly.

'Ease down, Cesar,' Anya implored. 'You'll get us all killed.'

Rojas' response was to take his foot off the accelerator, swing the wheel over and stamp hard on the brakes, bringing the Hilux to a shuddering, screeching halt at the edge of the busy road amidst a cloud of burned rubber and more angry horn blasts. Both passengers were forced to grab for the overhead handles to keep from being pitched forward.

'Jesus Christ! What's the matter with you, man?' Dietrich shouted.

'What's the matter with me?' Rojas repeated, clutching a Beretta M9 automatic in his hand. 'What's the matter? In the past hour I've been attacked, my home destroyed, my men killed and my life ruined. That's what's the matter with me.' His accusing gaze turned on Anya. 'Did you sell me out, Maras? Answer me now!'

Anya's shock was obvious, but she shook her head. 'No, Cesar. I didn't.'

'Then why did they come for me?'

'I don't know. Nobody else knew about our meeting.'

'Bullshit!' he snarled. 'You led them straight to my home, you bitch!'

Anya admitted nothing, but Dietrich sensed an undertone of doubt. She was starting to perceive the folly of her actions tonight, her underestimation of their enemies, and the lives that mistake might well have cost.

'Why would I do that? I came to you because I needed your help.'

'And you got it. How do I know you didn't send those bastards to kill me once you had the information you needed?'

She sighed. 'Because they are my enemies too.'

'She's telling the truth,' Dietrich said. He wasn't normally inclined to back Anya, but since he suspected both their fates hinged on how she pleaded her case, it was enough to change his perspective. 'Anya is many things, but not a liar.'

'Shut up, *idiota*!' Rojas growled. 'I want answers from *her*. I want to know what the hell you're really doing here in Rio.' He thumbed back the hammer on his automatic. 'And if I don't like your answer, you'll wish I hadn't saved you tonight.'

Anya was silent at first, obviously weighing up what to say, how much she could trust this man, and what their chances were if Rojas didn't believe her.

'You were right, Cesar,' she finally admitted. 'Things have changed since we last met. Things have changed a lot. A man I once trusted betrayed me, and now he is the director of the CIA. The assault team at the safe house were under his command.'

'You brought your war to my doorstep.'

Anya shook her head. 'That wasn't my intention.'

'But it's what happened. The entire Agency is after your blood, and you led them to me. What did you expect them to do?'

'I never wanted any of this.'

'Nobody ever wants to bring their problems with them, but they always do. And it's men like me who get fucked for it.' His eyes flicked between them, still keeping his gun at the ready. 'Why would you take such a risk for one man? This... Drake?'

'Because he never gave up on me, and I won't do it to him now. I owe him that much,' she answered. There was an edge to her voice, a strain that hadn't been there before. 'When he found me, I had been locked in a Russian prison for four years. I had not seen sunlight, breathed fresh air or spoken a word in all that time. I could barely even remember what those things felt like. I had nothing left, but he gave me something, showed me compassion, risked his life for someone he had no reason to trust. He did those things because he was a good man. I have to help him before it's too late.'

She watched Rojas' expression soften a little, the tide of his anger starting to turn.

'If you're lying to me...'

'If you don't believe me, then kill me now, Cesar. I'm ready. I've been ready for a long time.' Some of her defiance faded, a hint of regret now showing through. 'I'm sorry for what happened tonight, and if I could change it then I would. But I... *we* are not your enemy.'

'I was out, Maras,' he said, a bitter undertone in his voice. 'Gone for good. I'd left all this behind.'

'I know,' Anya said. There was little she could add to that.

Rojas eyed her for a long moment, then finally let out a vexed sigh, along with a muttered curse, and lowered his gun. Dietrich and Anya allowed themselves to relax fractionally.

'You have a safe house in this city, I assume?'

She nodded.

Rojas laid the automatic in the centre console and gripped the wheel. 'Then I hope they have tequila, because I need a drink.'

Chapter 47

All three occupants of the apartment were jolted by the urgent pounding on the door. Frost cautiously approached as the banging continued, removed the barricade and eased the door open.

'Get the hell out of the way,' Dietrich growled, storming past her. Frost was taken aback by his dishevelled appearance. The man was a mess, his clothes torn and bloodied, his body bruised and injured, his limp noticeable.

It was obvious he'd been in a serious confrontation. So had Anya, who barely looked any better off as she slunk in, exhausted and in pain. A bloody gash across her chest suggested she'd been knifed.

They were followed by a third man that Frost didn't recognize. Out of the three, he was the only one who looked somewhat respectable, dressed in a dark shirt and expensive shoes and trousers, his long dark hair swept back from a slightly aged but still handsome face. He might have been unharmed, but the man didn't look happy. He also didn't bother introducing himself, instead sweeping past imperiously.

Mitchell and Alex were in the living room, and both looked equally startled and relieved at the return of their bedraggled teammates.

'What the bloody hell happened to you two? Why have you been off comms all evening?' Alex asked, voicing their collective thoughts. 'And who the fuck is this guy?'

'Shut up, Alex,' Dietrich replied, pouring himself a glass of vodka and downing it in one gulp. It was quickly followed by a second.

Alex glared at him. However, his hostility abated slightly when he noticed the drops of blood that had pattered to the floor by Dietrich's feet. They had leaked through the makeshift dressings tied around his chest.

'You've got red on you,' he said matter-of-factly.

Dietrich looked at the stain and shrugged, saying nothing as he refilled his glass. He either didn't care about the mess he was making, or simply didn't have the energy to engage in conversation.

Rojas approached, snatched up the bottle and poured a glass of his own. Dietrich gave him a sharp look, which was reciprocated in kind, but neither man made a move. Having apparently reached the unspoken agreement that the drink was more important than further argument, they downed their shots almost in unison.

Rojas made a face. '*Tem gosto de urina*,' he decided with a disdainful curl of the lip. *Tastes like piss.*

'I presume your leads didn't pan out?' Mitchell remarked.

'You presume correctly,' Rojas acknowledged with a bitter look at Anya.

Mitchell folded her arms. 'And who are you?'

'His name is Cesar Rojas.' Anya sank into a chair, looking utterly drained. 'He helped us tonight.'

Rojas bowed sarcastically. 'A pleasure to meet you all, I'm sure.'

Frost regarded the three new arrivals with a combination of confusion and growing annoyance. 'Well, this is a beautiful little reunion, but would someone care to explain what the fuck happened tonight?'

Rojas cocked an eyebrow. 'Quite the firecracker, isn't she?'

'You have no idea,' Dietrich muttered.

'Shut the fuck up, Dietrich,' the young woman retorted. 'We've wasted half the day looking for your dumb ass, so if you're expecting sympathy, go screw yourself.'

This scathing retort delivered, she turned her attention to Rojas.

'And for the record, *she* has a name, asshole. And *she* doesn't appreciate it when some arrogant prick appears out of nowhere and acts like he owns the place. Now explain what the hell has been going on.'

'Back off, Frost,' Anya ordered, though her voice was lacking some of its usual authority. 'It has been a long night for all of us.'

'No shit. Enlighten me.'

Anya exhaled slowly, mustering the strength and patience to continue. Only with considerable effort was she able to marshal her thoughts into a coherent stream.

The others listened while she briefly related the events of the evening, from her contact with Rojas to the revelation about Cuatro's safe house and the subsequent ambush by Hawkins and his team. Anya ended with an account of their escape across the rooftops, and their unexpected reunion with Rojas.

'So in short, we're fucked,' Dietrich concluded grimly. 'Our cover in Rio is blown, and we've got no leads on Drake or what he's planning.'

'Maybe not.' Reaching into her pocket, Anya removed the cell phone recovered from Cuatro's safe house and tossed it to Frost.

Keira caught it more out of instinct than desire, and quickly identified it as a cheap unregistered burner phone.

'Run a scan of the call history, see if you can find where the last call came from.'

Frost frowned. 'Where did you get this?'

'Someone left it at the safe house for me.'

'Someone? You mean Ryan.'

Anya shook her head.

'So how do you know it was for you?' Alex asked.

Anya glanced at him. 'Because he called me on it. He must have been nearby because he saw me go in. I need to know where he is now.'

It was obvious from her expression there was more to this than she was saying, and Alex wasn't the only one to pick up on it.

'Who is he?'

'It's not important. What *is* important is finding him.'

'Bullshit it's not important,' Frost leapt in. 'We're supposed to be a team, although fuck knows, not many of us are acting like it. If you know something, spill it.'

Anya wasn't normally inclined to share details of her past life unless she absolutely had to, and certainly couldn't be cajoled or forced into giving away something she didn't want to, but this time at least she seemed to recognize the mood of the room was against her.

Her comrades weren't going to move on unless she gave them something.

'His name is Romek Karalius,' she said at last. There was an odd inflection when she spoke the name, as if she'd just lapsed into a different language mid-sentence. 'He was once a member of my unit.'

'You mean Task Force Black?' Frost prompted.

Anya nodded as she searched back through her memories. 'He was one of the original batch of recruits, trained with us since the very beginning. We fought together in Afghanistan and a dozen other places. When part of our unit went rogue and tried to stage a coup, Romek was right in the middle of the fighting. He stayed with us, even returned with us to Afghanistan during the US invasion. He remained loyal to the very end.'

'So what happened to him?' Frost asked.

'I don't know,' Anya admitted. 'When I left the unit in 2003 to go to Iraq, I left him in command until I returned. That was the last time I saw him. I was captured and imprisoned by the Russians before I made it to Iraq, and by the time you broke me out of prison four years later, Romek and the rest of the unit had disappeared. I never found out what happened to them.'

In truth, she had made sporadic efforts to re-establish contact with Task Force Black in the years since her escape, hoping against hope that some of its members might have survived and gone into hiding. Hoping that some day she might reunite with her former comrades. Hoping she wasn't truly the last of them.

But her efforts had come to nothing. None of her avenues of investigation had led anywhere, and she'd eventually resigned herself to the fact they were all gone. Now it seemed at least one of her former comrades had returned.

She didn't say it, but this revelation had kindled the wild hope that there might be others out there as well. The hope that she might still return to the men she had fought alongside, who had become more of a family to her than her half-forgotten parents and the time in her life she now referred to simply as Before.

Dietrich was stretched out on a couch, a glass of vodka balanced on his chest.

'So one of your old friends is back from the dead. Congratulations,' he said cynically. 'Did things just get better or worse for us?'

'I don't know,' Anya admitted. 'Romek was a remarkable soldier, and his loyalty was unshakable. But that was seven years ago. A lot could have changed.'

'A lot can change in one night,' Rojas snorted.

'You should try spending a week with her – Ow! *Verdammt!*' Dietrich growled, spilling some of his drink as Mitchell peeled away the bloody dressing covering his gunshot wound, taking some of the coagulated blood with it and exposing the raw, torn flesh beneath.

'Big boys don't cry, pal,' she said, patting him on the shoulder.

'Fuck you.' He had the distinct impression she'd enjoyed watching him squirm.

Mitchell gave him a wink. 'There's not enough alcohol in the world. Anyway, I'm keeping you from bleeding to death or dying from infection,' she replied as she examined the wound, touching around it with careful, probing fingers. 'Can't say I'd be too torn up either way, but you might start to stink this place up after a while. And you smell bad enough alive.'

A sweat-covered strip of shirt was no match for a proper sterile dressing, and if they didn't clean and bind the wound soon he'd be at real risk of bacterial infection. Judging by the size of the gash, he would almost certainly need sutures. Fortunately they'd anticipated the possibility of trouble, and had brought a couple of medical kits. Anya would likely also need treatment, though whether she would acquiesce was another matter.

Dietrich cracked a sardonic smile, the alcohol helping to dull the pain a little. 'Your bedside manner's shit, Mitchell. Anyone tell you that?'

'More often than you'd think.'

'Let's play this thing out logically,' Alex said, turning back to the group's larger problems. 'If your mate Romek is here in Rio and he's connected to the explosion at the lab, then it's safe to say he's not allied with Powell and Hawkins.'

'The enemy of my enemy,' Mitchell mused.

'More or less.'

Anya considered this, playing it out against their earlier phone conversation. 'He *did* warn me of the assault team's arrival.'

'A positive.'

'But he did nothing to assist our escape.'

'Christ. Talk about mixed messages,' said Frost.

'So either he was unwilling or unable to help during the fight.' Alex ran a hand along his jaw, which was bristling with stubble. 'The question is, are he and Ryan working together or against each other?'

Anya pondered. 'He was aware of Ryan's presence here, and I think he understood what happened to him. He said Ryan was beyond my help.'

A sense of foreboding fell on the room before Mitchell spoke up. 'Did he give you any idea what he was planning next?'

'He said this was the first step on the journey, and soon he would take another. And that when the time was right, he and I would meet again.'

Chapter 48

'You get in there, boy!' a voice roared, as low and powerful as the tractor engines its owner helped to repair and service.

Jason gasped as the hand clamped tight around the nape of his neck and shoved him forward with such force that he stumbled and nearly tripped. Mercifully he managed to stay on his feet, because he knew that such clumsiness would only earn him further punishment.

Like the time he'd dropped his plate on the way to the kitchen sink, and his father had nonchalantly thrown an open-handed swipe at the back of his head that left his ears ringing for hours afterwards.

The garage in which he now stood wasn't a big building. Low and squat, the floor little more than hard-packed dirt, the roof timbers sagging under weight and age, it was just big enough for his father's 1972 Buick Riviera to fit inside. Jason couldn't recall it ever being parked in there, though.

Instead, most of its space was given over to the kind of junk that always finds its way into garages: tools, engine parts, old lawnmowers, motor oil and paint tins that had long since dried up, broken furniture that lingered here in this curious state of half-life until it was eventually declared a lost cause and taken to the dump. The windows were barred on the outside for security, their panes cracked and fogged with age and dirt, so that only misty bars of sunlight managed to struggle through.

For most people, it must have seemed like a perfectly normal workshop and storage space. Old, dusty, familiar and even a little comforting perhaps. Like a well-worn jacket or shoes, past their prime but somehow better for it.

For most people, but not for Jason or his two siblings. For them, the garage was something very different. This was where they were brought when their father decided he had to 'give them one'. That's what he always called it.

Sorry son, but I gotta give ya one.

As if it were some playful little gift or keepsake that was being handed out. Never a beating, never a punch in the gut or an ass-kicking or a leathering with his belt that left black bruises and blisters filled with blood. Never those things, because that wasn't how Tyler Hawkins saw it.

He did what he wanted, and what he wanted today was to give somebody one. And by God, somebody was going to get one.

Jason's younger siblings were there too, having already been herded in there like the frightened sheep they were. Both boys stood near the cluttered work bench in the corner, and Jason was quite certain that was exactly where their father had put them. They wouldn't have moved an inch even if he'd left them there all day, because such wilful disobedience would earn them one too.

They were fairly close in age, less than two years separating their births. Nathan, the elder of the two, was nine. He was already tall like Jason, dark haired and well built, but in a way that tended towards fat rather than muscle. Porky, their father mockingly called him, despite being plenty overweight himself.

Nathan's eyes were screwed up in a squint now, as they so often were. He'd confessed to Jason one night that he struggled to see the TV at night, and often failed to recognize friends on the opposite side of the street. But their dad refused to even consider glasses.

No son of mine's gonna be a four-eyed bookworm.

No, sir. Instead he'll miss a DON'T WALK sign because of his nearsightedness, and get mown down by a Pontiac Trans Am while crossing the road two years from now.

Samuel, standing beside him, was the youngest of the three brothers, having just turned seven a few weeks ago. Short and scrawny, with coppery flecks showing in his buzz-cut hair and freckles marking the pale skin across his nose and cheeks. Samuel who always seemed to have a cold or a cough or a runny nose. The kind of kid who was never going to be big or strong or fast, never going to be picked for the football team, never going to withstand their dad's fists when it was his turn to get one.

'Well, shit, boys,' Tyler Hawkins said as he sauntered in front of Jason, placing his huge, calloused, scarred, muscular, indomitable man's body between the boy and his two brothers. 'We've got something we need to straighten out here today, and no mistake.'

Jason could feel himself shrink at the change in his father's voice. Some kids got that same feeling when their parents raised their voices in anger, but it wasn't anger that made Jason frightened. It was excitement. Tyler Hawkins liked nothing more than giving somebody one, and it really didn't take much to give him the excuse he needed. Jason thought sometimes he actually looked forward to one of his boys making some mistake or transgression that could be punished.

And he certainly had one today.

He turned slowly to look at Jason, looking down at him. Tyler was a big man, standing over six feet. Jason might grow to that size some day; he was certainly shaping up to be tall when he became a man, but he wasn't a man now. He was a 11-year-old kid, and he was frightened.

'Now, a good buddy of mine, Frank Reznik came to me today. Frank works nights over at the train yard. Man has eyes like a hawk, never met anything like it. And old Frank there, he says he saw you break into the night watchman's hut last night and steal the man's wallet. Now I said to him, that can't be right, my Jason knows better than to steal. And he says to me, it's the truth Tyler, I saw him with my own eyes. And old Frank's eyes don't miss much.' He clamped his jaw down, the muscles along his neck tightening as he stared at his son. 'Well, boy? What you got to say for yourself? Is old Frank a liar?'

Jason's heart seemed to have dropped into the pit of his stomach, because he knew he was in a hopeless situation. Old Frank was quite right of course – damn his fucking hawk-like eyes. Jason had indeed snuck into the train yard last night through a gap in the fence, had jimmied the lock on the night watchman's hut, found the guy's wallet with about 30 bucks inside, pocketed it and made good his escape. In and out, easy money. Or so he'd thought.

To admit his crime would mean taking the kind of beating that left you walking stiff and sore for a week. To deny it would be worse, because it would mean calling his old man's friend

206

a liar. And it would mean lying to his father's face. And there was nothing more disrespectful than a son who lied to his father.

With a supreme effort, Jason swallowed down his fear and spoke.

'He's right, Dad. I took the wallet.'

Tyler Hawkins closed his eyes for a second or two, then drew in a deep breath and exhaled through his nose, the air whistling though the hair in his nostrils. Nodding solemnly to himself, he turned away and removed the leather belt that he kept hanging on the wall above his workbench. A belt from which he'd removed the metal buckle, allowing him to use it with impunity, without worrying about causing the kind of injury that would involve hospital visits and paperwork and questions from suspicious doctors.

'Well, son, you know I can't let that kind of shit fly. My own son caught stealing, and me looking like an asshole who can't keep him in line. No, sir, I can't let that shit fly at all.'

Pulling on both ends of the belt with those big, square mechanic's hands that always carried a trace of engine oil no matter how much he scrubbed them, he turned to face his wayward son again. He looked him up and down, taking in the shoulders that were starting to grow broader, the arms that were growing thicker, the face that might soon start to show hairs around the chin and upper lip. The boy who was showing the first vestiges of manhood.

A man who would one day be strong enough to stand up to him. A man who might eventually give him *one. And perhaps that was what truly drove him to such acts: the knowledge that one day this boy would become more than him.*

'So tell me, son. Which one is it going to be?'

Jason frowned, wondering if he'd misunderstood. He'd expected his father to go at him with the belt while Samuel and Nathan watched. Tyler would want them to watch this humiliation, because he knew the two boys looked up to their older sibling, saw him as a kind of leader and protector. And deep down, maybe he even knew that they loved and respected Jason more than their own father.

But he hadn't expected this. And the question caught him off guard.

'What?' he asked before he could stop himself.

Tyler's arm swept around and clipped him across the side of his head, jarring it sideways, prompting a yelp of fright and pain.

'You answer my question, son. Somebody's gotta get one for this, and you get to decide who it's gonna be.' He pointed the belt at the two boys opposite, who shrank away from it in fear but didn't dare take a step backwards. 'Is it gonna be Porky, or Four Eyes?'

Jason's eyes opened wide in horror as his father's words sank in. He wasn't going to take out his punishment on Jason himself, he was going to make him choose which of his brothers took it in his place.

'Dad, please. I did it. You oughta give me one.'

The second blow dropped him on his ass on the hard-packed garage floor, his vision spotted with lights, and blood trickling from the corner of his mouth. He gasped as Tyler grabbed a handful of his hair and yanked his head backwards, forcing him to look into his father's face. The face that was so like his own, except marked by an extra 30 years of toil and failure and pent-up frustration.

'You don't never tell me what I ought to do, boy. Not as long as I'm breathin',' he warned. His face was just inches away from Jason's, his breath smelling of stale beer and

cigarettes. 'Now you go ahead and you pick one right now, or so help me I'll give it to all three of you twice as hard.'

There were tears in his eyes now as he looked at them both. He could take a beating if it came down to it. He'd done wrong, no matter the reason, and he deserved his punishment. But not them. They'd had nothing to do with this.

Only later in life, much later, would he begin to comprehend the brutal, calculated intent behind his father's decision, the beautiful simplicity of it. Why make Jason a hero in the eyes of his brothers when he could make him a villain through a simple choice? It was a lesson his father had never intended to teach him, but one that he would learn all the same and eventually apply in his own unique way.

'You better not be crying, boy,' his father warned him, pulling so hard on his hair that he was sure it was about to rip from his scalp. 'Don't you act like no faggot in front of your dad. You choose, right now.'

Jason's gaze moved from one sibling to the other. Both were frightened, both were shaking, both knew bad things were about to happen. But one of them met his gaze, one of them reluctantly understood and accepted that he was going to have to take it. Because he was bigger, because it would hurt him but it wouldn't break him like it would his little brother.

Nathan gave him a nod, tiny and barely noticeable. Not a nod of encouragement, but rather a nod of sad acceptance. Somebody was going to get one today, and that somebody was him.

Sorry son, but I gotta give you one.

'Nathan,' Jason said, somehow managing to force the word out. Hating himself for it. Hating even more the surge of relief he felt when his brother gave him the nod.

Tyler Hawkins' face split into a smile then, revealing a set of teeth that were already the worse for wear, and would probably start to fall out in a few years.

'Well now, that's better,' he said, letting go of Jason's hair and advancing towards Nathan with the belt at the ready. 'Now you watch this, both of you. I catch either of you looking away, and you'll both get one, and no mistake.'

Jason couldn't hide the tears in his eyes now as his father laid into his younger brother with that belt, the dusty garage resounded with the sharp crack of leather impacting flesh. His brother who knew what was coming and didn't run, but stood there and took it until he could stand no longer. For the rest of his life, Jason would always marvel at how long Nathan managed to keep from crying out.

-

Hawkins' face tightened with pain as the medic finished stitching the stab wound on his chest, the skin giving and resisting slightly before the needle slipped through his flesh, pulling the short length of suture with it. Blood from the deep laceration trickled down his exposed chest as the medic tightened up the thread, pulling the wound closed.

He didn't make a sound throughout the entire procedure, didn't groan or cry out or flinch; he just sat there and stoically took it. He'd been trained to take the pain, to absorb it and use it. He'd been taking pain all his life.

There was certainly no shortage of it to go around tonight. The stab wound combined with heavy bruising to his shoulder courtesy of Anya's German comrade, not to mention the impact of falling from the rooftop to the level below, was a potent combination of injuries that would linger with him for several days at least.

However, such physical discomfort was far less of a concern than the woman standing opposite him, who had listened to his report of the night's events and watched the medic going about his gruesome work with impassive eyes. She had always been hard to read, and that made Hawkins uneasy.

'So let me get this straight,' Powell said, pacing the room. Hers wasn't the fast, agitated step of someone struggling to contain their mounting frustration, but rather the slow, steady movements of a scholar pondering a thorny problem. 'I give you free rein tonight, I allow you to take *my* men off to pursue your own leads. I even give you authorization to conduct operations on foreign soil. And after all that, after killing civilians and compromising our presence here, you come back to me with nothing? Worse than nothing, you come back with several men killed and injured chasing a target I didn't authorize you to engage. Is that what you're telling me, Jason?'

'They were ready for us at the safe house,' he replied coolly. 'Our assault was—'

'Your assault was incompetent, for starters,' Powell interrupted him. 'You were disorganized and sloppy, and you lost to a *woman*.'

She practically spat that word out. Whatever Powell's attitude towards her own gender, she apparently didn't consider them worthwhile assets in the world of warfare. Certainly none of her research candidates had been female, though he had no idea whether that decision had been hers or someone higher in the chain of command.

Then again, her anger wasn't directed at just any woman, but at one particular woman. Hawkins and the others were products of her research, the fruits of her own efforts, the very best that Elizabeth Powell could create. And they had failed her tonight. They had failed against the very person they'd been intended to surpass.

'She's no ordinary woman.' Whatever animosity existed between himself and Anya, he wouldn't deny her skill and ability as a soldier.

Powell rounded on him, and Hawkins actually felt a sudden and unexpected surge of fear. For a moment, he didn't see the woman at all. Instead he could have sworn he saw Tyler Hawkins looming over him, those big square oil-stained hands clutching a well-worn leather belt with the buckle removed. He was looking at him with that same hungry, excited expression on his face that now so closely resembled his own.

Sorry, son, but I gotta give ya one.

'She's a dead end, an inferior specimen,' a female voice said, and suddenly it was Powell standing before him again. 'All you've managed to do tonight is screw up, waste time and squander resources. But then, you always were a disappointment, Jason. Because beneath all your bullshit, you're always going to be that frightened little boy cowering in your father's garage.'

Pushing the medic aside, Hawkins leapt to his feet and drew himself up to his full height. As tall as she was with those high heels of hers, Powell was still several inches shorter than him, and nowhere close to his strength and power. He could overpower her in seconds, break her neck with a single vicious twist.

And he wanted to. By God, he wanted to give her one in that moment. He knew that other men in his unit viewed Powell differently, saw her as almost godlike in her omnipotence and infinite wisdom. But he'd never felt that closeness, that desire to please her or win her admiration. He'd never felt it back when they were candidates, and he didn't feel it now.

As dangerous and powerful as his father had once been, Jason Hawkins had grown to become ten times worse. It had been bred into him, imprinted into his psyche from his earliest memories, honed and enhanced by careful training and conditioning. And all of it was focussed on the woman standing before him. Could she even begin to comprehend the sheer variety of ways in which he could kill her, both quick and slow, painless and agonizing, clinical and brutal?

But far from shrinking away from him or trying to protect herself, Powell simply stood her ground, as implacable as a statue.

'Stand down,' she said, putting extra emphasis on each word, speaking the order slowly and precisely as one might command an angry dog.

There it was. The urge, the *need* to obey her kicked in hard, as hard as he could ever remember. He felt as if he were choking, trapped without air and slowly suffocating, and the only way to draw breath was to do what she commanded.

And yet he resisted. The anger, the fury that lay deep within his soul leapt up like a fire doused in gasoline, raging with nearly unquenchable power, pushing defiantly back against the smothering darkness of obedience. Almost, but he knew the darkness could never truly be driven out.

'Stand down, Jason,' she repeated, firmer now. Her voice had somehow become deeper, coarser, more powerful. A man's voice. His father's voice.

Don't make me give you one, boy.

Stubbornly holding his ground for a few seconds, Jason Hawkins finally let out a slow, steady breath, then took a step back and lowered himself down into the chair he'd been treated in. And as he did so, his mind entertained the same thoughts that had sustained him in that garage all those years ago, as he watched his father beat his younger brother into the hard-packed dirt floor.

One day — maybe soon, maybe not — it won't be like this. One day you're going to take it a little too far, push a little too hard, and then we'll see who really gets theirs in the end. We'll see, and no mistake.

Chapter 49

Sitting on one of the stools that ran along the outer edge of the bar, security operative Greg Wheeler took a sip of his coffee – his third cup so far tonight – and glanced out along the main concourse without much interest. In the past four hours he'd witnessed thousands, maybe tens of thousands of civilians coming and going down that wide departures hallway.

Families, old people, young couples, students, tourists, businessmen, kids, even a group of nuns in full black-and-white habits. He'd gotten a chuckle out of that. They looked like something from a bad cop show, the kind of over-the-top innocent civilians who wander onto the scene just as a gun battle is about to erupt. But his mirth hadn't lasted long.

He'd heard it said that there was nothing quite so interesting as watching people. But whatever asshole had said that had clearly never been posted on watch duty in the busiest airport in Brazil looking for one needle in a haystack.

Wheeler had studied Ryan Drake's bio – or at least the limited information that his superiors were willing to share – and committed every possible detail of his appearance to memory. Late-thirties, medium build, tall but not unusually so, dark hair, a tanned complexion that could almost pass for southern European. He couldn't have asked for a more difficult target to identify. He looked like just about every other man around these parts.

Still, at least things had quietened down. Like most big international airports, Galeão never really closed no matter the hour, but this late at night the flow of human traffic had at least slowed so that only scattered handfuls of weary-looking travellers passed by now. The airport cleaning staff had even rolled out their floor buffers, their rhythmic hum a sure sign that the place had slipped into a state of nocturnal torpor.

Wheeler lifted the cup and took another drink. He didn't really want any more caffeine in his body but he'd been loitering here for some time, his laptop open to make him look busy, and he knew the bar staff would ask him to move on if he didn't keep ordering.

That was when he spotted something that made him sit up straighter. A man, heading down the main concourse towards him. Caucasian, late-thirties, dark hair and thick but neatly trimmed beard, average build. Lean and fit without being showy about it.

Dressed in casual clothes – jeans, loose cotton shirt, rucksack slung casually over one shoulder – he appeared on first glance to be little different from so many men Wheeler had seen tonight. Another tourist reluctantly trudging towards his flight home after a week or two in the sun.

First glances however rarely told the full story. He was walking with the deliberate, unhurried pace of a man with time on his hands, but Wheeler detected something about his demeanour that marked him out. A heightened awareness of his surroundings that most passengers in the sleepy terminal didn't possess. To Wheeler it looked an awful lot like the trained situational alertness of a professional operator.

He was wearing a pair of thick-framed glasses, but the way the light refracted off the lenses told Wheeler they were just for show. And his beard looked to be a slightly different shade from his hair. A bad dye job by a vain man of early middle age, or a fake hairpiece?

Wheeler couldn't rightly say whether this was his target, or just a random civilian who bore a passing resemblance to him. After watching people for the past four hours, he was even beginning to doubt himself.

Reaching for his cell phone, he quickly dialled a number for one of the other operatives stationed in the airport terminal. He would have preferred tactical radios, but they'd been forced to ditch any incriminating gear and weapons before passing through security. Fortunately those same restrictions applied to their target as well.

'Unit Two, I'm in the bar on the western concourse.'

'Go, Two.'

'Possible target sighted, heading north towards the departure gates. Male, Caucasian, white shirt and jeans. I'm going to tail him. Move in and cover my position.'

'Copy that. Moving now.'

Waiting until the target passed by, Wheeler closed down the laptop, replaced it in his carry bag and slipped out of his seat, following the man at a discreet distance.

The main concourse was long and fairly quiet, with most of the food and retail outlets closed until morning. Wheeler made sure to give the man plenty of space as he ambled along. Lacking a crowd to blend into, he kept to the side where he could at least pretend to be browsing shop windows.

Out of the corner of his eye he spotted Spears, his backup, approaching from the opposite direction. They were too far away to communicate, but he could tell Spears had seen the target by the way his posture shifted slightly and his pace slowed. He was hanging back, letting Wheeler take the lead, waiting to see what both he and their target did next.

As it turned out, not much of anything. Checking his watch, the man wandered over to a row of vacant seats and sat down. He was facing out onto the concourse, giving him a perfect view of traffic heading in both directions. Reaching into his pack, he fished out a paperback novel with a garish front cover, flicked it open and was soon engrossed.

Fuck, Wheeler thought to himself, by now very much aware that he was in the man's line of sight. There's only so long a man can linger in front of a shop window before he starts to look suspicious. Resuming his walk, he carried on through the departures terminal, angling over to another gate further up where about 30 passengers were waiting for their flight to be called.

Spears approached and sat down on the row of seats directly behind him so that the two men were effectively back-to-back.

'What do you think?' he asked under his breath.

'Hard to tell,' Wheeler acknowledged. 'Son of a bitch looks pretty shifty. If he sees us, he's playing it cool.'

'You want to do a walk-by?'

He thought about it for a short time. 'No, let's see what he does next.'

So they waited. For 15 minutes Wheeler sat there watching their target as he leafed through his book, his eyes occasionally glancing up at people as they passed by. Was he worried? Wheeler wondered. He looked a little nervous, his movements jerky and agitated as if he were filled with energy that could find no outlet.

Then, glancing at his watch again, he marked his place in the book, stood up and made his way towards the nearest restrooms.

'Heads up, he's going for the john,' Wheeler said, watching him vanish down the short corridor.

He watched, waiting for the man to reappear, but he didn't. The minutes ticked by, and Wheeler could feel his unease growing with each movement of the hand on his watch. Five minutes, six, seven.

'You got eyes-on?' Spears asked.

'Nothing yet.'

'The fuck's he doing in there?' Spears paused. 'You think we've been made?'

Wheeler said nothing. He had a bad feeling about this. From what he remembered during his brief walk by, the short corridor leading off towards the restrooms had only four doors: the men's, ladies' and disabled bathrooms, and a storage room for cleaning equipment. But what if he'd been wrong? What if there was another way out he hadn't spotted?

'I'm going in,' he decided. 'Cover me.'

He strode over towards the corridor leading to the restrooms, with Spears following a short distance behind. With the airport at a low ebb, there was nobody else entering or exiting the bathrooms.

To his relief, his memory hadn't failed him. The tiled hallway was marked by three doors on his left, and a small storage room on his right. A quick check of the handle confirmed that this room was firmly locked, and it was unlikely their target would have been able to pick it without being seen.

Next he advanced to the disabled restroom and tried the handle. The door swung open, revealing an empty bathroom beyond. That only left the men's and ladies' rooms.

Reaching into his inner jacket pocket, Wheeler produced a small gold fountain pen. A pen that contained something a little more potent than ink, however.

Unscrewing the cap, he removed the tip which actually did contain a small amount of real ink in case security wanted to test it, revealing a hypodermic needle protruding from the end of the device. The pen contained a healthy cocktail of compressed sodium pentathol and scopolamine – enough to incapacitate within seconds.

All things being equal, Wheeler would rather have a Glock 17 to back him up, but the syringe would have to do. He glanced around at Spears who was lingering near the entrance to the restroom corridor, ready to come running at the first sounds of trouble. Slipping his hands into his pockets with the syringe at the ready, he sauntered into the men's room.

The place looked pretty much like any airport restroom anywhere in the world. A retaining wall blocked the view from outside. Beyond this, a row of sinks and mirrors lined one wall, while a bank of urinals jutted out from the other.

There was no sign of the target at either the sinks or the urinals, which left only the stalls at the far end. Wheeler felt his heart rate increase as he advanced down the room, closing in on the stalls. There were four of them, and two at least were empty, their doors hanging partially open.

The third had swung closed, but wasn't locked. Gripping the syringe, Wheeler reached out and eased the door open. It swung back without a sound, revealing the empty cubicle within.

That left only one possibility. Taking a breath, Wheeler positioned himself off to the side, reached out and knocked on the stall door.

'Sir, I'm afraid we have to close this restroom for maintenance,' he said loudly, trying to sound suitably apologetic. 'I'll have to ask you to vacate the stall now.'

There was no reply.

Wheeler knocked again, harder this time. 'Sir, you must vacate the stall now.'

Finally something happened. The sound of clothes rustling, a toilet flushing, the click of a lock disengaging. Wheeler waited for the door to swing inwards before making his move, stepping quickly into the doorway and whipping the syringe out of his pocket. Go in hard and fast, don't hold back.

'Whoa!' the stall's occupant cried out, throwing up his hands in fear at his sudden appearance and trying to back away, nearly tripping over the toilet. He spoke with a distinctly East Coast American accent, probably Boston or New York. 'What the fuck? Take it easy, man!'

It's remarkable how different people look when you get up close and personal. Suddenly this enigmatic man he'd been following around the airport for the past 15 minutes didn't look like the dangerous, professional operative he'd been tasked with finding. Now the tall and athletic build had become spare and skinny, the face young and frightened, and even the beard looked different, more convincing somehow.

Wheeler quickly hid the syringe behind his back, masking his look of surprise and replacing it with one of severe authority.

'Let me see your ID, sir,' he said, thrusting out a hand.

'My ID?' the young man stammered.

'Yes, now!' he snapped. 'I'm a cop. We're tracking suspected drug traffickers.'

'Drugs? No, man. That's not me!' With trembling hands, he fumbled in his back pocket. 'I just came to Rio to party for a couple weeks. One of my college buddies lives here now, that's all.'

'Why were you in here so long?'

His already frightened face coloured noticeably. 'The food around here doesn't agree with me,' he said as he handed his boarding card and passport over. 'It's... well, been a rough couple of days. Know what I mean?'

Wheeler scanned the documents quickly. James Delvecchio, from Queens, New York. Twenty-seven years old. Fuck! Fuck!

He'd just wasted his time.

'Here,' Wheeler said, shoving the documents against the young traveller's chest and turning away in disgust. 'Wash your goddamn hands.'

Spears was waiting for him when he emerged from the restroom.

'False alarm,' he said in response to the unspoken question, already heading back towards the coffee shop to resume his frustrating and so far fruitless vigil. 'Dumb college kid with the shits. Let's get the fuck out of here.'

Preoccupied as they had been with their wasteful pursuit of the wrong man, both operatives were ignorant of events playing out at the Air Portugal check-in desk a few hundred yards away. It was, after all, on the wrong side of the security screen, so they had little reason to patrol that section of the airport.

It would prove to be a costly mistake.

–

Juliana Almeida held a hand against her mouth, stifling a yawn. Working nights at check-in was never a thrilling experience, and she was still a couple of hours shy of the end of her shift. Still, at least she was spared the frantic chaos of the morning rush, where passengers would be queued up beyond the lanes, waiting to collect their boarding passes. For obvious reasons, international flights between Brazil and Portugal were popular throughout the year.

She glanced up from her computer screen as a passenger approached her desk, dressed in cargo pants, trainers and a loose fitting T-shirt, his hair looking as if it had never seen a brush. He was carrying a small backpack over his shoulders, but otherwise seemed to have brought no luggage.

Almeida thought there was something a little odd about the way he walked, a certain jerkiness in his movements. His back was hunched, his shoulders slumped forward. She wondered for a moment if this might spell trouble, but she'd encountered enough drunk and belligerent passengers in her time to know this man wasn't intoxicated. Perhaps he was ill or impaired in some way.

'Good morning,' she said, putting on the best smile one could summon at 3 a.m. 'May I see your passport and booking confirmation?'

'I have a flight reservation.' There was an odd tone to his voice, which seemed to shift up and down at random. She also noticed that he avoided making eye contact.

She nodded. 'May I see your passport?'

He handed it over, still evading her gaze. Scanning it through the reader below her desk, Almeida waited while the booking system retrieved his details.

Lewis Bailey, booked on the next flight to Lisbon, departing in about an hour. He was cutting it pretty close for an international flight, she thought. The gate might already be closing. He'd have to run if he hoped to make it…

Her train of thought halted when she noticed something in the notes section of his reservation.

> Special assistance required. Passenger to be escorted to departure gate and given priority boarding.

Almeida glanced up at him again. 'Mr Bailey, yes?'

'My name is Lewis,' he replied in that strange, lilting tone of his.

'Lewis,' she corrected herself as the printer beside her desk whirred into action and churned out his boarding passes. 'I have a note here that you're to be escorted to your flight.'

'Yes, someone usually comes with me.' She noticed he seemed to answer questions by echoing them. 'I have autism. I don't like crowds or waiting in lines. I can get upset and that makes other people nervous.'

Almeida blinked, taken aback by the blunt, matter-of-fact way he said it. She'd dealt with passengers suffering from all manner of conditions in her time, but this was the first time one of them had informed her of it in such a direct manner.

'Of course,' she said, feeling a twinge of sympathy for the man. 'I'll have someone come right out to help you.'

'Thank you.' He looked purposefully at the name tag on her jacket. 'Juliana.'

It took a matter of minutes to put a call through to airport security and have one of their staff report to her desk to act as an escort, while she busied herself with the usual check-in procedures. As a precaution, she also contacted his departure gate to advise them he was on his way, and to give him priority boarding.

'Here's your passport and boarding card,' she said, handing the documents over. She pointed to the burly security guard beside the desk. 'Pablo here will make sure you get to your gate. Have a good flight, Mr Ba— Lewis,' she corrected herself.

He collected his documents, hoisted the bag a little higher on his shoulder and turned away. She watched as he followed the security guard, walking with the same jerky, uncomfortable movements, the stooped posture and furtive glances at his surroundings. She hoped for his sake that someone was waiting for him when he disembarked in Portugal.

Her fears were quite unfounded however.

As Drake had hoped, the guard escorted him through security and baggage check, making sure he bypassed the small queues of fellow passengers. He ignored the irritable looks that were cast his way as he walked by, throwing himself into the role of a man who was largely oblivious to the people around him.

Naturally his bag contained few possessions, and no weapons of any kind, so if he was unlucky enough to run into trouble beyond this point, he'd have a tough time fighting his way out of it. He could only hope that the young man he'd bribed to wander around the international departures terminal for a while had sufficiently occupied whatever operatives might have been stationed to look out for him.

He'd specified at least half an hour of distraction, impressing on the man the importance of fulfilling his mission unless he wanted another visit from Drake under far less favourable circumstances. Five hundred dollars had been enough to silence the man's questions.

Of course, he hadn't mentioned to his new friend that this decoy role entailed a measure of danger. It was unlikely that Powell's men would harm him in a heavily monitored airport, but there was a chance that things could get out of hand. There was always a chance.

Once through security, Pablo hustled him over to a door marked 'AUTHO-RIZED PERSONNEL ONLY', and showed Drake through to a service corridor that bypassed the shops and bars of the main concourse. He said nothing, merely gestured with his hands for Drake to follow. Likely he wasn't as fluent in English as the check-in girl had been.

Drake followed him, quite happy to let the man take the lead.

This whole ruse had been surprisingly easy to pull off. Most big international airports have a special assistance service to accommodate disabled passengers. Most of the time they didn't even require proof of the passenger's condition, perhaps wary of potential discrimination lawsuits.

When he'd called the airline about an hour ago to book the first available transatlantic flight, he'd made sure to explain that Lewis Bailey was autistic, suffered from a terrible fear of crowds and particularly couldn't stand being held up in queues. Hence he preferred to travel late at night when the airports were quieter. The woman on the booking line couldn't have been more helpful, assuring him she'd flag his reservation as a priority passenger.

And that was all it had taken. He had bypassed the most likely entrance routes to the departure terminal, and hopefully any operatives that might still be lurking there.

The service corridor carried on for a good 50 yards before meeting a set of stairs. As he walked, the guard spoke into his radio in Portuguese. At the bottom of the stairwell was another set of locked doors which faced out onto the jetway itself. A small shuttle bus was parked outside, apparently laid on just for him. Unlocking the doors, the guard ushered him forward.

He wasn't about to argue.

It took less than five minutes to reach the gate, where a big Airbus A340 was parked up, the jet bridge connecting its forward hatch to the departure terminal. A member of the ground staff was waiting for Drake outside, escorting him upstairs and along the jet bridge to the aircraft. Running his hands through his hair to smooth it out, he let out a relieved breath as he stepped aboard.

So far, so good.

'Welcome aboard, sir,' the flight attendant said after briefly checking his boarding pass, flashing a charming but professional smile. She was short and petite, and wearing a little too much make-up as cabin crew often did to hide the fatigue of long-haul flights.

'Thanks,' he said, dropping the 'special assistance required' act now that he was through the airport. 'Hope I haven't kept you guys waiting.'

The smile was more relaxed, more genuine this time. 'I wouldn't worry, sir. It's not exactly a busy flight.'

Drake saw only a handful of passengers scattered about, many asleep with masks already covering their eyes.

'This is just a return flight, so we can change crews for the morning run back to Rio. Most of the passengers work for the airline,' she explained. There was a hint of playfulness in her eyes. 'You may be outnumbered.'

Drake smiled back. 'Well, I'll try not to be too demanding.'

Her laugh was light and pleasant. She glanced about, hesitantly. 'You know, you could probably take one of the business class seats if you like. They're more comfortable, especially for taller passengers.'

Drake feigned concern. 'I wouldn't want you to get in trouble.'

The young woman leaned a little closer and lowered her voice, her expression conspiratorial. 'Well, I won't tell anyone if you don't.'

Before long the Airbus was rocketing along the main runway, the landing gear parted company with the ground and the big aircraft lumbered into the night sky. Rio de Janeiro was soon receding to a cluster of lights in the darkness behind as they headed east towards the rising sun.

Drake ordered a double whisky as soon as the seat belt light went off. No water, no ice, no fucking around. There would be much to do once he touched down, but for now he needed to sleep.

He was raising the glass to take his first sip when he spotted the pronounced tremble in his hand, ripples shivering across the surface of his drink.

Time was slipping away from him.

Don't think about it now. Just focus on the mission. The mission is everything.

With that, he downed his drink in a single gulp, then chased this liquid breakfast with a couple of painkillers from the tab in his pack. With his self-medication administered, Drake stretched out on his reclining seat, closed his eyes and eventually fell asleep somewhere over the south Atlantic.

Chapter 50

'Tell me you have something,' Anya said, looking down at Frost, who had been hunched over her laptop for the past hour, trying to interrogate the cell phone that Anya had recovered from Cuatro's safe house.

Frost's eyes were tired and bloodshot.

'Right now, I've got somewhere between nothing and fuck-all,' she admitted, looking at the cheap burner as if it were some implacable enemy. 'Your buddy Karalius used an encrypted satellite phone to contact you. A real bitch to break through even if you're using a cutting-edge workstation, which this isn't.'

She gestured to her laptop, which had multiple windows open, many streaming raw computer code that Anya couldn't begin to understand.

'In short, he didn't want to be found,' Frost concluded.

'So we have no leads on our mysterious friend,' Rojas said, glowering at them from the corner of the room where he'd been stripping and cleaning his sidearm to pass the time.

'Or Drake,' Mitchell added, downing a mouthful of coffee. She looked as strung out as Frost. 'He could be anywhere by now.'

A loud, unexpected outburst suddenly issued from Alex.

'Fuck, yeah! Get in there, son!' he cried, slamming a fist down on the table hard enough to knock over an empty can of Red Bull.

Aware that all eyes in the room were now very much on him, he removed his earphones, allowing tinny, high-tempo music to blast out. He looked jittery and wired, but nonetheless it was clear something significant had happened.

Mitchell frowned. 'Care to enlighten us, Alex?'

Alex stretched out his arms as if relaxing after some hard-fought victory. 'No big deal, I've just figured out where Drake's going.'

Whatever his faults, he rarely made unfounded claims. Anya was moving right away, quickly followed by the others.

'What exactly have you found?'

Grinning, he spun the computer around to face the others. The screen showed a scanned image of a man's passport, made out in the name of Lewis Bailey. However, the photograph was clearly Drake.

'Ryan checked into Galeão international airport about two hours ago, boarded an Air Portugal flight direct to Lisbon. Our boy is heading back to Europe. I can even tell you what seat he was allocated.'

Frost glanced up from the screen, looking both suspicious and annoyed at his apparent breakthrough. 'How the fuck did you get all this?'

'Because I'm really good at this stuff.'

'Alex...' Anya said, her manner making it plain this was no time for show-boating.

'Oh, all right!' Frost might have held little sway over him, but Anya was another matter. 'I hacked the booking systems of the major airlines operating out of all three airports in Rio. Most of them weren't that hard. Their firewalls were about three years out of date, backdoors all over the place—'

'I'm sure this is fascinating, but how did you find Ryan?' Mitchell asked.

Alex looked disappointed at being cut off. 'Once I was inside their systems, I could review every booking made in the last 24 hours. I set automatic search macros to filter out anyone of the wrong gender, age range, ethnicity, whatever else. Then all I had to do was run image recognition on what was left. Ryan might have changed his name, but he can't change his face. And Bob's your mother's brother, we've got our man bang to rights.'

Anya was stunned by what he'd accomplished. Their trail, which seemed to have run cold just a couple of hours ago, had suddenly picked up again.

'Good work, Alex,' she said.

'But what the hell would Ryan be looking for in Lisbon?' Frost wondered.

'He's not,' Rojas said. 'Rio to Lisbon is one of the most frequent routes out of this city. It's more likely he will take a connecting flight.'

Anya chewed her lip. 'Alex, can you hack the airlines based at Lisbon International? Find out if Ryan has booked another flight?'

'I can get into their systems, but I won't be able to search on facial recognition unless he checks in to collect his boarding pass,' Alex explained.

'Then run a search on the Lewis Bailey ID,' Anya instructed him. 'He has no reason to suspect it's been compromised.'

'Way ahead of you,' he replied, already switching tasks on his laptop.

'Not that far ahead, or you would have done it already,' Frost said, returning to her own computer and setting to work. 'We should combine our efforts on this.'

Alex shook his head. 'This isn't amateur hour, Frost. I don't have time to walk you through the process. No offence, of course.'

She flashed a dangerously polite smile. The kind of smile she offered before knocking someone out. Only Dietrich, who knew her best, might have recognized it for what it was, but he was fast asleep on a combination of vodka and sedatives.

'None taken, Alex. But there are 61 airlines operating routes out of Lisbon International,' Frost pointed out helpfully. 'You really want to try cracking them all yourself?'

'Let her help,' Anya advised him. 'This is no time to compete.'

'Fine,' he conceded. 'I'll send you the diagnostic suite I've been using. Try not to bollocks it up.'

'No need, I've already got it.'

That was enough to stop Alex in his tracks. 'You what?'

She smirked. 'I cloned your system and downloaded everything on your drives. Just as a precaution, of course.'

For the first time, his cocky smile faltered. 'Bull-fucking-shit. There's no way you could have gotten past my firewall.'

'Didn't have to. You left the system unlocked when you were in the john,' she reminded him. 'I mean, I hate to mention amateur hour again so soon, but—'

'Piss off. That's a dirty trick to play on anyone.'

She shrugged. 'That's life, pal. You don't get bonus points for playing fair. Now why don't you start at the top of the list? I'll start at the bottom and we'll meet in the middle.'

Alex gave her a hostile glare.

'Fine. Sounds great,' he replied brusquely, turning his eyes back towards the screen. His unhappy expression however suggested he wouldn't forget that little deception.

Anya, Rojas and Mitchell could do little more than watch and wait as these two experts went about their task, fingers dancing across their keyboards, occasionally exchanging information about their progress. Frost's injured hand impeded her typing, but each seemed to be making steady progress.

Watching the way each occasionally cast surreptitious glances at the other, Anya had the distinct impression that this had become a competition, a matter of honour and prestige to crack the problem first.

But in the end, only one of them would make the discovery they needed.

'Got him!' Frost cried out, pushing herself away from her laptop. 'You were right, Rojas. He's booked on a connecting flight from Lisbon to Tunisia with Tunisair.'

Anya scanned the booking reservation she'd managed to call up. After a layover of about five hours, Drake's flight was due to depart for Tunisia at around 9 a.m. local time, arriving in Tunis just before midday.

Tunisia. What could he want there? That was something they'd have to figure out en route. For now, they had what they needed to continue their pursuit.

'We know where he's going,' she said, clenching her fists in relief. 'Now we need to get there ahead of him.'

'That's not going to be that easy,' Alex said, having switched to searching local airports again, this time as a customer rather than a hacker. 'There are no direct flights from Rio to Tunis. And if we tried it Drake's way, we'd arrive about eight hours behind him.'

Mitchell shook her head. 'The trail could have gone cold by then.'

'That won't be a problem,' Rojas said.

'What do you mean?' replied Anya.

'I know a man in Rio with access to a private jet. He uses it to import… valuable cargo into the United States from time to time.'

Anya could guess the kind of 'valuable cargo' a man might want to transport clandestinely from South America into the United States, but that wasn't her concern now.

'Can we trust him?' she asked. Drug smugglers were hardly the kind of people one entrusted their life to.

'He and I have worked together many times,' Rojas assured her. 'He owes me a debt, and we had an agreement that if I ever needed it, he would get me out of the country. Use of his plane is his way of settling the score.'

It sounded promising, not that there were any other options on the table. 'And he will take us to Tunisia?'

Rojas nodded. 'He will. For a price.'

She had a feeling she wasn't going to like what he had to say. 'What is his price?'

The assassin folded his arms. 'Not his, mine. Once we find Drake, I want out. I want the men who tried to kill me tonight to be dealt with permanently. And I want your assurance that you'll never come looking for me again, ever.'

'Would you like a mansion and a yacht to go with that?' Frost asked sarcastically.

'No, I can get those things for myself,' he fired back. 'But they're not worth much to a man who must spend his life looking over his shoulder.'

Anya knew exactly what he was looking for: peace of mind. 'If you help us find Ryan, then I will do what I can to put an end to Hawkins and the others, and help you start a new life. That's the best I can offer.'

'Not much of a deal,' he remarked.

'But it's an honest one. And better than you're likely to get elsewhere.'

Rojas was quiet for a time, obviously weighing up whether helping her was better than cutting them all loose and taking his chances. In the end however, it was clear which choice offered better prospects for him.

'I'll make a call,' he said at last, reaching for his cell phone.

Anya nodded, more relieved than she was prepared to admit. They had a chance now. It was a slim chance to be sure, and one that could very well still lead to failure, but it was something. Drake might have given them the slip here in Rio, but he wasn't yet beyond their reach.

If they acted fast, if even a glimmer of luck was on their side, then perhaps they could still get to him in time. Perhaps they could still pull him back from the brink. She told herself this because she wanted, *needed*, to believe it.

But whether luck was with them or not, whatever obstacles or challenges got in their way, Anya knew one thing was absolute certainty: as long as there was life in her, she would never give up on Drake.

Chapter 51

It was a cold, blustery sort of afternoon in Virginia, the fitful breeze stirring up the desiccated leaves of last fall into little tornados that whirled and twisted across open spaces. The sky overhead was iron grey, threatening rain later.

Dan Franklin was on his way out to his car, which he'd deliberately left in a remote section of Langley's vast employee parking lot. As a divisional leader, Franklin had a private spot assigned to him near the main campus building, but he rarely used it, instead choosing spaces increasingly far away from his office. He wanted to walk, wanted to make the most of the opportunity to exercise, to push himself a little further every time.

That was how he'd painstakingly regained much of his former strength and fitness, how he'd recovered from the spinal surgery that had left him virtually paralysed for weeks afterwards. Single-minded determination and a refusal to accept the pessimistic advice of his doctors had seen him through. That hard work was paying off now, his stride confident and energetic, with only a slight limp betraying the old injury.

He should have felt elation at this new lease on life he'd been granted, but he could dig up no such emotions today. All things considered, it had been a shit week, beginning with the bombing that had killed George Breckenridge, just after their meeting about resurrecting the Shepherd programme. Matters had worsened exponentially with the release of a video in which the bomber had revealed himself to be Ryan Drake.

Ryan fucking Drake! His friend. His former comrade in arms. The man who had saved his life during the ambush in Afghanistan that had left him with life-changing injuries. The man he'd placed a great deal of trust and faith in.

Even now he could scarcely believe it, and certainly couldn't understand it. What was the man thinking? Why would he do such a thing?

Things had gotten progressively worse since then. Word had reached him of another attack, this time in Brazil. A factory destroyed, men dead, and one man responsible for it all. Franklin knew all too well who that man was.

Somehow, Drake had gone well and truly rogue. He had no idea where this was all leading or what the man's final goal was, but he could make one confident prediction: more people were going to die before this was over.

Spots of rain began to patter off the ground, the long-threatened downpour looking like it was about to start. Franklin's strides were quickening, his posture tense and agitated as he walked, his limp more pronounced. He needed to get the hell out of here for the day, needed time to think. Maybe he'd crack open that bottle of Scotch back home and put a dent in it tonight.

He was just reaching into his heavy overcoat for his car keys when he felt something vibrating in his pocket. His cell phone. Not his work phone, but the private burner he always kept on his person.

He stopped, oblivious to the cold wind and worsening weather, his car keys forgotten. Only a very few people knew his number, one of whom was Drake himself.

Fishing the phone out, he took a moment to collect himself and question whether this was really a call he ought to take, then pressed the green button.

'Yeah.'

'Franklin.'

The voice that spoke wasn't Drake's. This voice was female, tense and anxious, and carrying a faint trace of a foreign accent.

'Who is this?' he demanded, ready to hang up and destroy the phone.

'It's Anya.'

He heard a sigh on the line. He sensed this was a call she hadn't wanted to make, but she'd made it anyway because she had no choice.

'I need your help.'

Part III

Consciousness

Frank Olson, a scientist employed by the CIA on MK-Ultra, fell to his death from the window of a New York City hotel room on 28 November 1953 in an alleged suicide. Subsequent autopsy findings suggested he may have been assassinated.

The candidate was waiting for her as always. But he was different now, no longer restrained to the chair. His eyes stared off blankly into space, seeing nothing at all. A man finally broken by the wars that had raged inside his mind.

It had been a hard battle indeed, and even she had begun to doubt whether their conditioning would take hold, whether it was simple pride and hubris that prevented her from conceding defeat. But she had persevered, hitting him again and again with mental and chemical conditioning, breaking down his resistance, until at last she had won.

They had both won.

She took no pleasure in seeing him like this, but she knew it was a necessary evil. Like so much of what they did here, the rewards would ultimately justify the sacrifices.

'Good morning, candidate,' she said once again as she sat down. As she always did, never varying the routine. 'We're going to begin our next session. Do you know how many times we've met?'

He shook his head slowly.

'This is our thirteenth session together,' she informed him. 'I'd like to ask you a few questions before we begin. Would that be okay?'

'Yes.'

'What's today's date?'

'I don't know.'

'Who is the president of the United States?'

'I don't know.'

She made a note of his responses. 'Where are we right now?'

'I don't know.'

She smiled faintly. 'We're home, candidate. This is your home. This has always been your home, and you'll always be safe here. With me.'

'Home,' he repeated, a flicker of recognition showing in his eyes now.

'It took a lot of work to bring you to this point, Ryan,' she said, using his real name for the first time. It was the first step in re-establishing his identity, putting the pieces of his fragmented mind back together. 'It wasn't easy. In fact, it caused a lot of pain for both of us. Do you know why we did it?'

'No.'

'Because that's how we help people. We build them into something perfect, something beautiful. But before we can do that, we have to tear down what they were before. Like demolishing an old building to make way for a better one. You understand?'

'Yes.'

'That's what we had to do with you, candidate. It wasn't easy, but we did it together. And I'm very proud of you.' She smiled gently. 'Now we're ready to rebuild you into something better. How do you feel about that?'

She saw something in him then. A smile.

'I feel ready.'

Chapter 52

Drake jolted awake with a gasp, instinctively reaching for a weapon at his hip and finding nothing. Blinking, he looked up into the concerned face of the cabin attendant who had welcomed him aboard the flight.

'Are you all right, sir?' she asked, looking worried. 'You were... talking in your sleep.'

'Yeah, I'm... fine,' he lied, his heart rate slowing to something approaching normality. 'Bad dreams.'

'Of course.' She looked doubtful, but knew better than to press him. 'I'm sorry to disturb you, but we're starting our descent into Lisbon.'

Drake glanced around. His own window blind was closed, but he could see blue sky and clouds through one on the opposite side. He must have slept through most of the flight.

'I'll need you to return your seat to its upright position—'

'I know the drill,' Drake said.

The young woman made a face. 'Sorry,' she whispered. 'The galley's still open for a few more minutes. Can I get you anything before we land?'

'The blackest, strongest coffee you've got.'

A more relaxed smile this time. 'Coming up.'

Already Drake could feel the change of cabin pressure as the aircraft's nose tilted downwards and they began to lose altitude. In less than an hour he would be on the ground, preparing to start the final leg of his journey to Tunisia.

And there, finally, he would find his answers.

Chapter 53

Anya awoke to the slight lurch and shudder as their aircraft passed through a pocket of high-altitude turbulence. Rubbing her eyes, she looked at her watch – she'd been out for nearly six hours. She had no idea what time zone they were in, but it was obvious that most of her companions had seized the opportunity to grab some rest while they could.

They lay scattered around the rather cramped passenger cabin, stretched out on reclining seats or even lying on the floor.

Rojas had indeed made good on his promise to arrange a flight out of Rio. Within two hours of making the call, the small group were assembled at a remote hangar in Jacarepaguá airport, a smaller regional airfield about 20 miles outside the city, mostly reserved for private aircraft operating locally.

A sleek Gulfstream executive jet had been waiting for them, fuelled and ready to go, along with its pilot: a small, skinny man with long greying hair, an open red shirt and tinted glasses that made him look like he'd just walked off the set of a 1970s cop drama. He'd greeted Rojas with the enthusiastic embrace of a long-lost brother, which he very well might have been for all Anya knew.

In short order they'd stowed their limited gear aboard, closed the hatch and been on their way.

Drake by this point had a six-hour head start, but since he had to switch flights in Lisbon, they'd been able to make up some of that time. According to Alex's calculations they should reach Tunisia less than an hour after Drake touched down.

Of course, there was still the problem of figuring out what or who Drake was looking for in Tunisia, but Anya had someone working on that. She could only hope he came up with something before they touched down.

Sitting up in her seat, she rubbed her neck and stretched uncomfortably. Her body had taken quite a beating through various misadventures over the previous day, and was now fully intent on reminding her of every one of them. Bruised muscles had seized up, joints and tendons ached and strained.

There had been a time when she'd been able to absorb stuff like this. Anya was used to taking hits, but she'd usually been able to bounce back from them pretty quickly. She caught herself wondering when all that had begun to change, when the aches and pains had started lingering that bit longer.

She rose from her chair and crept through the cabin, steadying herself as they hit another pocket of turbulence, then eased open the cockpit door.

The pilot was reclining in his seat, a cup of coffee in one hand and a car magazine in the other, though it seemed to feature as many scantily clad young women as it did sports cars. As with most long-haul flights, the jet's autopilot handled the mundane tasks of maintaining their speed, altitude and heading, only requiring his input during take-off and landing.

Beyond the cockpit windows stretched a sea of scattered clouds, the sun high in the sky and dazzlingly bright at this altitude. They'd been travelling east for several hours, heading straight into the dawn. Chasing the new day.

He glanced up from his magazine, eyeing her over his tinted glasses.

'Good morning, young lady,' he said, his grin exposing teeth that were too white and straight to be real. 'You want some coffee?'

Anya shook her head, faintly amused. She certainly wasn't feeling very 'young' at that moment, and after sleeping awkwardly on a chair for the past few hours, was almost positive she didn't look it. Then again, a man who flew private jets for a living probably didn't have to work too hard on his repartee.

'Where are we?' she asked.

'The ocean.'

She hoped his piloting abilities were better than his navigation.

'Be more specific.'

The pilot checked his GPS system, making no great rush of it. 'Approaching the Strait of Gibraltar. We should be on the ground in two, maybe three hours.'

Three hours. She'd been asleep longer than she thought.

'So you're the girl Cesar cashed in his escape plan for?' he went on, taking a sip of his coffee. It was strong; she could tell from the scent.

'I am,' she acknowledged.

He tutted and shook his head. 'You sure you want to be mixing up with a man like him? He's a crazy guy, dangerous. A nice girl like you could get hurt.'

She honestly couldn't tell if he was joking. Then again, if he knew the circumstances behind Rojas' flight from Brazil and the part she'd played in it, Anya was quite sure he'd be less sympathetic towards her.

'I'll take my chances.' She pointed out the port cockpit window. 'And as for danger, I'm more worried about that F16 closing on our port side.'

His reaction – born of years of running illicit cargo – was as instinctive as it was abrupt. Twisting around to get a look at the jet she'd just spotted, he accidentally knocked his coffee cup against the edge of the magazine, spilling a good portion of its contents over his lap.

'*Filho da puta!*' he growled, tossing the magazine aside and wiping at his crotch.

Anya shrugged apologetically, masking her smirk. 'My mistake. Must have been a trick of the light.'

Leaving him to deal with the mess, she returned to the main cabin, seeking out the coffee machine in the compact galley. Gulfstreams were designed to cater to millionaires, corporate CEOs and celebrities, and many were kitted out with the very best luxury fixtures and fittings. This plane was quite different however. Its interior was dusty and dated, with much of the furniture stripped out to save weight, though fortunately she found the galley had remained largely intact.

As the machine burred away and black liquid began to dribble into Anya's cup, she heard footsteps approaching. Dietrich eased himself into a seat opposite, moving gingerly, clearly in some discomfort from the now heavily bandaged gunshot wound. Anya empathized with him on that, at least.

He was watching her, his expression difficult to read. The man seemed unusually adept at hiding his emotions, leaving Anya feeling uneasy and defensive in his presence.

'You wanted something, Dietrich?' Anya asked pointedly.

'You risked your life to protect me back in those favelas.' It sounded almost like an accusation. 'Why?'

Anya shrugged. 'You knew too much. You could compromise us all.'

'No,' he decided. 'If that was your only worry, you could have just killed me and saved yourself.'

'I was out of ammunition.'

He smiled thinly. 'Somehow I doubt that would have stopped you.'

Dietrich was right about that, though Anya decided not to pursue that line of thought. 'I could ask you the same question. You had a chance to escape, but instead you came back for me. Why?'

'Well, it's not because I like you.'

'That much is obvious.'

'We were fighting for our lives. At times like that, personal relationships are irrelevant. All that matters is getting out alive, and that means having the other person's back because sooner or later you might need them to have yours.'

Anya folded her arms. 'Your point being?'

'My point being, whether we like each other or not, whether we agree with each other or not, we're in this fight together. Maybe we should start acting like it.'

Of all the things she'd expected from a man like Dietrich, this wasn't one of them. He hadn't said it in as many words, but she sensed the intent. 'Is this your idea of an apology?'

'Don't flatter yourself,' Dietrich scoffed. 'This is my idea of pragmatism. We have a better chance of survival by working together instead of against each other. But the question is one of trust. I can't trust someone who keeps things from me, and...' He looked at her hard. 'I suppose you feel the same way.'

Anya was quiet, considering his words. Dietrich was hardly prone to empty compliments or pandering to vanity, but neither was he inclined towards outright deception. He spoke his mind, because he generally didn't care what others thought about him. But he remained, by his own admission, a pragmatist. And perhaps now he'd realized that his own interests were entwined with Anya's.

The ping of the coffee machine jolted her out of these contemplations, and she felt oddly relieved. That simple noise seemed to mark a definitive end to their conflict, as if it were an announcer's bell signalling the end of a boxing round.

'All right,' she finally agreed. 'No more secrets, no more deception, no more striking out alone. Agreed?'

Dietrich nodded. 'I can live with that.'

Chapter 54

Tunis, Tunisia

Even with the rental car's air conditioning running full blast, Drake was visibly perspiring as he eased the vehicle along the winding streets, dodging other cars heading the opposite way and ignoring their blaring horns.

A hot breeze whipped through the dusty street up ahead, forming little dust devils that whirled and twisted across the road. The ground shimmered in the late afternoon heat, buildings bleached white beneath the relentless onslaught of the sun, yet the locals scarcely seemed to notice. Drake had operated in neighbouring Libya a couple of years ago, and knew full well how lethally hot the Saharan sun could be.

Like most cities in North Africa, Tunis had been conquered and occupied many times in its long history, from the Spanish to the Ottomans, then the French, and even the Germans had held it for a while during the Second World War. With each successive empire leaving its own distinct architectural mark on the city, the result was an often bewildering array of homes, shops, mosques, cathedrals, temples, palaces, monuments to long-dead leaders and towering government offices, all crammed together in sweltering heat and thronging humanity.

Glancing left, Drake spotted an arched entrance, and caught a glimpse of hanging rugs and fabrics, bags and shoes of every kind, clothing and decorations of all shapes and sizes. It was a souk, one of the many covered street markets that criss-crossed the ancient city. They were popular tourist traps, with prices to match.

The traffic eased off at last, and Drake was able to pick up the pace. He checked his satnav unit and was relieved to see he was less than a mile from his destination.

He was just passing a big, bland-looking office building that looked to be government owned when he spotted a big group of men out front, easily 40 or 50 strong, chanting and shouting. They carried no banners or slogans that he could see, but they were clearly fired up about something and were determined to make their discontent known. Many had scarves and masks covering their faces.

Drake had seen enough civil unrest to know that people rarely went to the trouble of disguising their identity if they intended only a peaceful protest. These guys clearly had other plans.

Sure enough, he watched as one drew back his arm and hurled a fist-sized rock through one of the lower-floor windows, quickly followed by several more missiles from his fellow protestors. Within seconds, broken glass was raining down onto the sidewalk, and people inside began to flee and take cover.

No one seemed to take much notice. Most locals simply walked on by, their heads down and eyes averted, not wanting to get involved. Unrest was a fact of life around here.

Drake had no desire to get caught up in a riot and drove on by just as the protestors started to break up and disperse, making a quick escape before local police arrived. Hit and run. They'd probably reform later in a different part of the city to target other buildings.

Another five minutes brought Drake to his destination: a small, old-fashioned sandstone building that seemed to specialize in spices and exotic seasonings. Bags and jars of brightly coloured powders, herbs, plants and dried fruits lined the grimy window, crammed into every possible space so that the shop's interior was almost obscured from view.

Parking up, Drake got out and stood there for a few seconds, tuning into his surroundings. This was a quieter part of town, off the main drags and away from the tourist hotspots, so there was little traffic. He did catch a couple of old guys looking his way as they shuffled along the opposite side of the street, both sporting threadbare suits and respectable beer guts, but their interest appeared fleeting at best. Off in the distance he heard the faint wail of police sirens, probably responding to the attack on the government building.

Crossing the street, he made for the shop and slipped cautiously inside.

The first thing to hit him was the smell: what seemed like hundreds of different herbs and spices assailed his senses, from the fragrant and aromatic to the rich and earthy, to the fiery and hot, and every possible variation in between. It was a combination of scents that he could only describe as *absolute*.

The place was long in proportion to its width, extending back some distance from the entrance and so filled with stock that he couldn't quite tell where the shop ended. His difficulty was compounded by the fact the place was poorly lit with sparse electric lights. A couple of ceiling fans turned sluggishly overhead, the tired hum of their motors virtually the only sound to be heard in the warm, oppressively odorous interior.

The proprietor was seated behind a small counter to the right of the doorway. There was no cash register that Drake could see, just a set of old-fashioned brass measuring scales and various weights stacked up beside it.

A sombre-looking man in his late sixties with a pockmarked and deeply lined face, he was watching Drake, wisps of smoke from his cigarette curling lazily around his face. He sported a poorly trimmed beard, a dark suit jacket that had seen better days and a red *chechia*, the Tunisian equivalent of the popular fez hat but without the tassel.

'Looking for something, friend?' he asked in Arabic.

Drake nodded. 'Jamal sent me here. He said you had a package waiting for me.'

The man didn't react to this right away. Instead he lifted the hand-rolled cigarette to his lips and took a slow, thoughtful drag. Drake could hear the faint, hot rustle as the tobacco inside ignited.

'Jamal sent you, did he?'

'That's right. He said I should trust no other merchant in Tunis.'

Another thoughtful silence.

'All right,' he grunted at last, rising from behind the counter. Closing and bolting the front door, he turned to Drake. 'Come with me.'

Drake followed as the man led him through the shop with slow but sure strides, the smell of spice growing more intense with each step.

Drake tensed as a police car hurtled by outside, perhaps just one street away, its siren wailing stridently. The shop owner too had paused, only resuming his walk when the siren had faded into the distance.

'Trouble?' Drake asked.

The old man shrugged. 'People are always angry about something these days. The taxes, the police, the price of bread... I keep to myself and don't go out looking for trouble.'

Drake pressed onwards, finding himself facing a small doorway at the rear of the shop. He couldn't imagine this place needed much storage space since there was plainly enough stock to last for years.

The shop owner swung the door open, revealing a small room beyond. A bed stood in one corner: a simple metal-framed construction, complete with thin, threadbare mattress. A chipped sink and basic shower unit were positioned near this, while on the opposite side of the room was a small gas cooking stove, along with various plates, dishes and pieces of cutlery. Apparently this man's shop was also his home.

The shop owner bent over and dragged a large, heavy canvas holdall out from beneath the bed. The clink of metal inside gave Drake some idea of its contents.

'Everything is inside, it has not been touched. Take as long as you need,' the man said, backing away and giving Drake some space. 'No one will disturb you.'

'The man who gave you this,' Drake began. 'What did he look like?'

The old man offered a dry smile, exposing a mouth that was several teeth shy of a full set. 'That is one question I can't answer.'

Standing so close, Drake noticed that the man's eyes had a dull, faded, hazy look about them, like clothes that had been washed too many times. Cataracts or some other degenerative condition, he couldn't say.

'Give me a few minutes to check it over,' he said, deciding to change the subject.

The door closed behind him, leaving him alone in the relatively cool darkness. Kneeling down, Drake unzipped the holdall and pulled the top open, revealing the contents. Cold, black and lethal, exactly what he needed for the task ahead.

He smiled faintly. His contact had come through for him indeed, supplying everything he'd requested for this mission. Now it was time to make use of his new-found tools.

Chapter 55

'Luiz says we should be on the ground within 30 minutes,' Rojas reported, closing the cockpit door. He gave Anya a smirk. 'He also says you're a heartless bitch who doesn't appreciate an honest man's attention.'

'Right on both counts,' Anya agreed without much concern. Her mind was already on other matters, namely their imminent arrival in Tunisia and what they would do once they were on the ground.

The team had brought their weapons and tactical gear with them since it would be impractical to source new ones from local dealers. Naturally arriving at Tunis International with its security checks and customs officials was a big no-no.

Fortunately their intrepid pilot – in between sponging coffee out of his trousers and cursing Anya's name – had found them a solution in the form of Borj El Amri airport, a small airfield about 15 miles south-west of the capital that dated back to the Second World War. The place was now only used part time as a training field and had no dedicated ground staff, but it did at least have an intact asphalt runway that could – barely – accommodate their Gulfstream.

A fake report of engine trouble would be enough to get them permission to conduct an emergency landing there, and hopefully buy time for the passengers to hurriedly disembark before local police showed up. That was the plan, at least.

Anya turned her attention to Alex and Frost, who lately had begun to merge into one entity in her mind. Their domain was information gathering, and though each seemed to have particular strengths and weaknesses, collectively they represented a formidable if reluctant combination of intellects.

'Any leads on Ryan's next target?'

Alex's face made it clear the news wasn't good. 'Not yet. I've tried searching for any companies that might have a connection to Unity or Powell, but nothing so far. That being said, there's a fuck-tonne of US-affiliated companies in Tunisia, and Unity covered their tracks pretty well last time. It's possible we've missed some connection.'

'Thought you never missed anything, Alex?' Dietrich taunted.

Alex looked at him and held out his laptop. 'If you think you can do better...'

Anya nodded her acceptance of his disheartening report. It had been a forlorn hope, but there was always a chance his online forays might have yielded something.

'Sorry to add to the bad news parade, but shit's going down in Tunisia,' Frost added.

Mitchell eyed the young woman. 'Define "shit"?'

'Reports of civil unrest in most major cities, especially Tunis. Strikes, protests, riots – it's been growing for the past few months, ever since all that evidence of government corruption was leaked.'

It was still unknown where that plethora of classified documents had come from, but most of the major news outlets had received it within hours of each other. The results had been incendiary to say the least, spreading like wildfire across message boards and social media.

'How bad is it?' Mitchell asked.

'Bad. Police and military are cracking down hard, but it's only making things worse. The State Department's already issued a no-travel warning, and the word is the Tunisian government's close to declaring a state of emergency.' She looked up from her laptop. 'Apparently the president's not a popular guy these days.'

'Fucking dictators never are,' Dietrich sniffed.

Anya cocked an eyebrow. She might not have phrased it so colourfully, but neither did she disagree. President Ben Ali had taken power in a bloodless coup back in 1987 and had remained in office ever since, winning a string of landslide election victories that were either rigged, falsified or entirely uncontested.

Ben Ali had maintained his iron grip through a combination of heavy media censorship, a formidable secret police force and outright assassination of opposition leaders. But unlike his temperamental and antagonistic neighbour in Libya, he'd maintained a staunchly pro-Western foreign policy, which had in turn stimulated foreign investment and tourism. The result was an odd dichotomy. Tunisia had developed into one of the most economically advanced but politically repressive countries in the Arab world, with a growing tide of public discontent threatening to boil over into full-blown revolution.

'Fuck him,' Frost decided. 'He's somebody else's problem. The point is, we need to watch our asses on the ground. Police are everywhere and tensions are high. Tunisia's a fucking powder keg, and we really don't want to be around when it explodes.'

Dietrich leaned forward, scrutinising her curiously. 'We're a group of rogue operatives wanted for treason, mounting an unsanctioned mission into a foreign country to find a wanted terrorist. At what point would we *not* watch our asses?'

She opened her mouth to respond, but Anya held up a hand to stop her.

'We understand, Keira,' she said evenly. 'And we appreciate the warning.'

That seemed to pacify Frost.

'There's something else,' Alex added.

Dietrich rolled his eyes. 'More good news?'

'Not really. Rioting and police crackdowns could be the least of our problems,' the young man went on. 'I can't say for sure, but there's a chance Hawkins and Powell might be on their way here too.'

Anya frowned. 'How much of a chance?'

'Well, they have all the resources of the Agency at their disposal. They might have made the same guess I did about Drake leaving the country. It wouldn't take them long to figure out where he was going. They could even be ahead of us.'

A silence, brooding and ominous, descended on the group as his news sank in. Each of them was now privately contemplating the very real possibility that they might already be too late, that Hawkins and his team might be waiting to intercept Drake, that their mission might be over before it had even begun.

It was amidst this unhappy silence that Anya's cell phone started to ring. Not the burner phone that she'd recovered from the safe house, but her own personal cell. And she had a feeling she knew who was calling.

She retreated to the rear of the cabin to gain a measure of privacy. 'I'm here.'

'I might have a lead for you,' Dan Franklin announced from a Washington DC parking garage. She could hear his voice echoing in the cavernous space, mingling with the more distant drone of traffic outside.

Drake had supplied her with Franklin's emergency contact details in the event Anya ever needed to reach out to his old comrade. She'd never had occasion to do so until now.

Having met him only once, she remained wary of Franklin and unsure of his motivations. He didn't strike her as an overtly deceitful man, but neither did it mean he was free of Cain's insidious influence. In her opinion, he was a liability they could do without. But in this case, desperation had driven her to take the risk.

'I don't have much time,' Franklin continued. 'You ready for this?'

'Go on.'

'Wasn't easy, but I ran a search of all active Agency personnel embedded in Tunisia, and cross-referenced it with deployments to Afghanistan around the time Ryan and I served there. We got one hit back – Elijah Tenbrook.'

Anya's pulse quickened. Her hunch just might have been proven correct. Drake's target wasn't part of Powell's murky business empire – he was in all likelihood part of the Agency. If so, it was proof that the two entities were very much linked.

'Who is he?'

'Officially he's with the State Department, part of the US diplomatic mission in Tunisia, but he's one of ours. A field operative with Special Activities Division.'

That made sense. Embassies had been fronts for spying operations since the very concept had been invented, and virtually every US diplomatic mission had a CIA contingent.

'He used to be a liaison officer with military intelligence in Afghanistan, assigned to a joint CIA-Special Forces group. I remember the guy – real slippery son of a bitch. It's a safe bet Ryan remembers him too.'

The pieces were coming together now. Whatever mission Drake was undertaking and whatever his final objective might be, it all somehow tied back to his experiences in Afghanistan seven years earlier.

Up in the cockpit Luiz Santiago crumpled up the packet of potato chips that served as his breakfast, then keyed his radio to communicate with the ground controllers at Tunis International.

'Delta Six-Six-Two, contact approach.'

'Copy, Six-Six-Two,' came the smooth and efficient – if slightly bored – voice of the air traffic controller. 'Turn right on zero-eight-zero, descend to five thousand and wait for approach clearance.'

'Negative, tower. Six-Six-Two has loss of oil pressure in starboard engine,' he said, injecting the right amount of urgency into his voice. 'I have to shut it down.'

'Understood, Six-Six-Two.' His tone had gone up in tempo. 'Declaring an emergency. You're cleared for immediate approach.'

'Can't maintain altitude on one engine, tower. Request alternate landing site.'

Santiago could hear voices in the background, muffled and urgent. 'Stand by, Six-Six-Two.'

'I see a runway on my starboard side, five or six miles away.'

'Understood, Six-Six-Two. That is Borj El Amri airport. Your approach vector should be clear. Can you make it that far?'

'I'll find out, I suppose. Turning right onto heading... one-zero-five,' he replied, reaching out and adjusting the autopilot's course. 'Descending to five thousand for approach.'

'Understood, Six-Six-Two. Good luck.'

'Thanks, tower.' Clicking the radio off, he hit the internal intercom to speak with the passengers in the main cabin. 'We're starting our descent. Get strapped in, this might be a bumpy one.'

Anya stood with the phone pressed to her ear, ignoring the pilot's warnings. 'How much do you have on this man Tenbrook?'

'Everything. Photograph, location, cell phone tracker. We've got the guy nailed.'

Anya closed her eyes as the deck beneath her took on a noticeable slope. They were descending, every second bringing them closer to Drake. She could only hope they weren't too late.

'Send everything you have to me now.'

'Already have. It should be in your inbox.' He sighed. 'Wish I could be there with you guys.'

'No you don't. Even I don't want to be here,' Anya admitted, well aware of how dangerous Drake might be if he was unwilling to surrender. Franklin didn't dispute that. 'Oh, and Franklin?'

'Yeah?'

'For what it's worth... thanks.'

Silence for a time. 'Just find him. Good luck.'

Chapter 56

Emerging from the air-conditioned sanctuary of the central staff building, Elijah Tenbrook slipped on his sunglasses and strode towards the waiting SUV. The witheringly hot afternoon sun beat down and the dusty breeze whipped at his thinning hair.

He was dressed in a simple light-grey suit and open-collared shirt, a marked contrast to the protective operatives who would be accompanying him on today's mission. They weren't part of the Marine Corps detail attached to the embassy security staff. All six of them were private contractors, formerly employed by Horizon Defense Solutions. Their former company, once one of the world's leading private military contractors, had been shut down three years ago following the murder of its CEO and allegations of collusion with Afghan insurgents.

It had been a shit-storm indeed, with an inevitable public outcry and strident headlines calling for congressional hearings. But like all shit-storms it had passed, fickle public interest had shifted to fresh scandals and with it, the politicians' appetites for dredging up dirty secrets about an increasingly unpopular war. Horizon meanwhile had been quietly resurrected under new management, its vast pool of operatives and resources appropriated by a group who could make use of them far more prudently.

All six operatives were dressed in dark-blue polo shirts bearing the logo of their new company Nexus, cargo trousers, combat webbing and body armour, and packing M4 carbine assault rifles. Tenbrook knew the difference between wannabe mercenaries out to make a name for themselves and experienced operators who wouldn't cut and run at the first sign of trouble. These guys were the latter – serious players, each and every one.

'I want situation reports from all our humint sources by the time I get back,' he instructed the staff officer hurrying along beside him. 'And make sure they're on standby to bug out when we give the order. When this thing goes south, it's going to happen fast. We need to be ahead of it.'

'We're on it, sir,' the young man replied, squinting in the harsh sunlight.

'Where are we on data backup?'

'Almost finished. There's been a lot of State Department traffic all day, but we're sending the last of the data packets as soon as we get the satellite bandwidth.'

Tenbrook nodded. 'Make sure it gets done no matter what – I don't want any intel lost if we have to pull out. They give you any shit, tell them it's on me.'

'I will, sir,' the staff officer promised, though there was an uncertainty in his voice. These kinds of diplomatic dick-waving contests were just fine for established case officers with plenty of political clout to back them up, but a daunting prospect for someone at his level.

He nodded towards the city beyond the perimeter wall, where sporadic gunfire had been exchanged less than an hour ago, accompanied by a thick plume of black smoke that had drifted over the rooftops. Sirens were audible even now.

'You sure you want to be going out there?'

Pulling the SUV door open, Tenbrook looked at him. 'They're not paying us to play it safe, son. Better learn that fast if you want to work under me.' With that, he waved at the Nexus operatives gathered around. 'Let's go, boys!'

Two operatives accompanied him, while the remainder went in the lead SUV. In the event they were ambushed outside the compound, the men in that vehicle would provide cover fire while Tenbrook was safely evacuated. Both cars were heavily armoured and fitted with the latest countermeasures, making them tough nuts to crack with anything less than anti-tank rockets.

They headed for the main gate with its reinforced block houses and concrete anti car-bomb chicanes. The US embassy in Tunis was part office complex and part fortified military compound. Surrounded on all sides by a 12-feet-high perimeter wall topped with razor wire and monitored with CCTV cameras, the whole facility was heavily secured against potential insurgent attacks. The US had endured enough diplomatic hostage crises over the years, and was taking no further chances.

Worse, a deadly explosion in their embassy in Islamabad earlier in the year meant that new arrivals were subject to the strictest security checks. Tenbrook's more 'sensitive' meetings now had to be conducted off site, in safe houses around the city. Not that many places in Tunis were safe these days.

A pain in the ass, but one that he could live with. Especially now they were so close to their goal. The seeds of dissent and revolution carefully sown over the past 12 months were soon to bear fruit, and all his hard work would be worth it.

He allowed that satisfying thought to linger as the two-vehicle convoy turned onto the main drag, heading west.

Chapter 57

Santiago, whatever his womanising tendencies, proved to be a competent pilot, guiding them in towards the single-runway airfield on a smooth and even trajectory.

'Twenty seconds!' he called out, increasing flaps to slow their airspeed. The runway might have been paved, but it was designed for light aircraft rather than executive jets.

In the main cabin, Anya and the others sat tense and ready, hands clasping the release latches of their seat belts. They would have to move fast.

Anya glanced out of her window. Beyond the modest aerodrome complex lay a flat, rural landscape of dusty open ground and scrubland, interspersed with irrigated farmland: little patches of stark, vibrant green amidst the dun-yellow world of sand and rock. There were no large towns within sight, though she did spot small clusters of buildings further off, probably agricultural.

'Ten seconds!'

The aircraft banked slightly to the left as Santiago adjusted their heading. Beneath the starboard wing, asphalt rushed by impossibly fast, barely ten feet from the projecting landing gear. Five feet.

Two feet.

Anya braced herself against the sudden jolt as they touched down hard. A second later, a growing roar filled her ears as Santiago applied the brakes and full reverse thrust on both engines to slow their ground speed.

She was moving as soon as they touched down, unstrapping herself, snatching up her kit bag and hurrying towards the forward hatch. The others followed her example. Rojas beat her to it, being closer to the door, and grasped the hatch release mechanism.

'We're ready, Luiz!' he called out.

According to the satellite maps Frost had been able to dig up, the taxiway swung off to the right just as they approached the end of the runway, allowing incoming aircraft to head towards the main terminal, such as it was. That was where they would bail. They couldn't stop the jet entirely as it could arouse suspicion.

'Almost there,' Santiago replied. 'Pop the hatch!'

Normally the main hatch couldn't be opened unless the aircraft had come to a stop, but the emergency override switch took care of that. Pulling the red release handle, Rojas lifted it all the way up until it locked into place and the door suddenly swung downwards, the steps automatically extending.

The cabin was engulfed in a storm of noise and wind, the high-pitched whine of the jet engines deafeningly loud. Looking over Rojas' shoulder, Anya could see the rough blacktop of the runway sliding by just below the end of the stairs, still moving at a decent pace.

She leaned in close to her companion and shouted in his ear. 'Drop and roll once you land, Cesar,' she advised. 'Unless you want to end up inside the engine.'

He gave a dry smile. 'All this concern just for me. I knew you cared, after all.'

Anya went to reply but Rojas was already gone, clambering down the steps and pausing at the bottom to cross himself before leaping onto the runway below. She did notice that he followed her advice, rolling tightly to avoid being clipped by the low-slung wings.

Anya followed him down the steps, gripping the guard rails as they flexed slightly under her weight. She could feel rather than hear someone behind her, and snatched a look back at Mitchell. The woman's face was tight with concentration, and it was clear she was in no mood for last-minute words of encouragement.

Reaching the bottom step, Anya leapt without hesitation. It had always been that way for her when it came to jumping out of planes, whether at ten feet or ten thousand. The longer you waited, the more reasons you'd find not to do it.

She landed gracefully, bending her knees and dropping into a roll to bleed off momentum. The pack slung over her shoulders was an uncomfortable burden, but one that she was quite accustomed to.

Coming to a skidding halt with nothing worse than grazed elbows, Anya turned her face away from the hot exhaust gases still blasting from the engine outlets. The smell of fumes and burned rubber was strong and acrid.

As soon as she could look, she turned her attention back to the hatch, eager to see how the rest of her comrades fared. Mitchell had been right behind her, coming down at an awkward angle and landing in an uncomfortable sprawl, but nonetheless managed to pick herself up. Anya saw her lips moving and guessed she was muttering a curse.

Dietrich came next, stepping off the end of the stairs as if the Gulfstream weren't even moving. He didn't bother to drop, as if such things were unworthy of him, but simply ducked his head as the wings passed overhead.

Alex didn't hesitate to make his jump and made a surprisingly decent job of the landing, having watched what the others did. Frost meanwhile brought up the rear, rocking back and forward a couple of times, before finally throwing herself off the end.

She didn't roll to cushion her fall and instead landed flat on all fours like a cat, clutching at the rough asphalt. It seemed an oddly amateurish technique for someone well trained in parachute landings, but that was her concern.

Anya sprinted for the southern perimeter fence just as the jet swung north towards the terminal buildings. Reaching for the holster at her hip, Anya drew her M1911 and flicked the safety off as she ran, keeping low, the heavy pack bouncing and jolting across her shoulders. Keep low, move fast, eyes open – a sound principle to operate under, no matter the situation.

The coarse grass at the edge of the runway began to give way to a line of dry scrub about three or four feet tall that gradually thickened as it approached the chain-link perimeter fence. It wasn't much in the way of cover, but it would serve as a temporary rally point.

Kneeling in the dusty ground right at the base of the fence, Anya waited for the others to join her. The searing heat seemed to steal the very air from her lungs, and it was clear as her companions closed in that they felt much the same.

'Is everyone all right?' she asked, paying particular attention to Mitchell.

'Lovely. I want to do it again,' Alex retorted.

Dietrich looked at Frost, having witnessed her unconventional landing. 'What the fuck was that, Frost? Were you taking a shit when they taught you to jump?'

Frost gave him the finger. 'All our tech gear's in my pack, asshole,' she reminded him. 'Want me to land on it and break everything?'

That was enough to silence even Dietrich. Anya glanced up at the steel fence which now barred their way. It was easily ten feet high and topped with wire to deter intruders.

'Dietrich, we need a way through,' she said quickly.

'On it,' he replied as he pulled a set of bolt cutters out of his pack and went to work. In short order he'd snipped an inverted T out of the links, slithered through and held it open while the others followed behind him.

To their relief, a ditch of some kind ran parallel to the perimeter fence, about three feet deep and twice as wide, choked with rocks, brittle-looking weeds and bits of windblown trash that had found their way in over the years. It was likely a remnant of the construction process when this airfield had been laid down. Either way, it provided some decent cover.

'Which way now?' Alex asked, wiping a dusty hand across his brow. 'We're in the middle of—'

'Shh!' Anya hissed, straining to listen. The sound of sirens coming from the north-east, the direction of the capital.

'Police?' Mitchell queried.

Anya shook her head. 'Fire trucks, from the main airport probably. The police won't be far behind, though.'

'Then it's time we were somewhere else,' Frost suggested.

Anya nodded. 'Stay low and follow me.'

They struck out southwards, cutting through an irrigation field, the long wheat stalks helping to mask their progress. It also cut down visibility to almost zero, forcing the group to move in single file with Anya leading the way.

After perhaps half a mile the wheat finally parted, revealing a road running between their field and another identical plantation. The road was unpaved, and little more than a dirt embankment bulldozed into place, but it was obvious from the fresh tyre marks that it was well used.

Most of them knew what was to happen next, and by unspoken agreement ditched their packs at the base of the embankment while they checked weapons.

Crouching down, Anya fished her cell phone out of her pocket and dialled Franklin's number. It was answered on the first ring. 'Go,' he said brusquely.

'We're on the ground, about ten miles outside the city,' she reported. 'Do you have a location on Tenbrook?'

'He's on the move, just left the embassy complex,' Franklin reported. 'Heading west into the city centre.'

'Send the tracking data to Frost. We should be up and running soon.'

'Copy that.'

'Vehicle inbound!' Mitchell called out, having assumed a lookout position at the edge of the road. Slithering back down the embankment, she hurried over to join the others.

'I'll contact you again when we have him.'

'Understood. Good hunting.'

Closing down the phone, Anya looked at Mitchell. 'What did you see?'

'Pickup truck, maybe half a klick away. Moving pretty slow.'

That was as good a target as any, Anya decided. 'We go for it. Get ready.'

Dietrich switched to the team's technical specialist. 'Frost, come here!'

She crept over, irritated at being summoned. 'What?'

'We need bait.'

'So?'

'Want me to draw you a picture? You're a young woman. More or less,' he acknowledged grudgingly. 'They'll be more likely to stop for you.'

Frost looked at the others as if expecting them to refute this assertion. None did however. Further down the road, the sound of an approaching vehicle was now clearly audible.

Sensing he'd made his point, Dietrich nodded towards the road. 'Try to look small and pathetic. Shouldn't be too hard for you.'

Frost glowered at him but, with time running out, seemed to see the truth in his words.

'When this is over, you and I are gonna have a talk about mutual respect,' she promised, shoving her handgun down the back of her trousers.

Scrambling up the short embankment into the centre of the road, she reached for the neck of her T-shirt and, with a forceful yank, opened a wide tear down one shoulder. A couple of handfuls of dirt rubbed into her clothes and skin completed the look of someone who had narrowly escaped an attack.

Suitably dishevelled, she began walking towards the source of the noise. The others meanwhile settled for concealing themselves amongst the swaying wheat stalks.

It didn't take long for the vehicle to trundle into view, or for them to realize why it was moving so slowly. An old Toyota pickup truck that might once have been black, but years of sun and windblown grit had faded to a dull, washed-out grey. Its entire flatbed was taken up with boxes of fruit and vegetable produce, mostly tomatoes and citrus fruits by the look of it. The sheer weight of it was causing the vehicle to ride low on its rear axles.

Frost launched into the helpless victim routine with gusto. 'Help!' she called out, waving her arms and staggering towards the truck. 'Please help!'

The pair of young men in the cab spotted her and exchanged urgent words, but nonetheless the truck slowed its meandering progress and came to a halt about ten feet from her. The driver's door opened and a tall, gangly kid of no more than 16 leapt out, all broad shoulders and bony limbs and the fluffy beginnings of facial hair.

He was speaking to her in Arabic. She didn't understand the language, but he was loud and didn't seem altogether friendly. His passenger had also stepped out to join them, jabbing an accusing finger at Frost and adding his voice to the unproductive conversation.

'Please, you've got to help me!' she said, allowing her voice to break with emotion. 'My boyfriend and I were attacked, I... I don't know what happened to him. They took him!'

The wind whipped at her ripped T-shirt, exposing the bra underneath. As his adolescent gaze inevitably strayed, Frost judged that now was the perfect time to make her move.

Reaching behind her back, she drew her automatic and turned it on him. One quick and efficient motion, and it was done. It almost seemed too easy.

Most people take a second or two to react to such an unexpected threat, but this guy was clearly at the slower end of the spectrum. Frost watched the varying play of emotions as his brain slowly transitioned from confusion to anger, then to frightened surprise and finally to dumb, paralysing shock.

'Get your hands up, son,' she ordered, advancing quickly towards him. 'Don't be dumber than you look. Fuck with me, and I *will* put you down.'

Not much chance of that. The kid looked like he was about to shit his pants.

His friend however was a little more switched on, and tried to make a grab for the hunting rifle hanging from the rear window of the cab. He'd barely taken his first step when the muted thud of a silenced gunshot rang out. He flinched as a round slammed into the metal bodywork barely a foot away from him.

'Bad idea, my friend,' Rojas warned him, striding up the embankment with his weapon up and ready. 'The next one won't be a warning shot.'

Neither of these guys were going to put up a fight, Frost knew. They were just kids, dumb farmhands making a daily run into town to deliver their produce.

'Okay, boys. Get yourselves down to the bottom of that slope,' she said, gesturing with the barrel of her gun.

They might not have understood the words, but they got the message and scrambled down the embankment while the rest of the group closed on the vehicle.

'We need to lighten the load,' Mitchell remarked, surveying the boxes filling the truck's bed. No way were they getting anywhere like this.

Dietrich was apparently of like mind. Unhitching the tailgate, he clambered up into the flatbed. Rojas followed suit, and together they shoved and manhandled the crates until they toppled off the end, clattering and smashing onto the road.

The youth who had tried to grab the rifle shouted out in protest, but was quickly silenced by an elbow to the ribs from his companion.

Frost nodded in approval. 'Maybe you're smarter than I thought. Now... fuck off.' When they frowned at her, she gestured into the field behind them. 'Go on. Run, dumbasses!'

In the end it took a couple of rounds fired into the ground at their feet to get them moving. And move they did, quickly disappearing into the tall wheat stalks. If they had any sense they'd keep running until they ran out of energy.

As the last of their packs were hoisted into the truck's flatbed, Frost holstered her weapon and headed for the driver's door.

'Forget it,' Dietrich warned her. 'You can't drive here.'

'Watch me,' she retorted. She'd stack her driving skills against Dietrich's any day.

Dietrich however placed his considerable mass between her and the door. 'Sorry *mädchen*. This is a Muslim country, no women drivers. You'll draw attention to us.'

Frost chewed her lip. Her annoyance was made worse because she could tell how much he was enjoying this.

'He's right, Frost,' Anya said, busy wrapping a long piece of cloth around her head. It was a *safseri*, a traditional veil worn by Tunisian women to cover the hair and face. It would help disguise the team's ethnicity. 'Anyway, we need you to track Tenbrook's cell phone.'

Stepping up into the cab, Dietrich slammed the door shut and indicated the truck's rear bed with his thumb.

'Get in before I leave you behind,' he said, then glanced down at Frost's ripped, dirt-stained T-shirt. 'And cover up, would you? You'll give us a bad reputation.'

Frost glared at him for a second or two, her expression saying it all. *Laugh it up, asshole. There will come a time when you need my help. And I might not be there for you.*

She turned away, marched around to the rear of the vehicle and hoisted herself up, ignoring Rojas' outstretched hand. The others said nothing, sensing her smouldering mood.

'Give me the goddamn laptop,' she snapped, yanking it out of Alex's hands.

'We don't have much time. Let's go!' Anya called out, slapping the side of the cab.

'*Jawohl,*' Dietrich mumbled. Spotting a cheap and slightly battered pair of sunglasses perched on the dashboard, he slipped them on, then stamped on the gas. The Toyota accelerated away from the scene, leaving a pile of broken crates and a cloud of dust in its wake.

Chapter 58

Tamim bazaar was much like the dozens of other street markets dotted around Tunis. Occupying several streets and courtyards, it was packed with stalls and shops of all shapes and sizes, their owners eagerly touting everything from handmade rugs to food, spices, clothing, jewellery, watches and even pirated DVDs. Customers bustled from stall to stall, searching for bargains and bunching up at choke points, forming human traffic jams that even the most belligerent shoppers struggled to break through.

It was through this organized chaos that Tenbrook strode confidently, flanked by three Nexus security operatives. They'd left their assault rifles behind in the vehicles, knowing that such an overt display of force would attract unwanted attention, each man armed with compact MP7 submachine guns concealed inside their jackets. If the shit hit the fan, they could lay down close to 1,000 rounds per minute.

Seeing a wealthy-looking customer approaching, one clothing stall owner sparked up, launching into an enthusiastic sales pitch. He was an old man, well into his seventies, his face sagging and creased like old leather.

Tenbrook ignored him, and when he tried to step forward, one of the operatives blocked his path. 'Fuck off, pal,' he growled.

Tenbrook didn't even break stride. He had other matters on his mind. They had passed two big groups of protesters on the drive here, one of which was violently clashing with local police and military units trying to disperse them. He had watched petrol bombs and rocks being hurled at riot shields with a sense of mounting excitement, knowing that much of this was down to him.

After about 100 yards the bazaar opened out into a large square packed with narrow and crowded streets, and the smell of cooking meats, diesel fumes and tobacco smoke.

A large two-storey building occupied the eastern corner of the square – squat, old and weathered, with a flat roof supporting a huge, ancient satellite dish. At ground level, Tenbrook spotted a sign, written in both Arabic and English, announcing that this place was a tea house.

There were only a couple of windows out front, and they were shielded by wrought iron bars for security. Heavy wooden shutters had been pulled closed, blocking his view of the interior. The front door was also shut, though a quick check of the handle told him it was unlocked.

Naturally one of his security team went first, hand inside his jacket ready to draw if there was trouble waiting. When the second operative gave him a nod, Tenbrook followed him inside.

The room was low-ceilinged and dimly lit, with a dozen old tables and chairs dotted around, their wood stained almost black with decades of spilled drinks and cigarette smoke. The long serving bar along the opposite wall was unmanned. The smell of dried tea leaves and tobacco was pervasive; probably soaked into the very fabric of the place.

'Good of you to join us, my friend,' a voice announced.

His contact was seated at one of the larger tables, a steaming cup of tea in front of him. In his mid-forties but still lean and trim, he was dressed in a loose casual shirt and grey trousers, his dark curling hair cropped short, his beard just starting to show flecks of grey. He was smiling, but it wasn't the smile of a man greeting an old friend. It was cold, professional.

Tenbrook reciprocated. 'For you, Karim, it's always a pleasure,' he lied.

'Come, sit with me,' the Tunisian said, beckoning Tenbrook over. 'What do you have for me?'

Tenbrook helped himself to a chair, then reached into his jacket, lifting out a USB flash drive and placing it on the table just out of Karim's reach.

'This right here is the mother lode, Karim,' he said. 'Government budgets for the past year, classified emails between ministers, orders to discredit and assassinate political rivals, falsified testimonies, even an itemized list of the President's personal expenditures. You just wouldn't believe some of the shit his wife spends money on.'

Karim's eyes lit up. The information contained in that flash drive – if proven legitimate – could spark the revolution he'd been waiting a lifetime for. The government had outlawed TV shows, newspapers and publications critical of the regime, but even they couldn't control the flow of information over the internet.

As a prominent writer and reporter forced into digital exile, Karim had spent much of his life trying to expose the regime's excesses and failures. But without proof he could do little more than criticize and berate them. And that was precisely why Tenbrook had approached him.

You didn't need to drop bombs or send in troops to overthrow men like President Ben Ali – there was more than enough dirt in their own sordid history to do it for you. All you had to do was make sure it found its way to the right people. Information had become the newest weapon of war, the internet its most fiercely contested battlefield.

The men Tenbrook represented knew how to manipulate the ebb and flow of online opinion, how to disseminate the stories and beliefs they wished to espouse, and how to bury the inconvenient truths that could harm their cause. Whoever controlled information controlled public opinion, and ultimately the politicians who depended on them for votes.

After all, they'd been doing it to their own people for decades.

'This flash drive here contains enough information to change the course of history for your country. Enough dirt to bury Ben Ali and his entire government for all time.' He reached out and tapped the device with his finger. 'Not many men get to hold history in the palm of their hand, but right here, right now, we have that chance. And I'm offering it to you.'

–

Cesar Rojas had backed up against a coarse sandstone wall at the edge of the square, scanning the thronging crowd for any sign of either Tenbrook or Drake. It was no easy task, despite his keen eyesight and excellent memory for faces. The marketplace all around him was still busy with evening trade and stretched over a large area. It would be all too easy to miss someone amidst the sea of faces, which was probably why Tenbrook had chosen it as the meeting location in the first place.

His radio earpiece buzzed as a transmission came in. Half a second later, Anya's voice was relayed, sounding as if it were somehow inside his head. Not a comforting thought, on reflection.

'Rojas, what's your sitrep?'

Of all the members of their group, Rojas was the only one Drake had never encountered and so wouldn't recognize. He'd therefore been picked to recon the area while the others stayed in their stolen pickup truck about a block away.

'I'm at the south-west corner of the square,' he said quietly. 'No sign of him yet.'

Frost's voice piped up over the secure comms net. 'I've tracked Tenbrook's cell phone to a structure about 50 yards north of your position. It's big, probably two storeys.'

Rojas turned towards it. 'I see it. The sign says it's a tea house.'

'You got a visual inside?'

'No. The windows are shuttered.' He considered it for a few seconds before making his decision. 'I'm going in for a closer look.'

'Negative,' Anya said emphatically. 'Hold your position. You might tip them off.'

'Relax, Maras. You'll live longer,' Rojas replied as he pushed himself away from the wall and slipped easily through the passing crowds. He hadn't survived as an assassin for ten years by being clumsy or careless.

'*You* might not,' she warned.

He smirked. 'We'll see.'

–

Tenbrook could see the excitement written on his contact's face. Much as he wanted to take it, Karim knew better than to simply reach out for the flash drive. It was never going to be that easy. There was always a price for such information.

'I presume you want something in return?'

249

Tenbrook smiled. 'The men I represent don't deal in charity, I'm afraid. They invested a great deal of money and resources to get this information. It's an investment they expect to pay off.'

'I have no money to give you.'

Tenbrook actually laughed out loud. As if his employers needed handouts from shithole countries like this. 'It's not money they're looking for. We're interested in the future, Karim.'

'Whose future?'

'Come on, buddy. You're so preoccupied with bringing down Ben Ali's regime that you've never stopped to consider what will replace it?'

Karim's eyes narrowed. 'You obviously have.'

'Let's just say the only thing worse than a bad leader is no leader at all. We learned that from our old buddy Saddam. Chaos and anarchy does nothing but breed the next generation of terrorists, and that's not what we want for your country.'

'So what *do* you want?' Karim pressed him.

'We want a stable, democratic government running the show in Tunisia.'

Karim was a seasoned journalist, and clearly no stranger to bullshit. 'You mean a puppet regime?'

He shrugged. 'Think of it as… a government whose interests align with our own. They'd have aid, economic investment, education, healthcare, jobs for your people. Tunisia would become a land of freedom and opportunity, an example for other countries to follow. Not a bad deal in my book.' The legs of his old chair creaked ominously beneath his weight. 'And you, Karim. You'd have your place in history as the man who helped bring it all about. The fearless journalist who risked his life to expose a quarter of a century of corruption and political repression. Hell, might even be a Nobel Peace Prize nomination if you play your cards right.'

It's a well-worn cliché that every man has his price. The kind of thing people use to excuse all kinds of transgressions and bad compromises. But sitting there in that hot, run-down tea room in the midst of a crowded market, watching the varying emotions playing across his contact's face, the suspicion and hope rising and receding like waves on a beach, Elijah Tenbrook knew that it was also absolutely fucking true.

'You're a smart guy, so you don't need me to tell you that this is a limited-term offer,' he added. 'If you don't want to get with the programme on this one, there are plenty of other guys who will. Be a shame if you missed the boat.'

He couldn't truly say which aspect of the offer had finally hooked him, whether it was the prospect of reviving his country's fortunes and freedoms, albeit under a certain amount of foreign influence, or the possibility of the rewards and accolades that might be heaped upon him for playing his part in the upcoming revolution. Instinct told him it was the former. Karim was a good man, an honourable man who genuinely seemed to care for his people. And his kind were always easy to manipulate.

'What would you have me do?' Karim asked, shoulders slumping a little. A man resigned to accepting the lesser of two evils.

That was the sucker punch, the killer blow, and Tenbrook knew that from this moment on he had Karim in his pocket. It was just as well for him, since it wouldn't be difficult to make him disappear. Tenbrook had organized many such disappearances in his time, and would likely do so again. But perhaps he'd stay his hand on this one.

'When Ben Ali's regime goes down in flames, a new country's going to rise from the ashes, but it won't be an easy or a peaceful process. It never is. There's always going to be ambitious and ruthless assholes looking to step in and fill his shoes, but men like you will make sure the Tunisian people chose the right man for the job.'

He didn't have to say it; Karim knew well enough what was being asked of him. He would become a propaganda mouthpiece for Tenbrook's chosen successor, extolling his virtues and leadership potential while leaking damaging insider information on his rivals. He would become just another weapon in the information war that would rage in the chaos of revolution.

That was all he had ever been, really.

He didn't say anything, didn't even look him in the eye, but Tenbrook saw him nod. It was small, reluctant, almost shameful, but it was there. Karim had given his assent.

'Good to have you on board,' Tenbrook said, sliding the flash drive across the table to him and rising to his feet. He buttoned up his suit jacket and looked at the man still seated across from him, smiling pleasantly. 'We're going to do great things for this country, Karim. Just you wait and see.'

Tenbrook saw Karim's hand reach out and slowly close around the flash drive. Another little compromise, another little victory.

Turning away, Tenbrook strode towards the door, nodding to his three security operatives. 'Let's go, boys. Time's a-wasting.'

Chapter 59

Ascending to a rooftop on the opposite side of the square, Anya ducked between lines of washing until she reached the low brick parapet encircling the roof. She knew it was unwise to venture this close when Drake could be lurking, but she couldn't bring herself to hold back any longer.

She needed to be here, to see it for herself.

She reached into her pocket for a pair of binoculars, scanning the thronging marketplace below. It didn't take long to find the tea house. Sure enough, the windows were barred and shuttered, preventing her from seeing within.

Turning the binoculars downwards into the crowds of civilians, she traced a path back and forth, scanning dozens of faces until she spotted Rojas, slipping discreetly through the merchants and tourists, heading towards the target building. As always, the man was competent but overconfident, too trusting of his own ability to consider that anyone might get the drop on him.

Reaching up, she pressed the little radio transmit button next to her throat, the encrypted device hidden by the headscarf she was wearing.

'Rojas, what's your position?'

He didn't even break stride. 'Approaching the building now. Do you see something?'

'No, but—'

'Then stay off the line, Maras. Let me do my job.'

This situation was stirring a growing sense of unease and anticipation in her. Like a storm brewing, Anya could almost feel the change in the air.

'I don't like this,' Frost said, echoing her sentiments. 'What if we were wrong about this guy? What if he's not the target at all?'

Anya was wondering the very same thing. Had they misjudged Drake's intentions, misunderstood his connection to this man Tenbrook? Had he anticipated their pursuit and led them on a wild-goose chase?

She scanned the rooftops overlooking the busy square. Like her own, many were festooned with laundry and outdated satellite dishes, or cluttered with air vents and chimneys. But one in particular caught her eye, where she spotted a sudden flare of light as the evening sun reflected off highly polished glass.

She turned her binoculars towards it, and spotted a hunched figure near the edge of a roof about 100 yards away. And, cradled in his arms, the long barrel of a rifle trained on the crowds below.

Anya reacted as she'd been trained to act on sighting a sniper – get down and stay down. She held her breath, wondering if she'd been seen. Wondering if she or Rojas might come under fire at any moment.

Reaching up, she hit her radio transmitter again. 'Rojas, abort the approach now. Snipers in the area. Abort now!'

In the square down below, Rojas discreetly altered course, turning away from the target building and pretending to browse a nearby jewellery stall. His face bore an expression of mild interest, though his mind was racing.

'Where?' he asked urgently. He had scoped out the area carefully on arrival, finding nothing out of the ordinary.

'Rooftop, eastern edge of the square.'

Rojas resisted the urge to look up. The only thing an assassin truly feared was being in the crosshairs of another assassin, and he might well have just become that target.

'Is it Drake?'

'Can't tell,' she admitted. 'I only saw him for a moment.'

'Get the fuck out of there, Rojas,' Frost's voice cut in. 'You're too close to this.'

'Not yet.'

'You out of your goddamn mind?'

'If they were after me, I'd be dead already,' he reasoned, hoping it was true. 'Don't lose your nerve.'

'It's your head I'm more concerned with.'

'Your concern for my welfare is touching.'

'I couldn't give a shit about your welfare,' she snapped. 'But if you get yourself killed, we lose Tenbrook *and* Drake. Then we're fucked.'

Spotting movement out of the corner of his eye, he glanced over at the target building just as a man in a grey suit emerged into the evening light, slipping on a pair of sunglasses. He was quickly followed by three men in civilian clothes, though it was clear these men were anything but tourists.

Rojas had only seen Elijah Tenbrook's face in a couple of black-and-white file photographs on Frost's laptop, but he'd made a living out of committing men's faces to memory. You had to when there might be a window of mere seconds to identify your target.

'I see Tenbrook,' he spoke into his radio. 'He just came out of the building along with three bodyguards.'

'Where's he going?' Anya asked. Wary of drawing the sniper's attention, she didn't dare raise her head.

'Heading east, towards your sniper. Stand by.'

He tensed up, knowing that if the sniper was hostile and Tenbrook was his target, then it was going to happen now. It had to happen now. A head-on sight picture moving at walking pace was as close to perfect as anyone could wish for. If Drake intended to take this man out, then now was his time.

'What's happening, Rojas?' Anya demanded.

'Stand by,' he hissed, watching and waiting for the first shot.

Nothing happened. The seconds stretched out, and Tenbrook continued down a smaller cobbled street heading away from the central square, flanked by his three bodyguards. The hustle and bustle of the street market continued uninterrupted. Life went on as normal, like nothing had ever happened.

'Nothing,' he said at last. 'Tenbrook's still heading east. No contact.'

'What the fuck's going on out there?' Frost asked, plainly at a loss.

Rojas had no answers for her, and he wasn't likely to find any standing here looking at cheap jewellery. 'I'm tailing him,' Rojas decided, moving to follow the four-man group. 'Keep a trace on his cell phone.'

'On it. I've got a solid signal.'

'I'm circling around to intercept,' Anya added, her steps echoing in the stairwell she was descending. 'Bring the car around and be ready to move fast.'

'Copy that. We're moving,' Frost confirmed. 'Dietrich, let's go!'

–

Tenbrook was more than happy to climb aboard the second SUV, retreating into its darkened, air-conditioned interior. Away from the smell of food and sweat and shit and Christ knew what else. He'd be glad when his work here was finished and he could leave this goddamn city for good.

But for now, there was still work to be done.

'Let's go, Mike!' he said to the agent up front. 'They ain't paying you by the hour.'

The driver's eyes were hidden behind dark sunglasses, otherwise Tenbrook was quite sure he would have received an irritated glare in the rear mirror. *Let him glare*, he thought.

The two-vehicle convoy pulled away from the market entrance, accelerating out and merging into the flow of traffic. It was a 15-minute drive back to the embassy compound under normal conditions, but the evening rush was slowing things down a little, creating a stop-and-start effect that, combined with the oppressive heat, soon had drivers leaning on their horns.

Tenbrook withdrew one of the cans of Coke stowed in the car's central console and cracked it open. Another man might have kicked back with a beer, but Tenbrook was a strict teetotaller. Only a weak mind craved alcohol, and he most definitely wasn't the owner of a weak mind.

Taking a pull on the Coke, he fished out his cell phone and dialled a new number. This number was unlisted, and known only to a few select individuals. Fortunately he was part of this trusted cadre.

'Yes?'

The voice that greeted him was old, deep and smooth. A voice of wisdom. The voice of a man who understood how the world really worked, because he'd helped to make it that way. It didn't matter that Tenbrook had never met the owner of that voice. He didn't need to, because he understood what that man, and others like him, wanted and worked towards.

At least, those were the notions he flattered himself with.

254

'It's done. He took the bait, just like we knew he would,' Tenbrook reported. 'Everything's on schedule.'

'Well done. You've encountered no problems, I assume?'

He smiled, staring out through the windshield at the lead SUV. 'None at all.'

What Tenbrook hadn't noticed was the truck that pulled alongside the lead vehicle as it moved sluggishly through the heavy traffic. A big old flatbed, its bodywork scarred and dented, now inching slightly ahead of the lead SUV so that its rear bed was roughly level with the smaller vehicle.

The security operative seated in the front passenger seat glanced over at it, more out of habit than any real sense of danger. After all, they'd driven through the local traffic countless times and encountered nothing more dangerous than a minor fender bender when a driver in front had braked suddenly. He had nothing to fear from this battered old thing.

And yet, something about it seemed unusual. A heavy tarpaulin had been draped over the rear bed, secured by a couple of ropes at each corner so that it draped over the sides of the vehicle. But as the breeze rippled through this heavy canvas, it lifted one corner that had worked its way free of the restraining rope, exposing something beneath. Something small, olive green, fixed to the side of the truck.

Something with lettering formed into its plastic casing.

FRONT TOWARDS ENEMY

The world around him seemed to stutter and freeze in that single, horrifying moment.

'Contact! Get us out of here!' he shouted.

Seated in the cab of the truck that had pulled up alongside, Ryan Drake reached for a small metal device resting on the passenger seat with a single plastic-covered button on top. Its official name was the M57 firing device, but Drake, like most infantry soldiers, had always known it by its colloquial term of 'clacker'. Bracing himself, Drake gripped the clacker firmly and pressed down on its trigger.

The driver of the lead SUV had just stamped on the accelerator when the three M18A1 Claymore anti-personnel mines fixed to the side of Drake's truck detonated at almost the same instant, blasting more than two thousand 3.2mm steel ball bearings straight into the side of the vehicle like a trio of enormous shotguns discharging their load at point blank range.

The effect was utterly devastating.

The Claymore was designed more for anti-personnel work than for taking out armoured vehicles, but at such close range the sheer explosive power and number of projectiles was more than enough to defeat the SUV's Kevlar armour scheme. The ball bearings, travelling at close to 4000 feet per second, ripped through armoured doors and windshields, shredded seating, blew open the tyres and of course, decimated the fragile human bodies caught inside the SUV. All four men were killed instantly by this lethal steel rain, literally ripped to pieces by the sheer volume of shrapnel.

The heavy truck was rocked sideways on its axles by the recoil of all three mines detonating at once, but the smaller and lighter SUV fared much worse. The force of the impact hurled it sideways, flipping the mangled and blood-streaked wreck onto its roof as if some giant fist had taken a swipe at it.

Tenbrook and his remaining protective detail could do nothing but stare in shock and disbelief at the destruction and carnage that had suddenly been unleashed in front of them. Each of them had seen battle before and knew all too well that death could come without warning, but this was so sudden, so powerful, so close, that it took them a moment or two to process.

Tenbrook, oddly, found himself transfixed by a little chunk of flesh that had been thrown against the windshield like a bug and was sliding slowly down the glass surface, leaving a tiny crimson trail. He caught himself wondering which man in the lead SUV it had come from.

'Holy shit!' the agent up front called out. 'Alpha team's down!'

That seemed to snap Tenbrook out of his fugue, and he hammered the seat in front of him to get the driver's attention.

'Get us the fuck out of here!' he screamed.

The way ahead was blocked by the mangled wreckage that had once been their lead vehicle, forcing the driver to back up. Throwing the SUV into reverse, he twisted around in his seat. Even as he did so however, the truck that had unleashed such destructive firepower against their men suddenly rumbled backwards, diesel smoke flaring from its top-mounted exhausts, the huge mass of metal coming straight for them.

'Oh, fuck! Look out! Look out!' the operative up front shouted.

The truck's rear fender caught them just as their driver tried to swing the SUV out of the behemoth's path, the truck's greater mass ploughing straight into the front wheel arch with a screaming, rending impact. The wheel buckled right away, the axle and steering bar sheared away by the kinetic force of the impact.

Undaunted, the truck continued on, spinning the SUV around 180 degrees until it slammed into the bigger vehicle's flank. They were now side by side, pinned against one another by twisted wreckage and broken machinery, and facing in opposite directions. Though its engine was still running, the SUV had been effectively crippled by the crash.

–

'Holy shit!' Frost cried out, jolted up from her laptop by the rippling boom of the nearby explosion. 'We've got a contact in the area!'

'I see it,' Rojas confirmed over the radio net, sounding disconcertingly calm given what was unfolding in front of him. 'Tenbrook's convoy is under attack.'

'Jesus. Where did it come from?'

'Can't see much from here, but the lead vehicle has been destroyed.'

'It's him. It's Ryan,' Anya said. She had no doubt, no shock and little surprise. This was simply the confirmation she'd been waiting for.

Dietrich, at the wheel of their 4 x 4, stepped on the gas and forced his way between two slower-moving cars.

'We're one minute out. Hold position and wait for us!'

—

The truck had done its work well, permanently disabling Tenbrook's vehicle. Now it was time to get to the man himself.

Drake leaned out of his window, looking down on the SUV's roof with the long frame of a Barrett M82 anti-materiel rifle cradled in his arms. Bracing the weapon against the door frame, he swung the barrel downwards, sighting roughly where he estimated the driver and front passenger would be seated, and opened fire.

In the vehicle below, Tenbrook shook his head, scattering fragments of glass on the seats around him. The impact of the truck had jarred his neck, but that was the least of his concerns now. They'd been attacked, the lead car in their convoy had been obliterated and their own vehicle rendered inoperable. And the insane fucker behind it was still out there.

'Shit, we're pinned here!' the driver said, slamming his fist against the wheel. He looked back at Tenbrook. 'Sir, we're gonna have to—'

His sentence was abruptly cut short when something burst through the roof above. There was a sudden flash of red, a spray of something hot and wet that caused Tenbrook to turn away, and an odd bubbling, gurgling sound. When Tenbrook looked back at the man, he found his head and the left side of his chest were gone, replaced by a mass of pulped flesh and broken, protruding bones.

That was when all semblance of discipline fell apart. The professionalism of his security operatives, the training, the years of battlefield experience began to unravel as the terrible reality sank in. Every countermeasure set in place to protect them was failing. They were outmatched and unprepared for what had found them.

'Oh, Jesus!' the second operative up front stammered, his face dripping with his comrade's blood. He was pawing blindly at his door, trying to back away from the horror in front of him, trying in his own futile way to escape. 'Oh fuck, I—'

A second round penetrated through the reinforced roof with a crash, shattering the vehicle's centre console, destroying the transmission and carrying on right through to strike the roadway below. A third shot resulted in another spray of red, and the man convulsed visibly, staring at the ragged stump where his leg had just been amputated above his right knee.

He might have started to scream, but another shot blew through his torso barely a second later, destroying most of his internal organs in the process.

Drake was wearing ear protectors, mainly to prevent his eardrums from being shattered by the close-range blast of the Claymore mines. However, the change of air pressure inside the cab as each .50 calibre shell was expended was so powerful that it actually blew out the window opposite. The rifle's frame was designed to absorb most of the formidable recoil, but nonetheless he could feel each thunderous detonation travel up his arm every time he squeezed the trigger.

The Barrett M82 carried ten rounds in its detachable box magazine, and Drake carried on firing into the forward section of the vehicle until he'd expended the entire clip, even putting one through the hood to finally silence the SUV's engine. With this task complete, he withdrew the weapon from the door frame and laid it in the passenger footwell, then picked up the IMI Desert Eagle pistol on the seat beside it.

In the car below, Tenbrook gasped when the last remaining operative, seated in the back seat beside him, grabbed him by the shoulders in an iron-hard, desperate grip.

'We've gotta get the fuck out of here!' he shouted, flecks of spit flying from his mouth and mingling with the blood that already coated them both. 'We've gotta move now!'

There was no choice, he knew. Whoever was out there had more than enough firepower to get inside this car and kill them both. The only remaining option was to make a break for it.

Still gripping Tenbrook with one hand, the operative kicked the door open. Bright light and warm, dusty air cascaded in, mingled with the stench of cordite and burning plastic.

Drawing his MP7 submachine gun, then he practically dragged Tenbrook out onto the sidewalk, his feet scraping along the glass-covered ground. Turning his weapon towards the truck's cab, he unloaded its entire 30-round magazine in a single, deafening burst, peppering the door and cab with 4.6×30mm armour-piercing rounds.

But his target was no longer inside the vehicle. Even as they'd been deciding on their desperate course of action, Drake had opened the passenger-side door and leapt down to the road below. Waiting behind the mass of the truck's engine block until the panicked operative's weapon had run dry, he emerged from behind his cover and took aim with the Desert Eagle.

Designed by Israel Military Industries back in the early 1980s, the Desert Eagle was chambered for the massive .50 calibre Action Express cartridge, making it the most powerful semi-automatic pistol in existence. Normally Drake wasn't a fan of such overpowered weapons, considering them more suitable for action movies than practical military applications. But when it came to defeating modern composite body armour, there really was no substitute for raw stopping power.

The operative saw him coming as he ejected his spent magazine and reached for a fresh one. Drake saw the look of fleeting anger and fear painted across his bloodied face, saw the realization he wasn't going to make it, saw him turn away and try to flee.

Taking aim and bracing himself, Drake put two rounds through his back. He didn't trust himself to go for a headshot while dealing with the brutal recoil of the Desert Eagle, but the twin blood splatters as the rounds tore through his armour and exited through his chest told Drake it didn't matter. The operative went down in a limp pile, jerking feebly, the submachine gun clattering from his grasp.

Tenbrook, splashed with other men's blood but apparently unharmed, didn't seem to care one bit that his last remaining security operative had just been cut down. He was already running, sprinting away from the scene and probably hoping to take shelter inside one of the shops or restaurants that fronted the main avenue. Drake wasn't about to let him make it that far.

Opening a pouch in his webbing, he withdrew an M84 stun grenade, popped the pin and hurled it towards the retreating CIA man. Fragmentation grenades have a delayed fuse of up to five seconds to give the user time to take cover, but not so with stun grenades. They're designed to detonate almost immediately to enhance the element of surprise and prevent the intended target from throwing them back.

The device landed with a solid thump and bounced several yards beyond Tenbrook. Drake glanced away just as it detonated, though he could feel the faint tremble of the concussive wave rippling up through his legs. Such devices were really meant to be used in confined spaces, and naturally the effectiveness was diminished in an open environment like this, but it had detonated close enough to Tenbrook to do the job.

The man stumbled and fell to his knees, clutching at his temporarily blinded eyes. Advancing towards him, Drake passed the still-moving body of the operative he'd gunned down, casually drilling a hole through his head with the Desert Eagle just to be on the safe side.

Drake stepped over his corpse, holstered the Desert Eagle and drew a different weapon strapped around his right thigh. Resembling a chunky plastic handgun, it was designed to fire electric conductors rather than bullets.

Tenbrook had managed to get to his feet again and was stumbling blindly away, hands groping out in front of him. Drake pulled the trigger. There was a whoosh as the weapon's compressed air cylinder launched its two metal darts, which embedded themselves in the centre of Tenbrook's back, leaving a pair of thin conducting wires trailing back to the gun.

A quick press of the discharge button sent several thousand volts coursing through Tenbrook's body, shorting out his nervous system and paralysing his muscles. The man went down like a ton of bricks. Drake applied a few more seconds of current before relenting. Ejecting the spent power pack, he quickly holstered the weapon, bent down and got a good grip of his incapacitated target, then hoisted his limp body up over his shoulder.

Tenbrook wasn't particularly tall or muscular, but he was a good weight nonetheless, and Drake knew he'd be hard pressed to carry him any distance like this. A quick look at the truck confirmed he wouldn't be escaping in that. It was tangled up in the wreck of the second SUV, and the security operative's burst of automatic gunfire had likely destroyed the dashboard.

It didn't matter anyway. The big vehicle had served its purpose, but it was too slow and conspicuous to make his escape in. He needed something smaller and faster.

Fortunately, he had plenty to choose from. The roadway had been busy with traffic when he triggered the Claymores, and while the cars in front had wisely made a quick getaway from the unfolding carnage, those trapped behind it were largely unable to escape. Their owners had mostly fled to safety, leaving him with at least a dozen possible vehicles, some of which had even been abandoned with their engines still running.

That was fine by him. Hotwiring a car was considerably trickier and more time consuming than the movies would have people believe, and he had little enough to waste. The police would almost certainly have been alerted by now.

Quickly reviewing his options, he selected an old Renault that still looked reasonably solid, yanked open the trunk and dumped Tenbrook inside. He quickly rifled through the man's pockets, searching for any device that could be used to track him, but came up empty. Maybe he'd dropped them in the crash. Either way, it didn't matter much to Drake.

The man was moaning and beginning to stir as the effects of the taser started to wear off. Drake could almost sense the shock and confusion of his attack giving way to growing dread as he realized what was happening. Tenbrook was a CIA man through and through – he knew that hostile operatives didn't go to the trouble of keeping you alive unless they wanted something. Which usually meant you were in for a very unpleasant time.

Slamming the trunk closed, Drake raced to the driver's door and jumped in, swiftly manoeuvring past the wreckage in front before accelerating away as fast as the car's limited horsepower would allow.

He had Tenbrook. Now it was time to get some answers.

Chapter 60

Rojas was waiting for Anya near the site of the ambush. When she caught up with him, they surveyed the scene of carnage in solemn, contemplative silence. Vehicles lay burning and mangled, while the bloodied corpses of Tenbrook's security team were visible through the drifting smoke.

'One man did all this,' he said, astounded by the scale of the destruction.

Local civilians had emerged from shops and homes and were starting to drift cautiously closer, driven by the same morbid fascination that draws people to the site of a car crash. But this situation was different, the atmosphere slowly turning from grim curiosity to anger and hostility. Already they were casting suspicious glances at the two foreigners, as if sensing their involvement.

Anya could sense the changing mood and turned away, gripping her companion's arm. 'We can't stay here,' she whispered. 'We need to find Ryan before we lose him.'

Rojas blinked and nodded. 'Come.'

Traffic was at a complete standstill now as the growing tailbacks locked up all the major intersections. The only things still able to make headway were vehicles of the two-wheeled variety, able to zip in and out the narrow gaps between stuck cars.

One in particular was heading their way, the rider angling left to avoid the mess of fire and twisted metal that blocked much of the road. Crouching down behind a station wagon, Rojas waited until the motorbike was almost on top of him before leaping out, catching the rider by the shoulders and yanking him backwards out of his seat.

Uncontrolled, the bike carried on for another ten yards or so before toppling over, skidding along the asphalt with a horrible grinding screech.

'Sorry, my friend. But we need this more than you,' Rojas whispered as the downed rider, stunned but alive, looked up groggily.

Rojas let go of him and sprinted over to the fallen bike. It was an old Yamaha unit, the kind of cheap, rugged bike favoured for off-roading, its frame spotted with rust, dented and scratched up even before his hijack manoeuvre. The little 125cc engine was still running despite the rough handling, which was good enough for him.

Heaving it upright, he mounted it and beckoned Anya over. 'This way, Maras!'

Anya approached dubiously and slid onto the seat behind him, gripping him by the waist. 'Do you even know how to ride?'

He flashed a grin, testing the throttle. The engine rattled rather than roared, but it was functioning. 'We'll find out, won't we?'

Within seconds they were zigzagging between stranded cars, following the route Drake had taken less than a minute earlier. The engine might have been lacking in raw power, but the bike was so lightweight that it didn't matter, and Rojas was determined to push its performance to the limit.

Anya could do little more than cling on for dear life as other vehicles whipped past mere feet away from her, the heat of the exhaust system searing her leg. Windblown dust blasted their exposed skin, making their eyes stream, but still he wouldn't let up.

Chancing to let go with one arm, Anya reached up and hit her radio transmitter. 'All units, come in!' she shouted over the roar of the wind.

'Check your range, we can barely read you,' Frost warned her. 'What the fuck's going on there?'

'Ryan's on the move, heading south away from the ambush site. He has Tenbrook. We're in pursuit now. Where are you?'

'We're stuck two blocks away,' Dietrich growled in frustration. 'Traffic's completely snarled. And it looks like the locals are pissed over this. They just smashed up a police cruiser that tried to get to the ambush site. This place is about to go down.'

Anya had suspected as much. With tensions running high, it wouldn't take much to ignite a full-scale riot. And Frost and the others were trapped right in the middle of it.

'Copy that. Get out of there and try to rendezvous with us. And watch your backs! That sniper I saw back at the market might not have been Ryan. Alex might have been right – Hawkins and his team could have gotten here ahead of us.'

'Great, as if we need more problems right now.' Despite his bluster, he sounded uneasy, and Anya didn't blame him. 'But where the fuck are you heading?'

Rojas swerved left to avoid a car that was trying to pull out in front of them, narrowly missing it. Clearly he wasn't unskilled at riding, but Anya disliked someone else having control in such a dangerous situation.

'Track my cell phone. When we stop moving, you'll know we've found Ryan.'

'Or you've been killed,' Dietrich pointed out.

–

Hauling a now bound and restrained Tenbrook up the flight of well-worn steps, Drake paused to look up at the great arched doorway that stood in his path. It was big, easily eight feet high at the apex and almost as wide, constructed of thick planks of wood bound with iron. A thick chain had been passed between the metal ring handles, secured with an even larger padlock.

A formidable barrier for the casual thief, but one that had been easy for a man of Drake's training to defeat. He had already picked the padlock's simple pin tumbler mechanism, leaving the device in place while he went to retrieve Tenbrook. Now he unlatched it and unwound the great chains, allowing them to fall aside.

Hauling the big doors open on creaking, ancient hinges, Drake shoved his prisoner in ahead of him, drew his gun and followed the man inside. He closed and barred the doors behind him, sealing them both inside.

The room was huge, occupying almost the full length and height of the building. Rows of ornate stone pillars ran along both sides, rising up to a magnificent vaulted ceiling with big stained-glass windows set into the upper reaches. Shafts of sunlight streamed in through these gaps, casting their fiery orange glow on the east wall of the room.

It was a majestic, captivating place that had likely inspired feelings of wonder and awe in the generations of Muslims who had come here to worship. But whatever its illustrious history, even this holy place hadn't escaped the ravages of time.

Scaffolding had been set up around a number of pillars that had started to weaken under the immense weight of the roof, the rickety metal framework extending all the way up to the great dome overhead. Most of the stained-glass windows had been removed and lowered down to ground level via a system of ropes and pulleys, the gaping holes covered with nothing more substantial than billowing tarpaulins.

Judging by the layer of dust that coated everything, Drake was willing to bet it had been a long time since any workmen had laboured in here. Trowels, chisels, saws, hammers, mortars, brushes and myriad other masonry tools of all shapes and sizes lay scattered about on work benches and old wooden tables, abandoned weeks or even months earlier. Perhaps the worsening political situation had prompted the owners of this place to bail, removing whatever artefacts and valuables had once resided here until order was restored.

And yet, despite the neglect, there was something about this building. Drake didn't consider himself a religious man, but even he could appreciate the significance of this place. And for a moment, he actually allowed himself to feel some measure of the peace that others had once found here.

'Listen, pal, I don't pretend to know what you want,' Tenbrook said, his harsh and unpleasant voice breaking the spell. 'But I can promise you're fucking with the wrong guy. The men I work for are gonna be *real* pissed after the stunt you pulled today.'

Drake pushed him forward, steering him towards the far end of the room, saying nothing. They'd get down to it soon enough.

'Not that I ain't impressed,' the CIA man allowed. 'Not many guys could have done what you did back there, taking out an entire field team single-handed. Goddamn poetry in motion right there.' He snorted in amusement. 'But let's put our cards on the table, huh? My employers are gonna catch up with us sooner or later. Hell, they make a living out of finding people. So you want some free advice? Run, pal. Run right now and maybe you'll get enough of a head start to stay alive. Because if they get their hands on you, that little bloodbath back there will seem like—'

Raising his foot, Drake planted a firm kick in the small of his back. Tenbrook pitched forward, tripped over his own feet and landed in an ungainly sprawl on the bare stone floor, unable to use his bound arms to protect himself. He let out a grunt of pain as he hit the deck, leaving a smear of congealing blood on the sandy flagstones.

'Christ!' he snarled. 'The fuck's the matter with you?'

Drake looked down at the dishevelled prisoner lying on the floor. Stripped of his protective detail and his cocky arrogance, all he had left was his voice, which was just as well. He'd be needing it soon.

'It's time to confess your sins, you piece of shit,' Drake said, gesturing at their surroundings. 'And you've got a lot of confessing to do.'

Grabbing the taser from its holster at his thigh, Drake reached into his webbing for a replacement power pack. He'd expended the last one when he took Tenbrook down. Slotting it into place, he pressed it home until he heard the click as the conductors locked.

'What the fuck are you talking about?' Tenbrook gasped, shaking his head and blinking furiously. Blood was seeping into his eyes, impairing his vision. 'I don't even know who you are!'

Applying the device against his neck, Drake depressed the trigger. The X26 stun gun was a police- and military-issue device designed to be used in several different configurations. It could launch a pair of barbed conducting prongs at a distant target just as he'd done earlier, but the weapon could also be used at close range to administer intermittent shocks. Just hold it in place and taser away.

Drake gave him a five-second burst, watching as Tenbrook bucked and thrashed, groaning and crying out in agony as thousands of volts surged through his body. When he withdrew the weapon, the man was breathing hard, trembling and jerking spasmodically.

'You... you fu-ck,' he mumbled, struggling to form the words.

Drake lowered himself down to the stone floor so that Tenbrook could make eye contact with him. He said nothing, just allowed the other man to look at his face, to search back through his long years of memories and slowly home in on one particular day. One particular briefing room on a hot afternoon in Afghanistan.

'How about now?' he asked. 'Now do you remember me?'

It didn't happen right away. There was no dramatic change from confusion to understanding. But studying his facial expressions closely, Drake was able to watch as the fire of remembrance slowly began to kindle within Tenbrook's mind, gradually gaining strength as old memories resurfaced, until finally the flames caught hold and his eyes lit up with realization.

'There it is,' Drake said. 'Now it's coming back.'

'It's impossible,' the man gasped, shaking his head. 'It's not...'

'*This mission is going to call for the best we have, and as of now, that is you.* You remember those words, don't you? How many other soldiers did you feed that bullshit line to over the years?'

'W-what do you want?'

Drake leaned in closer, letting Tenbrook get a good look at his eyes, a glimpse of what lay behind them.

'I want answers,' Drake said slowly. 'I want to know what Operation Hydra was. I want to know what happened that day.'

Drake had expected to see fear, but instead he saw something he hadn't expected: disbelief.

'What the fuck are you talking about? You *led* the operation. It was your mission.'

Drake's mind flashed back to that day, seeing the same images that had plagued his thoughts and haunted his dreams for too long. He saw the bodies, the fire, the smoke, the blood-red sky, and most of all he saw the black sun. Darkness where there should have been light, stark and absolute, swallowing everything.

Screams. Darkness. Fear.

'*My* mission,' he repeated. 'Why?'

'We needed men who could do what nobody else could, men who could make the hard choices. That was you. That's why your unit was created.'

With a shaking hand, Drake pressed the taser against Tenbrook's neck and let him have a full ten-second burst, relishing the man's screams.

It took most of his remaining self-control to release the trigger. He needed the man alive. *Not yet*, he told himself. Withdrawing the weapon, he watched with a curious detachment as Tenbrook coughed and retched, leaving a trail of slimy mucus on the floor.

'Where did you send us?' Drake demanded, grabbing him by the collar. 'What did you make us do, you bastard? What was our mission?'

Tenbrook's mouth was working, but barely a whisper made it from his spittle-covered lips. 'It was... what you were... made for. Your mission... to take them out...'

Drake's brows drew together, his mind grasping as he tried to process what he was hearing. 'To take who out?' he demanded, shaking Tenbrook violently. 'What were we made for?'

'No,' the prisoner protested, starting to revive a little. 'You kill me, you... get nothing. You untie me... then we talk.'

'*Answer me, you fuck!*' he shouted, ready to give him another shot. This time however there was no clicking or buzzing as current arced between the two conducting rods. The power pack had been depleted.

Throwing the useless taser aside, Drake released his grip and strode over to a nearby work table, where various tools had been left by workmen.

Amongst them, Drake spotted a sturdy-looking claw hammer. Its wooden handle had been worn smooth, and it was coated in a good layer of dust, but its five-pound steel head still looked perfectly serviceable. Especially for what he had in mind.

'I'm not going to kill you, Tenbrook,' he said. 'You'll just wish I had by the time I'm finished.'

But just as he was about to lift the weapon from its long resting place, a voice called out, issuing a single command that echoed around the vast, empty space. A voice that Drake had hoped never to hear again.

'Stop!'

Chapter 61

The world around Drake vanished, his surroundings seeming to melt away into darkness, as if he were a performer on stage and the lights had just died. That single word cut through it all – a shard of memory driven deep.

He felt the briefest glimmer of something. Too brief, too primal to be a fully formed memory or thought, but something that was called up inside him all the same. Feelings of loyalty, of devotion, of completeness. And in the same instant, the agony of separation, the ache of regret and the burning longing for what could never be his.

She must have found another way in. Not the main doors, he'd barred them when he'd entered, and there was no way she could have gotten here ahead of him. Some hidden passage or doorway that had escaped his notice during his earlier recon.

Why did you have to come? Why now? God-fucking-damn you, Anya, why couldn't you just let it go?

Drake lowered his head, closed his eyes and let out a slow, meditative breath. A moment of deceptive calm and equanimity before the storm broke upon him.

'How did you find me?' he asked.

'Does it matter now?' her voice carrying across the room. 'You knew this was coming. You knew sooner or later we would meet.'

His hand strayed down to the weapon pushed down the front of his trousers. The Desert Eagle, its .50 calibre rounds able to punch through any armour she might be wearing. His keen hearing strained to listen out for the sounds of movement that would tell him where she was. When he went for it, he wouldn't have much time to take aim and…

'Don't even think about it,' she warned, guessing his thoughts. 'I have the drop on you. Lay the weapon down on the ground and slide it away.'

She was right. The acoustics made it near impossible to pinpoint her location. Not to mention he was caught out in the open with his back to her. Bad odds.

'Or what? You'll shoot me?'

'It won't be the first time I've killed someone I care about,' she assured him. 'Now take the weapon out slowly and slide it away.'

Laying the Desert Eagle gently on the stone floor, Drake gave it a nudge with his foot, sending it skittering away across the uneven surface. He was unarmed, save for a single weapon concealed in his webbing.

'Now turn around, Ryan.'

'What will I find if I do?' he asked. 'A friend or an enemy?'

'Someone who wants to help you.'

Sighing, he turned to face the woman who had hunted him across half the world. The woman who he'd once foolishly considered an ally, perhaps even something more, and who had now become his enemy by standing between him and his objective.

His eyes swept the room, searching for her, finding nothing but ancient stonework and deep pools of shadow. Had he been wrong? Was she trying to close in on him from another direction?

He saw movement amongst the murky shadows cast by one of the huge stone columns, and knew she'd at last chosen to reveal herself.

Anya stepped forward into a shaft of light slanting down from the windows high above, the glow of the evening sun casting her features perfectly.

Drake took in the curve of her lips, parted a little as she breathed deeper. She'd been running. Running to get here, to catch up, to reach him. Her hair was tied back in a haphazard ponytail, a few loose strands escaping to fall around her face. Her eyes, pale blue and daunting in their intensity, questioning, doubting, looking for the man she'd once known.

Drake saw all these things, but his attention was mostly focussed on the weapon in her hand. An M1911 semi-automatic. Her weapon of choice. Old, proven, reliable, powerful.

A weapon trained on him.

'I'm going to give you one chance,' he said, looking at her. Looking for that crucial moment of weakness. 'Walk away. Walk away now and forget what you saw here.'

'You know I can't do that. I *won't* do that.'

Drake shook his head, trying to banish the thoughts, trying to shake himself free of their insidious grip. His mind had been clear before, secure in its hatred. He couldn't allow her to cloud it now.

'This isn't your fight.'

'Yes it is, Ryan,' she informed him. 'Because I came to fight for you.'

Her statement was not delivered forcefully, but tenderly, with the quiet determination of a woman set on her path, resolved to reach its end no matter the distance or difficulty

'The Ryan Drake I know is worth fighting for. He's a good man, and even though you tried to destroy him, I know he's still in there. I came to bring him back.'

She's playing you, trying to make you doubt yourself just like she was trained to do. Don't believe her. Don't let her in.

'That man you knew never even existed,' Drake said, his teeth gritted. 'He was a lie. I'm the only truth that matters. Now I'm going to give you one chance to stand aside, then I'm going to make you shoot me.'

'Bad move, friend,' a second voice called out. 'If she hesitates to put you down, I won't.'

Drake's head snapped around.

268

He watched as a man lowered himself down from the scaffolding gantry above, using one of the ropes to descend gracefully to ground level. That at least explained how they'd made their way in here undetected, he thought with a pang of anger. The unsecured windows above had allowed them in, while the scaffold had provided an easy way down.

That was irrelevant now however as Drake concentrated on the new arrival himself. Mid-forties, long dark hair, lean build, South American features. Drake didn't recognize him, but he did recognize his gun. A Beretta 92. Fifteen 9mm rounds in the mag. More than enough to put Drake down if he opened fire.

She brought this man to finish the job if she fails. They're working together. You have to strike first. Do it now, finish your mission.

'Stay back, Cesar,' Anya implored. 'Nobody is going to fire.'

'You're wrong about that,' Drake said coldly. 'Only one of us is leaving here. Think it's going to be you?'

'Don't make me answer that,' Anya warned. The compassion in her voice had hardened into deepening resolve, but he sensed an undertone of doubt. This was one battle she didn't want to fight.

'You could have stayed out of this. You made the choice. This is on you.'

Drake heard the click as she thumbed back the hammer. 'Don't do this. This isn't who you are.'

Finish your mission. Kill her!

'You still don't get it, do you?' he said, knowing and accepting how this was going to end. 'This is who I've always been.'

It happened fast. Drake felt his hand close around the handle of the hammer he'd planned to use on Tenbrook. It would have to serve a different purpose now.

Swinging his arm forward, Drake took rough aim at Anya and hurled the hammer like a tomahawk. She twisted aside as the heavy missile hurtled through the air, narrowly missing her head and glancing off the pillar behind, gouging out a sizeable chunk of stone.

Drake was well aware of Anya's fast reactions and her ability to sense attacks coming. He'd guessed she would avoid the improvised projectile, but it didn't matter. He'd created an opening, giving him time to close the distance. He went for it, unsheathing his knife and rushing at her with explosive force.

He almost expected Anya to bring her weapon back into play and open fire, hoping to put a round in him before he got close, but instead she tossed the gun aside and clenched her fists, ready to defend herself hand to hand. Still not ready to kill him.

Drake swiped at her, drawing the knife in a deadly horizontal arc. Anya leapt away and tilted her weight backwards, allowing the blade to sail past her throat. Adrenaline was pumping through Drake's veins, investing his muscles with greater strength and slowing the world down around him.

The thoughts and doubts had vanished now, replaced by the simple, primal instinct to fight and kill. She was his enemy, and she had to be stopped. That was all he needed to know, the only truth that mattered now.

Anya whirled to face him again, and he could see the concern etched into her features. She was afraid. Afraid she'd taken on an opponent she couldn't defeat. She had made a mistake by not shooting him when she had the chance. Whether it was weakness or overconfidence, Drake couldn't say. But he knew one thing – it would be the last mistake she ever made.

Tenbrook meanwhile had not been idle. With his former captor locked in combat, the CIA case officer saw his chance to escape. Swinging his legs beneath him, he made to rise from the floor, only for a shadow to fall across him. Looking up, he saw a second man silhouetted against the light from the windows overhead, saw the gleam of a weapon in his hands.

'That would be a very bad move, my friend,' Rojas warned him. 'Stay down and don't move if you hope to live through this.'

'None of you will live through this, you dumb shit,' Tenbrook spat. 'Your friends have fucking lost it. Your only chance is to—'

Rojas silenced him with a sharp jab from the butt of his pistol. The blow wasn't enough to knock Tenbrook unconscious, but it did put him down hard, blood dripping from a newly opened cut over his left eye.

'Consider that a warning. There won't be another,' Rojas said, moving towards the desperate, one-sided battle now playing out on the other side of the room.

Gathering up his strength, Drake brought his knife against Anya again, slashing at her arm. The blade whirled down viciously, its keen edge gleaming in the light, to slice through clothing and flesh.

Anya let out a hiss of pain and pulled away, blood dripping from a deep gash across her right arm. As she backed up close to a stone pillar, Drake slashed at her throat to finish the job. Reacting with lightning speed, Anya caught his knife arm, muscles straining to hold back the blade.

Rather than try to overcome her with sheer force, Drake released his hold on the weapon and allowed it to fall between them. She saw it and tried to grab for the knife, but he was faster, catching it with his free hand and sweeping it up into her midsection.

She moved, slipping aside so that the blade missed her stomach and struck unyielding stone, breaking under the sheer force and jarring his arm.

Anya drove her knee into his chest, knocking the air from his lungs. She used the opportunity to deliver a hard elbow to the spine that dropped him to one knee. Drake lashed out again with the broken remnants of the blade, but she was already beyond his range.

Anya kept her distance, body taut and ready, pacing slowly around him. Spots of her blood dripped on the floor.

'I'm not your enemy, Ryan,' Anya said, breathing harder now. 'Don't you see? I came to help you. The man I know is still in there. The man who rescued me from prison, who showed me trust and compassion when no one else would. You are that man!'

Her words seemed to cut briefly through the haze of his anger, as if revealing something buried away in some distant recess of his psyche, something that should have been destroyed for ever. But it wasn't gone. It had been diminished and beaten down and buried, but it remained still.

A memory. A memory of the man he'd been.

He had no idea what the future held for this woman, but she would come to no harm while she was with him. That was one promise Drake was determined to make good on.

He was just turning to leave when she spoke up again.

'What is your name?'

He stopped and looked at her. 'Drake. Ryan Drake.'

The woman looked at him for a long time. Then at last she gave a nod of acknowledgement. Her expression gave away little, but the gratitude, the relief, the raw emotion in her eyes was impossible to hide.

'Thank you, Drake.'

'No,' he hissed, throwing the broken knife aside. 'It's a lie!'

Leaping to his feet, Drake threw himself at her again. He went in hard and fast, pressing forward relentlessly, keeping her on the back foot. His adversary moved and dodged, shifting her weight and posture perfectly, matching her movements with his attacks and parrying his blows when she couldn't dodge them. She was protecting herself, trying to hold him at bay, trying to buy time.

Drake knew that Anya had been endowed with an instinctive understanding of posture and body language. In effect, she was able to sense what her opponent was going to do almost before they did it.

But this skill was hindered by one fatal flaw today – Anya wasn't fighting to win. Worse, she was trying to defend herself against the man she knew, not the man who now came at her. A man who didn't move or fight like the one she'd sparred against.

A man who was set on killing her.

He caught her when, thinking her opponent was tiring, she finally went on the offensive and tried to strike at his legs to drop him. Drake, prepared for this, abruptly shifted position just as she moved in, catching her off guard, and lifted her right off the ground, throwing her backwards into scaffolding rig that encircled one of the room's crumbling pillars.

The dull clang was accompanied by a cacophony of noise as loose sections of scaffolding tubes tumbled out of their stack above. Anya fell to her knees as these metal spears clattered to the floor, narrowly missing both combatants.

She's beaten, she's down. Now... now move forward and finish her!

Drake felt fresh strength coursing through his body, his chest swelling as he drew in a deep breath, his heart pounding with the thrill of victory, eyes alight with the lust for death. Spotting an object lying near his feet, he stooped and snatched up the hammer he'd thrown at her earlier and closed in, fingers tightening on the worn grip.

'I gave you a chance to leave,' he said, drawing his arm back. One good, hard swing and it would be over. 'You should have taken it.'

Lips drawn back in a fearsome grimace, Drake brought the hammer down against her.

But at the same moment, Anya snatched up one of the fallen poles and raised it up, clutching it tight with both hands. Primitive weapon met improvised shield with an explosive impact that jarred both combatants' arms. Anya was almost knocked over by the force of the blow, while Drake felt and heard the crunch as the hammer's wooden shaft fractured under the strain.

A heartbeat later, Anya swept the metal pole into his ribs. Pain exploded out from the point of impact, followed by a second strike to the face that snapped his head back and caused white light to burst across his eyes. Drake staggered backwards and crashed into one of the window frames stacked near the centre of the room, shattering it. Broken glass cascaded across the floor, slicing his skin.

'Stop this, Ryan!' Anya shouted, hurling the scaffolding pole aside and forcing herself to her feet. 'You *know* me. Do you think I came all this way to kill you?'

Dropping the broken, useless hammer, Drake reached up with a trembling hand and wiped his mouth. It came away smeared with blood.

'You won't stop me,' he snarled, spitting bloody phlegm on the floor. 'This is my mission. This is all I have left.'

She was his enemy, she was standing between him and his purpose here. She had come to stop him, to obscure the truth and frustrate his efforts just as she always had. Anya, who always seemed to inspire others to fight for her. Anya, who was the source of everything bad that had overtaken him, every loss and sacrifice and death. It was all because of her.

Anya was the real enemy. She always had been.

'No, it's not. I can face anything in this world,' she said, her voice raw and pained. 'Anything but losing you.'

Another memory flashed before his mind's eye. A memory of a hot evening in Islamabad, mere hours before they'd risked their lives on a final desperate gamble. He saw an angry, heated confrontation with this woman, and an admission both had ached to make yet neither one had seen coming.

In all the time he'd known her, he had never once seen Anya show even a hint of fear. She'd been through too much to feel such an emotion. 'What could you possibly be afraid of now?'

He saw her swallow, saw the barriers start to break down. Her eyes were locked with his, and for once there was nothing masking what lay behind them, no steely resolve or calculating intelligence. He saw the fear and the regret for things left unsaid too long, the pain and sadness over what might have been, and the forlorn hope for what might still be.

'You,' she said, her voice wavering. 'I'm afraid of losing you.'

Anya seemed to relax then, making no move to raise her arms or protect herself. It was as if she'd simply given up. 'If this is your mission, then finish it,' she said sadly. 'I'm not going to fight you. Not any more.'

It's a trick! Don't let her in when you're so close to the end! Finish her now!

'No!' he shouted again, swinging a wild backhanded strike. The woman staggered sideways, seemed poised to fall to her knees, but managed to stay on her feet.

She looked up at him, blood welling up from the cut opened across her cheek. There was no anger in her, no fear or defiance. Just acceptance, compassion, and the same determination he'd seen earlier.

'Maras, stop this!' Rojas pleaded, disgusted by the spectacle he was witnessing. 'Stop it, or *I will!*'

'Stay out of this,' Anya ordered him without taking her eyes off Drake. 'Do nothing.'

'He's going to kill you!'

'Then that's what will happen. But if you interfere, I promise I will kill you.'

Rojas said nothing to this, but neither did he move to intervene. Knowing Anya as he did, he had little doubt that she would make good on her threat.

Anya tilted her head a little, looking at Drake, trying to understand him. Trying to reach him. 'Your name is Ryan Drake. You have a sister named Jessica.'

The breath seemed to catch in his throat as a different image leapt into his mind. An image of his sister, alone with him in her kitchen, tears reddening her eyes as he said farewell to her, perhaps for the last time. Going into hiding, leaving her behind, severing the ties that had bound him to his former life and family. The memory of her brought an unexpected surge of grief and longing and regret.

'Come back to us, Ryan,' Anya implored. 'Come back so we can finish this together, just like you said we would.'

Another memory. A memory of a grassy hill overlooking an isolated house. A memory of sitting with this woman, watching the swaying grass stalks and the tiny insects circling in the evening light.

He reached out and gently touched her hand. For once, she didn't move it away.

'Remember what I said to you once? I promised I'd be there for you even if you didn't think you needed me, that I'd do everything I could to help you, and that I'd never give up on you. Because this is my fight now as much as yours. We started this together, Anya,' he said. 'You and me. That's how we're going to finish it. Together.'

The woman said nothing, but at that moment he felt it. He felt her squeeze his hand just a little.

It was too much. Too many thoughts and memories that conflicted with everything he'd been conditioned to believe. The part of him, the fake identity he'd ripped apart and believed lost for ever was trying to come back, gaining strength, threatening to undermine him.

Threatening his mission.

Drake threw himself at Anya, tackling her to the ground. There was no yielding canvas ring to absorb the fall this time. Her body took the full bruising force of the impact

'You're lying!' he shouted. 'You're nothing to me! *Nothing!*'

Yet still she didn't try to defend herself. She didn't raise her arms, didn't try to push him off or slip free of his grasp. She lay there, pinned beneath him, her body bruised and bleeding, looking up at him with that same inexplicable, maddening look of quiet acceptance.

She would let him do whatever he wanted, he knew then. The choice was his.

'Why are you doing this?' he cried.

His mind felt like it was tearing itself apart. He wanted to hate her, wanted to destroy her, wanted to see her as another enemy to be eliminated. Then he could justify it. Then it would all make sense.

'I was with you when this all started,' she confessed. 'And I'll be with you to the end, Ryan. No matter when it comes.'

One final act and it's finished. DO IT NOW!

The opposing forces now at war for his soul had risen to an exquisite, horrific crescendo, a perfectly balanced scream of rage and fury, doubt and resolve, love and hatred. In between these two fractured halves of his identity, the centre of his being was trapped, pulled in separate directions, torn apart at the seams.

Drake snatched up a shard of broken window pane, oblivious as the sharp edges cut into his flesh, and with a furious, agonized cry he plunged the weapon towards her neck.

And there he stopped, the tip of the shard just pressing into the skin, drawing a tiny trickle of blood.

Anya looked him in the eye, ready to accept what was coming.

'You're a good man,' she whispered. 'My life is yours. Take it if you have to.'

Anya saw the change come over him. It was as if he were becoming an entirely different man before her very eyes. The coiled, bunched muscles began to relax, his expression of cold resolve easing as if some great shadow had been lifted. The shard of glass that was pressed in so tight against her neck was removed and hurled away.

Drake let go of his hold and slumped back on his knees as if stunned. He looked suddenly weary, as if the battle fought in his mind had caused scars on the body that housed it.

Anya picked herself up and stared hard into his eyes, searching desperately for the man she remembered and feeling her heart swell with relief when she found him.

He looked at her too, really looked at her this time, and recognized her.

'Anya,' he gasped, the word torn from a dry, constricted throat.

She had no words now. Throwing her arms around him, Anya buried her face in his neck as the emotions that had been held in such rigid check finally found a release. She could feel her hot tears moistening his skin, heard a pained, exhausted sob and couldn't tell whether it was from her or him. Maybe it didn't matter now.

'I'm sorry,' Drake whispered, ragged with grief. 'I'm sorry, Anya.'

She pulled back enough to look at him again and, seeing his anguish, knew that the man she remembered had truly returned.

Then she did something she hadn't done for a long time. She smiled. A true, radiant, beaming smile of relief.

'How did you know?' Drake asked, looking back at her with awe and thinking about that shard of glass pressed into her throat. 'How did you know you could bring me back?'

'I didn't.'

Just for that one moment, all that existed was the two of them. Hurt and bruised, holding each other with bloodied hands, the sun forming a curtain of golden light.

Drake reached out and touched her face, running his fingers down her cheek. Anya held his gaze, her lips slightly parted, her breathing coming faster. She wanted, needed to reach out to him, pull him to her, give in to what they both knew was coming.

She blinked suddenly at the sound of a cough from nearby. 'I hate to interrupt this moment, but do you think we could get the fuck out of here now?' Rojas asked.

Reality seemed to snap back into place like the crack of a whip, the more pragmatic part of her mind reasserting itself.

Much as she hated to admit it, Rojas was right. Drake might have been saved, but they were still in the middle of a dangerous country on the brink of armed revolution. If they expected to get out then they would have to leave fast.

'Who the hell are you?' Drake asked, irritated at the intervention. 'And how do you know me?'

Rojas flashed a terse smile. 'The name's Cesar. You're partly responsible for ruining my life these last few days, *babaca*.'

Drake quickly surmised this was a conversation best kept for later.

'Fine, whatever,' he decided. 'Can you move, Anya?'

'Better than you, I think.'

He didn't look convinced, but nodded all the same. 'We need to get Tenbrook out of here. This is all for nothing if I don't get answers from him.'

'Who is he? What answers do you expect?'

'Long story. The short version is that he knows what happened to me in Afghanistan. And he's going to tell us everything,' Drake explained, picking himself up painfully. 'It's Cesar, right?'

'That's right.'

'Get him ready to move.'

Rojas seemed poised to dispute Drake's sudden assumption of authority, but a look from Anya was enough to persuade him that cooperation should take priority over ego.

'*Filho da puta*,' he muttered, striding over to retrieve the prisoner.

Drake meanwhile held a hand out to Anya, who accepted it. He could feel the warm blood that had dripped down her arm, and winced in shame. He'd done that to her.

'That cut looks bad,' he said quietly. 'We need to get it seen to.'

'I'll be fine. I've had worse.' Anya's expression warned him against further questions about her condition.

Drake was just helping the woman back to her feet when everything started to unravel.

One of the scattered pieces of glass had landed near Tenbrook, allowing him to quietly grasp it without being noticed. And for the past couple of minutes he'd been working at his bindings with it, ignoring the gashes it had opened across his palms.

And now his hands were free. Rojas, unaware of this alarming development and believing him still securely bound, approached and hooked a hand beneath his armpit.

'Come on, *puta*. Time to go,' he said, heaving the man to his feet.

But as Tenbrook's arm popped free and whipped towards his midsection, glass glinted in the bright sunlight, and Rojas let out a cry of pain and surprise, doubling over with a hand clutched against his stomach.

'*Porra!*' he snarled.

Tenbrook didn't waste any more time on him. It was three against one, and even if he managed to wrest Rojas' weapon away from him, the other two would kill him before he could use it. That was a dumb move, and Tenbrook hadn't survived this long by being dumb.

So he ran, sprinting for the main doors at the other end of the room. He might have been pushing 50, but he was tall and lean and still exercised regularly. More than that, he was desperate to escape. All three factors allowed him to put on a startling burst of speed.

Drake and Anya knew they wouldn't be able to catch him in time. The only option was to put a round in him and slow the man down.

Both of them looked around in desperation, both sighted a weapon – Anya spotting the Desert Eagle and Drake the M1911 – and they dived for each simultaneously.

Drake swung the old Colt .45 around towards his rapidly fleeing target, flicking the safety off. Half a second later, Anya brought the Desert Eagle to bear, clutching the massive semi-automatic with both hands to brace herself against the inevitable recoil.

Even as they took aim, Tenbrook yanked back the deadbolt holding the door closed.

'Stop, Tenbrook!' Drake shouted. 'Stop or we'll fire!'

Tenbrook didn't even hesitate, swinging the massive door open. Bright light flooded in, and he took a step forward. To escape. To freedom. To salvation—

Their erstwhile prisoner jerked as something slammed into him, staggering as if being pummelled by unseen fists. Bright-red blood exploded from half a dozen wounds across his torso, staining his clothes and the wall behind him. The crackle of gunfire reverberated around the massive echoing mosque, rebounding off the ancient stone pillars and the towering dome overhead.

Tenbrook collapsed to the floor like a rag doll. One look was enough to confirm he wasn't going to be getting up again.

Shocked, Anya looked over at Drake, expecting to see wisps of grey smoke trailing from the barrel of his gun, only to find the same expression of shock on his face. He hadn't fired.

'One down!' Hawkins called out. 'Anyone else wanna try?'

Chapter 62

Another man might have hesitated, might have questioned how Hawkins had managed to track them down here, but Drake wasn't that man.

Survival instinct took over.

'Cover!' he yelled.

The piercing crackle of automatic gunfire filled the quiet air of the mosque, rounds howling against the ancient stone pillars and tearing through the decorative windows stacked in the centre of the room. One round hit the scaffolding pole less than a foot from Drake's head, snapping the metal pole clean in half and causing the heavy, unbalanced structure to list dangerously.

Drake backed up against the solid cover of a stone pillar, clutching the Colt .45 in a white-knuckle grip as his mind raced. The crackle of weapons fire was still ringing in his ears.

Hawkins was somewhere near the entrance, firing in through the open door and keeping them pinned down. But entrances were usually choke points that limited the firepower an attacker could bring to bear, not the choice he'd have expected from a seasoned pro like Hawkins.

Either Tenbrook's sudden escape attempt had caught him off guard before his men were in position, or…

'Shit,' he hissed, realizing this was a delaying tactic. Hawkins was keeping them pinned down, preventing them from fighting their way out while the rest of his assault team sought another way in. It wouldn't take them long to find the same route Anya and Rojas had used.

He glanced over at Anya, who leaned out from behind cover just long enough to survey the scene beyond the doorway. A volley of gunfire quickly forced her back behind the pillar as a line of fist-sized explosions traced their way across the ancient stonework, scattering broken chunks across the floor.

With the Desert Eagle held in a two-handed grip, she angled the weapon around the edge of the pillar and put a trio of rounds out through the open door, firing blind. The big .50-calibre gun boomed in the vast enclosed space, the recoil snapping back against her wrists.

Backing up against the pillar, she met Drake's gaze, held two fingers up to her eyes to indicate she'd seen something, then held three fingers up in the air. At least three operatives outside the door, with more almost certainly moving to encircle the building.

Drake nodded. He knew making a stand here would be futile, but neither could they break cover without being mown down.

277

Something was creaking and groaning ominously overhead, distracting his thoughts. Glancing up, he saw that the big, rickety-looking scaffolding rig extending all the way up to the domed ceiling was tilting over at an angle now that one of the poles was compromised.

It wouldn't take much for the whole thing to collapse. Not much at all.

Taking a step back from the pillar, he raised his foot and planted a solid kick on the nearest scaffolding pole. The structure shuddered and rattled, threatening to topple but not quite giving way.

A second kick was enough to tip the balance. With the long, painful groan of buckling metal, the overtaxed structure gave way and toppled towards the far end of the room like an ancient tree being felled. Wooden deck boards, loose tools, buckets and support posts cascaded from its upper levels, adding to the clamour. His last sight was of Hawkins throwing himself aside to avoid being crushed.

The roaring, crashing impact was loud enough to leave Drake's ears ringing as the entire structure disintegrated against the open doorway, scattering wreckage in all directions and raising a cloud of dust thick enough to obscure his view of the entrance. The doorway was well and truly blocked.

'Fall back! Let's go!' he called out, breaking cover and retreating towards the opposite side of the room. Anya followed him, facing backwards with the Desert Eagle at the ready to cover their retreat.

'What have you done?' she demanded angrily.

'Bought us some time. Got a better idea?'

'The scaffold was our only way out.' She pointed upwards, where the open windows that surrounded the dome now lay impossibly beyond reach. 'You've just sealed us inside.'

Drake didn't respond. Their first priority was to recover the injured member of their party, then they could look for another way out.

Rojas had managed to crawl behind the stack of window panes in the centre of the room, and though he was bleeding from a stomach wound and covered with broken glass, he was still very much alive.

'Come on, dickhead. Time to go,' Drake said, hooking an arm beneath the injured man and helping him up. Rojas bared his teeth in a painful grimace, but struggled determinedly to his feet.

'I had guessed as much,' Rojas replied drily.

'Ryan, we need an exit!' Anya called out.

Drake cast his eyes about the room, seeking an alternative way out. At the opposite end of the long prayer room was an ornate, decorated alcove. Known as a *mihrab*, it was intended to point the way to Mecca – the centre of all Islam. At prayer time, everyone in the room would face towards it and prostrate themselves before the potent symbol of their faith.

To the left of the *mihrab* was a small door leading deeper into the building, padlocked shut. He didn't know what lay beyond as there hadn't been time to investigate during his brief recon of the building earlier, but it certainly wouldn't have any religious function. Perhaps it was an administrative area or storage room.

278

Either way, it was better than remaining here.

'Door,' he said, pointing.

Anya hurried to investigate, hitting her radio transmitter as she went.

'Frost, Dietrich, does anyone copy? Over.'

It was Frost who replied. 'We're here, Anya. We've got you on locator. Do you have Ryan?'

'We have him. He's alive, but none of us will be for long if we don't get out of here. Hawkins caught up with us. We're pinned down inside an abandoned mosque. Unknown number of hostiles, heavily armed.'

'Shit! We're trying to get to you, but the ambush has stirred up protestors all over the city. The police and military are opening fire on them. It's fucking chaos out here.'

Anya could hear several long horn blasts in the background, even over the radio net. Probably from Dietrich as he tried to force his way through heavy traffic.

'We had to circle around to the north to avoid a blockade. They're trying to shut down all major intersections.'

Anya had neither the time nor the inclination to discuss the local traffic situation. 'How far out are you?'

'Five, maybe six minutes. We're doing everything we can.'

'Understood. Radio when you're on site, and watch yourselves.'

'Copy that. Hang in there!'

Clicking the radio off, Anya approached the door barring her way. A shot from the Desert Eagle was enough to defeat the lock securing it. Anya winced as the recoil felt like it was going to snap her wrist, and made a mental note to chastise Drake for his choice of weapons later.

Assuming they lived that long.

The door opened reluctantly, revealing a narrow stone staircase sloping downwards that disappeared into darkness. There were no lights or electrical cables. It was impossible to know how deep the stairs descended or what exactly lay at the bottom.

'What have you got?' Drake asked as he approached, Rojas leaning heavily on him.

'A staircase. It must lead to a basement or cellar.'

'Take him,' he said, handing Rojas over to Anya. 'I'll meet you outside.'

'Where are you going?'

The great cloud of dust that had been stirred up by the collapsed scaffolding was clearing, revealing the ruin of twisted pipes and splintered wooden deck boards partially blocking the main doors. It was impossible to know if Hawkins was amongst them – if he'd retreated outside to avoid being trapped without support, or if he'd been caught and impaled beneath the wreckage.

'Cesar's hurt, he'll slow us down. I'll cover you, try to buy you some time.'

Anya knew a lie when she saw one. She hadn't come all this way, risked everything only to lose him now.

'Ryan—'

'Don't argue! You risked your life to save mine, now let me help you.' He turned to her, pleading for understanding. 'Go! Go now!'

Anya sensed this was a bad move, but knew there was no time to debate the matter. They had a chance, and they had to take it.

'Be right behind us,' she said, leading Rojas down the stairs, the pair quickly swallowed up by the darkness below.

Satisfied that Anya was safe – for now at least – Drake turned back towards the prayer room. An ominous quiet had fallen in the wake of their recent confrontation. Bright shafts of light from the windows above slanted down through the plumes of dust, still hanging heavily in the air.

He advanced towards the ruined doors, keeping the M1911 up, his finger tight on the trigger, keeping to the shadows and using whatever cover he could find to obscure his progress.

Hawkins was in here somewhere. He knew it. That bastard was still alive.

Not for long.

He felt rather than saw the figure on the other side of the room, in a deeper patch of blackness amongst the shadows. Watching him, waiting for his chance. Drake caught the faintest movement out of the corner of his eye. The tiny shift of a weapon.

He reacted, changing direction, breaking into a run just as a burst of gunfire rang out, the muzzle flash incandescent, rounds zipping so close that they seemed to pluck at the folds of his clothing.

Drake turned the Colt .45 towards the source of this pyrotechnic illumination and squeezed the trigger, snapping off a rapid volley of shots as he moved. The weapon kicked back against his hand, gunshots echoing off the vaulted ceiling while brass shell casings bounced off the floor.

The exchange was deafeningly loud but all too brief. As Drake slipped beyond view behind cover, Hawkins abandoned his position and disappeared, melting into the darkness like a ghost.

Above the urgent pounding of his heartbeat, Drake heard the muted thump of boots on the hard floor, the metallic ping as an empty brass shell casing was kicked aside. And then a peal of sadistic laugher.

'Hey, Ryan!' Hawkins called out. 'How you doing over there?'

'Come over and find out,' he replied, ejecting the M1911's magazine.

'All in good time, buddy. All in good time.'

The crackle of automatic fire resounded again as Hawkins squeezed off a short burst, A trio of 5.56mm rounds glanced off a stone column nearby, carving out big chunks of masonry with each hit. Hawkins was probing, searching for him, trying to make him flinch and reveal himself.

'Nice work on Tenbrook's security detail, by the way,' Hawkins went on. 'I saw the whole thing. Always did enjoy watching you work.'

Drake swore under his breath as he looked at the empty magazine in his hand. He was using Anya's weapon, so there was no spare ammunition. Pulling back the slide on top, he saw a single brass round in the chamber.

One shot left.

'I'm glad you're impressed,' Drake replied, hoping to stall his opponent while his mind raced. 'But you were too late. Tenbrook already told me everything.'

Another laugh echoed all around him, cold and malicious. 'Oh, buddy, you're a bad liar. If he'd told you everything, we wouldn't even be having this conversation.'

There. Drake could see his attacker picking his way forward through the debris that now littered the floor. His eyes keen and eager, staring down the sights of the M4 assault rifle at his shoulder.

The sighting only lasted for a second, then there was a sudden flash of light from the barrel, and an instant later the stonework beside him exploded, peppering his face with flying debris.

Teeth clenched in pain, Drake backed up against cover and pressed a hand against the newly opened gash across his cheek.

-

Outside the mosque, Riley stared at the tangle of wreckage blocking the entrance, her lips drawn back in a grimace of fury and frustration. Two of her operatives were attempting to clear a path, but the scaffolding poles had bent and buckled, forming an impenetrable mass of twisted metal.

'Goddamn you, Drake,' she snapped, kicking the side of the SUV they'd rolled up in. Her boot left a dent in the door.

Disregarding the blocked entrance, her gaze turned to the roof of the building, where four minaret towers rose into the azure sky. In the centre there stood a big dome with windows set at intervals around its base. And immediately an idea leapt into her mind.

'Hickman!' she shouted.

One of the assault team leaders hurried over to her. Grabbing him by the arm, Riley pointed up to the roof. 'Get a team up there now. Make sure they have fast rope gear, and signal when you're ready. Move!'

Hickman looked up and understood right away. 'Copy that. We're on it.' He turned his attention to his own team. 'Conway, Serrano, Boyer. On me!'

The three men were just approaching him when they heard a wail of sirens. Riley watched as a pair of blue-and-white police cruisers rounded a corner and came roaring up the road towards them.

'Hostiles inbound. Get ready,' she hissed, standing her ground. Around her, weapons were hidden inside jackets and behind backs.

The lead cruiser came to a screeching halt barely ten feet away. Both doors flew open and a pair of officers in pale-blue shirts emerged, hands on their weapons, one already barking a report into his radio.

The other one was calling out in Arabic, demanding to know what was going on.

'It's okay, sir. The situation's under control,' she said, holding out a hand to stop him coming any closer. The other was on the Kel Tec P-11 pistol concealed at the small of her back. 'For your own safety, I'm going to have to ask you to leave.'

He was having none of it. His eyes narrowed with suspicion as he took in the cluster of men in tactical gear lingering around the team's vehicles. It didn't take him long to connect this mysterious group with the reports of a terrorist attack just a couple of miles away, and to go for his weapon.

Riley was ahead of him. Drawing the P-11 and flicking the safety off in the same movement, she took aim and calmly put a round through his head. His partner started to react, but Riley dropped him with the same clinical precision.

The men who had just emerged from the second cruiser tried to take cover within the vehicle, only to come under a furious hail of automatic fire from both sides as Riley's operatives opened up. Both men were shredded by this merciless steel rain, collapsing across the bloodstained seats.

It was over in seconds, with Hickman closing in to administer the *coup de grâce* with his sidearm. Riley however knew this was just the beginning. More would inevitably be on their way as news of the confrontation spread, not to mention local civilians who now seemed to be rioting throughout the city.

This situation was going downhill fast.

'Hickman! Get your team moving now,' she ordered.

'On it!'

As the assault team sprinted off, Riley touched her encrypted radio transmitter. 'All units, be advised we have local security forces in our AO. We can't stay here much longer. Over.'

–

Inside the mosque a frustrated Hawkins paused in the shadows of an arched alcove. He'd sensed this would happen, but hadn't expected such a quick response from local law enforcement.

'Copy that,' he whispered in response, his voice flat and calm.

He would have to finish this quickly, while there was still time to escape.

He heard the click of a magazine retaining lug disengaging, then a loud clatter as a spent clip slipped from its housing onto the hard stone floor.

Drake was reloading, leaving himself vulnerable.

This was his chance.

Hawkins went for it, sprinting forward with the M4 up at his shoulder, angling in from the left to get a clean shot at his enemy.

But as he did so, Drake suddenly leaned out from behind cover. Hawkins saw the weapon in his hand, saw the barrel turn towards him, and with a flash of indignation, realized he'd been played.

Drake had lured him in.

He changed direction, throwing his weight to the right just as Drake pulled the trigger. Hawkins felt something punch hard into his body armour, knocking him sideways a pace. But no second shot followed.

With his only shot expended, Drake dropped the empty weapon and charged at Hawkins, closing the gap with desperate speed. Realizing Drake was now unarmed, Hawkins triggered a burst that stitched through the air around him.

Drake felt something hot sting his arm but ignored it. He was committed now; it was all or nothing. Kill or die.

With a snarl, Drake ducked and drove his shoulder into Hawkins' midsection, tackling him like a rugby player. Caught off guard by this sudden close-range assault, Hawkins lost his grip and dropped the weapon.

Drake's momentum carried Hawkins into the wall behind, eliciting a grunt as the breath was punched from his chest. Every movement sent a stab of pain through Drake's injured body, but he was beyond that now. He was fighting for his life, fighting for Anya's, fighting for all the people he cared for who now lay dead because of this man.

He had him now. After so many months of waiting, his moment had come. He wanted to tear him apart, shatter his bones, crush the life out of him.

A savage uppercut jerked Hawkins' head back, followed up by a knee driven into his stomach with every ounce of hatred and violence that Drake could summon. He could feel something hot and wet coating his right arm, could feel a sense of hazy weakness taking hold, and knew at least one of Hawkins' shots had found its mark. But he forced himself to ignore it, push past the pain, to concentrate on the anger and bitter fury that was driving him.

Pinning one of the man's arms against the stone surface, Drake clamped his other hand around Hawkins' neck and tightened his grip mercilessly, trying to crush the man's windpipe. Their eyes met then in that moment of deathly struggle, and Drake stared deep into those twin pools of cold malice, knowing he would see fear in them at the last.

This is how you end, he thought. *I told you I'd get you, you bastard. I want you to look at me when the darkness comes for you, I want you to see the faces of all the people you killed.*

But his hand was now slick with his own blood, struggling to find purchase, and his fingers lacked their usual strength, as if his muscles were no longer fully obeying his commands. Anger and adrenaline would only carry him so far.

His adversary meanwhile had recovered from the sudden ferocity of Drake's assault. Hawkins knew his opponent was injured, and how to exploit it.

A fist slammed into Drake's injured arm. White-hot pain exploded and Drake's grip slackened. Leaning back, Hawkins butted him full in the face.

Drake was sent stumbling backwards, stunned and disoriented. His legs gave way and broken glass sliced into his skin.

Drake watched hazily as Hawkins straightened up, drawing a ragged breath, recovering his strength. He knew he somehow had to get up, do something to stop him.

'Holy shit, Ryan. That was fun,' Hawkins said, smiling euphorically. 'Almost makes me feel nostalgic.'

Feeling like he was moving through treacle, Drake rolled over and tried to push himself up, watching with detached interest as blood from his face dripped onto the floor.

It was a futile effort.

The surge of adrenaline that had carried him through the fight was ebbing now, his strength waning. A kick to the ribs was enough to send him sprawling.

'Look at you,' Hawkins said, staring down at him in disgust. 'You're the guy who was supposed to lead us? The guy who was chosen by Powell herself?' He shook his head. 'And now what are you? I always knew she chose the wrong man.'

Drake's world seemed to be rendered soft and indistinct, sounds and shapes appearing as if wrapped in cotton wool. And it was cold, colder than he knew it to be. Hawkins loomed over him, a dark and terrible presence.

'You were a mistake, Ryan. I'm doing the world a favour by ending you,' Hawkins said, snatching up the assault rifle dropped during the fight.

A single gunshot rang out, thunder echoing around the prayer room. But he felt no pain, no thudding impact, no sudden spray of warm blood coating his skin.

The round slammed into Hawkins' right shoulder. His finger tightened involuntarily on the M4's trigger, spraying a burst of uncontrolled automatic fire. The flash of the muzzle flare illuminated his face, full of rage as he stumbled and turned away, vanishing into the shadows.

Then, dimly, as if heard from the depths of a murky pond, Drake became aware of a voice near him. He couldn't make out what was being said, but he sensed great urgency – a forceful, authoritative edge that seemed quite at odds with the peaceful world his mind was lapsing into.

He dragged his eyes open and waited as the world of the mosque swam into bleary focus. Above lay the high vaulted ceiling, shafts of sunlight streaming down.

And then suddenly a face appeared in front of him: a woman's face, bloodied and bruised, but filled with concern. He was quite convinced he'd never seen a more perfect sight in all his life.

'Anya?' he mumbled, not understanding how she could be there. He'd told her to leave, watched her retreat down that stairwell.

'Get up, Ryan,' she ordered, her voice strong and commanding as she tried to pull him to his feet while covering the direction of Hawkins' retreat with the Desert Eagle. 'Get up now or we both die!'

Her words seemed to cut through the fog that had enveloped him, investing his tired body with a renewed sense of urgency and determination.

Summoning up whatever strength remained, Drake rose unsteadily. He felt dizzy and light-headed, and his right arm was disconcertingly numb, but he was able to focus on the woman by his side.

'Can you walk?' she asked.

Drake nodded, the movement seeming to require more effort than necessary. 'Yeah.'

'Good. Now come on!' she said, dragging him towards the back of the room.

Chapter 63

Together they ran towards the low arched doorway that Anya and Rojas had disappeared through earlier, Anya covering their retreat and Drake pushing himself hard to close the distance. Blood dripped down his arm, but at least his mind felt clearer now, better able to process what had happened.

'What the fuck are you doing here?' he asked, suddenly angry. 'I told you to leave!'

'You would be dead now if I hadn't come back,' Anya called back over her shoulder, her weapon sweeping the shadows behind them. 'Now shut up and move!'

Spotting something lying on the ground off to his left, Drake angled towards it, bent down and seized it up.

'What are you doing?' the woman demanded. They were almost at the door now.

'Lost property,' Drake said, pushing her discarded M1911 down the front of his trousers. 'You'd never let me hear the end of it.'

Anya was about to reply, but was interrupted by a call from high up in the domed ceiling at the centre of the prayer room. 'Contact! Ten o'clock low!'

Drake and Anya jumped sideways, moving deeper beneath the overhanging roof at the edge of the room as a string of rounds burst against the ground and columns.

High above, Hickman, who was leaning in through one of the empty windows, let out a frustrated curse. His targets had retreated to the edge of the room, the lower roof blocking his line of sight.

'Cover me! I'm going in!' he shouted, shouldering his assault rifle and stepping in through the window. His fast descent harness was already braced against a stone buttress at the edge of the roof.

As Conway and Boyer took up firing positions in the windows beside him, he threw himself into the void beyond and released his brake. The pulleys screamed as he descended practically in freefall, already bracing himself for the hard landing.

Drake heard the telltale high-pitched hiss of the descent harness. They had mere seconds before a new adversary arrived.

'Come on! Go!' he cried, clapping a hand on Anya's shoulder and sprinting the last few yards to the door.

Seeing them making a break for it now that he was at a lower angle, Hickman halted his descent, swung his assault rifle around and opened fire one-handed.

Anya had barely slipped in through the doorway before a storm of projectiles tore into the wall beside her, some of them punching clean through the thick wooden door panels. She hurried down the stairs after Drake, their feet slipping and skidding on the ancient steps.

Chapter 64

The light quickly tapered off as they descended, leaving them feeling their way in virtual darkness. Drake naturally moved more slowly, unfamiliar with what lay ahead and wary of walking straight into a wall or falling into some unseen gap. The walls changed in character as they went; rather than blocks of stone, this passage appeared to have been roughly hewn into the rock itself. The air was different here too, cool and dry as old bones, suggestive of great age.

'How far does this passage go?' Drake asked, his hushed voice echoing off the bare rock walls.

'We are almost at the bottom,' Anya replied, working from memory to estimate their position. 'There is a drop. Watch yourself.'

There certainly was. Expecting to find the next step, Drake's boot touched only empty space. He pitched forward, leaping onto hard-packed dirt about a foot below.

'I did warn you,' Anya remarked. It was impossible to know if she was smiling, but Drake had the distinct impression that she was.

'Fuck this *Indiana Jones* stuff,' Drake retorted irritably.

The acoustics and the flow of air suggested a chamber of considerable size, but beyond that he couldn't say. The inky darkness was absolute; Drake literally couldn't see the hand in front of his face. It was a disconcerting feeling to have no idea what was around him.

There was also a distinctive smell, different to that of the passageway. This one was newer, more pungent and quite unpleasant, reminding him of a stagnant pond or a muddy bog.

He removed a blue light stick from his webbing, cracked it and shook it a few times to let the phosphorescent chemicals do their thing. His surroundings leapt into solid reality, illuminated by the eerie blue glow. Drake held the source of illumination higher to get a decent view of the room.

The chamber was low-ceilinged and roughly rectangular, with the long axis angling away from them. He guessed it to be about 15 feet wide and perhaps 60 feet long, the floor sloping gently downwards towards the far end. As he'd suspected, the room appeared to be simply carved out of solid rock. Perhaps a natural cavern that had been enlarged and remade.

A series of low stone plinths sat at regular intervals along the length of the room, their size and shape making their purpose obvious even if they were now empty.

'What the hell is a crypt doing beneath a mosque?'

He was no expert on the Islamic faith, but he did know that there were almost never human remains or tombs located within the grounds of mosques.

'This room may be part of an older structure,' Anya surmised, glancing around. 'Early Christian, maybe. Or Judaic.'

The crash of a door being kicked open further up the passage reminded them their enemies knew where they had fled to, and would waste little time giving chase.

Drake reached for the Colt .45 retrieved during their escape from the mosque and held it out to Anya. 'Swap.'

She gratefully accepted her favoured weapon, drawing a fresh magazine from her pocket and pressing it home. Drake was less enthusiastic about the Desert Eagle, but it was better than nothing.

'Rojas must have found a way out of here. Where is it?' he asked, checking he had a round chambered.

'This way.' She led him past the row of empty plinths and towards the far end of the room, where the ground sloped downwards slightly, becoming rougher and uneven underfoot, suggesting that this more distant section had never been finished.

Approaching a narrow fissure in the rock wall, Drake began to understand where the distinctive smell was coming from. It was much stronger now that they were so close, and even less pleasant.

A large, heavy-looking stone block lay on the floor beside this break in the wall, having recently been cast aside. Its general shape suggested it had once been placed there to plug the gap.

'Follow me,' Anya said, turning sideways and shuffling through the gap.

Drake did as requested, the rough stone scraping his skin. It was a tight enough fit for Anya, who was considerably slimmer, and for one moment he feared he'd become trapped. Drake didn't normally consider himself claustrophobic, but he did feel the great immensity of rock pressing on him, and couldn't help but imagine what might happen if it gave way.

Nonetheless, he emerged into a low, arched tunnel beyond, his boots immediately disappearing into a moist, slimy substance that coated the floor to a depth of several inches. The stench of organic decay was pervasive, the air humid and heavy with a nauseating miasma that tickled the throat and brought to mind dead bloated things rotting in the darkness.

'A sewer?' he asked, peering off into the gloom.

An ancient sewer system belonging to the distant past by the looks of things, and likely long supplanted by far more modern arrangements. He imagined these tunnels hadn't been used for their original purpose in decades, maybe even centuries, but still the smell of ancient waste lingered.

Anya nodded. 'They must have broken through when they were excavating that crypt. They had covered it over with a blocking stone. It was Cesar who found it.' She cocked an eyebrow. 'Apparently he is no stranger to escape tunnels.'

Drake might have laughed if their predicament hadn't been so perilous. He imagined there was nothing quite like breaking through into a tunnel filled with the city's shit and piss water to ruin the sanctity of a holy place. No wonder they'd abandoned the place.

'Where is he now?' he asked, changing the subject to more immediate matters.

Anya turned her eyes to the black, decomposing detritus on the ground. Deposited there over the centuries, it resembled dark, boggy looking soil, the kind of stuff that was impossible to move through without leaving an obvious trail. And sure enough, a clear set of prints was visible in the blue glow of the light stick. It led off to the right, where the tunnel appeared to be sloping upwards.

'This way,' she said, leading.

'Wait.' Turning back, Drake ran off in the opposite direction for about 20 feet, then turned and hurried back to her.

She understood what he was doing, leaving a trail that might confuse their enemies and buy them some time to escape. Not much, but enough perhaps.

No sooner had he completed his task than a cacophonous boom echoed from the fissure in the wall, causing the ancient bricks around them to tremble and sending fine shivers of dust down from the ceiling. A couple of pieces of stone, weakened by centuries of damp and exposure, broke away and fell to the floor with a loud clatter. Their pursuers had just stormed the abandoned crypt, using stun grenades to clear the way before making entry.

Nearby, several rats nesting in a small alcove, disturbed by the commotion, let out an indignant squeak and retreated along the edge of the tunnel, their tails slithering through the decomposing effluent.

'We must hurry,' Anya whispered, echoing Drake's own thoughts.

Together they ran off, following Rojas' trail.

–

'Clear!' Hickman called out, having conducted a brief sweep of the crypt and found it empty. The dry, cool air reeked of burned phosphorous.

'Clear!' Conway agreed, lowering his weapon but staying alert. Their two targets had retreated down here, so here they had to be.

Both men parted, making way for Hawkins as he strode into the room. His eyes swept the ancient cavern, lit now by the electric glow of the team's flashlights, taking note of the roughly hewn walls, the sloping floor, the empty plinths long since vacated.

An empty room, with no sign of Drake or Anya.

'Anyone care to explain this?' he asked, his anger turning on the two operatives who had accompanied him.

Neither had an answer.

His earpiece buzzed as a garbled transmission came through. 'All units, we have to pull out,' Riley snapped. 'Local military units are moving to secure the area.'

His face impassive, Hawkins reached up and pressed his transmitter. 'Copy that. We'll meet at the rally point when we're finished.'

Riley hesitated. 'You understand we can't support you now?'

'I understand. Alpha, out.'

Hawkins turned his attention back to his two comrades, their uncertain expressions making it obvious they'd heard the same report he had. They were well and truly committed now; unless they found another way out of here, the only option would be to surrender to the Tunisian military.

'They didn't vanish into thin air,' he said, striding forward into the room, galvanized by the determination to prevail.

Remembering their brief fight earlier, he recalled that Drake had been injured, both by fragments of broken glass and gunfire. None of those injuries were likely to prove fatal, but they had resulted in serious bleeding.

Bleeding...

He turned his flashlight beam downwards. The floor was spotted with blood.

'Got you, Ryan,' Hawkins said, following the trail.

The floor was sloping downwards, and as he moved further away from the site of the grenade detonation, he detected a new scent on the air, foul and decaying.

'On me,' he whispered, raising his weapon as he picked his way carefully forward.

The two operatives took up flanking positions. His flashlight dipped briefly, illuminating a large slab that seemed to be lying discarded near one corner of the room. And then, sure enough, Hawkins' eyes fastened on what lay beyond.

Peering into the narrow crack in the wall, his flashlight beam illuminated the slimy moss-covered walls of an old sewer tunnel. 'They're in there. Find them.'

-

Anya and Drake ploughed onwards, following the course of the tunnel, bent uncomfortably low to avoid the ceiling. They must have covered at least 100 yards, though it was hard to know for certain.

The only time they dared slow down was when they came upon the intersection of several tunnels. With Drake shielding the glow stick, Anya crouched down, studying the tracks at her feet for a second or two. It appeared Rojas had changed direction and veered off to the right, though she couldn't say for sure why.

For a time, the only sounds to be heard were the soft and deeply unpleasant squelch of their boots in the damp muck of the tunnel floor, the rasp of their breathing and the occasional sharp hiss as one of them stumbled on some unseen obstacle.

'How did you know I was in Tunisia?' Drake asked, keeping his voice low.

Anya shrugged, knowing the full story could wait until later. 'Hard work, and some good people who still care about you.'

Drake could scarcely imagine what he'd put them through. 'They're going to be pissed off with me, aren't they?'

'They are,' she agreed. 'How's that shoulder?'

'It works,' he said, deciding not to mention that his right hand was numb and tingling. 'You?'

'The same.' Drake had caught her pretty well with his knife, carving a deep gash in her upper arm.

'Would it make you feel better if I apologised?'

'Not really.'

Drake couldn't hide a smirk. 'Good, because if we're tallying up injuries, you've got some catching up to do. You did shoot me in the stomach, after all.'

'You are still angry about that? It's been three years.'

'Only when I look in the mirror.'

'I missed the vital organs.'

'That supposed to make *me* feel better?'

'Not really.'

Drake snorted with grim humour. 'Figured as much.'

'Wait!' Anya whispered, coming to a halt.

Drake stopped beside her, holding his breath, straining to listen.

It didn't take him long to make out the distant sound of footsteps echoing down the tunnel. Glancing back the way they had come, he was able to discern the faint glow of flashlights – not the direct beams yet, but the reflection of them against the moist walls of the tunnel. They were gaining.

He saw movement beside him. Anya had lowered herself to her knees to present a smaller target, preparing to open fire on their pursuers. He heard the distinctive click as she drew back the hammer on her weapon.

He gripped her shoulder then knelt down beside her. 'Bad idea.'

'We can't outrun them,' Anya pointed out quite logically. Armed with flashlights and with little care for concealment, Hawkins' men could afford to run them down just as fast as they could move. 'But we can meet them on our terms.'

'And we'd die on our terms. They outnumber and outgun us.'

They might get lucky and take down one of their pursuers with a well-timed ambush, but the others would quickly respond. The sewer tunnel offered nothing in the way of cover or concealment, and the muzzle flash of their weapons would quickly betray them.

'What do you suggest? Split up?' Anya replied, her voice restrained but urgent. Having two trails to follow might delay their pursuers, but would also mean they couldn't watch each other's backs and might very well never find each other again.

'Fuck that,' he retorted immediately. 'We push on, turn right at the next two junctions and look for a way up.'

'Double back on ourselves?'

'They won't expect it.'

'Because it's a stupid idea,' she pointed out.

'You'd be surprised how many times a stupid idea saved my life,' Drake said, letting go of her and forcing himself up again. 'Let's go.'

–

Fingers flexing and tensing against the grip of his assault rifle, Hawkins dashed down the narrow, low-hanging corridor, his flashlight beam jumping with each step. They were closing in. They might not be able to follow the spots of blood from Drake's injury, but their targets had left an easily identifiable trail in the black mulch underfoot. It was like tracking an animal through deep snow – you simply couldn't miss it.

His shoulder burned where the round had glanced off his body armour and torn through the flesh beneath. He could feel hot sticky blood coating his back, but he pushed past the pain, using it to his advantage the way he'd been taught, allowing the anger it kindled to burn bright within him.

He stopped suddenly at an intersection, where their own tunnel joined up with another running almost directly across its path. Here the trail turned abruptly right, taking the side passage. Hawkins stared at it, considering the situation and what might have prompted it.

Then a smile began to form as Drake's plan became apparent.

'He knows he can't outrun us. He's trying to shake us off.'

Turning to the two operatives following him, he trained his flashlight on the shorter of the pair. Trevor Conway, short and compact but a lightning-fast sprinter, often chosen to take point and scout ahead.

'Conway, double back and take your first left. Move your ass. Hickman, stay on me.'

Conway nodded, immediately grasping what he was saying. He would be the hammer, and Hawkins and Hickman the anvil. 'Copy that.'

As the operative sprinted back the way he'd come, Hawkins resumed his pursuit with Hickman right behind him.

Drake had escaped by the skin of his teeth, but he was hurt, and he was moving slowly. Hawkins had the advantage of speed, firepower and numbers, and that was all he needed. He'd kill that bitch Anya for sure, swat her quickly like the irritating fly she'd become, but maybe he'd take his time with Drake.

After all, nobody was going to interfere with them down here.

–

Drake couldn't say when he first became aware of the growing ambient light. He'd grown so accustomed to using the sounds of their movements and the feel of the walls around them that a kind of mental picture of their surroundings had already developed in his mind. But gradually he became aware that it was more than just a visualisation; details, still vague and indistinct, were starting to become visible to his naked eyes even without the glow stick.

He glanced left and saw the shadowy form of Anya moving beside him, bent low. He saw the shape of her slender arms, the brighter shock of her hair. He looked up at the curved roof of the tunnel, caught a fleeting, tantalising glimpse of daylight through a tiny crack in the brickwork.

'Light,' he whispered.

'I know,' came the reply.

The tunnel was still sloping upwards, despite their change of course. Whether through intuition or sheer blind luck, they were heading in the right direction, ascending slowly from the depths of the old sewer network. Even the air seemed to have changed, becoming less damp and fetid as they progressed.

The increased visibility, not to mention the prospect of escaping these dark, claustrophobic tunnels was enough to spur both of them on to greater efforts. They quickened their pace, pushing through the pain and fatigue.

Only Anya still harboured doubts.

'Rojas could still be down here,' she said quietly, her voice tinged with guilt.

It had been her decision to leave him and go back for Drake. Though injured and bleeding, he'd still been capable of moving under his own power, and she'd considered it a risk worth taking at the time. They had certainly seen no further sign of him, but there was no reason to believe he wasn't still alive.

A man could wander for hours, maybe days in this network of abandoned underground tunnels, faltering as blood loss took its toll. Dying slowly, alone in the darkness.

Drake nodded solemnly, understanding her conflicted feelings. 'He doesn't seem stupid. He'll find another way—'

With a sudden, unexpected lunge, Anya threw herself at him, grabbed him by the shirt and pulled him to the floor. Drake landed amongst the accumulated muck with Anya on top of him, trying to stifle a cry of surprise and pain as his injured arm blazed.

But before he could utter a word, the tunnel was filled with the deafening boom of automatic gunfire. Drake looked up as tracer rounds sailed right over them, arcing down the tunnel like angry hornets before ricocheting off the ancient walls further down.

Instinctively he turned towards the source of this unexpected gunfire, and was just about able to make out a figure leaning out from around a bend in the tunnel. Taking advantage of the dim natural light, he'd killed his under-barrel flashlight so that he could approach unseen. Somehow Hawkins had anticipated their course and moved to intercept them.

Another burst rang out, the flash of the weapon illuminating their target.

Startled they might have been, but neither Drake nor Anya were out of the fight. Both returned fire simultaneously, the boom of their semi-automatics adding to the ear-splitting din. Drake's big .50 calibre pistol leapt upwards with each shot, and he flinched as an ejected casing from Anya's weapon, still red-hot, bounced against his neck and seared the skin.

Their loud show of defiance was enough to force their attacker to retreat around the corner, but poor visibility meant that neither side was able to score any decisive hits. They had bought themselves a reprieve, albeit a fleeting one.

'Fall back!' Drake yelled, taking advantage of the temporary lull. Scrambling to his feet, he retreated the way they'd come, covering Anya by snapping off another shot. He was down to his last mag, and there couldn't be many rounds left in it.

To try to fight their way through would be futile. They were both injured and low on ammunition. Their best chance was to get to the next intersection about 30 yards back and take a different tunnel, hopefully avoiding another—

He skidded to a halt, hearing the echoing sounds of footsteps up ahead. More than one attacker, closing in rapidly. Drake and Anya drew back, flattening themselves against the wall as a short burst sliced through the air from just around the corner, narrowly missing them and instead chewing up ancient brickwork just yards away.

It was an ambush, two groups closing off both ends of the tunnel.

They were trapped.

'Tangos in sight!' they heard a voice call out from their right. 'Watch yourselves, they're still armed.'

Just a few scant yards away, around a curve in the tunnel, Conway pulled a fragmentation grenade from its Velcro pouch. He was a veteran of the tunnel and cave fighting in Afghanistan, and knew there was no quicker way to flush an enemy out than a grenade or two.

Hooking his thumb into the pin, he jerked it back, withdrawing it from the housing. The fuse handle, held in place by a coiled spring, detached and flew across the tunnel to ping against the wall opposite.

Drake and Anya both tensed up at this distinctive sound. By unspoken agreement, they prepared to push off the wall and make a break for it, preferring to take their chances against their enemies than be torn apart by shrapnel.

Then something happened, something neither side had foreseen.

As Conway stepped away from the wall to hurl the grenade, a second figure emerged from the shadows behind him. A man who had crept up close unseen and unheard, using the darkness and the urgency of battle to his advantage.

The first shot he fired hit Conway between the neck and shoulder joint just as he was winding up to throw, blasting through the muscles and nerve bundles and sending a jolt like electricity down his arm. The grenade flew from his grasp just as he was about to throw it, bouncing off the wall about ten yards away as he let out a cry of pain and surprise.

The next two rounds hit his upper torso as he twisted towards this unexpected new threat, trying to bring the awkward assault rifle to bear. Too late. A fourth round went through his right eye, abruptly ending his fight. He crashed against the tunnel wall, leaving a smear of blood as he slid down the stones.

His comrades had of course heard this commotion too, and each began to react according to their own understanding of the situation.

Hawkins was the first to move, realizing something was wrong.

'Go! Go!' he yelled, pushing himself away from his narrow area of cover and rounding the bend in the tunnel, weapon up, searching frantically for a target.

Anya was next, turning towards the source of the gunfire. She had recognized the distinctive crackle of a 9mm pistol, and knew such a weapon was unlikely to belong to their enemies. As she approached, she saw Conway stagger backwards and collapse against the wall.

Drake meanwhile had heard the grenade ricochet off the wall close by. He couldn't see it in the dim light cast by the glow stick, but he knew it was there, and it was already fused. If the device was of US origin, it would have a five-second delay. It had to be at least two seconds since he'd caught the distinctive ping of the fly-off handle detaching, giving him maybe three seconds in which to act.

Three seconds, if he was lucky.

He went for it, diving towards where he guessed the grenade would have landed, and crashing to the ground amidst the mulchy detritus. He could hear movement to his left, loud voices, urgent footsteps pounding towards him, but he ignored them. All that mattered now was the grenade.

Two seconds.

His hands moved frantically, searching, feeling small rocks and other pieces of unidentified debris. Desperately seeking the smooth, rounded metal casing. He could smell something above the stench of centuries-old decay – an acrid, chemical tang. The scent of the grenade's internal fuse burning.

One second.

'Contact!' he heard a voice yell out to his left. Hawkins' voice, flushed with excitement and triumph. He would be swinging his weapon up to fire.

There! Drake's fingers brushed against something smooth and round and heavy, lying partially embedded in the soft loamy ground. He had it!

Without thinking, he hurled it towards the sound of Hawkins' voice.

His last sight was of a darkened figure diving aside, then there was a bright flash in mid-air, and suddenly the tunnel was filled with a terrible roaring, deafening thunder. Drake curled into a ball in a feeble effort to protect himself as the roar intensified, breaking up into individual blasts and rumblings that carried on far longer than a single explosive detonation should have allowed.

He felt a wave of something cold and gritty wash over him, and squeezed his eyes shut, choking and coughing as dust was sucked into his lungs. He felt several small, hard lumps of rock pummelling his body, and could do little more than pray nothing larger hit him.

Only when the rumbling at last abated did he dare to move, stretching his limbs experimentally, then raising himself up. It would be wrong to say he was unharmed, since he'd endured almost nothing but harm today, but he didn't feel like he'd broken any bones. With the dust now beginning to settle, he chanced to open his eyes.

What he saw left him speechless.

The entire section of tunnel around the site of the grenade detonation had collapsed, the concussive blast proving the final straw for the old and neglected structure. It was impossible to tell how long a section of tunnel had been destroyed, but the entire height and width of the passage was now blocked by rocks and loose earth. The loss of ground stability had also opened up a hole overhead that allowed bright daylight to stream in. Peering up through the swirling dust, he could make out blue sky and the walls of some kind of building.

'Ryan!' Anya called out.

Turning around, Drake was just in time for Anya to throw her arms around him, the warmth and softness of her body a welcome contrast to the falling rocks that had assailed him. He closed his eyes and let out a relieved breath, and could happily have spent the rest of the day right there.

'Will you two please save it for later?'

Drake opened his eyes as Rojas limped over to him, one hand pressed against his abdomen. He looked drawn and pained, and like Drake and Anya he was covered in dirt and dust from the collapse, but he was still very much alive. A 9mm Beretta was clasped in his other hand. He also noticed the dead operative slumped against the wall, and realized it was Rojas' handiwork.

'How did you find us?'

The former assassin flashed a grin. 'It wasn't hard. You made enough noise that a blind man could find you.'

Fair point, Drake thought.

Rojas pointed up at the hole that had now opened above them. The tumble of debris now filling the tunnel was steep and unstable, but it looked like it might just be climbable if they were careful.

'I'm no expert, but a street collapsing into the ground will probably attract attention,' Rojas remarked drily. 'Maybe we should consider being somewhere else?'

Drake wasn't inclined to argue. The sooner they got out of this dark, confined, desperate place, the happier he'd be.

'You go first,' he said. 'I'll help you up.'

Rojas cocked an eyebrow. 'Thought you'd never ask.'

Chapter 65

The Hawkins household had settled into a deep, exhausted slumber. All of them except Jason, who lay awake in his bed listening to the patter of rain against the window, staring at the patch of discoloured damp on the ceiling. There was a hole in the roof. Several of them, in fact, that his father hadn't gotten around to patching. Every time it rained the stain would grow just a little bigger as more moisture soaked through. He imagined sometimes that he could see it creeping outward at the edges. How long, he wondered, would it be before it took up the entire ceiling?

And how many of them would still be around when it did?

His father had given Nathan one, all right. He'd given him a good one, working him over again and again with the patient, methodical approach of a carpenter taking on a challenging project. His shoulders, his back, his ass. He'd kept going until Nathan's legs had buckled and he'd collapsed to the dirty garage floor. He'd kept going until Nathan started to whimper, until the tears came, until finally he was crying out in pain and begging for him to stop.

Jason could still see his eyes screwed shut as he lay curled up in a pathetic ball, tears streaking his face, whining and choking back sobs. And all the while, his two brothers had just stood there watching. Watching, saying nothing, unable to look at each other. And secretly, horribly, feeling glad that it wasn't happening to them.

His father had been sweating and breathing heavily when he'd finally had enough. And yet, despite his fatigue, there was an odd, flickering light of excitement in his eyes. The perspiration seemed to have come from this sense of elation rather than the exertion. And as he'd turned away, Jason had noticed a bulge in the crotch of his work trousers that hadn't been there before.

He'd instructed his other two sons to help Nathan up and carry him back into the house, while he'd carefully set the belt back on its peg, loosened his shirt and left without saying a word. While Tyler Hawkins was stretched out on his recliner chair sipping back a beer and watching TV, his eldest son had been slowly peeling off his clothes to reveal blackened skin and bruises that would linger for weeks. Bruises so deep he had to sleep on his stomach for the next several nights.

Jason had gone to bed without speaking to either his father or his two brothers. He'd lain there angry, furious, disgusted and most of all, ashamed. Ashamed he hadn't stood up for Nathan. Ashamed that what had happened was doubly his fault. Ashamed because in some inexplicable, intuitive part of his childish mind, he knew Tyler Hawkins wasn't going to stop. There would always be another transgression, another mistake, another rule broken. Another reason to give them one.

And sooner or later he wouldn't cease his beating. He would get caught up in the moment, go too far, keep on working over his victim until the crying and the screaming ceased. Would he even realize? Would he even care?

Jason waited until the lights had gone off, not even pretending to go to sleep. He waited until all movement in the house had ceased, until his father was sure to be asleep.

He looked over at the alarm clock by his bed – 2:12 am.

If a man's got himself a problem that's bustin' his ass, then by God it's up to him to fix it – that was what Tyler Hawkins confidently declared. His father wasn't much of a philosopher, but after a few cans he was apt to give his opinion on a range of subjects regardless of his knowledge or understanding. Who was going to argue with him? Three frightened kids? No, sir.

If a man's got himself a problem that's bustin' his ass, then by God it's up to him to fix it. Well, Jason Hawkins had himself one big motherfucker of a problem. It was bustin' his ass to be sure, and his brothers'. And that problem wasn't going to go away by itself. That much was clear. Something would have to be done.

Reaching beneath his old, lumpy mattress, he felt around until his hands closed on the ridged plastic frame of a box cutter. He'd swiped it from one of his father's toolboxes, kept it hidden for weeks, months now, hoping and praying he'd never need it, but secretly knowing that someday he would.

Someday. Today.

Pulling off the covers, he eased himself out of bed and crept across his room, opened the door a crack and looked out into the hallway. The faint flickering glow of a TV was coming from the lounge, accompanied by soft snoring.

He pushed his door open further, slipped out into the hall and crept towards the sound, heart pounding in his thin chest, the box cutter already slick with cold sweat. He slowly emerged into the lounge.

Tyler Hawkins was there, stretched out unconscious on his recliner in front of the TV, with several crumpled beer cans lying around him.

Jason crept closer, instinctively avoiding the loose floorboards, and rounding the chair so that he could look down at the sleeping form of his father.

Considering this man had been there almost every day of his life, Jason spent remarkably little time actually looking at him. Really looking at him. To do so for too long would provoke an indignant question of what he was staring at, maybe even an excuse to give him one.

But not now. Now he could look all he wanted, and Tyler Hawkins would know nothing of it. He couldn't quite resist the voyeuristic temptation.

He'd seen photographs of his father in his younger days. Happier days, when he and Mom used to go cruising in his Chevy convertible that he'd restored himself – always a point of fierce pride – and drive down the coast to Mobile, Orange Beach, even Pensacola. When his father had looked young and slim and energetic, when he had long hair and big sideburns and wore T-shirts that showed off his muscles. He'd looked invincible in those pictures, Jason had always thought. Like a hero. A guy who could take on anything. A guy who was afraid of nothing. A guy a kid could look up to.

Tyler Hawkins didn't look like much of a hero now, he thought with a sudden, aching sadness. The sadness of a kid who finally sees their once godlike parents as the flawed, weak humans they really are. Sprawled out on the threadbare recliner, his stained T-shirt riding up to reveal a bloated gut and sagging chest, his once strong jaw starting to go jowly, his hair crudely buzz cut and flecked with grey, and starting to recede at the sides. Smelling of stale sweat and stale beer.

No, he didn't look like much of a hero at all. He looked like the kind of thing a hero was supposed to fight against. A villain, a tyrant, a monster. A monster who beat up his own kids for any reason he damn well pleased, and who got a hard-on when he did it. A tyrant who sooner or later was going to kill one of them. Or all of them.

Sorry, Dad, but I gotta give you one.

Jason's thumb worked the little plastic latch on top of the box cutter, and the small, clinically sharp blade emerged. He moved closer, bringing the little knife in, changing his grip on it then changing it back, unsure what way to hold it. Was there a right way to kill a man with a box cutter?

He tried to think back to the movies he'd seen, the action flicks that made it all seem so quick and easy and painless. When he'd watched John Wayne catch a Vietcong sentry from behind in The Green Berets, big John had just drawn his knife across the guy's throat and he'd gone limp within seconds, falling from sight. Dead. Forgotten. Move on.

Was it really that easy? His eyes travelled over his father's stubble-covered throat. Should he cut the windpipe? Then he saw the thick jugular vein at the side, pulsing ever so slightly in time to the beat of his heart. He knew about that, at least. Lions bit down on the jugular of their prey, didn't they? That was the way to end it. And it was so close to the surface, even the little box cutter blade would be able to cut it.

He brought the knife fractionally closer, his hand trembling visibly now. It had seemed so simple and logical when he'd resolved to do it. A necessary step — that was what he'd told himself. A sacrifice to protect his brothers. He didn't doubt there would be trouble after that. Cops, social workers, maybe even prison. But he could live with that, because then he wouldn't have to be afraid any more.

Sorry, Dad, but I gotta give you one.

The blade moved closer, edged in so far, but no further, stopping a clear foot from his father's neck as if it had hit some invisible wall. Jason found that he could do no more. Thinking about it was one thing. Fantasising about doing it was another. But actually going through with it, actually cutting his father's throat, murdering him, taking a life... was that really something he could do? Was that what a hero was supposed to do? Kill the monster, overthrow the tyrant, vanquish the villain?

He didn't feel like a hero at that moment. He didn't feel like big John taking on the Vietcong, he felt like an 11-year-old kid. Small and weak and frightened and sick to his stomach and desperate to run away and pretend none of this had ever happened. More than that, in some pathetic, anguished part of his mind he still loved his father. He hated him sometimes, he was afraid of him most of the time, but part of him still loved him. That little boy part of him that remembered the man from those old photographs who looked so strong and young and happy. The hero. His hero.

Almost without thinking, he felt himself thumb the blade back into the knife's frame and slowly straighten up from his father's chair. But as he did so, he heard a sudden horrified gasp from the other side of the room.

His head snapped around, fear flooding his body, to see the small skinny form of Samuel standing in the doorway, looking obscenely small and young in his pyjamas. He was staring at Jason, at the knife in his hand, his eyes huge and frightened, his mouth gaping open.

Oh Christ. Oh no, Samuel, please don't make a fucking sound or he's going to wake up and see me. Please, Samuel, this isn't what you think it is.

Jason acted without thinking, taking a step towards his younger brother, wanting to reach out to him, talk to him, explain to him what was really going on. But he should have thought, should have remembered there was a crumpled beer can beside his foot, should have taken just a second to consider what might happen.

If he had, Jason Hawkins' life might have turned out very differently.

–

Hawkins' eyes snapped open like someone had turned a switch on inside his head. He practically leapt up, scattering pieces of rock and ancient cement that had settled over him. He drew in a breath, craving oxygen but instead finding hot, dusty air that clogged his lungs and started him coughing immediately. The sudden shock of it was enough to bring his mind fully conscious again and, like a computer rebooting, his others senses began to light up too.

He was hurting – that much was obvious. His ears were ringing, his skin and clothes grey with dust, mingling with sticky dark patches of blood from various injuries. His body felt as if he'd just been sealed inside a steel drum and rolled down a hill.

Drake had given him one, all right. But he was used to that. He'd taken worse.

He glanced over at where his enemy had been, finding instead a wall of rubble. The tunnel beyond was gone, collapsed in on itself by the grenade blast, with only a few thin shafts of daylight peeking in.

Fucking Conway, using explosives in an unstable tunnel like this. If the man wasn't dead already, he soon would be when Hawkins caught up with him.

'Sir! Sir, are you okay?'

Hawkins turned slowly to regard Hickman who had appeared from further down the tunnel, looking relatively unharmed, probably because he was further away from the blast

'Where's Drake?' Hawkins asked.

The operative shook his head. 'I don't know, sir. Probably killed in the collapse. It's a miracle you're alive yourself.'

Hawkins didn't believe in miracles, nor did he believe Ryan Drake was dead. The man was too fucking stubborn to be killed by something like this. He'd lost him. A perfect opportunity, and he'd watched it slip right through his fingers.

He should have felt anger at this failure, but oddly something else stirred in the depths of his mind. Something Jason Hawkins hadn't felt in a long time. A slight, barely detectable kernel of fear.

The man he'd faced today hadn't been the same man he had so easily overpowered in Pakistan several months ago. He was harder, stronger, more savage than almost any he'd gone up against in his life. A man who fought and killed without mercy or remorse, who had once been strong enough to lead Hawkins' own unit.

He began to wonder if that man had finally returned, if it was possible he had underestimated Ryan Drake.

'We have to get him,' he said. 'We have to finish this.'

Hickman cocked his head, listening as a radio transmission came through. Hawkins' unit had been broken in the explosion.

'Copy that,' he said at length, then looked at his commander. 'We've got Tunisian army units inbound, sir. We've been ordered to pull back.'

The military would almost certainly have responded to the fire fight at the mosque, and it wouldn't take them long to find the underground crypt and the entrance to the sewers. Not to mention the tunnel explosion had caused a portion of a city street to suddenly collapse into the ground. Even the most bone-headed of commanders couldn't fail to connect those events.

Hawkins held out a hand. Regardless of the risks, nobody was going to order him to break off now. 'Give me that fucking radio.'

Unclipping his radio unit from the attached earpiece, the operative tossed it to him.

'We need confirmation Drake's dead,' Hawkins said firmly. 'We're not leaving until we have him KIA.'

He'd expected to hear Riley or one of the other assault team leaders over the net, trying to convince him to give up the hunt. Instead the voice that responded was deeper, smoother, calmly commanding.

'Negative, Jason. You'll withdraw now,' Powell instructed. 'I don't need you being captured and exposing us.'

'We won't get another chance at this.'

She paused, and he sensed something coming. Like a fighter drawing back their arm to deliver a haymaker.

'Jason, you've created enough problems already. Don't make me give you one.'

Her words were like pressing the rewind button on his life. In the blink of an eye, he had skipped backwards through the last three decades, back to another time when he hadn't been the man he was now. Back to that living room with the rain pattering off the windows and a box cutter clutched in his sweating hands.

His silence told her that her message had been received.

'You'll withdraw now,' she repeated. 'Say it, Jason.'

Hawkins closed his eyes. The fire of anger and lust for revenge was still there, but it had dimmed now, smothered by the cloying hold she still had on him. The power her voice commanded.

He held the radio up, his hand trembling a little, and pressed the transmit button. 'We're withdrawing.'

Chapter 66

The climb was neither easy nor fast. Each of them was tired and injured, and the debris pile was dangerously unstable. Rocks and chunks of stone gave way beneath their feet, tumbling down the steep slope into the darkness below. Anya had to swing aside as a large piece of stonework slipped free and rolled past her, rumbling and crashing onto the floor of the tunnel.

'Sorry,' Rojas called back over his shoulder.

Anya gave him a hostile glare.

Slipping and clawing his way up while keeping one hand pressed against the wound at his abdomen, Rojas let out a gasp when a pair of big hairy hands suddenly appeared over the lip of the hole, reached in and grasped his outstretched arm. In a matter of moments he'd disappeared, hauled right out of the tunnel.

Drake froze, his hand going instinctively for his weapon. Then a face appeared in the gap above, big and broad, the stubble-coated jaw giving way to a thick muscular neck. An equally large arm, heavy with slabs of corded muscle, reached in towards him.

The man grunted a word in Arabic that Drake was pretty sure meant 'reach'. Drake however wasn't inclined to blindly trust his life to a stranger, and pulled back from him.

'It's okay,' he heard Rojas call down. 'It's civilians up here.'

The man repeated his command, still holding one massive hand out. Reluctantly Drake reached out and grasped it.

The effect was like being attached to a mechanical winch that was suddenly spun up to maximum speed. With one mighty heave, the man pulled him right out, rocks and sandy soil sliding beneath him as he emerged, blinking, filthy and bloodstained, into the evening light.

Drake could see that a crowd had indeed gathered around the collapsed tunnel, mostly men of various ages but a few women and children as well. Some, like the big guy who had just pulled him out, were obviously no strangers to emergencies and had come here to help. Most however were keeping their distance, watching the drama play out, while a few regarded Drake with open suspicion and hostility. A couple were even recording the events on their cell phones.

Releasing his grip, the man who had pulled Drake and Rojas free turned his attention back to the hole, and within seconds Anya appeared in similar fashion, virtually lifted right off her feet.

It was easy to see why he'd had no trouble with heavy lifting. The man was quite simply huge – not tall but massively built, with a heavy barrel chest, broad muscular shoulders and thick brawny arms. His physique wasn't the lean form of an athlete, but rather the big, bulked-out frame of a power lifter.

'Anyone else down there?' he asked in Arabic, peering down into the gloom.

Anya shook her head and looked down. 'I hope not.'

He frowned. 'Who are you? What happened down there?'

She had no time for explanations, and doubted he'd believe any lie she might spin anyway. Turning away, she hit her radio transmitter.

'All units, come in. Does anyone copy me?'

'Goddamn it, where the hell have you been?' Frost's voice was unmistakable, as was her relief and anger. 'We've been trying to raise you on comms.'

'We were out of radio range.' The full story of their escape could wait. 'We're in a civilian neighbourhood.'

She glanced around, spotting the distinctive minaret towers of the mosque situated halfway up a hillside in the distance. Even from here she could see the flash of blue lights around it, not to mention a couple of olive-green military trucks.

'We're about a quarter of a mile north of the mosque. We need extraction now.'

'Copy that. Keep the comms open, we'll track your signal.'

'Wilco. Out.'

Drake on the other hand had his attention on matters closer at hand. The tunnel collapse had caved in a portion of the street about 15 yards long, running roughly diagonal across the roadway and extending all the way to the edge of a residential block opposite. The outer wall was badly cracked and a portion of it was sagging downwards with nothing left to support it.

'Get away from that building!' he called out, pointing to the small group of civilians who had gathered to inspect the damage. 'Move back! It could collapse.'

They stared at him blankly, but one at least seemed to understand enough English to catch the gist. Quickly explaining the situation to the others, they began to move away from the compromised structure.

'We can't stay here,' Anya warned, hurrying over. 'The police will connect this explosion to the attack earlier. They've already sealed off the mosque.'

Drake nodded, well aware of the danger. None of them were in any shape for another running battle, especially against the Tunisian military. Not only that, but their appearance had attracted more attention from local residents, who were leaning out of windows and doorways to watch them.

Another group was approaching from the west, this one looking decidedly antagonistic. Many had their faces covered with masks, and a few were carrying improvised weapons of various kinds: bats, clubs and even bricks. Protestors on their way to smash up the nearest government building, and perhaps attracted by rumours of an explosion here. The kind of people Drake had no interest in tangling with.

He nodded down the street which headed east, away from the mosque, away from the rioters, away from the shit storm they'd just stirred up.

'We move. Front it, no sudden movements. Go.'

The group started at a brisk pace, which was about as much as any of them were capable of at that point. But if they'd expected to slip away unnoticed, they were to be very decisively proven wrong.

Within seconds the big guy was calling out to them, demanding to know where they were going, who they were and what they were doing in the city. Anya turned and tried to offer an excuse.

'Our friend needs help,' she said, pointing to Rojas. 'We must find a hospital.'

That at least was true. None of them were looking particularly good.

Whatever the lie, he wasn't buying it. A renewed volley of shouting hounded them as they retreated, quickly joined by other voices, both male and female, all increasingly angry and fired up.

'This crowd is turning ugly,' Rojas warned. Word of their presence was spreading, and the mob coming in from the west were starting to take notice.

'Tell me something I don't know,' Drake shouted over the growing catcalls and angry yells. 'Just keep moving.'

There's nothing quite so frightening as watching a hostile mob forming, especially when that hostility is directed against you. Drake had seen it for himself in places like Iraq, where peaceful protests could turn into violent waves of destruction in a matter of minutes. All it took was for something to set it off.

As it turned out, that thing came in the form of a glass bottle thrown down at them from one of the upper floor windows. Drake couldn't tell exactly where it came from, but he saw the missile come sailing in towards them and dodged aside. It smashed on the ground by his feet.

That was it as far as he was concerned. There's a time to tough it out, and a time to break and run. This was the latter.

'Move,' he said, urging his companions on as more improvised missiles rained down, one striking Anya a glancing blow between the shoulder blades and another hitting Drake in the thigh. Neither hit was serious, but sooner or later they were bound to be struck by something more substantial.

'You all right?' Drake asked, drawing protectively close to her.

Anya's face was tight with pain. 'None of us will be unless we get out of here.'

As one young man darted forward to pelt them with pieces of brick, Drake decided it was time to act. Drawing the Desert Eagle, he aimed a few feet above the youth's head and capped off a round.

The sight of the weapon alone was enough to extinguish whatever fire of courage he possessed, but the booming gunshot quickly sent him scurrying for cover. His retreat was accompanied by screams and yells from the assembled mob, some frightened, others angry. All focussed on the three foreigners trying to beat a hasty retreat.

This show of force was enough to make the crowd draw back, but Drake knew it was a temporary reprieve at best. The use of weapons would only escalate the situation. Bring a gun to a rock fight, and soon enough the other side will fetch their own guns.

The three of them were ducking down as a renewed volley was hurled from upper windows, when suddenly a vehicle came to a screeching halt at the intersection up ahead. Drake's first instinct was to turn his weapon on this new arrival, thinking the local police or military had decided to join the party.

Until he saw the driver.

'Well?' Dietrich called out, flinching as a bottle rebounded off the truck's hood and shattered on the road. 'You want a ride or what?'

Drake couldn't say he and Dietrich shared a good history. But that didn't change the fact he could have kissed him at that moment.

'Go! Go!' he said, urging Anya and Rojas towards the vehicle while he covered them, firing off another warning shot at the crowd who sensed their enemy was about to escape.

He was the last member of the bedraggled party to clamber up into the truck's rear bed, with rocks and bottles and other missiles raining down around them. Thrusting out a hand, Frost helped him up, then hammered on the driver's cab.

'They're in! Get us the fuck out of here!'

Dietrich did just that, and with a squeal of skidding tyres and a cloud of burned rubber, they were on their way, leaving the frustrated mob to vent their anger somewhere else.

Chapter 67

After driving due south more or less flat out for about 20 minutes, with the hot desert wind snapping at the clothes of the small group clustered in the back, Dietrich decided they'd gone far enough. He turned off the main road and pulled in behind a low rocky escarpment covered with dry scrub, hiding them from view. The sun was just going down, its light blazing across the sky. He killed the engine and slumped back in his seat, letting out a weary but relieved breath.

Against the odds, they'd located Drake and made it out of the city with him in one piece. More or less.

Reaching into his pocket, Dietrich found his pack of cigarettes and lit one up, taking a deep and well deserved draw.

The others clambered down from the rear cargo bed on aching limbs. None of them had said much during the journey, the situation being too fraught, the wind too loud, their minds too weary.

Instead they had busied themselves dressing wounds and stabilizing injuries as best they could, particularly Rojas. Constant pressure had helped slow the bleeding. He would certainly need more attention, but barring infection the wound was unlikely to prove fatal.

Drake however knew that there were other more pressing matters to attend to, starting with an apology to the rest of the group. They deserved that much at least.

He first approached Frost. 'Keira, I wanted to—'

She swung around abruptly and socked him hard across the jaw.

'That's for being a fucking selfish asshole, Ryan!' she shouted. 'Goddamn you, we've travelled halfway across the fucking world looking for you, nearly got ourselves killed for this shit. Don't you have any idea what you've put us all through? Don't you know how worried we were? We thought you were gone for good, you prick!'

Rubbing his throbbing jaw, Drake looked at her sadly. She was shaking with rage, her voice wavering towards the end of her tirade, her eyes glistening in the orange sunset.

He understood why she'd done it, and didn't blame her one bit. He deserved it. Deserved a lot more, come to think of it.

He glanced around at the others, who were all watching him closely, waiting to see how he'd respond. Likely few of them trusted him after everything he'd done, and he wouldn't blame them for that either.

'You might as well form a line, guys,' he said, managing a pained smile. He was pretty sure she'd split his lip.

Rushing forward, Frost threw her arms around him in what might have been considered a bear hug if she'd been bigger. As it was, she clung to him so hard it hurt.

'Ow! Take it easy!' he implored, though he couldn't help but smile with relief. 'There's not much of me left that doesn't hurt.'

'Goddamn you, don't ever do that again,' she whispered, her voice close to breaking. 'You die, I'll fucking kill you.'

Drake closed his eyes, hugging her back just as tight. 'I'm not going anywhere.'

Frost finally released him, her face flushed with embarrassment. It wasn't often she let her guard down, and for once she seemed to be at a loss for words.

She might have been the most vocal of the group, but it was obvious to Drake that the others harboured similar thoughts. They needed – more than that, they *deserved* – to hear something from him. Some explanation that might justify the insanity of the past few days, some reasoned account of his actions that would make all this worth it.

He wished he could give it to them.

'You all took a huge risk coming here, and an even bigger one trying to bring me back when I was... not myself.' He paid particular attention to Anya when he said this. 'I know it doesn't add up to much now, but I'm grateful for what you did. All of you. And I'm... sorry that I put you through this.'

He was right. It didn't sound like much at all, woefully inadequate considering everything he'd done. But it was pretty much all he had left at that point.

'Explanations, Ryan,' Dietrich said as he took another drag on his cigarette. 'Apologies can wait. For now, I'd rather hear your side of the story.'

Drake eased himself down onto a jutting rock. Dietrich wasn't wrong, but answering his questions wasn't going to be easy. He looked at each of them in turn, at this group of people who had risked their lives to bring him in. Some of them he'd served with for years, others he barely even knew beyond their names, yet here they all were, gathered in a loose semicircle around him, waiting expectantly for answers.

'What do you want to know?'

For the next 15 minutes he talked and they listened; Drake doing his best to explain the change that had come over him, the resurrection of some shadowy dormant persona from the depths of his mind – this was a particularly hard element to relate, and just the thought of it was enough to make his skin prickle – his desperate and ruthless hunt for answers that always seemed to be just beyond his grasp, his brief phone conversations with his mysterious benefactor, and finally the mission that had brought him here to Tunisia.

'Tenbrook was supposed to be the final link in the chain,' Drake said, bringing his dark tale to a close. 'He was the CIA liaison who handed out our mission objectives in Afghanistan. He knew what Operation Hydra was all about.'

'And now he's dead,' Rojas reminded him.

Drake nodded. Whatever answers the man might have provided had gone with him to his grave. 'He never got a chance to tell me what he knew.'

He looked down at the sandy ground, feeling the full weight of his actions, the deaths he'd caused, settling on him like a physical presence. He might not have been in full control, but neither was he without blame. The people he'd killed to get here might have been good or bad, but they'd died for no other reason than because they'd been unlucky enough to get in his way. And that was a shitty thing to live with, in a life already filled with regrets.

'This was all for nothing. Rio, the lab, Tenbrook… A lot of people are dead, and I'm no closer to answers than when I started.'

'You might not be, but we are,' Anya said.

Drake turned to her. She was sitting on the tailgate of the truck, having stayed quiet during Drake's summary of events. Her clothes smeared with dirt, her arm wrapped with an improvised dressing, but her gaze was just as keen and sharp as always.

And it was concentrated on Drake.

'The man who contacted you, who sent you to kill people… I know this man.'

Drake could feel his body tensing up. 'How?'

She swallowed briefly. 'His name is Romek Karalius. He was a member of my unit for nearly 20 years. When I was captured by the FSB, I lost contact with him and could find no trace of him after I escaped. I believed he was dead like the others. But somehow he survived. He was with us in Rio, he helped Dietrich and me escape that safe house.'

'And he's been feeding me information,' Drake finished, stunned by the revelation.

'So what does this mean? Is he the enemy of our enemy?' Rojas asked.

Anya wasn't convinced, and her expression showed it. As she'd learned, the enemy of my enemy could be a whole host of things. Friend was rarely at the top of the list.

'That remains to be seen.'

Drake however was more interested in how Karalius had come into contact with him. 'But if you're right, how would this man even know who I was, or where to find me?'

Anya shook her head. 'I don't know, but Romek was resourceful and well connected. Maybe he has been watching us, planning this for a long time. Or maybe he found information on you through the Agency.'

'Then we need to meet with him. If he's your man, then he answers to you.'

If only it were that simple, Anya thought bleakly. 'He would not agree to meet with me. He said it would only happen when the time was right, when you had finished your task.'

'Jumped through fucking hoops for him, you mean,' Dietrich added.

Rojas looked at Drake. 'Losing Tenbrook wasn't part of his plan, I assume.'

Drake's mind was already racing ahead. 'Tenbrook was a link in the chain, but he wasn't the end. Powell's the one he really wants, the one everything leads back to. But only he knows how to get to her.'

'I thought *you* got to her in Rio?' Mitchell reminded him.

He shook his head. 'I did, but it was a mistake and he knew it. He tried to warn me against it. He knew what would happen.'

Dietrich frowned. 'And what *did* happen?'

Drake didn't respond. He had no desire to relive that particular encounter.

'Ryan, this is a hell of a time to be holding out on us,' Frost warned.

Drake sighed, knowing they weren't going to like what they heard. 'She stopped me.'

Frost sat up straighter. 'What do you mean, she stopped you?'

'It's hard to explain. Maybe I don't have the words. But it's like… she was able to reshape the world around me, just by speaking. Whatever she said became real in my mind. If she'd told me the sky was green and the ocean was red, I'd have believed her. If she'd told me to put a gun to my head and blow my brains out… I think I would have done it. I couldn't kill her, I couldn't even disobey her. For those few minutes we were talking, she had me under her control. And I couldn't resist… I didn't *want* to resist.'

His words failed quite to convey the true terror of those few minutes, the devastating war that had raged within his mind, but even his limited description was enough to give them some idea. That alone was a disturbing prospect, and it showed in their nervous glances.

'So who is she?' Dietrich asked. 'How exactly do you know her, and how did she get this kind of control over you?'

Drake frowned, striving to recall those memories. He couldn't say for certain, but he felt like he was close to a breakthrough. Almost, but not quite.

'She was there,' he said, his voice small and quiet. 'Back during my training, when I was part of 14th Special Operations Group. I don't remember much, but I see flashes… moments. A white room. A table. Bright light. She's there, talking to me, asking me questions. Smiling at me.'

The pieces seemed to be coming together, like fragments of a jigsaw drawing closer to each other, the pattern almost discernible. Almost. And then in a flash they had broken up once more, and the pattern was lost. He let out a frustrated sigh.

'It's like trying to replay your earliest memories,' Drake fumbled to explain. 'There's no sense of order to them. All you see is pieces.'

'Elizabeth Powell is head of a major pharmaceutical research group,' Frost said, hoping it might help him sort through his chaotic thoughts. 'They've got divisions working on new medical treatments, drugs, gene therapies, you name it. And if someone with her background and expertise is connected to the Agency, well, join the dots. What you're describing sounds an awful lot like brainwashing to me.'

Mitchell seemed to see the connection, even if she wasn't convinced by the young woman's conclusion. 'So you were conditioned to… forget her? How is that even possible?'

'Come on, don't you watch *The X-Files*? It's like that MK-Ultra shit they did back in the 60s,' Alex said, quickly picking up on the idea. 'Mind control, drug-induced hypnosis, mental programming… They had hundreds of people researching all that stuff, trying to create the perfect spy or the most effective interrogation tools.'

'Nothing but bullshit if you ask me,' Dietrich said. 'Just Cold War nonsense. It was shut down decades ago.'

Alex snorted. 'You think? Who's to say they didn't just move the whole thing overseas, someplace without any oversight or superiors to answer to? Someplace like Brazil? Or what if they were just biding their time, waiting for technology to catch up? Or for some ambitious young research scientist with no morals to come along and finish what they started? If that's what they could do 40 years ago, imagine what they'd be capable of with twenty-first-century tools and all the dirty money they could ask for.'

Dietrich had no answer, so instead he took a final drag of his cigarette and flicked the glowing butt into the sand.

None of the others could refute his idea either. Alex's words seemed to hang in the air around them, refusing to be dispelled by the fitful desert wind. The implications were as frightening as they were profound. If his wild supposition was right, then Drake was a living example of a highly secretive, highly unethical and highly illegal programme to reshape the human mind itself.

What had they done to him? And what might they do to others if left unchecked?

Chapter 68

Jason's foot came down on the beer can, sending it clattering across the room. It wasn't much really, but in the deadened night silence of the lounge, it was like the pealing of church bells. He heard a grunt from the recliner, looked down in horror as his father's eyes flickered briefly, then shot open, wide and alert and suspicious. He saw them snap to him, then to the box cutter in his hand.

'What the fuck?' he mumbled, then seemed to assemble the disparate pieces of information and mash them into a stark and infuriating conclusion.

'Dad, I was—'

Tyler Hawkins' fist shot out like a piston, slamming into his chest so hard that Jason crumpled like a paper bag, dropping the box cutter, gasping and straining to breathe, feeling like his entire ribcage had been caved in.

'You little sneaking, pussy-assed son of a bitch,' his father snarled, kicking him hard enough to send him sprawling. Through blurred eyes he saw his father bend over and snatch up the box cutter, working the blade backwards and forwards a couple of times as if considering its purpose carefully.

He turned towards Jason again. 'You gonna kill me, boy? Is that it? You gonna kill your old man in his sleep, you cowardly fuck?'

Jason saw the huge booted foot swing back, braced himself as it impacted his stomach, and immediately doubled over, throwing up a thick trail of vomit over the rug.

'Goddamn you, boy. Always knew you was trouble,' Tyler Hawkins growled, planting another kick in his already bruised ribs.

Jason was really panicking now. He tried to cough the chunky vomit and mucus out of his throat, but there was no breath in his lungs with which to shift it. He tried to breathe in, only to find his airways clogged, his chest aching, his lungs sagging like deflating balloons. He tried to roll over on his back in the hopes it would make his breathing easier, but his father planted another hard kick right in his ass. A fresh wave of pain exploded inside him, and he let out a scream that emerged instead as a terrified, choking whimper.

'Dad, please no!' Samuel screamed, terrified. 'Don't hurt him!'

Tyler Hawkins rounded on his youngest son. 'You get back to your room, you little bastard! Get back now and don't come out, or I swear by Jesus you'll be next!'

He must not have noticed Samuel when he first awoke, Jason thought with a flicker of relief, hadn't connected him to the events that had been about to play out. That was something at least.

Jason had taken plenty of beatings at his father's hands before — some deserved, most not — but never like this. Tyler Hawkins might have taken a perverse pleasure in meting out violence against his sons, but there had always been a limit to his rage.

Not now. Now there was real, towering fury as he seized Jason by the T-shirt and dragged him across the room towards the kitchen, to the door leading out to the garage.

'You come with me, boy. You're gonna get one,' his father said, speaking almost to himself as he yanked the boy behind him, the fabric of his T-shirt ripping and straining. 'Oh by Christ you're gonna get one tonight.'

He threw the door open and hauled Jason outside. He felt rain lashing down on him, soaking his clothes and chilling his skin, before his father opened the garage door and hurled him in.

He pitched forward, slammed shoulder-first into a shelving unit that rattled and swayed alarmingly, scattering tools and other implements on the floor around him, with one hammer in particular barely missing his head. He was too frightened to take much notice of the pain.

Jason looked up fearfully at his father, standing big and square in the doorway, breathing hard, water dripping from him. He didn't look like the broken-down, ageing, pathetic man he'd watched sleeping on that recliner chair. It was as if his consciousness had returned, and now that he was fully himself and roused to anger, he became more somehow. More than just flesh and blood. He was Jason's father, the man who would always be bigger, stronger, meaner and tougher than he could ever be.

Holding up the box cutter again, he slowly extended the blade and looked at it, turning it over slowly in his hand.

'I can tolerate a lot of shit in my life, but there's things I just can't let fly,' he said, speaking slowly, laying down each word solid and firm. 'I really don't know what's worse — that you thought about using this, or that you were too much of a faggot to go through with it.'

Pressing the knife against the workbench beside him, he snapped the blade off and tossed the useless plastic handle at Jason.

'Goddamn, that a son of mine would end up like this,' he said, shaking his head. Turning away, he reached for the leather belt hanging on its special peg beside the hammers and saws, bringing it down carefully, reverently.

He turned back towards Jason with such purpose, he knew immediately this was going to be no playful beating behind the pretext of discipline. There was a new light in his eyes. A cold, detached, soulless kind of light.

His dad knew that Jason had meant to kill him tonight, and even if he'd lacked the resolve to see it through, they both knew that sooner or later it was going to happen again. He understood only one of them would be leaving this garage alive.

Jason was a problem that was bustin' his ass big time, and by God he was going to take care of that problem once and for all.

'You know I gotta give ya one,' he said, wrapping one end of the belt around his meaty hand. 'I gotta give ya a real big one for this.'

But before he'd taken a step, the door suddenly flew open. Was it a cop? Had Samuel called the police? Had a neighbour heard shit kicking off in the middle of the night and come to see what was up?

'What are you doing?' a small, timid voice asked. A child's voice. Nathan's voice.

'I told you and your brother to stay the fuck out of this!' Tyler growled. 'You get on out of here before I give you another one!'

Nathan shrank back from him, and Jason's heart sank. Nathan had taken one good beating already because of his actions; there was no way he could endure another. He'd run, retreat to his room and hide under the bed if he knew what was good for him, praying his father didn't come looking for him.

But he didn't. Rallying what little reserve of courage remained to him, Nathan stood his ground, his hands clenching into fists. He looked hard at his father, squinting a little with his bad eyes, his jaw jutting defiantly.

And then he did the dumbest and bravest thing he'd ever do in his short, unhappy life.

'No,' he said.

—

'Your ability to fail is impressive, Jason,' Elizabeth Powell remarked sourly as Hawkins finished his report. 'At least you're consistent, I suppose.'

Rather than risk venturing into Tunisia, which by all accounts was rapidly descending into anarchy, she had chosen to base herself safely offshore. A luxury yacht had been chartered, its sleek white hull cruising smoothly through the Gulf of Tunis even as Drake and Hawkins had been battling through ancient mosques and festering underground sewers.

Hawkins had cleaned himself up and changed before coming aboard, but even a shower and clean clothes couldn't hide the bruises and cuts that marked his face. Neither did the opulence of his surroundings or the moonlit waters beyond the cabin's windows help to calm the anger that burned inside him. He'd failed in his objective, been forced to abandon his pursuit rather than risk capture, and having his authority undermined still rankled.

'Tenbrook's been handled. He didn't give away anything that could compromise us.'

It wasn't much of a consolation prize, but it was something at least. Though he doubted Powell would see it that way.

She raised a perfectly sculpted brow. 'And you know this *how*?'

'If Drake had learned the truth, it would have destroyed him.'

'Really? I think you underestimate him. Nasty habit of yours.' She watched him closely, studying his reactions. 'Or is it something else? Could it be jealousy?'

Hawkins ignored that barbed remark with difficulty.

'Drake might still be KIA,' he ventured, even if he didn't truly believe it. 'The explosion collapsed a good section of the tunnel. If I'd been able to confirm—'

Powell silenced him with a raised hand. Hawkins looked at the slender wrist, the long elegant fingers, the lighter tone of the skin on her palm.

Elizabeth, do you have any idea how easily I could snap that pretty wrist of yours?

'Don't waste my time,' she said, having turned her attention to her tablet PC. Bringing up a video file, she turned the screen around to face him and hit 'play'.

Hawkins watched as the jerky video, clearly shot on a handheld camera and uploaded to a video-sharing website, played out. He watched as a man, injured and dishevelled, was pulled from a collapsed hole in the ground. A tall, slender, Hispanic-looking man with long dark hair. A man he'd believed killed in Brazil.

'Rojas,' he said, hiding his surprise. *What the hell was he doing thousands of miles from home?*

The answer presented itself a few seconds later when a second man was pulled from the hole, looking equally beat up and exhausted, but infuriatingly alive.

His hands curled into fists as a third survivor emerged from the collapsed sewer tunnel. A woman, blonde-haired and tall, blinking in the harsh sunlight. Bearing the scars of a recent confrontation.

Powell cocked her head slightly to one side.

'You were saying?'

He had to draw in a slow, calming breath before answering. 'You saw the footage, it must be obvious. Drake had help. First Anya in the mosque, then Rojas in the tunnels.'

'All loose ends that *you* were supposed to tie up.'

'I warned you not to underestimate Anya,' he reminded her irritably. 'That seems to be a habit of *yours*.'

Powell's dark eyes flashed. 'Careful, Jason. We both know what happens when you speak out of turn.'

Hawkins was wise enough to back down a little. He had learned, painfully, the penalty for disobedience at Powell's hands.

'She's highly trained and dangerous enough by herself,' he elaborated. 'And she won't give up on Drake.'

Powell's lips curled into a mocking, sardonic smile. 'Of course she won't. Which is exactly what I'm counting on.'

Hawkins frowned. Not for the first time, he had the distinct impression that he was a pawn in a larger game whose grand strategy only Powell understood. He could kill her physically in a dozen different ways without breaking sweat, yet he was no match for her intellect.

'Relax, Jason,' Powell said, rising from her chair. 'You played your part, like I knew you would. Just as Ryan played his.'

'What do you mean?'

Her smile was still there, but it was a cool, calculating one. 'Do you really think I'd depend on you alone to end this?' she asked. 'You have your uses, but you're a sledgehammer. You always were. Strong and powerful, but blunt and crude. I need something more precise.'

Lifting her cell phone from the table, she dialled a number. It was answered on the second ring. 'Have my flight standing by. We'll be there within the hour.'

Hawkins folded his arms across his broad chest. 'You plan on telling me where we're going?'

'To meet Ryan. And to end this once and for all.'

He was annoyed at her evasiveness. 'How do you know he'll be waiting for you?'

She'd turned her back to him, staring out across the placid waters of the Mediterranean with her back straight, her head high and shoulders back. A master chess player, always thinking ahead of her opponent.

'Because it's what I told him to do, Jason.'

Chapter 69

After driving west for several hours and crossing the lightly patrolled border into Algeria, the exhausted group halted for the night in the small fishing town of El Kala, about ten miles from the frontier. Tomorrow was a new and unknown challenge, but today they needed to rest and recover.

A brief recce of local hotels and guest houses landed them several rooms in a small, rather run-down establishment overlooking the sheltered bay and the fishing port that likely provided most of the town's employment. It wasn't much of a place, but the husband-and-wife team running it were happy to take their money without asking too many questions. They did however survey Drake and Anya suspiciously, eyeing their cuts and bruises and probably wondering if they were inviting trouble under their roof.

The situation was only ameliorated when Anya explained that they'd been attacked by thugs while visiting Tunisia, and that they were unlikely to return. Given what had happened, her summary of events wasn't exactly a lie.

Despite the late hour, the kitchen was reopened for the plainly famished group. Food and wine was brought out, and they quickly fell upon a meal of spiced lamb, flatbreads, couscous and stewed vegetables as only the ravenously hungry can, each privately remarking that the hotel's food was far better than its exterior suggested. Then again, hunger was always the best seasoning.

Liberal quantities of wine contributed to the celebratory atmosphere, and the day's tumultuous events were temporarily forgotten as they drank and ate together, even cracking jokes and erupting into gales of laughter that seemed at odds with their predicament.

Most of them knew why it was happening of course, especially Drake and Anya. They'd been in enough battles to know that humour so often surfaced in the direst of circumstances. It was a way of coping, a way of pretending just for a moment that everything was all right. It felt good to be together, to be out of danger – at least temporarily – and for one night, to act like normal people.

'Okay, here's one,' Mitchell said, taking a drink of her wine. She looked at each of them with mock seriousness, even if her eyes were a little bleary now with a heady mix of drink and fatigue. 'What's your worst night out ever?'

'You should have this one nailed, Keira,' Drake said. 'That time in Frankfurt when you got abducted, shot and ended up in a car crash?'

The young woman gave him the finger, but also flashed a wicked grin as an idea occurred to her. 'I don't know, Ryan. I think I can beat that.'

'This ought to be good,' Dietrich remarked, reclining in his chair.

'Amsterdam.' She said it slowly, really laying into each syllable.

It meant nothing to the rest of them, save for Drake himself. His eyes lit up, both with recollection and alarm. 'Oh, fuck off! We agreed we'd never talk about that again. Ever.'

'You owe me big time after today,' she pointed out. 'So I'm calling it in.'

'What the hell happened in Amsterdam?' Alex asked, intrigued.

'Nothing. Keira can't hold her drink,' Drake evaded. 'There's just not enough of her.'

'Now I'm definitely gonna tell them,' Frost said, grinning mischievously.

'Someone better tell it before I pass out,' Alex coaxed them. 'Start at the beginning. So you were in Holland...'

'Fuck no, we were in New Jersey. Atlantic City, New Jersey,' Frost corrected him. Seeing his look of confusion, she elaborated. 'Amsterdam was the name of the nightclub.'

Alex threw up his hands, lost already.

'So somehow I convinced Ryan to go out drinking, told him I knew the place like the back of my hand, which was kind of bullshit in retrospect. Anyway, there are plenty of shithole drinking places in Atlantic City, so we hit it hard. And there we are at about one am, a little worse for wear, trying to get home, but there's no fucking cabs anywhere and pretty soon it starts raining. Ryan spots this club called Amsterdam and suggests we go in for a few drinks to finish up the night. I sure as shit wasn't gonna argue, so in we went, got our drinks and started talking shit as usual. More than usual, I guess. But then Ryan spots a couple of tall blondes over by the bar eyeing him up. I mean, like supermodel tall.'

'Peter Dinklage is tall from your point of view, Keira,' Drake cut in.

'Bite my ass, and stop trying to derail my story,' she fired back, clearly enjoying his discomfort. 'Anyway, so he downs his drink and swaggers over to join them, and starts putting the moves on. And before too long, one of them whispers in his ear and all three of them disappear into one of the chill-out rooms. And I thought to myself, "Goddamn, this guy must have some killer lines. Sure as shit isn't his looks".'

In spite of himself, Drake was grinning.

'There weren't many dudes there, and I was starting to get kind of a weird vibe from the place. So I'm getting ready to bug out and call it a night, when all of a sudden Ryan comes running over to me, looking like he just fucked his cousin, and tells me we're leaving right now. "What's wrong, man? Are they a couple of nut jobs?" I ask him. Ryan shakes his head and says,' – she applied her best impersonation of Drake's British accent – '"No, mate. They're a couple of fucking blokes!"'

The eruption of laughter from the others was almost enough to drown out Frost's voice, and she had to repeat herself to be heard.

'Turns out that Amsterdam was a cross-dressers' bar,' she explained, struggling to keep it together. 'I've seen Ryan under fire with stray rounds breaking up the ground around him, I've seen him chasing targets through busy streets, but that's still the fastest I've seen him move in my life.'

The laughter continued, and even Drake couldn't help but join in. He had to admit it was a funny story, especially now that a few years had passed.

They stayed there a little longer, finishing their drinks and swapping a few more anecdotes, as if reluctant to break the unexpected sense of camaraderie that seemed to have developed. They knew that when they next met, things would be different. The urgency, the creeping sense of danger, the paranoia would be back.

Tonight was a glimpse, fleeting though it was, of a different life. A life they might have had if things played out differently. A life each secretly knew they would never truly possess.

Time marched on, and one by one they began to drift off to their rooms. Alex was the first to go, rising up from his chair a little unsteadily.

'I'll see you losers in the morning,' he said. '*Late* in the morning. Try not to have any emergencies before ten am.'

'We promise nothing,' Mitchell called after him, prompting a mumbled response that was probably not complimentary. However, she too was aware of the late hour, and soon made her excuses and departed.

Dietrich downed the remainder of his drink and laid his glass down firmly on the table. He looked at Drake. 'You're an asshole, Ryan,' he decided. 'But it's good to have you back all the same.'

'That's what I've missed, Jonas – your sunny disposition.'

The normally dry and sardonic German flashed a thin semblance of a smile before taking his leave.

Rojas was next to go, rising stiffly from his chair. His midsection was swathed in bandages, hidden only by the dust-covered shirt he was wearing. Nonetheless, he gave Anya a nod.

'Stay out of trouble, Maras. Or at least, keep it away from me.'

Despite herself, Anya smiled. 'Thank you, Cesar. For everything.'

Frost remained behind a little longer, waiting until the others were out of sight before standing up. 'Goddamn, I'm gonna sleep tonight.' She glanced at Drake and grinned. 'You try to stay away from nightclubs.'

She was just turning away again when Drake spoke up. 'Keira?'

When she looked over at him, he was holding his hand out to her. She hesitated only a moment before clasping it tight. Neither of them said anything more. There was no need.

Frost released her grip, turned away and retreated upstairs to her room.

Only Drake and Anya were left, hanging in there until the end, seated on opposite sides of the table like adversaries in some great game. But they weren't adversaries any longer. It had all changed today.

Drake could feel it, as if the air around them was charged with electricity, growing heavy with anticipation, with building tension.

'You know, if you'd told me a few days ago that we'd be sitting together talking about all this over a bottle of wine, I'd have said you'd lost your mind,' Drake

318

remarked, idly turning the wine cork over in his hand. He studied her expression, trying to gauge her mood. 'I suppose a lot can change in a few days.'

Drake glanced over his shoulder. The owner of the hotel was waiting near the restaurant entrance, clearly impatient to close up for the night. Drake didn't blame him, and didn't want to impose any further.

'We should go,' Anya said, echoing this thoughts.

He nodded, and together the two of them headed upstairs. Whatever needed to be said between them, Drake guessed it would have to remain unsaid for now.

Chapter 70

The hotel was too small to accommodate a group of this size with their own individual rooms, forcing them to double up. Mitchell and Frost had taken one, while Alex, Rojas and Dietrich were in another (the latter making his displeasure known to anyone willing to listen, and a few who weren't).

Drake and Anya had opted to take the final room. This seemed to work to everyone's advantage since most of the group were understandably reluctant to share a room with either a dangerous man whose mental state remained questionable, or an equally dangerous woman who had inflicted various injuries on them in the past.

Anya at any rate hadn't objected, and Drake could guess why. She wanted to keep an eye on him.

'Someone should keep watch,' he said, easing out of his shirt with difficulty, the knotted muscles and torn flesh hindering his progress. 'I'll take the first shift.'

He doubted Hawkins or Powell would track them here, but as he'd learned over the past few days, they weren't to be underestimated. Neither was Karalius, whom Anya had once thought of highly enough to appoint as her second in command.

'No, I'll go first,' Anya countered firmly.

He glanced at her. 'You took a beating today. You could use the rest.'

'I can take just as much as you can. And I'll be the one to decide when I need rest.'

'Jesus, do you have to fight against everything I say?'

'Only when you put bravado ahead of practicality. Here, let me help.'

She helped him out of his shirt, taking note of the dark and ugly bruising that marked his back and shoulders, the cuts and grazes that had been hastily cleaned and still glistened with freshly clotted blood. The sight of it was enough to make her wince.

One particularly deep cut across his left shoulder blade had reopened and started bleeding again.

'Sit down, I'll see if I can clean this up,' she said, easing him onto a chair. Retrieving a washcloth from the bathroom, she pressed it into the cut, prompting a sharp intake of breath.

'It hurts,' she said quietly.

'Rough day,' he admitted. 'Some woman tried to beat the shit out of me.'

'You probably deserved it.' The wine Anya had drunk tonight engendered a slightly more relaxed frame of mind. 'This woman. Tell me about her.'

'Well, she's probably the biggest pain in the arse I've ever dealt with.'

Drake hissed as she pushed the cloth in a little harder than necessary. A little reminder to choose his words carefully. He let out a controlled breath, muscles slowly relaxing, then continued.

'She's also the most… unique person I've ever met in my life.'

'Unique. Interesting choice of words,' she observed. 'How, exactly?'

Drake considered it for a few seconds. 'She's brave, smart, strong, beautiful… and *good*. Sounds like a stupid way to describe someone, but it's the only word that makes sense. There's no doubt with her. I never question if she'd do the right thing, I just know. You don't meet many people like that in this life.'

Anya swallowed, feeling an annoying flush rising to her cheeks. She was glad that Drake was facing away from her.

'She sounds… special,' she said, feeling uncomfortable, like she'd taken it too far.

Drake turned around then, looking her in the eye. 'She is to me.'

Her heart was beating stronger and faster now, as she recalled some of the great outpouring of emotion she'd felt in that mosque today, holding Drake, able to forget everything else around them. Feeling and wanting only him.

Having finished her task, Anya stood up and backed away. She needed to put some distance between them, to calm down, to regain her composure.

'That should be enough,' she decided, laying the bloodstained cloth aside. 'If the wound won't close by itself, it might need stitches.'

'That's the problem with old wounds. They never really close.' Drake seemed poised to add more, but decided to let it pass. 'Don't stay on watch too long, Anya. Even you need to rest eventually.'

He rose stiffly and made his way towards the bed at the other end of the room.

'Why didn't you do it?'

Drake was struck by Anya's unexpected question. She was watching him just as before, but her expression had changed. He could almost feel the tension and worry radiating from her. She was afraid, but of what? Of him? Of what he might say?

'Do what?'

'Kill me,' she replied. 'You had the chance today, you could have done it. But you stopped yourself. Why, Ryan?'

'You know why.'

'No, I don't. But I want to… Please.'

It was then that he understood. The final barrier that stood between them, withstanding everything else that had happened these past four years. The admission he'd longed to make, the truth he'd known for so long but never articulated, always held back by circumstances, or by fear.

She'd sensed it too, and he realized that she'd pulled away from him not because she was rejecting him, but because she didn't know what to do. She'd never allowed herself to get this close, never opened herself to someone in this way.

Anya, the woman who had faced uncounted dangers and hardships in her life without fear, was afraid of this. She needed him to take that final step, because she couldn't.

And in the end, he did.

'Because I love you, Anya.'

There were a million different things he could have said, uncountable possibilities to more artfully express what he felt, but in truth he could think of no better answer than those five simple, honest, heartfelt words. Never in his life had he meant something more.

After all this time, these years of separation, of painful longing, of coming together only to be pulled apart again, of heartache and triumph and loss, he'd just come right out and said it. It almost didn't seem real.

But real it was. He knew that much when Anya let out a shuddering, ragged breath. Her eyes were wide and staring, her face pale.

She took a step towards him, and he towards her until they were standing together in the centre of the room, so close they could feel the warmth of each other's bodies. He saw her reach out, felt her hand rest lightly against his chest as if afraid of the touch

She looked at him as she never had before. An entire lifetime that passed in a single look. No barriers now, no masks, no walls between them.

Just her.

And him.

Drake was barely aware of what happened next; it all passed in a blur of sensation and movement. He felt her arms around his neck as his encircled her waist, the warm firmness of her body pressed hard against his, the urgency of her kiss. He was aware of them stumbling backwards, falling onto the bed together, the soft spring of the mattress beneath them as they pulled and fought at each other's clothes. This was no tender and careful act, but a desperate and urgent search for release.

Her hands were at his belt, unbuckling it, pulling it apart, her breath hot in his ear as she reached inside, while at the same time he pulled her T-shirt up and over her head. He felt his hands tracing the contours of her body, the arch of her back, the smooth musculature of her shoulders, the soft curve of her breasts.

He bent down and kissed her cheek, her neck, feeling the pulse beating hard and fast just beneath the skin, then her breasts. He felt a shiver run through her, realized that she was trembling. And that realization brought such an upwelling of emotion that he almost wondered if he should stop.

But he didn't. He couldn't.

Neither could she.

'Now,' she whispered. 'Now.'

Her hands laced around his neck, pulling tight as he entered her. He heard her sudden exhalation, felt her body tense beneath him, recoiling from his sudden entry, only for her hips to press forward, pushing against him, pulling away, then thrusting forward again.

Drake closed his eyes, moving with her rhythm, their bodies in harmony, striving to reach each other, aching for release. For a moment he remembered the only other time they had come together like this, what felt like a lifetime ago. Two people with dark pasts and uncertain futures, alone and vulnerable, finding comfort in each other the only way they knew how. He felt that moment closing with this, the past and the present, the circle of their lives so long entwined, at last joined.

Their movements were growing faster, more forceful, more powerful as the need within them rose, as they sought and strove to reach what they both needed. Anya gripped him hard as he thrust in deep, her whole body seeming to rally behind this final, great upsurge of pure feeling.

And then in an explosive release that was so intense it was almost painful, she finally came. She bit his shoulder to keep from crying out, and felt hot tears moistening her cheeks. He carried on a few more times before finally collapsing beside her, breathing hard, exhausted, spent. She felt a fleeting sense of loss, of emptiness as he slipped free of her, and instinctively reached out, pulling him close, feeling the heat that still radiated from their naked bodies.

And for the first time in a long time, Anya closed her eyes and felt complete.

They lay together like that for a while – naked, entwined, wanting and needing nothing else in the world. Neither could say how long the spell lasted; they only knew that they were each unwilling to break it. One or both might have dozed lightly, their thoughts of watch-keeping and other precautions forgotten. They were together. After everything, all the dangers and losses and sacrifices, they had found each other again.

Somehow they'd both known it would happen eventually, as if each exerted some unseen force on the other, pulling them inexorably together. They couldn't explain it, couldn't rationalize it, but they knew they didn't have to. It made sense, it felt right in a way that so few things ever did.

Drake ran his fingers idly down Anya's body, tracing the gentle swell of her hip, the firm musculature of her stomach, the soft and yielding curve of a breast. Her breathing deepened a little when his finger brushed a nipple and he felt a twinge of renewed arousal at her response.

But when his touch strayed to her back, to the slight puckering and indentation of scar tissue that he knew criss-crossed that expanse of skin, he felt her tense a little, stiffen and shift position slightly. An instinctive reaction, born from bad experiences.

He opened his eyes and looked at her, her face so close to his own.

'It still hurts?' he whispered.

Anya shook her head. 'Just the memory of them.' She hesitated before speaking again. 'Does it... Do they bother you?'

He'd only witnessed the spider's web of scars on a couple of occasions; he knew she was reluctant to let others see them. She didn't want to answer the questions they inevitably provoked, probably didn't want to be reminded of the man who had given them to her. She had suffered at his hands to be sure, had endured things that would have broken most other people. But she'd survived, withstood what few others could.

And she was asking *him* if they bothered him?

Drake looked at her hard, really seeing her in a way he'd so rarely been able to. She was worried about his answer, maybe even a little embarrassed by the question. God, she was beautiful, he thought. It had been a long time since he'd allowed himself to think of her that way, to let those thoughts in.

He knew how important this moment was, what she was really asking him. It wasn't just the scars, it was everything that came with them. Everything that she was, everything she'd been and done.

She was asking if he accepted *her*.

'They're part of you,' he said, taking her hand. 'And you're part of me now. Don't ever be ashamed of that.'

She nodded, squeezed his hand hard and moved closer to him, her flesh pressed against his, their foreheads touching. Knowing that the last barrier between them was finally gone, Drake closed his eyes and at last allowed sleep to come.

Chapter 71

Nobody was feeling particularly energetic the next day, and it was late morning before the group rose and drifted downstairs in search of breakfast. Drake's suspicions about his body seizing up overnight had proven all too accurate, and it had been an effort just to get out of bed. Only after popping a few painkillers and turning the shower temperature up to maximum had he been able to ease the knotted muscles.

The atmosphere around breakfast was a curious one, Drake noticed, with only stilted conversation and furtive glances between his companions. He had the odd impression that he'd just walked into a party he hadn't been invited to.

'You guys sleep okay?' Alex asked, taking a drink of coffee to hide his face.

Drake frowned. 'No worse than you, I suppose.'

'Not a bad place to stay,' Dietrich remarked with a wry smile. 'Comfortable beds.' He paused then, and Drake could tell something was coming. 'Thin walls, though.'

That was too much for Alex. Drake heard him snorting with laughter, nearly choking on his coffee in the process. He was quickly followed by Rojas and Mitchell, both of whom were struggling to hold it in.

He glanced at Anya. The woman was looking down at her plate, her face noticeably more colourful than before, though she did have a knowing little smile that he'd never seen before.

'It was a long day,' he said, shrugging. This only seemed to add to their amusement.

He was spared further embarrassment when Frost hurried into the room, clutching her laptop. Her expression made it obvious that something of considerable importance was going on.

'Guys, you've got to see this,' she said, hurriedly sweeping plates and cutlery aside and setting the computer down in the centre of the table.

'Jesus, Frost. Aren't you ever off the clock?' Dietrich said irritably.

'Shut up,' the young woman replied. 'Just look at it.'

Their eyes swept the screen, scanning the news headlines that confronted them.

PROTESTS SPREAD ACROSS NORTH AFRICA

STATE OF EMERGENCY DECLARED IN TUNISIA

GOVERNMENT UNDER PRESSURE TO RESIGN

CROWDS GATHER IN CAIRO

SYRIAN GOVERNMENT UNDER FIRE

'What the fuck…?' Alex gasped.

Frost looked at them. 'It's spreading all across the region,' she said. 'Protests in every major city from here to Syria, governments declaring emergencies, police units refusing orders. The entire thing exploded overnight. The whole of North Africa is about to go down.'

'How did this happen?' Mitchell asked, stunned by the scale of what they were witnessing. This could prove to be the biggest political shift since the fall of the Iron Curtain.

Frost looked at her. 'Well, it wasn't an accident, I'll tell you that much,' she confirmed. 'Social media's on fire with this. It's everywhere. Thousands of accounts just sprang into life in the past 24 hours, calling for demonstrations, organizing protests, demanding resignations. This shit was planned.'

'Planned by who?' Rojas asked.

Drake knew the answer, even if he'd rather not have. 'The Circle,' he said. 'That's who Tenbrook was really working for, what he was doing in Tunisia. He was helping spread dissent, undermining the government, whipping up a revolution.' He let out a breath, staggered by the scale of their plan.

'Two years ago they tried the same thing in Libya,' Frost said. 'They wanted to bring down Gaddafi's regime, but we stopped them.'

'Libya was just the beginning. We didn't stop anything, we only delayed it.' Drake could see it all too clearly. The vast machinations of which they had become a part. 'This was their plan all along – regime change from Africa to the Middle East. Replace dictators with pro-Western governments. No bombs and invasions this time, no accountability, no investigations. Just information. That's all it takes now.'

'Jesus Christ,' Dietrich said, at last recognizing the implications. 'If they can trigger something like this, what will they do next?'

Nobody had an answer.

–

A short time later, Drake found himself alone, walking along the edge of the fishing harbour that the town was clustered around. It was a bright, warm morning, the sun rising into a cloudless sky. A fair breeze was blowing in off the sea, but it was already shaping up to be a hot day.

He needed time alone to think, to consider everything that had happened and where it might lead them.

The Circle's plans were coming to fruition regardless of Drake's actions, or perhaps even because of them. Perhaps their armed confrontation yesterday had lit the fire of a revolution that might otherwise have fizzled out, or perhaps it was inevitable. Perhaps an organization as vast and powerful as the Circle simply couldn't be stopped.

Perhaps they had become caught up in a war they could never hope to win.

This gloomy introspection was interrupted by the buzz of his cell phone. Someone was calling, and he had a feeling he knew who.

He didn't have to answer this call. He could let it go, throw the phone away, pretend none of it had happened. But it *had* happened. And Karalius would always be out there, and the answers he needed would forever elude him.

Steeling himself, he pressed the green phone icon to receive the call.

'I'm here.'

'You've been busy, I see. An entire continent is burning because of your actions.'

It was the same voice as before. The same digitized, electronically distorted voice that had always spoken to him. And this time he could detect an edge to it. A hardness, a tension that hadn't been there before. They were coming to the end of their journey now, and they both knew it.

'One disaster at a time,' Drake said. 'That's the best I can do.'

'Enough jokes. Do you have Tenbrook?'

'Tenbrook's dead. Just like everyone else, Romek.'

This statement was met with silence. A puzzled, questioning silence.

Drake knew he could have held back, could have feigned ignorance and hoped to lure Karalius into some false sense of security, but deep down he knew it would have been a futile effort. The man he was speaking to was better than that.

'Yeah, I know who you really are. Or should I say, *were*. Romek Karalius, second in command of Task Force Black. One of Anya's trusted few. And now what are you? Just a coward who hides in the shadows and uses other people to do his dirty work. I don't know how you found me or what you expect to get from this, but I can tell you one thing: I'm done being your fucking puppet.'

'Well, well,' Karalius said at last. It was hard to know if his digitized voice carried a trace of mockery or grudging respect. 'You've come further than I expected.'

'Far enough to see through your bullshit. It's over, Karalius.'

Karalius chuckled to himself then, the sound coming out of the phone as an eerie, discordant jumble of electronic mush. 'No. It's not over yet, Ryan. You've come a long way, but you still have one last step to take. One last person who must answer for her crimes.'

It wasn't hard to guess who Karalius had in mind.

'Powell.'

'Bring her to me, and this will all be over. You'll know the truth, and you'll be free of your past. And in the end, isn't that all you ever wanted, Ryan?'

'Why the hell would I do that?' Drake demanded. 'So you can kill me?'

'You're not my enemy, Ryan Drake,' Karalius promised him. 'And I won't force you to do anything. All I offer is a choice – walk away, or see it through to the end. Are you really prepared to abandon it now, after coming so far?'

Drake shook his head, refusing to be drawn in. 'Even if I wanted to do it, it would be suicide. You said it yourself, I can't kill Powell.'

'You won't have to. Bring her to me, and I'll take care of the rest. We can end this together, but I need your help.'

Drake closed his eyes. Despite everything, despite his logical mind telling him this was a bad idea, he could feel himself being drawn back in. Not because he was compelled to obey, but because he knew if he didn't he would never be free of Powell's insidious influence. He would forever be a liability, a weak point, a man who could never be fully trusted.

He couldn't live like that. Not again.

'Where would this happen?' he asked.

'You know where. Every good journey should come full circle,' Karalius decided. 'Bring Powell to where this all started, and I'll be waiting for you.'

The line went dead then, and Drake lowered the phone, lost in thought.

–

'Tell me you're not seriously considering this,' Frost said about an hour later. Drake had finished relating his brief conversation with Karalius, along with the hastily conceived plan he'd concocted to make it possible.

She knew that look on his face, and she didn't like it. It was the look she'd seen in countless planning sessions and operational briefings during their time as Shepherd operatives, where Drake was applying his formidable knowledge and experience to solving a particularly difficult problem.

Now he had the mother of all problems to tackle.

'If we want to find Karalius, this may be the only way,' Anya reasoned.

'Fuck Karalius, and fuck his bullshit "journey". I can tell you where this journey's going to end, Ryan. It ends with you lying face down on the ground with a bullet in your head,' Frost declared. 'That really the end you want for yourself?'

Frost could understand why Anya was contemplating Drake's insane plan, why she was so eager to reunite with a former member of her unit, but that didn't mean the rest of them had to be sacrificed for it. His plan was without a doubt the most risky, borderline-insane scheme they had ever contemplated.

Drake's expression hadn't changed however. If anything, his resolve seemed to be strengthening.

'I have to know, Keira. I've carried this with me for a long time. I'm tired of running.' Drake shook his head, resigned. He looked suddenly older, as if years had passed during their conversation. 'One way or another I have to face it.'

Anya nodded, subdued but resolute. 'Ryan is right. If Karalius can give us the answers we need and put a stop to Powell, then I think it is worth the risk.'

'Suppose you're right, not that I think you are,' Dietrich prompted. 'Where does he expect you to meet him?'

For Drake, the answer was as clear as day. 'He told me this would end where it began. It began with Operation Hydra.' He sighed, facing up to the final leg of his journey. 'He wants to meet me in Afghanistan.'

Anya nodded. 'Then that is where we'll go.'

Alex folded his arms, unconvinced by what he'd just heard. 'That's all well and good, mate. But tell me something – how do we know you're actually you?'

The group's attention quickly switched to him. Nobody said a word however, and the silence stretched out, but it was clear his question had hit home with some of them. Their expressions ranged from flat rejection and denial to simmering disquiet and doubt.

'Oh, come on. Do I really need to be the one to say it?' Alex asked, responding to their unspoken censure. 'You're telling us all this stuff now, Ryan, but how do we know this isn't some kind of bullshit act? You said yourself, Powell can control everything you do, everything you *think*. And even if it's not an act, Karalius seems to make you dance to his tune. What's to stop you going all Bruce Banner on us again? One wrong word, one phone call and, before you know it, we're right back where we started. I don't know about you, but I'm pretty sure we can't keep doing this.'

'Shut up, Alex,' Frost snapped. 'You don't have a goddamn clue what you're talking about. You're not one of us.'

'No, I'm not. And maybe I'm seeing this clearer than the rest of you,' he retorted, in no mood for being lectured. 'And, for the record, I took the same fucking risks you did by coming here.'

'What the hell do you know about risk? You're a fucking keyboard warrior.'

'The man is just saying what we're all thinking,' Rojas observed. 'Even if you don't want to hear it.'

Frost rounded on him. 'He doesn't speak for me.'

'No one does, it seems. But that doesn't mean he's wrong.'

Dietrich was next to wade into this argument, though to Keira's surprise he actually leapt to her defence. 'Maybe you should shut your mouth, Cesar. We don't need the opinions of every waif and stray we pick up.'

'Goddamn it, stop this!' Mitchell interrupted. 'Fighting each other isn't the answer.'

The others were starting to raise their voices, each vying to be heard amid the growing clamour as simmering tensions and grudges rose to the surface. The unity and camaraderie of the previous evening had vanished as differing opinions threatened to break them apart.

'That's enough!' Drake shouted.

Their attention turned towards him, waiting, knowing something was coming.

'Alex is right,' he said, his expression betraying the sombre acceptance of someone coming to terms with an unpleasant truth. 'I'm a liability to you. All of you. Might as well be honest about that. As long as Powell and Karalius are out there, there's a chance I could go back to… what I was before. I couldn't live with myself if that happened. None of you will be safe until I've beaten this thing.'

'None of us are safe without you.'

The others stopped and turned to the woman who had spoken up.

Anya took a step towards Drake. 'You have shown faith in each one of us, Ryan. You have risked your life for us more times than I know. If we can do the same for you now, then I'm prepared to do it.'

'I almost killed you once already.'

'But you didn't,' she reminded him. 'Maybe that means something, maybe it will help when the time comes.'

'And maybe it won't,' Drake countered. 'You really want to take that chance?'

Anya's eyes flashed dangerously.

'I'm not yours to command, Ryan. I never will be.' She calmed herself, pushing back a strand of hair that had come loose in the breeze. 'But we both have questions that must be answered. Yours started with Powell, and mine will end with Karalius. So we go together, we find our answers together, and we finish this together. That was what you promised me.'

Drake studied her closely, seeing in her a mind and a will as unyielding as his own. The others might protest and argue against his decision, but in the end he knew they would understand and abide by his choice. But not Anya. She wouldn't bend, wouldn't give up on this, because she needed it as much as he did.

He'd always known it would come down to the two of them.

They were going to Afghanistan, each seeking their own answers.

Neither could imagine what was waiting for them.

Part IV

Identity

Nearly all records pertaining to MK-Ultra were destroyed by the CIA in 1973. The full extent of the programme may never be known.

Drake wasn't seated patiently at the table this time, waiting for her arrival. Instead he was strapped to a hospital bed that had been set up in the centre of the room, his wrists and ankles securely bound. Even then, the skin around them had been rubbed raw by his frantic efforts to break free. Only heavy sedation had finally subdued him.

Elizabeth Powell took a breath as the door slid open, allowing her to enter. Normally she was utterly composed during these sessions, her mind focussed and analytical. But not today. This session was something very different.

This session could mean the end for both of them.

She had disabled the security cameras. Nobody was going to see or hear what was discussed during this session. Just this once, they were truly alone.

'Good morning, Ryan,' she said, feigning calm as she entered the room.

Drake looked groggily towards her, but even through the haze of sedatives she saw the recognition in his eyes. He began to struggle again, muscles standing out hard against his skin as he strove to break free of his restraints.

'Stop that, please,' Powell said.

His struggles eased, even if that frightened, angry look in his eyes hadn't changed. He was still capable of receiving commands, she thought. There was hope.

'Do you know why you've been brought here, Ryan?'

Drake's jaw clenched. 'You sent us in there,' he spat. 'You knew what we'd find. How could you do that?'

'That wasn't my decision to make,' she responded, keeping her tone quiet and even. 'You're here because you stopped obeying orders, Ryan. Abandoned your unit and tried to leave. Why?'

'You know why!' he shouted, furious. Even the sound-absorbing walls couldn't dampen the sound of his anger.

'Limit your emotions,' she ordered.

Drake let out a breath, calming himself against his will.

Powell reached out and laid a hand on his chest. 'I'm disappointed in you,' she admitted. 'You're the first anomaly we've had in this batch. My colleagues warned me you weren't taking to the conditioning like the others, but I ignored them. I believed I could make you even better than the others.' She sighed, knowing what had to come next. 'I may have been wrong.'

'What are you going to do? Kill me?' Drake asked contemptuously. 'Terminate me like some failed experiment?'

Powell shook her head. 'No, Ryan. I won't do that. But I can't risk you telling anyone what really happened.' Reaching into her pocket, she produced a syringe loaded with a compound of her own making. 'So I'm going to give you something instead. A gift. A gift that will protect us both.'

Finding the vein in his arm, she pushed the device in and depressed the plunger, giving him the full load.

'You're going to forget, Ryan,' she whispered as his eyes dimmed and the drugs took hold. 'You're going to forget everything that happened.'

Chapter 72

'How much further?' Drake asked, turning the wheel over as he fought to negotiate a path along the jolting, potholed dirt track. Their Toyota 4 x 4 slewed sideways, wheels skidding in a patch of icy mud before finding purchase.

It was as well they had, since there was literally nothing to their left but a drop of several hundred feet down to the floor of the valley below. Above them, great snow-capped peaks rose high into a steel-grey sky, flecks of sleet drifting down around them on the fitful wind.

'Not far now. Just beyond the next ridge,' his passenger replied, bracing herself as they hit another bump.

Anya had no map to consult, no GPS system, no artificial means of navigation whatsoever. It was all done by memory and dead reckoning – two factors which Drake would normally be reluctant to put his faith in. With Anya, however, it was different. She knew this place like most people knew their hometown.

'Didn't you say that about the last ridge?' he asked with a playful glint in his eye.

Anya glanced over. 'When you learn how to drive properly, you can start questioning my sense of direction.'

He shrugged. 'Fair enough.'

Afghanistan was a tough enough place to reach anyway, but it was made even worse for two people already on the Agency's most wanted list. Flying commercially was impossible, and even privately chartered flights were closely monitored by Coalition radar. Air travel was out of the question.

The only option had been to travel to neighbouring Tajikistan, secure a reliable car and drive south across the sparsely patrolled border zone, charting a winding course through tortuous mountain passes and barely discernible jeep trails known mostly to local farmers. It was slow going, but it was the only method of reaching their destination undetected.

Their plan, such as it was, had succeeded. They'd been able to slip across the border without encountering any military checkpoints or border patrols. The region was sparsely populated and only nominally under the jurisdiction of the Afghan government, who rarely deployed troops here in large numbers. And for good reason.

This was made readily apparent not long after crossing the border, as they passed a pair of burned-out vehicles lying abandoned by the side of the road, their frames charred and twisted. They might have been there for days, months or years, it was hard to tell.

They were however just the first of many such wrecks that littered the main roads, some torn apart by explosions, others peppered with bullet holes. One, chillingly, appeared to have been a school bus. As difficult as the mountain trails were to negotiate, Drake was relieved to see the back of those grim wrecks.

This was as lawless and dangerous a place as any on the face of the earth. The Taliban might have been ousted from power, and even al-Qaeda's back broken after years of attrition warfare, but such groups were as resilient as weeds – where one was removed, others soon took root.

The result was a constantly shifting, treacherous political landscape where petty rivalries were often settled in blood. In the absence of government or law enforcement, tribal warlords rose and fell, carving out swathes of territory, clashing with rivals, raiding villages and inevitably being supplanted by someone stronger, more ruthless or just more opportunistic. But no matter who was in charge, the civilian population usually lived in poverty, hardship and constant fear for their lives.

Drake turned his head upwards, uneasily scoping out the rocky crags overlooking the trail. Plenty of places that provided an excellent field of fire over the road below, making this place an ideal spot for an ambush. It was no wonder the government avoided the area.

'Not that I'm doubting you, but what makes you think we'll get a friendly welcome?'

According to Anya, the village that lay beyond the next ridge was under the protection of a friendly militia commander who might be able to aid them. 'Friendly' however was a relative term in these parts, and Drake was well aware of how easily loyalties could shift.

Anya's answer was simple. 'Because we're still alive.'

Drake once again surveyed the bleak landscape, seeing little but rocks and damp, windblown snow. 'I don't see anything.'

'That's the point,' Anya assured him. 'Every one of these passes is watched.'

'How comforting.'

They carried on up the trail for another half-mile or so, staying in low ratio in case they needed a sudden burst of power, but encountered no obstacles or difficulties to speak of. Until they approached the crest of the ridge.

Suddenly a pair of armed men sprang up onto the road, seeming to materialize out of thin air. In moments they were blocking the way, the long barrels of their bolt-action rifles trained on the 4 x 4.

'Stop,' Anya commanded him. 'Make no sudden moves.'

He stepped on the brakes, bringing them to a halt. Escape would have been a dicey proposition anyway. The mountain road was narrow, offered little room to manoeuvre, and absolutely no cover. Not to mention that two more men had emerged behind them.

They were boxed in, surrounded and outgunned.

'Hope you know what you're doing,' he muttered as the two men in front approached them, rifles up at their shoulders. After all the shit they'd been through to get this far, being gunned down by a pair of guerrilla fighters would be pretty disappointing.

'I do. Now kill the engine.'

Drake did as she asked, and an uneasy silence descended on the vehicle's cab. The two men had stopped about five yards ahead of the Toyota, permitting Drake a chance to evaluate them. Both were kitted out in old-fashioned but nonetheless effective mountain camo fatigues and mismatched webbing that seemed to have been cobbled together from half a dozen different sources.

He couldn't be sure since they were pointed right at him, but their weapons looked like Mosin-Nagant rifles. He almost hadn't believed it possible, but it seemed he'd finally encountered a weapon older than Anya's favourite handgun. The Mosin-Nagant had been around in various forms since the 1890s, which technically made it older than the country in which they now sat. Simple, rugged, accurate and powerful, they'd proven themselves formidable weapons in every major conflict for the past 120 years, and showed no signs of slowing down even in the twenty-first century.

The two men motioned with their rifles for Drake and Anya to disembark. This they did, keeping their hands in view and their faces turned slightly away from the driving sleet. It was cold, the temperature falling along with the sun, and wind chill was adding to the grim conditions.

One kept them covered while the other moved forward and frisked them for weapons – none too gently, Drake noted with annoyance. Nonetheless, he seemed to relax fractionally when it became apparent neither of them was carrying.

Now that he'd established the new arrivals weren't an immediate threat, the one who'd searched them barked out a question in Dari, the language most common to the northern districts of Afghanistan. Drake understood enough of it to know he was asking who they were and why they had come here.

They were looking to Drake for a response, but it was Anya who answered. She, after all, knew the man they'd come here to find.

'We have come to speak with Malak. Tell him Anya wishes to see him.'

'You speak when spoken to, woman!' he growled, raising the rifle as if to hit her with it. Afghanistan was hardly known for its progressive attitude towards women's rights, and the remote tribal areas were the most conservative of all.

Anya didn't flinch at this naked provocation. Instead she stood her ground, passive but undaunted.

'He knows me, and will welcome us,' she assured him. 'Please give him my message.'

The man considered this. Clearly he resented taking instructions from a woman, but he wasn't about to risk pissing off his commander by turning away or even executing a potentially influential guest.

'Wait here,' he said, backing away and pulling a bulky-looking walkie-talkie from his webbing. Neither of them made a move, though they weren't exactly enjoying the freezing wind and stinging sleet.

Drake kept his eyes fixed on the radio man, studying his posture and expression carefully as he went from irritation to suspicion, surprise and finally realization.

Stowing the radio, he approached them both, his rifle pointing downwards. He barked an order to his comrade, who similarly lowered his gun.

'You can go ahead,' he informed Drake, studiously avoiding Anya's gaze. 'The village is on the other side of the ridge. Drive slow and don't try anything.'

Drake nodded. 'Fair enough.'

Gratefully sliding back into the Toyota, Drake fired up the engine and turned the heaters on full. 'Nice guys,' he remarked as the two militia men moved aside deliberately slowly.

'This country has known nothing but war since before you were born. I don't blame them for being what they are,' Anya replied.

Drake said nothing. He eased them onwards, ascending the last 50 yards to the crest of the ridge. Ahead they found a relatively flat plain about a mile across, roughly bisected by a small river, swollen by recent snows. Straddling this waterway was a small village. Electric lights glowed here and there, probably running off generators, but most of the houses were lit against the gathering gloom by simple lamps and wood fires.

It was an isolated and backward little settlement, about as bleak and remote a spot as one could imagine.

Drake brought them into this cluster of manmade structures at low speed, watching as a few children stopped to stare at them as if they'd come from another world. Perhaps in some ways they had, he reflected.

'There. That building there,' Anya said, pointing towards the largest of the buildings where a few rugged looking 4 x 4s were parked.

For better or worse, they'd arrived.

They stepped out into swirling snow.

'You want to ring the doorbell?' he asked, casting his eyes around dubiously.

Barely had he spoken than the front door swung open and a trio of men strode out to meet them. Unlike the two they'd encountered on the road, all three were dressed in civilian clothes and appeared to be unarmed.

The two at the back were Drake's age or younger, still strong and in their prime, one clean-shaven and the other sporting a light, neatly trimmed beard. There was enough of a similarity between them that Drake guessed them to be brothers.

However, it was the man they were following who was clearly in charge. He must have been well into his seventies at least, with a thick grey beard. Despite moving a little uncomfortably on joints that had seen better days, he still possessed the tall, rangy build of a man used to covering distance. One eye, sharp and intelligent, was focussed on Anya, the other was simply an empty socket lined with old scar tissue.

Drake recognized him right away. Malak, the weapons trader who had supplied them with most of their gear for the doomed mission in Islamabad last year. This place was, it seemed, his home.

He grinned, revealing the oddly perfect set of teeth that had caught Drake's eye last time they'd met, and moved forward to embrace Anya.

'Anya,' he said, letting go to look at her. '*As-salaamu alaikum.*'

She nodded and gave the customary response. '*Wa-alaikum-salaam.*'

Malak beamed. 'When I heard your name, I thought my men must have been mistaken.'

'It's no mistake,' she confirmed, her expression turning more serious. 'Forgive me. I would not have come here if there were another choice.'

Malak was perceptive enough to realize this was a matter best discussed in private. 'Come. We'll talk inside.'

Chapter 73

Drake's experiences in Afghanistan had naturally made him wary of venturing into the homes of strangers; especially strangers who led rag-tag mountain militia units. Still, the freezing temperature and gathering darkness were enough to overcome these reservations, and he followed Malak and his two companions inside.

The interior of the dwelling was surprisingly comfortable and well appointed given its drab and impoverished façade. The floor was lined with thick rugs, the stone walls plastered and freshly painted, and what little furniture there was seemed to be of good quality. A fire burned brightly in the hearth opposite, adding to the warm and comfortable feel of the place. Drake could smell tea being prepared somewhere nearby.

'You have not met my sons,' Malak began. He indicated the man with the beard first, which told Drake he was the elder. In Afghan families, sons were always introduced in order of seniority. 'This is Farjaad, and his younger brother Jammas.'

'*As-salaamu alaikum,*' Drake said, going with the traditional greeting. *Peace be upon you.* Somehow he doubted either man had lived a life of peace, but such was the way of things. He was hardly one to judge.

'*Wa-alaikum-salaam,*' they each replied. *And upon you, peace.*

Malak might have been all smiles, but his sons were a different matter. Neither looked pleased, and regarded Drake in particular with thinly veiled suspicion. Still, opposing your father's wishes in front of guests was a massive no-no, so neither made further comment.

'Please, sit,' Malak urged them, switching to English for the sake of convenience. There were no couches or chairs as such, but rather a series of stuffed pillows laid out around the periphery of the room, facing towards the hearth.

Drake lowered himself into one, with Anya seated beside him. Malak and his two sons settled themselves opposite.

A young woman came in bearing a tray of tea. Too young to be Malak's wife, she couldn't have been more than 15 or 16, short in stature and nimble, almost birdlike in her movements. Likely a granddaughter, born from one of Malak's sons. Her hair was covered by a *tsādar,* but since they were in her home it was permitted for her face to be uncovered.

Drake waited in patient silence while she poured him a cup of tea, careful to avoid making eye contact, or indeed paying her much attention at all. Malak's sons were hardly his biggest fans anyway, and any overt interest in their daughter would be seen as an outright provocation.

338

There was no talking while this was going on. Matters of importance wouldn't be discussed while the girl was present. She was no doubt aware of this too, and hurriedly finished up and departed. Drake felt a twinge of pity for her as she scurried from the room, wondering what kind of life awaited her in a place like this.

His thoughts were drawn back to matters at hand when Malak opened the conversation.

'The last time I saw you both, you and your people were going to Islamabad,' he commented. He took a mouthful of tea before continuing. 'Tell me, what happened there?'

'Nothing good,' Drake replied tersely. The less said about that disastrous attempt to capture Marcus Cain, the better. 'We're here on other business.'

Malak watched him shrewdly. 'And what business might that be?'

'We need a place to stay for the night,' Anya said, jumping in before Drake said something they'd both regret. 'In the morning, we will be on our way.'

'No weapons? No equipment?' Malak asked, surprised.

Anya shook her head. 'We have everything we need.'

She didn't offer to compensate him, Drake noticed. Offering any Afghan payment for their hospitality was seen as a grave insult.

'You have everything, you say?' Farjaad, the eldest brother asked. 'Money, transport, supplies. Why then do you come here asking for help?'

Malak quietly advised his son to simmer down, but didn't fully reprimand him. Which told Drake he wanted to know the answer himself.

'We have enemies, in Afghanistan and elsewhere,' Anya explained. As far as understatements went, that one was up there with the best of them. 'I would rather put our safety in the hands of a friend.'

'And take *his* safety away with the same breath,' Farjaad scoffed. 'You would bring your problems here with you.'

'A real friend is one who takes the hand of his friend in time of distress,' Drake said.

Farjaad looked at him sharply, having picked up on his choice of words. Afghans are particularly fond of sayings and proverbs, particularly when underlining points and settling disputes. A good proverb, properly employed, could carry a great deal of weight.

'And if a forest catches fire, dry and wet alike will burn,' his brother Jammas responded.

'Enough,' Malak said sharply, realizing that sniping would achieve little. He turned his eye on Drake and Anya again. 'This village has been my home since I was a boy. It's a peaceful place, and we work hard to keep it that way. Allah knows, there are few enough of them in this country as it is.'

'And that's the way it will stay,' Anya promised. 'You have my word.'

Malak exhaled slowly, the air whistling through the hairs of his beard. His sons had made their feelings plain, and while it was clear who held sway over this family,

Drake knew that in Afghan culture only brave or foolish men made enemies of their sons. There was no reason to believe he'd take them in out of charity.

'I have known you a long time, and you have never placed demands on me,' he said at length. 'If you come seeking help today, I will give it to you.'

Anya nodded, her relief obvious. Jammas and Farjaad looked pissed off but wisely held their peace, deferring to their father's wishes. The decision had been made. They had a place to stay.

Despite the rocky start, Malak proved to be a generous host, even inviting them to share the evening meal with him and the rest of his family. Tradition and honour dictated that he show the utmost hospitality, and he was apparently a man who took such things seriously.

Neither Drake nor Anya was inclined to object. Given that they'd been subsisting on bottled water and protein bars since their departure from Tajikistan, the platter of freshly baked naans, tandoored lamb and spiced potatoes brought out to them was like a banquet by comparison. Simple food cooked well, seasoned even better and provided in more than ample quantity.

There was no dining table as such. Rather, a large tablecloth was laid out on the floor in front of them, and the various dishes placed on it. Neither were there any cutlery or utensils for their personal use. Meals were expected to be eaten with the hands – only the right hand – with the naan bread usually acting as a kind of crude spoon for mopping up.

No alcohol was served either. Instead they were given a local drink known as *doogh* – a mixture of water and yoghurt flavoured with mint. Drake had sampled the concoction before, and while the flavour wasn't exactly appealing to his palate, it was nonetheless cold and refreshing, and a good counterpoint to the spicy meat dishes.

Given what they were about to attempt tomorrow, Drake would have preferred something stronger, but he wasn't about to complain now. Anyway, he'd brought a little something along in his backpack for just such a contingency.

Talk flowed in a mixture of Pashto and English depending on who was speaking to whom, though Malak was careful to keep the conversation away from the darker aspects of Drake and Anya's lives, for obvious reasons. Drake couldn't guess how much his family actually knew of their father's profession – his sons were likely not ignorant of his arms-dealing enterprises – but whether they understood how he made his money or not, it was clearly not to be discussed here.

The young woman who had poured the tea earlier had returned, along with another girl of comparable age but considerably fuller build, and a younger boy who had barely seen five years. He seemed to find Drake particularly intriguing, and spent much of the meal staring up at him with big, solemn brown eyes.

The family gathering was completed by an older woman who was introduced as Malak's wife. The girls spoke only amongst themselves, never addressing or even looking directly at Drake or Anya, though they seemed quite fascinated by the latter's blonde hair. The older woman was not so constrained, however. As the matriarch of the house and with her husband present, she was permitted to converse freely.

Her name was Asal. A short, rotund woman of late middle age, her rounded face bore a severe expression that suggested she wasn't someone to trifle with. More than once she snapped out a curt word or command to the young women when they started to make too much noise. It was easy to see where her sons got their temperaments from, Drake thought.

Asal seemed particularly interested in Anya, and quizzed her in depth about her own history, her experiences in Afghanistan and even specific people she might know. Anya did her best to answer vaguely but truthfully, tactfully leaving out the fact she'd once been a covert operative for the CIA sent behind enemy lines to fight alongside the Mujahedeen against the Soviets. That was probably a little heavy as far as dinner conversation went.

Unsurprisingly, it eventually transpired that Asal knew a couple of men from Kabul with whom Anya had once associated. Drake had encountered many different peoples and cultures in his life, but none who spun such complex webs of kinship ties and family associations as the Afghans. There was even a joke that a man in debt could move from Kabul to Herat and still run into someone demanding his money.

Nonetheless, keeping up such a façade under intense questioning was clearly a taxing experience for Anya, and Drake decided it was best to bring matters to a close.

'Thank you for dinner, but it's been a long journey. We should get some rest,' he said, speaking in Pashto so they could all understand. He also made sure to leave a little food on his plate as a token of respect.

Malak nodded, guessing his intent. A room had been set aside for them, and he instructed one of his granddaughters to show Anya to it.

With Drake however, it was plain he had something else in mind. 'I like to stretch my legs after dinner,' he said, rising up from his pillow with surprising grace and dignity given his age. 'Will you walk with me a ways?'

It was obvious this was no idle suggestion, and it would be unwise to decline. Nodding agreement, Drake followed Malak outside.

Darkness had fallen across the mountains. A few stars were even visible between the thick ribbons of cloud overhead, shivering cold and hard in the night sky.

Malak progressed slowly down what obviously passed for a main street around here, moving with no great sense of purpose or direction. A pair of boys ran across the street up ahead, shouting and laughing, their long thin sticks doubling as toy swords that they swung and parried. Kids horsing around without a care, lost in their fantasy world.

Malak smiled fondly as they disappeared down an alley between two houses. 'My brother and I used to play just like that when we were boys, heroes in our own stories,' he remarked with a wistful tone. 'That's what we thought when we rushed off to fight the Soviets 30 years ago. From boys into men, and men into heroes. Yesal died still believing that.'

'And you?' Drake asked. 'What do you believe?'

'I lost half my sight to a Soviet sniper,' Malak said. 'His shot punched straight through the wall I was crouched behind. I still remember it even now. The sound of the blast, the darkness, the hot blood.' He allowed that thought to linger a moment before continuing. 'But I think Allah took my eye so he could give me something better in return – perspective. My generation rode off proudly to war seeking honour and glory, and my sons' generation had to live with the consequences. I think Afghanistan has had enough of young men trying to be heroes. Maybe the next generation will grow up into something better.'

'I hope so,' Drake said.

'And you, Ryan Drake?' the old man asked. 'What did you come here to be?'

Drake offered a wry smile. 'Been a while since anyone called me young. And I'm no hero. I never was. I'm just trying to stay alive.'

Malak nodded thoughtfully. 'Spoken like a man who has seen war.'

'More than you know,' he replied, watching as the two boys emerged from behind another house, still play fighting, one pursuing the other. Another generation of warriors in training.

He turned southwards. Somewhere out there, beyond the mountain peaks, lay Kabul. And somewhere in that city was Powell. He knew it as surely as he knew the sun would rise in the morning.

'There are people out there who want to kill me.'

'And yet you still live,' Malak observed.

'I should have died so many times. Better men than me didn't make it this far.' Drake sighed. 'Do you ever ask yourself why you made it back and your brother didn't? Why you deserved life more than him?'

'It was God's will. I may not understand it, but it's not my place to question it.'

Drake didn't respond, and Malak was quick to guess why.

'You're not a believer, Drake.'

He grunted. 'If there is a god, he's making a bit of a mess of things, wouldn't you say? Living through the things you've seen, how can you still believe in him?'

Malak's boots crunched on the ground as he moved to stand beside Drake. 'God does not make men good or evil. He gives us the wisdom to choose for ourselves. You might live or die tomorrow, that's not your choice. But you *can* choose what kind of man you want to be.'

If only he knew, Drake thought. It wasn't a matter of choosing which kind of man he wanted to be. There were already two men within him – one good, and one evil. It was only a question of which one would prevail.

'The night is cold,' Malak said, sensing he'd made his point. 'And my old bones feel it more than yours. Come, let's go back.'

Drake began to wonder about Powell, what she was doing at that moment, whether she was thinking about him, whether she knew how this was going to end.

One way or another, they would find out tomorrow.

With this thought weighing heavily on his mind, he turned away and followed Malak back to his home.

Chapter 74

Like many Afghan homes, Malak's residence was roughly rectangular, with most of the rooms overlooking a central courtyard. Extended families were common to many households in this country, several generations often living together under the same roof. This naturally resulted in a degree of overcrowding for many Afghans, but Malak at least possessed the means to build a home of appropriate size.

Drake and Anya had been furnished with a guest room in the most remote corner of the compound – a sign that their presence here was tolerated but hardly welcomed. Unlike the more frequented areas of the house, this was a plain and functional living space, sparsely decorated with mismatched and decidedly outdated furniture.

One feature that both intrigued and amused Drake was an old vinyl record player set proudly on a wooden stand in one corner of the room, as if it were some miracle of modern technology. The shelf beneath was laden with discs, some still in their cardboard sleeves, most without. Judging by the worn and frayed covers, most were from local musicians he'd never heard of, and none seemed to have been produced in the last two decades.

Still, it was warm and dry, and a roof over their heads for the night. Both he and Anya had seen their share of Afghan winters and had no desire to repeat the experience.

'This is a map of the eastern districts,' Anya said, unfolding a big printed graphic on the floor in front of her. 'It's not military grade, but it's the best I could find.'

She was sitting cross-legged on the floor, since there was no table in the room big enough to accommodate it. Searching for a while, she reached out and marked their current position in the northern mountain range with a red pen.

'I'll forgive you,' Drake replied, pouring the contents of his hip flask into a chipped glass he'd found in the bathroom. 'All right, so working on the assumption Karalius is already in Afghanistan, where could he be?'

'Kabul would be the logical place,' Anya remarked. 'High population, plenty of Westerners to help him blend in.'

'Lots of police and military units too.'

Anya pursed her lips. 'He said this would end where it began,' she recalled. 'What do you think he meant by that?'

Drake had initially taken it to mean Afghanistan in general. It had been the first place that Anya and Karalius had deployed to a quarter of a century earlier, and for Drake it had been the staging place for Operation Hydra. But now he began to suspect there was more to it, something more specific.

'Where did you operate from when you served here?'

'Here.' She indicated a swathe of mostly mountainous terrain along the Pakistani border, running from Jalalabad in the south to the Wakhan Corridor in the east. 'Sometimes we would go as far south as Khost, and west to hit convoys on the way to Bagram.'

'Sounds fun,' Drake remarked. 'How was it done? Splash-and-dash ops?'

Anya snorted with amusement. 'Are you joking? We never had that level of support. Our mission was to fight alongside the Mujahedeen, not jump in and out when it suited us. Once we were in, we stayed in until we exhausted our supplies.'

'Ballsy.' The Agency back then had clearly been a very different place to the one he'd served in. 'Dangerous, but ballsy.'

'It was our job, Ryan.'

Drake glanced at her. She was sitting close to him – an easy, companionable closeness that had developed between them over the past couple of days – but there was something else in her expression too. A kind of fierce pride at what she and her team had accomplished, a memory of the hardships and dangers they'd shared.

He turned back to the map. 'All right, so if you were operating here for long periods, you must have had a FOB.'

A forward operating base was any location from which a military force could deploy, often serving as a combination of supply depot, planning centre and communications point. Drake had seen them range in size from small towns with their own airports and recreation facilities, down to a few tents hacked out of a jungle clearing.

'We had lots of them. We never stayed in one place for too long.'

Made sense. He would have conducted such operations along similar lines.

'Show me.'

Using the pen again, she marked nearly a dozen points on the map, mostly amongst the twisting valleys and mountain passes that defined the eastern edge of the country. The kind of places that would have been a nightmare for the Soviets to deploy forces into, where ambushes would be easy to set up and impossible to predict. No wonder they'd been able to operate for lengthy periods.

'Stop,' Drake said, suddenly clasping her hand.

Anya was struck by the expression of intense recognition and understanding on his face. He'd seen something on that map, something that had jogged a long-buried memory.

'What is it?' Anya said.

Releasing her hand, he reached out slowly, reluctantly, and pointed to one of the marks she'd made. One that lay about 50 miles north-east of Kabul.

'There. That's where we'll find him.'

Anya frowned. He'd spoken with such certainty, such absolute assurance, as if he'd just seen Karalius with his own eyes, yet she saw no reason to believe that spot was unique amongst all the others they'd used over the years.

'How do you know this?'

'It's where we were sent. That's where it happened.'

His voice carried a frighteningly disconnected undertone, as if she were only hearing the echoes of his words.

'What happened there, Ryan?' she asked.

He didn't respond. He was staring at that point on the map, his eyes glossy and unfocussed. A man haunted by a waking dream.

'Ryan.'

She gripped his arm. He blinked, coming back to himself, and turned to her with an expression of puzzlement, as if trying to understand.

'I don't know,' he whispered. 'But *he* does.'

Chapter 75

Drake awoke to the sound of music.

Old and melancholy music, playing softly. It was instantly familiar to him, yet strangely antiquated. Music that belonged to a different generation.

'I can see clearly now, the rain is gone.
I can see all obstacles in my way...'

It was cooler now, and the breeze running through the room raised goosebumps on his exposed skin. A window was open somewhere.

He rolled over, seeking Anya.

She wasn't there.

He opened his eyes and glanced around the darkened room. Cast in pale silvery moonlight and deep shadow, the place seemed almost ghostlike, as if he were still caught on the edge of a dream.

But he was awake. He knew that for certain.

'Gone are the dark clouds that had me blind.
It's gonna be a bright, bright, bright sun-shinin' day...'

Pulling the sheets aside, he rose from the bed and crossed the room, his senses unusually heightened, eyes straining to pierce the darkness. He almost thought to retrieve his gun, but instinct told him that no weapons were needed. Whatever was happening, he wasn't going to take up arms tonight.

'I think I can make it now, the pain has gone.
All of the bad feelings have disappeared...'

He found Anya reclining on a chair by the open window, her long legs stretched out and resting on the sill.

She was wearing his loosely buttoned shirt, but aside from that she sat unashamedly naked. She looked peaceful and relaxed as she allowed the music to wash over her.

Drake said and did nothing, feeling a little guilty for intruding on such a personal, intimate moment. Not for the first time he caught himself wondering at the soul that lurked behind her intimidating façade, at the triumphs and tragedies that had shaped her.

'Look straight ahead, there's nothing but blue skies...'

Raising a glass to her lips, she took a drink, her chest rising beneath the thin material of the shirt. He could see the soft curves of her full breasts, the nipples standing out hard in the cool night air.

Such a strange dichotomy, he thought. That inexplicable contrast of firm unyielding strength and tender vulnerability combined in one body. A woman created to bring forth life, who had made a career out of taking it.

'You can come closer, Ryan,' she said. 'I know you're there.'

Of course she knew. She seemed to sense the presence of others more acutely than anyone he'd ever encountered. Relaxing, Drake crossed the room and eased himself into a chair opposite her. He gestured to the record player nearby, the scratched old vinyl disc still turning on it. Old music playing on old technology.

'You found something in that pile worth listening to.'

He saw a smile, faint and bittersweet. 'It helps me remember.'

'Remember what?'

'Absent friends.' She took another drink. Drake could smell vodka. She must have brought it with her, just as he had.

It was then that he noticed something around her neck: a simple link necklace, with an identity tag at the end. A dog tag, its metal surface stamped with Anya's unit number, blood type and religion. But no name. She had no name in the eyes of the men she'd served, no identity beyond her role as an operative.

She'd explained that the tags had been issued on an informal basis, their use in the field strictly forbidden. Such people were never supposed to be identified. They were ghosts whose very existence could be expunged if they were ever captured or killed. And yet still they'd acted as soldiers, as a unit, a family who lived and fought and bled together.

It wasn't hard to guess what was on her mind. 'You're wondering what will happen when we meet Karalius tomorrow.'

'I had told myself he was gone like the others. I mourned him, and I let him go. Now... so much time has passed, so much has changed, I don't know if I will even recognize him. Or if he'll recognize me.'

She laid the glass down, thinking on those words. To say it out loud made the doubts and fears suddenly real.

'When I came back from Afghanistan, I told myself I had ten good years left as a soldier. That was two decades ago.' She chuckled then, both in disappointment and bleak amusement at the way things had turned out. 'I'm older now than my parents ever got to be. I've outlived them, even outlived the world I was born into.'

He saw the toll it had taken. He caught a glimpse of the weariness that now weighed on her spirit, the grief for comrades fallen, the regrets for mistakes made and opportunities missed. The sorrow of love lost.

'You never asked me why,' she said, coming back to herself.

'Why?'

'Why I did it. Why I became a soldier.'

Drake shrugged. 'You'd tell me when you were ready. Not before.'

She smiled, acknowledging the mild dig at her stubborn personality, then took another drink. It was a while before she spoke again.

'You might find it hard to believe, but I thought one day I would be a doctor, a healer. That was the future I saw for myself.' The smile faded as she spoke, her gaze growing unfocussed as old memories resurfaced. 'Then the State came. They took my parents, made them "disappear" like they did with so many others. They died in prison, the same one you rescued me from 30 years later. My old life, the future I imagined... it died with them.'

He'd expected to hear pain or anger, but there was nothing, as if the entire experience had torn some hole in her psyche and all of the emotions she should have felt had long since flowed away.

'I became someone very different after that. I didn't want to help people any longer. I wanted to hurt them, punish them, take everything they had taken from me. It was a raw wound that I never allowed to heal. So I waited, and I let it fester inside me, and when my chance came, I took it. I begged the Agency to take me, and it was Cain who did it. Cain who took pity on me, perhaps even wanted to help me in his own way.'

Even she could allow him that.

'I didn't care about the danger or the mission, I only wanted revenge. And for that, I was rewarded. And in the end, I came to the attention of the real power behind the Agency, behind everything.'

'The Circle,' he said quietly.

Anya nodded. 'They said I could play a part in reshaping the world into something better. And in my arrogance, I believed them. I flattered myself that I could make a real difference at last, not as a soldier but as something else. I thought I could *be* something better, and I could help them to be better too.'

'That was the future I saw for myself. Everything from the day I lost my parents until then seemed to make sense at last, like it had all been for some greater purpose. For one moment it all seemed possible. And then... it was gone.'

She looked at him, emerging from her reverie. 'After everything I did, I was still just a pawn in someone else's game. My part was over. And I would never, ever get that chance again.' She drained the last of her vodka and laid down the glass.

'I've known you a long time,' Drake said at last. 'You've never spoken like this before. Why now?'

'I wanted you to know who I really was, why I did the things I did. I hoped that if you knew what brought us to this... you wouldn't repeat my mistakes. Maybe you wouldn't end up like me.

'This belongs to you now,' she whispered, placing his hand on her heart. 'All I have left. All I can give you.'

Drake was silent, struck by her gesture. Anya, who had survived for so long by withholding her trust, by never opening up, by never lowering her guard, had finally laid herself bare before him. No pretences, no deceptions.

Just her honest admission.

'There's one thing I have to ask from you,' he said, knowing he could avoid this no longer. 'A promise I need you to make.'

Anya stared back, waiting.

'If I... change again. If I lose myself like I did before—'

'That won't happen,' she said firmly. 'I won't let it.'

Drake shook his head. Her words were determined enough, but he could sense a lack of conviction. She could no more control the balance of his mind than she could control the weather.

'Whatever happened to me... it's not gone,' he confessed, hating each word. 'It's beaten, it's locked away, but it's still there. And I might not be able to stop it a second time. If that happens, I want you to end it. Don't hesitate, don't let anything else get in the way. You... understand why I'm asking this, don't you?'

'Ryan...'

'Promise me,' he said, his tone harder. 'I can't become that man again. I'd rather die than live like that.'

Anya could tell he wouldn't be swayed. She also knew that if she made this promise, it would be binding.

She swallowed, but finally nodded. 'I promise.'

Drake pulled her into a fierce embrace. They stood there by the window, holding each other tight until the scratched old vinyl record reached the end of the track and stopped.

Chapter 76

They had come down to it at last. The final leg of their journey.

The weather at least had improved for their departure, the clouds breaking up during the night and the wind easing off. It was still cold, but it was better than what they'd fought through yesterday. They needed the weather to be on their side today, not to mention a healthy portion of luck.

Malak and his two sons had come out to see them on their way, and a good number of other villagers had found reason to be outside as well.

'You're sure this is everything you need?' Malak asked, surveying the meagre provisions loaded into the 4 x 4. 'Not much for what you're planning.'

Drake shook his head. 'Weapons won't help us now.'

The old man was clearly of a different mindset, but nonetheless relented.

'*Khoda hafiz*, Anya,' he said solemnly. *May God protect you.*

She nodded, repeating the gesture and the phrase. Whether she believed in a higher power or not, she respected Malak enough to bid him farewell on his own terms.

With the matter concluded, both travellers moved to mount the vehicle, but Malak caught Drake just as he was opening his door.

'Think on what I said last night, Drake,' he advised, speaking so that only the two of them could hear it. 'A man can choose what he will be. I hope you choose well.'

Firing up the engine, Drake tackled the uneven road at a slow pace until they were clear of the village.

'What did Malak say to you?' Anya asked.

Drake shrugged, keeping his attention on the road. 'Just a reminder.'

Leaving their mountain refuge behind, they descended the narrow trail and turned towards Kabul, moving at a steady pace once they found a better-defined road.

They slowed a little to stare at the rusting hulk of a tank perched on a nearby hill. Its long gun barrel was now lying at its maximum declination and its tracks missing, but the sloping hull and rounded turret were unmistakable. It was a Soviet T-34 – a relic of a different war, now standing as a silent monument to the failed aspirations of its masters. He'd heard the Red Army had deployed some of these veterans of the Second World War to Afghanistan during the invasion, but he'd never seen one until today.

Anya in particular seemed to bristle at the sight of the ancient war machine, as if its engine might suddenly rumble back into life and its rusted gun track towards them.

'Old news,' Drake said quietly. 'We missed that party.'

Anya didn't respond.

After driving for almost an hour, their journey carrying them well out of range of Malak's village, Drake knew it was almost time.

Anya was sitting with her boots up on the dashboard, her eyes on the towering mountain peaks. Her expression was thoughtful, pensive, troubled. Maybe some part of her sensed what was going to happen today, the end that awaited them.

Drake reached down and felt the sidearm holstered at his hip. A single handgun wasn't much to fight with, but perhaps it didn't matter now. This was a battle that wouldn't be decided by firepower.

'There's something I wanted to ask,' he said at length. He sensed this might be his last chance to speak with her. 'About what you told me last night.'

Anya waited for him to go on.

'You said you once wanted a different life for yourself.'

'I did,' she acknowledged. 'A long time ago.'

'Maybe you still could,' he ventured. 'When this is all over.'

'No.' Her voice was distant and weary. 'It's too late now.'

'It's never too late.'

She shook her head. 'I am what I am, Ryan. This might not be the life I wanted, but it's the one I was given. I can't run away from that. I won't.'

'You don't have to, but you can make peace with it and move on. This has to end for you some time. There has to be something after.'

She thought on that, perhaps sensing what he was hinting at, what he was trying to make her see. A life beyond. A future to strive for.

'I have to follow my path to the end. After that… I can't say.'

Drake didn't have an answer to that. Instead he eased off the accelerator and turned off the road. He brought them, bumping and jolting, down a gentle slope into the dried-up remnants of an ancient riverbed. Well out of sight of anyone who might pass by on the main road.

'Why here?' Anya asked.

'We've driven enough. Let's stop for a minute, yeah?'

Anya nodded and together they stepped out into the new morning. It was invigorating, the mountains empty and splendid.

A hard, beautiful country, Drake thought.

Stepping over precariously slanted rocks, Anya halted in a patch of long grass and bent down, lowering herself to her knees so that she was sitting amongst them, her eyes closed, hair fluttering in the breeze. Reaching out, she allowed her hands to brush lightly across the stalks, still wet from last night's sleet and rain, then brought her hands up and wiped them slowly across her face.

She inhaled, drawing deep from the cold air of the new day. And there came across her face an expression of such peace and tranquillity that Drake was captivated. It was a glimpse, the briefest vision of the woman she might have become, the life she might have lived.

'I did my best,' she whispered.

She opened her eyes, and rose up slowly from her place of refuge. The spell was broken. The look of quiescent serenity had faded, replaced by hardened resolve as Drake approached.

'You're a good man, Ryan,' she said as his hand clenched into a fist. 'Remember that.'

Drake swung fast and hard, catching her with a solid blow to the side of the face that almost knocked her off her feet, blood running from a cut opened across her cheek. He moved in closer, getting ready to strike again, to do what he'd been waiting three days to do.

What he'd been ordered to do.

Chapter 77

Bagram Air Base was an immense military stronghold whose sheer scale and complexity defied belief. It was home not only to the veteran 82nd Airborne Division and its support elements, but also to marine and air force companies, and even contingents of the British and German armies. The base also served as the headquarters of ISAF's (International Security Assistance Force) Regional Command East, making it a vital element of the Coalition's presence here.

The US might have scaled down active combat operations in Afghanistan in recent years, but their presence was still very much felt.

Being the hub for all military traffic in central Afghanistan, the place was a hive of aircraft activity. An incoming Globemaster heavy-lift transport joined a contingent of four C-130s parked side by side on the north side of the runways, with more cargo haulers lurking in nearby hangars.

Set apart from the transports were the fast-strike aircraft. Half a dozen A-10 Warthogs were parked side by side, maintenance crews hard at work, while further away rose the distinctive twin tail booms of F-15 Strike Eagles.

An impressive display of military might, but one which meant little to Elizabeth Powell as she stood in her office, staring out across the base. Let the army have their tanks and their planes if it made them feel better. Their means of waging war were rapidly becoming obsolete. She had something far more powerful. She had the keys to the future.

She watched as a Black Hawk helicopter came in to land, downwash from its rotors kicking up a storm of water from last night's rain. A range of barren, windblown mountains reared up into the clear blue sky, dominating the horizon.

An ugly country, she thought. Cold, bleak and backward looking. God only knew why armies and empires had fought so hard over such a worthless patch of ground for centuries. Powerful, ambitious men carrying their dreams off the edge of a cliff as they strove to outdo each other.

She heard the door open, footsteps on the carpeted floor behind her.

'The team's set up and ready to go,' Hawkins reported. 'We've increased drone flights and electronic surveillance around the border zones. Nothing so far.'

Powell didn't expect there to be. Drake was smarter than that. When they found him, it would be because he wanted to be found.

'How does it feel to be back in the old stomping ground, Jason?' she asked, keeping her back to him. 'Bring back fond memories?'

'We did what we were made for. What you trained us to do.'

'Of course you did.'

She heard him come closer. Perhaps he was trying to intimidate her. She didn't turn around, however. He could come as close as he wanted; they both knew he was incapable of doing her harm.

'You should have come out with us, seen what you helped us become.' His voice was low, quiet, almost sensual as he spoke. 'Even you might have been surprised.'

She chuckled derisively. 'If I order a steak for dinner, I don't need to see the cow getting slaughtered,' she informed him. 'That's for lesser people to take care of.'

'Lesser people, huh?'

'That's right.' Only then did she deign to turn around and face him. Hawkins was tall, but standing in heels she was almost a match for him. 'Soldiers don't change the world, Jason. There'll always be more soldiers. It's the people who direct them, give them purpose that really make the difference. Just like I gave you purpose. And Ryan.'

'Ryan's not here.'

She smiled. A patient, knowing, confident smile. 'Not yet.'

Her phone was vibrating on a nearby desk. She strode over and picked it up. She felt her pulse quicken. The call was coming from an unencrypted number.

'Yes?'

'It's done,' Drake reported. 'I have her.'

'Condition?'

'Not exactly unharmed, but alive.'

Powell closed her eyes, allowing the moment of triumph and elation to wash over her. The gamble had paid off. Her plan had come to fruition, just as she'd known it would.

'Well done, Ryan,' she said. He had come through for her in the end. After all this time, he had come back to her. 'Where are you?'

'In the mountains north of Kabul. Follow this phone signal.'

'We're on our way,' she said. 'I'm looking forward to seeing you again.'

As the call closed down, she tossed the phone to Hawkins. He caught it, his surprise clear.

'Get a trace on that last call, divert any active drones in the area to that location, and have your strike team gear up.' She paused, considering her position. 'And make sure the choppers are heavily armed. When we go in, I want to be backed up to the fullest extent.'

'You're coming with us this time?'

'What's the matter, Jason? You wanted me to come into the field with you, see the results of my work. Well, today's the day.'

–

'Move it! Go! Go!' Hawkins shouted, his voice echoing around the cavernous aircraft hangar as the assault team fell in around him, checking weapons, securing body armour and performing last-minute equipment tests. Ten men in total, all supplied with the latest generation body armour, secure comms and enough firepower to decimate an entire platoon.

Not to mention their airborne backup.

A pair of Black Hawk helicopters sat on the aircraft ramp just beyond the hangar entrance, low and squat and dangerous looking. One was serving as the troop deployment chopper, the other outfitted with rockets, air-to-ground missiles and automatic cannons, providing devastating airborne fire support if it were needed. In addition, a pair of Predator drones had been vectored towards the target area and were expected to arrive any minute, one of which was armed with Hellfire missiles for additional target suppression.

A lot of firepower and technology at their disposal, and yet that gave Hawkins little comfort. He was simply unwilling and unable to believe that Drake had given up. But Powell wouldn't listen, wouldn't hear his objections or doubts, wouldn't countenance the possibility she was wrong. She was like a train bound for its destination, unable to stray from its tracks.

He felt a touch on his arm and turned to face Riley, who had approached unheard while he was absorbed in his thoughts.

'I want to go in with the assault team,' she said bluntly.

Hawkins shook his head. 'Not this time. I can't have you there.'

If she was seen, Hawkins would lose his most vital play. No, Riley had to remain out of sight for now. Until she was needed, until it was time for her to do what Hawkins couldn't.

Her jaw jutted defiantly, her fists clenched. Fiery and defiant, she wouldn't be cowed by a single command. 'I owe Drake.'

Hawkins ran a hand down her cheek.

'You know why I need you here.'

She looked up into his eyes and, despite her anger at being denied her prize, he nonetheless saw a flicker of excitement at what lay in store. She might not get what she wanted today, but the consolation would be worth it.

Hawkins was sure she wouldn't let him down. Breaking away, he turned towards the others. Preparations were almost complete, the Black Hawk's engines were already spinning up, whining as they began to generate power.

He reached up and keyed his secure comms unit.

'We're ready here. Bring the boss in.'

Chapter 78

The interior of the chopper was extremely loud, and smelled of engine grease and gun oil and carefully controlled tension. Powell watched the range of arid mountain peaks floating by a couple of thousand feet below, while on their starboard flank the second chopper hovered protectively, a brooding and reassuring presence.

Packed into the crew compartment around her were almost a dozen men in full combat gear. Big and bulked out by their armour and equipment, faces grim, weapons clutched in gloved hands. There was no chatter, no joking or laughter. They were serious and cold. Ready to go into battle, mentally preparing themselves to kill and be killed.

It was the first time she'd witnessed an active operation up close, and even she had to admit there was a certain intimidation that came with such an overt display of size and physical power. She might have felt uneasy in their presence if she weren't secure in the knowledge that they'd each been conditioned just as Hawkins had.

These men could neither harm nor oppose her.

Her bulky headset unit crackled as a voice spoke up over the aircraft's intercom. 'Predator drones are on station, we have confirmed target acquisition,' Hawkins reported. The other men around him tensed up. 'Drake and an unidentified second target.'

'Right where he said he'd be,' Powell remarked. 'Is there anyone else in the area?'

Even she recognized the possibility of an ambush in such a rugged, isolated spot. Their choppers would make large and tempting targets for a hidden surface-to-air missile.

'Thermal scans are blanketing the whole area. So far nothing.'

'Good. How much longer?'

'Three minutes out.'

Their course was changing, she realized. The deck was tilting under their feet, the nose rising up to slow their forward momentum.

'What's happening? Why are we slowing?'

'This is the failsafe point,' Hawkins responded. 'We hold position here while the gunship scouts ahead and clears the area.'

Powell shook her head. 'No. Take us in.'

A few uneasy looks were exchanged amongst the assault team now.

'If this is a trap—'

'It's not,' she said confidently. 'Take us in, Jason. I want to see him myself.'

Hawkins switched channels to speak with the pilots. 'Alpha One is going in. Alpha Two, cover our approach.'

'Are you sure, Alpha One?'

'It's my call. Alpha One has lead. Everyone else stay frosty. If he so much as twitches, you waste the entire area.'

'Copy that, Alpha One. You have lead. Alpha Two is on overwatch.'

The big, heavily armoured gunship peeled away, climbing above them as their own Black Hawk began to descend towards a broad, rocky plateau nestled amongst the mountains.

Powell watched as something shot skywards from the midst of this plateau, and felt herself tense up for a moment, only for it to burst harmlessly into a ball of red light half a mile away. It was merely a signal flare fired by Drake to indicate his position.

The Black Hawk dropped lower, the wide-open space resolving itself into discernible details: tangled boulders and patches of sparse trees growing near water sources, with areas of rocky but flat ground in between. And standing there patient and unmoving, a pair of figures.

'Hello, Ryan,' she whispered as the chopper swung in for its final descent.

'Gear up!' Hawkins called out, removing his intercom. 'Twenty seconds!'

Powell was oblivious to the frantic last-minute activity going on around her as the big aircraft descended the last 50 feet, the pilot bringing the nose up to slow their momentum.

'Brace for landing!'

They came down hard and fast, the impact jolting her in her seat, the thump of the landing gear making contact rattling through the fuselage.

The assault team were moving within moments, unstrapping themselves and hauling the sliding door open. Dust kicked up by the rotors whipped in through the doorway as the team piled out, weapons up and ready, spreading out to take up defensive positions all around.

Drake held his ground, making no move. Just as she'd known he would.

'Clear!' she heard one call out.

'Clear!' another confirmed.

The engines were spinning down now, the rotors slowing, allowing easier communication.

Hawkins looked over at her. 'Sure you want to do this?'

Powell unstrapped herself from the secure harness and stood up, having to duck slightly because of the chopper's low ceiling.

'I'm ready,' she said.

Hawkins went out first, his weapon trained on Drake. She approached the edge of the chopper, gathered herself up and leapt down carefully onto the rocky and uneven ground below. Powell might have earned a life of comparative ease and comfort in recent years, but it hadn't always been this way. And she hadn't forgotten the experiences that had made her who she was.

Straightening up, she looked over to Drake. He was standing barely 30 yards away, hands by his sides. The bound and hooded prisoner was there with him.

She started forward, her feet finding a path through the rocks and sharp stones waiting to trip her up. Hawkins was by her side, weapon up at his shoulder, covering Drake. A caged lion aching to strike at its prey. The rest of the assault team had spread out to form a circle around both the aircraft and its passenger. A wall of guns facing outwards.

Still Drake made no move to strike or retreat. Powell looked up and down, seeing no obvious weapons on either him or his apparent prisoner. He was well aware of the guns pointed his way, and that any move might tip an already fraught situation over the brink.

She halted a few yards from him. Almost close enough to reach out and touch. And for a couple of seconds, no one spoke a word or made a move. The two of them just stood there, each taking stock of the other, each trying to discern the other's thoughts.

'You know the drill,' Hawkins said. 'Let's see those hands. Slowly.'

Drake glanced at him and smiled. 'Nervous, Jason?'

'Should I be?'

'Depends what you came here for.'

He didn't respond, but Powell could practically feel the hostility emanating from him. Every instinct in his body was telling him to open fire, and yet she knew he wouldn't. Not without her permission.

Drake raised his hands up, proving to them that he was unarmed. He had come to this meeting with nothing.

'That's enough,' Powell decided. 'Let's not get started on the wrong foot. Ryan's come here in good faith, and so have we. Lower your weapon.'

Reluctantly the operative complied.

Drake smiled again, apparently amused by how easily she controlled him.

First things first. Powell nodded to his hooded prisoner. 'Let's see her.'

Drake grasped the prisoner's hood and yanked it off. A ripple of tension ran through Hawkins and the other operatives as the hood came away, and Powell saw their weapons raised a little despite their orders to stand down. She saw the fleeting look of surprise in Hawkins' eyes, the relief that Drake hadn't betrayed them, then the growing realization of what this moment truly meant.

Anya.

The woman who had eluded them time and again, who had defeated Cain and all his intrigues and strategies, who had given Hawkins the facial scar he still bore today, who had somehow fought her way out of every trap they'd laid for her, was standing helpless before them now. A prize offered up willingly by Powell's most powerful creation.

It was absolute perfection.

–

Rio de Janeiro — four days earlier

Powell leaned in close to Drake and spoke quietly, persuasively, reasonably in his ear, outlining what she needed.

'You'll leave here tonight, you'll go on your way and resume your mission. Sooner or later, Anya and the rest of your friends are going to find you, and they're going to try to convince you that I'm your enemy. And they're going to succeed.'

Drake stared at her, shocked and confused by what she was saying.

'At least, that's what you'll make them believe. You're going to make them think they've got you back, that you're back to being yourself again. And you'll play this role for a time to gain their confidence. You'll even tell them there's a danger you could lose yourself again, and that they shouldn't trust you. But Anya will. She'll insist on staying with you. Then when the time's right, you'll bring her to me, alive. And then it'll be over. You'll have completed your mission, and we'll be together again, Ryan. I promise.'

–

'Well I'll be damned,' Hawkins said under his breath, his familiar sneer returning. Even he was surprised by this turn of events.

'Oh, Ryan,' Powell said, savouring the moment. 'It's good to have you back.'

Drake was triumphant. 'It's good to be back.'

She embraced him warmly, and he returned the gesture in equal measure. The man she'd created, whom she had built and perfected, whom she had loved as if he were her own son, had returned to her.

She let go and backed off, turning her attention to the prize that Drake had won for them. Powell grasped the edge of the duct tape covering Anya's mouth and ripped it away, eliciting a gasp of pain.

So this was the woman who had stolen Marcus Cain's heart, Powell thought as she looked Anya up and down, surveying her as one might consider the merits of a sculpture.

She was tall, standing almost eye to eye with Powell herself, and fuller at the breast and hip. Probably stronger too, judging by the compact but efficient muscu-lature. An attractive, albeit conventional example of her gender, Powell decided. But then, Cain's taste in women had always been characteristically predictable.

Anya could do little but glare back at her with impotent fury as Powell looked her over. A tiger without teeth, rendered helpless and impotent by that most devastating of weapons — trust.

'I imagine you're feeling pretty let down right around now,' Powell remarked. 'Thinking you'd won Ryan back, that you had this game all figured out, only to realize you were the one being played.' She shook her head, almost feeling sorry for this woman who had survived so much only to be undone by her own emotions. 'Don't you see? I was there long before you, Anya, and I'll be there long after you're gone.'

Anya arched her head forward and spat straight in Powell's face.

Hawkins was moving immediately. Placing himself between the two women, he reversed his grip on his assault rifle and slammed the stock into Anya's unprotected sternum.

'This isn't exactly how I pictured us meeting again,' he said, looking down on her as she coughed and struggled to draw breath. 'But I'll take it.'

'Wait,' Powell called out as he raised the rifle to strike her a second time.

Wiping her cheek, Powell turned towards Anya again, displaying no sign of anger or discomfort at what had happened. She did however keep her distance.

'Pick her up. Now.'

Hawkins complied, grabbing a handful of Anya's hair and hauling her up from the rocky ground. She stubbornly refused to cry out, defiant to the last.

'Pretty good. Not exactly original, but full marks for effort,' Powell acknowledged with grudging respect.

'You're a monster,' Anya snapped. 'The things you've done—'

'Spare me the self-righteous routine. I doubt someone as limited as you could even begin to understand my work.' For the first time, Powell's composure had slipped a little. 'You've caused a lot of problems for a lot of people over the years, Anya. Including my employers. I can't imagine how many of them would like to see you dead.'

'I'm used to that.'

'I'm sure you are, but I think you've kept them waiting long enough.'

Reaching into her jacket, she withdrew a Kel-Tec P-11 automatic pistol, designed for concealed carrying. She didn't normally carry firearms, finding them brutish and crude, but her presence in one of the most dangerous countries on earth had prompted a rethink.

'We don't need her any longer,' Powell said, holding the weapon out to Drake. 'Deal with her, Ryan.'

Anya backed away a step, and even Hawkins looked at her in surprise. 'Cain's orders were to bring her back alive.'

Powell shrugged. 'I don't take orders from Cain. Anyway, he always was too weak and sentimental with Anya. Better to deal with it ourselves.' She nodded to the gun. 'Take it, Ryan. Finish this.'

Hesitating just for a second, Drake took the weapon, checking that the safety was disengaged before turning it on Anya. She stared back at him, standing her ground, unwilling to show weakness even now, at the end.

'Ryan, remember what I told you,' Anya said, speaking softly, almost reassuringly. 'I meant it. You're... my life.'

Something seemed to pass between them then. Something even Powell couldn't fully articulate. A kind of unspoken understanding, an acceptance of what neither could avoid. A forgiveness.

'You're my mission,' Drake said as he took aim.

Anya closed her eyes, inhaling a final breath, one last gasp of life before the end.

And with that, Drake pulled the trigger.

Click.

Anya flinched as the sharp, precise sound of the weapon's firing pin hitting an empty chamber rang out. Opening her eyes, she looked at the weapon in Drake's hands, as if convinced she must have imagined it, as if she would see the telltale curls of grey smoke.

'Well done, Ryan,' Powell said, easing the empty weapon from his grasp. 'Forgive the cheap trick, but I had to know.'

'I would have done the same thing.'

She nodded, pleased by his reaction. 'Good. Now, there's something else I need from you. Your group, the ones who helped you escape Tunisia. Where are they?'

'I don't know.'

Powell's expression darkened. 'Are you sure about that, Ryan?'

'They didn't trust me. They knew there was a chance I could turn again, so Anya and I separated from the others.' He nodded to Anya, who was still glaring at Powell with murderous eyes. 'Only she knows where they are.'

Powell's smile returned. 'Then we'll find out. Jason, prep the prisoner for transport.' She turned towards the waiting chopper. 'We're taking her home.'

As Hawkins snatched up the hood and threw it over Anya's head, Drake moved close to Powell. 'Where do you want me?'

'You stay by my side, where you belong. We're going there together.'

Chapter 79

Forward Operating Base Pegasus was located about 50 miles due east of Kabul, on the western edge of a mountain range that threaded a tortuous path all the way to Jalalabad. Technically this placed it under the authority of ISAF's Regional Command East. However, Pegasus was no ordinary military installation, appearing on no official maps and belonging to no recognized command structure.

It was a black site, created by the CIA and maintained under the highest possible security. No military or government representatives had set foot inside its high walls, no journalists or reporters would ever witness the events that took place within its underground holding cells and interrogation rooms.

The facility certainly wasn't a purpose-built encampment, Drake thought as their Black Hawk came in to land. Roughly pentagonal in shape, with circular guard towers set at each corner and ancient stone walls overlooking the plain below, the structure belonged to a different era of warfare.

Appearances, however, could be deceptive. Despite its antiquated façade, the entire fortress was protected by a state-of-the-art electronic surveillance system, from thermal imaging to motion sensors covering every square inch of ground for miles around. The flat, open plains surrounding it offered a perfect field of fire for the remote-controlled heavy machine guns mounted on each of its five watchtowers, allowing their operators to identify and engage targets from the safety of the base's heavily protected control centre. There was also a surface-to-air missile battery for engaging low-flying aircraft, while sub-surface seismic monitors even guarded against the possibility of tunnelling attempts.

These formidable measures combined to create one of the most secure, heavily defended outposts in the entire country. It was quite simply impossible to enter or leave Pegasus without being seen, whether on, above or beneath the ground.

The armed personnel on duty were almost exclusively private contractors, employed by the newly resurrected Nexus Security. Men who would follow orders and asked few questions as long as the money was good. And, as for the rest of the staff, Unity Pharmaceuticals provided a cadre of carefully selected doctors to carry out their own dark work.

Sweeping in low over the ancient walls, their Black Hawk touched down in the wide open courtyard that occupied the centre of the fortress. Drake, Powell and the other passengers waited until the engines had shut down and the dust subsided before opening the main doors.

As they exited the chopper, a man in civilian clothes strode confidently forward to meet them. Late-fifties, medium height, thinning brown hair, and with a noticeable gut straining against his shirt.

'Ms Powell,' he began, shaking her hand. 'I'm Tom Deans, the director of this facility. It's a pleasure to have you here.'

'Likewise.' Powell's thin smile indicated the feeling wasn't mutual. 'You've been briefed on the package we brought?'

Hawkins was escorting the hooded prisoner none too gently out of the Black Hawk.

'Yes, ma'am. There's an interrogation suite prepped and ready.'

'Good. Get her processed and set up. I'll be in there to start the interrogation shortly.'

The director hesitated. 'Are you sure you wouldn't rather our team handle this? It's… not exactly a lab environment down there.'

Powell's look told him everything he needed to know. 'Just get her processed.'

He complied, knowing better than to push.

'Now, I assume you have secure satellite communications?' Powell went on. 'I need to put a call through to Langley.'

She was already moving towards the facility entrance. Drake followed, staying by her side just as she'd instructed. 'Jason, take the prisoner downstairs. And have both choppers refuelled and ready. I want you and your team standing by to deploy as soon as you get the word.'

Drake could feel himself being watched as they left the courtyard, and turned to look back. Sure enough, Hawkins was observing him, his expression wary, hostile and, to Drake's satisfaction, jealous.

He gave his former comrade a wink before following Powell inside.

Deans led them down a short corridor, where they passed a couple of offices and smaller meeting rooms, all modern and meticulously maintained, before passing through an electronically locked door into what was clearly the heart of the facility.

Drake had seen a lot of ops rooms in his time, from improvised field set-ups that were little more than a cluster of laptops tied to a satellite uplink, all the way up to the mammoth operations centre at Langley, which put NASA's mission control to shame. This, though, was a serious set-up.

Technicians worked diligently at computer terminals, their monitors displaying everything from camera feeds to thermal- and motion-sensor networks beyond the perimeter walls, to the remotely operated turrets and the facility's internal security systems. The surveillance feeds also extended down to the lower levels of the facility, which functioned as a prison and interrogation centre.

He caught a glimpse of Hawkins leading Anya along a narrow corridor with two armed guards in tow. She wasn't resisting, which was as well for her since Hawkins wouldn't hesitate to use force again. The small group carried on before disappearing off the edge of the screen.

'Our comms suite is over here,' Deans said, leading the way into a private conference room set away from this hive of activity. 'Satellite uplink is live and good to go. It's completely encrypted and soundproofed.'

A long table ran down the centre of the modest room, with a communications and data terminal installed in the middle, allowing users to connect quickly to the facility's secure network.

'Thank you,' Powell said after surveying the room. 'See to it that we're undisturbed until further notice.'

As Deans departed, Powell closed and locked the door behind him. She turned towards Drake and gratefully shed the jacket she'd worn since their reunion in the mountains earlier, tossing it idly onto one of the chairs.

'You're going to report in to Cain?' Drake said.

'Someone has to tell him what a good job you've done.'

Drake smiled. He was standing close now, so close she could smell his scent, almost feel the warmth of his body. There was a different look in his eyes now, a look he'd been careful to keep hidden thus far. A look of excitement, of anticipation, of desire.

Powell could also clearly see the changes that seven years of active and dangerous living had wrought on Ryan Drake. Always a handsome man, his features were harder now, more definite, etched with fine lines around the eyes and mouth, his skin roughened and marked with small cuts and bruises, but it didn't matter to her. If anything, it added to what she already felt about him, *knew* about him.

She reached up and caressed his stubbled jaw, delighting in the feel of it. Drake had never been a pampered and preened pretty boy, but a tough, coarse and uncompromising man. A man she'd been drawn to right from the first, whose strength had set him apart from the others, whose potential she had understood and nurtured, and whose life she had protected.

'Well, there's no rush, is there?' he whispered, leaning in and kissing her neck, drawing a shiver of delight.

Allowing her hand to stray behind his head, Powell gripped his hair and pulled his head back, kissing him forcefully, passionately. She felt his response right away, hard and urgent against her. She pressed herself into him, pushing him backwards onto the table, her hands already working to undo his belt.

Yes, she'd waited a long time to get Drake back, to have him the way she used to have him, body and mind and soul utterly bound to her. A man who had fought, killed, betrayed everything for her.

Drake was hers now, and she wouldn't lose him again.

Chapter 80

CIA headquarters, Langley

Marcus Cain's phone was ringing, the call coming through the encrypted Agency network. He had a feeling he knew who it was, and felt his pulse quicken as he lifted the receiver.

'Cain.'

'Hello, Marcus.' Powell's voice was smooth, relaxed and, he thought, just a little out of breath. 'I thought you might want to hear my report.'

'Depends what you have to tell me.'

A silence stretched out. Not because of some encryption error, but because she chose to make it so. She was making him wait. She was enjoying this.

'You'll be pleased to know I've solved our little problem.'

Cain froze, struck as much by the nonchalant way she'd delivered her news as he was by the realization that the woman he'd pursued for so long had finally been captured. It didn't seem possible. It *couldn't* be possible.

'You have her alive?' he heard himself ask.

'She's in one of our interrogation rooms right now.'

'And Drake?'

She chuckled, enjoying her chance to toy with him. 'Who do you think delivered her to us, Marcus?'

Cain couldn't believe what he was hearing. Ryan Drake, the man who had become almost as much of a thorn in his side as Anya herself, who had derailed plans, defeated strategies and risked his life on countless occasions for her. Drake had simply handed her over to Powell?

His silence was telling, and she was quick to pick up on it. 'Oh, Marcus. You and your Agency with all your schemes and your plans, and the one thing you never understood was the people you were fighting. You should be grateful I was around to clean up your mess.'

Cain didn't appreciate being patronized at the best of times, never mind by someone like Powell who had never sacrificed a single thing in her entire life, who had never had to make the choices he'd been forced to make.

'I want Drake out of the picture as soon as you're finished.'

'Not going to happen.'

'That wasn't a request, Elizabeth.'

'Neither is this,' she fired back. 'Ryan knows where his loyalties lie now.'

'He didn't before,' Cain pointed out.

'That was an error, easily corrected. We have Anya because of him, and him alone. I'm not going to hand him over to you so you can put him down like some rabid dog.'

'If you don't, I'll find someone who will.'

She was silent for a moment or two. 'That door swings both ways, Marcus. It would be a shame if something happened to Anya during her interrogation.'

Her threat wasn't lost on him. 'You wouldn't do something like that.'

'Relax, Marcus. Our methods are a lot more efficient than the CIA's torture chambers,' she promised. 'Once she gives up her people, I'll have them dealt with, then I'll ship Anya back Stateside so you can... finish the job.' There was an edge of distaste in her voice. 'Meanwhile, I leave with Ryan, and you back the hell off for good. Do we understand one another?'

Cain didn't have to be a strategist to realize he'd been backed into a corner. Powell, for now at least, held all the cards. However, the deal she was offering wasn't entirely unacceptable: Anya and the collection of allies she'd somehow amassed in exchange for Drake's life.

It wouldn't be the first time he'd been convinced to spare Drake's life by a woman with a vested interest in his survival. But he knew one thing for certain – it *would* be the last.

Chapter 81

Anya was alone in darkness. Bound to a chair and with a heavy hood covering her head, she was forced to rely on her other senses instead.

After leaving Powell and the others, she'd been taken in for 'processing'. Stripped, forcibly showered with cold water and scrubbed with brushes so hard they'd left her skin raw, she'd been issued with the familiar orange jumpsuit of the US military prison system, then hooded once more and escorted downstairs to the detention centre.

Anya had endured her share of prisons, torture, and years of solitary confinement, but even she was unnerved by what she'd heard as she was dragged to this interrogation room.

Anguished screams echoed out of the cells on either side of the central corridor. The kind of screams that only madness or agony could produce. She'd smelled the ugly stench of prisoners who had voided their bowels, mixed with the acrid tang of sweat and filth and fear. Dark acts committed in dark places. Desperation and animal instinct.

And yet once she was placed in this room and the door was sealed, she found herself alone. Not just isolated from the presence of others, but isolated from everything, as if the world itself had ceased to be. There was no obvious smell, no movement, no sounds of any kind. Even her own breathing seemed to be swallowed up by the walls around her, producing not the slightest reverberation. It was a strange and decidedly unnerving feeling, as if she were in a void of infinite nothingness.

At least Hawkins had obeyed Powell's command to deliver her unharmed. Whatever control that woman exerted over Drake apparently extended to his nemesis as well, because she was certain he would have done her serious harm if left to his own devices. A small mercy perhaps, but one she was under no illusion would last for long. She'd been kept alive for a reason.

She tensed up as the door clicked and unlocked, swinging open with only a silent rush of air. Footsteps approached her softly, and suddenly the hood was torn off.

She blinked, looking around, quickly taking in her surroundings as her eyes adjusted. She'd expected harsh, intense light to flood her eyes, intended to blind and dazzle the prisoner, helping to keep them off balance.

The lighting here was soft, subdued, almost restful. The walls were plain white and lined with foam tiles that deadened ambient noise.

In front of her was a table. Metal, fixed to the floor, its surface uncluttered. No weapons or tools of torture, no bloodstains or dents. A simple, austere, clinical piece of furniture. A chair sat unoccupied on the opposite side.

One thing that wasn't surprising was the woman standing beside her. Elizabeth Powell had discarded her heavy outdoor jacket, but her clothes still looked like they belonged more in a corporate boardroom than a cell in Afghanistan. She was holding a small plastic case.

'Sorry to keep you waiting,' she said, smiling pleasantly. 'Business. You understand.'

Anya looked away. 'I'm not going anywhere.'

Powell chuckled. 'And here I was thinking you had no sense of humour.'

'What would you know of me?'

'A lot, as it happens. I reviewed your old CIA psych evaluations on the flight over here. Makes for some pretty interesting reading, believe me. Then again, I always did find myself fascinated by other people's minds, understanding what makes them tick. And learning what breaks them down.' She paused, bringing up something from memory. 'Know your enemy and know yourself, and you can fight a hundred battles without fear. Wouldn't you say?'

She was looking for a reaction. The quote from Sun Tzu's *The Art of War* was her way of demonstrating how well she knew her.

'Reading about someone is one thing. Understanding them is another,' Anya replied. Her double meaning was clear.

'Then let's understand each other. Before we get started.'

She laid the plastic case down on the table. Unlatching it, she flipped the top open and reached inside, carefully lifting out a syringe.

Anya felt her pulse quicken, her body tensing up as the instinct to fight back asserted itself. Her hands strained against the plasticuffs, but she was unable to find leverage, unable to break free.

'I'm going to let you in on a little secret, just between us,' Powell said as she checked the syringe was properly primed. 'I hate this country. This miserable little patch of mud and rock at the end of the world. It's a mystery to me. It has nothing of value. And yet somehow, it's become the hill that everyone chooses to die on.'

Powell was slowly pacing the interrogation room, taking it all in. 'Take this place. The British built it two centuries ago, then the Soviets made it their own. And now... here we are. Another empire fighting over a country nobody cares about.' She halted on the opposite side of the table, resting her hands on its polished surface. 'Surely you of all people can appreciate the irony of that, Anya.'

Anya felt herself stiffen. Powell did indeed know a lot about her, knew that she'd fought in Afghanistan 20 years ago, that she'd been captured and tortured by the Soviets, that she'd sacrificed almost everything she had to give for this place. A pyrrhic victory in a forgotten war.

'Tell me. How does it feel, knowing you gave up so much to achieve so little?'

She was gloating, laughing at her for her foolishness. A silly, idealistic girl who had run off to war with a head full of heroism and glory, only to find a far harsher reality awaiting her.

Anya raised her chin, staring her adversary down. She might have been that girl once, but no longer. 'I don't measure the value of a place by how rich its people are.'

'How noble of you,' Powell remarked sarcastically. 'Personally, I tend to base its value on what it can do for us. So you see, even a place like Afghanistan can be made to serve a purpose. An active war zone where people disappear easily, where nobody asks questions, and where we can go about our work undisturbed.'

Anya thought again about the tortured screams she'd heard as she was dragged down here. They hadn't just come from prisoners being interrogated, she realized. Their suffering had been caused by something else, something more insidious.

'You're using the people here,' she said, appalled. 'Experimenting on them?'

'They're assisting with our research.'

'You're torturing them. I heard their screams.'

Powell snorted derisively. 'You're really going to lecture me about ethics and humanitarianism, Anya? How many people have you killed in this country alone, hmm? Fifty? A hundred? At what point did it become easier not to keep track?'

'It was war. Both sides knew what they were fighting for. What you are doing here is barbaric.'

'Scientific advancement comes at a price. It always has. You think human civilisation got to where it is by holding hands and singing peace songs? It's painful, and chaotic, and it requires sacrifice on a scale even you could barely understand.' Powell took a calming breath. 'It takes a certain kind of person to acknowledge that and push forward anyway.'

'I know exactly what kind of person you are,' Anya replied coldly.

'Really?' Powell asked. 'Is this where you give me some inspiring speech about how you and I are not so different?'

'No, because we *are* different. You crave power because you were born into a life that gave you none. You were looked down on, ignored, mocked. People were never going to give you the chance you thought you deserved. You learned to fight instead. You learned to take without asking, use people for your own ends, stand on their shoulders to reach higher and then get rid of them when they served their purpose. All that matters is the reflection of your own success, the illusion of your own power. It's not a means to do good any more, it's an end all of its own.' She shook her head. 'No, Elizabeth, you and I are nothing alike.'

Powell slammed the Autoject onto the table between them, her smile gone. She wasn't toying with Anya any longer.

'Do you have any idea how many people owe their lives to me right now? The number of new treatments we've developed? Diseases we've cured? There are children alive today who would have died before they were even born if it wasn't for our gene therapy programmes. Women who were told they would never conceive, paraplegics who were told they would never walk again, schizophrenics who would never live independent lives. *None* of that would have been possible without the work done in places like this. Hate me all you want, but none of it can change the fact my work *saves lives*. My work is the future of our species.' The smile, mocking and disparaging, had returned once more. 'And you... What are you, when you get right down to it? The past. A soldier with no war left to fight, and no life left to live. Who are *you* to judge me?'

Anya almost felt pity for this woman standing before her, railing against her, demanding her understanding. Powell really did believe that what she was doing was justifiable, that the suffering being inflicted in places like this could be washed away.

'The difference between us is that I know who I am, and what I've done,' Anya said, her tone quiet, controlled, reasonable. 'I know this, but I take no pride in it. And I don't delude myself into thinking a few good acts can undo it.'

Powell didn't rise to this bait. Instead she smiled, as if another piece of the puzzle had just fallen into place, as if Anya had just given her exactly what she wanted.

'You know, I've dealt with all kinds of people, broken them down into their psychological components. It's not unlike taking a watch mechanism apart piece by piece, learning how they all fit together. But you... you're something different. A woman who became a soldier, a soldier who became a spy, a spy who became a fugitive. So many layers clouding the picture. But who are you really, Anya? What are you beneath all that?'

Anya could do nothing to fend her off as she brought the Autoject towards her neck.

'Let's find out, shall we?'

Anya braced herself, trying to harden her mind against whatever was coming. She heard a faint hiss as the pressurized syringe's contents flooded into her bloodstream, and squeezed her eyes shut as the potent combination started to take effect.

Chapter 82

Such was Tyler Hawkins' shock at his son's refusal to leave, that for a good couple of seconds he actually didn't utter a word. It was as if the mere notion that not one, but two of his boys would openly defy him was beyond his comprehension.

'What did you say?'

Jason could see his brother swallowing hard, forcing down his terror. 'I said no,' he repeated. 'You leave Jason alone, Dad. You're the reason all this is happening, not him. You brought all this on yourself. Leave him alone!'

It took Tyler three seconds to make up his mind about what to do next. The belt suddenly whipped around, whistling through the air and catching Nathan across the side of the face with an audible, sickening crack.

His plump body fell to the floor just inside the doorway, crying out in pain. There was going to be no enduring this one with quiet dignity; that impact had probably broken teeth and knocked him half unconscious.

But Tyler Hawkins didn't stop. There was a wild, terrifying look in his eyes now. It was as if something, some emotional spring or cog or gear that made up the complex machinery of his mind, under strain for a long time now, had finally snapped.

He went in on Nathan, raining blows on his son's helpless form, screaming and howling like an animal. Such was his anger, he couldn't even form words. It was pure, unfettered rage.

But Nathan's sacrifice, horrific though it was, had diverted Tyler Hawkins' attention from his most defiant, most dangerous son. Thinking Jason cowed and beaten, he had switched the focus of his rage, leaving him lying on the dirt floor of the garage.

But Jason was neither cowed nor beaten. Something had awoken in him as he watched his father raining blows on his helpless brother, something that had been stirring for some time, something that had tried to reveal itself earlier only to be held back at the last by childish notions of love and loyalty.

How flimsy those things seemed to him now, how weak and insubstantial. He saw the world now with a piercing, absolute clarity that he'd never experienced before.

Jason's gaze turned from his father to the object that had fallen from the shelf when he slammed into it. It was lying just a few feet away now. A claw hammer. Not one of those flimsy old-fashioned ones with a wooden handle. This one was forged from a single piece of steel, with a moulded rubber grip that was starting to wear and fray a little at the base.

With an odd sense of detachment, Jason reached out and picked it up. It felt good in his hand, felt solid, right somehow, like he was some ancient warrior examining a well-balanced sword.

He stood up, testing his weight, making sure he had solid footing. The pain of his injuries seemed to have faded, becoming merely an inconvenience that he could attend to later. For now, he had a problem that needed solving. A problem that had been bustin' his ass for too long.

A problem named Tyler Hawkins.

He walked towards him, taking his time, making sure he didn't make too much noise. Now that he needed to worry. His father was wholly focussed on laying into Nathan, who had by now ceased all pretence of trying to protect himself. Now he was just lying on the ground, jerking a little each time his father cracked him with the belt.

'I'm gonna give you all one,' Tyler Hawkins growled, having recovered his senses enough to speak at least. He was glistening with a mixture of rainwater and sweat, spittle flying from his mouth with each word. 'Whole fucking family turned against me. Well I won't have it. No fucking way will I tolerate this shit. You're gonna get one. Oh yes, you're gonna—'

Jason's swing was perfect, like one of those slow-motion instructional videos of a baseball player hitting a home run. The hammer came down in a clean, graceful arc, making just the slightest whirring sound as it parted the air, then buried itself two full inches into Tyler Hawkins' skull.

Jason was surprised by the sensation as he drove that hammer into the top of his father's head. He'd expected to feel or hear some kind of crunch or crack as if he were breaking an egg, but it wasn't like that at all. Instead it felt and sounded like a sort of wet pop, as if he'd just burst a balloon filled with some thick, viscous substance.

He yanked the hammer free and felt something warm and wet splash on his face.

Swinging the belt one more time at Nathan, Tyler straightened up and turned slowly towards his other son, then simply stood there, swaying a little on his feet, his mouth hanging open slackly. Blood ran down his forehead into his eyes, which were staring in Jason's direction, but not really seeing him. The wild fury had vanished, replaced by a look of vague puzzlement.

Gripping the gore-covered hammer, Jason swung again. His second blow landed with less force because he was having to aim upwards, but his aim was true all the same, and the first hit had already opened a hole for him.

Tyler Hawkins, who had been too angry to realize he'd been dealt a mortal blow, and too dumbfounded to recognize he was already dying, finally succumbed to his devastating brain injuries and fell. He didn't topple backwards like some mighty oak tree, or the great titanic beast Jason had always imagined him to be. Instead his legs simply ceased to support him and he crumpled to the floor in a fleshy, tangled heap. Jason could smell the distinctive odour of faeces and realized with a vague sense of disgust that his father had soiled himself in his last moments.

He was gone.

-

Hawkins ran his knife edge along the surface of the whetstone, listening to the satisfying rasp as another tiny layer of steel was scraped away, the edge brought to a sharper and sharper point. A patient noise, a comforting noise that he'd always found useful for focussing his mind.

But not today. Today was very different.

His mind was in turmoil, trying to make sense of everything that had happened in the last few hours. The sudden reappearance of Drake, the capture of Anya without a shot fired, the imminent destruction of what remained of their enemies – it should have been a cause for relief, even celebration. But something gnawed at him, festering, refusing to heal. It was all too easy, too simple.

Too good to be true.

And yet, Powell had control. His subconscious warned him against questioning her, instinct reminding him that she was right. She had always been right, about everything. How could she ever be wrong? She was the foundation of all their worlds. The thing that united all of them. Their actions, their minds, forged together as one by her will.

He looked up and saw Drake approaching.

He seemed to have changed somehow in the past few days, becoming a very different man from the cowed, broken prisoner that Hawkins had so easily tormented just a few months earlier. It was as if he'd grown in confidence, in presence, in sheer power and authority.

And, for the briefest flash, Hawkins saw a shadow of his father in the man standing before him. Not their physical likeness, but something far more fundamental: the feelings they evoked in him.

His grip on the knife tightened as they faced each other down. Men who had fought, tried to kill each other, bled because of the other. Here they stood, in the middle of a country at war, both of their worlds turned upside down.

'Well, well,' Hawkins said, forcing his doubts aside. 'What brings you here, Ryan?'

'We both know why I'm here. You and I have unfinished business, Jason.'

Laying aside the whetstone, Hawkins rose slowly to his feet, drawing himself up to his full height so that he could look down a little on Drake. He still had the knife in his hands, ready to whip it upwards at the perfect angle beneath his ribs and into Drake's vital organs.

All he needed was an excuse. His body was ready, heart beating fast and strong, muscles swelling and tensing in anticipation. Yes, they certainly did have unfinished business.

Just make one move, Ryan. One move is all it'll take, then I'm gonna give you one in return. Oh yes boy, I'm gonna give you one.

Drake did make a move, but it wasn't one that Hawkins had foreseen.

'I owe you an apology,' he said, looking Hawkins dead in the eyes. 'For all the shit I've put you through. I wasn't myself, I lost sight of who I really was. But I'm back now and I'm never leaving again.' He sighed. 'We were friends once... brothers. I'm not pretending we ever will be again, but I at least wanted to make peace with you.'

Hawkins stared, taken aback by this attempted reconciliation. Despite himself, he could feel his doubts starting to fade, melting away like ice beneath a spring sun as suspicion vied with trust.

374

Drake waited, giving him time to make his choice.

Chapter 83

Anya lay on her back in the long grass, staring up into the endless blue sky overhead. No clouds marred its perfection or measured its vastness. It was a warm, still summer's evening, with just the faintest breeze rippling through the yellow stalks around her. The kind of evening that made her feel grateful simply to be alive.

High above, she spotted the contrail of some aircraft tracing a line from north to south, straight as an arrow. It was hard and definite near the tip, seeming almost solid, but breaking up and dissipating as her eyes followed it northwards.

Where was it going? She didn't know. But lying there staring upwards, the sky seemed to carry on for ever. She felt so small that she could almost lose herself in it.

She inhaled, tasted the scent of pine needles, grass and wild flowers, rich loamy earth and other growing things. She loved to lie out here on evenings like this, feeling part of the world around her, having nowhere to go and nothing to do. She was at peace.

Her thoughts were disturbed by the rumble of a car engine crunching up the rocky road to the house.

Rising up from her little refuge, she looked down the slope towards her home, haunted by a sudden but painfully familiar sense of fear and worry. The sense that something bad was about to happen, that some wrenching change was about to be wrought on her young life. The feeling that this had all happened before.

But she was wrong. Instead she saw her parents' familiar old car, worn and unreliable and kept alive through the determined efforts of her father, chugging along towards her.

'Mother!' she cried out, running down to meet it. She was seized by a sudden, powerful upwelling of joy and relief, as if she'd been separated from her parents for a lifetime.

She flitted through the grass, nimble and full of energy as only a child could be, inhaling the hazy summer air, watching the tiny insects buzzing around her from flower to flower.

Anya reached the woman just as she was emerging from the car, throwing her arms around her and hugging her tight, burying her face in her chest, wishing she would never have to let go. Was she crying? Why was she crying?

How long had they really been gone?

'I've missed you so much,' she managed to say, her throat so tight that it hurt.

'It's all right, child,' her mother whispered back, running a hand through her tangled blonde hair. 'It's all right. I'm here with you now. And I'll never leave you, Anya.'

Anya looked up at her, looked up into a face that was so like her own. A face that meant love and security and understanding. The face of her childhood.

'My little Anya,' her mother said, smiling down at her. 'Always with your head in the sky, always looking for the next adventure. Sometimes you miss what's right in front of you.'

She reached down and tickled the tip of Anya's nose, prompting a giggle from the girl. A delightful, uninhibited sound from one who had never known loss or pain.

Hunkering down beside her daughter so they were eye to eye, she took Anya's hand in her own, holding it gently. 'There's something I need from you, Anya.'

'What?'

'Your friends have gone missing. Their parents are very worried about them, and they want them to come home. Will you help us find them?'

Anya frowned, confused. 'My friends?'

'Yes. Don't you remember? Alex, Olivia, Keira and the others.'

A memory flashed before Anya's eyes then, as if some veil obscuring it had been ripped aside. Of course she remembered her friends. Keira, fiery and temperamental; Alex, with his love of computers and technology; Olivia, who always seemed so mature and reasonable. And yet her mind still played tricks on her. Why did she keep picturing them as grown-ups?

'They went out and they haven't come back,' her mother continued, patiently and gently explaining to her. 'They're playing a game, hiding from us, but it's getting late and it's time for the game to end.'

Anya glanced over her shoulder, to where the sun was just touching the horizon in a final display of radiant brilliance. It would be dark soon. The thought of her friends out there alone sent a shiver through her.

'I think you know where they might be hiding. Will you tell us?'

Anya did know something, and yet it was difficult for her to articulate her feelings. She wanted to help, wanted never to keep secrets from her parents, but some part of her was reluctant to speak. Some tiny fragment of her mind warned her to say nothing. Why was that? What was bothering her?

Her mother's hand tightened around hers. 'Think, Anya.' Her voice was firmer now. 'We don't want anything to happen to your friends, do we?'

Of course not, she thought. Her mother was right. She knew something, and it was her responsibility to help.

'I... don't know where they're hiding,' she said, concentrating on the memories that seemed to flit and weave in her mind like butterflies fluttering to avoid a net. 'They wouldn't tell me. They didn't want people to know.'

'But you do know *something*,' her mother pressed her. 'Something you're reluctant to say. It's all right, Anya. You can always tell me the truth. I won't ever be angry with you.'

That was enough to break through the final barrier in Anya's mind.

'A number,' she said. 'They gave me a number.'

'A phone number?'

She nodded.

'Good girl. Now tell it to me.'

Her mother listened carefully while Anya recited the number, even making her repeat it again to be sure it was right. As she said it, Anya had some hazy, confused mental image of her friends carrying phones around with them that resembled little squares of plastic, but that couldn't be right. Such things simply didn't exist.

She was getting confused, and tired. The sun was going down, night was falling. And soon she would go to bed, sleeping a deep and contented sleep such as she hadn't known for a very long time. She wanted that. She didn't want to be afraid ever again.

'Will they be all right, Mother?' she asked, looking hopefully at the woman who so resembled her.

Her mother smiled. 'Yes, of course they will, child. We'll take care of them.'

Taking Anya's face in her hands, she leaned forward and kissed her on the forehead. Anya closed her eyes, delighted that she'd done the right thing, even as she felt an uncanny sense of loss and sadness rise inside her.

'*We'll take care of them.*'

Anya's eyes snapped open, finding to her dismay that her mother was gone. All of it, the field, the house, the car, the sunset... it had all vanished. She was in a room, white and clinical, almost suffocatingly empty. Her hands were bound tightly to the chair she was seated on.

And facing her, smiling in gratitude and triumph, was Elizabeth Powell.

'Thanks for your help, Anya,' she said, tucking a notebook into her pocket. 'We'll make sure your friends are taken care of.'

'No,' Anya gasped, realizing how easily she had been deceived. 'No! No!'

The dead walls absorbed her cries, oblivious to the dawning horror of what had just happened.

Powell left the room, no longer listening. Powering up her phone, she quickly dialled the ops centre as she strode down the bare, sterile corridor.

'Deans.'

'We have what we need. I'm sending you a cell number. Run a trace on it and get me a location right away,' she instructed. 'And have the choppers ready to lift off.'

She closed down the phone without waiting for a reply, smiling to herself. One final step and her work would be done. And she could be out of here with Drake and put this godforsaken country behind her.

Chapter 84

'All units, we have a confirmed location. Repeat, we have a confirmed target location. Assault team, prepare to deploy.'

Hawkins pressed his transmit button. 'Copy that. I'm on my way.'

'Duty calls, right?' Drake remarked as he closed down his radio.

Hawkins studied him. 'We're going to kill your friends now. You know that, right?'

He shrugged, showing no trace of remorse. 'They're not my friends. Not any more. I know where my loyalty is.'

'Glad to hear it.' Hawkins slid his knife into its sheath and looked up at his former comrade, still undecided about what he'd become. 'We'll see how things play out today, then we'll talk.'

'Fair enough.' Drake nodded, and as Hawkins was moving off, added, 'And Jason?'

He halted briefly and turned to face him once more.

'Good hunting.'

Hawkins strode off to rejoin his team.

Most of them were already assembled in the fortress's wide courtyard, awaiting his arrival. Long shadows stretched across the open, dusty ground as the sun descended towards the western horizon. Darkness came early to Afghanistan at this time of year.

'What have we got?' he demanded as he emerged from the main building, throwing on a set of body armour and hastily fastening the straps in place.

'NSA just locked in a location for the target's cell phone, sir,' Hickman reported. 'It's an abandoned village about 30 miles north of here.'

'Do we have real-time satellite?'

The man shook his head. 'Not yet, but we've got a Predator inbound right now. Should be over that area before we arrive.'

'Good. What's our status?'

'Give the word, and we're gone.'

Hawkins looked at his team, and nodded. 'The word's given.'

With the choppers fully fuelled and standing by for the go command, it took mere minutes for the assault team to embark, for the engines to spin up and the rotors to start turning. Five minutes after getting a confirmed cell phone triangulation from the National Reconnaissance Office, the two Black Hawks lifted off and peeled away northwards, heading for their target at full speed.

It would take them just 15 minutes to reach it.

'How much longer?' Mitchell asked impatiently, surveying the darkening mountains and shadowy valleys that lay beyond the open doorway. Night was falling on Afghanistan, bringing with it a gathering breeze and a noticeable drop in temperature. Somehow this inclement weather seemed to worsen her already fraught mood.

Time was running short. If this insane plan was to have any chance of success, their efforts here absolutely had to pay off.

'Five minutes,' Alex replied without looking up from his laptop.

'You said five minutes ten minutes ago.'

Frost, who was likewise preoccupied with her own tasks, gave the woman a sharp look. 'We're trying to access one of the most sophisticated systems on the planet using a pair of laptops barely powerful enough to run *Minecraft*. You want to take over?'

Mitchell tensed and relaxed her grip on the AK-74 assault rifle cradled in her arms.

'The problem's not us, it's the bandwidth,' Alex explained more reasonably, pointing to the portable satellite dish they'd rigged up outside. It was, at best, a jury-rigged system of limited power and questionable reliability. 'Connection isn't exactly reliable here. It's making everything twice as hard.'

'God, I'd fuck somebody for a proper multi-screen workstation and a fibre optic connection right now,' Frost said.

'Too much information, Frost,' Alex shot back, prompting a wry grin from the young woman.

Mitchell piped up. 'Can't you boost the signal or something?'

Alex looked at her disapprovingly. 'No. One, because this isn't *Star Trek*. And two, why would you think it's not at full power already?'

Mitchell's cell phone buzzed with an incoming call. Enabling her Bluetooth earpiece, she hit the 'receive call' button.

'Go.'

'I'm in position,' Dietrich reported, his voice occasionally cutting out as the encrypted signal struggled to reach them. 'But I can't stay here long. When are we moving?'

'Stand by,' Mitchell said, looking expectantly at the two technical experts.

'We're working on it,' Frost promised. 'Just give us a little more time.'

'Almost there. Hold position and wait for the go command.'

'Easy for you to say. You're not sitting here with your dick hanging out.'

'Then hold it tight and stand by,' she snapped.

The call cut out, and Mitchell's gaze returned to the world outside. She didn't like this. She could feel something was wrong, and that they were all going to suffer for it.

Just a little more time.

Time was one resource they were rapidly running out of.

Chapter 85

Powell leaned forward in her chair, glued to the feeds being transmitted from the assault team's helmet-mounted cameras. The effect was to make her feel as if she were almost there in the chopper with them, getting ready for the attack.

In that respect, this was about as close as she wanted to come.

The interior of the Black Hawk was bathed in red light for night flying. Outside, the world streaked past at dangerously low altitude. The two choppers were using the winding valleys to mask the distinctive sound of their engines, trying to get as close as possible without alerting their enemies.

'We're almost over the target,' Hawkins reported. 'Predator has positive thermal signatures around the village.'

Another window on Powell's computer showed real-time coverage from the unmanned Predator drone orbiting the area at higher altitude, unseen and unheard by those below. The target area was a cluster of small stone huts nestled in a narrow river valley, the remains of a village abandoned during the civil war that had wracked the country in the wake of the Soviet withdrawal. According to the decryption team at Fort Meade, the cell phone was still active inside one of the buildings.

Even without this positive tracking, thermal imaging from the drone's downward-pointing cameras told its own story. Three separate buildings glowed brightly against the dark-green background, indicating multiple heat sources within each, possibly camp fires or space heaters. Likely such heat sources were invisible to the naked eye, but with infrared they were as bright and obvious as signal flares.

'Understood,' Powell replied. 'Remember, Jason, this is a search and destroy mission, with the emphasis on the second part. I want no survivors.'

'Music to my ears,' he promised. 'Gear up, gentlemen! Thirty seconds!'

Weapons and equipment shifted and clicked as final checks were made.

Another voice came over the radio net. The voice of the drone's pilot, operating out of a locked room at Bagram Air Base where no details of this operation would ever be officially recorded.

'Overlord at Angels Two-Zero. Target locked. Awaiting go command.'

A third voice followed this up.

'Bravo Two, Angels Zero-Five. Ready to move in.'

Powell didn't respond to either message. She'd already given her assent to the mission and would play no further role in its execution. Ultimately Hawkins now had tactical control of the situation, so he called the shots from here.

'Overlord, you are cleared hot,' he instructed.

–

There! Mitchell had served in Afghanistan before, and knew all too well the acoustic tricks that the country's tangled valleys and towering mountains could play. But she now heard the distinctive, frightening *whop-whop-whop* of an incoming chopper.

Two incoming choppers. One providing fire support, the other holding the assault team. Standard attack pattern for an air and ground attack.

'We're out of time,' she said, moving away from the doorway. 'Whatever you're going to do, do it now!'

'Almost there,' Alex replied, staring intently at his screen. 'Two more minutes.'

The noise was getting louder.

'We don't have two more minutes,' she warned him.

Somewhere up in that darkened sky, their enemies were approaching. And they were out to end this once and for all.

–

The command was given; the pilot in his locked room at Bagram depressed the trigger on his joystick to begin the assault.

A pair of AGM-114 Hellfire air-to-ground missiles detached from the Predator's wing pylons, angling downwards automatically before igniting their rocket motors. Each was independently guided, locked onto a separate laser guidance beam that they followed all the way down to their targets.

Both were hardened against electronic countermeasures, and even included an autopilot feature to reacquire their lock if they somehow lost track of their target. In this case however, neither feature was required. Both missiles flew straight and true, with no interference.

Accelerating to Mach 1.3 under maximum power, both missiles broke through the sound barrier as they descended from 20,000 feet, impacting shortly before the sound of their approach reached the ground.

The twin explosions, amounting to a combined mass of 40 pounds of high explosive, obliterated the two buildings they had targeted, dropping in through the roof and detonating inside. The blast pressure wave shattered the walls like porcelain, the shockwave visibly rippling through the ground as broken pieces of rock were hurled outwards, forming a hail of shrapnel that would have shattered any human bodies within 50 yards.

'Overlord, splash two. Good hits. Bravo Two is cleared to engage.'

'Copy that, Overlord. Bravo Two is cleared hot.'

With the Predator's ordnance spent, the MH-60 fire-support Black Hawk swooped in next, unleashing a salvo of Hydra unguided rockets into the smoking ruins. What the Hydra lacked in accuracy, it more than made up for with devastating explosive power. Nineteen of the weapons departed from their launching tube in automated sequence, landing amongst the ruined buildings and erupting in further plumes of fire and shrapnel.

As a final measure, the Black Hawk's M230 automatic cannon swept what was left of the ruined village, pumping out 600 high-explosive incendiary rounds per minute in a single deadly strafing run.

'Bravo Two has good hits,' the pilot confirmed as the chopper wheeled around and gained altitude, sweeping the area with its thermal cameras. 'No movement in the kill zone. Standing by on overwatch.'

'Confirmed, Two. We've got nothing here. Lot of smoke and heat sources.'

'Bravo One, you're cleared to deploy.'

Hawkins smiled as the transmissions came in, confirming the destructive impact of their attack run. In all likelihood, there would be nothing left for his team to do except count up the dead bodies. Or what was left of them.

'Bravo One is moving in.'

As the chopper swept in to disgorge its cargo of troops, Hawkins turned to the men under his command.

'Remember, I want a solid perimeter as soon as we touch down. Assume nothing, take no chances and no prisoners. Clear?'

'Clear!' they replied in unison.

'Ten seconds!'

One of the troopers leaned over and hauled open the sliding door, and then the cabin was filled with the rush of wind and the thudding of rotor blades. Hawkins was first to hook on to the descent wire and then disappear out into the darkness. The rest of the team followed in short order.

Powell could see nothing on her screen except blurred movement as they slid down their fast-rope descent harnesses. The images soon returned to normal as each of the troopers touched down with a bump and unhooked themselves.

'Watch that left flank! Get me a perimeter now!'

On the live Predator feed, Powell watched as the glowing blobs of the assault team fanned out to encircle the smouldering remains of the village, occasionally obscured amongst the multiple heat sources. Overhead, the Black Hawk peeled off to give the assault team room to work. Still there was no movement.

'Perimeter secure!'

She switched her attention back to Hawkins' helmet camera as he picked his way through the smoking ruins, making for what remained of the first target building. Other men were approaching the remaining two structures.

'Walker, cover left,' he said, as he crouched down beside a shattered wall. 'Montez, on me. Ready?'

'Roger.'

Powell peered eagerly at the screen, wondering what grisly sights might await her. She'd seen the human body in all states of decay and damage, and felt nothing for such things, but it would be interesting all the same.

Hawkins rose from cover, weapon at the ready. 'Go!'

The team converged on the ruined structure, leaping over walls and rushing in through the remains of doorways, their weapons sweeping left and right.

'Clear!'

'Clear!'

'Talk to me!' Hawkins snapped.

'I got nothing!'

'Nothing in the other buildings either.'

'Wait, there's something over here.'

'What you got?'

Powell scanned the screen, looking for the soldier who had found something. Half a second later, she found it. He had retrieved the charred and broken remains of some kind of device from the rubble, roughly the size of a small briefcase. The blasts that had so thoroughly flattened this place had wrought similar damage on the machine, flattening its casing and blackening it with scorch marks, but even she recognized its function well enough.

It was no weapon or piece of military equipment. It was a basic portable heating unit. The kind of thing civilians might leave running in their garage to keep the temperature above freezing in winter. The kind of thing that gave an abandoned building a noticeable glow on thermal-imaging cameras, making it seem like it was occupied.

'They're not here,' Hawkins growled down the radio. 'We've been fucking played!'

Chapter 86

Elizabeth Powell wasn't the sort of person accustomed to being caught off guard. She'd forged a career and built a life out of foreseeing possible outcomes, calculating risks and planning for every contingency. But even she could do little more than stare at the screen in uncomprehending disbelief.

'Get out of there,' she ordered, her voice sounding oddly disembodied. 'Pull out and get back here right away.'

Hawkins started to respond, but just as he opened his mouth the feed abruptly cut out, replaced by a blank screen with two simple words: NO SIGNAL.

'Jason. Talk to me,' she commanded him in mounting panic. 'Come in, goddamn it!'

An instant later, she started in fright at the distinctive, booming sound of heavy-calibre gunfire outside, followed by a series of thunderous explosions that shook the walls around her, fine streams of dust shivering down from cracks in the ceiling.

The fortress was under attack.

The lights suddenly cut out, plunging the room into darkness. And then, hard and urgent and chilling, came the sound of alarms blaring around the facility, the echo of screams and frantic shouts, and the crackle of gunfire.

Oh Jesus, her mind screamed at her as the enormity of what was happening at last settled on her. Whoever had hit them had already found a way inside. How was this even possible? This place was protected, shielded against every possible weapon.

As dull red emergency lights powered up, the door to her office flew open and Drake rushed in, clutching an automatic. He looked at her, relieved at finding her unharmed.

'We have to go,' he said, taking her by the arm and leading her towards the door.

'What the hell's happening, Ryan?' she demanded as they hurried along the corridor outside, even as panicked medical officers and technicians fled past, having abandoned their posts. 'Who's attacking us?'

'No idea, but the security system's failing all across the facility. Doors are open, cameras are down. There's nothing between us and the detention levels now.'

'Oh Christ,' she gasped, barely able to comprehend what those desperate prisoners could do to anyone they got their hands on.

Drake thought it best not to comment. 'This place is going down. We need to get outside, find a vehicle and get the hell out of here.'

Powell was in a daze as she stumbled after him, still struggling to understand how such a catastrophic security breach could have come about. The systems here were state of the art, impenetrable from the outside…

'Anya,' she hissed, realizing at last where this trail of disaster inevitably led. 'She did this. She led our team into a trap.'

'And she'll pay for it with her life when the other prisoners find her,' Drake promised. 'Right now we need to worry about ourselves.'

Powell was inclined to trust to Drake's superior training and experience. She had, after all, moulded him into the best combat soldier he could be – a fact he'd ably proven many times over. If anyone could get them out of here safely, it was him.

'Get security down there! Lock the doors!' she heard Deans frantically shout as they passed by the operations room.

'Can't, sir, the whole system's down. We're fucked!'

'Then switch to – hey! Where are you going? Get back to your post, goddamn it!'

Drake pulled Powell aside as a technician sprinted out right in front of them, skidding into the wall opposite before pushing himself off and fleeing blindly down the corridor.

'Stay close to me,' Drake urged her, rushing on.

Unlatching the big steel doors that led outside, Drake threw them open. Powell stumbled up the steps after him, emerging into the fortress's wide-open courtyard.

The scene that confronted her was, if possible, even worse than the nightmare unfolding below. All five of the watchtowers were ablaze, sparks and smoke drifting across the open space beneath, the automated gun turrets that could defend against virtually any foe on land or air reduced to twisted, smouldering scrap. Occasional explosions rocked the ancient walls as stored ammunition cooked off in the intense heat.

The armoured gate was open, having been retracted on its automated winch mechanism to allow a vehicle to enter. And enter it had.

It was sitting now in the centre of the courtyard, engine rumbling. A civilian 4 x 4, old and dented but apparently still sound.

The driver, a grim-faced middle-aged man with dark hair, leaned out of his window to shout to them.

'Ryan! Get your ass in here now!'

'What the hell is going on here?' Powell demanded.

Turning towards her, Drake raised his weapon, taking aim at her. 'Get in the car, Elizabeth. It's time to go.'

Powell backed away, daunted by the sight of the weapon but furious as the realization sank in. *He* had done this. Somehow Drake had made this happen, had betrayed her, had ruined everything.

'You can't hurt me, Ryan,' she retorted defiantly, staring him down as smoke and sparks drifted around them. 'You never could.'

'You're right.' He lowered the gun, then nodded over her shoulder. 'But *she* can.'

Powell turned instinctively, glimpsed a woman with blonde hair and an orange prison jumpsuit, then a fist rushing towards her. Pain and blinding light exploded through her head as she fell.

Her last thought as darkness swallowed her was to ask the same question that had dogged her ever since the lights went out.

How could this possibly have happened?

Chapter 87

'All right, listen up because this is the last chance we'll have to go over the plan. After today, we're committed,' Drake said, taking in each member of the group in turn. 'In order for this to work, a lot of things have to happen at the right time, in the right sequence.'

He took a breath, visualising the chain of events, imagining how each step in the process would feed into the next.

'First of all, I deliver Anya to Powell and the others.' He looked at her, his expression faintly apologetic. 'We'll need to rough you up a little first…'

—

'You're a good man,' she said as he formed a fist. 'Remember that.'

Drake swung fast and hard, catching her with a solid blow to the side of the face that caused a cut to open across her cheek. He moved in, getting ready to strike again, to do what he'd been waiting three days to do.

What he'd been ordered to do.

Anya straightened up, shook her head and reached up to touch her face. Her fingers came away smeared with blood.

'Are you all right?' Drake asked, hating what he'd had to do.

The woman offered a dry, brittle smile. 'It's not the first time a man has hit me. Do it again, and mean it this time. It has to look real.'

Drake took a step forward to strike her again.

—

'Once I hand her over, Powell should be convinced I'm on her side again. She'll almost certainly want to know where the rest of you are, so she'll take us back to a secure location for interrogation.'

—

'They didn't trust me. They knew there was a chance I could turn again, so Anya and I separated from the others.' He nodded to Anya, who was still glaring at Powell with murderous eyes. 'Only she knows where they are.'

Powell's smile returned. 'Then we'll find out.'

Drake could guess what she had in mind, and she could see the thrill of excitement in him. Out of all the men she'd trained, he'd proven particularly adept at interrogation.

'Jason, prep the prisoner for transport,' Powell commanded, turning towards the waiting chopper. 'We're taking her home.'

–

'Once we're inside the facility, we'll need access to their security system,' Drake carried on. 'That's where you come in, Alex.'

Reaching into his pocket, Alex handed him a micro-memory stick. Nothing more than a USB connector with a tiny sliver of solid-state memory attached. The entire unit was less than half an inch in length, and easily hidden in a fold of clothing, the lining of a jacket or other less savoury places.

'It's loaded with the most aggressive worm Frost and I could come up with, and that's saying something because we're brainy as fuck,' he explained. 'We called it Downfall. It'll override their security system from the inside and allow us to take over remotely. Insert it into any networked terminal with a USB port inside the facility, and Downfall will do the rest.'

'If everything's going according to plan, Powell should have me by her side. I'll distract her and find a place to upload your program.'

Alex eyed him shrewdly. 'How exactly do you plan on distracting her?'

'I'll find a way,' Drake promised.

–

She reached up and caressed his stubbled jaw, delighting in the feel of it. Drake had never been a pampered and preened pretty boy, but a tough, coarse and uncompromising man. A man she'd been drawn to right from the first, whose strength had set him apart from the others, whose potential she had understood and nurtured, and whose life she had protected.

'Well, there's no rush, is there?' Drake whispered, leaning in and kissing her neck, drawing a shiver of delight.

Allowing her hand to stray behind his head, Powell gripped his hair and pulled his head back, kissing him forcefully, passionately. She felt his response right away, hard and urgent against her. She pressed herself into him, pushing him backwards onto the table, her hands already working to undo his belt.

As the woman worked to remove his clothes, Drake reached behind him, blindly feeling for the encrypted communications terminal installed in the centre of the conference table. Mounted along its side were a row of USB ports for laptops and presentation devices to connect to the network.

He gently pressed Alex's memory stick into the port. No sooner had power started to flow through its tiny digital pathways than Downfall automatically booted up and went to work.

'Once we have control of the security system, we'll be able to disable cameras, unlock doors and shut down any defensive measures across the facility.' Drake looked over at Anya again. 'In the meantime, your job will be to give up just enough information to send most of Powell's forces on a wild-goose chase.'

–

Powell's eyes scanned the screen, looking for the soldier who had found something. Half a second later, she found it. He had retrieved the charred and broken remains of some kind of device from the rubble, roughly the size of a small briefcase.

It was no weapon or piece of military equipment. It was a simple portable heating unit. The kind of thing civilians might leave running in their garage to keep the temperature above freezing in winter. The kind of thing that gave an abandoned building a noticeable glow on thermal-imaging cameras, making it seem like it was occupied.

'They're not here,' Hawkins growled down the radio, his barely concealed fury obvious. 'We've been fucking played!'

–

'While they're occupied chasing ghosts, Alex and Keira will shut down the internal security system remotely, so I can get in and free Anya from her cell...'

–

Drake halted outside Anya's cell, and glanced up at the security camera that was trained on him, giving a faint nod. It was now or never. If Alex's worm had failed, he'd soon know about it, and everything they'd risked their lives for would be for nothing.

The door clicked once and quietly slid open for him, and he let out the breath he'd been holding.

As expected, an armed Nexus Security operative was waiting for him on the other side. Anya was considered a maximum-security risk, and therefore was under constant observation both by cameras and by a physically present guard.

Not for long, however.

'Sir, this is a restricted area,' the guard warned him.

'Powell wants a status report on the prisoner,' Drake replied, moving forward to examine Anya. 'You want to tell her why she can't have it?'

As Drake stepped forward, the guard moved to block his path, laying a hand firmly on his shoulder as he reached for his weapon with the other.

Big mistake.

'Listen, asshole, you can't—'

Grabbing his arm, Drake twisted it around and dropped to his knees, pulling the man right over his shoulder so that he pitched forward, landing with a heavy thump on the sound-dampening floor.

'Fuck! Security breach!' the man called out, trying to scramble to his feet and clearly missing the fact this cell was soundproofed.

An elbow to the base of his skull dropped him like a stone. Removing the keys from his belt kit, he hurried over to Anya and unlocked her cuffs.

'Are you okay?' he asked, smoothing the hair back from her face so he could look at her. 'Talk to me, Anya.'

She didn't respond. Her shoulders were slumped, her eyes blank and staring. Though she was physically unharmed, it was clear she'd been hit with something strong, and Drake could guess what. He also knew the effects would take time to wear off by themselves. Time they didn't have.

Reaching into his pocket, he produced an Autoject liberated from the facility's medical stores minutes earlier. 'I'm going to hit you with a shot of adrenaline. It's going to feel... intense.'

Jabbing it against the woman's neck, he depressed the trigger.

The effect was profound and virtually immediate. Her eyes flew open wide and she took a deep, gasping breath, her back arching and muscles tightening as her heart rate went into overdrive.

'It's all right, Anya. It's okay,' he whispered, holding her down.

She looked at him, her gaze wild. But he saw a flicker of recognition all the same. 'Ryan?'

'That's right. It's Ryan.'

That seemed to cut through the last of the confusion clouding her mind. Anya threw her arms around his neck, her kiss hard and insistent, and filled with relief at seeing him again.

'What took you so long?' she asked.

'You know me. I like to make a big entrance.'

She pulled away, looked at him for a second or so, and whispered something he'd never heard from her in all the time they'd been together.

'I love you.'

Even Drake struggled with that. Just hearing her say it was enough, but *seeing* it in her, knowing how strongly she felt it was almost too much. He couldn't say why he did it, but he laughed. Not in mockery, but a sheer expression of joy and exhilaration. They were together, they were alive, and they had a chance.

But it wouldn't stay that way for long if they didn't act fast. Forcing his mind back to the present, he handed her the guard's weapon.

'How do you feel now?'

She was struggling to keep herself under control, the adrenaline doing its job and more. 'Alive,' she replied, breathing fast. 'Very alive.'

'Good. Because we're probably going to have to kill a bunch of people now. Are you ready?'

Anya's fierce, eager smile as she accepted the gun provided all the answer he needed. 'Let's find out.'

–

'Anya and I will make our way upstairs, but we'll need a distraction to get clear of the facility.' Drake's gaze rested on the German operative seated opposite. 'That's where you come in, Dietrich. You're our way out.'

'If I don't get blown to pieces first,' he remarked sourly.

Alex folded his arms. 'I'm... reasonably confident that won't happen.'

–

'Yes! Get in, my son!' Alex shouted, punching the air. 'We're through the firewall.'

Mitchell was immediately over by his computer. 'What do we have control over?'

'Cameras, doors, motion sensors, defence systems. You name it, it's ours,' Alex said, grinning triumphantly.

Mitchell was in no mood for celebration. There were still a lot of things that had to pass without a hitch if their audacious plan was to succeed.

'About goddamn time,' she muttered. 'Where are Drake and Anya?'

Frost was scrolling rapidly through the security camera feeds, abruptly stopping when she found what she was looking for. 'Anya's in cell 32. Looks like there's an armed guard in with her.'

'Kill the feeds for that room and disable the door lock. Drake will have to handle the guard.' Mitchell had a feeling one guard would present little difficulty.

'On it.'

'Hope to Christ this works,' she whispered as she dialled Dietrich's number.

'Tell me we're in,' he said right away.

'We're in! Start your run now.'

'Copy that.' He paused. 'Hope I'm not driving into a fucking firing squad.'

Mitchell's gaze was on Alex and Frost, both working feverishly to complete their act of digital sabotage. 'Yeah, so do I.'

Several miles south of Forward Operating Base Pegasus, Dietrich started the engine of his Ford 4 x 4. It struggled once, caught, then came to life. Though he wasn't a Catholic, he paused to cross himself before releasing the clutch and starting out, bumping and jolting across the rough ground towards the distant fortress.

–

'Alex, it'll be your responsibility to make sure Dietrich makes it through the defences in one piece,' Drake said. 'This plan's no good if we can't get beyond the perimeter.'

Alex nodded. 'I can't do anything about the soldiers on base, but he won't have any problems with automated defences. I can promise that much.'

In the operations room of Pegasus, Chief of Station Deans frowned when one of his security chiefs called out from his workstation.

'Sir, we have an incoming tango!'

He was moving right away, striding across the room to the man's terminal.

'Where?'

'Here, sir. Approaching from the south,' the chief explained, pointing to a digitized map of the area. 'Motion sensors picked it up when it hit the perimeter. Range is down to two thousand yards.'

Within their zone of engagement, Deans thought. 'Can you identify it?'

Bringing up a separate window, he indicated video feeds from one of the infrared cameras mounted topside. Sure enough, a civilian model four-wheel drive was bouncing and jolting across the open ground towards them, moving fast despite the rough terrain.

'It doesn't have an access transponder,' the man confirmed. 'And the driver's not answering to radio hails.'

Deans chewed his lip, considering his options. 'Put me on loudspeaker.'

Loudspeakers had been set up around the perimeter fencing for contingencies just like this, but thus far any locals passing through this area had been wise enough to give the fortress a wide berth. Not so this driver.

Flicking several switches on his terminal, the security chief handed him a radio headset. 'You're on, sir.'

'Attention unidentified vehicle. This is a restricted area. Turn around immediately or you *will* be fired upon. I repeat, turn around now.'

There was no response. The vehicle carried on without slowing or changing course.

'What are your orders, sir?'

Their standing orders were clear in situations like this. In the event of an incursion into their security perimeter, they were authorized to open fire.

'Bring the point defence guns online.'

'Roger that.'

Up above, all five of the remote-controlled 30mm defensive cannons – one in each of the fortress's watchtowers – whirred into life, their long barrels tracking left and right, automated feed mechanisms clanking and rattling as their first rounds were drawn into the breech.

'Turrets three and four have positive lock,' the security chief reported. 'Permission to engage, sir?'

Deans looked at the infrared camera feed. The 4 x 4's range was down to just over a thousand yards now – well within the auto-cannon's range. Whatever the driver was thinking, he clearly had no idea of the firepower that was about to be unleashed on him.

'Open fire.'

But instead of unleashing a deadly torrent of 30mm high-explosive shells at the incoming vehicle, the two gun turrets began to rotate, turning away from their target.

'What's going on?' Deans asked, watching as the feeds from their targeting cameras began to track left.

'I'm not sure, sir.' He was inputting commands, but nothing seemed to be happening. It was as if the guns were moving of their own accord. 'Both turrets are non-responsive.'

'The others are moving too,' another technician reported, his face suddenly etched with worry. 'All five of them.'

Deans stared in disbelief as all five of their defensive turrets tracked slowly left, pointing away from the approaching vehicle, away from the perimeter altogether, until each of their cameras centred on something else. Something that sent a chill of foreboding and disbelief through him.

'Oh, shit,' he gasped. 'They're targeting each other.'

Each weapon was now pointed at the one to its left, their targeting apertures centred dead on the next turret in line as if they had formed some kind of group suicide pact.

'Shut it down! Shut the system down!' Deans cried out.

His command, even if it hadn't come too late, would have been useless anyway. The system was no longer under their control. It had been hijacked by a young man with a second-hand laptop about 40 miles away. A young man who grinned in victory as he input a single command.

As one, all five turrets opened fire, spraying each other with a destructive hail of high-velocity projectiles that tore through their lightly armoured covers and detonated amongst the delicate machinery inside, shredding targeting mechanisms and blasting apart the ammunition already stored in there, which quickly added to the explosions now rocking the ancient fortress.

In the space of just a few seconds, the base's point defence guns had obliterated each other in a deafening cacophony of destruction.

Forty miles away, Alex watched as the feeds from the turrets crackled and went out one by one. 'Fuck, that was fun! That takes care of the defence systems,' he said, leaning back a little from his machine. 'He's good to go.'

Mitchell let out a breath she'd been holding for far too long. 'Dietrich, you're clear to move in. The perimeter gate's open for you.'

'Copy that, looks like World War Three just started. I'm almost inside,' he replied. 'Ryan better fucking be there!'

Frost, seated opposite, was now ready to make her contribution. She had already watched Drake take out the guard covering Anya and free the woman from her restraints.

'Now it's time for lights out,' she added, inputting a command to shut down the facility's power grid.

–

'Last of all, we need someone to cover our escape,' Drake concluded, turning his attention to Rojas, who had sat in brooding silence, listening as the other's roles were dictated. 'Someone who's a good shot and cool under pressure.'

The assassin flashed a wolfish smile. 'It's your lucky day.'

–

Standing in the smoke-filled courtyard, Drake looked down at the now unconscious Powell lying sprawled on the dusty ground at his feet.

'You probably didn't have to knock her out,' he remarked.

Anya shrugged. The drugged-up, unfocussed look had faded from her eyes. Now they shone with righteous anger. 'Yes I did, Ryan.'

Now was no time to debate the finer details. This entire facility was soon going to be overrun. They needed to be somewhere else, fast.

'Help me carry her,' he said, hooking his arms beneath Powell's. Anya took her feet, and together they carried her over to the waiting vehicle.

'Targets in the open!' a voice called out from above.

Drake and Anya both looked up through the swirling smoke at an operative standing on the high stone wall that encircled the fortress. They saw him switch into a firing stance, saw the barrel of an assault rifle raised towards them, and braced themselves for the burst that they knew was about to cut them down.

But it didn't come. Instead something whizzed past the man's head. Or rather, *through* his head, carving out a ruinous chunk of skull and brain matter as it went, before burying itself in the old stonework opposite. The man instantly pitched sideways and tumbled off the parapet, landing with a sickeningly wet thump below.

Lying flat on a low hillock 1,200 yards away, Cesar Rojas worked the bolt action of his McMillan TAC-50 sniper rifle, drawing a fresh .50 calibre round into the breech. The rifle's working parts clicked with satisfying precision. This was by no means the longest-range kill he'd made, but firing at night with smoke partially obscuring his vision presented unique challenges.

'Still got the magic,' he mumbled as he leaned into the powerful rifle, already scanning for his next target.

Drake and Anya heaved Powell's unconscious body into the back seat before clambering in themselves, weary and shaken but still very much alive.

Dietrich glanced over at Drake as he slammed the passenger door shut, breathing hard, fired up on adrenaline and sheer willpower.

'Shall we go?' he enquired.

'Don't make me kill another person tonight,' Drake returned. 'Fucking drive!'

Smirking in amusement, Dietrich threw the old Ford into gear and accelerated out of the burning, ruined compound, heading for the open country beyond the perimeter.

Chapter 88

'Someone give me a sitrep!' Hawkins snarled over the Black Hawk's intercom as the aircraft raced southwards at maximum cruising speed. 'What's going on there?'

Realizing that they'd been led on a wild-goose chase at the abandoned village, he had immediately ordered his strike team back into their transport chopper and lifted off, heading back to Forward Operating Base Pegasus. They had lost communications with Powell, and everyone else on the base.

It was like the entire facility had gone dark.

'Still no response by radio,' the pilot replied apologetically. He wasn't part of Hawkins' unit, but he knew a dangerous operative when he saw one. 'We should have visual contact any time now.'

Unstrapping himself, Hawkins made his way forward as the chopper rose from the valley it had been hugging, affording them a good view of an open plain, and in the distance, the base, alight.

'Jesus Christ,' the pilot gasped, staring at a giant plume of smoke and fire that now illuminated the landscape for miles around. 'Pegasus has been hit.'

Hawkins' jaw tightened. Drake had fucked them, betrayed the trust that Powell had foolishly shown in him.

'Take us in.'

'Sir, there could still be hostiles—'

The big operative laid a hand on his shoulder, squeezing a little harder than necessary. 'I said take us in, son. Now.'

His expression was enough to forestall further doubts, and Hawkins returned to his seat as the big aircraft swept in towards the burning facility, landing outside the perimeter walls rather than risking the smoke-filled courtyard. They could already see that the main gate was standing wide open. It didn't seem to have been destroyed or demolished, but rather opened automatically.

Hawkins and his team disembarked the chopper, advancing inside with their weapons up and ready.

'Look sharp,' he hissed, peering into the smoke.

As they passed beneath the main walls, he glanced up at the smouldering mass of twisted metal that had once been an automated gun turret. It, along with all the others, appeared to have been destroyed, rendering the base defenceless.

'Don't shoot!' a voice called out.

Hawkins and the others wheeled right, weapons sweeping around to focus on the bedraggled, bloodied man who had emerged from the arched doorway that led below. His hands were up, his shirt smeared with soot and blood, and torn to reveal his sagging gut.

'Thank God you're here!' Deans gasped, moving towards them. 'I thought nobody would get to us in time.'

'What happened?' Hawkins asked, unmoved by the terror on his face.

'Our system was compromised, the prisoners escaped, rioted, destroyed the place and killed anyone they could find. They're all dead, all of them...'

'What about Powell and Drake? Where are they?'

Deans shook his head slowly. Traumatized by the destruction of his world. He had no idea what had become of them.

Sighing, Hawkins took aim and put a single round through his head, dropping him instantly. 'Dumb shit,' he said under his breath as the man's body quivered. 'Hickman!'

'Sir?' Hickman responded, unmoved by his act of cold-blooded murder.

'Get hold of Cain, tell him we need backdated satellite tracking of the entire area for the past two hours. Drake left this place with Powell, and I want to know where the fuck he went, right now.'

–

Lifting the bottle of water to his mouth, Drake took a deep pull, eager to slake his ravenous thirst. Part of him couldn't even believe they were still alive, that they'd made it this far, that their plan had somehow succeeded against the odds.

If only that was it. If only they could escape now, put this all behind them. But they couldn't. Not yet. There was still one more thing to do.

The 4 x 4 had joined a main road about ten minutes after escaping the base, allowing Dietrich to pick up the pace. The surface was potholed, but it was a hell of a lot better than what they'd been driving over.

He was in little doubt that their enemies would pursue them. They didn't have much time to reach their final destination.

He passed the bottle to Anya, who was watching him from the back seat, partially hidden in shadow.

'How are you feeling?'

She didn't respond until she'd drained the bottle, and Drake could guess why. The subject was clearly not a pleasant one for her.

'Better now,' she said, casting a dark gaze at Powell, who was bound and unconscious on the back seat beside her.

'What... did she do to you?' Drake couldn't help asking.

Anya sighed. 'I understand now the kind of power she had over you.'

And that was all she had to say on that subject.

In any case, Powell was beginning to stir. Anya had socked her good and hard, which Drake didn't exactly blame her for, but the last thing he needed was for their prisoner to end up with a concussion or worse.

Powell tried to move her arms, only to find they'd been tied. An uncharacteristic moment of panic surfaced.

'I'd ask how you're feeling, but I think we both know your well-being isn't top priority right now,' Drake said, finally allowing his true emotions to come to the surface.

Realizing the futility of her situation, Powell ceased struggling. She looked at both her captors, then licked her split lip where Anya had punched her.

'You hit like a pussy,' she said derisively, before turning her eyes on Drake. 'Well Ryan, I have to admit even I didn't see this coming.'

'I'm happy to disappoint you.'

'How did you do it?' she asked, her analytical mind still trying to process the events that had led to this. 'Break your conditioning?'

Drake turned his head to the side and pointed to a tiny device inserted into his ear canal. None of the others could hear it, but the device issued a constant pulsing tone, like a car alarm going off in his ear. It was uncomfortable and distracting to say the least, but that was exactly the point.

'It was Rio that changed everything,' he explained. 'That was where I understood your weakness.'

–

Something happened then that neither of them had anticipated. Instead of Powell's quiet, wonderfully convincing voice, the room was suddenly filled with the deafening blare of an emergency alarm.

The effect on Drake was akin to throwing a bucket of freezing water over a man just as he's drifting off to sleep. The spell was broken in an instant. He started with shock, his mind painfully torn out of the hypnotic, dreamlike state that it had lapsed into.

–

'The alarm. The noise, the distraction. That's what broke your hold,' Drake went on. 'That's why all your interrogation rooms are designed to block out everything except your voice.'

Powell smiled. The bitter, reflective smile of a defeated player considering the decisions that had led them to disaster. 'You were willing to execute Anya.'

Drake looked her hard in the eye. 'I knew you wouldn't trust me with a loaded gun. Just like I knew Cain wanted Anya alive.'

Powell glanced at Anya, apparently torn between anger and respect for the risk she'd taken. 'And you? You were willing to risk everything on Ryan's hunch?'

'Some people are worth risking everything for. Not that you would ever know.'

'I expected as much,' the older woman remarked cynically. 'So what happens now? You're going to kill me?'

Drake shook his head. 'No, Elizabeth. We're going to kill your life's work.'

At this, he gave Anya a nod and she quickly fixed a gag around Powell's mouth.

Drake looked over at Dietrich, who had kept himself focussed on driving throughout the exchange. 'How much further, mate?'

'Not far. The others are waiting for us.'

Chapter 89

Dietrich turned off the main road not long after, taking them down a rough trail that even the 4 x 4 struggled to manage. Still, they didn't have to venture far through this difficult terrain.

A couple of vehicles were waiting ahead. And clustered around them, standing in a loose semicircle, were his friends. Alex, Mitchell, Frost and Rojas had all made their way here for the final rendezvous. And, mercifully, they had all made it here unharmed.

'Well, fuck,' Frost said, grinning at Drake as he emerged from the vehicle. 'I can't believe that shit actually worked.'

Drake embraced Keira, filled with relief. He shared her sentiments and more.

'Well done. All of you,' he said, moved by the risks they'd all taken on his behalf. 'None of this would have been possible without you.'

'You're making me all misty-eyed, Ryan,' Dietrich said in his usual dour tone, prompting a laugh from the others.

'I just wanted a free trip overseas,' Alex added. 'Seriously though, I'm glad you made it out, mate.'

Rojas meanwhile approached Anya, touching her arm gently. 'Are you all right?'

'I will be when this is finished.'

Frost's smile faded as her attention turned to their prisoner, still seated in the back seat of the 4 x 4. 'So that's the bitch who's been messing with Ryan's head?'

'That's her.'

The young woman's expression hardened as she took a step towards her. 'I say we waste her now and be done with it.'

Drake gripped her arm, preventing her getting closer. 'Not yet. Remember the plan,' he said. 'We see this through.'

Frost went to protest, but realizing it would be a wasted effort, reluctantly nodded acceptance.

'Bring her out!'

Gripping the bound prisoner, Dietrich escorted her over to where the group was gathered. Alex had already set up his laptop on the hood of their vehicle, with a familiar memory stick inserted in the side. That was displaying the same warning box that had so confounded Drake several days earlier in Rio.

Access restricted (Executive level only). Enter password.

Drake tore away Powell's gag. 'I think you can guess what we want, Elizabeth.'

Her eyes flicked from the screen to the man facing her, her mind quickly assembling the facts. She knew exactly what was on that laptop. A copy of all their research records, all the work they had done, every experiment, every subject, every death carefully recorded and catalogued. Information that was never supposed to be seen by anyone outside her company.

'You're out of your mind. There's no way I'm giving you that code.'

Drake smiled. 'I thought you might say that.'

As he said this, Dietrich reached up, grabbed a handful of dark hair and yanked her head back, eliciting a gasp of shock and pain. Drake reached into his pocket and produced a little Autoject syringe, just like the one she'd used on Anya.

'You've spent a good portion of your life testing this stuff on other people,' Drake said, bringing the device up in front of her. 'I suppose we should be grateful to you for making this so easy.'

She was really struggling now, trying to twist away, to fight, but Dietrich was having none of it. He held her firmly in place as Drake pressed the device against her neck.

'Now, let's begin our first session,' he said. There was a hiss as the Autoject did its thing, and Powell's struggles quickly eased off. She shook her head as if trying to clear her vision, but there was no fighting off the effects of the potent drugs. Her eyes slowly lost their focus, her breathing slowed. Dietrich released his grip of her, but she made no attempt to flee.

'Can you hear me?' Drake asked.

'Yes.'

'Good. Tell us your system password, Elizabeth.'

He saw the conflict in her, her conscious mind trying to rally itself and fight back. Her great intellect working to preserve and defend itself in one last great effort. But it wasn't enough.

'Hydra-16309.'

Drake looked over at Alex who was standing by at the computer, and gave him a nod. They held their breath as he entered the code, paused for a moment to check it was correct, then clicked 'confirm'.

The warning screen disappeared, replaced by a vast folder structure of projects, initiatives, testing programmes, drug experiments. Every dark secret of Unity Medical Group laid bare.

'It worked!' Alex gasped. 'Holy shit, it actually worked. We're in!'

Powell's expression was passive, but Drake noticed a tear had rolled down her cheek. She was witnessing the beginning of the end of her life's work, and even if she couldn't consciously react to it, part of her knew what that meant.

'Jesus, there's more data here than we could sift through in a year,' Alex said as he scrolled through the list of files.

'It'll have to wait,' Drake decided, looking at Anya. 'We've got one more place to be.'

'We've got something, sir!' Montez called out, studying the video footage that was downloading to his laptop.

Hawkins strode over to join him. 'Talk to me.'

'National Reconnaissance Office just sent us through footage of the attack. Lucky for us, they had a bird overhead at the time.'

Hawkins watched as the scene unfolded. As he'd suspected, the point defence guns had been commanded to open fire on one another, crippling the base's defences. The resulting heat blooms and clouds of hot smoke temporarily obscured the image, before stabilizing again, allowing him to watch a vehicle drive in through the main gate.

Shortly after, a trio of bright points of light emerged from the building, with one apparently injured or unconscious individual being dragged towards the waiting vehicle by another. In short order the car was loaded up and sped back out the gate, heading east.

'Where did they go from there?' Hawkins demanded.

Montez looked at him fearfully. 'We lost the satellite not long after that, but they're trying to draw footage from other birds in the vicinity and pick up the trail from there.'

'Fuck,' Hawkins said under his breath. 'Let me know as soon as you find them. In the meantime, pack everything up. We're leaving!'

Chapter 90

They were close now. Drake could feel it as much as Anya.

It was akin to returning to one's home town after many years' absence. The place had changed, but the sense of familiarity was uncanny.

However, it was clear they'd come about as far as they could go by vehicle. The terrain had grown more and more difficult, and despite Anya's best efforts to negotiate a drivable path, it was clear she was fighting a losing battle.

Bringing the 4 x 4 to a halt, Anya turned to Drake. 'We walk from here.'

He nodded. 'How far is it?'

'A mile. Maybe less.'

It was a clear, almost cloudless night as they stepped outside. The stars were bright, thousands of tiny points of light, shining cold and hard and remote in the darkness. It was a beautiful and awe-inspiring sight.

Anya had brought Powell out of the back seat, rather unwillingly as it turned out, but with her hands bound she was in no position to resist. She had recovered somewhat from the drugs they'd dosed her with, but was still a little unsteady on her feet.

Drake turned to look at her. 'Hope you've got your walking shoes on.'

Since Anya knew this area better than him, she led the way. Drake followed behind with one arm around Powell, leaving roughly a five-yard gap between them as they advanced up the shallow rocky valley towards their destination.

It was a quiet night, broken only by the shuffling of boots on rocks as they climbed up a rocky, brush-covered slope at the head of the winding valley. The moon was little more than a thin sliver of ghostly light, providing little illumination, but dawn didn't seem to be far off judging by the gradual lightening of the sky in the east.

Both Drake and Anya were physically fit, but their endeavours tonight had sapped their stamina, and both were breathing hard as they approached the crest of the slope.

When they reached the top, Drake froze, struck by a sudden, intense recollection.

Black smoke, the sky on fire, the sharp rattle of gunshots...

'What's wrong?' Anya asked.

'I've been here before,' he whispered. 'I've seen this place.'

Anya's face was pale and cold in the wan moonlight. 'We have to keep moving. There's a cave on the other side of the plateau.'

'I'm afraid, Anya. Afraid of what we'll find in there.'

She looked almost as frightened as him: not because of what lay ahead, but because of his reaction to it. 'We've come too far to turn back now.' She laid a hand on his shoulder. 'We're almost there, Ryan. I'll be with you.'

He forced himself to move forward, to keep going. She was right; whatever truth awaited them, there was no sense running any longer. One way or another, he had to face it.

The plateau was about 100 yards across and lower in the centre, forming a wide, bowl-shaped depression in the ground. Possibly it had once been a lake or pool of some kind, but its natural formation provided some shelter from the prevailing wind. As they picked their way through it, Drake began seeing more images, more flashes of a battle he couldn't remember, more echoes of feelings without context. And a voice, pained and stricken, asking him a single question over and over again.

Why?

Anya's assertion was proven correct, and the two of them halted before the low cave entrance at the eastern side of the plateau, overhung by a shelf of rock that would make it difficult to spot from the air.

'He's in there,' Drake said, his voice hushed.

'How do you know?'

He didn't answer, instead reaching into his pack for a couple of light sticks, their glow soon illuminating the area around them.

With Powell between them, they ducked down and ventured into the darkened mouth. Though the cave entrance was low and narrow, it soon opened out into a larger passage that sloped down into the mountainside. Moisture-covered walls sparkled as they picked their way forward, careful to avoid hidden fissures and crevasses.

Their path continued downwards for perhaps 30 yards before splitting into several side tunnels. There was no obvious clue as to which was the correct path. Drake was all too aware of how extensive and confusing the cave networks in places like this could be. Unwary travellers could easily become disoriented in this strange subterranean maze, walking for hours in a vain search for an exit.

But Drake experienced no such confusion. He knew where he was going. And they were almost there now. The long and difficult journey that had brought them here was almost at an end.

'Let's go,' he whispered.

Together they pressed forward, side by side, their weapons at the ready, following the winding and uneven cavern as it descended ever deeper into the rock. They could hear a rushing noise up ahead, the sound of flowing water coming from around a turn in the passage. An underground spring.

'Are you ready?' Drake asked, almost wishing Anya would say no.

He felt her hand on his arm, warm and reassuring. 'I'm with you.'

With that, they rounded the final turn.

It was clear right away that they had emerged into a far larger cavern whose size and scale dwarfed the narrow passages they had negotiated to get here. The glow of their light sticks barely even reached the vaulted roof, where towering stalactites stretched downwards like the long bony fingers of immense hands, reaching for similar formations rising out of the floor.

They had been right about the underground river. They could see it flowing along the wall to their left, maybe 20 yards away, while the rest of the cave disappeared off into some indeterminate distance that the feeble light couldn't hope to reach.

'This is it,' Drake whispered. 'This is where it ends.'

Anya's eyes scanned the shadows and ghostly rock formations, the hairs on the back of her neck prickling. 'Where is he?'

'Right here,' an echoing voice called out, the words reverberating off the walls, everywhere and nowhere at once.

Drake tensed up, his weapon sweeping the darkness. 'We're here. This is what you wanted.'

'This is what we both wanted. You've done well, Ryan.'

'Then show yourself!' Drake challenged him.

'All right. If you're ready.'

A figure emerged from the shadows, staying just beyond the light of their glow sticks, its head covered by a long hood, leaving his face drowned in darkness. He seemed to have appeared out of nowhere, but Romek Karalius' presence was all too real now.

Drake couldn't see it, but he felt it. He knew that Karalius was smiling at him.

'It's good to see you again.'

Chapter 91

'Sir, just got word in from the NRO,' Montez called out. 'They've picked up the trail. Took a while to lock it in, but the target vehicle's stopped in a mountain valley about 40 miles east of here.'

'Show me,' Hawkins ordered.

Montez brought up a satellite map of the area, zooming in far enough to show the abandoned 4 x 4 sitting near the head of an old river valley. The heat signature told them the engine was still warm.

Poring over the image of the wider area, Hawkins spotted something and jabbed his finger at the screen. 'There! Enhance that area.'

Montez did as instructed, and the picture zoomed in on what looked like a small plateau further up the valley, with a darkened cave entrance at one end. Partially obscured, it would have been easy to miss if they hadn't known to look for it.

But Hawkins did know.

'Son of a bitch,' he whispered.

'What is it, sir?'

'Where it all started.' Reaching for his intercom, he keyed the pilot's radio frequency. 'Listen up. Our target is on heading zero-nine-zero, range 40 miles. Grid reference is seven-two-one. Get us there, and haul ass. We don't have much time.'

'That's near the limit of our operational range, sir,' the pilot warned.

'You have an emergency reserve, don't you?'

'Yes sir, but—'

'Then use it. Just get us there!'

'Roger that.' Already the Black Hawk was altering course.

With the deck tilting beneath him, Hawkins turned to the assault ream awaiting his commands. 'Listen up, gentlemen! We have a fix on our target and we're going in. Our enemy is armed and extremely dangerous, so you're authorized to shoot on sight. Clear?'

'Yes, sir!' came the unanimous reply.

As the engines throttled up to full power, Hawkins settled in his seat and waited. Every second was bringing them closer to their enemies, closer to the revenge he'd been denied for too long.

I'm coming for you, Ryan. I'm coming for you, and today I'm going to give you one.

Chapter 92

'Freeze!' Drake shouted, covering the man with his weapon, his finger tight on the trigger. 'Don't move a fucking muscle.'

Karalius chuckled, entirely unperturbed by his threat. 'Really? After everything we've been through together, that's all you have to say?'

'What do you mean?' Drake demanded. 'We've never met.'

'Ryan...' he heard Anya say, but tried to ignore it. Karalius was his focus now.

'You still don't remember me? Well, I suppose I shouldn't be surprised. Memories aren't all they're cracked up to be, Ryan,' Karalius informed him. 'You of all people should know that.'

Drake let out a breath. 'How do you know me?'

-

Afghanistan – 18th March, 2003

It was a bleak, gusty and overcast evening typical of early springtime in Afghanistan, with a chill breeze whipping across the mountains and whistling through rocky crags. Already the temperature, which had barely struggled above freezing for most of the day, was starting to fall as the sun descended towards the western horizon.

Huddled beneath grey cloaks and clustered in small groups, the 20 or so men who had made camp in a shallow depression halfway up the side of a mountain were barely distinguishable from the scattered, wind-scoured boulders that littered the area. Only the occasional movement or muttered voice betrayed some sign of life.

Camouflaged sentries ringed the area, carefully concealed amongst the ample cover that the rocky hilltop provided, the long barrels of their weapons slowly tracking back and forth across the forlorn landscape.

There was little talking, and no laughter or jokes as there had once been. This was a group weary in both body and spirit, worn down by months of stinging defeats and hollow victories. A group that had been sent to fight a war it couldn't hope to win, against an enemy willing to make any sacrifice to defeat them. An enemy they had inadvertently helped to create two decades earlier. Worst of all, it was a group without its leader.

A lone figure rose from his resting place with a weary grunt, made some excuses and retreated from the others.

He withdrew to the edge of the meagre encampment and sat down on the lee side of a boulder, trying not to acknowledge the pain in his knees and back as he lowered himself to the ground. He was getting older, he realized, as were they all. His hair and beard were flecked with grey. Aches and discomfort were becoming harder to ignore, old injuries starting to flare up again.

Laying his weapon on his lap, he reached into his tunic and pulled out a small, battered leather notebook. His journal, which he had been privately recording for almost a year now. He knew it was strictly forbidden for them to bring anything like this on active deployment, but he no longer cared. He'd fought too long and hard, lost too much to worry about rules and regulations now.

Anyway, deep down he sensed the necessity of what he was now doing. He and the men he'd fought beside for 20 years were coming to the end of their time. They all knew it, whether they admitted it or not. But each of them had spent most of their adult lives fighting in one form or another. They would fight until they could fight no longer, and then they would die and be forgotten.

History would never record their deeds, sacrifices and accomplishments. The world would never know the great and terrible events they had helped to shape, the disasters they had helped avert. He accepted this, but he'd also resolved that they wouldn't be entirely forgotten.

The little journal was filled almost from cover to cover with everything he could think of, from the unit's earliest formation to their training and deployment, their first missions together, the things they had seen and done, the losses they'd taken and the victories they had achieved. Perhaps one day when it was all over, someone would find this journal, read it and understand something of the man who had compiled it.

It wasn't much, but it gave him a small sense of comfort to think part of them might live on after they were gone.

Maybe the book would even find its way into the hands of their leader, wherever she might be now. He knew Anya would never willingly abandon them, yet as the days wore on without word or contact, he'd begun to harbour doubts over whether she would return. She was the glue that held them together, the rock around which they rallied, the implacable authority on which they could always depend.

Removing a pencil bound to the spine of the notebook, he opened one of the few unmarked pages and began to write his final entry. It took him less than five minutes.

He hardly considered himself a poet or student of literature, but his words, such as they were, had at least been heartfelt.

He had just folded the book away and replaced it inside his tunic when he spotted a red glow alighting the rocks and crags. He saw that the setting sun had dipped below the roiling cloud base overhead, its rays highlighting them in vibrant red and iridescent orange, a final display of heavenly glory before nightfall.

Staring at it, he wondered how many soldiers crouched in muddy trenches or surrounded by the wreckage and ruin of war had paused to witness such a sight.

He didn't hear the missile as it streaked its way in. It was moving faster than the speed of sound, and reached its target before the roar of its rocket motor. Even if he had heard it, he never would have had time to react, much less shout out a warning to his comrades.

All he was aware of was the bright flash of a high-explosive detonation directly ahead of him, followed an instant later by an ear-splitting roar. He saw rocks and dirt thrown outwards, and suddenly his world disintegrated into pain and chaos and violent movement.

He was aware of being picked up and hurled backwards like a rag doll, of the world spinning and tumbling, and then at last the crushing impact as he landed. Darkness closed in.

He awoke slowly, his mind emerging from a painful red fog some time later. He had no idea how long it had been. A few seconds or a few hours, it meant nothing to him. All he knew was that he was still alive. He raised his head slowly, dirt running off his hair and clothes as he moved.

The camp was gone. In its place, a smouldering crater had been gouged out of the rocky hillside. Fires burned here and there, while acrid smoke drifted across the entire area. Overhead, above the smoke and flames, the sun continued to cast its blood-red glow on the dark storm clouds.

He cast his eyes around, trying to understand the nightmare that had just enveloped his comrades, yet could see little except death and destruction. In some places he caught the unmistakable shapes of men sprawled on the ground, some charred and smoking, others reduced only to pieces that were barely identifiable.

Men. His men. His brothers, who had fought and killed and bled alongside him, now lay dead and dying all around. Killed by a cowardly rocket or artillery strike before they even had a chance to fight back.

Anger and grief welled up inside him. He instinctively reached for his weapon, but couldn't find it. It must have been torn from his grasp.

Only his distance from the camp had saved his life, he realized. Had he not retreated to complete his journal, he too would have been killed by the blast.

He had to go to his companions, had to search amongst the grisly remains in the hopes of finding survivors. Maybe someone else had survived the explosion. Maybe he wasn't alone.

He tried to scramble to his feet, but fell back to the ground the moment he tried to put weight on his right leg. He could feel the broken ends of his shattered femur grating against each other. He'd endured many hardships and injuries in his long life, but the agony that lashed through him then was almost overwhelming.

Drawing breath, he pulled himself upright against the boulder.

That was when he saw them: a line of soldiers just visible through the swirling smoke. They had emerged over the edge of the depression in which his men had camped, their silhouettes horribly visible against the blood-red sky. He understood it all in a single, terrible moment. The weapons, the uniforms, the shouted commands and acknowledgements.

He watched as one of them slowed down to examine a figure that was still moving, albeit pitifully in a pool of blood at his feet. He watched as the man raised his weapon, took aim and pulled the trigger without hesitation.

These men hadn't come to win a victory, to take prisoners that could be interrogated later. They were here for one reason only – to kill every living thing in this camp. Including him.

He could do nothing for his companions now, he realized, heartbroken at the thought. Unarmed, injured and alone, he stood no chance. His intervention wouldn't even delay these men in their chilling work, much less prevent it.

All he could do was survive. Survive, and perhaps one day return to take revenge.

–

'Your unit was ambushed here,' Drake said. 'They were killed, but you survived. You survived and now you're out for revenge, Romek.'

'Ryan, this isn't—' Anya began.

'Don't!' Drake pleaded. 'I have to know the truth.'

The hooded figure shook his head. 'No, Ryan. Romek Karalius didn't survive. He died seven years ago, not far from this very spot. You know this.'

–

He was moving almost before he knew it, sliding off the boulder and crawling away, his broken leg dragging behind him, fighting down the pain and grief and horror at what was unfolding. He crawled, tears streaking his dirty and bloody face, his fingers clawing at frozen rocks as more gunshots echoed behind him. His comrades' final, wrenching sacrifice would perhaps create enough of a distraction to mask his escape.

He continued to crawl, vowing that this final treacherous act would not go unpunished.

However, he had made it barely a dozen yards before he felt a shadow fall across his face, and looked up to find a man with a weapon trained right on him.

He looked his killer in the eye, hating him and yet somehow pitying him as well now that he finally understood the system that had created them both. A man who had been sent to destroy what had once been great, and who in turn would eventually be destroyed by another.

His final word was a simple, heartfelt question.

'Why?'

–

Drake's heart was pounding. Images and memories swirled and intertwined as he struggled to make sense of it. To hold it all together.

'If you're not Romek Karalius…'

'Say it,' the man prompted him.

'No. Please.'

'You knew this was coming, Ryan. Don't hide from it any longer. Say it.'

Drake let out a shuddering breath, facing up to it at last. 'Show yourself to me.'

He felt a hand on his arm, and looked at Anya. She was watching him, her eyes wide with fear. Not fear of the stranger who had found them, but fear of Drake himself. Fear of a man she no longer understood.

'Ryan, there is nobody there,' she whispered.

Her words tore into him like a knife. In disbelief, in denial, in horror, he turned back towards the stranger just as the man pulled back his hood, revealing a face that he knew well.

Drake's face.

–

Drake shivered as another chill blast of wind hit, flexing and tensing his fingers as he prepared to move. Their enemies were just over the crest of the slope, encamped in their mountain refuge, believing themselves safe. He and his men had spent most of the day approaching slowly, staying out of sight of the sentries posted around the area.

And now it was almost time.

'Weapons free, weapons free,' his radio earpiece crackled. 'Ten seconds to impact.'

He looked up at the sky, knowing the drone which had just deployed a laser-guided missile was too high to be visible, but he pictured it all the same. He imagined the missile streaking down towards them, picking up speed with every second.

At that moment, the setting sun broke through a tear in the clouds, setting the sky and the mountains around them alight in a blaze of colour. It was a spectacular sight, mesmerizing in its vividly crimson glow.

The explosion as the precision-guided munitions detonated seemed to rumble through the mountain, shaking it to its very core. He opened his mouth as the blast wave rocked him and the men crouched beside him, and looked up as a great column of smoke rose into the sky.

The command went out a second or so later. 'Move! Go! Go!'

Scrambling to his feet, Drake rushed up the slope with his weapon at the ready, into the haze and smoke. After the ear-splitting explosion, a sense of unnatural calm had descended on the mountain plateau as he and his comrades advanced.

He almost jumped at the sound of a single gunshot, then relaxed when he heard someone call out, 'Tango down!'

'Call out your targets when you see them!'

'Clear here!'

Something was lying on the ground off to his right. Looking closer, he saw the remains of what had once been a man, one entire side of the body blasted away, leaving only burned flesh and shredded clothing. No need to confirm that kill.

Drake pushed on.

A few more shots echoed across the open space, but no return fire. The Predator had done its work well.

But then, through the gradually clearing smoke, Drake saw movement. One of the enemy, wounded but alive, trying to crawl away from the scene. Trying to hide himself, hoping they might miss him.

No prisoners. That had been their order.

Moving with the easy grace of a natural athlete, Drake looped around in front of him. He could hear the man's laboured breathing coming closer, the faint gasps of pain, the rustling of a body being dragged over loose stones.

Checking his weapon one last time, Drake leapt out. The face that confronted him wasn't the face of a Taliban or al-Qaeda fighter. It was the face of a soldier just like him, twisted in pain and grief, and a dawning realization that his time was up.

Drake raised the rifle up to his shoulder with leaden arms, taking aim. From this range he could barely miss.

It was then that the wounded man uttered a single word that seemed to stop everything else around them. A single agonized declaration of betrayal.
'Why?'

–

Drake could see it now. The images that had been so fragmented, so fleeting, starting to coalesce into a horribly vivid chain of events. He remembered the thunderous explosion as the missile came in, the charge up over the hill, the smell of smoke and charred flesh, the moans of the dying and the echo of the gunshots.

Killing their own people. Anya's people.

He'd always thought his suppressed memories were of some terrible ambush or catastrophe that had befallen his unit, some lost cause he'd barely survived, but now he saw it in a sickening new light.

'No,' he moaned, falling to his knees. 'It's not possible. It's not.'

The other man, the other Drake, had stepped forward to meet him. Now he stood over him, looking down at the man he'd become.

'Look at me, Ryan,' he said gently.

Drake did, finding himself staring into a face that was a perfect reflection of his own. A face that looked down on him now with pity and remorse. He managed only to gasp the same word he'd heard all those years ago.

'Why?'

'Because ever since that day, you've been at war with yourself, Ryan. Fighting to remember the truth, fighting to be free of her control.' He raised an arm and pointed towards Powell. 'But you couldn't do this by yourself. So you created me. A man who would guide you, show you the way forward, help you understand the truth. A man who could do the things you couldn't.'

'This is impossible...'

'Is it? I'm you, Ryan. A man with all your memories and abilities, and none of your limitations. All those days you lost, all those times you woke up in your bed not knowing where you'd been or what you'd done. You weren't living in a dream, you were living as me.'

More images now, more memories that had remained carefully beyond his reach until now. He saw himself in Washington DC, crouched in George Breckenridge's driveway as he finished wiring up the remotely operated bomb beneath the man's car.

Not long after, he was seated before a video camera, his face obscured by a black mask as he explained his reasons for the upcoming attack, even revealing his true name. Knowing it would be enough to attract the attention he needed.

Another flash and he was in the sweltering heat of Tunis, handing over a bag of weapons and explosives to a blind shopkeeper on the promise that a 'friend' would come to retrieve it within a week. Making the man promise to reveal nothing of his visit here.

Yet another rapid shift, and he was on a rooftop in the favelas of Rio, watching Anya through a pair of binoculars as she entered the safe house that Drake had so recently departed. He saw himself reaching for the encrypted cell phone by his side, getting ready to speak with her, knowing he would need her presence.

'You were still fighting against it, of course, so you didn't always follow my instructions. Stubborn as always. You tried to confront Powell before you were ready, almost got yourself killed.'

–

'Didn't work, did it?' the voice asked. 'I warned you. We could have avoided this.'

'What the fuck did you bastards do to me?' Drake demanded. His adrenaline was spiking as if preparing for another fight. He was desperate for an enemy to lash out at, for a face he could pound into mush.

But he couldn't. The awful truth had already dawned on him.

You want to see your real enemy, Ryan? Go look in the mirror again.

–

Drake's world shattered. Everything he'd believed, everything he knew about himself, the whole basis of his identity just broke apart. He staggered, his face blank and uncomprehending as the memory played out with terrifying clarity.

It had been there all along, he knew now. All this time. All these years he'd been living a lie, deluding himself he was a good man, that he knew his own mind, that he understood himself. It was all wrong.

'You spoke to Anya, you knew things about her...'

The man smiled sadly. 'Because *you* knew.'

–

'Why?'

Drake stopped, his finger resting on the trigger of his weapon, staring down the sights at the man lying before him. The man he'd just taken everything from. The man who even now couldn't understand what was happening to him, couldn't understand why he'd been betrayed.

It was like a layer was being peeled away from his psyche, exposing something new beneath. All the cold, malicious fury that had been instilled in training, the absolute conviction that everything they did was right and true and justified, all of it seemed to fade away.

Why?

His questions were shattered by the sharp, painful crack of a single gunshot. The man jerked once, body convulsing as his old heart beat one final time, then went still.

Lowering his smoking weapon, Drake knelt down, spotting something inside the dead man's tunic. Reaching inside, he pulled out a small, leather-bound journal. Old and battered and frayed, heavily used.

Almost without realizing, Drake quickly stowed the journal in his pocket and rose to his feet once more. Sparing the dead man one last glance, he called out to his fellow operatives.

'Clear!'

Drake found his hands clawing at the loose soil that coated the cave floor. Sediment from the nearby stream that had built up over millennia, forming a layer of dirt beneath them.

His fingers pulled and shovelled until finally they touched on something. Something firm and rectangular. A journal, leather bound, small and battered and frayed with age and long use. He held it for a moment, staring down at it.

'Ryan?'

It came out as a small, tentative sound. Barely a whisper.

His gaze turned slowly over to Anya, who was staring back at him, her eyes pleading, begging for an explanation. Maybe she would even believe him if he lied to her, force herself to accept a fantasy rather than live with the truth.

He couldn't do it. Even now, knowing what it would mean, what it would do to her, he couldn't live a lie any longer. She had to know the truth.

'It was me,' he whispered. 'I was here seven years ago. It was my unit who destroyed Task Force Black. I was the one who killed Karalius.'

The effect on her was worse than he could have imagined. Romek, the final member of her unit, the last remaining link to the brotherhood, the family who had once protected her, was dead.

Killed by the man kneeling before her.

She seemed to crumble then, sinking to her knees. The expression of loss and desolation on her face was absolute.

'Why?' she now asked, her voice little more than a murmur. 'Why, Ryan?'

'I never could tell you what my unit was created for,' Drake said, speaking both as himself and the other man. Two fractured minds coming together as one. 'It's so clear to me now. We were replacements.'

Her head was down, her shoulders slumped. 'For what?'

'For you. For Task Force Black. That's what Operation Hydra really was. We were created to be better in every way. Stronger, faster, more ruthless. Soldiers who would obey without question, kill without hesitation. We were supposed to be your... evolution.'

She looked at him with utter, crushing grief. 'They were loyal soldiers! Why kill them?'

'Only she can tell us,' Drake said, approaching Powell. He could feel the other Drake's presence still, could feel the anger and rage within them both. 'Tell us, Elizabeth. Tell us why they had to die.'

The woman stared at him, seeing the fury and knowing there was little to be gained by holding back the truth.

'The order came from Marcus Cain,' she admitted. 'He said Task Force Black had become a liability, that they were a threat to us. There was only one option – elimination.'

Anya could feel her heart ache as she pictured her unit, her men, her family, callously murdered by men serving the same masters.

'What threat did they pose?' Anya demanded.

'The threat *you* created, when you risked exposing everything Cain had been working towards. Don't you understand?' Powell asked. 'Their deaths and your capture were all part of the same deal. The Russians didn't just capture you – you were given to them willingly. By Cain.'

Anya fell silent, struck dumb by the sheer scale of Cain's betrayal. Not only had he ordered the destruction of her unit, but he had engineered her capture by the Russians. Four years in solitary confinement in Siberia. All because of him.

It didn't seem possible. Surely even he couldn't have been capable of such cruelty.

'So you sent us in to kill our own men,' Drake spat. 'And you forced me to forget.'

'We had to!' she protested. 'Your conditioning was breaking down. I did everything I could to salvage it, I tried to repair the damage, but your mind wouldn't accept it. The only choice was to wipe the whole thing.'

'You erased everything I was.'

Powell let out a breath, closing her eyes before speaking. 'I saved your life. They wanted to terminate you. I couldn't bear to see you killed, Ryan. I wouldn't let that happen.'

'So you made me forget the whole thing, cooked up a fake court martial to get me out of the military,' Drake finished for her. 'And Cain made sure I found my way into the CIA, where he could keep an eye on me.'

Drake perceived at last the chain of events that had led him to the CIA, the Shepherd programme, and even the mission to recover Anya from a Siberian prison. It had seemed so logical at the time, a stroke of good luck that an old army buddy had recommended him for the job where his skills could be put to good use.

But like everything else about his life, it had been a carefully concealed lie. All of it had been orchestrated by Marcus Cain and Elizabeth Powell. The entire course of his life had been dictated by someone else.

–

'Two minutes to target!' the pilot called out.

The Black Hawk chopper dodged and weaved its way through the valley, the deck lurching dangerously as the pilot wrestled with the controls, keeping them at low altitude to minimize rotor noise.

Hawkins clenched his fists, readying himself for what was coming. They'd found Drake and Anya, they had them cornered, and soon they would put an end to this. Drake was going to die at the site of his greatest triumph, while Anya would join the rest of her unit in their final resting place. It would be poetic justice indeed.

'Get ready!' he snapped into his headset.

Chapter 93

'I brought you here for a reason, Anya. I didn't understand it before, but I do now,' Drake said. His mind was clear now, set in its purpose. 'I brought you here to do the one thing I couldn't.'

He reversed his grip on his weapon and held it out to her. Anya, roused from her shock and grief, looked at the weapon, then at its owner.

'Take it.'

Anya closed her hand around the butt and pulled it from his grasp. Drake stepped back, his alter ego seeming to watch and encourage him, just as he'd always done. His work was almost complete. There was no need for him now.

Anya stared at him in shock, waiting for an explanation.

Drake let out a breath. 'I'm tired, Anya. Tired of running, tired of living a lie. I have to be free of this. Only you can do it.'

He nodded to the gun.

'What happens next is up to you. Knowing what you know about me. But no matter what you decide, I want you to know that... I'm sorry. About everything.'

With trembling hands, Anya raised the gun towards Powell. The woman's fear was naked and powerful. No more pretences, no haughty self-control. She was cornered and out of options, and she was afraid.

'Anya, please. I... I was just doing what I had to do,' she protested, pleading for mercy. 'Think about everything I told you. The work I've done will save lives, change history. Please don't do this, I know you're better than this. I can answer for my mistakes, I can make it right.' She choked back a sob. 'I'm sorry for what happened to you. Please, I don't want to die here.'

She was no threat. She was frightened, cowed, broken.

Anya turned the weapon towards Drake. The man who had destroyed her family, killed her friend, torn her apart inside, betrayed her in the most absolute way possible.

He was silent and subdued. It was as if all the emotion had been drained out of him, as if he had nothing left.

'What would you have me do?' she asked.

Drake shook his head slowly. His face was still impassive, but his eyes reflected the full depth of his loss and grief.

'Remember what you said to me once? You told me I was a good man. And I believed you, I *wanted* to believe you. But it wasn't true.' He swallowed, raising his chin a little, facing up to it at last. 'I understand now, Anya. And I'm not afraid. Not any more.'

He could feel the other Drake leaving, his presence fading away, and felt a fleeting sense of satisfaction and completeness. He'd done what he had to, had carried Drake all the way to the end. There was no more need for him now.

As Drake had said, it all came down to a simple choice.

Hot tears stung as Anya's finger tightened on the trigger. She knew what she had to do, what was coming to them all.

'I'm sorry, Ryan,' she whispered.

–

The Black Hawk swept up over the edge of the plateau, nose flaring upwards to slow its airspeed before the pilot reduced engine power, preparing for the impact of a tough landing. Above them, the second chopper circled protectively, its cannons sweeping the area for targets.

'This is it!' Hawkins shouted as they bumped down, straining the undercarriage to its limit. 'Get ready!'

'Bravo Two is bingo on fuel. We can't stay here long.'

'Hold position, Two!' Hawkins ordered. 'On my authority.'

Leaping up, he hauled open the crew door.

'Go! Go!'

So preoccupied were they with rushing out the door that none of them saw the lone figure behind a stone covering about 500 yards away, his presence masked from overhead satellite recon, and his thermal signature disguised by the heavy insulated camo suit he was wearing.

They didn't see the long barrel of the .50 calibre bolt-action rifle swing towards the gunship orbiting overhead, or hear the click as its operator thumbed off the weapon's safety. They didn't even hear the thunderous boom of the first round as he opened fire. Not until it was too late.

The heavy-calibre armour-piercing round punched straight through the Perspex canopy, striking the pilot in the centre of his chest and killing him within seconds.

Cesar Rojas hurriedly worked the weapon's bolt action, reloading with haste.

'Oh Christ!' the chopper's co-pilot called out. 'Bravo Two is taking fire! We're—'

A second round blew out what was left of the canopy, shattering his helmet and skull. With nobody left to maintain control, the aircraft tilted slowly to starboard, heeling over under its own weight and throwing the remaining crew off their feet.

'Good night, my friends,' Rojas whispered as the doomed aircraft tumbled out of the sky.

Looking up, Hawkins watched as Bravo Two slowly pitched forward, gathering speed, the rotors still clawing at the air. He watched the big aircraft soar right past them and impact the side of the mountain about 200 yards further up the slope.

He turned away as the bright, bolt-like flash lit the sky, followed by the thunderous detonation as the chopper's munitions ignited in the fireball that had just enveloped it.

Chapter 94

A tremor seemed to run through the very core of the mountain. The cavern shuddered violently as the shockwaves reached them, dislodging rock formations and breaking apart walls.

Hearing a crack up above, Drake looked up as a stalactite detached itself from its millennia-old roots and fell through the air towards them.

'Anya!' he screamed, throwing himself at her. Barely had he knocked her aside before broken chunks of rock rained down all around them. The pair landed in a shallow pool of water, Anya pinned beneath him, her weapon disappearing beneath the surface. Drake's groans of pain told her that Drake had taken the brunt of the impacts from above.

Powell meanwhile had seen her chance. With Anya and Drake temporarily down, she turned and darted away from them, back up the passageway through which they'd entered.

Anya, shaking the freezing water out of her eyes, struggled to get up, her back bruised and cut. But even as this was happening, she saw a figure retreating into one of the passages leading back up to the surface. Powell, fleeing while they were distracted.

Drake had seen it too. Spotting something glimmering beneath the surface of the pool, he reached out and grasped the weapon she'd dropped, tossing it to Anya who caught it instinctively.

'Take it!' he cried, knowing that only Anya could end this. 'Don't let her get away!'

There was no time to argue. Scrambling to her feet, Anya took off in pursuit.

She could hear the woman's footsteps up ahead, fast but erratic, that of a hunted animal fleeing its predator.

Anya's foot caught suddenly on an unseen rock and she pitched forward, landing hard, cutting both forearms. Ignoring the stinging pain and the warm blood seeping down her arms, she struggled to her feet and carried on.

The passage was getting lighter as they approached the surface. Already Anya had passed the intersection where it had split apart earlier, and it must have been approaching dawn because she could see bright light up ahead as well as hear a heavy thumping sound. The roar of her own heartbeat as she pushed herself onwards.

Only as she neared the entrance did she realize the truth. It wasn't the light of a sunrise she was seeing. It was the glow of a searchlight.

Powell was barely 20 yards ahead, running for her very life, gasping for air, ignoring the pain of the bruises where she'd slipped and fallen, or banged her shoulder against the rock wall.

She ran, hearing something up ahead. The roar of an aircraft, the sound of voices. With a final push she staggered from the cave entrance and into a row of weapons.

'Stop! Get down on the ground!'

'Do it or we fire!'

She threw her bound hands up. 'I'm on your side, you bastards!'

And suddenly Hawkins was there, stepping in front of the others. Smoke was drifting down around them, and she could smell burning aviation fuel. One of their choppers must have come down. That must have been the source of the explosion.

'What the fuck's going on?' he demanded.

'We're leaving,' she barked, unwilling to spend another second in this place. 'Get me in that goddamn chopper.'

'What about Drake and—'

'I said now!' she screamed. 'Move now!'

Hawkins bristled with anger, yet still the old compulsion to obey was too much for him. Gritting his teeth, he turned towards the others.

'We're leaving. Bravo One, prepare to lift off.'

As Powell was led towards the waiting Black Hawk, Hawkins cast one final glance towards the cave mouth, trying in vain to pierce the darkness. He couldn't see anything, but he would swear to his dying day that Anya was there, watching him from the gloom.

He was right. Hopelessly outnumbered and outgunned, Anya could do nothing but watch as Powell was escorted on board the chopper. Hawkins was the last to go, reluctantly turning away and retreating from the scene.

The engines roared with increased power and the aircraft lurched skywards, disappeared into the early-morning sky.

Chapter 95

Anya was still there when Drake emerged onto the plateau a short time later. She was standing with her back to him, her hair unbound and lifted by the morning breeze. Surveying the spot where her unit had met their end.

No monuments would ever be built to mark this place, no one would remember the men who had died that day. Except her.

'Powell?' he asked.

Anya let out a breath. 'Hawkins came for her. I couldn't reach her in time.'

Drake felt himself sag. There would be a reckoning for Powell one way or the other. They had already seen to that, but it troubled him that she would live, that her money and power and influence might yet buy her a way out of this.

He stepped up beside Anya, holding out something to her. An old, leather-bound journal. The book that Karalius had written, which Drake had buried here, knowing that one day he would return to retrieve it.

'He wanted you to have this,' he said quietly. 'It was his last wish.'

Anya reached out and gently took it, flicking through the crowded pages, the stories of their time together, the triumphs and losses and hardships they had faced together, until at last she came to the final entry. The message Karalius had addressed to her personally.

> *Sesele,*
>
> *I don't hold much hope that you will ever read these words, but it gives me comfort to put my thoughts down like this while there is still time. I don't pretend to know why you left or where your path took you, but I trust that you were trying to do the right thing, as you always have. If this book somehow finds its way to you, then know that we never lost faith in you or the cause we serve. We fought to the end, did our duty and respected your wishes.*
>
> *As for myself, I can say only that I did my best. Wherever you are now and whatever happens, I wish you well.*

Anya closed the book and bowed her head. A teardrop landed on the worn cover, moistening the old leather.

'We can't stay here,' Drake said, glancing up the hill at the wreckage of the crashed chopper, still burning. 'They'll be back.'

Anya didn't answer. She was still looking at the journal.

Drake reached out tentatively and touched her shoulder.

She twisted out of his grip and backed off, looking at him differently now. The trust, the belief, the openness he'd so recently sensed in her was gone. She regarded him as if he were a stranger.

'Don't, Ryan,' she warned him. 'I can't...'

She shook her head, unable to find the words.

'I have to leave. I can't be here with you.'

She was slipping away from him. Piece by piece, the strands that had bound them together were breaking apart, the gulf between them opening wide.

'Don't do this, Anya. Please.'

She backed up another step, withdrawing, cutting herself off from him.

'I have to. Things are different now. I... I am different.' She pointed off to the east, to the border where the others had agreed to meet them. 'Go, be with the others. They'll need you now.'

Drake felt as if a knife had just slid into his chest.

'What about you?'

She merely shook her head, backing away.

'Don't come looking for me.'

With those final, haunting words, Anya parted company with him.

Chapter 96

Jason dropped the hammer, allowing it to land on the dirt floor with a heavy, significant thud. It felt celebratory, like it marked the start of a new life. A life without Tyler Hawkins. A life without fear. A life without regrets.

He felt different. Renewed, refreshed somehow. And lighter. He'd discarded something tonight, something that had held him back. Now he felt free as he never had before.

Nathan was just beginning to stir. He'd been beaten hard, whipped close to unconsciousness, but he recognized that the attack had ceased. The agonizing blows were no longer hammering in on him, and the garage which had been filled with his father's terrifying roars was now quiet, with only the patter of raindrops on the roof to break the silence.

'It's okay, Nathan,' Jason heard himself say. 'It's over now. Open your eyes.'

He did, staring short-sightedly up at his brother.

'Jason? What happened?' His words were slurred. 'Where's Dad?'

Then he caught a glimpse of the body lying in a heap nearby, and his dull eyes opened wider as shock and horror began to dawn in them. Jason instinctively moved in front of him, blocking his view of the grisly sight.

'It's okay, Nathan. Don't look at it. It's going to be okay now,' Jason said, smoothing his brother's hair back from his forehead.

'You k-killed him?' Nathan stammered.

Jason nodded. What was the point in lying now? So he told the truth, and held his brother while he broke down and cried. He wept, mourning the loss of their father, the loss of life as they'd once known it, the end of their childhoods.

Jason for his part said and felt nothing.

'Listen, I need you to promise me something,' he said once the boy's sobs had abated a little. 'I need you to look after Samuel for me. He's not strong like we are. He'll need someone to protect him.'

Nathan wiped his nose. 'What about you?'

Jason offered him a sad, knowing smile. 'The police are gonna take me away soon, maybe for a long time. A kid who kills his old man...' He shook his head. 'They're not gonna just let that go.'

He'd known it would happen, of course. In the few seconds before he'd swung that perfect blow, he'd known what the consequences would be. But he'd done it anyway, because it was worth it. Samuel and Nathan would live. They'd be sent to live with someone else, hopefully someone better than Tyler Hawkins had been, and maybe they'd learn to live normal lives.

And as for himself, he had a different path to walk now.

'No!' Nathan protested. 'No, they can't! I'll tell them. I'll tell them everything, they'll understand. They can't take you away, Jason.'

It was too much. Jason held him again as the tears returned, more intense, more raw than before. He hadn't felt anything when Nathan wept for their father, but he felt something now. Their lives were set on different courses, and soon the separation he felt in his soul would become all too real. Soon he would go indoors, calmly call 911, and report that he'd killed his father. Then he'd dry himself off with a towel, drink a glass of water and wait in the living room for the police to come and take him away.

Soon, but for those last few moments he knelt down on that dirt floor and held the brother he would never see again. And, at last, he allowed tears of his own to come.

—

Bagram Air Base, Afghanistan

'Goddamn it!' Powell shouted, striding across the almost empty hangar with Hawkins following behind. 'Where the fuck were you, Jason? You were supposed to prevent this from happening.'

'This was your fuck-up, Elizabeth,' Hawkins said, calm and controlled. Her anger had only exposed the cracks in her façade, shown him that she was merely human after all. 'Your arrogance and your ego made this happen. Men are dead, and Drake's gone. And what do we have to show for it?'

Powell drew back her arm to slap him, but he caught it before it could connect. The other members of the assault team quickly stopped what they were doing and gathered around to watch.

'Let go of me, you fucking bastard!' she snarled. He complied, as she knew he would. Still the obedient lapdog. 'I could have every one of you kill yourselves right now if I wanted. Maybe that's what I ought to do, clean house and start over again. Would you like that, Jason?'

'I'd like for you to get what's coming.'

'Really?' she sneered. 'And who do you think is going to do that? You?' She turned and jabbed a finger at Hickman. 'You?'

None of them answered.

'That's what I thought.' She shook her head, hating them for their dumb obedience. Only then did she perceive what she'd lost in creating these men, these soldiers who were supposed to be better than any who had come before. Blindly obeying orders wasn't enough. She'd diminished them rather than improving them. They were failures, flawed creations. 'None of you fucking bitches can touch me.'

To her surprise, Hawkins didn't rise to the bait. Instead, he smiled.

'You're right, but this bitch can,' a voice said from behind.

Powell spun round just in time to see steel flash before her, followed by a sudden surge of hot pain and spreading warmth. She looked down, in disbelief, in incomprehension, at the sword blade now impaled in her chest.

Riley relished pushing the blade in further. The same blade that Hawkins had liberated from Brazil several days earlier. He had kept it all this time, promising Riley they'd find an appropriate use for it. And so they had.

422

Powell opened her mouth to cry out, but nothing seemed to come. Just a kind of crackling groan.

'You see, Elizabeth, you were right after all,' Hawkins said, moving around to stand before her. He watched as the life drained from her eyes. 'Sometimes the best person for a job really isn't a man.'

As Riley withdrew the blade, the woman collapsed in front of them, her blood staining the concrete floor. Hawkins looked at Powell, the woman who had held such absolute control over him, who had moulded and made him into what he was. She was gone, removed from his life and his psyche, and it felt good.

He reached out and touched Riley's eager face, seeing the excitement in her eyes, feeling the connection that bound them together. She had wanted this as much as him, had understood how important it was. And in the end, she hadn't let him down.

'Clean this up. Make sure nobody finds her,' he ordered, walking away with Riley. Leaving Powell's lifeless body behind. Starting a new life.

A life without rules and laws imposed by others. A life without control.

A life that he would reshape as he saw fit.

Chapter 97

Wales, UK – one month later

Drake walked slowly down the grassy hill, still covered with a dusting of snow from the previous day, a heavy winter coat pulled up against the chill February wind. How strange it felt to be back here, he reflected, surveying the gently rolling landscape that felt at once comforting yet alien.

It had been a long time since he'd been here. So much had changed, he wondered if the person he'd come to speak with would even recognize him.

Much had certainly changed since the tumultuous events in Afghanistan four weeks ago, both for him and for the world at large. The wave of protest and revolution which had started in Tunisia had now spread to engulf all of North Africa. Governments were falling, dictators were being overthrown and countries were descending into civil war as rival factions vied for power.

This great popular uprising was already being referred to as the Arab Spring, with many hailing it as the dawn of a new age in the region. Well, they would see how long that spring lasted, Drake reflected. If the shadowy group known as the Circle were indeed behind it, their power and influence had grown to truly global proportions.

There was no telling what they might do next.

The Unity Medical Group was faring little better than these embattled African dictatorships, with revelations of illegal human experimentation whipping up a very public storm of controversy and scandal. Already people had begun dissecting the complex web of shell companies and proxies that they'd used to disguise their illegal activities. The apparently accidental death of the company's CEO and founder Elizabeth Powell had only added to the chaos, and according to the latest news reports, the entire multinational enterprise was soon to go into liquidation.

Drake wasn't sad to see them go, and was even less upset by news of Powell's death. Yet even he couldn't help but wonder at the brilliant but flawed mind that had allowed her to achieve such successes at such costs. Had she truly believed she was serving a greater good, that her work would ultimately benefit all humanity, and embraced the darker aspects of her work as necessary evils? Or had she simply been another greedy opportunist, hungry for profit and success no matter the cost? Perhaps no one would ever truly know.

All he knew for certain was that she was gone now, and with her the last vestiges of her insidious influence over him. Never again would he have to fear falling under her control.

His own group had also seen their share of upheavals in the days since that final, chilling confrontation in Afghanistan. He had finally reunited with them just over the border with Pakistan. And there he had told them everything, sparing no detail, wanting them to know exactly who he was and what he'd done.

He'd foreseen the result of this confession, but he hadn't shied away from it.

Rojas had left them not long after, deciding his work was done and that he would have no further part in their conflict. Drake knew well enough why he'd left, knew that his loyalty lay with Anya rather than the others. She was the only thing that had bound him to them, and she was gone now.

Alex too had left not long after, deciding he could no longer follow Drake in good conscience. Drake didn't blame either man for his decision, and part of him hoped they were each able to move on and make new lives for themselves despite the uncertain world in which they now lived.

He had of course obeyed Anya's wishes not to contact or search for her, not that he would have had much luck anyway. She had gone dark, selling her property in Switzerland, liquidating any assets Drake was aware of and disappearing from the world. She had become a ghost, neither seen nor heard, only remembered.

The pain of losing her was still too raw for him to fully deal with. There would come a time when he could process it better, could begin to understand it. For now, he knew only that she had left an aching void in his life, and that he would wake often in the night, reaching out and hoping to find her there. But she never was.

And as for himself, things felt different now. The sense of conflict within him, the feeling of not being quite whole, was gone. There was no 'other' Drake lurking in the dark recesses of his mind, waiting for a chance to come out again. Whether that part of him had died with Powell's legacy, or whether he had somehow found a way to make peace with himself, he couldn't say for sure. All he knew was the truth of his past was his to own, for better or worse. He knew at last who he was, where he had come from, how he'd become the man he was today.

The question was, what was he going to do with that knowledge?

And so here he was on a cold morning in late February, approaching a house he'd left behind two years ago, thinking he might never see the owner again. But he had to come. Only here would he find the one clue that offered him a chance of understanding the Circle's true motives and intentions. And it had come from the most unlikely source.

He tightened his grip on the mysterious key in his coat pocket, the metal warmed by his hands. It had been left to him by his late mother; the only material possession he'd inherited following her death, its purpose and intent left frustratingly unexplained. For almost two years he had kept it, never knowing what it was intended to unlock, what secrets it might reveal about the woman who had entrusted it to him.

Until now. The answers he sought had been waiting here all along; he'd simply lacked the vision and understanding to see them. Now he saw clearly at last.

Approaching the front door, his boots crunching on the gravel driveway, Drake paused to reflect on where this final quest might take him, what answers he might unearth about his mother and the enigmatic group she'd served, how this journey might drastically change or perhaps even end his life.

After all this, after everything he'd been through, it was a risk he was willing to take.

'Coming!' a voice called out as he rapped on the door. He heard footsteps in the hallway beyond, the sound of someone approaching light and fast.

Drake held his breath, bracing himself as the door was unlocked and swung open, revealing a face that bore a certain resemblance to his own. A face that froze in shock and disbelief as it alighted on him, bright-green eyes widening with amazement.

His sister's face.

'Jessica,' he said quietly. 'I've missed you.'

CPSIA information can be obtained
at www.ICGtesting.com
Printed in the USA
BVHW030932091120
592841BV00008B/1505